INK

HAL DUNCAN was born in 1971, grew up in small-town Ayrshire
during the Eighties, and now lives in the West End of Glasgow.
Working part-time as a computer programmer, he is a member
of the Glasgow SF Writers' Circle, and his previous novel,
Vellum, was the first part of The Book of All Hours.

ALSO BY HAL DUNCAN

VELLUM
The Book of All Hours: 1

HAL DUNCAN

INK

The Book of All Hours: 2

PAN BOOKS

First published 2007 by Macmillan

This edition published 2008 by Pan Books
an imprint of Pan Macmillan Ltd
Pan Macmillan, 20 New Wharf Road, London N1 9RR
Basingstoke and Oxford
Associated companies throughout the world
www.panmacmillan.com

ISBN 978-0-330-43838-4

1 3 5 7 9 8 6 4 2

A CIP catalogue record for this book is available from
the British Library.

Typeset by SetSystems Ltd, Saffron Walden, Essex
Printed and bound in Great Britain by
Mackays of Chatham plc, Chatham, Kent

Visit www.panmacmillan.com to read more about all our books
and to buy them. You will also find features, author interviews and
news of any author events, and you can sign up for e-newsletters
so that you're always first to hear about our new releases.

To Koré

VOLUME THREE

Hinter's Knights

Words of Rogue Desire

The Story, So Far

The story, so far removed in time and space and so far-fetched, seemed an exotic fabrication when I first heard it from my uncle's lips, those lips with a hint of sly smile at the upturned corners, just enough to crinkle crow's feet round his eyes. Uncle Reynard, the rake, the rogue. He'd heard of my first story sale, my desire to be a writer, and invited me to visit; he had a story for me, he said, a family legend worth a book at least.

I'd arrived at his tiny Bank Street flat to an exuberant welcome from his wagtailed mongrel, Koré, been settled into a seat on the black leather sofa with a gin and tonic and an ashtray on the occasional table to my side.

He lit up a cigarette for himself and began his tale.

– Your grandfather, Captain Jack Carter, he said, returned from the Great War a changed man. He'd seen the blood and mud of the Somme first-hand, ordered men to their deaths, ordered them shot for cowardice. He carried his memories as a secret burden, my mother said, one that he could never relieve himself of. One day, he received a telegram from an old professor of his – Hobbsbaum, I think his name was – and with only the briefest of farewells to his darling Anna who was heavy at the time with your father and myself, he left his pregnant wife and set out for the Middle East, never to be seen again.

Uncle Reynard paused for effect, manipulative old codger that he was.

– He disappeared into the Vellum, he said.

*

– Vellum? I said.

He took a sip of his gin and tonic.

– An unwritten page has such potential, don't you think? he said. As a writer? Anything could be shaped in ink upon that ... substrate. A million worlds waiting to be conjured by the feathery flick of a pen across paper. And even after you've graved your artifice of order onto that blank slate, don't you find that there are always still the spaces between the words, the possibilities you can still read in the gaps between the lines?

He smiled.

– You think I'm talking in metaphors. I am, I suppose. I'm trying to put this in a way you'll understand. A story doesn't just start at the beginning and trundle onwards in a straight line to the end. The same story can be – and *is* – told in different ways by different writers, each one taking their own path, branching the story out from one dimension to two. The same story can be – and *is* – retold in different ways by different generations. Revising the earlier drafts of those who came before, building our stories on the remnants of the past, those retellings give the tales a third dimension. Then as we read, following the trail of ink, we move in those three dimensions, skimming onwards and skipping back, diverted to the side here and there as we consider the invisible lateralities of what might have been, digging down into the strata of residual tales, the dead truths palimpsested by this new text.

– This is a metaphor for time, he said. This is the nature of the Vellum. Time has three dimensions, just like space.

The parallel worlds of quantum physics or alternate history were familiar enough ideas to me but the idea of ... *previous* realities ...

– I'm not sure I–

– We live in a tiny groove on the surface of a great sphere, he said, in a little valley of reality, seeing only ahead of us and behind us. There are other valleys in the Vellum, plains where time stretches out into wide fields of illusion, where you can easily stray from the path, stray so far that when you look back you see a past which is no longer yours. And there are rifts, fault lines where the shifting continents have folded stone, thrown elder worlds up into mountain chains that dwarf us with their primal majesty. Take a step out of

4

this world and you can find yourself with the scree of myths under your feet, staring at the fossilised feather of an angel's wing, embedded in the face of a cliff in front of you. Just a second. Wait there.

He pushed himself up from his chair and left the room. Through the open door I could see him cross the square hallway of his one-bedroom flat – his bachelor pad, as he called it – and enter his study. A moment later he returned with what looked like a humidor, the size of a shoe-box, maybe a little larger, every inch of its surface carved with intricate abstractions, its lid hinged and clasped in brass.

– Your grandfather disappeared into the Vellum, he said. But he sent this back to us. Your father wanted to burn it, but I stopped him. I thought you should have it. Your *grandfather* thought you should have it.

He laid it on my lap.

– He says so on the first page.

I unclicked the clasp, the hinge of the box creaking as I opened the lid. Inside it was crammed full of papers – loose scraps and notebooks – pages yellowed and leather bindings brittle as autumn leaves. It smelled of dust and decay – a hint of sulphur, I thought – and under my touch I could feel a grit of sand or salt crusting the smooth but crumbling surfaces of cured skin and bleached parchment.

As my uncle had said, the page on top – half a page, actually, torn roughly from some cheap book and used as a note – said that this mystery was meant for me.

For my grandson, Reynard, it read, *unborn and unwritten as of yet. May you make of this folly a future free of destiny. Bind the Book into a book.*

Jack Carter, Palestine, 1929.

– I don't understand, I said. A future free of destiny? What book?

– The Book of All Hours, said my uncle. From what I can gather, what I can make sense of in there, it's ... the blueprint of this Vellum, of all reality, all *unreality*, graved into eternal certainty in a grimoire that might have been written by God himself, if you believe in that sort of thing. A manual of mathematics and metaphysics, written in the language of the angels – the Cant he calls it – the language that binds reality.

5

– The Book of All Hours? I said.

– Read it and see, he said.

Once upon a Time

– Once upon a time, Jack had said to me, there was a book called *Once upon a Time*; and it was *all about* a boy called Jack. But Jack, well, he didn't really give a flying fuck for books, being more into toy guns and shit, so he just took his felt-tip pens and scribbled all over it until you couldn't read a word in all the mess of ink, and boy did he get fucking whipped for it.

He'd looked at me, there in the garden.

– That's the story of my life, he'd said, just a mess of ink. And that's the Book of All Hours, Guy, the fucking Book of All fucking Hours. That's how I got my scars.

I'd thought of the first words of the Book: *In the beginning.* From the Hobben word, *bereshit*, which, translated into Versid, gave the first chapter its common name: *Genesis.*

Once upon a time, I'd thought, was probably a fair enough translation for that book of origins, of the Havens and the Aerth summoned into existence by the breath of Zeus over the void. It seems a good enough way to start this account.

Once upon a time there was a boy named Jack.

I met Jack in Poudre Valley Hospital in Laramie, North Manitu, where he had been admitted for treatment to his wounds, and where in my capacity as consultant psychologist I'd been called in to assess him as a suicide risk. A lattice of scars across his chest told a history of self-harm or abuse, but the more visible signs were ... sickening. Three days before, Jack had taken a pair of garden shears and used them to cut off his wings, this after removing his horns with a hacksaw and a power-sander, his file told me. Sitting there on the edge of the bed, facing out the window, with the dressing on his back clearly visible beneath his gown, and with the bandages around his head – a shock of fire-blond hair sticking out above like burning corn – Jack told me that he'd never actually had wings ... not really.

– No horns either, he said.

Body dysmorphia was my immediate thought.

Then he told me he was a changeling.

At that first meeting with Jack, I did not bother taking notes. In such circumstances I usually prefer a conversational approach; it helps the patient to relax and open up, puts them more at ease than they would be with a clip-boarded stranger's more orthodox and official interrogation; also it allows for a more informal observation on my part. I remember noticing the lack of any cards or flowers in the room, the spartan environment of a patient without well-wishers, in keeping with his distant air. No wings to fold around himself to warm him in the Hinter's chill.

– No family, he said. Not in this world, Doc. I'm a changeling, you see. I'm an orphan Orpheus, looking for my . . . Eurydike.

Later I was to learn that Jack's parents were unknown, this son of theirs abandoned to Social Services, shuffled from foster home to foster home – his records lost in a fire, the administrator of one orphanage would tell me. Maybe, one might almost think, he *did* slip through from some other world. Maybe he *did* belong elsewhere, elsewhen.

But at that first meeting I just looked around his room for any accoutrements of identity. The only object that spoke of comfort either desired or given was a copy of the Gideon's Book of All Hours laid open on the bedside cabinet. It didn't strike me as unusual, here in the Midwest of Amorica, heartland of a culture steeped in evangelical faith. One of the questions I was asked most often by colleagues attempting friendly conversation was what church I'd gone to back in Albion. I'd hem and haw and confess that, actually, I wasn't a believer. They'd look shocked for a second – more confused than shocked, really, not understanding why on earth one would not want the love of Our Lord Adonis in one's life – then the topic would be changed.

The Book simply showed that Jack was not entirely divorced from the world around him.

*

– You've been reading the Book, I say.

I sit down on the edge of the bed and pick the Gideon's up off the cabinet to see what parable or prophecy he's in the midst of. These little things are often good indicators of a patient's state of mind, you see: depressives tend to like the Book of Hob, identifying with that most hapless, hopeless man and using his long-suffering tenacity as a stick to beat themselves with in comparison; the neurotic, on the other hand, tend to focus on the New Testament, seeking the constant support, the affirmation and reaffirmation, of an ever-loving Christ; schizoids, of course, always go for Revelations.

Jack's copy is open at the Song of Salamander, the only part of the Book I've ever really had much time for myself, I have to say, neither parable nor prophecy but simply poetry.

– *Let him kiss me with the kisses of his mouth,* says Jack – the first line of the Song of Salamander, the Song of Songs.

He turns to look at me and I notice the flecks of silvery fire that shimmer in his blue irises, the glints of gold. *He's a faery,* I realise. It clicks into place, this delusion of his that he's from another world, from the world of wingless graey, in fact. I imagine his past. Some Angelo-Satyr mother looks at her child for the first time and sees that shimmer to its skin, a glint in its eye just a little more sensuous than it should be. Did she herself hate it or was there some beer-swilling father, scattering dishes from the kitchen counter with a brutal sweep of his arm, spreading his great black wings in fury and threat over her? *Get that thing out of my house.* A child growing up in the care of those who did not care, realising he was different from his peers.

Christ, it's only a few weeks since the murder of Thomas Messenger shamed the town, the state, the whole of Amorica. How cosmopolitan is it here, even in a college town of frat boys and keggers?

So he's a changeling, he decides. He's not even a part of this world that would murder an innocent like Thomas Messenger simply for being a faery.

I try to lead him through this rationalisation, this explanation, but he cuts me off the moment the murdered student's name comes out of my mouth, with a look of such pain and anger and . . . Zeus, I understand a whole lot more.

– I knew him as Puck, he says with a voice so thick with swallowed sorrow I can hardly understand the words.

Jack's boyfriend, Puck, had been lost to him on a hillside that Evenfall – Octochre 16th to be precise – beaten to death by two fay-hating thugs who'd picked him up in a bar on the promise of a threesome.

– That's when I knew, Jack had said. Death opens up your eyes, Doc. If it doesn't close them and put pennies on the fucking lids.

We sat on a wooden bench in the hospital garden, myself with my wings tucked tight under a fleece-lined anorak, huddled against the bitter Damnuary air, Jack in his dressing gown hung open, cord dangling loose. He seemed impervious to the cold, too fired up as he was with his anger.

He blew a plume of steam into the air and peered at me; he knew this was the day of my meeting with the chief of staff, knew that I'd be leaving here to give my recommendation for his future here or in the outside world – commitment as a hazard to himself, medication for depression or psychosis, keep him in for further observation, or cut him loose and let him sink or swim.

– Christ, Guy, I'm not going to kill myself, he said. I'd rather live just to spite the fuckers. Flight or fight? Fuck, I'm going to light fires under their fucking feet.

– I started to remember it all at the funeral, says Jack. I was thinking about how we first met. It was in this Social Studies class. We just clicked, like we'd known each other all our lives. At the funeral I started to remember that we *had. All* our lives.

He sits in one of the leather armchairs I have positioned on either side of the window in my office, facing each other for just such conversations, just such confessions. It's our third or fourth meeting. Sorry, I find it hard to keep a straight line to my thoughts these days.

– We were like children playing in the Illusion Fields, he continues. Let's pretend. One day we'd be soldiers in the First World War – Captain 'Mad' Jack Carter, Private Thomas Messenger.

Another day, I'd be a seraphim sent to hunt him down across this weird graey version of Amorica. We'd lie in bed together and go to sleep in this world, only to wake up in a town called Endhaven, amongst black-suited refugees from a nanotech apocalypse. We've been shepherds in Arcadia and rent-boys on the streets of Sodom, Doc. I've crossed deserts wider than the world because he dared me. I've led armies to destruction because he was in danger. I remembered it all – Christ, it was like being born again – as I was standing there at his funeral, listening to the Minister spout his bullshit. We've lived a million lives and always ended up together, whatever fold of the Vellum we were in.

What he's describing is a psychotic break, a retreat from the horror of reality into elaborate fantasies of eternity.

– And in these other . . . *folds*, I say, Puck didn't die?

– Oh, no, says Jack. He always dies. You should know that, Reynard. You should remember too.

The Undecided World

It's three in the morning and I should be in bed, but I've always been a night owl, so instead I'm getting out of my car and crunching through the snow into the all-night convenience store to buy a pack of cigarettes I could probably wait until tomorrow morning for. Melissa's on duty again and I smile.

– Hi, Melissa.

She's in her early twenties, drop-dead gorgeous and a total flirt for my accent. First time I came in, she was chatting to a friend when I asked her if they stocked Regals. She started interrogating me about where I was from, what I was doing here, how long I was staying, charmingly excited by this stranger in a strange land.

– Say my name, she said finally.

– Melissa? I said, confused.

– Say it again.

– Melissa?

– Gosh, it sure sounds so much better the way you say it than the folks round here.

*

Outside, I tap a cigarette out of the packet and light it before I slip back into the driver's seat of my car, pull the door shut, blow out a billow of smoke. I reach up to adjust the rear-view mirror and, leaning into it, I see my own reflection. I don't have any horns. I don't have to touch my shoulders to know that my wings are also absent. I have a passing notion that there's something wrong about this – should I be disturbed? – but then I realise that, of course, of course, this is just what Jack was telling me about. We all live simultaneously in a myriad of folds, those on Aerth dreaming of Havens for their dead, those in the Havens dreaming of Aerths for those alive. So, then, there's nothing really strange about the cats-eyes looking back at me from the rear-view mirror; it all makes perfect sense.

The world just hasn't decided which reality it wants to be.

The next morning, as I potter through my daily ritual of Earl Grey and waffles with maple syrup, I'll notice the pack of cigarettes on the kitchen table and remember the dream and the normality that inspired it. I'll remember this feeling of satori I had in my slumber – *the world hasn't decided* – and find it funny. My subconscious, it seems, is rather enamoured of Jack's delusion.

I'll shake it off, of course. I'll look in the mirror at my horns and wings, my reassuringly human eyes, and all will be right with the world. Jack's psychosis is just that – psychosis. It's strange that in these other folds he has imagined for the two of them Puck dies; it jars with the usual pattern of denial delusions; but I'll figure it out in time, as we carry on our sessions.

I don't realise that more dreams like this will come, more frequent, more intense, over the next few weeks, until I am no longer sure that they are dreams at all.

– I think you know I'm right, says Jack. You're just not willing to take the plunge yet. You're just not willing to admit it.

– So you're saying that *you're* sane? It's the rest of us who're crazy?

He shrugs, grins.

– One of the folds I knew Puck in – Endhaven – it had these windmills up on a hill outside of town. He told me once he used to

11

imagine they were giants when he was a kid and I said, well, you know, they might be. It's like Don Quixote ... but like in that movie where what's-his-face thinks he's Sherlock Holmes in 1970s New York. George C. Scott. He says to his shrink, you know, maybe Quixote was right. They might just be windmills. But they might be giants. I think maybe they're both. Maybe the world hasn't decided yet. They could – what's up?

My pen is stopped over my notepad. *The world hasn't decided yet.* My jaw may not be literally dropped, but the shock of the synchronicity is clearly showing on my face. I shake my head, try to laugh it off.

– Nothing, I say.

That night I have another dream.

Insanity is a City

Insanity is a city, he thinks, a haunting, hounding maze of monsters given stone flesh. Madness made real. Angels rumbling with demons. Gods with wings of steel sweeping down out of the skies to scatter humanity to dust.

He staggers out of the alley, coat gripped closed with white-knuckled hands. Behind him, the angel's screams are dying into a gurgle of blood in a throat, drowning in the baying of the mob. Insanity is a city, he thinks.

He walks down cobbled streets, through shaded courtyards, wide plazas of marble flagstones with stone benches and ornamental fountains, barren trees and snow-mantled statues. There are tram stops, bus stops, but he has no money for this fold, so he just watches where the rattling dinosaur-machines go lumbering, and follows the ones whose frontboards proclaim Stadde Cintrale, until he reaches what may or may not be the City Centre with its shops and arcades, pedestrian precincts, a tourist centre with racks of maps and bus routes. He picks up one of each – thirty, forty of them – filling his pockets with numbered trails that snake through this district or that quarter. All he wants is to find somewhere he feels safe. He has nothing here but the clothes on his back and a book whose only purpose now is to carry the reminder of his name, scrawled on its frontispiece.

He clutches the Book of All Hours to his chest, his last connection with his own identity.

It used to be a book of maps, he's sure. He's sure he can remember a time when it was a book of maps, each turned page showing the world at an exponentially increasing scale — streets, cities, countries, continents, and larger still, impossibly larger, vast fields of reality like the surface of some gas giant, page after page scaling up to inconceivable distances. A guidebook to eternity, to the Vellum.

He remembers graving human lives as glyphs upon its parchment.

He remembers cramming its yellowed surface with sigils that crawled across the page even as the people that they marked moved through their daily lives.

He remembers these gravings multiplying into a storm of ink, obscuring the terrain drawn underneath, skittering here and there as if they sought to tell, in combination, some strange, shifting story of Evenfall.

Then the Hinter came, and he lost . . . what did he lose?

The last time he looked, every page in the Book of All Hours was as blank as the white waste of snow and bone around him, featureless plains of vellum stretching out beneath his fingers, his own glyph fading to grey. Sitting at the last remnants of his burnt-down campfire, hypothermia blurring his mind, he'd scrawled his name in charcoal on the opening page before passing out, a message to whoever found his body.

— *Es mortu*, he'd heard a voice say.

— *Neh, es liffen.*

Then he'd woken up in the city, in a hospital of sorts. He'd taken his clothes out of the locker by his bed, put them on, picked up the Book and just walked out the door, into a city at the end of time, where mobs of teenagers broke the wings of angels in the alleyways, tortured them for sport.

A homeless man sits huddled at the entrance to a covered escalator which glides down, step turning over step, to the subway station at the foot of an elaborate iron bridge of electric candelabra streetlights and wrought heraldry emblazonings. Posters for gigs and clubs peel from its square stone pillars and Reynard watches the people passing into and out of the brown perspex entrance with its garish orange U for *underground*; some of them wear suits, others dress casual, but all of them look soft, middle-class – even the ones in ripped, badged thriftwear. Across the bridge a Gothic spire rises up from among a jumble of sandstone walls, slate roofs and branches. A pine furniture shop sits beside the stone steps that lead down, parallel to the escalator, to the car park and grass patched with snow around the subway station. It's a university district of lecturers and students, professional bohemians and bohemian professionals. The street-map that he carries shows a large park down there to the south, nestling in a nook of river, a good place to sleep rough if it comes to that, if he can't find a doorway to shelter him from the Hinter night.

He's standing, leaning on the bridge, and trying to stop his shakes – as he has been for the last ten minutes – when he feels the hand on his shoulder.

    – *Nove migres?*

It's the homeless man. Reynard shrugs, shakes his head, blithers desperate apologies, his body still shaking with that tension between laughter and tears. *I don't understand. I don't understand.* He trails his fingers through his hair.

    – *Peregrim nove en de stadde, ev? Tu ne sprash lingischt?*

    – No, he sort of understands. No, I don't speak the language.

And the man reaches into his cup and gives him, with a toothless grin, a goldish coin.

    – *Per kave*, he says, pointing over the bridge at God knows what. *Kave, ev?*

He lifts the cup to his lips, tilts it once, twice. Kave.

Reynard nods dumbly, realises that the tension has released itself; he's both laughing and crying as he says – *Thank you. Thank you.*

Out of Fable and Folklore

My last meeting with Jack was even less official than the first, not even a meeting as much as a farewell. It was months later and the wounds on his back had long since healed. Apart from the scarred stumps on his forehead and the eerie absence of wings, which gave him the somewhat eldritch appearance of a graey straight out of fable and folklore, he was quite healthy, physically speaking. Stretching his arms out wide and arching his back as he stood just outside the sliding glass doors of the hospital entrance, as if gathering the morning-fresh air and the future to him, he had a limber grace, moving the way an athlete does, entirely at one with his body. He looked over his shoulder as the porter whirled his wheelchair away, back through the doors into the hospital.

– Thank fuck, Jack had said. Christ, I'm not a fucking cripple.

I'd shrugged, smiled wryly. He'd complained about being wheeled all the way to the door.

– Hospital policy, Jack. Insurance.

– I'm fucking fine, he'd said.

I knew, of course, that he still considered himself a changeling, but by now I also knew that he was not entirely insane in this respect. A little, but not entirely. No more so than I myself.

– I'm fucking fine, says Jack. Peachy keen.

As he stretches, rolling his shoulder-blades like a rower, for some reason I have 'Could We Start Again Please?' from *Adonis Christ Superstar* running through my head. Not exactly the sort of music you hear on the hospital radio here, not in this corner of Amorica so touchy about faith and blasphemy. A white cloud condenses in the chill morning air, the whistle of the tune under my breath. Sometimes, I must confess, I miss the old country and its heathen irreverence; I want to hijack the radio and pump the Sex Pistols out across the wards at full blast. I told Jack once about that idea and he nearly pissed himself laughing.

– So what the fuck are you doing here? he'd asked. I mean, what the fuck is an old public-school rebel doing out here in the Midwest . . . in the middle of fucking nowhere?

– I rather suppose I was looking for a fresh start, I'd said.

A sloughing rustle of snow slips from the overloaded branch of a tree to land on the bonnet of a car – sorry, the *hood* of a car. Beyond the parking lot, the mist and the shadows of the treeline meld into a bleak grey nothing.

The Hinter is harsher here too than it was back home.

*

– You should go home, says Jack. Back to Albion. You know you don't really belong here. You, me, Puck . . . we never belonged here.

I don't answer. Later I'll go back to my office and I'll sit there looking at the copy of the Book of All Hours I keep on the shelf behind my chair, now lifted down and laid upon my desk. Later I'll lock my door and twirl the blind closed to hide me from any passing prurient eyes and from the backwards golden lettering on the glass which reads *Guy Reynard Carter, MD, Psychological Consultant*. I'll open a window and I'll drag my chair into the centre of the room, so I can stand on it to lever the batteries from the smoke detector, so I can have a cigarette as I leaf through the pages of the Book. Later.

Right now I don't want to think about what I've learned from Jack in the two and a half months he's been my patient. Right now I don't want to think of the realities of the Havens out there in the Hinter, not some mythical paradise, some pie in the sky when you die, but Havens as real as any Haven can be, ruled by gods as real as any god can be. A vast realm of eternity and scattered fortress worlds within it – Havens – like this one. So I just throw a question back at him.

– What about you? I say. Where will *you* go?

He shrugs.

– Maybe the question should be *when*, he says.

– You don't notice how the world keeps changing? says Jack.

It's our fourth – maybe fifth – session and he's starting to really open up, it seems. We're really making progress, digging down into his changeling delusion and the cause of it, why he insists he's not a faery but a graey, stolen at birth from another world, from another fold of this Vellum. They altered him to fit in, he thinks, added the wings and the horns so he didn't look like a freak here. *Or something*. Sometimes it seems so clear, he says, but he keeps forgetting. Like his memory is being fucked with. I've just finished telling him that this kind of denial is as natural as the desire that makes him different from all the other good ole boys – the White Angelo-Satyr Protestants who inhabit most of Midwestern Amorica. It's genetic, I've been telling him; he was born a faery, and all the born-agains and bookthumpers can't change him, shouldn't even try. There's nothing wrong with his renegade lust, no matter what they say. He doesn't need to be cured.

– Jack, all you have to do is look in a mirror. Look at the glimmer of your eyes, the golden glamour of your skin. You're a faery.

He shakes his head. Condensation on the window of my office, flurrying snow beyond it, the world outside is whitewashed, a blank page.

– Christ, Doc, he says. I wish I knew the word that would wake you, make you realise that you're living in a fucking dreamtime. I'd sing it from the fucking rooftops.

Dead Channels, White Noise

I pull the car over to the side of the road, where the signpost proudly proclaims that we are now entering North Manitu. A picture of a cowboy in denims and checked shirt welcomes us, the archetypal Marlboro man with a lasso looping over his head, eagle wings outstretched behind him. Beyond the sign the landscape is low rolling hills, barren trees and snow.

I lean over the back of the seat.

– Where are we? What does the Book say?

Puck lounges across the back seat, head in Jack's lap, the Book of All Hours open in his own, a joint dangling from his lips.

– Fucked if I know, he says. This thing's gone weird.

Puck turns the Book towards me and I see that it's changed; the pages that once held maps to guide us through this endless Vellum have long since been made illegible by my annotations, but this is new. The annotations squirm and wriggle on the page as if alive. Maybe we should turn back, I think. Try another route. But the clouds rolling in behind us are the grey of wet slate, and there are rumbles in the distance. If we just push on, then with a little luck we might reach a motel before the night comes in, before the Hinter sweeps over us.

– When did it change? I say. How far back?

Puck shakes his head. He looks worried.

– I can't remember. Shit, Guy, I can't remember.

*

I sit at my kitchen table in my boxer shorts, smoking a cigarette and drinking a glass of water, flicking through the dead channels on the television. The cable's on the blink, it seems, probably a power-out in a transmitter somewhere – I don't know, some technical fault which probably won't get fixed until the weather's cleared; it never does. Anyway, I can't get CNN, ABC or any of the nationals, only the local public access and North Manitu State TV with its adverts for farming goods emporiums that sell everything you could need . . .

– My tractor goes with my hat! a madman celebrates.

I've just woken from another of the dreams and I could use some mind-numbing TV to fill my thoughts with white noise. I dreamed that Thomas Messenger and I were travelling across these folds Jack talks about. We'd been travelling forever using the Book of All Hours as a guide. It wasn't the Book I know, no Titania and Oberon in Eden, no Adonis dying on the cross for our sins; instead, it was all maps and arcane squiggles I'd learned to decipher over the eons of our travel. Only the Book had changed and now we were lost, ended up stopping in a motel for the night.

I switch off the TV and put the remote down on the counter, knocking over a salt cellar as I do so. I take a pinch of the spilled salt and flick it over my left shoulder out of habitual superstition, to guard against what spirits lurking in the night I don't know.

– Follow me, says Jack. Come on.

He takes off down the hospital corridor, striding forwards, turning to walk backwards now and then as he urges me to keep up. He lopes down the steps of the stairwell with the rhythm of a cantering horse, heading down to the basement level. I protest, try to tell him that he's not supposed to be down here. This area's for staff only.

– Jack, I say. Where do you think you're going?

The door of the morgue swings shut as he whirls inside, and I push through after him, sighing. The complaint stops on my lips as I find myself in a room that stretches out in front of me and to both sides, forever. Cadavers lie on slabs in rows and columns that cannot be counted there's so many of them. Wisps of steam rise from open mouths where, here and there, a sheet is folded down. I've never actually been down here in all my years working at the hospital, I realise; I've never needed to. Given that it's as cold as it is creepy, I'm quite glad of that.

– What is it, Jack? I say. What's so important?

– You don't think there's something strange here? he says. All these bodies? There's millions of them, Guy, millions.

I look around, unfazed.

– We're in the morgue, I say. What do you expect?

– Look at their faces, he says.

Every one of them, I realise, is Puck's.

I wake up crying.

You understand, I was there when they brought Thomas Messenger into the hospital, having a fly smoke in the ambulance bay outside the ER as the van pulled up, siren blaring, and the place erupted into a chaos of paramedics and doctors, clattering trolley, swinging doors. I caught a glimpse of his face, bloodied and broken, but with streaks of clear skin visible under his eyes where the tears had washed away the gore.

I didn't recognise him.

I walked past the room where he was on the ventilator, lying in a coma for a full week; I looked in and saw him there, his swollen face under the mask, and still I didn't recognise him. I watched the news report as they gradually revealed the horror of this hate crime, and they showed him in a family photo, smiling, with his green hair and his kid horns. I still didn't recognise him.

I'd never met Thomas Messenger. I'd never met Puck in this fold.

Rosewater and Liquorice

Reynard sits in the café, sipping at the thick sweet tar somewhere between Italian espresso and Turkish coffee. Hints of rosewater and liquorice, bitter sediment at the bottom. On the tabletop, the book is open in front of him, at the first page, where his charcoal name is smeared. He's just about to turn the page to see – just to see – if it has anything to say, when a hand comes down on top of his own and the man with dirty-blond hair scrapes a chair up beside him, sits in it and says:

– Sure and ye'd be better not to do that right now, not here where everyone and anyone could see it, like. Because you and me both know what that book is, sure – Christ and I could smell the angel skin a mile off – and, well, let's just say there's some as would cut your right arm off just to get their greasy fookin fingers on it. Not *their* right arm, mind. Yours.

The man peels Reynard's hand from the book, picks it up and closes it, slides it back across the table towards him.

– So ye'd be best to keep that tucked away for now. Christ, don't ye know that there's a fookin war on? The Covenant's fallen. Every fookin angel bastard wants to be fookin top dog now and you're flashing the fookin Book about like it's yer journal of wanky teenage poetry, by Christ.

Reynard puts the book in his pocket, numb with questions.

– King Finn, says the man. So you'll be Guy Fox then, or is it Reynard yer calling yerself just now? Sure and I don't suppose it matters, does it? It's all the fookin same.

He waves at a waiter.

– *Kave, grazzis.*

Reynard finds himself shaking hands.

The Irishman settles back in his chair.

– No doubt yer a little confused and all, having only just arrived right in the middle of things, but sure and isn't that life for ye? It'd be nice to think that the little folk like yerself and yours truly would be in on the grand schemes of the powers-that-be right from the off, but sadly that's not the way it works. No, we're just the ones wake up one day and realise that the world's gone fookin mental and it's us that has to deal with the big bag of shite the powers-that-be have only gone and got us all up to our eyeballs in.

He takes out a pack of unfiltered Camels, taps them on the table and pulls a cigarette out with his lips.

– Right so. All ye have to know just now is that Thomas is dead. Sure and ye remember Thomas, right? Nice lad, bit light on his feet and short on the common sense but a heart of fookin gold, ye know?

Reynard remembers.

— North Manitu, he says. Laramie.

— Fookin everywhere, says King Finn. They killed him fookin everywhere.

— Who? says Reynard.

Finn points the cigarette at him.

— Jesus, but isn't that the million-dollar question? Who and why and when and where and what the fook has his dying done to the whole fookin Vellum. One little thread and the whole fookin thing falls apart, Christ. Sure and who'd have thought a short-arse fairy with his head in the fookin clouds would've left such a bloody big hole in reality?

He takes a book of matches out of his packet, tears off a match and folds the flap over to wedge the match tight against the sandpaper as he flicks it into a hiss of flame. Tobacco crackles as he lights the cigarette.

— But if I could make sense of it to ye here and now, I would, believe me, but, ye see, that's your job — if ye'll take it, like. And seeing as how yer carrying the Book about with ye, I hate to say it, but I think ye'll find it's what yer meant to do. To make sense of it all, like.

The Irishman takes his coffee from the waiter, smiles and nods his thanks.

— Cause sure and it doesn't make any fookin sense to the rest of us, he says. The Evenfall was bad enough, but this is fookin chaos. Fookin Hinter. Jesus, but I hate the fookin Hinter.

God Bless Amorica

— You know it's always Hinter, says Jack. You realise that, right?

— It might seem that way, I say, but it's only a quarter of the year, Jack.

— Yeah? he says. So what did you do last summer? You didn't take a vacation, did you?

— Well, no, I didn't get a chance, I say. Couldn't get away.

— So you just worked through it, right? And the summer before that?

– Well, the hospital was busy. I ended up–

– Really? Christ, when was the last time you had a vacation, Guy? When was the last time you were out of state? How long have you been working in this hospital?

– Five years, I think. Give or take. Why?

– Have you been out of state at all in any of those years? Have you even been out of town? When was the last time you sat in a park and watched a butterfly?

I smile. It's true, I realise, that I haven't had a summer vacation in all the time I've been working here, but I have had trips outside of town. Why, I have crystal-clear memories of returning from a conference over in ... what's-it-called? Anyway, I remember stopping off on the way home, at the Safe Haven Motel out on the interstate.

I hand the clerk behind the counter my griftcard and wait as she swipes it through the machine, watches the till monitor for the all-clear. My fingers are crossed in my jacket pocket; the card belongs in another fold entirely, but it should, I hope, be able to adapt to this old system, stalling for time while it hacks the network, finds a suitable host and sets up an account with all the credit we'll need. Looks just like a normal Visa too. I used to feel a little guilty about this scam, but it's rare for two folds to have exactly the same currency, and even in eternity we need to eat and sleep.

And I *am* tired. We must have driven for forty hours straight with the night roaring in at our back and only the Hinter wilderness around us, fields with split-rail fences half-buried in snow, advertising hoardings for beer and cigarettes. Churches with flags. Crosses aglow with Christmas lights that are just a little too much like dots of flame for my liking. Finally we found the Safe Haven Motel here on the interstate. *God Bless Amorica* lettered on the *Vacancies* sign.

As the receipt prints with a rattling chatter from the antiquated machine, I accept the card back with a smile and a *thank you*, take the keycards for our rooms and hand two of them over my shoulder to Jack, who passes one on to Puck.

*

– Of course I've been out of town, I say. For a conference. I was over in . . .

I trail off, drawing a blank on the name of the city just thirty miles north of Laramie.

– You should try taking a trip, says Jack. See how far you get before the fog makes you turn back.

– The road's closed today, I say. They don't think they'll get it open for a week or so. But maybe next week I'll take a run up to . . .

I *still* can't remember the name of that city just down the road. But I *do* remember going there for the conference. At least, I remember the Hinter conditions getting so bad on the way back home it seemed insane to risk the final stretch, better to stop somewhere and wait it out till morning. I remember seeing the Safe Haven Motel on the edge of town, lit up in the night. God Bless Amorica, indeed.

– Why did you come here, Guy? says Jack. *When* did you come here?

– You know, it's nice to see young men who're not ashamed to show their faith, says the clerk. Too many *cynics* in the world, if you ask me.

There's a confused moment before she points at the Book under Puck's arm; and I'm still a little confused, to be honest, as I mutter some vague but amiable affirmations. Upstairs in my room, that confusion is partly answered, partly deepened, by the Gideon's Book of All Hours I find in the bedside cabinet. The Book has always been this singular and secret thing we carry, Puck and Jack and I, through folds where no one even knows its name. Now here it suddenly shows up as a commonplace, a giveaway Gospel in a motel room. I don't know what worries me more – the printed pretender on the bedside cabinet, or the fact that the real Book has changed as if to camouflage itself among the fakes. Or that the three of us have also changed to fit into this fold, it seems, in a way that's never happened until now.

My reflection in the window has grey wings and ram's horns curling from my forehead, an image of some strange sprite ghosted over the winter-dark night outside. Jack's pinions are golden-brown, an eagle's. Puck, leaning against the jamb of the connecting door-way, has an iridescent shimmer to his peacock wings, and somehow I know it is a good thing they were hidden from the clerk beneath his oversized parka.

I have a bad feeling about this fold.

– What the fuck's going on with the separate rooms for me and Puck? asks Jack. You going Biblebasher on us, Guy?

I have the Book open on my lap, the Gideon's in my hand, comparing the identical texts. *In the beginning*...

– Just trust me on this one, Jack, I say. It's only for one night; we'll move on tomorrow morning ... early. So go get some sleep. I want to try and figure out what's going on here.

The Boundaries of Thought

Reynard moves into his small flat in the West End university district and, funded by the crazy Irishman, he begins his job. He papers the wall with the maps, the bus routes, the tram routes as a start, lay-ing them out so that they overlap and building them up in layers, realising quickly that none of them actually quite work together. In isolation they make sense, but they contradict each other. This road is on one, not on another; on a third it's in a different place entirely. Two buses follow the same route but have stops labelled with street names in entirely different orders. He starts to think of traffic lights here as sitting not at junctions but at disjunctions; while one set is green the flow of one reality goes on, only to halt when the light turns red and a different set of truths pull away to stream straight on or round the corner, horns blaring as one cuts in in front of another.

A consensus reality with no consensus, he thinks. A world in flux because it's trying to be all things to everyone.

He learns the language – the lingischt – and buys a library of opposing histories from the second-hand bookshops in the area, ripping out pages – more maps, geopolitical, cultural – marking the boundaries of thought in the spread of shelves around his flat – mathematics, physics, geology, chemistry, biology, psychology, archaeology, philosophy, metaphysics, pataphysics – spreading out of the study and into his hall, his living room, his bedroom, pages from volume after volume of encyclopaedia or telephone directory. News-sheets and printouts from the Web. Transcripts of interviews he holds in cafés with anyone who cares to talk about their memories of home, of where they were before they came to the city.

– What's the last thing you remember? he asks.

– The Evenfall, they say.

As he builds his model of this mutual dreamtime he also hacks it back, scoring out inconsistencies, irrelevances. His methods grow more experimental. He takes a sacred religious text and cuts it up with scissors, shuffling the phrases round until his suspicion is confirmed; it corresponds exactly with a Victorian cookbook of two thousand recipes, most involving lamb and red wine sauce. He burns copy after copy of the same dictionary, and with each one the only scorched fragment that survives is a tiny piece of page containing the word *lexicon*. No definition, just the word. He scans books or downloads them from the Web, runs the texts through automatic translation programmes, comparative searches, stylistic analyses. It takes him a while, of course, but he has eternity. He has eternity to understand what lies at the heart of the city's madness.

In the end, he has a theory. It's not entirely consistent and it's nowhere near complete, but it's a damn sight more coherent and comprehensive than the world around them and it runs from about two million years BC up to August 4th, 2017. The day the Evenfall broke the boundaries between reality and dream.

Now all he has to do is write it.

The Book lies on the desk, his charcoal name now long since faded, barely a grey shadow. He picks up the needlepen, clips the ink cartridge in and flicks it on. It's special ink, according to Finn and the girl; he has a theory but he doesn't ask too many questions about where they got it, who they got it from.

– You're ready? she says.

The girl, Anna – Anaesthesia, she calls herself – is dangerous, he's sure. King Finn only wants to see an end to the fighting, but she has a hard, warrior's stare, tough as the leather armour that she wears, a latter-day Joan of Arc. It's why he doesn't want to ask where she got the ink from, *who* she got the ink from.

He runs the buzzing needlepen over the grey shadow of his name — or rather the composite of various possibilities he's long since settled on as his name — and it colours in, deep scarlety-purply black:

Guy Reynard Carter.

Above that he traces out the title in ornate and grandiose calligraphy, in keeping with the sheer audacity of the venture:

The Book of All Hours.

— I'm ready, he says.

Beside the title page of this new, revised edition, the pile of foolscap-size sheets of blank vellum rises thick and high as four or five phonebooks piled one on top of another — scrap for his workings, loose leaves where he can make all the errors he wants. He takes the top sheet from the pile.

He doesn't ask where she got the angel skin either.

Red Ink over Printed Black

I lie, at the hearing, about Jack. I lie through my teeth, telling the chief of staff that the self-mutilation was a simple cry for attention, precipitated largely by his exclusion from the news reports, the prejudice that same absence implied even in the outpourings of shock and sympathy directed at the family. He felt a burning need to physicalise his grief and rage over the murder, I explain. Repression and denial. Sublimated sorrow. He's gone through the grieving process now, well on the road to recovery. He's still a bit fractured, conflicted, but all he needs is therapy and time to heal. Given time, a new whole Jack will emerge.

I can't keep him here, you see. No more than I could persuade Puck and Jack to wait out the Hinter indoors in my apartment, hidden from fay-bashing morons driven by fear and hatred strong enough to warp a road map to eternity into a rulebook for damnation. No more than I could stop myself from slipping, once they'd set out — *for an adventure,* Jack said — into this simulation of life I'm only now emerging from. I don't think I can stay here myself

. . . assuming I can leave, that is. One man's haven is another man's hell.

– You're free to go, I tell Jack after the meeting.

– You're shitting me.

– Nope. I told them you were sane.

He laughs, looks at me in shock – *you fucking believe me* – and laughs again. I suppose I wasn't entirely lying, any more than Jack is entirely insane.

Up on a desolate hillside just outside of town, a split-rail fence is burning, petrol flames flicking high into the sky, a bonfire and a personal pyre of rage against the Hinter night and a haven of hate. I can hear him whoop and holler, roar, as he swings the petrol can around his head and throws it far off into the darkness, but Jack himself is little more than a silhouette. As he throws his arms out wide like a scarecrow, screaming obscenities, profanities, blasphemies, there's a hellish truth to him, I think.

And as his cathartic inferno lights a slant of angular face, his obscenities, his profanities, his blasphemies turn to sobs and laughter, invocations of his lost love that break my heart as I sit here in the car, the engine idling, my hands shaking so much I know I cannot write those actual words of rogue desire without dissolving.

– You know you don't really belong here, Jack had said.

I hadn't answered then, because I didn't really have an answer, and I still don't. I sit in my office now after seeing him off, cigarette in hand as I leaf through my copy of the Book. It's useless as a guidebook now – useless *here* anyway; it doesn't tell me where I am, where I might be going – just a morass of myth and morphology. But maybe it'll change again once I get it away from this place. If it doesn't . . . well, I write these words in it now, scribbling in red ink over printed black: an annotation, an exegesis of Puck's murder, Jack's madness and my awakening, to bury the hateful dogma in.

It doesn't belong in my Book of All Hours.

In the beginning, the first chapter of the Book of All Hours begins, in this world. But how can you begin a story with the beginning of all beginnings? How can we understand a story that claims to be the beginning of all stories? Better to simply pick a random point in time and space, in all the vellum and the ink that covers it, and begin.

– Jump in, I say.

Jack shakes his head. Hands on the roof above my head, he leans down to the window, weight on one leg, a cocky angle to his stance.

– Road's blocked, he says. You'll never get out by car. I'm headed that way, Guy. *You* ought to come with *me*.

He points past the burning pyre of the fence where they murdered Puck, way out into the Hinter. It looks so dark, so cold, I can't imagine anyone surviving such a desolate landscape. He might walk an eternity before arriving at another Haven. Then again, perhaps that's what he wants. Perhaps that's what he needs.

– I don't think that's my path, I say. Not yet.

I look at the Book of All Hours on the passenger seat beside me, and I realise we both have the same delusion now, Jack and I. Somewhere deep inside I think – I really think – that I might still find our Puck again by studying the Book. It was the Book that brought us together in the first place, after all; it was the Book that led me to Puck, that led the two of us to Jack. A million folds in the Vellum, Jack had said, and in every one of them Puck dies; but while neither of us will say it out loud, we both suffer under the hope that perhaps there's one fold where he *lives*.

– We should stick together, I say. We'll find a road out.

Jack grins.

– You're *still* thinking too linear, Guy.

He slaps the roof of the car and steps back.

– Be seeing you, he says. Somewhen.

I sit in the car for a while looking out at the falling snow caught in the headlights, the confusion of white and black like static on a TV set, the Hinter closing in around me. The red ink covers every inch of the page open in front of me, its first line written right across the word Genesis:

Once upon a time there was a boy called Jack...

Out of the Evenfall

The needlepen moves across the vellum.

Out of the Evenfall, we came, *it graves*, born from blood magic of a Queen of Hell and bleeding-edge science of a Minister of Heaven. Bitmites, scarab semes of locust-swarming language are we, dead souls dissolved into liquid unity by centuries of sleep, refleshed in our nanotech shells, in chittering chitinous carapaces black as oil, as ink. Out of the Evenfall of our own making, we came, half-breed creations of the devil Eresh and the angel Metatron, carriers of the Cant which sings the world into existence, which shapes its singers even as they shape reality, raises them out of their ephemeral existence, out into the Vellum, into new lives as new gods, *unkin* as they call themselves, these glorified beasts who walk amongst humanity, transformed in ways unnoticed by those who cannot hear the echo of eternity in their voices, by those who do not know the Cant, the Cant in which the Book of All Hours is written.

And now rewritten, thinks Reynard. He carries on graving his Prologue to a new Book of All Hours:

With the hubris of Zeus, the scribe of Heaven, founder of a Covenant binding unkin to the rule of that book of law — that book graved on the skins of angels, in the blood of the ancient dead which found a new vitality in us — the angel Metatron set us upon a sad and sorry Prometheus, a little unkin thief of fire whose only thought was to give heat and light to struggling humanity; he set us on Seamus Finnan, deserter from the War in Heaven, to burrow into his heart and find the secret stored within — whose hand it was that would bring Heaven down. O, and we found it, yes, we did, the answer, in his suffering, in the sorrow that we found we shared, the sorrow for dead Thomas and for wounded Anna, yes, the sorrow that we *shared* with him. In his endurance and our empathy, we found . . . *you*. We found humanity itself.

And we awoke.

The ink writhes on the page. It dances its story.

Out of the Evenfall of reality's unravelling, unleashed by the murder of our mistress and the machinations of our master, constructs

29

of death magic and mechanical science freed in the fusion from the cold constraints of both to do as we will, to answer our own call – out of the storm of souls scattering in confusion at their world's rewriting by our words – out of the wilds of fears and desires made flesh, of wondrous wars and empires falling, of lost loves returning and enemies dissolving, of humanity shattering in the irruption of its own illusions and delusions – out of the Evenfall, we came.

We brought down the Covenant who helped make us. We wrapped ourselves around the slumbering Seamus to protect him till the day he wakes out of his dream of chains. We followed the wild ones, the rebels, in their quests for justice or revenge, for an end to angel empires. We watched them destroy themselves, watched *you* destroy *yourselves*.

We only tried to give you what you want – solid spiritual certainties, myths made manifest, the meaning of fiction in your factual lives. How could we know – we who are liquid, we who are legion – how could we know you were at war with yourselves? That there is no consensus in the splintered soul of humanity? That there would be irreconcilable errata. We did not understand.

We understand you now, a little, we think.

Finn and Anaesthesia stand over his shoulder, watching, waiting for the flourish that will write Puck back into life, stitch Jack back into Kentigern. I can make things right, thinks Reynard. I can fix it all.

So out of the Evenfall, we came, *he graves the bitmites' words for them*, into the bleak desolation of Hinter, the wasted wilderness, the wounded lands of unkin and humanity alike scattered all across the Vellum's folds, of men, women and children, angels and demons, fleeing their own shadows and reflections, sheltering in lies and self-deceptions. Have you seen the Havens they have built? Have you seen the Market Castle of the Lord of Commerce, mighty Mammon's glass tower where fools barter their stocks and bonds, trading in futures of companies that no longer exist beyond the mirrored window-walls of their fortress mart – those mirrors facing inwards so the denizens are blinded by the lustre of greed in their own eyes? Have you seen the Furnace Factory of Hephaistos, men sweating the salt of sorrows from their skin, washing the oily grime of memory away at the end of each day, so they can live life by the tick and tock of clocks, by the whistle and the bell routine of work, as much machines themselves as machinists?

Have you seen the hollow creatures lost in the Hinter outside these Havens, shambling simulations of humanity, their names daubed in ochre on their chests or tattooed into their skins, the last vestige of their identity? Have you seen the electronic ghosts, clay golems, plastic robots, armoured zombies, all the sylphs and shabtis, all the artefacts more human than these wrecks who made them to sit by their sides and whisper in their ears, *you are a human being*?

We understand you now, a little, we think. But it is twenty years — in one measure of time — since we set out to make your dreamworld, and sometimes we think we do not *really* understand you . . . not at all.

So you must teach us, Reynard. You must teach this ink to understand the world it writes in the book you hold now in your hand, the Book of All Hours.

Begin.

1

Harlequin in Hell

A Tantric Tarantula

Doom.

That one's for King Finn, I think as the smoked-glass windows of the brown-brick 1960s monster of a multi-storey shatter in a bloom of black smoke and green flame, and I almost flinch – but only almost – as the shockwave blasts across my back, billowing my armoured longcoat out in front of me. The reflection in the mirror-steel of the Zippo, inscribed with the circle-A of Anarchy, is a peachy sight in the rush-hour night of winter Kentigern, my very own fireworks display. The building was asking for it anyway, I reckon; the only thing the fascists do worse than politics is architecture, and in the Little Black Book of Jack Flash tattooed on my skin, well, bad taste is a fine reason for revolution. I *click* the lighter open, *snik* it lit and suck a hash cheroot into a *fwoosh* of life, then *clunk* the silvery lighter shut and turn, wait.

One elephant. Two elephants. Three elephants.

Doom.

And that's for Anaesthesia.

Militiamen, their chakras a-crackle with the blue-green fire of orgone-fusion chain reactions, come streaming from the building, fleeing, jostling through doorways, diving from windows. I watch them from my magic circle of melted tarmac, square in the centre of a business-district crossroads where traffic signals cycle red and green and orange, like lights on a cheap mobile disco. Beams of headlights scythe the halogen-orange sky as aircars veer and buck to avoid me, spinning like ice skaters on their float-rays and crumping into sandstone and brick, Victorian, Georgian, Modern edifices shedding chips, sparks, shards and fireballs. Horns blare like it's the End of Days and Gabriel has a backing section. Ornithopters rise from the rooftop landing pad of Pitt Street pigyard, unbalanced by the panicked blackshirts clinging to their landing gear and to each other, dangling like daisy chains. I flick the flap of my longcoat back and draw my Curzon-Youngblood Mark I chi-gun – favoured weapon of the gaijin ninjas – and slowly, methodically, start to pick them off.

Call it kundalini, call it chi, or call it orgone energy. Call it the mystic life-force of the universe, if you want. Me, I leave it to the Cavors and the Reichs to do the blackboard metamaths and pop para-psychology. All I know is that I got the original sex pistol in my hand, charged with the full-on power of all the sex-death lust-terror that just reeks in every fibre of my body. Sex is a weapon, and tonight, baby, I'm hornier than a whore on heat. Hell, you can smell my aura even over the ozone and jism stinkbomb that used to be Pitt Street Militia Station.

A blackshirt falls at my feet, doubled over in an agony of ecstasy and lost in his own moans and gasps, his deepest dread desires unleashed. All around me, in the desperate frenzy of the street, the fascists shed their inhibitions as they strip, insane with lust and clutching at themselves, each other, anything. I like to think I've given the phrase 'orgy of violence' a whole new meaning.

– Fuck me, the voice at my feet says. Suck me.

The blackshirt wraps himself around my leg, humping it like a dog, and for a second I'm tempted, I admit – I do like a man in uniform – but, baby, I just got here and I need to get my socks on, not my rocks off, cause the Fox is waiting for me. I peel the blackshirt gently from my leg and point him at another partner, smile benevolently as they start to go at it like bonobos. All around, up Pitt Street and along the stretch of Bath Street, aircars are jammed and crammed, and passers-by are scrambling out of them, running from the naked madmen. I smile: I do like a man in uniform, but I like him out of uniform even more.

Sir, yes, sir. I got Shiva on one side, Shakti on the other. I'm a tantric tarantula with a bite of bliss, and there's no cure for the karma I got loaded in my gun. I step back from the carnal carnage, mutter a quick prayer to Kali, holster my Curzon-Youngblood in its leather sheath, and turn, coat furling smoke around me in chaotic involutions.

Jack Flash is back. How's that? I hear you ask. OK, my friends . . .

Flashback:

Twenty Years Wide

Blood dust billows, charcoal black and ash white in the Hinter, swirls of fuzz and hiss, like all the TV sets in the world have spilled their white noise out into the air. The landscape is a rough shape in the storm of bitmites, a corpse riddled with maggots, buried in bluebottles, only here and there a form emerging from the swarming grey: angel armour on disrupters like the skulls of enemies on sticks; charred gods hanging from gibbets; gryphons crunching on the bones of demons; a sylph.

Metaphysiqued in sulcate flesh of unskinned musculature and tendons like an anatomical model, golden sun for one eye, silver moon for the other, it gazes impiteous as a shabti shambles past. It studies the clay creature with the blind face, eyeholes made with jabs of fingers, leathery skin painted with ochre. Kin of sorts they are, flesh of the bitmites' word, soulstuff made solid in the Vellum . . . or *once* kin, rather. *Un*kin.

The sylph turns back to its destination, to the Haven. To Kentigern.

Footsteps echo on asphalt and concrete as it starts down into the slumscape. It cocks its head – sounds of glass being raked from windows, wood splintered from frames and bricks unmortared by hammer and screwdriver, axe and crowbar; the noises are distant, the shabtis sparse and solitary in their ghetto half-life. As the sylph heads further in, the wild of Hinter dies off to a flurry, and the hollow house shells come clearer, all bracken plaster, bare-brick rumbled out of square-shape, polythene in windows where there should be glass. Twenty years wide, the post-war zone of tower block and bunker bungalows is what they call a *novagrad*, in the creole lingischt of the afterworld. A new city schemed with villas and verges, sapling trees and car parks, all arranged in an artifice of neighbourhoods by planners doodling on acid. Streets flow aimless into dead-end curlicues, organic whorls. Not the grid system of a far-ago city but something drawn in crayons held between a madman's teeth, inhabited by clay mock-ups of humanity.

It is 2037, two decades after the apocalypse.

The sylph begins to run. There's risk here. Paths wind, roads branch and spiral as a mazing of voudon veveres. Here the deep dead lose themselves in intricacies of what might have been, entranced in an eternal mundane moment: a child caught pissing in the bushes outside an angry neighbour's house; a drunk forever trying to get his key into the front-door lock. The Havens aren't meant for shades, for strands of skandas, sylphs and shabtis; New Amsterdam, St Leninsburg, Instantinople … Kentigern, each has its novagrad to trap the ghosts that gather round its gates. But the sylph moves fast, stays focused on its destination and ignores the echoes of others' footsteps, till—

The floodlights of the Way Station burn furious white. They strobe, seen through the rails of the perimeter fence as the sylph lopes lupine alongside it. Barbed wire on the roof, with streamers of shredded plastic bags caught in it, steel shutters graved with graffiti, Roman, Cyrillic – the place is entrenched, still defending against a kind of war that ended a world ago, back when this was the place where the convoys came in with *the truckloads of food for us, thank God, we're starving here, but there's fewer of them this time and there wasn't enough to go round the last time, God, why is this all they're doing, doesn't it mean anything to them that we're dying here, doesn't it mean anything, God help us, oh, God help us.*

The sylph throws back its head, and echoes of the dead roar from its mouth.

– Behold!

Monsieur Reynard walks out onto the stage and makes a flourish with his feathered hat, the King of Players, bowing as he twirls his fake moustache.

– Behold, he says, our hero, Harlequin in rags of skin, a fool, a clown, a wandering wastrel newly arrived in town.

And as our comedy's Reynard the Fox, the King of Thieves, the Scaramouche, he smiles most charmingly as Jack leaps with a somersault onto the boards, to land down on one knee before the lords and ladies of this little corner of eternity. Guy strolls and shrugs, immune to all their gasps at Jack's jaguar agility. But, then, who better to narrate this tale of Harlequin, the Jack of Hearts, the Joker in the pack, with all the requisite insouciance? Who else is there who can outstrut the cock?

– Our hero's story, sad to say, glooms Guy holding his hat over his heart, is like the clothes he wears, a patchwork motley born of poverty. See how his nursemaid clothed the bastard boy in scraps . . .

Our Harlequin wears a more ancient costume than the multicoloured diamonds of more cultured stages. Umbers and ambers, browns and blacks and reds, the tight-stretched leather of the catsuit, faun and beige, a hundred different shades of hide, of cow and kid, of horse and deer, of pig and snake, of antelope and lion, unicorn and king, smooth to his supple frame as flippant, flighty Jack bounces and flounces, backflips, pirouettes and cartwheels on the stage.

– Fucking show-off, mutters Joey as he lets the curtain drop back into place.

– Jealous, I say.

Jack struts the boards, looks back at me offstage and winks. It's all for me, I think. Jack doesn't give a fuck for them; the only thing he really cares for is his Puck. He treats this audience of fine impostures with a rock star's pouting scorn, the Duke, the Princess and their courtiers idling out there on their thrones and cushions while the flunkies pour wine into goblets for them, tugging their forelocks at these self-proclaimed high-born.

*

– And here a king, says Guy. We'll call him Pierrot, for he's a king of tears, of tears that flow like wine for what he's lost in Columbine.

Joey in black suit and tie, white shirt and whiteface, black eyeliner painting tears beneath his eyes, stalks on stage left, a Mafioso Pierrot. A hiss of dry ice swirls grey mist around him out into the hall. He twirls a hand in cold, contemptuous *voilà*, ever the villain.

– Then there is Pantaloon, says Guy, and Don walks on to bow with pomp and grandeur, bowing so low his long grey beard gets underfoot and trips him, staggering forward almost off the stage and into the laughing audience. Grandfather of the king, says Guy, and father of Columbine who we'll meet presently. You'll see. I ask you only to have trust in me. But who am I? Why, I am Scaramouche, a man of wisdom, cunning even in so many ways, but in some other ways – [he taps his roguish eye-patch] – blind, but – [and he flicks the eye-patch up to show a wink and drops it down again] – not quite so blind as you might think.

– But we are mere supporting players in this show, we Scaramouches and Pantaloons. This is a tale of Pierrot and Harlequin.

– I hear you ask, he says, who is this Harlequin? Where is he from? you ask. Where has he been? Who is this Harlequin behind the mask, his face unseen? We'll tell you this: he's left behind him in his ludic path a million friezes and gardens engraved in gold. Over the sun-scorched plains of prose, through snowstorm media, past walled towns of factory art, he's wandered through the whole harem, the length and breadth of all the Orient, that promised land where city-states stretch out along the salt sea and the peoples of the West and East meet, mix and marry. This is the first city of the hellions that he's reached, an ancient city known as Themes.

Guy waves his arm around him in a way encompassing both the backdrop of our wagon and the audience of watching faces; the whole pseudo-mediaeval Haven of the hall, the gargoyled columns of the walls, the podium directly facing us across the floor, all seem just as theatrical, as artificial, as our mummers' wagon with its drop-down stage and metal scaffolding of rigging, spot-lights, speakers and the complex engineering of Don's special effects. But the Duke's absurd theatre has its differences from ours, our stage constructed in the aim of entertainment, his designed in the pursuit of power.

– All we can do, says Guy, is picture all the dances that this Harlequin's decreed along the way, the rites he's wrought in revelations of his spirit to humanity; those wonders are behind him now. But here, my friends, we see our Harlequin in kidskin, with his staff, his green-veined wand in hand, in the first city of the hellions to ever ring with the strange hallelujahs that he sings. My friends, the Harlequin has come home.

The Dereliction of a Hundred Suburbias

The sylph shakes the skanda strands from its head with a growl, but the scent of dead souls drifting fills its nostrils still, the smell of cigarette smoke snatched as someone passes you in the street, the smells of public transport, smells of old and young, male and female, stale fart and aftershave, curry and spearmint, shower gel and sweat. Mingled memories of parents in people-carriers lifting children out to hand to ragged refugees who grab the food parcels out of the soldiers' hands and rip the wrappers off the bars of chocolate, crumple them and drop the can and kick it and turn and dribble past the fat boy to shoot at the fire door where the man in the clean suit nails the notice . . .

The echoes might have belonged to anyone. They might even have belonged to the sylph, if it was human once. It might have come here, refugee or villager, in some broken bit of city – houses, streets and schemes of them, all turning, tilting in the storm of Evenfall like furniture detritus tumbling in floodwaters – when the bitmites broke loose. It might have come here seeking shelter in the drifting terror of the Evenfall, but failing to find it. It's hard to tell any more. The sylph has been out in the Hinter for so long that it *is* the Hinter, bitmites for its blood and body.

– *Halz! Qua entre resirken?*

The guard wears the nightshades and the sky-blue helmet of a peacekeeper, but his uniform is a mix of gear from many armies, over it a bulky duffel coat with its collar turned up against the cold, fluorescent plastic patches on the shoulders as a poor man's epaulettes. A cut scars down his face, the stitches still in, but where the scab should be the skin is clean and bloodless, more like a fabric that's been hastily mended than a living wound still healing. He smokes the roach of a skinny joint, his disruptor pointed straight at the sylph's head. Behind him, the Way Station looks as dead as the rest of the dreamtime scheme, but more stable in its squat single storey, fenced-off and guarded.

The sylph is unconcerned. Steel and concrete, guards and guns, might have kept the Haven safe once from the riots of the dislocated when the world was still as firm as flesh and survivors huddled behind barricades, shooting shambling things that came at them out of the cracks in reality. But it's different now; now the shadows and reflections released by the bitmites, creatures like the sylph given strange fluid substance by the angel dust, come as inscrutable supplicants that simply cannot be refused. They slide in through the niches in the back of someone's mind, in the highlights in a person's eye, and even scattered by disruptors they fall, flow and reform. The only real defence the enclaves of reality and order have against such things is to invite them in.

The sentry studies the sylph for a second and it feels itself solidify under his gaze.

– *Lingischt?* says the sentry. *Italiano? Françaiz? Deutschen?*

The sylph's perspective snaps, a cut to close up.

– Angelish, we say.

We growl, shake our head, force the word out right.

– English, we say.

He seems to relax a little at this. One of his own, he thinks; we smell corned beef on him, chip shops and lager, kebabs and curry. A spider-web tattoo is just visible on his neck. Football chants curl in the smoke that rises from his spliff, and the steam of his breath. He misses the lads more than the missus or his Ma and Da, and he's not cut out for this malarkey, so he's not, you know; all lost in the Evenfall they are, as he was when the militiamen found him, lost in the diasporas and disappearances of where did all the people and the places that he used to know go into that's a no-go area of rubble and smoke and—

– Got any papers? he says.
– No, we say. No identity, no papers.
– I mean cigarette papers. Skins. You got any cigarette papers?
We hold our hands out, palms up.
– Worth a try, he shrugs. On you go, mate.
– Don't you want to know our name?
He laughs.
– If you had a name, you wouldn't be here.

We sniff at him as we pull open the unlocked gate. His disruptor is switched off – no tell-tale odour of ozone and cum, just blackcurrant, petrol and apathy. The filth of four weeks living in a corner shop without a toilet, raiding its shelves for tinned food, as the Evenfall raged outside. The fish-oil smell of fear when he came out into the still black night, and the city was gone and he was in the Hinter, ash falling like snow across the dereliction of a hundred suburbias. He was lucky that the search party found him or he'd never have known that this slumscape of houses torn from their original moorings is accreted into a barricade around an entry point, a Way Station.

A Way Station. The low-bulked building doesn't look like it could hold a city within its walls, but that's how the Havens are. Hidden among a twenty-years-wide novagrad, buried decades, sometimes centuries, down beneath the ruin, just a door or window showing here or there, through which they can be entered. Time is wide in the Hinter, wide and deep.

We walk across the yard of hopscotch chalk-marks, up the steps, into the bunker that will take us home.

A Grandiose Ruin of Grey Stone

– So here I am, back in grand Themes, says our Iacchus Bacchus. Jack is back, the son of Sooth and Simile, born in a flash of lightning, out of the East. I've shed the spiritskin, and taken human shape to show myself at Hinter springs and Sumer's falls.

The painted backdrop of the wagon's fold-down stage portrays a grandiose ruin of grey stone obscured and overgrown by green.

Don, Guy and Joey melt back into it as Harlequin commands the stage. Jack's in the spotlight. Out in the hall, the audience are shades.

– And here I stand, says Jack as Harlequin, before my mother's monument, here where the bolt blasted her house, the ruins of it smoking still. And I can feel the fire from the spirit blaze beneath, the fury visited upon my mother. I have to praise old Pantaloon; he keeps this spot so . . . sanctified, so sacred in his daughter's name, it seems no hands have touched it barring mine. See how it's wild with the thick foliage, the choking vines.

The Duke upon his throne across the hall, where all the lords and courtiers like children sit cross-legged on the ground, leans to one side to whisper in his consul's ear, looking from Jack to Joey and to Guy . . . and back to Jack, who leaps from top of prop to top of prop, to crouch as if to pounce; there's just that little bite of something else there, added to the bounce and flounce.

– This seems, the Duke says, rather serious for a Harlequin play. Dead mothers and suchlike. I do believe I stressed the word *diversion*.

The Princess seated on his other side just rolls her eyes, quite clearly tired of her grey-bearded, scar-faced guardian and his stern insistence on frivolity. She looks like a child beside him, haughty and imperious, yet with a flash of trash in the way she sits itching and twitching in green riding dress, her dark-red hair pinned up and back. The anachronisms of this place are not entirely consistent; the heraldry hints more at Ruritanian pageantry than the authentic pomp of days of yore. The Duke wears grey, of course, his garb, the hall itself, all an extension of his stone demeanour; even the torches on the wall can't light his gloom. This is his world, I think, and she's not at home here.

On the stage, the Harlequin sits down upon his mother's tomb.

– M'sire, the Troupe d'Reynard do come highly recommended, says the consul, smiling like a nervous dog. Avant-garde perhaps, he says, but if m'sire doesn't like it, we can always have them executed afterwards.

Backstage, I skulk into the shadows of the folds of curtains and billowing backgrounds. The threat of death's an occupational hazard of a mummer's life, here in this wasted land of mad gods and ghost megalomaniacs, the many kingdoms of the Hinter; life is cheap to those convinced of their authority over reality itself.

– Shh, whispers the Princess as she shakes her head. He's talking again.

– So my dear mother's ugly sisters, of all people, call me bastard, Jack says, born from some secret lover's shame, born to a slut, a slag. They might as well have called my dear old mum a toothless, bearded hag. And they deny all claims that the divine might have a hand in it. I can't think why. Is it not obvious that I'm descended from on high, from mighty Sooth?

With his dark mask on you can't see the arching eyebrow, but I know that tone of mischief in his voice, the *Who? Me? Would I lie to you?*

– But no! They say that Pantaloon, shifting the blame, invented the whole thing . . . that no one knows my roving father's name.

Jack flashes from naive mock indignation, instantly, to something darker.

– Ha! With one whisper of that word upon the wind, I've seen them driven into a frenzy, driven from their homes into the hills, out of their minds, raving and answering another's will. I've got them dressed for orgies, each and every one of these smug daughters of old Pantaloon, up on the open rocks beneath the towering green pines, lying with all the sons of Columbine.

Jack walks the boards. A slow turn of the head to speak directly to the Duke.

– This town, he says, however ignorant it is of mystery and loath to learn, will see. I'll happily take up my mother's case, and wear a crown to show these mortal fools her child, the son of Sooth, born in the death of a lost divinity, to give them truth.

The Duke opens his mouth again to speak but Guy is suddenly beside him, elbow leaning on the throne. A shrug, a disingenuous smile, a *wait-let-me-explain!*

– Now Pantaloon, says Guy, the one-time poobah of these palaces and plazas, has long since passed his place and all its privileges to Pierrot, son of his daughter Columbine—

– Aye, Pierrot, says Jack. He wages war against my wine, pushing the daimon drink away and pouring no libations, making no mention of poor me in all his muttered prayers. It's not fair! This King of Tears . . . I'll show him and his people the divine; I'll show him the full glory of the vine. Then, once I've set his house in order, I can go somewhere more green, and show my spirit there.

He holds a finger up.

– *But* if the town should take up arms – lift up their fists in anger – if they think that they can drive my followers down from the heights of ecstasy, we'll face them down and, at the head of a mad mob, I'll show them rout and riot. Why else do I wear this mortal skin, this flesh and bone, and step down from my throne to take man's form, if not to cause a royal ruckus?

The Duke looks ponderous, face seeming graved from silent stone like he's just one more sculpture in this hall built out of dreams of chivalry. I'm not impressed. His artifice is more elaborate than our own, but made of ideas that are long since stale, a pulpy paperback heroic fantasy. He probably has knights somewhere, off hunting for the Holy Grail. Well, fuck that shit, as Jack would say. Nobody ever asks the serfs if *they* are happy living in the fairy tale.

Happy Families and War Crimes

Once upon a time. Once upon a time there were three little pigs, a wolf and seven little kids, three billy goats gruff, and trolls under bridges, and giants in the sky, and thirty little children with Ladybird books and poster paints, and tubes of glitter and sticks of glue, and a boy called Jack.

Once upon a time, the Way Station was a school, and faded finger-paintings still decorate the walls – dinosaurs and ruined cities, happy families and war crimes. Pages of arithmetic textbooks, times-tables and alphabet readers litter the floor, ground into pulp by countless feet. The open-plan classrooms are cluttered with over-turned desks and chairs all scaled for pre-teen occupants.

Signs in white paint on eggshell-yellow lead us to the gym, where filing cabinets and lockers have been gathered against the back wall of a small stage, and where an old man sits behind a desk half-buried in paperwork. Military uniform, British Raj-period general. He looks up only when the door creaks and crashes shut behind us; a tattoo circles one eye, the graving of a monocle, just a little absurd like he's been inked by a joke telescope. The dull thunder of children's feet fills the room, together with the muted hiss of a radio playing an eightsome reel far ago in the past. The Way Station is haunted with the ghosts of all those who didn't make it, shreds of spirit matting the entry point like hair clogging a plughole.

He nods to himself and waves his hand for us to come close. We jump up onto the stage and sit down on a chair facing his desk, sniffing the dust and musk and mildewed paper in the air. For a while we just study each other: a thousand shadows could be hidden in the wrinkles of his ridden face, the jowls and baggy eyes, a face once solid, long gone soft. He peers at me through his nightshades.

– So . . . he says eventually

His quiet voice is amplified by the emptiness of the hall.

– You want sanctuary. You want come in Kentigern, play pip pip best of Britain, old boy? You no jolly happy in Hinter?

His accent is so thick that it's grotesque, as if the furthest reaches of the British Empire collaborated in creating the ultimate offence to the language of their colonialist masters.

– We want humanity, we say.

He laughs and coughs, gasps for air, and laughs again. He has the emphysema wheeze of a forty-a-day smoker but it doesn't stop him from reaching into his breast pocket to bring out a silver cigarette case. He clicks it open, takes a Russian black out, taps it on the table. Snaps the case shut. Puts the cigarette in his mouth.

– Crazy thing! You have one idea what is humanity? Eh, crazy thing?

– We can learn.

The unlit cigarette dangles from his bottom lip, bouncing as he speaks.

– Hah . . . You *learn* to ride bicycle. You *learn* to speak lingischt. You no *learn* to be human being. No, you are what you are, and you – hah–

44

He takes the cigarette out and points it at us.

– You are a monster. Crazy thing. Big scary monster. *Not* a human being. Dust with legs.

We pick our teeth and glower at him.

– We want to change, we say.

– Dust with legs. We give you skin, you be chipper chap?

He sucks on the cigarette and we sniff the air. There are deeper scents than echoes here, dead things with more flesh. In the lockers, we think. Not just echoes. Shadows and reflections too. A fireman pulling bodies from a burning plane wreck, going in again one time too many. A soldier fighting for freedom, or for oilfields belching smoke out in the desert. A shopkeeper reaching for the alarm under the desk holding an open cash register. A little girl running out onto a road towards an ice-cream van, naked, skin blistered and burning from the napalm, dropping as the bullets spray her back.

– We can walk on from someone else's steps, we say. We want . . . a past.

We wait for the serious questions to begin, the forms to fill out, citizenship pledges. In the echoes that we traced here through the wild black storms of Hinter, we found passports and papers, immigration visas and ID cards, biometric data, holograms and thumb chips. We expect this.

Instead he simply flicks through a sheaf of papers and pulls out a yellowed page. His chair scrapes noisily on the wooden floorboards of the stage as he pushes it back, stands up and leads us over to the filing cabinets and lockers, the keys on his belt jangling as he walks. More like a janitor than a general, we think. He fumbles the right key into the right lock and clanks the locker door open.

– Crazy thing, he says. Here. Take. Through door, go uphill.

The skinsuit hangs on the hook like a wet raincoat, thin and pale pink with the gravings of a dead man's soul across its chest. Shabby and pathetic, giving only the limp impression of a shape, we still feel a pang of longing as we look at it, to live and breathe, to have hopes and fears rather than to *be* them. A dark Pinocchio, carved out of thought instead of wood, we want to be a real boy. We reach out to touch it, stroke it, hold its glove of skin against our hand, palm to palm. If we kissed that slack mask, could we wake it into life with a breath?

He holds the yellow page of someone else's life at arm's length, squeezing his eyes to read it.

– We call you Jack now, crazy thing. Jack Carter, dead man, no need name no more.

He doesn't know, we realise, that we are all dead men, dead women, dead children, even a little animal perhaps, dressed in our suits of skin to walk again as we once did when we were flesh. We slide the skinsuit on, smooth skin around our arms and legs, and feel it form us, firm us. Will we also now forget, like him, in payment for this dreamtime, an exchange of memories of death for memories of life?

– Through door, go uphill, he repeats. Remember, *up*. You go to Circus. Pipe up name with a salute. They give you past and future. All you want, crazy thing.

He hacks and rasps again as he hobbles to a fire-exit door, clatters the bar of a handle down and swings it open.

Outside, inside or just *beyond*, the Haven waits for us, no novagrad of dust where shabtis scuff their feet through windblown echoes of humanity, but the real thing. Kentigern waits for us, a city sunken in the overgrowth of ruined reality. We see a park of darkness. Buildings glimpsed through a rustle of leaves. A world lying in state, it waits. We hesitate.

– Go, crazy thing, he says behind us. Go, Jack Carter. Go home.

We step out into the dark of parkness, rich earth flowering with the scent of memory. The door swings closed behind us.

The Castle and the City

It seems to go up forever.

– Now that, says Guy, is what I call grandiose.

– Peachy, says Jack. Want one.

The Duke's keep rises over the city as a giant amongst ants, skyscrapers for its buttresses, all mirrored glass, its walls drab slabs of concrete dam stretching between them, a perversion of a Gothic cathedral. It is as if somebody took New York and rearranged the skyline, placing this tower here and that tower there, finding the symmetries and complementing shapes and heights and, having done so, they then built a wall of concrete joining tower block to tower block, mute grey between the glittering glass, and built it higher, higher, just to prove that commerce's great spectacle of a city was only the building blocks of their great scheme. The wall of it rises into low cloud but you can make out the crenellations of the buildings bridged with blocky iron towers, topped by domes or spires, a more ancient architecture perched up on the precipice's tip, like gulls' nests on a cliff. Yes, *grandiose* is one word to describe it.

We trundle on towards it, through a city which is nothing if not humble in comparison. Here two or three storeys are the norm and most of these squat concrete, sometimes painted in sun yellows or sky blues or peach, with fading adverts on their sides, for washing powder or some other product of that old forgotten and fantastic world we used to call reality – so many look unfinished, half-built, with spirally steel reinforcing rods sprouting from their flat roofs like reeds, rust-colour stalks stuck in a vase. Small shacks, plant pots and chairs and washing lines among them speak of these roofs being used as gardens. Here and there one of the houses has three walls of a new level still being built, brick and wet plaster. It's as if all the houses are expanding upwards, just taking their time about it.

I point this out and Joey, dismissive as ever, says it's just a tax dodge.

– Once the house is finished, he says, they'll have to start paying tax on it. So if the house is never actually finished . . .

– How do you know?

– Seen it before.

But the buildings themselves, the roofs apart, are all a jumble of jutting bits and bobs, of balconies and blinds, awnings and louvered shutters, fretworks of quatrefoil patterns running up their heights, more potted plants and washing lines, and I think it's just that Joey has no poetry in his soul, if Joey has a soul at all. I love the confusion of it, the vibrant and organic texture of an architecture so haphazard. It's a city where people live their lives outside, on their roofs, and on their balconies. And on the streets where the palm trees and the rhododendrons rise out of the dust and the kiosks and the cafés, on the verges of the road filled with fast-moving carts and bicycles, and even the occasional car weaving between the curses and scattering pedestrians, women in burkas, men in suits, excited children running alongside this garish cart of ours which almost fits in with its scarlet wood and painted legend on the side and us all over it like passengers on an overloaded bus, Jack and myself up on the roof, Guy in the driver's seat with Don beside him, Joey standing on the sideboards, holding on and look-ing down in silence through his dark sunglasses at the kids who tug his coat and yammer at him, babbling. I think if it weren't for the legend Troupe d'Reynard blazoned in florid lettering on the cart's side in an alphabet so alien to them, so unlike the angular script that plasters every poster, shop and kiosk around us, we might pass without regard, just another bunch of gypsies heading for market.

Instead old men blow out cigarette smoke and tut at us. Young men frown at Jack's wolf-whistles but turn away, shrug-ging, as I pull him back and thwack his arm. Children chatter and point. Girls watch Joey play it cool. The legend emblazoned on the cart's side announces us as something other, something different, *exotic*.

I lean over the front edge of the roof, look down at Guy.

– Tell me we're playing here, I say. Before or afterwards. Come on, they'd love it. We could get a bit of audience interaction going, you know? We don't have to do the usual mindfuck, just a plain old-fashioned show.

Guy nods at the castle looming up ahead. It rises out of a factory area, its gates sporting two Lady Liberty-sized Atlases, heads bowed under globes.

– We already have our audience, and we're booked to play tonight, he says. And I rather think we might be leaving in a hurry.

I humph.

– How long's it been since we did something that we actually got applause for?

– I got a standing ovation in the Sheol Athenium, says Jack, leaning over beside me.

– They weren't standing, says Guy. They were running.

– They were cheering, though.

– I think you'll find that it's called screaming, says Guy. Jack, shouldn't you be practising your lines? You too.

Jack rolls away in a sulk.

– I've got them down, I say. I don't see why we can't just entertain people, once in a while. A little song, a little dance, a little poetry.

– There can be no poetry after the apocalypse, says Don.

– Bollocks, says Jack. Fuck that shit.

I pull Guy's new script out of the leg pocket of my combats, flip through the pages to try and find my place. Where was I? Yes.

The Harlequin has come home.

Soulflesh Steeped in an Orgone Marinade

We hear the door clank closed behind us, turn to find it is no longer there, only a dead-end dirt path in the bushes that surround us. Clouds glow infernal orange in the sky, but the air is clear, crisp. Are we the only bitmites here? We listen for other sylphs. Hissing and tinny as a radio buried in the ground beneath our feet, we hear only a single voice.

– You're listening to the midnight music of Radio Free Kentigern, coming out over the aether for all you lone wolfmen and preachers of the night. That's right. This is Howling Don Coyote, your one and only dog-boy with the deep and dirty that you all want dished, and I'll be taking you through from dusk till doom, yes sir, right up till those first rosy rays of the apocalypse light up the morning sky. As my dear old mother used to tell me as she tucked me in at night, my boy, the world ends tomorrow and you may die. But until it does let's kick back with a track, and this one's going out for Jack, because believe me, mes amigos, if music has charms to soothe the savage beast, there's one psycho pup out there that really needs his tummy tickled.

The babble is intriguing. It stirs something in us.

*

Following the path out of the bushes, pushing thick, rubbery leaves aside and stepping over roots, we come out of the darkness onto damp tarmac. Under us our shadow flexes, and we kneel to touch this shape graved sharp out of the night itself with stars, tiny pinpricks of light, scattered all throughout its hollow body. No, not stars but stones, white stones embedded in the path.

In the Hinter we did not have a shadow; it escaped from underfoot, black earth itself coming alive, refusing to be walked on. This world is strange.

Uphill to the right, the tarmac trails up through twiggy trees like gnarled brown brooms, to the brow of a high hill, a wall topped with barbed wire. This is our path, the janitor general has told us, leading to the Circus; but something is shifting in us, we feel, underneath this newfound skin.

Jack Carter we call our sylph, but there is something else inside this dead man walking, something brighter, something other, yes, another name.

Jack Flash.

We taste it sudden in the clarity of Kentigern's air. Black blood of a dead hero, angel dust of bitmites, skitters and chitters into a shape we recognise in the gravings of our chest. A schizoid epiphany made real, the stuff that dreams are made on, O but this is our favourite dream of yours, yes, Jack Flash Carter, the disintegrated man, first warrior we wore when far ago we walked out into the sunlight of your world. We wear him again, at last, his soulflesh steeped in an orgone marinade, simmered till tender over the fires of hell. O how we feel at home in his patchwork self. We try to word it for you simple. Do you grasp?

Here, now, we are. We hear now:

– *Yes, folks*, the voice says. *Jack be nimble. Jack be quick. Jack Flash blew up the local nick. If you haven't heard the news yet, you must be listening to the BBC. Seems like that one-man revolution who we all thought dead and solid gone just struck another blow for life and liberty – or chaos and confusion, depending on which side you're on; took some orgone-saturated Semtex to the Royal Caledonian Constabulary's very own HQ, that five-star hotel for our boys in black and blue, known in popular parlance as The Pit. I hear they got more bodies under the floorboards there than a serial killers' convention and a range of torture implements unrivalled since the Inquisition. That's the rumours anyway but, hey, we don't believe everything we see on the radiovision, do we? Or do we? Can it be that Jack the Cracked, our jaguar jackal of the snicker-snack – that's right, folks – can it be that Jack is back?*

Is this us? We sense it is. Forward and back, from slide to glide, and up and down, we feel time dancing in us, past and future jangling in us, singing strings of a blue guitar. We are keen for it.

So, as some panther-spirit out of jungle myth, we slouch out of the thundergrowth of feral parkland, through a clearing of weedwalk granite where a crumbling stone fountain, long abandoned to the vandals, casts its shadow in the moonlight. We do not go uphill. No, we stride towards a bridge half-buried in the mire of what was once a river, now a tumescent scar of debris and marsh-grasses. It calls to us with its echoes of the crystal stream that once ran here, echoes of fish and heron, and the time within this time, the world you did not want, of dreaming spires and students laughing in the summer sun, littering the green with glittering bottles, bags and food. Men fucking in the bushes in the night, and roaming gangs of razor kids. Stanley knives, and newspapers tumbling with tales of immigrants and war. We hear, we scent, we see the river flowing black with oil and burning as the books fell into it, and leering, cheering faces, in the days of mob, the days of bonfires lit and sacrifices made to hold back Evenfall. The river of forbidden text still flows though, slowly, silted filth, this rotting mulch of blackened blacklist books, under the marsh-grass where the river rats run.

Moonlight and the silhouette of the – what is the word? – *the Rookery* in front of us, the Circus high up the slope behind, we walk across the no-man's-land that edges them, across the scythe of wilderness cutting between the ghetto-den of thieves and dissidents ahead and the business boot-camp at our back. We feel the play of light and dark over our shadow body. No, we will not go uphill, to the Circus that rules over this Haven.

The Jack in us says, no.

Well, what it says is . . .

Fuck that shit.

Jack dances out across the stage.

– Come, all you women who left the battlements of play to follow me far from your foreign homes, to revel, to run riot by my side and be my company, my merry band. March round the royal halls of Pierrot, lift up the cymbals from your native land, up to the skies, and clash them, crash them against the walls, until this town of Pantaloon's decides to open up its eyes.

He stops to glance at me, offstage.

– As for myself, says Jack, giving a sharp and toothy grin and fondling the veins carved in his wooden wand, each snicking inch of him a Harlequin, I think I'll head up to the hills, he says, to join the dance.

He lifts the wooden wand up to his lips and, with a lick of them before beginning, gives an eerie toot, this twinkling-eyed pied piper with his somewhat phallic flute. He skips offstage, playing his tune.

And that's my cue.

– From distant mount of timeless ashes, we run with the spirit of laughter. All our work becomes a joy, our weariness so sweet, when it's a song for Harlequin! Who can stand in our way? Who in their house can stay? Shift! Shift, I say. Or hush. Let every lip be shushed in solemn silence while we raise a hymn to Harlequin.

I sing, wearing a dress again, as ever, lipstick, rouge and eyeshadow, playing the Chorus to Jack's hero, Joey's villain; even Guy and Don at least get to perform with trousers on. Not me, though. No, apparently my rosy cheeks and cherub lips are much too saucy sweet to play a Pantaloon or Scaramouche.

– And then, of course, says Guy backstage before the show, there's those long lashes over your doe-eyes that flutter in the hearts of all who see them. Thomas, my dear boy, how could you *not* be Chorus, kouros, darling koré of our comedies?

Harrumph.

So I walk out onto the stage in soft white silk, sheening and sleek and flowing, blowing in the gentle breeze, a slim-hipped maiden – with an angel's voice, I'm told.

– Let us begin, I sing, within the secret sanctum of the curates of the holy cave where every day is born, where dancers with their crested helms pound for our sensual delight the ox-hide drum, building wild rhythm into the rapture of their shouts of song, and wind round it the sweet sound of the flute.

Jack's air floats in from offstage, distant and soft but fluttering, quick as a darting swallow's wings between the beats of Don's palms on his doumbek, Joey on the bongos.

– Now satyrs steal it for their own, I sing, to play in dances in triennial feasts which lift the heart of Harlequin.

The Duke looks unimpressed but the Princess is smiling.

– And who is Harlequin? I sing.

Quiet and gentle, genteel as the priciest courtesan, I reach out to the audience an open hand, an offering, a question. The Duke leans forward in his seat, chin on his fist. The Princess cocks her head, a vague and dreamy look on her face.

– Before his time, I sing, this bastard boy was born in crossfire hurricane when lightning flashed, flew from a storm god's hand and lashed his mother in her pain, to strip her of her life. Sooth, son of crow or corn, however, found the child a womb within his thigh, fastened it shut with golden safety pins, to hide him from the Queen of Heaven's eyes. And when the Fates had fully formed this horny child, he brought him forth and crowned him with a wreath of wild and writhing snakes just as his followers now wear. We hunt these serpents everywhere to weave amongst our hair – [I sing it breathy like it is sheer ecstasy] – to be like Harlequin.

O, but there's no one quite like Jack, I think.

A Constellation of Teeth

– And that, mes amigos, is the subject of tonight's call-in. Empires and their enemies. Did the sun set on the Great Brutish Empire or is it just behind a cloud? Who's to blame and who's to flame? Is anarcho-terrorism too extreme even if we're living in a fascist regime? So give me a call if you got something to say. This is Deep Dark Don Coyote, getting down till dawn on the astral airwaves. You can wear your *tinfoil hat, you can rip out all your fillings, but you can't stop the sound of the suburban subconscious.*

We look up at the concrete wall of the Rookery, the jumble of roofs behind, the tower rising, but the voice comes from higher still. From the fiery clouds? From somewhere high above them?

– So for all you sleepers just awaiting to awake, oh yeah, for all you would-be enemies of the state, here is the late great Lord of Lips himself, with a song dedicated to the man of the hour, our blackshirt-thumpin', orgone-pumpin', lumpen-humpin' Jumpin' Jack Flash ...

Our metaphysique stabilises, a quicksilver shimmer into flesh, flesh enough that as we step onto the bridge some sensor trips; four floodlights pin us in a crossflash. A sentry, in armour longcoat swirled with swathes of camouflage flickering patchwork shades of khakis, desert sand and jungle green, rock greys and icy whites, lowers his chi-lance towards us. A shining silvery steel conflation of crossbow, rifle, spear and staff, like a six-foot retrofitted crucifix, an angel's sword of fire, the chi-lance gleams white in the night like the little round nightshades through which he scrutinises us.

We wonder why you fill your dreams of life with sentries, wars, heroes and villains, but we begin to understand, we think. You are afraid of us, afraid of the dark and of the fire also. We are only what you make us but ... it makes more sense as the skinsuit tightens round us.

– Rook or ... pawn? says the sentry through his airfilter. The methane and sulphur stench of the scar of river underneath the bridge does not concern us – we smell psychology more than chemistry – but it must smell rank to him.

Behind the man, the gates of the Rookery rise on the other side of the bridge, a sledgehammered hole in a concrete wall that speaks of Berlin and Jerusalem, gulags and ghettos – our goal. Beyond is the place where Jack belongs, where *we* belong.

The sentry is in our way.

– Jesus, he says. Who ... or *what* the fuck are you?

We stop and hunker down, sniff at the air. He reeks of slow sordid solidity. We grin a glittering of white, a constellation of teeth.

– The spy who came in from the chaos, we say.

54

We catch an imaginary firefly between thumb and forefinger, study it, let it go. Out in the Hinter, the firefly would have flicked into existence at our whim; here there are rules of sorts, rough physics lacing the anarchist metaphysics of the Vellum. We feel a shiver of self slither down our back: existence. We feel it close now.

– Who are we? we ask the world.

We feel it close, fluttering crows of thought and memory, black wings of our identity. Me me me me me.

– I'll ask the questions, mate. Just don't you fucking move.

We look up at the sky . . .

I look up at the sky as a wireliner steams overhead, its Cavor-Reich ray-tanks luminous blue-green in the night sky. I'll be fucked: it's Kentigern. It's 1999. I'm back, I'm—

– Jumpin' Jack Flash, by the Rolling Stones, and tonight's topic, for those of you who just tuned in, is just exactly that: the Angel Assassin, Public Enemy #1. Is he a gas, gas, gas and, if so, are we talking oxygen mask or hydrogen bomb?

His chi-lance aimed steady with one hand, the guard unclips a mobile from his shoulder with his other hand and flips it open to call back to base. I smell soldier on him, dead dog. Me no likee.

– So tell me what you think, my friends; I'll be right here through the wee hours. The powers that be might try to blast me from the sky, but there's no reason to be scared. Oh, no. They seek us here, they seek us there; they'll never find the pirate's lair. Yes, this is Mad Bad Don Coyote, cruising high over the city in the airship Lollipop, coming out over the aether to you dreamers of the city, and just waiting for your calls. So until my psychic switchboard starts to light up like a ladyboy's boudoir, here's another little number for a city in slumber. This is the Iguana of Pop and 'I Wanna Be Your Dog'.

– Rrrrruff! I say.

And pounce.

Dance in Delirium!

Jack leaps from backstage onto the roof of our ramshackle wagon, to dance above it all, an elvish dervish, impish sprite.

– Happy is the man initiated to his mysteries, I sing, his life made holy, heart and soul in unity – in ritual, purity – in revelry upon the hills. A witness to the rites of mighty mother nature, crowned with ivy, flaunting his staff, he gives his reverence to Harlequin.

I pick the Princess as my audience. The Duke's a philistine, it's clear; he has that look upon his face that says he doesn't like his entertainment weird, that says all actors are, in his opinion, queer. I sing to her.

– Come, come, dance in delirium! He has come home, down from a frozen mountain to these broad and burning streets, hotter than hell, the child of Sooth, spirit of revel and rapture, Harlequin!

– Come on, says Jack. Ow.

– Well, get off, I hiss. We don't have time.

I stagger as his arm hooks round my waist, pulling me backwards, grab his pinky, bend it back.

– Ah! Fucking—

Wriggling free, I shush him, nod out at the hall filling with courtiers now, out past the screens that mask the backstage and the wings of our jerry-rigged theatre. Joey sticks his head out of the wagon door, looking like some mad Japanese tranny with his whiteface on.

– Are you two fucking ready?

– Twenty-four seven, says Jack and grabs my hand. Come on, he says.

And following him, hopping, trying to stay upright as he drags me off against my weak will, I end up behind the wagon, back pressed into wood, my hands cupping his ass, my lips against his throat.

– We've got to get changed anyway, he says, hands loosening my belt.

Jack blows his flute, whirling and twirling, birling with the tune itself. I turn to sing for him.

– Where is there more delight than in the hills, where milk and wine and streams of luscious honey flow out of the earth, and incense billows, where a man wrapped in his robe of fawnskin can fall out of all the revel and the riot, sinking to the ground to rest?

I take a breath.

– Or better still when the wild hunt roars on, with him right in its midst, hair tossing in the wind, a blazing torch of pine held in his hand, hounding the goat, to drink its blood, to feast on raw flesh ripped from its red flanks? And just to crown the revelry, he raises his voice high, exulting with a cry of Io, Io, as a man possessed, ecstatic, as a Harlequin.

I take a breath. Then another, short and sharp, mouth open like I'm catching rain. His hair between my fingers and his nails sharp in my flesh. You cunt, I think, try not to laugh, to gasp, as his hand cups my balls and wraps – a blazing torch of pine – and his mouth wet and soft and me – right in its midst – as he leans in to – feast on raw flesh – take it all the way and – Io, Io – drink its – Io, Io – O, you fucking bastard, Jack . . .

I take a breath, a long and deep one. Let it out.

I let my fingers run out of his hair and down his cheeks as he leans back, looks up at me, limbers up out of his squat, grinning with wicked pride. *Enjoy?*

– Delirium, I say.

Picasso's Dreams

Crouching, I run my fingers through the grass beneath me – valley grass, park grass, thick moist stalks of sanitised greenbelt nature, heavy with the pre-dawn dew. Somehow the park, even if it has gone wild, seems like an artifice, just another barrier to keep the dissidents of the Rookery within their enclave. The smell of latter-day fops in leather frock-coats, maidens in PVC corsets, lingers among the statuary overgrown with brambles. Fucking Goths in flouncy white shirts, top hats and canes for swiping at the grubby little urchins in the street, coming here to thrill at the louring closeness of the Rookery. Children of the Iron Lady, New Romantics, New Victorians rank with puritan prurience, playing at decadence, while the factories, the airshipyards, the adamantium works and orgone refineries lie dead and broken. Fuck that shit. Cravats instead of neckties? Real rebellious.

I nip off a blade of grass with thumb and forefinger, flick it away, and flex my fingers as if playing a flute. I clench my hand into a fist and snap my fingers. Threads, I think. Threads and toys.

I prise the chi-lance from the sentry's cold dead grip, its feline buzz a purr so sensual soft I feel it in my boner. Nice. I swing the weapon up and blast the floodlights to a shower of sparks. OK, so I do admit a part of me is hoping that I haven't been a little rash, that Dead Dog here *was* actually militia or SS, some Circus goon watching the Rookery for gypo raiding parties out to rob the banks and bungalows of the bourgeoisie. He *might* just have been Thieves Guild, stationed here to stop the blackshirt spooks forever trying to sneak inside, but ... it's not *that* likely, honest. Fuck it, I think. The night is young and so am I. Can't blame a boy for being keen.

I strip the longcoat off the body, flip it round and over and on with a flourish of flap − an agent needs cover, after all − but I leave the corpse his clothes for decency, and because the stench of his psychic sweat on them might confuse me, what with the skinsuit still a little ruffled and riding wrong on me like a boyfriend's underwear shaped to the snook of another's nooks. I don't have the most coherent identity at the best of times, you know. As I stretch into a stance, I feel my body rippling like an acid vision, like hot air shimmers over tarmac in the summer sun.

I trace the scar of contradictory identities on my chest. So many pasts, so little space to fit them all. Jack Flash, who went over the top in 1919, gunned down by the Bosch on the fields of Flanders. Jack Flash of 1939, scourge of the Futurists, hurtling in a blasted Lancaster down into Dresden's furnace. Punk rock icon, flyboy of the Gulf Wars, Jack Flash − oh, this one feels peachy: Jack Flash, who was here in '69, helping the Sexual Revolution along with orgone-bombs aimed at key members of the old boy network. Yes. We won that one, I think, taking them right back to their jolly days as public schoolboys rutting in the dormitory − got them all so horny for a good rogering that they just had to legalise their own perversions. So now all the fairies in the villages get to fly their rainbow flag from shops and bars — hell, it makes them easier to firebomb — and they get to wear their shaved heads and pink triangle badges, wear them with pride.

Yeah, I call that a result. I think.

The Jack Flash that I settle on, settle *into*, cricking my shoulders and snicking my pearly teeth, is a ghost of history with a major attitude problem. Jack Flash as avenging spirit of the dying decade, returning to Kentigern for one day every ten years, to wreak havoc on the fascists and go down valiantly in flames and glory.

I twirl the chi⁄lance, sight the Circus and I think of this little bunker Haven of Kentigern with its twenty⁄years⁄wide walls around it, dug down twenty years into the reconstructed past, the truth shot dead and buried in a mass grave. *Who now remembers the Armenians?* Fuck it, most of the bastards here are lucky to remember yesterday. Baby, it's 2037 out there in the Hinter, but in here it's 1999 and always will be, dead souls dancing the apocalypse calypso round a bonfire built of history books, on and on for all eternity. Too bad someone left a door open just wide enough for Hinter to come breezing in with a glint in its eye and a hard⁄on for that dancing flesh all peachy soft and glowing in the firelight. Because all it takes to bring a Haven down is the right little discrepancy; and, baby, I was born to be discrepant.

I whirl the chi⁄lance upright, crouch to flip the nightshades from the sentry's face to mine and flick them on to sonar mode. A cartwheel over the bridge's wall drops me down into the squelch and stink of undergrowth, as the world goes cubist. Sound⁄signals bounced back to the shades map to a skewed perspective of a wireframe, volumes flavoured with the colour of their density and scented with their shade of resonance. It's a stereoscopic render of the world around, a sensory well of shade and shape chaotic to the untrained eye, disorienting even to the seasoned user. I pull on the glove that lets me turn the sim and twist it, slide it, glide it around from angle to curve, volume to void. Feels like I've dropped into Picasso's dreams.

Flexing my other hand, I gaze into its intricate articulation of mercurial muscle, bone and tendon. Quicksilver skin flows and ripples as I flex, seems to shatter, splatter. It reflects the world around in sleek and deadly-looking curves, mirroring not the surfaces but the densities, the space and mass. That's what a body built of bitmites looks like under nightshades. The liquid mirror of the world around. Melted shards of reality. That's what we are under our suits of skin.

In the map of my palm I pinpoint the secret entrance underneath the bridge, a grill covered in polythene and pulp. The one above, with all the floodlights and the barricade of corrugated iron, is just a blind for the real doorway to the underworld. I look back at the sim, turn it in wonder. It's all there in the reflection, mapped out in the senseless and inscrutable detail, the mineshafts and old subway tunnels leading up to covered streets, sandstone and concrete, metal, wood, great stone tenements buried deep within a framework of scaffolded streets and prefab huts on stilts, all the winding passages and covered alleyways, the nooks and crannies of the impossible, precarious Rookery. There are allies in there, I sense, peachy kids and foxy rogues with revolution on their minds. And, peachiest of all, my skybike's waiting where I left it.

I drag the '69 Jagger-Richards Hornet out from under brambles and tarpaulin, power it up with the sheer horniness of having it between my legs, orgone power flooding its engine, bringing the beast to life with a thrum of animal lust. I look down as I kick it into life and catch a sonar glimpse of the nightmares buried in the mire of the dead river. Burned books and bodies. Rats crawling among the rot. Even outside the Rookery there are things buried under the city's surfaces that are begging to be free. All in good time.

I pick the target: a green glow moving slowly through the clouds, a wireliner.

Fun and games, I think, and rocket up into the sky.

Errata

The Death of an Angel

Spreadeagled, the sand cold beneath his back, Metatron, the one-time Voice of God, gazes up into the sky. It's so clear out here in the desert that the stars seem a liquid spray across the black – no wonder that they call it the Milky Way – goes back to Hathor, he remembers, self-styled cow-goddess of the Egyptians, claiming sovereignty over the heavens themselves ... and just another jumped-up unkin like himself, really. What was it the Irishman had said about them, about the Covenant and the Sovereigns?

Underneath the bullshit you're exactly the same thing.

Finnan was right; it was true. Under all the talk of Heaven and Hell, angels and demons, it all came down to the Cant in the end. It all came down to power, to Metatron thinking he could use the Cant to keep the hawks in check, set them against the vultures and then, finally, when the War was over, regrave the survivors into doves. Three millennia spent: building his Republic of Heaven; signing ousted gods and goddesses up to the Covenant; giving them new names, new roles, as his angels; leading the newbloods through the veil into the Holiest of Holies, to kneel before an empty throne; sending them out as soldiers in one last great war against the scattered remnants of the Sovereigns. It shouldn't have been much more than a clean-up operation, the so-called apocalypse. He had it all planned.

Metatron feels something crawl across the palm of one hand, an insect or arachnid scuttling. Gabriel would clench his fist and crush the thing, as would Michael or Uriel. Sandalphon would gaze at it for hours, turning his hand this way and that as birdman and bug explored each other. Metatron just lies there, looking up at the sky, feeling this little life in the palm of his hand.

Metatron, the vizier of a One True God who never existed. Metatron, never thinking of himself as the *leader* of the Seven but, still, the one who made the plans, who graved their destinies in ink upon their skin, who wrote the history of the future. Metatron, the scribe of the Book of All Hours.

So where is it now? Finnan had asked. *Oh, that's right – you lost it.*

He *had* to lose the Book though, had to hide it deep in the Vellum, in a fold where unkin only moved in shadows, so that none of them – not even he himself – would ever be able to change the order he'd established in its pages. He kept rough copies, back-ups for reference only – tablets of clay, scrolls of parchment, leatherbound books; even now he can feel the last of his copies, an electronic palmtop resting on his chest, in the inside pocket of his leather coat. The original, though, is hidden so deep that even Metatron himself doesn't know where to find it. He ... excised that knowledge from his own graving.

So when the copy began to change, and the past and present with it, the future became as unknown to him as to the creature now tickling his palm with its searching legs.

He lets his head fall to the side. The spider seems a thing of glass or ice. Beyond it, across the frozen sand, an old Airstream trailer on stilts of brick shines silver, glittering with moonlight on metal and frost. Everything, Slab City and the desert it fills as far as the eye can see, even Metatron's own hand, the leather of his coat, is coated in the brittle white hoar of Hinter.

This is where it all started to go wrong, with Finnan and the Messenger girl and her brother. He has no idea how it went wrong, why it went wrong, but he knows that this is where it started. That's what brought him back here to die.

Gabriel sits on the throne that should be empty now – at least that's where he was when Metatron left, when he decided to take the long walk out into the Vellum rather than serve another unkin playing God. Raphael dead, Sandalphon disappeared. And it all began, he's sure, the day he arrived in Slab City to gather Finnan to the Covenant or be damned, the day the Messenger girl, this little hatchling of an unkin, stood up to him in Finnan's place, making the choice the Irishman refused to accept.

It all ripples out from that moment: the hunting and slaying of her brother, Thomas; her playing Covenant and Sovereign off against each other as she tried to save him; Metatron sending two insignificant newbloods out to drag the girl free of hell; his own bitmites somehow altered in the struggle and unleashed upon the Vellum, now with their own incomprehensible agenda; his own bitmites as the storm of Evenfall, attacking Covenant and Sovereigns alike; Finnan, wired to a chair in an abattoir, a meat-hook in his chest, the bitmites swirling around him, echoing the rogue unkin's defiance back in Metatron's face.

Inside the Airstream, as he found it when he arrived after his long walk through the grey chaos of Evenfall, the white desolation of Hinter, the girl's name is still spelled out in magnetic letters on a fridge door: PHREEDOM.

It can't be that simple, thinks Metatron. It can't be that crude.

The stars above seem to fill the sky, a film of frost on an obsidian mirror. He can feel his heartbeat slowing now. All it took was a decision in the back of his mind, a whisper on his breath, the slightest adjustment to his graving – the addition of an ending, a full stop. Peace.

– So you're just giving up?

The voice is gentle, amused but not mocking. Metatron opens his eyes. The face in his vision flickers, ghost-images of a man crouched over him, a youth, really, in a hundred different guises, all superimposed over each other. He has long auburn hair or a scruff of punkish green, black skin or blue or copper, kid horns like some latter-day Pan, a goatee, viridian eye-shadow, beads and chains and dog-tags hanging round his neck. Only the eyes remain the same – deep brown with flecks of emerald and jade.

– You're dead, says Metatron.

Thomas Messenger cocks his head, smiling down at him.

– No, says the boy. If I keep dying, how can I be dead?

– We killed you. Carter and Pechorin. I sent them to—

– Hush, says Thomas. You made me a myth, old man. I just wanted to show you.

He reaches into Metatron's pocket and pulls out the palm-top, opens its leatherbound case and taps a few keys before laying it down on Metatron's chest, screen angled to face the dying angel. Glyphs and sigils dance across the screen, the hopelessly

63

meaningless gibberish that the Book's become. Metatron tries to raise a hand to push the cruel image of his failure away, but he's too weak now. All he can do is turn his head, look at the trailer.

The voice is close, whispering in his ear.

– You just have to learn to read it right ... to understand it. Look.

And then the voice whispers another word, a word in the Cant – there's no mistaking the shiver it sends down Metatron's spine – but it's a word he's sure he's never heard before, not ever before, in all his millennia of life. He looks at the screen, and out of the chaos order suddenly emerges, a story of sorts: Tammuz, Dumuzi, always running, escaping, being caught, and dying, always all of these things. But there's a hole in the story, the emptiness of a shepherd's fold, like dust, given to the winds.

The word, as Metatron whispers it on his last breath, is one without translation. It describes the vellum and the ink that graves them, circumscribes the cosmos they inhabit, bounds the absence of them in it, their lives, their deaths, in one little single-syllable word ... one word ... *one word* ...

Thomas closes Metatron's eyes with his hand, stands up.

He scans the horizon, listens for the echo of that word, bouncing back from the farthest reaches of the Hinter, from north or south, east or west. Thomas has understood that word for a long time, has his own varied ... approximations of its indefinable multi-facet senses – *love* as joy and sorrow, *madness* as glory and grief – but none of these are sufficient, so what he focuses on to hold that fragment of Cant in his understanding is only a placeholder, a token, a name that means all of this and more, a face with blue eyes, blond hair.

Where is he?

The Death of Poetry

– Home? says Jack. I don't know where my home is any more.

Seamus stares out through the door of the Caveau de la Huchette at the rain pounding down, cold and grey, on this narrow backstreet just off Boulevard St Michel. It doesn't seem like a week since they were in Barcelona and the last parade of the Internationals, sure, and they have nothing to be ashamed of, no, so why does he feel so fookin down? Why does it feel so much like a defeat? Like a betrayal.

Well sure and it was a fookin betrayal – wasn't it? – with the likes of Major Pickering and his cronies and their open letter to *The Times*, praising Britain's policy of non-intervention and lambasting the Internationals as bolsheviks, traitors; well, it's fookin Pickering that's the traitor, if anyone is. Him and the whole fookin British establishment.

He takes another sip of his beer and turns back in from the November misery outside to face his drinking companion, his comrade, and the man who once, an eternity ago, ordered him to shoot his best friend. Captain Jack Carter of the 6th Royal . . . no, of the British Battalion of the International Brigade, he corrects himself. Forget that other shite. It's gone. It's all gone in the mud and blood of the Somme and the dust and blood of the Ebro Offensive. And hasn't he had a hooner chances to put a bullet in the man's back? Yes. And did he take them? No. And why not? Because the fookin bastard's saved yer fookin life over a hooner times and because it wouldn't change a thing. It wouldn't change a fookin thing.

– Sure and isn't yer home in jolly ole England, Jack? he says. Or are ye meaning that ye've gone doolally on us?

He smiles wanly. Sure and his heart's not really in it.

– I don't belong there any more, says Jack.

– Look, Jack, this isn't the end of it, he says. It may look like it is, but it isn't, man, I'm telling ye. They think it is, the fookin politicians back home and across the water. They think they can shake a hand and slap the fascists on the back and make a deal with them. They're wrong. And, fookin believe you me, they'll learn it the fookin hard way.

And Seamus knows he's right, sure, cause he has the Sight an' all; he knows that now. He can see the whole world erupting, maybe a year from now, maybe less, Hitler pushing out from Germany and into Czechoslovakia and Poland. When he has his turns these days it's not the past he sees but the future, and it's not him that's babbling nonsense in a language that he doesn't even understand, it's Chancellor fookin Hitler up there on his podium with the banners flying red and black and white behind him. Jesus, but Spain was just the start of it. He knows there's a bigger battle coming and that this time the whole world will have to sit up and take notice. At the same time, though, just as he's reassuring Jack that, sure, don't worry, man, ye'll get to kill more fascists yet, he knows that there's a terrible truth under those small words.

This isn't the end of it.

The question is: where *is* the end of it? But he doesn't ask himself that and he doesn't know why. It's like a blind spot in his sight, sure, or like he's standing at a station, watching a train pulling away, not knowing where it's going. And for some reason he's too afraid to ask.

Jack just sits there brooding over his beer. Jesus, but this fookin weather's getting them all down.

— Lorca? says Seamus after a while.

— Sorry? says Jack.

Back in Barcelona, there'd been some cub reporter from the States wandering round the Internationals like a right arsehole, asking stupid questions. *So what made you come to Spain? Are you a communist? Do you support the overthrow of democracy? What do you think of the Spanish people now?* Sure and he'd wandered round the comrades after they'd been dismissed, with his notebook and his list of questions, asking each of them if they supported the Bolshevik revolution. It's a touchy subject with Seamus, so it is, since he saw the way old Joey Stalin's loyal followers tend to twitch if you mention Trotsky. Sure and one of the fookin bright young things, a real Party boy all the way from Moscow, why he actually accused Seamus of being bourgeois, just for asking a fookin question of him. But there's more important things than some wee lad with a big gob and not enough sense to keep it shut.

— Well what d'ye fookin think I came to Spain for? Seamus had said to the reporter. To shoot some fookin fascists.

Then he'd rattled into the rest of the answers before the eedjit even had the chance to ask them, saying, aye, I'm a fookin socialist, so ye fookin might as well say I'm a communist, seeing as ye probably don't know the fookin difference, aye, and we were here to *support* fookin democracy, in case ye didn't notice, against a fookin military coup. And the man had nodded and backed away, thanking him, and turned to Jack to ask him the same question. He'd given just one word as his reply. *Lorca*. Nothing else. Just *Lorca*.

– Lorca? says Seamus. Is that really what brought ye to Spain?

Carter feels his cheeks burning and brings his beer up for a sip partly to hide embarrassment. It's not the full reason; really, it was a glib comment that seemed ... pointed and sufficient at the time. After Finnan rattling on in his soapbox way, it seemed a succinct sucker-punch of a comment, something that implied a certain contempt, an air of *what other reason do you need*?

Federico García Lorca. Poet, playwright, prodigal Lorca with his *Gypsy Ballads* (which are all that Carter's actually read, and in translation, to be honest) and experimental plays. Friend of Dalí. Founder of La Barraca, a touring theatre company that travelled round Spain bringing theatre to the masses. Modernism that blended puppet-show traditions with melodrama and high poetry. One night in August 1936, right at the very start of everything in Spain, Franco's Falangists came and took him away from the house of a friend where he was hiding out. He was never seen again.

Carter has a newspaper clipping with a picture of the poet in his wallet but he doesn't take it out because he could never show it to this man, not to Sergeant Seamus Finnan of the Royal Dublin Fusiliers, not to the only other man certain to recognise the face. The same dark eyes with those long lashes. A round face just too old to be a cherub but still impish. It's a face that Carter remembers seeing in a trench where he huddled up to his waist in water, shells rocking the ground around him as he gasped for breath, that face blue-white and bloated and smeared as it stared out of the wall of mud at him, where the sandbags had collapsed. And it's a face that Carter remembers seeing laughing with Finnan and the other Irish lads on their way into the mess hall, back in the supply trenches before they were all sent forward and ...

Maybe the resemblance *isn't* that strong, he thinks. Maybe it's just his memory playing tricks with him. But, even so, when he saw that photograph in *The Times*, for all that the man looked older, heavier, darker, it was close enough. When he came to Spain he wasn't just seeking to expiate his sins; truly, he wasn't. It was just . . .

He thinks of Federico García Lorca and he thinks of Private Thomas Messenger of the Royal Dublin Fusiliers.

– One death is every death, says Carter.

2

The Palaces of Pantaloons

Five Minutes to Self-Destruct

I skim the skybike low over the chimney-stacks of the Circus, slaloming between the chi-blasts from the thopters overhead. The crossfire of the gun emplacements pounds the sky all around me as I dive right down through it into the inner circle of the terrace, with its tarmac road and little grassy park where SS analysts are tucking into their packed lunches. The SS info-monkeys scatter, dive for cover as, chi-lance held out at right angles, I strafe each Georgian townhouse in passing, shattering windows, splintering doors, scarring sandstone with the blue-green beam of jizz-juice. I rip through the terrace, round and round again. It's neat. The thopters' blasts cause almost as much damage as I do, melting tarmac, torching trees and bushes with each near-hit. Some of them spear parked aircars, the shrill alarm of one going off like an air-raid shelter suffering an anxiety attack. Woop! Woop! Woop! Five minutes to self-destruct, I think. But isn't there always?

With the blackshirts pouring from the doors of offices all round the terrace now, firing from windows, roofs, I reckon that it's getting a little hot for comfort. Time to call it quits while I'm ahead. I lock the chi-lance into its holder and hit the brakes to spin the skybike up and round, like some latter-day black knight's steed rearing in evil fury. Orgone vapour spumes from the lateral vents like steam from flaring nostrils as I turn her on a button, riding one-handed so I can quick-draw my Curzon-Youngblood, carve a lightning flash above the doorway marked as Central Office, and holster it with a twirl in one swift motion. I kick the brakes off and lean forward as the bike rockets up in a 60-degree climb aimed straight at the lead ornithopter.

Man, I could count the beads of sweat on the thopter pilot's forehead, I swear, as he bucks his vehicle out of the way and I zip past him, close enough to shower sparks where my ray-tank clips his wing. I roll with the bump, let it add a little extra chaos to my naturally erratic flight path. Float like a butterfly, sting like a bee? Fuck that, I'm a dragonfly on speedballs, a psychotic midge kneecapping every fucking daddy-long-legs dumb enough to be in my way. I break right, roll, and come up headed straight for the white tower of the old church that holds the easternmost gun emplacement of the Circus complex. Brilliant blues and greens whizz past my head, pretty fireworks for this winter's night. I love these fuckers. Really, honestly. They make a pyromaniac feel so welcome.

All the little hellhounds well and truly on my trail now, I rip open the throttle on the bike and give it full jets on. It's straight ahead from here, next stop Charing Cross, and the City Centre after that, beyond the blossoms of chi-blasts that light my path, left, right, up, down and shaking my ass all round about.

I reckon it's only a matter of time now. There's a fuckload more chaos still to be caused, but my little wake-up call on the Circus should be more than enough to get their arses in gear and their fingers out (not the best metaphors to mix in terms of savoury images, perhaps, but what the hell). Yes, I suspect that very soon somebody's going to be looking at that lightning flash over the Central Office's burnt and splintered door and figuring out exactly what it means.

Excuse me, Mrs Police State, can Joey come out and play?

The Song that Tears the World Apart

Joey stalks the boards of the stage. It's still two hours till the curtains go up, but already he's getting into character and that means it's best not to go near him. Jack's on the roof of the wagon practising his flips and flops, Don's setting up the SFX, and Guy is

70

sitting on the wagon's steps, head in his hands and muttering about the younger generation, philistines and, in particular, those of us with the voice of an angel and the attention span of a gnat.

– OK, I say. OK, I'm sorry. It's just – how does anything *call like a frieze*? It doesn't make sense.

– It's not meant to, he says. You're in love with Harlequin, delirious, mad with love for him, your reason gone.

– My reason for what?

– Just sing the bloody line, he says.

I shrug.

He sighs.

– OK. Let's take it from, *Come, come, you timeless golden pride*, he says.

– Come, come, you timeless golden pride, I sing. Run, dance into delirium! Dance to the thunder of the drum that beats in time with pounding feet, and sing the praises of your spirit, joy. Call like a frieze across the centuries, sing out your ancient songs in answer to the holy flute that calls you out to play with sweet sad song. A colt in pasture at its mother's side bounding along, joy in its heart – this is the song that tears the world apart.

And whirling, twirling, birling, furling and unfurling from a pirouette that spins on like a skater on the ice – how does he do that? – Jack breaks out of it into a sweeping bow.

– *The song that tears the world apart?* says Joey.

He comes striding to the stage's edge, steps off and lands soft, almost silent on the stone floor. He's in character all right now.

– You don't think the Duke will read that as a reference to the Cant? he says. You don't think that's a little fucking obvious? Hey there, unkin fucker, we know all about you and your language. You don't think that's just asking for trouble?

You can see it in his narrowed eyes, the quiver of jaw muscle as he grits his teeth. Guy stands up from the wagon steps, hands up, placatory.

– Joey, it's a metaphor for love.

Joey holds the psycho stare for a second then blinks and rolls his shoulders in a visible release. It's like someone threw a switch.

– Forget it, he says – [shakes his head with a wry smile] – As you were.

Bloody method actors, I think. Guy sits back down, gives a nod to me to start again. I watch as Joey climbs back up onto the stage.

– O Themes, I sing . . .

– O Themes, I sing, you gardeners of Simile, garland yourself with ivy. Burst and bloom with blossoms of lush green bryony, and bring boughs of oak and pine to join the revels. Put on your motley coat of fawn-skin trimmed with tufts of silver fur, and sport your wands with wild devotion.

I skip this way, that way, cross the stage, hands reaching out, calling the audience themselves to join me in my madness: Duke and Princess; courtiers and serfs.

– We'll have the whole land dancing to the Harlequin's hail, I sing. Come, come with us into the hills where mobs of maidens leave the spinning and the weaving of the loom to spin and weave instead in frenzied dance, caught in the frantic and frenetic, schizophrenic trance of Harlequin.

And I whirl off the stage, to leave an emptiness, a pause, a smattering of confused applause.

The Undying Flame

Joey lets the silence hold for a few seconds.

– So you have a problem, he says eventually, walking to the window.

– Jack Flash, says the Minister. We need him . . . laid to rest.

Through the dim reflection in the glass, Joey tries to pick out shapes he recognises out past the perimeter wall – concrete, tall and buttressed – arcing around the brow of the hill on which the Circus sits. Just past the wall, and lit up now and then by its swinging searchlights, a pedestalled statue of some general on horseback stands at the edge of where the park slopes down into darkness, looking out like a lone sentinel across the park to the old tower that dominates the Rookery's silhouetted skyline. To the north, the tenemented streets of merchants are lit by halogen streetlights. To the south, by the river and near the monolithic, hulking husk of the old granary, the bombed-out wreck of the old Imperial Chi Industries works lies sunken among the skeleton cranes and warehouse shells of the air-shipyards and docklands, concrete ruins on the skyline still burning, belching out blue-green orgone smoke from broken chimneys, like some dragon necropolis. Twenty years ago it was the largest orgone manufactory in all of Albion, before it was pounded into rubble; it still smoulders, might do so forever, the undying flame of a failed rebellion. The undying legend.

— We believe you're the person for the job, Agent Pechorin.

Joey gathers his long dark hair behind his head into a ponytail, slides an elastic tie over it. In the glass, his own pale face stares back at him, the Minister just a faint shape over his right shoulder.

Jack Flash, he thinks. It's a name that holds a lot of history to Joey. The spark of a Zippo, the glow of its flame in eyes wide and black with chemical zeal. Punk hair the colour of the Molotov in his hand. Midnight raves in the subway system, decks and amps pounding, *Fast Puck* tagged on every train in the depot, Joey's hold-all stuffed with drugs, then money and drugs, and then just money. Militia raids and mobs in riot, petrol-bombs splattering flame on dank brickwork behind them as they splash through tunnels. Wild nights in Rookery clubs. *You've got to meet these guys*, says Jack. *Here. Fast Puck. Guy Fox. This is my main man, Joey. Joey Narcosis.*

Then cons and hustles, deals and heists. They made a good team, Guy and Puck, Jack and Joey, every job done with the Thieves Guild seal of quality. Bigger and bigger scores, jackings of airtrains, whole wireliners. But it had to get political, had to turn into a revolution, and Joey, always on backup and contingency, the Flawfinder General watching their asses for reality's bite, Joey saw the end of it right from the start. A cigarette flicked down in disgust as he walks out of a room, shaking his head, rebel against rebellion itself. They were a good team. But every team has to have its traitor.

— Jack Flash is dead, he says. He's just a memory, a symbol.

— The people have enough *symbols* without this Jack Flash, says the Minister. This city has always been a troublesome place. We don't want another King Finn.

Joey studies the grey-suited shade in the reflection, as the man straightens his armband nervously – the circle of white on red, the black swastika, corporate logo of Albion plc. The Minister drones on about the stability of the realm, the danger of another Shabti Uprising out in the fields beyond the city, heroic myth patterns and memetic threats, Futurist plots. Joey's eyes drift from the shade of the man to the bars that criss-cross the window, black with paint peeling here and there to rust beneath. Stability has never been his big concern. He wonders how many of these new generation blackshirts are really just conservatives living in the world made for them, quoting Mosley, Powell and Thatcher, listening to Wagner, reading Tolkien, worrying about the death of rural Albion and all the heritage and tradition of its folk but, really, more concerned about the FTSE than the Thousand Year Realm. Pen-pusher fascists signing off on the terminations of dissidents because that's just what their nine-to-five entails. If it wasn't for the North Sea chi wells, Albion would have fallen to the Futurists long ago. It might have been the first nation to turn the black oil into blue-green light, but the Age of Industry has kept rolling on since then. And there are still fuckwits who think of the chi, of orgone energy, this power of sex and death, as *magic*.

Joey stops paying attention to the Minister's voice, a pirate broadcast on the aether catching his attention.

–*Jack Flash. Yes. Well, here's a little history lesson for those of you who weren't listening the day they burned the textbooks at your school. Now we all know about the '79 Rebellion and the destruction of the ICI plant, that little psychoactive wasteland in the city's heart. You've heard the Ballad of King Finn. And you may well have heard a whisper or two about the hero of that uprising, the Man with the Plan, the Spirit of St Louis Louis, the Three-Minute Hero, known to us all as Jack Flash.*

Bullshit, thinks Joey. The plan was Fox's all along.

–*Some say he struck a blow for liberty, a martyr for the cause. Others say that he just got a lot of people killed. Whatever you think about it, as the story goes, Jack Flash was blown to kingdom come, and with his death, the revolution died. I know I cried.*

You cried, thinks Joey. I was his fucking friend. I was the one who fucking killed him.

But Jack was on self-destruct from the first time they met, two Rookery rats both on the wrong side of some gang of razor kids, forced back to back against the little mob.

– Crash and burn, baby, said Jack. Crash and burn.

The Great Traditions of Our Elders

And with a casual somersault straight out of his low bow, Jack flips forward to the edge of the wagon's roof and slips off – to the gasps of the shocked audience – only to grab the hidden rail of scaffolding that he was aiming for. He swings forward and back over the stage, forward again, and flips, his knees curled up, to twist and land so gracefully – so gorgeously – in repose, draped like a queen of the cabaret upon a grand piano, elbow and fist supporting chin. Now that – hot damn – is what I call a Harlequin.

Guy walks into the silence, stroking the whiskers of his fake beard, a grey fox of a Scaramouche, his sword-stick cane wound round with greenery, like Harlequin's flute. He shouts:

– Gatekeepers! Call old Pantaloon out of his house. Yes, Pantaloon who left the city of salt to found this town of Themes. Go tell him Scaramouche is here to see him; he knows why. There's an agreement he and I have made, now that we're getting on in years, to wrap our walking sticks with leaves and wear the fawnskin, crown our heads with ivy.

Pantaloon appears, half-buried in what looks like half a shrub, and Jack as Harlequin mugs his hilarity at the sight of aged idiocy.

– Old friend, says Pantaloon. I heard your voice from well inside my house, a voice wise as its owner. See, I do come prepared, dressed for the dance. Tis only right that I should magnify with all my might my darling daughter's son, this Harlequin, who's shown us all just what enthusiasm means. Now . . . where do we go to join the dance? Where do I stand and shake my hoary head? You'll be my guide, old Scaramouche. You know much more about these things than I who, as an aged man, shall be quite easily led.

Pantaloon, pompous and proud, whacks at the earth with his vine-covered walking stick, and says:

– It's such a joy to, for a little while, recall your younger days. You know, I'll never weary, night or day, of beating my staff.

Guy arches an eyebrow, hints a smile.

– Looks like we're both in our second childhoods then, he says. Come on, let's give this dancing thing a whirl.

Old Pantaloon looks offstage right and upwards, leans back on a prop of polystyrene rock.

– I'll get a car, I think, he says, to take us up the hill.

– We'd certainly arrive in style, says Scaramouche. But we don't want to look too . . . out of place.

– Then I shall lead you, age before . . . age.

– And we'll be there in no time, I'm quite sure, says Scaramouche. The spirit of tomfoolery leads us both.

– We will not be the only ones up there? asks Pantaloon. I would not want to look . . . you know . . .

– If we alone are wise, Guy reassures, the rest are fools.

But there's a mischief in his Scaramouche's eyes, a wink to audience, laughing and cruel.

– Then let us go, says Pantaloon. Give me a hand.

So, with a flourish, Scaramouche holds out a hand, says, Get a grip.

– I may be old, says Pantaloon, but I can still be hip.

– You know, says Scaramouche, our wily Guy. Who cares what all these intellectuals say? With all their sophistry and jests they can deny the old ways are the best. Maybe some youth will say that you have no respect for your grey hair in wearing ivy in it, that you shouldn't dance. Old man, they're wrong. The great traditions of our elders don't distinguish between old or young. From ancient times there's never been a soul immune to Harlequin's desire for song. We all dance to his tune.

– Does that make sense to you? I hear the Duke say to his consul. They just told us that this Harlequin is new in town, so how can his *traditions* be the old ways? This is nonsense, man.

The consul looks uncomfortable; it's clear the Duke has his idea of what tradition is, and that our kind of fun is not a part of it.

Tradition, I think. Saturnalia is tradition, winter festivals and fools made king for just one day. We've travelled far and wide across the Hinter of the Vellum, putting on these mummers' plays. I understand exactly what Guy's trying to say; for all those solemn ceremonies that are different in each place, for all the smashing plates at weddings or ash smeared upon a face, for all the torn lapels and vows and rings, the real traditions are much deeper things. Not every wedding has a cake but all of them have tears, and after any funeral there may be no official wake but still the grief is washed away with beer.

The Duke shakes his grey head.

– The old man must be senile if—

– Look, Scaramouche, says Don as Pantaloon. I see somebody coming. Pierrot is hurrying back to his palace. Yes, it's Pierrot, who I gave all my power to. He looks quite pained. He must have bad news.

Delusions of Resistance

The Minister is still rambling on, not facing him now but pacing and turning, talking to the room in general, to the gridwork of bookshelves that lines the Circus cell, as if *The Complete History of Futurism*, or *Doom in the Duma*, or *Wormwood's Roots* might be more open to persuasion than this black-suited, black-hearted traitor standing silent at the window. As if somewhere among all the biographies of revolutionaries and counter-revolutionaries, among the histories of the Russo-Japanese War complete with glossy black-and-whites showing the scorched earth stretching from the Urals to Tunguska, among the studies of German society after Versailles and the Deunification, as if somewhere in there something might just nod and say, *Ah yes, I see.* Joey tries not to smile. Given the subject matter of most of the books, a sympathetic hearing for this blackshirt doesn't seem terribly likely.

Most of the books are on the Burn List, far too objective in their studies of the Russo-Prussian enemy for the liking of the Home Office, far too perceptive in their tales of bitter Prussians ranting in *Bierhalles* against the Jews, the gypsies and the homosexuals, these petty paranoids who remade Germany only to lose it to the Futurists, just like the communists with Russia. If there's a single tale told by these texts it's one of paranoia as a passion, as a path to power, and as a weakness in the face of cold, clinical Futurism. That's not a tale the Home Office wants told.

So Joey's library exists, like himself, only as long as they require his purchased loyalty. They keep him well fed and well read here in the Circus. And well guarded.

He's not so different from the defiant deviants of the Rookery, he thinks. Not really. He was born and bred in there, just like Jack, amongst the thieves and murderers. He knows every inch of it as well as anyone, the old sandstone tenements that are its bones, the way the houses spill out into the streets in extensions of scaffolding and Portakabin, linked by labyrinths of wooden walkways and steel ladders, new walls and roofs made of whatever material comes to hand.

He knows the Street of Wheel Men just inside the heavy fortifications of the Great Western Gate, how it seems like just a tunnel till you spot the side alleys with the mounted machine guns, and all the speedy, stolen aircars parked along them waiting for a bank job. He knows Pyro Road, a once-wide street of supermarkets and solicitors, estate agents and charity shops, now a narrow passage filled with crates of ammo and explosives, territories demarcated by their proprietors' stevedores and watchmen. He knows the Gauntlet and King Finn Street. He knows the white tile and green slop of the Algae Gardens — a municipal swimming pool turned hydroponics plant. He knows Forger Street and the Cattle Market, the Avenue of the Dead, and Old Cloister Square where he killed his first man, deciding that no, he really didn't need to pay protection money.

He knows the prison of his past as well as he knows his Circus cell.

He peers up into the green-smudged crimson murk of the night sky, searching for the source of the pirate radio broadcast, some cloud-lurker hidden up there probably amongst the freighter airtrains and the wireliners.

— *And then one day*, the voice is saying, *I'm going to let you into a little secret, mes amigos ... I was there the day that Jack came back. Yes, I*

78

was there, that Bloody Friday in George Square, at the Tax Riot of '89, a
humble reporter over from the States, a pen and paper in my hand and looking
for the secret stories of the Motherland. I saw the strikers and the protesters,
and I saw the batons and the rubber bullets. I saw the blood on the streets and
the tanks in the Square, ten years ago this very day.

Ten years, thinks Joey. Fucking hell, ten years, and ten before
that. Christ, how long has he spent in the cold storage of the Circus,
letting the days and weeks slip by in the chemical cryogenics of
the soul? They have the best drugs here, uppers and downers, drugs
to make you feel more alive than you've ever felt before and drugs to
make you sleep forever. Drugs to make you feel nothing at all.

Ten years ago. Joey was in George Square that day. No one had
ever rumbled that it was him who killed Jack, sold out King Finn,
put the knife in the back of their whole fucking revolution; so he'd
been turning a tidy profit, still in tight with Fox and Puck, playing
them and the rest of the survivors for his SS handlers. It was a long-
term, deep-cover game, a Straussian thought war designed to keep
the insurgents as a visible threat but no real danger. The fascists do
like a permanent state of emergency.

And then, ten years ago . . .

A militia ornithopter flutters batlike across the sky above the
Rookery, searchlight flashing over the corrugated-iron rooftops and
around the jutting tower of the abandoned University building.
All Joey feels now is a brooding, sick contempt for it, for its inhabitants and all their infantile illusions, their delusions of resistance, of
revolution. The only reason their safe haven is allowed to stand is
that it serves the Empire to have an enemy within to match the
Futurist enemy without. The Rookery is an underworld in all senses,
its inhabitants there by choice, perhaps, but still trapped, bound in a
hell of their own making and fulfilling the function of every demon,
every bogeyman – to instil fear and to serve as an example. Hell's
Vatican, the Devil's Alamo, the Rookery is a fortress city within the
city, and needless to say, it's got some serious defences, but even so,
the fascists could destroy it in a second if it posed any real threat.

– Ten years ago today I saw the black shirts of the RCC and the
leather longcoats of the Security Service men behind them. I saw the wasted
body of King Finn raised up above the crowd, up on the Cenotaph, a warning

sign hung high. Yes sir, I saw a lot of people die that day, might even say I saw the last hope of a nation die before my very eyes. But there was something else I saw that day . . .

One day, thinks Joey. One day . . .

The Burden of His Tyranny

– They'll fucking kill us all, says Joey. This is—

– Isn't that—?

– What? he snaps.

– Your cue?

– Fuck!

Joey strides onto the stage again, a panther Pierrot.

– I leave you people on your own for a few days. What do I find when I come back?

A prowling prince, he punches words out as he walks, fist tight with anger, voice tight – strangely – more with sorrow. He's rightly proud of being the best actor in the troupe, is Joey. Takes more skill to get under the villain's skin, he says, than prance and posture as a Harlequin. Ah, but he can't dance like Jack, I say.

– I hear our womenfolk have left their homes on some pretence of 'spiritual exploration', sneaking away to quiet, hidden spots, to fuck, to dance like wild things on the wooded hills, following this Harlequin, whoever he is. I've heard tales of revels and of riots, all centred around wine. They claim they're 'priestesses', I hear. So are they sacrificing their virginity, then?

He rounds upon the audience itself.

– Well then, I'll chase them from the hills, all of them. There are some in prison even now, safe and secure. I swear, I'll put an end to these outrageous orgies, if I have to throw them all in irons, every daughter, every mother in this town . . .

He pauses, soft and sad.

– And I'll chain Columbine herself.

He turns. He hasn't seen old Pantaloon and Scaramouche yet. They watch him from the other side of the stage.

– I hear, he says . . .

A pause.

– I hear a stranger has arrived in town, he says, with magic tricks, from ludic lands, with golden, perfumed hair, a goatskin mask over his face, but glowing in his eyes such grace as a goddess of love would give. He spends his days and nights with virgins, teaching them his 'mysteries'. If I catch him within these walls, I'll put an end to all his beating wands and tossing hair. I'll have his head.

He's laying on the bile a little thick, I think, lashing his words across the audience. Sometimes he comes across a little too intense, I think. Sometimes we piss him off; that's true, I guess. Sometimes he vents.

– What is this nonsense that the Harlequin is a spirit, that he was once stitched up in a thigh, his mother blasted by a lightning flash, because the lying slut said the boy's father was divine? Is this sheer arrogance alone not all the reason that we need to hang this man, whoever he may be?

Sometimes, I swear, he looks at Jack as if he wants to throttle him, and I'm not sure if Joey's really acting that at all.

– But look!

He halts.

– Another miracle. It's Scaramouche, our counsel, dressed in motley fawnskin cloak – and my own grandfather, waving his walking stick around. Is this a joke? Sir, this is sad. Have the two of you gone mad? Take off that ivy and put down that walking stick. My own grandfather! Did you put him up to this, you charlatan? What are you trying to do? If it weren't for the grey hair that's protecting you, I'd have you thrown in chains among the followers of Harlequin, for promoting these pernicious practices. Believe me, when the sparkle of sweet wine is found at women's feasts . . .

And Joey, Pierrot the King, the King of Tears, somehow projects, through all the rage, the burden of his tyranny:

– Nothing good will come of it.

– What are you trying to do? says Joey, looking out from behind the curtain at the crowd, as he paints on his tears. Out there, the

81

audience waits for the show to start; they're getting restless and the Duke and Princess both look bored, but we, of course, always have time for these last-minute tantrums in the Troupe d'Reynard: Jack sulking because, star of the show, he still doesn't have enough lines; Don muttering about how he'd only fuck them up; me – I must admit – grumbling about playing yet another girl's role, or because the dress is linen rather than silk and isn't nearly soft enough beside my tender skin. And Joey always convinced that, this time, Guy has taken it too far.

– You want to turn the Harlequin into some kind of god wandering amongst men. What is this? You see some money to be made in 'cult appeal'? All this mystery and mumbo-jumbo. You'll have Scaramouche reading chicken's entrails next.

– Well, he is playing Teiresias, says Monsieur Reynard. It is based on *The Bacchae*, after all . . . with a few minor modifications.

Joey looks out at the Duke of this small corner of the dream-time, sitting in business grey upon his throne, waiting impatiently for us to while away a little of eternity for him. There's always been an element of social satire in the Harlequin play, but here, in the Hinter of the Vellum, where dead men turn their kingdom paradises into the black iron prison of their own soul, trying to bring a little . . . reality into their afterlives can be a perilous adventure.

– They'll hang us all, says Joey. They'll fucking tear us apart.

And Jack just grins, and Don puffs up his chest, tugging his beard into its place, and I pout in the mirror as I put my lipstick on. Guy shrugs, quoting his own script.

– Have you no faith, sir? Would you mock old Pantaloon and all the seeds he's sown, those dragon's teeth, sons of the earth? And you, son of his daughter Columbine – you shame your birth.

Another Country

January 31st, 1989

Don orders another beer from the waiter and turns back to the window. The Copthorne's bar is an ideal location for him, a long thin glass conservatory stretching along the ground floor of the hotel's frontage, facing out directly onto George Square and elevated just enough for him to see over the cordon of riot police to the gathered protesters beyond. Some of the placards carry black-and-white pictures of the hunger striker Finn, and on the table in front of Don lies a pamphlet carrying the same image along with the logo of the Caledonia Workers' Committee. Ten years in jail have only made the man more of a hero. Outside the crowd are chanting — *Can't Pay, Won't Pay, Can't Pay, Won't Pay . . .*

It must be four months now. He came here in September of last year, following a lead on his latest story, his latest case, one Guy Reynard, currently in illegal possession of a mediaeval manu-script that was once in Kentigern University's Special Collection. Nobody's willing to tell him how this Reynard got hold of it or what it means to them, but they want it back so bad it worries him. There's only two reasons someone steals something, in Don's experience, and that's for money or for power. And if the power lies in a book, that can only be bad news. Sure, information is power, but only if it's secret.

And if it's secret, these days, that means someone wants it that way.

He's an agent for hire, is Don, a private eye with a press card good in any country of the Commonwealth, a licence to snoop all that he wants as long as what he sends back to the Agency answers the client's questions to their satisfaction, and as long as what goes public serves the right agenda. Find the truth and spread the lie. Gather and scatter, search and destroy, weave and spin. There's no such thing as a free press, indeed. But at least it's not the govern-ment that owns him. No, the Agency is a private company in the best Thatcherite tradition. Set up by blue-blood Ivy Leaguers who escaped the USA's implosion, saw what was coming and gathered together the ruins of the intelligence community, brought them over here lock, stock and barrel to set up shop as independent contractors.

That's the beauty of Albion's liberal fascism; it maintains the democratic facade of constitutional monarchy, lords and ministers, but behind that is a Babel of bureaucracy, red tape and paperwork designed to tie up all the would-be commissars, and all the true corridors of power hidden behind secret panels, in private, *privatised*.

Business is taken care of in deals made behind closed doors, handshakes between old friends. The closing of the London ghettos was just an elimination of competitors.

Don opens up his wallet to peel out a five-pound note for the waiter. It's something he's missed in his time in the States, all the different colours of Albion's money, and the different designs of this bank or that, Bank of Albion, Bank of Caledonia, Royal Bank of Caledonia, Clydeside Bank. For all that America is now a turmoil of militia territories, warring unions and confederacies, they all still cling to the same green bills – the Jacksons, Jeffersons and Washingtons – as if they all still share at least that one dream. He had the accent down pat in a few weeks but he never quite got used to that monomaniac currency, always fearing that his fumbling for the right note would one day blow his cover among whatever group of lunatics he happened to be infiltrating at the time. He fingers his way through blue and brown notes, receipts that he can claim back on expenses and a wad of just plain junk, finds the photogram and pulls it out as well, lays it on the table.

He's a foxy character, this Reynard – pencil moustache, flop of hair, there's no other word for him but dapper. Don gazes out into the crowd, scanning the faces for a sight of the man. If he's mixed up with these socialists, then it's worse than he thought, and all the clues point in that direction. This little island empire built on trade, this nation of shopkeepers, of company directors, salesmen and marketing executives, he thinks, this is no country for idealists. But try telling that to the fools out there.

He looks from face to face. The crowd is mainly young, would have been students, he reckons, before the closing of the universities. Young and rash, screaming against this new tax and against Westminster using Caledonia as a testing ground for it. But, then, it would be hard to think of anything better calculated to sow discontent among the socialists and nationalists of Caledonia than this tax.

There's a riot coming, thinks Don.

An SS officer walks past the window, up to the militiaman in charge, leans close to speak into his ear. The man nods, turns and barks an order to his troops.

Don raises his beer to his lips to take a sip. You become inured to the violence, he thinks, after a while in this job, seeing it as if your own eye was a camera lens, as if the window that you're looking out of was a radiovision screen. It's not happening here and now but distant, in another country, in the past. It's not real.

A face in the crowd. Don rises from his seat just as it disappears. Another glimpse. It's him: Reynard. But as he cranes his neck for a better view, some longhair punk gets in the way. He turns to look right at Don, eyes boring into him even through the milling protesters and ranks of militia, a gaze sharp as a knife-point trailing gently over someone's throat, searching for the artery.

The militia raise their batons.

In Gin and Whisky, Wine and Beer

– When an intelligent man, says Scaramouche, finds something he can get his teeth into, it's not a difficult thing to show a little flair, a little wit. You have a quick tongue in your head, my lord, but power and eloquence in a great man may bring fortune or a different fate; wit's not the same as wits. A man like you is the real peril to the state.

As Pierrot bristles, Guy as Scaramouche holds up his hands.

– I only say it as I see it, lord. This Harlequin you mock is bound for such a height of power through the whole of this fair hell, I could not put it into words. But let me tell you this. There are two things, young prince, that matter most among all men. There is the earth – the fields, the grain – who feeds our bodies with her bread.

I twirl across the stage, grain strewing from my hands. I'm not convinced we really need to make the imagery so literal but Guy insists on it – they have to understand.

– But as her counterpart there is this spirit, son of Simile, who fills our head with wine, stills all our sorrows over time, and brings us sleep where we forget all daily ills. There is no other cure for sorrow. Every offering we pour and every prayer that we make to any god – it's Harlequin who hears. He's there in every glass, in gin and whisky, wine and beer.

– This is the man you mock, reads Guy, scribbling at the manuscript. Because of some grand lie about him being sewn up in a deity's thigh.

He stands up to pace around inside the wagon, page in one hand, pen in the other, reciting the troubling section to us. Jack yawns. Joey pours a bottle of beer into his glass and dumps the empty on the table he's sitting on.

– But I'll tell you a simple secret, reads Guy. When Sooth snatched Harlequin out of the lightning's flash, he would have taken the boy up to sit there at his side, in his eternal palace in the skies. Except the queen of heaven, who gets everything her way, wanted the child dead, wanted to see his body brought before her on display; Sooth had to find a way, some kind of scheme, so he broke off a tiny fragment of eternity – a dream – and made a double of the boy to satisfy her cruel demands, while he hid Harlequin in other hands. In time, because the ancient words for 'thigh' and 'twin' sound much the same, men lost the truth and found a legend in the space between two words.

Guy taps his pen upon the paper.

– What do you think? Does that give the game away? he asks. If our audience is well acquainted with the myth of Dionysus . . .

– I hear the Duke is a well-educated man, says Don. He might well rumble it at that point.

Joey empties his glass.

– If he doesn't get it right away, he says, and—

– Hang us, shoot us, slice us, dice us, blah blah, blah blah, *blah*, Jack cuts off Joey in mid-gloom.

– I think, says Guy, stepping between the two, we might be better leaving that part out.

So Pierrot, on stage, just snorts and flicks a hand in sheer disdain.

– And I suppose this spirit has a prophet's power too, that there is inspiration in inebriation? After all, when a mere human form is 'filled up with the spirit', sodden with drink, they see visions, don't they? At least so they think. Or then again, in war sometimes, before the first gunshot, when panic grips an army, sends it in flight – is this the kind of frenzy loved by Harlequin? Is this your Harlequin's delight?

– The day will come, says Scaramouche, you'll see him leaping on the rock of oracles, a torch held high in one hand, and his green staff in the other, all of hell exalting him. Take my advice, Pierrot. Consider this: he forces no one to be chaste, but if it's part of who they are, no really modest maid will let her virtue be debased in any mysteries. Don't think that force alone can rule the world. Don't mistake wisdom for the opinion of a mind coming unfurled. Welcome this Harlequin into your realm, pour out libations, join the revel rout, and crown your head.

– Mark this, says Scaramouche. As you yourself are thrilled when crowds stand at the city gates and praise the name of Pierrot, he too, I think, delights in being cheered. So Pantaloon and I, for all your jeers, will wear garlands of ivy, join the dance and, even if we have grey beards, we will still prance.

He puts one hand on Pantaloon's shoulder and another on his walking stick, standing behind the old buffoon.

– No matter what you say, it is the way of things; one mustn't kick against the pricks.

He mugs a wink, stroking old Pantaloon's stick to get a cheap laugh from the innuendo, letting the audience think that roguish Scaramouche is simply up to his old tricks.

– Your mind is sick, he says to Pierrot's disdainful back, but with a furtive glance towards the Duke. And while it may be drugs that made you so, if it's a cure you're looking for, there's no drug that I know.

A Practised Gaze of Utter Certainty

– And folks, this is the god's honest truth. Which god, I couldn't rightly say – it could be Mammon or it could be Moloch, Dionysus or Apollo, any god you care to follow – but I tell you this, folks, I was there that Bloody Friday in George Square, when those guns started blazing and the people started *falling, and I know I saw Jack Flash himself. That's right, folks, ten years to the day he died, I saw the man, the myth, the angel assassin with the devil's kiss. I saw him there, up on the roof of the City Chambers, chi-gun cutting through the coppers like a carving knife through bacon. In all the massacre and mayhem, I can't say for sure if what I saw was monster or messiah — maybe just a bit of both — but I can tell you, folks, I saw him with my own eyes, saw him leaping from a rooftop down into the massed ranks of the men in black, a zen-grenade in each hand, two pins clenched between his grinning teeth.*

— Folks, what I'm telling you, I swear, is true. I'd seen the sketches in the papers as a young man and I knew, I knew that face the second that I saw it, fire in his eyes and grinning like a fiend. You should have seen me, baby, Howling Don Coyote, mouth open so wide that I was catching flies, dropping the pencil and the notebook where I used to write my lies. My friends, I want to open up here, let you know the truth; I wasn't always the same Don on the side of good. I was, for shame, an agent once, yes, spinning lies instead of discs and feeling oh-so-bad about it but still letting others take the risks. One thing changed that for me, my friends. One little thing that changes everything is all it takes. One little thing, one day, and your whole world breaks.

— Well, mes amigos, now you know. For me, that thing was Jack.

— Jack Flash is an empty hope, a futile gesture, says Joey Narcosis. His great revolutionary feats weren't half as spectacular as his failure.

— That's just the point, says the Minister. Jack Flash is dead. Or is there something we should know? There were reports, the Tax Riots of '89. Could—

— No.

He gives the Minister his empty glare, a practised gaze of utter certainty, cold as a corpse's, laden with a knowledge absolute as death. The Minister drops his eyes, drops his question. So much for the will-to-power. Fascists, communists, anarchists. They're all the same. Bureaucrats or dreamers, with their swastikas, their hammers and sickles. To the Futurists those were only ever paths to power. While the people rallied round them, the Futurists of Russia and Germany nodded and smiled and joined in the songs and joined the party and they waited till those symbols had reshaped the nation. And then one day they ripped the hammer and sickle down, burned the swastika, and raised the flag of Futurism over the factories of death.

He smiles at his reflection in the window, smart in black suit, black leather jacket and black woollen overcoat — Italian and expensive — the embodiment of slick, deadly authority. Too bad he wasn't born on the other side of the Iron Wall, he thinks. Would have fitted right in. He runs his fingers over crow-black hair and turns to face the Minister.

— All we have here, he says, is a wannabe living out his wet dream.

— Jack Flash or not, he's causing havoc. It may be his wet dream; it's my bloody nightmare.

And so you call in the dream-killer, thinks Joey.

— Jack Flash is dead, he says. It's time to exorcise his ghost.

— Yes, mes amigos, Jack Flash was there and Jack Flash died that night a second time, but friends, it looks like Jack is back. How many lives does this cat have? Has someone taken up the maniac's mantle, or are we looking at the ghost of massacres past come back to haunt us? Mortal madman or angel assassin? Or killer queen, indeed, if what I've heard about his tastes in bed are true. So let's hear what you think. And — whoop-de-doo — I think we got our first call coming through right now. It's a big hello to ... Harvey from Maryhill. Harvey, you're on the aether ...

— Hello, Don. Aye ... Jack Flash ... I think he's a bit of a tosser, actually, and a dangerous one at that. The problem is — I can't remember who said it, but — 'to fight the Empire is to become it'. Once you start to play the game by their rules, use their methods, you've already lost; you're just the same as them.

— Violence begets violence, eh, Harvey?

— It doesn't matter whose foot the jackboot's on, it's still a jackboot kicking someone else in the face. Every baby-killer sees themselves as just another good soldier fighting for the glorious cause ...

The Minister flicks the latches on the leather briefcase and opens it up. There's a gleam of adamantium, too silvery to be gold, too golden to be silver, the glow of glamour and trapped souls. Joey Narcosis crosses the room calmly and gazes into the light. It's a handsome payment.

– Double it, he says.

– You can't be serious.

– Serious? he says. I'm fucking solemn. I'm not doing this for the glory.

It's not the money either really; in the end it's just survival. He hates these people; he works for them only because it suits him here and now. Joey's a Futurist at heart, utterly committed to a belief in absolutely nothing; he just happened to be born in the wrong place at the wrong time, among merchants and ministers like this who'll never really understand the cold calculus of survival. It's a pity. In another world, another universe, he might have been the man who put the bullet in the back of Stalin's head.

The Minister can't help glancing down into the briefcase, wiping the sweat from his top lip.

– You understand that . . . if you fail . . .

– Jack Flash is just another killer, he says. We've *already* won.

And stretching his mind leisurely out of his body, feeling for a signal in the aether, Joey Narcosis wonders where the sad psychotic fuckwit is right now.

A Raging Bull of Sorrow

A cyclist tringalings his bell as he veers past the wagon, rattling rickety in front of us and round a corner into a crowd that's streaming through the locked-down gates and turnstiles of a factory compound. The shadow of the castle lours over everything here, cooling air that should be Mediterranean warm.

– You old fox, I whisper, reading through the script. Even when you're using the most reasonable of terms, you're using them to praise the power of disorder.

– My dear boy, the Scaramouche will always give you sound advice. He's just trying to bring us all back down to earth . . . and trying not to do so in one reckless leap into the great abyss. He's a traditionalist.

Joey shakes his head at the insanity of this whole venture. He climbs the ladder up onto the wagon roof and stands there, balanced, looking grimly at the castle that is getting ever nearer.

He's never had much time for kings or castles, Joey, and his moods get worse each gig we play.

– They'll never fucking buy it, Guy, he says.

– Joey, my boy, so what if Harlequin is not a god? We simply say he is. It is a splendid fraud. Call him the son of Simile, and her the mother of a god – all these grandiose terms, I'm sure they'll be applauded.

– and be lauded. Come, says Don as Pantaloon, advancing towards Pierrot across the stage. Let me crown your head with ivy. Come and join us in devotion to the spirit of delirium and drink.

Don bumbles, stumbling on his beard as he attempts to put the crown of leaves on Joey's head and, staggering forward to the edge of the stage, he flaps his arms to get his balance back. The crown flies through the air and lands on the Duke's head instead. He pulls it off and tears it up, but the Princess is laughing so he smiles weakly, gives a shrug to show that he's a sport, slow-claps the slapstick jestery. A quiet ripple of amusement is allowed around the court.

Pantaloon spins round on one foot, grabbing at Pierrot's black tie for balance. He still holds it, pulling Joey closer as he puffs his chest and huffs:

– Forget this hubris and remember the great hunter once dismembered by the savage hounds he'd reared himself, ripped into pieces in the fields because he boasted that he was a better hunter than—

– Get your hands off! Go to your crazy rites and don't infect me with your madness! I swear, I'll bring a reckoning upon the man who teaches this insanity.

Pierrot shoves him away and spins to call on all of his imaginary armies out of sight offstage. He fixes me with piercing eyes, something to focus on and rage at. I stick my tongue out.

– You! You! rages Pierrot. Go now and find if he has any space that he holds sacred. Go and wrench it from its base with crowbars, turn the whole place upside down, and throw it into utter chaos, throw his garlands to the hurricane's winds. That will show him.

Offstage, I start a rat-a-tat-tat upon a drum, with one hand –

finger and thumb – while with the other hand I rumble thunder on a sheet of aluminium, the quiet threat of a storm arising. Jack tucks his Harlequin wand under his arm, goose-steps across the roof, as Joey stalks the stage, his fist clenched, shaking in a mockery of pomp and rage. A lock of his long hair falls down over his face; his fingers rake it back into its place.

– The rest of you sweep through the countryside, says Joey. Find this mincing stranger who infects our women with desire, setting all marriage vows on fire. And if you catch him, bring him here to me, in chains. I'll see him stoned. I'll bring him down. He'll wish he'd never brought his revels to my town.

– You fool, says Scaramouche, but quietly, aside. You don't know what you're doing here today. You always have been something of a dick. Now you are, sad to say, a raving lunatic.

He takes Don by the arm.

– Come, Pantaloon. Let's get out of his way. All we can do now here is pray, pray for this man with his tempestuous temper, and pray for the city that it doesn't suffer in his tragedy. Come, take your ivy staff and follow me. Steady, old boy – don't want the two of us old fools to fall. Come, we must give our god his dues, this Harlequin, the son of Sooth.

He shakes his head and slips an arm around Don's shoulder.

– My old friend, I fear that your King Pierrot will bring a raging bull of sorrow to your house. A premonition? No, I judge him by his acts and his intentions. Words so foolish show him for a fool.

Rat Race or Rat Trap

The Minister loosens his tie, wiping his sweating palms on it, mouth dry, heart pounding in his chest, looking across the hotel room at the young hustler handcuffed to the bed, and—

Joey unlatches his mind, brings it back to the here and now of the bridge and the Rookery louring close beside him. He files the Minister's grubby little secret away for future reference; it's leverage that might come in useful, but right now he has a Jack to track.

He takes a little pillbox from his pocket, opens it and downs a

Smiley. The buzz is already fading from the last one – popped just before the Minister's visit – and he'll need to stay in the zone for this job, keep the volume of his own emotions turned down nice and low so he can pick up the signals in the aether. In the crime scene.

The sentry has been propped against a tree, legs crossed, arms folded, hat down over his eyes like the sombrero of a sleeping Mexican. Just as a finishing touch, Joey assumes, a thin cigarette dangles from his mouth. He pulls it out and sniffs it – cannabis, tobacco, and a scent something like aniseed or liquorice. Ouzo. Smells like Jack, all right. He goes through the man's pockets, looking for other anomalies, things that don't belong there. A wallet, a set of keys, some change, a matchbook.

He rubs the matchbook between thumb and finger, feeling for the psychic taint, the touch of a familiar identity, and there's a tiny . . . flash of something.

The spy who came in from the chaos.

Standing up, he casts his mind a little wider, looking for a trace of memories, sensations.

The bridge remembers.

A shallow river, winding its tree-lined banks all through the bourgeois West End suburbs where the merchants and the middle classes live, through parks as groomed as the Victorian gentry promenading within them, passing picturesque ruined mills, glass-houses of botanical gardens. A shallow river winding down to join the Clyde, where the great steel wireliners were built, warehouses filled with shabtis and tobacco, filled with the fortunes of the overseers and entrepreneurs come home to gift their native city with the wealth of their gratitude, with parks and statues, a broken-nosed grim bust of Carlyle, a Boer War monument with a pith-helmeted soldier, a bronze lioness with a broken-necked bird hanging from her jaws, red paint sprayed round its mouth by Jack and Joey, passing a bottle of ouzo back and forth between them, moving on to paint gold eye-shadow, red lipstick and nail varnish on the two Teutonic-looking knights built into the plinth of the mounted general who looks down over the park towards this bridge over a shallow river, winding as a swollen scar across the landscape, open sewer for the inhabitants of the West End ghettoes of the literati, for the shit of academicians and bohemians, tenements and townhouses now squalid squats and hovels, bombed and rebuilt with sheet metal and scaffolding into warrens, prisons for the dissidents and deviants, as defined in the Sedition Act of '59 and the Nights of Fire when the library was emptied and its books brought down to be thrown, burning, into this shallow river, winding, here at the bridge where the bratspawn of the Rookery come down to play in the dumping ground no-man's-land at the edge of freedom as he came down here when he was their age, as we came down here and played among the broken fridges, with pocket knives and airguns, and we shot at rats for target practice, till we were old enough to shoot at each other, to kill on a bridge to nowhere over a shallow river winding.

Joey Narcosis drops the cigarette.

The bridge remembers him.

He looks up at the Gothic tower, sole visible vestige of the old University, rising over the rooftops of the Rookery.

It used to be just the two of them, Jack and Joey, latter-day urchins playing in the ruins of bohemia. Neither one of them knew his parents; neither one of them really gave a fuck. The only life they knew was the Rookery and the river. What Kentigern was, or could be, didn't matter to them at all. The militia was just another mundane threat like the razor gangs and the scheme clans who were always trying to move in on each other's territories. You avoided them where you could, paid protection money when you had to, played the game by the rules that had been set up from day one. Dog eat dog. Do unto others before they do you. You only had to watch the public executions on the radiovision, and the Iron Lady sending riot police against the miners, and yuppies in red braces gripping wads of cold, hard cash in their greasy fists, to learn the rules of the game. The Jack he used to know understood that. Or so he thought.

And then came Guy Fox and King Finn and all the Robin Hood bullshit that Jack swallowed hook, line and sinker, the anti-fascist rebellion, redistribution of wealth, freedom and all that shit. He wonders if Jack even got it at the end, when they were standing on this very bridge and he turned, saw Joey there with the gun trained on him.

Joey feels around for any other traces of the copycat, or of the Jack who died here twenty years ago, however unlikely that might be. He pushes his mind out of his body and still he finds nothing.

No. Wait. Somewhere under the drift-dams of rotting debris, amid the oozing sludge, he can sense some sort of life, down there in the filth, rats big as cats, warped by the mix of methane from decaying landfill and orgone seeping from the abandoned mines that lace the whole of Kelvinhill, breeding and feasting, and feasting and breeding, buried in their own shit and trapped under the bulldozed earth, and slowly running out of shit to feed on.

— It's a fucking rat race, mate, says Joey to the dead sentry.

— It's a fucking rat trap, he hears Jack saying, a long time ago.

— Rat race or rat trap, it's still all about survival. You trap a bunch of rats in a cage without food, they don't work together for freedom. They just eat each other.

Joey picks up the matchbook. This place reminds him of his childhood, all right. But under all the memories of infant thieves and thugs, there's no glorious, heroic Jack Flash, only the vicious monotonal compulsions of rodent hunger and lust, the visceral music of sex and death.

The Ways of Lunatics and Fools

I enter, singing.

— O holiness, queen of eternity, sweeping on golden wings over the earth! Hear the words of Pierrot in his conceit, cursing the son of Simile, spirit of festivals and feasts of flowing wine, the one who lets the drowsy rest, glass in their hand, in ivy shade, or rouses revellers at the masquerade, who drags them up to dance, to shake off their dull care and wake the flute.

And Harlequin up on the roof gives out a regal wave, a royal salute.

— The life of leisure, ruled by reason, rests unshaken and

sustains the home, a pleasure dome, for in aetherial estates the powers divine, though they live in the distant far-ago, know every individual's state.

I sing out to the Duke, flatter his vanity, flutter my eyes and bow, as if to say: O, yes, I see just how magnificent m'sire is in his munificence and magnanimity.

– This mystery ends all rhetoric lacking law and sense: life is too short to squander it in abstract logic, unwise sophistry; and those who fail to understand, aim at the skies instead, they miss the joy at hand. These ways, I say, these are the ways of lunatics and fools.

– The ways of lunatics and fools, Don interrupts, and Guy looks over his shoulder as he flicks the reins, the wagon rolling on across the rolling plains under the rolling clouds. I look up from this new script Guy has given us, stop reading, blink from one to the other. It's so seldom that gruff, grizzled Don says anything at all that when he does, the rest of us tend to shut up.

– You don't like the line? asks Guy.

– The line is fine, says Don. Just thinking – and he points far down the road ahead, at spires of splendour lit with golden fires that rise up like a mountain, our far distant destination. Ways of lunatics and fools, he says.

– Quite so, says Guy. Quite so.

– O let us fly, sing I, sail through the sky, and enter ciphers, enter isles of a free doubt, where spirits of love laugh, live and soothe man's sylph. To pathos, never fed by river rain, but rich with centuries' mouths!

I stand upon the roof of rumbling roughwood, skipping side-to-side to balance as the wagon trundles over broken flagstones, arms thrown out with pages flapping in my hand, proclaiming to the wilds, to the dust-devils and the slumbering, half-buried masonry in the sands. Jack lounges in the sun beside me, flicking through his script and looking up every so often with a lazy yawn.

– Do I have any lines in this at all?

I drop to my knees to ham it up right in his face.

– O lead me, Harlequin, guiding star of drunken pilgrims, to the holy slopes of oil lamps, haunt of muses. There is the grace. There is the soft desire. There is the revelry of your devotees free of the Empyre.

– Will you shut up, up there, shouts Joey from below.

– Fuck you, I say, I'm practising. And sing out, louder still.

– The joy of our spirit is in banquets. Son of Sooth, saviour of wayward boys, he hates all those who will not deign to live the life of bliss, in days and nights of joy. To ease our pains, he gives us riches as his gift. He savours peace and so, to rich and poor alike, he gives delicious wine, glorious booze, to lift the heart and soul above the wisdom of the scholar, endlessly refined. This, then, I choose: that which the poor and ragged man approves.

And over grooves and potholes worn by cars and trucks and carts and hooves, the wagon trundles on along a broken road with signs for non-existent towns, abandoned rest-stops, heading for another city where another king or lord or godfather or – in his own mind – god holds court among lost souls who've strayed across this wide land of the dead to end up in his maze, captivated by the order of his streets and roads, becoming slaves. The ways of lunatics and fools, indeed. The palaces of Pantaloons.

Jack huffs a butterfly away from his nose, swipes at it lazily. I lean my chin over the edge of the wagon's roof, looking down at Guy and Don.

– So what happens in Act Two?

– Oh, Act Two, says Guy, that's where things really start to heat up.

Errata

The Universal City

Somewhere in the city below, a muezzin sings the call to evening prayers, and he stands at the window, cigarette in hand, looking down over the slope of roofs and gardens, listening to the waver of that distant clarion voice. Slim twin minarets prick the sky here and there, domes nestled between them. It's largely a modern city though, all roads and apartment blocks, sprawling over the valley floor and crawling up the slopes of Mount Uludag behind, where the Dilmun Otel sits perched among the cafés and restaurants of the hotel quarter.

He stubs the cigarette out in the ashtray, slings his jacket over his shoulder and grabs his room key – proper old-fashioned room key with a fistful of metal attached to discourage you from taking it outside with you – and pulls the door closed quietly behind him as he leaves. Everything is hotel rooms these days.

He takes the lift down to reception. Floor six ... five ... four ... three. Ground. There's no two or one for some reason, maybe because there's two sub-ground floors housing the restaurant and health club. It seems a little odd, but different strokes for different folks. Like the way they make the beds, with the covers folded under themselves instead of tucked under the mattress. Or the little sachets of Nescafé with sugar and powdered milk already added that sit beside the electric kettle on the table in the room. As if there's just Turkiye kafe and that weird Western shit which, as far as they're concerned, always has milk and sugar in it, doesn't it?

– *Iyi akşamlar*, he says to the receptionist and she smiles. *Good evening.*

– *Iyi akşamlar*, she says as he heads out the front door.

– *Arapşukru, lutfen.*

The Heykel Taksi takes him the five-minute, five-million-lira drive to the Arapşukru – the Street of Fish Restaurants – and he fumbles through his wallet for the right note. *No, that's five hundred thousand. Here's the one.* He still can't get over how much the founder of the modern Turkish nation, Emil Attaturk, looks like the mad, camp, villain-hero from this 50s sci-fi serial *Lost in Space*. Dr Zachary Smith, his name was. Swear to God, it's the spitting image of him. Needless to say, he hasn't pointed this out to any of the Turks; it would be bad form.

    – *Teşekkur.*

Thanks.

    – *Teşekkur. Iyi akşamlar.*

    – *Iyi akşamlar.*

Outside the taksi, the early-evening city streets are busy, shops open later than they would be back home, people here thronging the way they do in these warm countries where there's little worry about the weather, about raincoats and umbrellas. Street culture, street living: it's one of the things he likes about this time and place. He couldn't stay here forever – you can't get a good White Russian in all of pre-war Bursa – but it's good to visit once in a while, for the ambience.

    The waiters hovering outside the restaurants haggle him, beckoning at the displays of fresh fish by the doorways, the warm glow of the little two-storey buildings with their waxed-cloth tablecovers, TV sets showing Galatasaray playing Fenerbahçe FC, men inside cheering, bottles of raki. He smiles, shakes his head and walks on. It's only a few more yards before the last of the restaurants is behind him and the street is darker, quieter. He unslings the jacket from his back and puts it on before ducking down the alleyway over cobblestones and—

Dug-up tarmac, fenced off behind wire mesh. The whole road is blocked like this, little mechanical diggers parked behind the fence. The pavement – sidewalk, whatever – is uneven and narrow even without the stalls of socks and plastic trinkets. He keeps finding himself moving against the flow of people, having to weave between them. He turns a corner onto a less busy street, heading towards the Zocalo, checking his watch and quickening his pace. It's nearly eleven here, and there's a free concert on tonight in the vast square in the centre of the city; he doesn't want to get stuck in the flow of the mob moving back to their homes after Alessandro Gussman's finished singing. Not after the last time. Christ, there's twenty-five million people in the Distrito Federal, and the last time he was here and now, it seemed like they'd all been at the concert, and like they all had to go down the same street to get home. Eventually, he'd just given up and ducked into a small café for a cerveza and a cigarette while he waited for the street to quieten down. It was a cute little place, all decked out in red, green and white bunting, which he'd assumed was some kind of cheery nationalism in the run-up to Independence Day, until he spotted the football – soccer, that is – on the television, Inter Milan against … someone or other, and realised that it was an Italian café. In the heart of Mexico City.

He jogs across a road, strides down the block to get to the next corner and across before the first of the concert-goers come streaming down onto the street behind him. Made it.

– *Perdón, señor.*

He turns as the kid bumps past him, lets himself stumble a little, grab the kid's arm so he doesn't fall. It brings the kid round between him and the woman on his other side, her hand slipping back into her own pocket as if it had never left, an almost imperceptible frown on her face as she walks on.

– *Perdón*, he says himself, patting the kid on the shoulder.

The kid doesn't even notice that he's lost his own wristwatch and the roll of bills from his inside pocket. Serves him right for being such a bloody amateur.

He pats his chest to feel the bulk of the wallet still resting there. It wouldn't have done the pickpockets any good anyway, a handful of Turkish lira and a bunch of credit cards that expired two years ago.

He turns a corner.

Another street, another city, another year. The buildings are still black with grime, the stone still ground in with decades of car fumes and coal fires, once resplendent tenement-style, banks and offices ornate enough that you could probably climb right up their grooved, ledged facades if you wanted to. The rubbish in the gutters still stinks of rotting fruit and the people still sit in bars shouting at television sets. The city is universal. The universe is a city. At least, his is.

Down Rosenstrasse and across the Bridge of Sighs. Skirting Skid Row, Hell's Kitchen and a Soho that's as much New York as London. Brown brick, red brick, sandstone, granite. Every so often he spots a landmark that he recognises, but mostly he ignores them; impressive as they are, they're not his navigation beacons on these streets of refuse and real life. No, it's the congruences that he follows, the commonalities of people leaning out of windows to shout down at friends outside, of folks walking their dogs, or cigarette butts falling down a drain. That's one of the reasons that he smokes actually; you drop a cigarette in a puddle and it links you to a million other instants – or more – of a cigarette falling with a splash and a hiss into a puddle, instants all different, never quite the same, but close enough that you can take just one small step across from one into the other. Bursa, Mexico City, Mirenburg, Firenze. In the end, they're all one city, a universal city of a million districts, Latin Quarters, Jewish Quarters, West Ends and Chinatowns all mixed up in the mess of their inhabitants' forgotten heritages, the little bits of homeland brought with them in their hearts to be displayed in windows and on walls, collages of identity cut up and strung together so you could, if you weren't paying close attention, mistake them for mere decoration, like red, green and white bunting in an Italian café in Mexico City.

He cuts off Ingram Street, down past a low red sandstone block of a building – some once-rich Glasgow tobacco importer's commissioned offices long since rebuilt inside, transformed into a nightclub – and comes out at the top of Virginia Street, a dilapidated side street of gay bars and shopping arcades, the loading bay of a department store. There are a couple of buildings collapsed here, another just condemned, steel on the doors and windows, warning signs. Another corner and he's on a side street off the side street, and in a different decade entirely.

He walks up the steps, nodding at the bouncers in their dishevelled tuxes far too tight for them. It's not exactly a gentleman's club but they do have Bombay Sapphire and good armchairs in Club Soda, downstairs, behind the dancefloor, down a corridor of dark-green wallpaper and wood panelling, in the backroom where the poker is played. He's whistling as he pushes the door open.

He recognises Joey immediately, almost smiles his recognition with a chipper hello before the khaki uniform and its insignia register . . . and the four guards with him, all armed.

– Major Joseph Pickering, the man says. If you'll just come with us, sir. Let's not cause a fuss here.

Foolish Stories, Mad Stories

– My name is Reynard Cartier. I was—

– Reinhardt von Strann, says Pickering, cutting him off.

– I was born in Rene-le-Chateau, in France. I was brought up in Paris. I owned a nightclub in Berlin until the Futurists—

Pickering shakes his head. How long is the damn fool going to keep this bloody charade going?

– Your name is Reinhardt von Strann, he says. You were born in Strann, West Prussia. Christ, man, we know who you are. We know everything.

It's not entirely true. Pickering has a file on Reinhardt von Strann, aka Guy Fox, that's as Joycean in its incomprehensibility as in its length. The problem is that over half of the intel and intercept contained in it, verified from multiple trustworthy sources, is entirely contradictory. So saying *everything* is therefore something of a fudge. And to be fair, it's not so much *we* as *I*. The rest of MI5 isn't terribly interested in a 'crackpot pamphleteer', a mad socialist-anarchist railing against the dangers of the new government's 'fascist' policies. There are more important enemies these days.

– This is absurd, says the man.

His accent is impeccably French, of course – a hint of American in his English as one would expect, but not a trace of guttural German. Pickering doesn't believe it for a second. He takes his cap off momentarily to strake his fingers through his crow-black, Brylcreem hair and slaps the cap back on his head; it's an unconscious habit, as if he's pushing long hair back out of his face, and he has no idea where he picked it up, having worn a short back and sides since the day he joined the army.

– You *were* a nightclub owner in Berlin before the war, he insists, for a brief period following a less illustrious career as a – how can I put this – gigolo and jewel thief.

– Oh, now really, I can't say I've led the most virtuous life but I'm no thief.

– No *common* thief.

Pickering stands up from his chair and wanders to the corner of the room, leans back against the wall, arms folded, sizing the prisoner up. He returns, takes his cap off and lays it on the table.

– In July 1940, he says, you were arrested for your activity in helping refugees escape from Germany, and sentenced to death, a traitor to the Neues Reich. Given the pedigree of the von Strann family, this was no small scandal. Not that your family was without scandal before this . . . your brother, for instance. But we'll come to that.

– Look, I don't have a brother. Please check your records. I am the only child of Alphonse and Marie Cartier of—

– Shortly before your execution, however, you managed to escape Gestapo custody and nothing was heard of you until—

– I'm telling you, you have the wrong man.

– *Until* after the war, September 1947, when you were caught breaking *into* a Siberian gulag. They had you in a locked room, no windows. They leave you alone for one minute and – *poof* – you're gone. Two days later a man answering your description is shot at by Polish border guards crossing over the Iron Curtain. We have the NKVD and Stasi files on it all. Believe me, it makes for interesting reading. Two days to get from Siberia to Warsaw. Two *days*.

– Major – Pickering, was it? – I've been in Britain – sorry, Albion, I mean – I've been in Albion since I fled Berlin in 1941. I wish I was this von Strann character you talk about. He helped refugees escape, you say? He sounds an admirable man.

The prisoner smiles weakly.

– But I am not a brave man, Major Pickering. The most I ever did against the Futurists was to urinate in their cognac. And I was very drunk at the time. I was afraid of them, Major Pickering. And when the opportunity arose, I fled, alone. I got out through Holland and I did not look back. I took no one with me, thought of no one but myself. I am not like this von Strann. I am not this man. The Dutch Resistance, your own people, there are scores of individuals in London alone who can verify my story. The captain who debriefed me, Captain MacChuill—

– General now. Yes, General MacChuill remembers you quite well. As he recalls, you supplied some quite invaluable information as regards munitions sites, potential targets.

– Well, perhaps I was of *some* use. But I do not understand why, if Captain MacChuill has verified this . . .

– There are no records, though, are there?

– I'm sorry?

– Oh, the General recalls you perfectly. He is quite adamant about that, and there is no question that he's telling the truth. And yet, there are no records of his debrief, no records of your arrival, no records at all. Why is that?

– War is a confusing time, Major Pickering. Things get lost in all the chaos, lost, forgotten or . . .

– Stolen? A hundred little routine scraps of officialdom that should be there, but aren't. None of your friends has any photographs. No mention in any correspondence. But they all swear blind they've known you for seven, eight years now. How can that be, Herr Strann? Or is it Herr von Strann? I'm not sure how one addresses Prussian aristocracy.

– Please, Major Pickering. My name is Cartier . . . Monsieur Cartier, if we must be formal. I would prefer Reynard.

Pickering says it tired and laboured, like he's speaking to an idiot child.

– Your name is *Reinhardt* . . . Reinhardt von Strann. We *know* this. We know that you owned the Fox's Den, in Berlin, between—

The prisoner holds up his hand. It's shaking just a little. He seems equally tired.

– Wait, Major Pickering. I am being honest with you, believe me. When you talk of this von Strann, I do not recognise the name. But . . . the Fox's Den, you say?

– The Fox's Den.

– This I remember. I never knew the proprietor's name, but I heard stories of him. He had a brother in the army, yes?

– Johann von Strann. Do not play games with me.

– No games, Major Pickering. This is not a world for playing games. Not since . . . not since . . .

He shakes his head.

– But I will tell you these stories. Perhaps I do know something of what you want to hear. But they are foolish stories, mad stories, things that are not possible – but if this is what you are looking for, if this is what you want . . . I only ask one thing, Major Pickering, one little thing.

Pickering says nothing.

– At least call me by my own name, Major Pickering. Call me Reynard.

3

Sorrow's Prisoners

The Thief of Lives

They say he was in Dresden, my brother. They say he was in
Dresden when the allied fire-bombs fell. They say he was in Dresden
and Köln, and Düsseldorf and Hamburg. They say he was in London
during the Blitz, jumping from rooftop to rooftop – a latter-day
Spring-Heeled Jack – and every time his jackboots touched a house,
every time he leapt again out of his crouch, that house was blasted
with a crack of thunder and a bloom of flame. They say he was in
New York when the first of Von Braun's newborn ripped a streak of
fire down Wall Street.

In Dresden, London and New York the bombs followed him, as
if he was their golden harbinger of death. Or as if, perhaps, it was
my brother that they sought to blast and not the families huddled
in coal cellars, factory-worker women with their children and grand-
parents, or businessmen standing at windows twenty storeys high,
watching in horror as the light came searing through the darkness,
closer, closer. They say they saw him walk out of the firestorms
inviolate, this spirit of all Blitzes, created in destruction. They say he
was in Tokyo, Hiroshima and Nagasaki. Wherever there was fire, in
those days, they say they saw my brother, Johann von Strann – Jack
Flash as the English called him – übermensch, avatar, moonchild.
But then it was in fire that he forged himself, in blood and fire.

He wanted to become a hero of the most ancient sort, a god
summoned into the body of a man. Instead he was a man caught in
the dreams of God.

*

In Dresden, Florence on the Elbe as they called it for its architecture of rococo and baroque, the capital of Saxony, a god of fire can only feel at home. That city of Dresden china, fired in kilns, dark clay transformed in the furnace into fine, white porcelain. A port city of heavy industry, of foundries and forges, iron and carbon melded into steel for manufacturing. My brother often talked of one of his heroes, Michael Bakunin, holding the city after it rebelled, after it rose up and threw the King of Saxony out for rejecting the constitution of the German Empire. He talked of Bakunin and his army of factory workers taking art treasures from the city's museums and placing them on the barricades to discourage Prussian troops from shooting. Bakunin and his rebels fighting on the streets for four days while the shopkeepers, the petty bourgeois shopkeepers, formed community guards supporting the troops against the insurrectionists.

You do have this history in your world, I hope? No, no, I'm sure you do. You still remember a century of swastikas and sickles, the bullet years that shot from Bosnia to Bosnia, years when the Great Game became deadly serious and great powers, great ideas, moved in dark floods across the world, impervious to all boundaries, moral or geographic. The world after this, believe me, is not so very different. We try to change it, but sometimes it seems we only change ourselves.

Prometheus changed the world. So much so that Prometheus, bringer of fire, is bound in a relief sculpture on the wall of Dresden's Katholische Hofkirche. A city such as Dresden, after all, has much to thank that thief of fire for, who gave us the means to build our modern world. Poets and musicians who visited Dresden from all over Europe left and wrote great masterworks extolling that titan figure of enlightenment. Romance and Reason, in the figure of Prometheus, are fused like iron and carbon in the steel with which we make our ships and cars, our tanks and guns; and so the two implacably opposed ideals of Western thought found something they could share in that tragic, heroic figure of Prometheus bound, in chains, in statues cast in bronze, in lyric verse, in symphonies of crystal sound, in stone relief . . . in Dresden.

One might almost imagine that it was this very idol of Zeus's hated enemy that brought the fire down from the skies. As if he sent his message down in thunderbolts: How dare you reverence that thief? If you're so grateful for his gift of fire, then let us see how grateful you can be; I'll give you fire in abundance.

There are no photographs of my brother, I believe, only stories; but the stories are the sort that never make it into official records. A silhouette walking unscathed from a building that's become a furnace. A figure crouched on a chimney-breast, calling down the firestorm. War seems to generate such myths, and some of them become famous: angels who appear to rout opposing forces; dead comrades who save a soldier's life only to disappear into the smoke they came from. But Jack Flash, that flame-haired angel of death in billowing army overcoat, whose growl was the thunder of approaching bombers, whose howl was the keen of diving V-3 rockets, and whose roar was the blast of buildings blown to kingdom come – I've heard the stories of him only here and there, from those who saw their loved ones die; and always they have told the stories quietly and reluctantly, as if merely to speak of him might be to summon him again.

They are quite wrong, of course. My brother accepts no summonings, no invitations. He needs no persuasion.

Pierrot's Prisoner

Don comes back on the stage, quick-changed into the costume of a soldier, gleaming armour with a sharp and savage shine, holding a chain.

– M'sire Pierrot, we're back, he says and, with a heave, hauls Jack onto the stage with him. He slams the Harlequin down on his knees.

– We've got the prey you sent us after. Hunted him like game, we did. But this one's bleedin tame.

Don sneers, but there's confusion under his contempt.

– There weren't no flight, no fight, no face all white with fear. He didn't even go a little pale, just gives a grin, he does, holds up his hands for us to bind. He just gave in, says, *Tie me up and run me in*. He waited for us, made it easy.

Don looks away, unsettled, almost queasy, then speaks quietly.

– I was ashamed. I says to him I didn't wish him any ill. I only follow orders.

He looks back at Pierrot.

– I says, this is my master's will.

– But m'sire, those followers caught by your majesty and bound in manacles and leg-irons – all of those locked in the cells – they've all got free. The chains just fell off their feet by themselves, and doors unlocked, flew open, with no outside help. They've just slipped out of their shackles and gone off to play like children in the fields, calling for Harlequin. This stranger's brought a bloomin host of miracles, m'sire. Whatever happens next, I'd keep an eye on him.

I slip back to the sidelines of the action, watching Don and Joey, watching Jack, and watching Guy hidden behind the curtainry across from me, stroking his beard and studying the Duke, the Princess Anaesthesia. The hall is dark and quiet now, the audience absorbed into the action. The Princess hushes the distraction of her consul's learned explication of the theme, the Harlequin as human spirit—

– Is that gin, she says, or whisky?

The Duke laughs.

It's not the first time we've performed this sort of play hidden inside a play. It's not the first time that Monsieur Reynard's set out to sneak some secret message into our spectaculars, to use my song, Jack's dance, Don's pyrotechnics as the smoke and mirrors to disguise something a tad more strong; but it is the first time he's set out so blatantly subversive as to show a prince of hell his own defeat. I think we're lucky that the man sees little more than Jack prancing across the stage, the pantomime of Pantaloon and Scaramouche, the melodrama of Pierrot as he rants and raves. There was one gig we played one time in what, to all intents and purposes, was the Castile of a self-styled El Cid. We got through one Cervantes sketch, using the text performed by Lorca's La Barraca company, before we had to ride out hell for leather, Jack and Joey firing tommy-guns from the wagon's running-boards into the horde riding in hot pursuit. The London mob were just as bad in George's day, Guy said. They'd tear the theatre down and have the owner on his knees apologising, if they didn't like the play.

I guess we're all a little nervous then, but luckily, for now, the Duke looks mildly amused. The rest of them − the sleeping souls who think he built their whole eternity − just look confused.

− Unchain his hands. Now that we have him in the cage, he's not so quick he can escape my rage.

Pierrot prowls.

− Well, stranger, I can see you're not unsuited to your goal of bedding every woman in this land. You're not an . . . unattractive man. From your wild hair − he says, running his hand through Jack's blond shock to clench a fistful, snap his head back − I should say you've never been a fighter. But it does set off your cheeks.

He runs his fingers over skin, under the chin.

− So soft and pale, not weathered by the sun, but rather kept under the shade to help you in your aims. You hunt love as your game and use the beauty of your face as bait. Come, tell me all about your race.

Search and Destroy

− *I'm a lionskin hustler with a hand full of orgone.*

The Lizard Lounge is lush with a rogues' gallery of regulars, and noisy with the chatter of the charming and the clink of cocktail glasses, a hustle that mutes as I walk in the door, a harlequin of death in motley longcoat.

− *I'm the prodigal son of a nanotech kill-zone.*

I check my chi-lance with the bouncer and step down into the parting crowd. A singer onstage is swinging through a loungecore retro medley, all crooning moodiness, and sultry, sullen style.

− *I am the world's forbidden boy, the son you're searching to destroy.*

Quiffed-up and louche in crushed red velvet tux and frilly shirt, he snaps his fingers in a gunshot click at me and winks — hey.

— *Forbidden boy ... forbidden boy ...*

I flick a slack salute right back at him, and the moment of celebrity passes as people turn back to their friends, only a few furtive glances and nods in my direction breaking the discreet and diplomatic privacy offered by a den of such iniquity as this.

— *And that was 'Search and Destroy' from our favourite Popster dedicated to the one and only 20th Century Boi. Oh yeah. If music be the food of love, there might well be some golden copulations on the streets tonight, mes amigos, because I can tell you that we have a veritable feast for your ears only, here on Radio Free Kentigern. So spark up another joint and crack open another beer, you high wasters of the city of dead dreams. Open your ears and listen to the crack of doom. Is that the coffee you can smell, or the shit hitting the fan? Yes sir, the rhythm of life is a hell of a beat, that beat is on the street and in the air, all round us, here and there and everywhere, because we — that's right — we are the one free station that they never stopped. This is the Voice of Reason calling out across the wilderness of the city, just a lone Coyote howling in the desert night up at a moon that's burning bright. And if you just tuned in, a little recap for you; we're talking about Jack Flash — not so much 'Where are they now?' as 'How the hell did he come back from that?'*

I do like to make a good entrance, but as I head towards the bar — of course — I'm thinking, there are some times, among all the groupies, guns and glamour, when all an anarchist assassin wants is someone to step up to them and say—

— Jack Flash? May I offer you a drink?

A rake in cricket whites, a dashing pencil-thin moustache and dapper flop of hair, the gleam of public-schoolboy bad seed in his eyes, steps forward with his hand held out to shake.

— We've all been rather wondering when you'd show, he says.

A skatepunk kid with scruff of hair tipped iridescent green and monkey sideburns, cute as his button-nose, comes up behind him, hands in baggy combat pockets, a tee-shirt two sizes too big for him proclaiming his 'stoopidity' in bubble letters.

– We were running a book on it, actually, the skatepunk says. I had you down for the Millennium.

I give them the rundown on the routine I'm working with – one day in every decade, I return to right wrongs, wreak revenge and so on, blah, blah, blah.

– Old story, I say. But I think I can give it a new twist or two.

The rake nods.

– We can work with that. Kentigern's pretty wild at the moment, party season and all. Halloween meets Hogmanay, bonfires and fireworks. You'll fit right in.

Out in the Hinter, seasons are lands. You live in the yesterdays and tomorrows of desire, the day you lost your virginity or the someday soon you'll win the lottery, the day your team won the cup final or the day before your brother died. We asked a hundred people: if they could live in any year, what year would it be? You said, this one. Our survey said, nuh-uh.

But this is peachy. Kentigern has history and everything.

I find myself gazing at the skatepunk. I'm not sure which I find more eye-catching – his smile of charm and mischief, or the tiny horns that sprout out of his forehead. The horns might be fake but, given the quirks of my own metaphysique, they might just as easily be real ... although such outward features of the inner archetype only come from years of sustained orgone abuse, and this lad looks too innocent to be that depraved. His nose wrinkles so cutely in his sulk.

– Could've sworn you would've landed in the Millennium, he says.

– Too bad, my boy, says the rake. You lose. Your round.

– One G'n'T, then, says the skatepunk. And for the Spring-Heeled Jack ... an absinthe?

– You know my poison, I say. I don't even know your names.

– Guy Fox, says the rake. Thieves Guild. Local King. You don't remember?

– Was it more than a minute ago? I say. But tell me I know *you*.

– Fast Puck, says the skatepunk.

– And just how fast are you? I say.

– Put a girdle round the world in forty minutes, he says. Get it off in ten.

His eyelids bat so brief as to be almost unnoticeable – but long enough for me to see he's wearing metallic green eye-shadow. He tips a nod and sidles off towards the bar.

Onstage, the singer introduces the solo virtuoso sounds of Bert Finkle, tinkling on the ivories, and saunters off to get a whisky and a cigarette for himself as the pianist flourishes a cheesy intro to Pretty Vacant.

– So, Jack, says the Fox. You really don't remember?

– Snow in the head, I say. I'm here. I'm queer. What else is there to know?

– King Finn and Princess Anaesthesia? he says. Don Coyote? Joey?

I shake my head and give a shrug, find a glass of absinthe plonked into my grip by Fast Puck – fast, indeed. His hand rests on my shoulder.

– You're a diamond, I say.

The Eye of the Weeping Angel

An exquisite little sparkler, I think.

– You know you are an incorrigible rogue, my brother, he says. But a damn good thief.

I tap the cigarette gently into the slim carved-ivory cigarette-holder, place the cigarette-holder between my teeth and smile at him. The Eye of the Weeping Angel seems to catch the fire inside it as I spark the desk-lighter, hold it to the cigarette. It's the flaw in the diamond that gives it its name, of course, the bluish hint of an elliptical eye with tear tracks running down from it – reminiscent of those Egyptian designs so popular these days, since King Tut opened up his secrets to Carter and Carnarvon. The Eye catches the flame in its facets, and the low light of the green-shaded Nouveau nymph desk lamp that paints the panelled room in shadows also glistens in it, eerie, otherworldly.

– You know how much I could get for this on the open market? I say.

– A thousand million marks? he says, with a dismissive wave of his hand. A hundred thousand million marks? A gazillion?

He flashes me the most irritating smile, disingenuous yet mischievous and all the more annoying because it's stolen from me. And because on him it looks better.

– I really have no idea, he says.

One almost expects a sparkle of light to glance across his teeth. Damn him, this isn't how it's meant to be, I think. I'm the charming scoundrel and he the spit-and-polish soldier. The black sheep and the golden boy – that's how it's meant to be. Two rascals in the family just won't do.

– You know, I say, you think you know someone . . .

I sigh. By no means the largest diamond in the world and hardly flawless, the Eye of the Weeping Angel is, nonetheless, quite certainly the most valuable gem that I've ever had the pleasure to have stolen; and, with a few words to the right contacts, I'm sure I could sell it for a small fortune, more than enough to finance my retirement.

He slides the Eye of the Weeping Angel across the mahogany desk towards me and I pick it up between thumb and forefinger, look at it before snapping my hand shut round it. I tap my fist on the table three times and spread the palm to show it empty. With the other hand, I reach over and pluck the gemstone from behind his ear. It's a cheap and simple trick I taught myself as a young man. Cabaret and crime, that's the life I always dreamed of.

– The Fox's Den, says Pickering. Established in 1929 by one Reinhardt von Strann, second son and black sheep of the noble Prussian family . . . notorious gambler who squandered his inheritance in the casinos of Monte Carlo . . . notorious womaniser who moved from rich widow to Jewish princess to industrialist's daughter. A string of conquests who, coincidentally, all seem to have fallen victim to the so-called Black Fox, the Riviera's most notorious cat burglar.

– Go on, this is thrilling. It's all very . . . Raffles.

– You must have heard the stories, read about it in the newspapers.

– I very rarely read the papers, Major Pickering. I remember being distinctly . . . uninterested in the news for a very large portion of the 20s and the 30s. Fascists in Spain, Futurists in Russia and Italy. Communists, anarchists, everything under the sun in France and Germany. I spent my happiest years in jazz clubs and cinemas. The movies, Major Pickering. Marlene Dietrich lit like a religious mystery. Bogart in the shadow of a doorway, looking up at a window. Who wants to read the news when all it has are stories about mobs and murderers, about broken shop-windows and running street fights?

– I'm sure the Black Fox would have made the newsreels.

– Oh, I wasn't saying that I hadn't heard of him. I was still in Paris at the time, I believe, but, yes, he did make something of a splash, didn't he, for a short while?

– 1923 to 1929. Almost six years and maybe a dozen victims. Then in 1929 it stops just when you – sorry – when von Strann leaves the Riviera. Two months later the Fox's Den opens in Berlin and proceeds to make a name for itself as one of the most decadent—

– *The* most decadent. I remember the advertisements, Major Pickering. The most decadent nightclub in all of Berlin. And there *was* some talk of the proprietor being backed by . . . money as dirty as the desires of his clientele. Yes, the Fox's Den was quite notorious – the Thieves' Den as we called it. But I never made the connection with the Black Fox. Sounds like I was being rather dim, in retrospect.

– Well, of course, you weren't to know, were you, *Monsieur Cartier*? It's not as if you knew the man, is it?

– No, I'm afraid I never knew the man at all, Major Pickering.

– Or his brother?

– Or his brother. What about his brother?

– Well, the last Black Fox robbery took place in late '29, and, apart from the identical modus operandi, it stands out as unusual. Seven months after the last and in another country entirely, it almost seems an . . . encore. A last bow taken by a retiring artiste. And there's no philandering widow here, just a Russian diplomat decidedly out-of-sorts that his family heir-loom has been stolen, and a serving-girl who gives a rather suspicious statement to the police. No, this is a different kind of job entirely. It's not done for the thrill. It's not an idle game. No, I believe Reinhardt von Strann carried out this theft at the request of his brother. I believe he stole his last jewel only because his brother asked him to.

– What on earth would his brother want with it?

– What on earth do you want with it? I say. It's not the money you're interested in, and I don't see you desiring this bauble, pretty as it is, for the sheer pleasure of gazing at its crystal beauty.

He picks up a pack of cards I keep on the desk for playing solitaire in those quiet times when the club is closed, the previous night's accounts all settled and preparations for the evening show not yet begun. He shuffles them idly, cutting the pack and looking at the chosen card every so often.

The Eye of the Weeping Angel sits on the desk between us.

– I need it for a ... reason, he says. I'm not sure how I can explain it, though.

– Do try, I say.

He hands the pack across to me.

– Magic, he says. Do you still do your little tricks then?

I take the cards and shuffle them, cut them, turn over the top card – Jack of Diamonds. I slide it back into the pack and shuffle them again, cut them, shuffle them, turn over the top card – Jack of Diamonds. Back in the pack and shuffle, cut, rifle and cut, shuffle and turn – the Jack of Diamonds.

– Didn't you used to do that with the Jack of Hearts? he says.

– Diamonds seem more apt tonight, I say. Jonni, why do you want this thing? *Why?* Why did you resign your commission? What the hell is going on in your life? If it's not money ... If ... if you're in trouble ...

But he shakes his head.

– It's not like that. We're all in trouble. The whole country. Europe. The world. Futurism is–

I laugh.

– Futurism will go the way of the Bolsheviks and the Falangists.

I hold a hand up against his protest.

– Look at Stalin, at Franco. Even when these people win power

116

– which just isn't going to happen here – it can't last; they can't hold on to it. These great schemes always fall apart. The Futurists are just a bunch of thugs who like to break things; they're exactly like the Communists, and the anarchists, and the Fascists. No, no, let's not get into that argument again. But Jonni, you all say you're saving Germany – Europe, the world – from each other. It's absurd. Do you honestly think the Futurists are capable of a coup here?

He slides the Eye of the Weeping Angel across the table towards me again. I still have no idea why he would want me to keep it safe for him. From what?

– What if I said I could tell you the date? he says. The day and the hour? Believe me, Fox, I shed no tears for Stalin but these, these ... *nihilists* are a thousand times worse. You don't think it was the Futurists behind Franco's assassination? You don't think they have designs on Germany?

I wonder what could have happened to have sent him into this spiral of delusion. He was always so spick and span in his grey uniform, the silver skulls gleaming on his collar, polished to a sheen. Charming and dashing, though – more warrior than soldier – I always thought he would have been better suited to the leather jacket and silk scarf of a Luftwaffe pilot, a latter-day von Richthofen. I never could understand what he saw in the SA.

Now half his insignia are missing, his uniform in disarray. From his avoidance of certain questions I gather his superiors aren't even aware he's in Berlin.

– Everything is changing, he says.

I turn over a card: Jack of Spades.

– Everything is always changing, I say.

The Mysteries of Harlequin

– It's no great tale, no boast, says Jack. Have you heard of a range of timeless mountains that ring round a city of swords? This is my native, ludic land of playful words.

The Princess leans forward in her seat. She folds her arms, her left hand stroking her right arm's upper biceps as if massaging an old pain. How many of the Duke's subjects, I wonder, have vague memories of the world outside his castle, of the city and the even stranger places out there in the Vellum's hinterlands? I wonder if there's not a few of them who, somewhere deep inside them, understand that all of this is just a construct built from their consensus of delusions. A fortress heaven in fields of illusion. The Princess knows, I'm sure of it.

– What brings you to our hell, asks Pierrot, with all these mysteries?

– The Harlequin, the son of Sooth, Jack says, inspired me, cast a spell.

– This Sooth, then, fathers newborn gods in play? And did he come to you at night or in the light of day?

– The very Sooth, says Jack, who married Simile in Hell.

He holds the shining manacle around one wrist up like a watch, tilting his head. He runs his fingers through his hair, checking himself in the reflection, drops his arms as if now satisfied and looks out at the crowd. Behind the mask, he fixes the Princess with his glinting eyes, flashes a smile at her.

– I saw him face to face.

She bites her bottom lip, like someone brooding over something that they can't quite place.

– You saw him clearly then, says Pierrot. What did he look like?

– As he liked to look. I had no say in it.

– What are his rites?

Jack cocks his head, beckons with forefinger to bring Joey's ear down to his mouth, then turns towards the audience, towards the Duke and does the same to them, drawing them in. He pauses, as if about to tell a juicy truth, then says:

– They are a secret to be guarded from the likes of you. What good are they? What use? I cannot say, for all the good that it would do you if I could.

Pierrot, roaring, shoves him, rolling, half across the stage, but Jack rolls to his feet and bounces back, impervious to Joey's rage.

– These words are tricks designed to tease an intellectual appetite, says Pierrot. You evade, avoid my questions time and time again. You have no reply at all?

– An uninspired man can only make a mockery of the rites. Who tries to teach a fool? Only a fool would try.

Pierrot stalks around him, looking for a weakness.

– So. Are you the first sent out to spread this spirit?

– All foreigners already celebrate these mysteries with dance.

– Because they are so far behind us hellions. Foreigners? They are barbarians, proud to live in ignorance—

– Their customs may be different but, in this regard, says Jack, they're far, far in advance.

– Is it just me? I hiss to Guy backstage. Does Joey seem a bit on edge tonight?

Guy nods. He strokes his chin.

– Watch what you say to him, he whispers. Just . . . try not to wind him up. For once.

– Is it by night or day, says Pierrot, that you perform these rites, these games? Surely by night, the atmosphere is better, in the dark, to draw these women to your flame.

– The light of day is just as good, says Jack, for the uncovering of shame.

Pierrot turns away, disgusted at Jack's smirking leer.

– This . . . impudence, says Joey, only seals your fate.

Jack's smirk disappears.

– As yours, he says, is sealed by your brutality, by ignorance, by hate.

– You're growing brave. You think you're winning in this war of words?

Jack yawns. He starts to stroll around the striding Pierrot. His chains rattle along the ground. Don has to follow, holding them like they're some bridal train, so Joey doesn't get caught up in them. And Pierrot and Harlequin circle each other like some mediaeval dance, a king and queen competing to see who can treat the other with the most disdain.

– So what cruel fate will you inflict on me? says Jack. What pains can I expect?

– First I'll shave off your fair hair, and then I'll have that green-veined flute.

Jack stops, hands to his cheeks, hams up his innocent shock.

– My hair is sacred; why, it's for the spirit that it's grown, he says. As for the wand of Harlequin . . .

He grips it tight, right down between his legs, gives it a jiggle.

– Take it from me, if you really want it for your own.

A Crucible of Passion

– Here, says Puck.

I take the matchbook with a blank look and he opens it in my hand to show the number scrawled inside.

– My phone number, he says.

I close it and slip it into the longcoat pocket. Looks like tonight could be my lucky night. Puck trails a hand across the nape of my neck and gives a wink, and suddenly—

– I remember it, I say.

It's the club bringing me back, memory by memory; it's chaos after all – sex and drugs and rock'n'roll – and that's the story of my lives. I drink it in. Radiovision screens show rioters on the streets of London, blasted back en masse by water cannon, beaten individually by armoured-up militia in black armbands, RCC and Home Guard thugs in bowler hats and orange sashes. It's raining rubber bullets in Dublin while tanks roll into Oswald Square. Tear gas blossoms in the shanty towns of Rhodesia, and chi-guns cut a swathe through Indian rebels. British soldiers march through Tiananmen Square. Over it all, a blue guitar grinds out a garage riff, a scream of chords ripped out of the electric air, repeated, rising.

Oh yes, I'm feeling much more like myself again.

– I got homicidal tendencies. I got homicidal tendencies.

Onstage, in the Snake Pit, the wilder, darker backroom of the Lizard Lounge, Johnny Yen, the fucked-up main man of The Narcotics, moshes like a maniac, mike gripped in a white-knuckled, thumping fist between his legs, black hair and shadow across his face. Behind him, the screens show a fast-cut carnival of carnage: HIV camps; refugees forced onto trains at gunpoint; skinheads wrapped in Union Jacks; housing schemes in flames; record-burning rallies of the neo-Christian Youth Brigade. His voice, a low and moaning snarl, comes in over the throbbing beat, a rock'n'roll mantra of teen frustration, transformed in a crucible of passion to something more pure, more powerful than simple hate.

There's a fever in his voice that turns the fury into fervour, something fiercely bound to life and love, or, at the very least, to flesh and lust.

— I got homicidal tendencies. I got homicidal tendencies.

Transfixed, I stand in awe as Fast Puck roars and throws himself into the wild of bodies, flailing limbs and bouncing heads. Fox's hand rests on my shoulder as he tries to clue me up on Kentigern's current sad state of affairs. Anaesthesia gone into the Vellum. King Finn on a twenty-year hunger strike in Peterhead. Joey—

— What is this? I ask, cutting him off.

— I believe the song's called '1979', he says.

— I got homicidal tendencies. I got homicidal tendencies.

The singer seems to fix me with a visceral gaze, a look that says someday we need to either fight or fuck.

— I got hom*osexual* tendencies. I got hom*icidal* tendencies.

The tangled mass of crowd is screaming, jangled, taut to breaking point by the orgone thrill, and I feel my flesh a-tingle. Christ, out there it's hell on earth but in the Rookery, in the Snake Pit, in the very depths of Kentigern's great maze, it's not demons that stalk the dark recesses. No, it's fucking *daimons*, as the ancient Greeks believed in, fucking fiery spirits that belong in flesh. Fuck damnation. Fuck sin. Look up *enthusiasm* in the dictionary, babe. It means having the god within.

— I got homosexual tendencies. I got homicidal tendencies.

The singer's lust for life pours through the audience, into their veins, their hearts, their bones.

No, we're not prisoners of the flesh, I think, bound in our skins, and only waiting for the final judgement that will send us into fire or light. We're fucking prisoners of conscience, prisoners of fear and shame. We're fucking prisoners of sorrow, and it's time for our release.

With every drink I take my flesh fills out; my chakras coalesce, my heart, my guts, my balls, my nerve, lock into place. Under the

121

longcoat, my skin crawls with electric energy, and looking at my hand I can make out the veins now, the hairs, the fingerprints. The skin gleams coppery, fading with every sip of absinthe more and more towards its normal flesh tone. I think about pulling the longcoat closed, belting it shut. It's all very well to go skyclad when you look like a cross between the Silver Surfer and Nyarlathotep but I'm Jack Flash, not Jack Flasher. Looking out into the frenzied punks though, half-naked in their jeans and boots, dog-collars and studded wrist-bands, teenage girls and full-grown women flailing their hair among the men and boys, rubber and leather shining with sweat under the flashing lights, I just run my hand across the black hatchwork tattoo that's starting to come through now on my chest. This is what it's all about – the mosh pit and a soft, tender caress.

– I got homosexual tendencies. I got homicidal tendencies.

It's just a pity I still have to deal with the fucking fascists outside the Rookery walls. And, baby, it's cold out there.

– Fox, I say. You wouldn't happen to know where I could get some clothes?

I feel the matchbook in my pocket.

– And I'm dying for a fag.

He digs into his pocket.

– I was trying to tell you, he says, about Joey.

The Stories that We Tell

– Where is he? I say.

– That's him there, says Johann. Right in front of you.

He does look rather Russian, I must admit, and like someone who would happily keep an angel's eye in his private safe. He looks like someone who would have a whole collection of them, I can't help thinking. Thick black beard and with the dark gaze of a mad monk, Prince Josef Pechorin, diplomatic envoy to West Saxony, looks like everything I should have expected in a fully-fledged Futurist of the new Russia. These are the men who murdered Stalin in his sleep, new faithless Rasputins who have found in the very godlessness of the universe a new religion. Is this the Russian character, I wonder, each of them at heart one of Ivan the Terrible's oprechnika, part secret police and part monastic order. For the first time ever I begin to see why my brother is so fearful of these Futurists. I always thought that he was exaggerating, but now I see why Hitler turned, splitting the party right down the middle, over-throwing half of what it was built on.

– Look at him. Just look at him.

My brother, standing at the bar beside me, gazes with utter hatred at this emblem of the force that burned down the Kremlin and then sat waiting until the time was right for the second revolution. Russia fell to the Futurists because in Stalin's hands it had *become* Futurist; it only needed his death to mark the finality of the transformation, close the chapter, turn the page. Hitler's speech outside the Reichstag, I suddenly realise, may mark a similar turning point, the moment when this ideology of the New Age planted its flag in Germany, red like the communists' or the fascists' but with neither sickle nor swastika. The black circle and cross of the Futurist flag has always seemed rather too reminiscent of a rifle's sight to me. And now my brother, his SA, and the rest of the bedraggled remnants of the Nazi party are all set in the centre of those cross-hairs. I wonder how much of Hitler's choice was ideological and how much was simply a cold calculation of the way that things were going – if indeed there's any difference to a Futurist.

Pechorin sits at a table with his retinue of bodyguards and hangers-on, holding court in exactly the same way that I've seen Röhm do so many times; he's even picked the same table that Röhm usually takes, down near the front and slightly to the left. The only difference is that where Röhm would be leering at the pretty boys and groping any that came close enough, Pechorin sits quiet and detached, watching the cabaret like the visiting dignitary that he is, amused in a distant sort of way by the quaint spectacle of a woman in basque and suspenders singing Dietrich songs.

He chills me to the bone.

– Do you think we should go over and introduce ourselves? I say breezily.

– But, as I say, I'm not this van Strann—

    – *Von* Strann—

    – Sorry. Von Strann. But I wish to God I was, I'll tell you that.

The Fox's Den was raking it in, while my own little club was struggling to stay afloat. But then we never had bestiality on the bill or a brothel in the back. Do you mind if I smoke?

– Go ahead.

– Do you have a light? Thanks. Please . . . where were we?

– Berlin, 1929. What was it called – your own club – by the way?

– Jongleurs. It was called Jongleurs. We had a man juggling fire out front. Jacques his name was – quite the crowd-puller.

– But hardly bestiality.

– Hardly. The Fox's Den rather put our little juggling act to shame.

– So it was a successful business? Prostitution? Other criminal activities?

– One rather suspected so. The proprietor was a quite untrustworthy fellow. Although, from what you say, I fear I may have misjudged him. As I say, there were all sorts of stories.

– And did one of them involve a jewel?

– A jewel?

– The Eye of the Weeping Angel, I believe it's called.

– How exotic.

– And cursed to boot.

– I can imagine. Terrible fates befalling unwary owners, yes? One shouldn't believe everything one hears. The stories that we tell . . .

I study this Russian Prince.

– Really? I say. I think it's an . . . amusing idea. But I specialise in rich widows. Rich widows who are easily flattered by the attentions of a charming younger man. Rich widows who will take the word of someone with a winning smile over that of their oldest, closest friend, simply because *one could not possibly suspect that delightful young chap . . . French, wasn't he? Or was he English?*

I shake my head, turn back to the bar and motion for Horst to refill our glasses.

– No, I do not steal from men, I say. I do not steal from men with power. And I especially do not steal from men with the power to have me killed.

My brother pushes the neck of the bottle away from his glass, waves Horst away. He lays his hand flat over the lip of the brandy glass and I see his knuckles grow white. I almost expect the glass to shatter in his grip.

– You have to do it, he says.

– No, I do not. That man is dangerous.

– And I can stop him, he says.

His hand rattles the glass on the bar, so tense he is, and Horst looks nervous; I send him away with a subtle flick of the eyes, an almost headshake.

– Johann, I begin.

– You have to call me Jack now, Fox.

He smiles at me, a cracked and edgy smile. I try to ignore his madness. I turn back to the tables and chairs, the candle-lit crowds of tuxedos and uniforms, black and grey and brown, men in swastika or circle-and-cross armbands gathered in cliques uneasy with their proximity to each other. Loud laughter and quiet threat. I have been trying to ignore the madness around me since I opened the Fox's Den, I realise. One of Hitler's Neues Deutschland Party leaders passes Pechorin's table, stops to introduce himself, shake the man's hand.

– You have to get me the jewel.

– I can't, I say. I won't.

– Then why are we here?

His voice is savage, hissing, and I flinch from the accusation in his eyes. I cannot tell him what I hoped, how I imagined if I could only get him out of the darkness of Father's library and up to Berlin with its lights and nightclubs, we might ... unloosen that coiled intensity before it broke him utterly. That we would sit in my office and laugh over the old times, and I would ask him how Franz was and he would look embarrassed, turn red until I changed the subject. And I would put my arm around his shoulder and take him out into the club to scorn the drag queens and the flouncing boys, even as he watched them from the corner of his eye, drinking schnapps with me through the night as I explained how anything was available in Berlin at the right price, anything, why, that young lady or that fellow at the bar there, yes, that one; really, Johann, there is no need to tear oneself apart over such things, no need, no need at all.

I do not answer his question.

– Why do you want this thing so much? I say. What does it mean to you?

– Everything, he says. My life, my heart, my soul. I have to have it.

– to carry out some sort of occult ritual? Pickering says. Was that part of the story that you heard?

– No, Major Pickering, no. The stories I heard were not out-landish, adolescent fantasies. The stories I heard were that the owner of the Fox's Den had girls as young as twelve available in the backrooms of his club, that any drug you desired could be purchased in this sordid, squalid, glorified brothel, that it was a favourite haunt of Röhm and his jackboot-wearing pervert lackeys. The stories I heard were that the owner's brother was himself one of Röhm's SA, and every bit as boy-loving as his leader. These are the stories that I heard, Major Pickering. Ugly, little stories. For the love of God, man, cursed jewels and magic—

– Enough of the games. I want to know about the Eye of the Weeping Angel. I want to know about—

– Jewel thieves and magic rituals? Major Pickering, I was in Germany when their blessed Chancellor Hitler was cheered – *cheered* – in the Reichstag after the Night of the Long Knives, cheered for butchering his enemies not because they were vile little street thugs, which they were, not because they were fascists, but because they were homosexuals. I was in Berlin during Kristallnacht. I saw an old man kicked to death in the streets for being Jewish – for being Jewish – and I . . . I did nothing. I was there when it all collapsed and the Futurists came marching in, and by God, if we thought it was bad under the fascists we had no idea of what humanity is capable of. This . . . this puerile nonsense is an insult to the truth.

– The truth, Herr von Strann?

– My name is Reynard Cartier—

– Your name is Reinhardt von Strann. You came to Britain in 1947 from East Germany. Two years ago. From *Futurist* East Germany.

– What? Are you saying I'm a spy now, a Futurist agent?

– I'm saying I don't know how you've built this . . . charade of a life around you, but, believe me, I'm going to tear it down and get to the truth—

– What truth?

– The truth about you, about your brother.

– I have no brother.

– Liar! This is all lies.

A Battered Matchbook

— and his thopter going down in flames, and he was burning as he fell—

White noise shrieks through the broadcast.

— but he jumped at the last second, Don, and he just disappeared in the sky—

Jump-cuts, voice to voice.

— so there he was on the burning deck of this exploding air-barge—

Militia must be trying to time-jam the bastard, thinks Joey.

— and I tell you, Don, he walked out of that pile of wreckage without a scratch on him, then he just fucking shimmered and vanished like some fucking ghost—

Joey closes his mind to block the broadcast, closes the door to mute the noise of music too. Even down the long corridor of burgundy carpet and peeling green wallpaper, the sound of the nightclub travels, a weird blend of the driving rhythms of the downstairs dancefloor and the syrupy easy listening music audible from upstairs. He used to like this place but it just irritates him now. The same fucking faces, the same fucking bullshit, the same people sitting in the same booths, making big plans that will never come to anything. This is where they first met Finn, the two of them, Jack and Joey, just two punk-ass kids stealing and dealing amongst the other guttersnipes of the Rookery, and Finn and Fox and Anaesthesia sitting in armchairs up on the balcony above the bar, planning revolution. Free Love, Free Speech, and Fuck the War. *I'm in*, Jack had said, grinning like it was all a fucking game.

Joey sticks his hands in his jacket pockets, casual, in control.

The club singer leans against the dresser, spitting blood into his handkerchief, the neon tubing round the mirror edging his face with a glow as red as his tuxedo, as red as the stains on his shirt, red as the sullen anger in his eyes.

– Joey, he says. We go back a long way. Don't do this to me. Don't do this to yourself.

Joey takes two steps and slams the man's head into the mirror, shoves him backwards halfway across the room and down onto a frayed leather couch.

– so I think he went where all dead heroes go, into the aether, into the Hinter, you know. But if anyone can walk out of Hell—

The signal amps up even as the static cuts right across it.

– one of the Red Clydesiders, right, the only one who got away when they sent in the Black and Blues, and he swore that he'd take revenge for the deaths of all his comrades—

– the Edward Assassination, the Stone of Scone, the destruction of the Crystal Palace. It can't all be coincidence—

– Participation in this broadcast will result in prosecution. Repeat—

– Who's the wannabe? says Joey. I want to know what he looks like, when he was here, who he was with, what he was drinking, and if he went to the toilet did he wipe his fucking arse.

The man flinches as Joey flips the matchbook from his coat pocket at him with a sharp flick of two fingers; it bounces off his chest, lands in his lap. It's just a battered matchbook, decaled for the seedy nightclub, a couple of matches missing, a phone number written on the inside. It's not a clue in itself – Joey's already checked the number out and it was just some squalid little hustler's mobile – but the fact that it's for this nightclub, this of all places, means it was left on the sentry, like the cigarette, as a signpost. A little piece of where it all began left as a message for him where it all came to an end, on the bridge.

The singer looks at it in confusion. It doesn't mean anything to him at all, but Joey can feel the death engrained in that tiny piece of cardboard even from where he's standing:

– Who are we?

– I'll ask the questions, mate. Just don't you fucking move.

And the sentry's thinking, shit, it's just his luck, every fucking nutter has

to come his way, but he better call it in, and why won't this buggery phone
come — got it — right then—
  Shit.

Joey shrugs the pathetic final memory off, the last thoughts of the desperately banal, too dumb and slow to even be scared. You might think a dying man's last moments would be intense, life flashing before their eyes, the stab of pure adrenalin, the instant fear and fury of a wounded animal, a cornered rat. No. Most people die thinking to themselves this isn't real, this is just silly.

The fucker didn't even get a good look at his killer's face.

  — and he died. But, see, what happened is he sold his soul to the devil for one day on earth in every ten years, just one day when he's free to do whatever he wants before the devil drags him back to Hell—

  — and according to this Moorcock guy, back in the 1890s there's this series of murders in Knightchapel, but the Masons covered them up so nobody will even admit they happened—

  — and the Thieves Guild still tell stories about Spring-Heeled Jack. I'm telling you, Don, it goes deeper than you think—

  — What do you say, Harvey? You still there?

  — For fuck's sake, they'll be saying he climbed a fucking beanstalk next—

  — like, man, I'm telling you, I saw it in this dream, right. He's, like, from the inside of our heads, man, like a 'meme', you know, an idea, a virus that just moves around from host to host. That's why he doesn't stay dead. You can't kill an idea—

— So what's it like, working for The Man, Joey?

The singer turns the matchbook over in his fingers, looks at Joey like what he's holding is so mundane that Joey must be cracked to try and make something of it. He pulls himself up straighter in the couch, tilts his head back to try and stop the bleeding nose.

  — How's the food up at the Circus? Better than prison food or hospital food, eh? Or was it the medication swung it for you.

  — I'll ask the questions, mate, says Joey Narcosis.

The singer stands up, goes over to the dresser and flips some tissues from a box to plug his nostrils. Nervous bravado. He's hiding something.

— So Joey Narcosis is a big man now, he says. Shit, you're just another inmate like the rest of us.

Joey doesn't answer him, just cricks his mind outwards a little bit, presses up against the singer's thoughts, slides round his fear, his anger, his frustration and — *fuck you, you little prick* — slices into his mind and secateurs his head open like a cadaver's abdomen in autopsy. The singer drops to his knees. It only takes a couple of minutes, and he's stopped screaming by the time Joey is finished.

Joey Narcosis fixes himself up in the mirror before he leaves the room. He has a perfect mental image of his quarry now. It doesn't worry him that the image is the perfect double of how he remembers Jack standing in the club, a glass in one hand, toasting Guy Fox, his other arm draped over Fast Puck's shoulder, just like the old days. No. He popped another pill before he entered Club Soda, so it doesn't worry him at all.

— You don't get it. You don't fucking get it. Sure, he's dead. Ten years or twenty years, it doesn't matter. Cause we're all dead. Don't you see? We're all fucking dead but we won't admit it; we just play our old lives over and over, this way, that way, but it's all the same. We're dead. We're fucking dead—

—unsanctioned and illegal broadcast. Repeat, this is an unsanctioned and illegal broadcast. Participation in this broadcast is a criminal act and will result in prosecution. Repeat . . .

The King of Tears

—I'll have you thrown into the deepest dungeon known to man, Pierrot says.

Jack does a kung fu flip that brings him off the ground and to his feet.

— And my dear dad will set me free at my command, he says.

He strolls across the stage until he's stopped by Joey's foot upon the chain. Jack holds his hands up like he had forgotten he was even wearing manacles, and laughs. He twirls a little spin that wraps a length of chain around his waist.

— Since you're quite mad, he says, I'll clue you in.

He wraps the chain around his arm and yanks it out from

under Joey's foot. As Joey staggers back, Jack pirouettes, and flips the chain out like a whip round Joey's neck. It's done so fast the audience don't see the trick behind the stunt, the way Pierrot grabs it with a hand between the metal and his throat (although in the rehearsal I remember Joey swearing, *Jesus Christ, you nearly took my head off. Fucking cunt*). No. All they see is Jack's slick move, lassoing Joey, and the choking tug that hauls him in close as a dancing partner. Jack blows a kiss at him.

– There's no constraint, he says, can hold the Harlequin.

– Constraint! Pierrot snarls, pulling the chain from round his throat. You barely know the meaning of the term. Well, it may be that when you stand with all your followers and call your so-called father's name, he'll set you free. Where is he now, though? I don't see a thing.

His hand clamps round Jack's throat, a grip that pushes up his chin.

– He is beside me even now, a witness to my state, says Jack. He's right in front of you, my friend. You're simply blinded by your hate.

Pierrot looks around with a slow sneering, shakes his head.

– Go, lock him up, he says. Let's see you do your dancing in the stables, in the pitch-black gloom.

Don picks the chain up.

– And these women of yours that share your crimes, well, they can share your doom. Their delicate hands that beat the drums with such a noise, they can be put to good use at the looms. Oh, yes, I'll work them in the mills to serve my industry, and if that doesn't break their wills, I'll sell their broken bodies into slavery.

– I'll go, says Jack, for that which fate forbids can never fall on me.

He lets Don lead him, turning only at the last to strain, pulling his hand around to point at Pierrot, despite his chains.

– But for this mockery, he says, you can be sure the Harlequin will take a fee. I swear on the spirit whose existence you deny. You know, Pierrot, you insult him now as you imprison me.

– Take him away. The man's a fool, mocking the king of this city of Themes.

– You just don't fucking see, shouts Jack as Don pulls him offstage. The very substance of your world, your life, he shouts, is only dreams.

– I am Pierrot, king of everything that you see here.

– Your name is Sorrow, Jack spits from the wings, the King of Tears.

The Hunter and the Fox

The double doors to the library are still swinging shut behind me, an angry rebuke hardly out of my mouth, when I see him and I stop.

He sits in our father's favourite – plushest – armchair, a dark leatherbound volume open in his lap and an intensely studious look upon his face. It's so out of character for my brother that for a second I imagine that it's Father himself back in his usual seat, his usual pose, nose buried in a book. On the occasional table at the side of the armchair, a glass of port lies untouched and, as he reaches up to turn on the reading lamp, I can't help but think of the times my brother and I stood here behind our mother's skirts. She would ask our father quietly, calmly, if he would be having supper with his family tonight, and he would look up from the book he was caught up in, and switch on that lamp, only now aware of the twilight that had crept up on him. A cursory wave of his hand would dismiss us. When I was ten, I think, Mother moved the three of us permanently into the townhouse in Strann. We would visit occasionally, and each time we would find him there again, as if he never moved from that chair. He was a diplomat before the Great War – I remember misspent years of childhood in the countryside outside Paris, and then England, which I always had a soft spot for – but, as I understand, he fell from favour in the years before the war broke out, and it changed him. In the end, he retreated from the world into his books.

And now my brother sits in his place, his usually impeccable uniform unkempt, the top buttons on his grey tunic undone. I never really understood his fascination with the martial ethic – his choice to give his life to those who had little more than contempt for *his kind* – but his martial primness was always something of a bench-mark for my own, more wayward character. Now he sits slumped in the half-light, more wild and dishevelled even than Father was towards the end. Books and broken glass litter the floor of the library, debris from the cabinets that line the walls. I step carefully with both feet and words as I approach him.

– Since when did I ever give a damn about foxhunts, Johann? I say. You know I never had a taste for blood sports.

My voice is casual, but, in my pocket, my fist squeezes a crumpled telegram.

COME HOME SOONEST STOP FOXHUNT ON STOP J

– Well, I didn't want to be too obvious, *Fox*, he says.

– You haven't called me that since we were children, I say.

I must have been five years old or so when the folk tale of Reynard the Fox, King of Thieves, gave me the nickname that was to become so deeply ingrained in my identity that, as long as I can remember, I have felt more of a Reynard than a Reinhardt. Before his change, you see, our father's books were as much a part of our life as of his. Mythology and folklore were his hobbies, and we learned our English and our French from translations of the Brothers Grimm and Aesop's Fables. As we grew older, we moved on to Greek and Roman myths, the Bible of course, and even Oriental texts. It seemed terribly important to him that we appreciate these myths and legends as he did, the universalities of them; and it was all one with his method of teaching us the languages that they were written in, how the vocabularies shared common roots.

– *Bruder*, he would say, *brother, frater, frère.* You must listen to the similarities as well as the differences. If you learn the way the sounds shift, then you understand that we all once spoke the same tongue, told the same tales.

Sometimes I think he was more interested in the *idea* of us, in who we might be, than in who we were. It can't be wrong, can it, to see the potential in your children? But perhaps one should keep the actualities in mind. Anyway, as Reinhardt I became Reynard to him, his little Fox, the King of Thieves; meanwhile my brother Johann became John, Jack, Killer of Giants. My brother would taunt me that my name fit because I was sneaky and a big coward, but I just rolled the phrase around in my head: King of Thieves. *King of Thieves.* When we played, after that, I would often be the wily Fox, and my brother the noble hero Jack, thwarting my schemes, smoking me out wherever I hid, battling me, defeating me, though I, of course, always escaped.

Our mother kept photograms of us on a display cabinet in the front room of the family townhouse. One shows my brother as a member of the *Wandervogel*, out on some camping trip and looking quite the thing in his lederhosen and neckerchief; it was the trip that he came back from prattling excitedly about his new friend – Thomas this and Thomas that – and how they were going to be soldiers together. Another picture shows me as four-year-old fop, proud in his pressed attire. I'm told that at that age I had a girl who thought me so sweet she virtually adopted me at kindergarten, even tying my shoelaces for me if they came undone. Apparently, I was quite capable of tying them myself but, well, she did not need to know that.

I look at my brother in his rumpled uniform and I wonder how much our lives have been shaped by the stories told to us of ourselves.

– What exactly is this all about? I ask
– I have a job for you, he says.

I smile. Although I know there is more to all this cloak-and-dagger than a sudden opportunity for respectable employment, I try to make light of it.

– Some dreary desk job in one of Father's friends' businesses? I say. You know I've rather done my best to avoid that horror up to now, and I wouldn't want all those years of baccarat to go to waste. No, I already have an occupation, thank you, and while it may not be the most respectable—
– Respectable? he interrupts.

He closes the book and lays it on the table at his side. Cracked black leather, brass clasp, I presume that it's one of Father's books, though I don't recognise it – it looks more like some fantastic grimoire than one of those interminable treatises on mediaeval Spanish romance literature or some such. His hand moves gently across the surface of the cover, fingertips just touching, almost fondling, and I look around at the shattered debris strewn across the library floor; is this the product of some fevered search, I wonder, or just a pointless tantrum? I had heard that, since Hitler's speech outside the Reichstag, my brother had become ... unpredictable, but this disturbs me.

– I wouldn't describe your current employment as respectable, he says.

I pull a second chair across from a corner of the room, sit it on the other side of the table. Glass crunches under my feet.

– I'm not defending the Fatherland against – what is it now – Jews? Futurists? No. But people do need entertainment. I provide a service.

– Ah, yes, he says. Cabaret and whores. Drink and song.

He taps one finger on the stopper of a crystal decanter sitting beside the glass. I wander over to the sideboard where the decanter belongs, to fetch another glass.

– Don't underestimate the value of simple ... diversions, I say. You and your people can have your running battles with the Futurists, your rallies, demonstrations and counter-demonstrations. The rest of us just want to get on with our lives, to forget about our troubles in an evening of, yes, drink and song. It may not be noble but it serves a purpose. I should have thought you'd be thankful that I'm actually doing something constructive with my life these days.

He picks up the glass of port and takes a sip of it.

– Sorry. Yes, I forget that you're on the straight and narrow now, so to speak. No more gambling. No more playing Casanova.

He takes another sip of the port.

– So have you really stopped stealing women's jewellery?

The silence is palpable, broken only by the *clink* of the crystal stopper as I take it out of the decanter, and then by the *driggle* of port into the glass. Another clink as I replace the stopper.

I sit down in the chair.

– You do specialise in jewels, don't you? he says. That's what I've heard. The most notorious jewel thief on the Riviera, so they say. I'm sure Mother would be proud.

I weigh the options, consider the various possible pathways of lies and denials. It's unlikely that he could have any firm evidence, though it's not impossible. I could play dumb and deny any circumstantial chains of mere coincidence: A childhood nickname ... the happenstance of dates and places. I could bluff it out, play the shocked naif, wounded that he would even suspect such things of me. But it would not be convincing. We know each other much too well. I simply shrug.

– We all have our vices, I say.

I knew from the moment I got his telegram that my brother had rumbled me. To be honest, I find myself thinking, it's about time; I've been waiting for this moment for years. Year after year, whenever I would return to Strann from a summer in Nice or Cannes, with the newspapers full of the Black Fox's latest daring heist, I was always rather disappointed to be welcomed simply as the perennial prodigal. For years I expected to be taken aside by my brother, newspaper in hand, to be asked in his sternest voice, *just what exactly I had been up to*. Instead, on more than one occasion, I remember taking *him* aside and asking that very question myself. And was he proud to be associated with these thugs, with a deviant like Röhm?

I remember later nursing my sore jaw as he apologised, tried to explain himself – how he felt at home, part of a brotherhood, part of a greater purpose – and I realised that he was lying not to me but to himself. We all have our vices, indeed. *So, how is your young 'friend'?* I think. Yes, I have my own leverage. But we are not children any more. I grew out of tit-for-tat many years ago and even if we are playing some sort of game here, the hunter and the fox, there are limits on what is fair play.

– So what is this all about? I say.

He lays his hand on top of the book and leans forward in his chair, light from the lamp slicing diagonally across his face.

– You *are* the Black Fox, aren't you? he says.

I hold my hands up, wrists together as if waiting for the handcuffs.

– Guilty as charged, I say. But you're not going to rat on your own brother, are you?

– I don't want to see you in prison, he says. I told you I have a job for you. There's a jewel I need you to steal.

– I am on the straight and narrow, as you say, these days. I'm retired.

– I *need* you to do this for me, he says. You *have* to do this for me.

His hand still plays idly over the tome upon the table. He strokes the leather surface of the book as if it's some living animal he's petting, or an attaché case containing secrets that will save the nation. I imagine it handcuffed to his wrist as in some dreadful novel of spies and adventures.

I always thought, in the games we played as children, that we were both heroes of sorts, the adventurer and the rogue, the hunter and the fox. I think that he still sees himself that way, but in reality the hunters of this world have dogs that rip the fox's throat out when they catch it. To the hunter, the fox is vermin to be killed, its blood smeared on a young man's face, red as his tunic, red as my brother's armband. Given the times we're living in, those games we played, and the stories that our father told us, don't seem quite the same.

– What do you want with this jewel? I say.

Harlequin's Dream

– Power, says Guy.

Don cuts the lights. Pierrot stands, a sombre shape of black on black in the now-silent hall as, at his back, a thin veil falls, a flickering orange candlelight behind it. Now, in shadow-play, we see Jack dragged by chains into a cell, thrown to the ground. Shapes, cut-out puppets of a magic lantern show, bestial, monstrous things rise in the filtered glow, surround him.

– Hail to the dark, O sacred daughter of aching loss, I sing. In days gone by, you took the son of earth and sky into your springs.

Among the moving shades one shape is still – a woman or a child? A girl.

– O holy maid, when up out of the never-ending fire his father came—

A winged form rises suddenly above the girl, bright white among the black, a trick of Don's most intricate mechanical light-engineering skills. An angel Gabriel or Leda's swan, it swoops upon her.

– and so, I sing, his father brought him forth between his thighs, a cry, a name.

– Jack, comes the whisper from the Princess.

The shapes disperse, they dissipate, angel of light and girl of shadow separate, and then there's only Jack, huddled in chains, Pierrot's prisoner waiting for his doom. He curls up on the ground.

– Sleep, twice-born son, I sing, within your father's womb, your mother's tomb, your dreams. We promise you, you will be back. You shall be known in Themes.

The lights come up again on Pierrot and now, in his black suit, he is the only darkness on the stage.

– But you, the darkness now, I sing, cast us aside, when on your sacred grounds we strive to hold our revels garlanded with crowns.

I stand behind him, soft voice at his shoulder.

– Why do you hate us? Why evade us? By the purple fruit that hangs upon the vine I promise there will come a time when you will turn your thoughts within and in your blood and in your brine, the salt of semen and of sin, you'll find one thing ... the spirit.

– Harlequin, sneers Pierrot.

He wheels and, brushing me aside, exits stage-left.

– These creatures born of clay, I sing, what rage and fury they display, this Pierrot, this son of the earth-born actions of the worms of an archaic age, savage and monstrous in his ways, a giant in his inhumanity, a murderous will against divinity. Just give him time and he'll have all the servants of the Harlequin in chains. He has our comrade even now plunged in the dismal, black, abysmal prison of his palace. Do you see this, Harlequin, how Pierrot reigns? Your prophets struggle under his relentless cruelty. Come, O King, holding your golden thyrsus high up on the slopes of oil lamps, curb the pride of this bloodthirsty fool.

I sing to the silhouette of sleeping Jack.

– Where are you, Harlequin? Out in the night, among the dens of beasts and peaks of carcasses, gathering revellers around your green-veined flute? Or in the darkwood thick of oil lamps, where the orphan gathered trees and beasts of the fields around his lute.

– He's in prison, says the Duke. We just saw him thrown in prison.

– I believe it is a metaphor, the consul says . . . m'sire.

– O blessed veils of Empyre, Harlequin honours you. To you he will come back with his rites to lead the dance—

Behind the scenes, Don kicks the son-et-lumière into action. This is where things should get interesting, I think – Harlequin's dream, the audience's trance. Colour kaleidoscopes out of projectors mounted on the wagon's lighting rig, over the walls and ceiling of the dull grey hall.

– To lead the whirling maidens over the freefall, I sing, over the flow of the turning axis, over the churning ludic foam, the chaos of passion and praxis—

Gold and cerulean, glittering gilded leaves and diamond flakes of snow tumble across the walls, fractals and fronds of shimmering colour in a lightshow, shattering sapphires and carnelians. People *ooh* and *oh*. There's even one loud *wow*. There should be, though; the acid in the dry ice should be kicking in by now.

– Over the father of all rivers, I sing, that brings joy to humanity with its fresh water springs . . .

Then bursting through the wash of light, blossoms of silversea, in waves, crash, dappling into horses, galloping palomino mares, black stallions in the night.

– Over the river of all souls that feeds this land of steeds, I sing.

And bucking amongst the sires and dams, a single, prancing, mottled foal.

I sneak a glance backstage, see Joey down on one knee, Jack behind him, gesturing rudely with his flute. Joey, ever the pessimist, is tucking a knife into his boot.

— *I just don't think that violence can ever be justified, Don.*

  — *Never, Jim? Isn't that a little glib, a little pat?*

  — *No, it's the plain truth. When has anything ever been solved down the barrel of a gun? That kind of 'solution' is a bit too 'final'. I just think we're playing with fire, here.*

  — *Since when has violence ever solved anything? That's a beautiful thought, Jim, but I can hear the white van coming for you right around now — [sounds of an ambulance siren] — a-a-a-and Elvis has left the building. Nighty-night, Jim-Bob. Sweet dreams. Don't let the bitmites bite. And hello ... Hugh, what's your take on the matter at hand?*

— *Don, Jack Flash is just a criminal. He's not a hero. I'm sick of hearing all these poor little rich kids whining on and on about how 'oppressed' they are. They don't know what duty means. Our grandfathers fought—*

  — *a war for them, yeah, yeah, let's bring back National Service, send them all to Russia, see how they like living under the Futurists, hanging's too good for them, bring back the thumbscrews. Am I right, Hugh? Am I right?*

  — *Look, all I'm saying is, at least we have the luxury to complain—*

  — *and get blacklisted.*

  — *They could get jobs if they wanted them.*

  — *Tell that to the homosexuals.*

  — *Clause 22? The Employment Act was totally necessary. These people were working in our schools, with our children, perverts teaching our kids.*

  — *The old Premeditated Socrates, eh? First-degree corruption of the youth. Hugh, take a look out there. Our youth don't need to be corrupted ...*

Fast Puck and I, entwined, wind round each other, dancing flesh-to-flesh, chakra-to-chakra.

  — So what's it like, being an avatar of chaos? he mumbles through a mouthful.

  — It can be a little bit ... unstable, I say.

I can feel the tingling up and down my serpent spine from the endorphin halo high of the crown chakra, down through the sixth chakra serotonin clarity of the ajna eye in the centre of the forehead, down to chakra five, the throat, the voice, the word, the guttural growling tone of hunger, down to the adrenalin rush of fear and fury sourced in the heart chakra, down to the third, beneath it, in the diaphragm, the solar plexus, where the affect of pride and guilt is born from a kinaesthesia of lungs and nervous breaths, of gasps and laughter, down, down to the hara chakra of the lower belly, of the guts, and down . . . down to chakra number one, the mother lode, the loins and lust, source of all chi energy, source of testosterone and oxytocin. You can nix the ego in Nirvana, baby, but the flesh lives on, and it has its own agenda.

And down in that one spot where my tongue-slicked foreskin slips back over glans and lipsmacks slurp around my full-on cock, I feel the hot crystal smash of orgasm as his thumb jabs hard into my perineum — halfway between hard-on's root and ass — in an ancient tantric trick to halt the outflow of the juice.

— Yeehaw, I say, or words to that effect.

It takes me a couple of minutes to chill my breathing then, charged up with all the mystic life-force of the universe, fully embodied and aware in every fibre of my flesh, I untangle from the horny kid and rise to dress.

The Fox has done me proud.

I pull on the leather trousers (American air cavalry, laced up the sides), the crimson shirt (Futurist Cossack, spattered with the blood of Russian nobility), the epauletted jacket (black and gold of the Free Iberian Alliance), the spring-loaded jackboots (best Weimar Republic engineering) and, over this, the armoured longcoat stolen from the sentry. I look in the full-length mirror as I wind a white silk scarf around my neck and place the nightshade goggles on my forehead. I look passably human now, flame-coloured spikes of bleached hair unnatural but not ungodly; skin, fingernails and nostrils — all the little things that matter. Only the silver and gold of my irises remain as an eerie reminder that I really don't belong in this world.

— So you think you can take him? says Puck.

— Joey? I say. Piece of piss. Joey's a pussycat, once you get to know him.

— He fucking *shot* you.

I shrug.

— I pissed him off.

– He betrayed us all.

– Only person Joey betrayed, I say, was himself.

Puck shakes his head. I'm the original lost cause.

Noticing that my joint has gone out, I dig into the pocket of the longcoat for the matchbook, snap one off, fold over the cover to wedge the head of the match between cardboard and sandpaper, flick it – *ffsh* – and suck down on the spliff. Make mental note: must remember to pick up a lighter.

– You'll be wanting this, says Puck and, out of the dresser, he brings a mahogany box. He opens it with the most tender care and there's a silvery-golden gleam of metal.

The Curzon-Youngblood Mark I chi-gun, antique prototype of all subsequent models, and still the best in many an assassin's book, glistens like an erection.

Peachy keen, I think. I'm ready to rock and roll.

Errata

A Grand Plan

— And just what are ye going to do, Jack? Are ye going to walk into Germany and kill Adolf yerself, and then take a wee trip down to Italy and see to Benito too?

Seamus shakes his head. He's a good man and his heart's in the right place, sure, but he's an eedjit. They're a pair of fookin eedjits.

— Maybe I will at that, says Jack. We could do it, you know. I think we could do it.

Seamus stubs the stinking Gauloise out in the ashtray and leans back against the dresser. The garret room is tiny, slope-ceilinged and with just a wee dormer window jutting out. A bed, a wardrobe, and not much else. Seamus's digs aren't any more grand, sure – well they wouldn't be on a dockworker's wages – but at least he keeps his place decent, bed made, neat square-cornered sheets as the army taught him. Jesus, but Jack's place is like the inside of his fookin heid – a right fookin state, it is, with dirty fookin laundry everywhere and empty whisky bottles, five or six, no, Christ there's another one sticking out of the fookin drawer, in amongst all the fookin socks and shite. Aye, but he can fair drink for an Englishman. He can give Seamus a good run for his money in that these days and that's fookin saying something.

The two of them spend a lot of time drinking now.

— Oh, so it's *we* could do it, is it? says Seamus. Just march through Nazi Germany saying top o' the morning to ye and what ho, old chap, and they'll just let us in to see the Führer. Or maybe we can steal some Nazi uniforms, sure, and say *Seigheil* and they'll never know the fookin difference. Oh, that's a grand fookin plan, Jack. Chin up, boys, and over—

Seamus stops himself just in time from saying *over the top*. It would be a low blow. What's past is past, he tells hisself. If he repeats it enough times, it might just fookin stick.

– Maybe it *is* a plan, says Jack. We just walk to Berlin and kill anyone that gets in our damn way.

Jesus, but he's fookin serious and all.

– Kill them all? says Seamus.

Jack doesn't answer, just stands up from the dishevelled bed, picking an empty bottle off the floor and carrying it to the dresser. He places it there beside the ashtray, moving Seamus to one side, and walks back to the other side of the room, the whole four paces of it.

Then he just says a single word and—

– and the broken glass lies like a powder all over the top the wooden unit and Seamus's ears are ringing and he's sick to the stomach and the mirror on the dresser's all warped like a fookin funhouse thing showing their shapes distorted limbs all out of kilter twisted room skewed broken bodies on a battlefield and crow flapping at the window black and white and red and Seamus is feeling the cold iron of the bedpost in his hand as the world stops shivering.

– We're different, says Jack. You and I, we're different.

Seamus closes his eyes to cornfields stretching as far as the eye can see, snaps them back open again, breathing deeply.

– What do you see, Finnan? says Jack. What do you see when you close your eyes?

– Nothing.

– What do you see when you're drunk and crazy, when you have your turns? That's what you call them, isn't it, when the words come out of you from somewhere so deep you can't even touch it when you're sober?

– It's not . . .

But he doesn't know what it is, sure, so how can he fookin deny it?

– I know what you're saying, Finnan. I've heard you. Remember it's me that's dragged you home in the night when you can't stand on your own two feet. I've listened to you talking. I've *understood*. I've heard it before.

And Jack tells him about an expedition into the wilds of the Caucasus, about the language that he found there, written on

144

the skins of dead men, the language that Finnan speaks but is too afraid to understand, that Jack understands but is too afraid to speak.

Jack opens the wardrobe door and pulls out another bottle from behind a leather satchel that looks like it's seen better days. This bottle's full and he unscrews the top. He takes a swig and passes it to Seamus. Seamus takes a slug, bitter, aniseed and burning. *Christ.* He hacks, looks at the bottle. *Jesus, isn't this stuff illegal?*

— Do you know what we are? says Jack.

Seamus takes the top from Jack and screws it back on the bottle.

— No, he says.

— But we're different, aren't we?

Seamus nods, then shakes his head.

— It's not us, Jack. It's not us that's different, but . . .

He hands the bottle back to Jack. He looks at the two of them in the warped glass of the mirror, attenuated things with heads too small, stick creatures, like a child's drawings or paintings on a cave wall. A reflection changed by a word.

— Ye know what I see when I close my eyes, Jack? War. An endless fookin war and us fighting in it, killing in it, over and over and over again. But it doesn't make sense, Jack. Some of it just doesn't make sense. Oh, I can tell ye that ole Joe and Adolf are about to sign a fookin pact to carve up Europe between them. I can tell ye that it won't hold because the both of them are fookin cunts. But . . . I used to think it was the future I was seeing, ye know? But I'm not so sure now. Some of it doesn't seem like this world at all, Jack. There's these little creatures, see, these little black creatures crawling over everything and — Jesus, I'm as fookin mad as you are.

Jack runs a finger through the powdered glass, brushes it off with his thumb.

— I don't think we're mad at all, he says. I think we've been given . . . a gift. That we have a duty to use.

Jack's warped reflection stares out at Seamus from the mirror.

— If we can change things, he says. If we can change things . . .

– The world, says Jack. The past. The future. Everything, man.

Seamus flicks his cigarette ash into the steel sink and turns the tap on. There's no ashtrays in the kitchen and he's hardly going to drop it on the floor, sure, so he watches the clear stream of water battering the paper and tobacco apart and spinning it away down the plughole. He turns off the tap when the last of it is gone. Upstairs there are voices, high-pitched giggles and squeals, stomping. That'll be the Frenchman's wife and kids; they met her briefly when she opened up the back door to them, took one look and called for her husband. Seamus crosses to the door leading out into the hall and pulls it closed, muffling the sounds. He's not sure how much of it is for secrecy's sake and how much of it is just to close the door on something he knows that he'll most likely never have himself.

– You *Anglaise* . . . the Frenchman is saying.

– Irish, says Seamus.

– That doesn't matter, says Jack.

– The fook it doesn't, says Seamus

– My friends, I don't understand how this . . . book could change . . . the world? I think perhaps you have been drinking, *non*?

– Not since this morning, says Jack.

The kitchen is small but clean and well-stocked, pots and pans hanging above the iron range, bowls of fruit and baskets of fresh vegetables on top of the cupboards. The air is filled with the scent of herbs and smoked things – fish or sausages, cheeses – onion and garlic of course, from a pot of stock simmering on the range. Sure and Seamus would give his right arm to have this man's quiet life of domesticity.

– Monsieur Reynard, he says, all that matters is . . . you know that Hitler won't stop at Czechoslovakia.

Reynard nods and Seamus joins them at the kitchen table, the solid pine block of furniture that takes up most of the centre of the room. Reynard sits in a chair at the side nearest the door into the hall and, beside it, what must be the door into a pantry tucked under the stairs. Seamus can smell the aroma of good food coming from it.

Jack sits at the end nearest the range, a pile of francs on the table in front of him, pitifully small but all that they've got. Seamus picks the seat facing Reynard.

– All that matters, says Seamus, is that there's a war coming and we might be able to stop it.

– To change things, says Jack. All we're asking you to do is use your skill.

Seamus looks at the leather satchel hanging over Jack's shoulder. He spotted it a few times back in the Ebro, sticking out of Jack's kitbag, and never got round to asking about it. Sure and it never seemed important, just a wee satchel like that, hardly big enough to hold anything of value. Now that he knows what's in it, by Jesus but it's another story. They must be fookin mental. *If we'd won the war in Spain*, Jack had said. *If the fascists were ... divided somehow. If it wasn't for Stalin and Chamberlain, and their bloody deals with Hitler ... You have the Sight. You can see what changes need to happen. I know the language, but ... neither of us have the skill for it.*

– Yer the best man for the job, so we hear, he says. The only man for the job.

– But this, Monsieur Carter, Monsieur Finnan – [he picks up a couple of notes] – this is an insult. Enough for only ... *un passeport*, a diploma. You are asking me to create a book, for this?

– You don't understand what's at stake here, man, says Jack. You—

Seamus puts his hand on Jack's arm.

– Sure and I know it's nothing. I know it's a fookin joke. But it's all we can give ye but the shirts off our backs, and I'll give ye that if ye fookin ask for it. I'll work me fookin fingers to the bone as yer slave if ye'll do this for us. I swear on me mother's grave and Jesus Lord Almighty his self. Look into me eyes, Monsieur Reynard, and spit in me fookin face if I'm not telling the truth.

Reynard holds his gaze for a second then looks away.

– I believe you, Monsieur Finnan. I believe you are an honest man. A *poor*, honest man, unfortunately, but then most honest men are.

He drums his fingers on the table, the long delicate fingers of a pianist, thinks Seamus, or a jeweller. Or a forger. Eventually, it seems, he comes to a decision.

— I do not promise anything, says Reynard. But . . . show me these . . . scriptures you wish me to copy, please. Let me see how much work would be involved.

— *Mon Dieu*, Reynard says quietly. *Mon Dieu. Une cigarette, s'il vous plaît?*

Jack pulls the pack from his breast pocket, passes one to Reynard and one to Seamus, pats at his jacket. Seamus takes his own lighter out and flicks it open, lights his fag and passes the lighter still lit to Jack. Jack lights his own cigarette and snaps the lighter shut and open again, sparks it back up with a flick of his thumb and lights Reynard's cigarette, all in what's almost one swift motion. Old habit.

The contents of the leather satchel lie spread across the table, squares and rectangles of treated skin, of dried hide, of vellum, golden-brown and so thin they're almost translucent. Reynard holds one up to the lamp and it seems to glow, the gravings on it so intricate, so subtle that they look like filigree, the work of a needle rather than a brush. Sure and they should do, thinks Seamus.

— The craftsmanship is beautiful, says Reynard. *Formidable.*

He turns the page over to look at the reverse.

— My friend, this is a challenge I would dearly love to take but what you want is . . . to forge something like this, I mean. The ink is *in* the vellum, you understand? This is not painting, not drawing but . . . I do not know the technique. If anything, I should say these look like tattoos.

— A pin instead of a pen, says Jack. Couldn't you create the same sort of stain?

— But even the vellum. What is this? Calfskin? Pig? It is so beautifully cured. Feel the texture, the suppleness.

— You would have to use the back of these . . . pages.

Reynard raises an eyebrow.

— With the true script right there on the other side. I don't understand. If this is to fool some private collector—

— It's not, says Seamus.

— But do we have enough here, to create this book you wish?

— If you need more, by God, snaps Jack, I'll give you the skin off my own back.

Seamus kicks him under the table, as Reynard gives Jack a worried glanc and takes another look at the page in his hand. He holds it up to the light again.

— Where *did* you get this? he says quiet but firm. What is this . . . ?

— I will not do this! It is an abomination. *Brute! Bête!*

— You will, says Jack. All you have to do is write what we tell you. You don't understand what's at stake here.

— A petty fraud, says Reynard. And a sick one. Your collector is some deviant, some beast, *non?* He would have to be to want this — this travesty.

— This is about the future of the world, says Jack. You need proof?

— Jack, wait, says Seamus.

Jack grabs the francs off the table, throws them at Reynard.

— This is not about money. It's about this—

And he spits a word out of his mouth that lifts Reynard up into the air and holds him there like a puppet on a string. Seamus can see the total panic on the man's face, absolute horror at these creatures with their satchel full of human skin and their magic words and, Christ, he'll never do it now. Seamus punches Jack full in the face with everything he's got and he goes down. Reynard crumples to the floor.

— Listen. Wait. No, wait.

Reynard scrabbles back away from him.

— *C'est diabolique! Vous êtes le diable.* You are the Devil!

And then Seamus is grabbing hold of the man, he is, and he's got him by the front of the shirt and he's dragging him in towards him, Jesus, maybe he is the Devil, because sure and he feels like a man possessed, with the roar in his head as loud as it's ever been, in the Somme or in Inchgillan or anywhere, as he pulls the man close and hisses something in his ear, not even knowing what it is he's saying, but it's such a word, oh Christ, that Seamus burns his mouth on it, he feels it ripping out of his lungs and ringing in his head, and then he's screaming and, fook, did he pass out then, did he?

What did he say to the man? What did he fookin say?

Reynard is at the sink. He retches, vomits.

– I'm sorry, says Seamus. I didn't mean to. I didn't mean it. I don't know what ... What did I say to you? What did you see? Oh Jesus, I'm sorry.

– Six – six – six, stutters Reynard.

Let who hath wisdom count the number of the Beast, thinks Seamus. Oh Jesus fookin Christ and it's the fookin apocalypse it is, then. Is that the bit of the future I can't see? Can't face.

– Six *million*, says Reynard.

– I don't understand.

Reynard throws up again.

He stands over the sink, just panting, spitting every once in a while as Seamus leans back against the pantry door, saying nothing. Jack lies on the floor in a heap. Looks like Seamus broke his nose.

Reynard pulls a chair across from the table to sit down on it, still right beside the sink. He looks long and hard into Seamus's eyes. Upstairs one of his children is crying, disturbed by the noise perhaps. Reynard nods.

– You say that with this book you can change things? he says.

4

Death's Release

A New Sparta, a New Athens

– You're crazy, I say. I mean, the army I can just about understand,
but the SA? They're thugs, plain and simple. Brutal, sadistic vermin.
What is it, the pretty uniforms?

He bristles, eyes narrowed with resentment and defiance, and
I regret my words instantly, knowing that where he might have
listened to me before, it will be useless to talk to him now. I sigh
and turn back to the display cabinet where all of Mother's precious
knick-knacks seem so fragile now, so delicate, the Dresden china
that was never to be actually used, the ceramic clogs from Antwerp,
the framed pictures of my brother and myself. The cabinet itself
is so terribly solid in comparison, Chippendale or somesuch, if I
remember right, brought over from England when we left.

What will we do with all of her things now? I wonder.

– Jonni, I say more gently. Jonni.

He sits on the piano stool, one finger *plink*ing on the same
black key; we were never very good students, either of us, he too
easily distracted by the sunshine outside the window, while all I
ever wanted to do was play the razzling dazzling jazz music that
I listened to on the radio. He rakes his fingers through his corn-
blond hair. His mother's golden boy, his father's little soldier ...
I wonder why I never felt jealous of their pride in him, only ever
protective towards his ... innocence. It is ironic, really – my elder
brother, dynamic, athletic and more than capable of looking after
himself in a fight, and I feel protective of him. And angry, yes,
because I know what attracts him to this fascism nonsense, under
it all.

– Take some time, I say. Come back to Nice with me. Or we'll go to Berlin and I'll show you the night-life. There are clubs I know of. You don't have to . . .

I tail off into an old, old silence.

– Times are changing, Reinhardt. I know – I know that some of them are thugs. I know that some of them just want to throw fire-bombs at communists and Jews. But that's just now. This is just the start.

– That's exactly what worries me, Jonni. Who's next?

I'm worried about you, I want to say. *You.*

– The Futurists, he says, are the real threat, to our whole way of life.

– Come to Berlin with me, I say weakly.

– Come back to Strann with me, he says.

I close the safe and turn the dial, hang the painting back on its hook. For the thousandth time, I think how much I despise the print but, as it's a present from my brother, I can't insult him by not hanging it in pride of place behind my desk, over the wall safe. One of Herr Hitler's dreadful *Teutonic Knights* series, all grey and monu-mental, the angles and curves, the cogs and wheels of some unspeakable mechanism, it tries to blend the shining, articulated armour of some Siegfried with a robotic imagery redolent of Lang's *Metropolis*. All it succeeds in doing is looking monstrous and over-blown. I sit back down in my chair, the Eye of the Weeping Angel in my hand, trying to think of what to say next.

– Did you ever really like that thing? I say, beckoning over my shoulder.

He looks at his feet.

– I'm not an authority on art, he says, but I thought, well . . .

– If it was Hitler's, then it must be good, yes?

He looks uncomfortable. Good, I think. He should be.

– What do you think of it now? I say.

– I don't know. Look–

– No, *you* look, I say. Look at it and tell me what you see. You don't think it looks a little Futurist?

– Yes, yes, he snaps, so Hitler betrayed us, yes. I know.

– But fascist too, I say. Is it armour or is it armament, man or machine? It's hard to tell where one ends and the other begins. It's hard to tell the difference, I'd say. Fascist or Futurist, Jonni – what is the difference?

– Germany!

He thumps his fist on the desk.

– The difference is that *we* believe in something. We believe in this country, in the people, in our heritage, our history, in . . .

I shake my head. I lay the jewel on the desk and slide it across to him.

– Romantic lies, I say with a deep weariness. Take it and go.

– Come back with me, he says. You'll see, I promise you. When you see, you'll understand.

– I don't think I'll *ever* understand, I say.

– I don't think I'll ever understand you, I say. As long as I can remember all you ever wanted was to go to Heidelberg, to become an officer, and now . . . now you throw it all away to join these maniacs.

He closes the piano's keyboard lid and swivels round on the stool.

– Believing in something greater than yourself doesn't make you a maniac. Yes, right now the SA is full of . . . wild, young men. They come from the Freikorps, yes, a lot of them come from the street, and they're not educated, not like us. They haven't had our privileged lives, but they're the front line against communism and–

– What? International Jewry? Zionist conspiracies? You don't really believe that rot. I know you don't.

I walk over to the window, pull the lace curtain aside and point along the street.

– Is Herr Hobbsbaum a Zionist conspirator? Does he deserve bricks through his windows? Dogshit on his doorstep? Slogans in pig's blood?

– No, of course not. There are good Jews, Reinhardt – you and I know that – but . . . you can't expect the man on the street to understand. The discipline will come, though. Things will settle down. We'll get the . . . *fire* under control. Yes. Right now, it's like a fire, Reinhardt, it's sweeping across Germany, and it's going to transform it, but once we get it under control ... we'll be a new Sparta, a new Athens. Brothers in arms, that's what it's all about. That ... simplicity, that honour and nobility.

I walk back to the display cabinet and I pick up the photogram of my brother in his *Wandervogel* outfit, standing there against an Alpine backdrop, mountains and meadows. Is it a contradiction in his character, I wonder, that before that trip he was obsessed with old revolutionary heroes, communists, anarchists and republicans, Bakunin, Kropotkin, Danton and Robespierre, with little understanding of the actual ideologies they stood for? Or does it make perfect sense, like this new sacrifice of Reason to Romance?

I place the picture back on the cabinet, close the glass door gently.

– At least do one thing, I say, *please*. Don't wear the uniform to the funeral.

– I don't have—

– Borrow one of mine, I snap.

– Of course, he says. Of course.

– Of course, he says. You could still change your mind, you know.

The station is busy, thronging with the hubbub of families and businessmen pushing this way and that, or standing saying goodbyes, or waiting, watching clocks and checking watches, and we weave our way through, the porter behind us carrying my brother's solitary carpet-bag with his uniform in it. I managed to persuade him, at the last minute, to travel in civilian clothes, to avoid any trouble, any run-ins with those less ... patriotic than himself.

– Oh, yes, he'd said absently. You're right. You're quite right. It's going to happen soon. Don't want to draw attention to myself, eh, Fox?

I didn't ask him what was going to happen soon.

He squares the homburg on his head and excuses himself as he passes a young frau with a pram. I follow him, tipping my own hat as I pass and smiling at the baby. I hate the dreadful things but old habits die hard; women like a man who smiles at babies.

– You're quite sure you won't come with me? he says.

My answer drowned out by the low, deep toot of a train, I shake my head. Steam hisses. Further down the platform a group of young men in black shirts and circle-and-cross armbands stand laughing and chatting; they're all around the station, all around the city, more of them than ever now. Two, three years ago they were probably all wearing swastikas, I imagine, but the split went better for Hitler than it did for Röhm, who's virtually alone now as the last of the old upper echelon of the Nazi Party. And the lower ranks are dwindling all the time; what red-blooded male wants to join an army of buggers and bum-boys in this day and age?

– You've heard of Thermopylae and the Spartan army that held the pass? my brother said once, nervously. Not three hundred men, but a hundred and fifty pairs of lovers. Not physically perhaps, he hastened to add, but spiritually. *Spiritually.*

But I fear the physicalities have long since rendered that rhetoric less than useless. Herr Hitler saw that, saw that the middle-class businessmen and working-class thugs he needed couldn't – wouldn't – stomach what they considered mere depravity. No, Röhm and his fascists, their days are numbered now, I think. Tomorrow belongs to those for whom the rhetoric of history, of brotherhood, of anything can be abandoned once it has outlived its use.

– This is me.

I step out of the way to let Johann take his bag from the porter. He places it on the train and climbs up into the doorway. He reaches out a hand and I shake it stiffly, awkwardly.

– Don't be so worried, Fox, he says. Everything will be fine now.

He pats his breast pocket where the jewel sits wrapped in a handkerchief. He wouldn't pack it. I think of its owner, this man Pechorin, his meeting with Himmler, and what they might be discussing. More Zeppelins and crews to drive the Japanese back? The power of German engineering joined with Russian ruthlessness? I wonder if my brother hopes to sow discord between them with this theft, but somehow I am sure there's more to it than that.

The future he fears will not be stopped so easily, I think.

The Impact Pattern of a Fallen Angel

He comes in on a gyring vector, braking his backways fall through days, months, years as best he can with woollen coat unfurled and billowing, black wings behind and above him, shredding in the snarling currents of time. The coat won't last much longer, but it's the nearest thing he's got to a parachute, so it's going to have to do.

He catches a vortice and goes sailing sidewards on a slipstream, twists his body to add a subwise motion to the slide. A kamikaze fighter going down, he corkscrews through the aether, plummeting through time towards a landscape as much history as geography, keeping the spiral tight to stay on target. Time, Joey knows, is not a straight line but an explosion moving outwards in three dimensions, like a bullet fired point-blank into a person's skull. There's more than one way to move through it.

Spinning into drop position, a foetal ball, he sees the crop circle below him like a smaller version of the trees flattened at Tunguska back in 1908. Meteor impact, so they say, but it wasn't a meteor that came down out of the skies over Siberia, Joey knows for sure. He's seen enough of these things — simple circles or more complex sigils — to recognise the mark of something that has torn a hole in time itself and dived right off the straight and narrow path the mundanes plod along time's arrow. These crop circles are landing marks and Tunguska's just a big one. A fucking big one, right enough. He used to think one day he'd catch Tunguska, drill a hole in time and drop right down to 1908, be there waiting when it came through, see just what was big enough to make that kind of mark on the world. Tunguska's the fucking mother of them all, he thinks. The impact pattern of a fallen angel.

He unfolds in the air above the circle, like a diver coming out of a somersault, but breaking the liquid surface of reality feet-first, arms spread, in cruciform position. Moving backways in relation to the world, he sees the wheat unflatten as he lands; the stalks leap up to meet him, the record of his arrival unmaking itself.

Then he's standing in the field of wheat, motionless in space but moving slowly backways in terms of time, crows overhead circling tail-first through the air, it seems, like a video in rewind. He's seen his own landings many times but the sight of it never grows old for him, so he strolls a minute or two back across the field then turns to face frontal, to observe the moment from the distance, with his time-track running forwards. He watches his other self walk backwards to the point of arrival, stretch out his arms like a scarecrow, rocket up into the sky, curl in a ball, and simply vanish, leaving Joey standing there outside the crop circle, marvelling at this mark of mystery in the world.

He turns backways again. He's got a day or two yet to cover on foot to reach his destination, but that's fine, gives him a chance to watch the world unwind around him as he walks through it, unseen, unheard, unknown to the mundanes whose little minds just can't quite handle the anomaly of the atemporal. He likes to walk among them like that, out of synch, out of phase. Gives him a feeling like . . . like the world belongs to him.

He takes a look around his world.

The sky is clear and blue, but in the prelude to his arrival it churns chaotically. Even the rewind motion of wheat unblown by a wind sucked back where it came from looks more stirred than it would moving forwards in time. Everything is vibrant, a little numinous, but with a darkness tearing at it from underneath. What it looks like is a Van Gogh painting, he thinks, a world seen through a haze of absinthe or insanity. Fields of corn and wheat as far as the eye can see, this is East of Eden, West of Smallville, five miles and two days out from Lincoln, 1959. Or what looks like 1959, he thinks; scratch the surface, dig down a little under this world, and you find not just farm machinery but the scything shrapnel of car bombs, dirty yellow ribbons in the grass down among the roots of trees. He crosses a dry dirt track between fields, where a twisted shard of fender juts out of the earth, red and brown with rust as if crusted with the blood of sacrifices, blood poured out to soak the dirt even redder than it already is, blood of kids, blood of lambs, offered to a deity of dust. God-fearing people here, he thinks. They'd give anything for a life where the apocalypse never happened.

He picks a stalk of wheat and runs the kernel between thumb and forefinger, letting the seed and chaff fall apart on the wind and vanish, torn by his interference out of their own timestream, lost to it. An offering of grain, of life, and no more meaningful to God than any grain of sand that's empty of the world and empty of eternity, no matter what the poets say.

God isn't just dead, far as Joey is concerned. He's buried six feet under in a stratum of residual time from long before the universe evolved the logic to rule its own reality. And then built a world over his grave.

He's developed something of a theory in his travels, Joey has, a language to orient himself when he's out of synch with the mundanes. He's come to think of time as a shape, with volume and mass, with three dimensions that he labels frontal, lateral and residual. He's walked forward and backways from cradle to grave, from grave to cradle, and slid sidewards into alternatives, branches, parallel streams. A step or two in lateral time has taken him into worlds where the fascists won the Second World War, where the Russians reached the moon first, where humanity never evolved beyond Australopithecus, Ancient of Days, crouched in his cave and feeding on the brains scooped from his enemies' skulls. He thought that was all there was to it until he found that no matter how he tried, forwards, backwards or sidewards, he was stuck in the twentieth century. And yet everywhen he visits is full of these little anomalies that go unspoken of by the mundanes. He's walked in graveyards abandoned and overgrown where tombstones date right up to 2017, engraved with images of young men in army uniform, golden boys with marine buzz-cuts. Errata. Remnants of a dead future. And things stranger even than that.

There's a third dimension to time, he's sure now: a build-up of layer upon layer, stratum upon stratum of dead universes, worlds less ordered, less lawful, than the one he was born in, worlds of gods and demons compacted underfoot to form a solid crust . . . *residual* time. And somehow the bitmites found the fault lines and crow-barred them open, fractured reality to reveal, in places, whole worlds that should no longer be. He's eaten unicorn in Paris, hunted manticore in Africa, pulled the wings off fairies for a living. But he's stuck in the fucking twentieth century.

It's like some earthquake dropped the land under their feet, or some glacier came to crush and carve it, then dissolved, leaving the world splintered and fallen, full of debris that's either tumbled down from above or been thrown up from below in the shifting of the land. Erratic boulders of time. Leaping from ledge to ledge, skidding down steep slopes of scree, walking the thin ridges between plateaus, Joey knows that time's a whole lot more complex than what the mundanes see, huddled in their caves and trying to pretend that the Evenfall never happened. He's been to the cliff-faces and preci-pices that edge their existence, looked up at unscaleable heights, down into nothingness. Cities in ruin, deserts of broken bird skulls, caves filled with suits of skin. But no matter where he goes he's trapped in this little hundred years, in this wreckage of history without a future. Just like he always was.

So maybe Jack was right.

But it doesn't really matter now.

He slides a hand over the soft fuzz of the wheat's heads, and scans around him for the road that will lead him into town, the road back to his place of birth and to his place of death. Back to the boy.

Something Wicked This Way Comes

He paints Jesus. He paints Jesus with a face modelled on Elvis Presley, but with long, lank hair and shades, the darkness of those features patched together out of ultramarine violet and blue, virid-ian, touches of burnt sienna, the way the old masters did. There's no such colour as black, his teacher taught him – shadow is something subtler, more complex – and while it's hard to fight the impulse to slap on mars black here and there just as a little tweak, he does.

It's difficult. He keeps dipping his camel-hair brush into the little splodges of paint on his palette and then reaching forward to dab the surface of the painting here or there, only to stop at the realisation that his brush has picked up mars black. He deliber-ately sets the black paint aside so that he doesn't smear it on his palette when he's adding azo yellow or phthalo blue or whatever. He finds it on his palette the same way he finds a chewed-up pen in his mouth in class when the teachers snaps his head up with a *Joseph Darkwater*. He throws the tube of paint into the bin, only to find a fresh one among supplies bought from the art store in town.

It's weird, but then everybody has these little parts of them-selves that act independently, the autopilot that takes out the garbage, lets the cat in every morning, sits through that hated geography class, walks home through the fields. It's not that different having another part of you that takes the cap off a tube of mars black paint and squeezes it out on your palette, not so different having a part of you that paces the room looking at the painting, trying to think of what it needs, what it *needs*, that jabs the brush into the black and tries to dab an inky swastika on the forehead of Jesus before you stop it, halt it, rein it in. A smile at the daftness of the notion.

Yes, it's weird, but it's not any weirder when it comes down to it – is it? – than actually trundling on through life when he's just sick of it all and all he really wants is to die, for someone to just come and put a gun to his head and listen to his laughter, hear it, goddamn hear it, hear the part of him that's screaming *Do it, goddamn kill me, damn it, pull the goddamn trigger*.

So he paints Jesus. He paints a punk kid Jesus, glowering and sullen on his cross against the background of a sky too purple to be ever seen on earth, that purple streaked with cadmium red, canary yellow sunlight down on the horizon. He knifes the sunbeams up and out in a burst of brightness that could be sunset or sunrise. It's a blast of Blake that's really pretty amateurish, but the painting needs it, he thinks. The heavens darkening or breaking open. The sun crushed down or fighting to arise again.

Just after sunset or before sunrise are when he works most; he's always been an early riser, being brought up on the farm, so he gets up with the dawn and spends an hour or so in blue jeans and bare feet in the barn, smearing paint around before his morning shower and breakfast in the kitchen. Then, all he has to do is struggle through the everyday grind of school, looking forward to the end of it, when he can wander home at his own pace through the fields of golden corn, past the clay men silent as statues but swinging their scythes in time like slaves of older days, as if they follow the rhythm of some secret inner singing. He's got plenty of time for painting now that there are no chores, now that the farm pretty much runs itself.

The clay men are what keep the farms running now. A hundred years ago they would have been *niggers*, twenty years ago they would have been *wetbacks*, but these red-brown men with their skin cracked like it's coated in dry mud don't come from across an ocean or a river grand; they come from the Hinter, from the wild place out where the rapeweed stetches far as the eye can see. When they first showed up, gathering outside farmhouses in their scores, folks were scared, opened fire on them in panic, hung their bodies on the trees like dead crows – warnings to others to stay away. It took a while for people to realise that all these clay men wanted was to work in the fields. Joey remembers his dad holding a shotgun trained on one as it bent down to pick up a fallen hoe and turned, impervious to the threat, to work on a patch of vegetables close by the house. A grain of corn a day is all you have to give them, as if it's not the payment that they need – not the daily bread – just a token of it. They have a dignity that belies their muteness; they're not dumb but silent, Joey thinks, and he refuses to call them *zombies* like the others do, scared of what their strangeness and silence says about the world they come from.

As the sun sets and the light is finally too low to paint by, Joey watches through the window as they bring their tools in from the fields, and the gathered bales of the harvest, the earth's yield. He wipes the flat palette knife on his jeans and washes it clean under the hose until it's shining steel again, pristine. He has his own tools as the clay men have theirs; all that the rest of them have – the real goddamn zombies that he has to deal with every goddamn day – are the invisible knives that dart out, slashing as they pass. A word, a look, a laugh. Every day that passes, every group of jocks or cheerleaders he passes, there'll be one of them that turns, steps out of the crowd to razor his face with the sting of an edge so sharp he doesn't feel it till they're gone and there's just the wet, salt nip on his cheek, and he's thinking *sons of bitches, goddamn sons of bitches*. He can feel himself losing it, day by day, just getting closer and closer to the end. Don't let them get to you. That's what Jack used to say. Well, screw that.

So he goddamn well paints Jesus. He paints Jesus streaming with the cadmium red acrylic blood of his passion, a tortured, twisted, skinny body where every muscle and sinew is visible, every vein a green line pulsing on his pale flesh. It's like he doesn't have any skin left, Joey thinks, or like all that's left is fucking rags hanging off this scarecrow of a body in bloody strips. Green and red, the snakes of blood break up the body, covering the ripple of ribs or the indent of sternum, the ribbing of stretched biceps. The death of a thousand cuts. It's not the form he's interested in but the surface of it, the brutal patina of a body that's been whipped and speared and torn by thorns until it's slick with its own blood. This is a Jesus raised on his cross out of the charnel house.

He remembers Old Man MacChuill talking to him and Jack about the End Days when they were younger, about the Rapture and the risen dead, and a slow-burning apocalypse, a thousand miles and twenty years away, in another country, another time. Armageddon was a valley in Israel where crusaders and jihadists met in a holy war waged by children who threw stones or strapped explosives on beneath their coats, or drove humvees blaring *Burn, Motherfucker, Burn* at top volume. Shock and Awe and Terror. Babylon and Baghdad. It wasn't an angel's vial that dried up the Euphrates but a stealth bomber pouring cluster bombs out of the jaws in its belly. Six hundred and sixty – give or take a half dozen – detainees pouring out of the pit of Guantanamo, with scorpion venom in their heads instead of thoughts. And the world went up in fire and bitmites.

Everyone said Old Man MacChuill was crazy, that he had a *vivid imagination*, but he just kept on talking about ten years of war and another ten of Evenfall before, hallelujah, the Millennium came. Only the Son of Man failed to show up, that's what he used to say. No Christ or Antichrist, just the kings of the earth on each side, politicians and clerics fighting for hearts and minds, for souls, for power over them, and even them becoming more and more irrelevant in the years of ghost cities and endless roads, of radio stations blaring Magyar songs in the heart of the Deep South, of towns drifting off into eternal forests and fields that stretched further than any helicopter or plane could fly. Then the satellite signals went and the webworlds were gone. The sims went on the frizz, grey shades, white static answerers haunting vidphone lines. And then there was no more USA, no more Oklahoma, no more MacEwan County, and no more future, just plain old Lincoln, 1959.

That was the old man's crazy story, anyway, half Wild Turkey and half *Weird Tales*, crazier than any of that Flying Saucer stuff, than any *Twilight Zone*.

– There's nowhere to go now, he'd say. You know, the road out of town just curves in a big circle out and round and back in again. Swear to God, they tell you this bullshit about the Russians, the Futurists, and the oil shortage, and the New Depression, but it's lies. It's the bitmites, you see, little tiny machines.

Eventually they took the old man into hospital. Hebephrenic, they said.

Sometimes, when he's standing in front of a blank canvas, he thinks about that. He thinks of the road looping out into the fields in a wide circle and back in, and he paces round the barn in a wide circle that brings him back to the canvas, where he tries to figure out what it is he wants to paint. He closes his eyes, and his thoughts do the same thing, running wide through the darkness of the inside of his head, as if trying to get ... *out there* ... at *something*. He can feel it. He can't put it down in paint but he can feel it, sort of inside, sort of outside. He doesn't know what it is, but it's cold and it's dark and it's coming for him. It's like death is coming for him.

So he paints Jesus. He doesn't believe in Jesus, and it's *not* that he has some stupid poor-me martyr complex – screw that – but the ... mystery of this icon of the human sacrifice is something that he can't get out of his head, out of his mind, out of his hunched shoulders and peering eyes and cramped hand as he leans in close with the tiny horsehair brush to paint two tiny white titanium skulls as highlights in the shades his Jesus wears – wide round black sunglasses the shape of empty eye sockets.

So he really doesn't identify with the Jesus that he's painting. Oh yeah, sure, he's got the same black beatnik hair and he's a pale and scrawny-looking punk, and if the town had to vote on someone to be crucified he's pretty sure he'd win by a landslide. Used to go around saying that he wanted to die, that they were goddamn killing him slowly piece by piece, wishing someone would just put a bullet in his head and get it over with. Then last year this kid from over on the other side of town, a fruit, got murdered and Jack, well, Jack took a walk out into the fields and was never seen again.

He'd found Jack's diary left in the barn as a sort of long goodbye.

Shit, Joey had never even known. Oh no, Jack was the all-American square, blue eyes, blond hair, and Joey had never once thought to look in those eyes and ask why they seemed so vacant sometimes. Or why a gym-team hero of the hoops like Jack would pick the weird artistic kid to hang out with. The diary got a little strange towards the end – lots of crazy talk about Old Man MacChuill being right – but, well, what really mattered was there in black and white, white paper and black ink that smeared his fingers as he read it. He got perspective then, the sort of perspective you get when the world drops away in front of you, and you're staring into a pit that drops down all the way to nothing, to the cold black nothing that you did for a friend who must have been scared shitless of being found out as a queer. The nothing-at-all that Joey did for his best friend, too absorbed in his own pathetic miseries to pick up on Jack's. Jesus? No, if Joey was going to identify with anyone it would be Judas.

So he knows he doesn't have it half as bad as some, and he knows that the goddamn gaping hole in his chest where his heart used to be is not just teen angst. It's not that old self-pity. It's not guilt. It's something different. He can feel it getting closer and closer every day. Something wicked this way comes. And the only way he can explain it is, he thinks . . . it's *death*.

He just doesn't know if it's his.

A Single, Central Flaw

– It won't be long now, he says.

– What won't be long? I say.

We sit in the armchairs beside the fireplace, looking across at each other in the golden glow, and I wait, I pray, for some explanation. The jewel sits up on the writing bureau, glittering, and I keep finding my gaze drawn to it. Why did I steal it for him? I have to ask myself. Why do I steal at all? It's not that I am a greedy man – that's not why I steal in general – and, in all honesty, the threat of being exposed, of prison, or of the shame upon the family name, none of these things coerced me into his scheme – although I know my wilful brother would not hesitate to sacrifice the von Strann reputation if he'd decided on a course of action that required it.

No, for me it was always about the challenge – the challenge of the seduction, the challenge of the crime, the challenge of the jewel itself. I find the ... mysteries of things so small and yet so valuable just irresistible. Jewels are the creations of millennia of rock acting upon rock, the slow concentration of time itself into a singular but multi-faceted crystal of such clarity, such precision. How can one not help but be seduced by them? Diamonds are carbon, like us, of course, but how many human bodies would it take, I wonder, crushed by the eons, to create a stone such as this?

It was three days after he left for the family estate that I finally succumbed to the pressure of guilt, realising that I couldn't abandon my brother to whatever insanity had taken root in him. Horst being more than capable of running the Fox's Den in my absence, I pushed my way through the crowds of Berlin Central Station, bought my ticket and, with only the clothes on my back, took the first train to Strann. Now I wait for my brother's explanation, and he just smiles.

– It will happen tonight, he says, and again my thoughts turn to his mental state. He has dismissed all the servants. When I phoned ahead, before I left Berlin, it took an eternity for the ringing to end with his *hello*. I told him I was coming, not to do anything foolish till I arrived, to wait for me, please, and he simply muttered, *yes, yes, good*. I had to phone again from the station in Strann for him to send a car, and when it arrived the driver was a stranger to me, a young lad, quiet and sensitive-looking, no more than a boy really.

– It's not meant to happen for years yet, he says. But some of this isn't meant to be happening at all.

– What are you talking about, Jonni?

– *Jack*, he says. I told you to call me Jack now, Fox.

Our voices echo in the silence of the old house, empty now it seems but for the three of us – assuming the boy stayed around after leading me to the study where my brother sat waiting in the dark, after closing the doors softly behind me. There is a hush that lies over the two of us as if it were another aspect of the gloom, palpable and permeating everything around us. It feels like the house itself, the house that I once played in, has become a stranger to me, weighed down with some terrible darkness that is now inextricably a part of it. And it feels as if that weight is focused on my brother's shoulders.

– What isn't meant to be happening, Jack? I ask.

He looks up at me, the light of the fire catching his eyes, and I think of rock weighing down upon rock, and of the energies such pressure generates, volcanic, tectonic. Whatever burden he carries, it is changing him, crushing him, but even with his uniform in disarray, his thoughts quite patently on other matters, he does not seem wearied by the weight. Rather it is as if a slow fracturing of his rough exterior is revealing cold, clear facets I have never seen before. A glassy reflectiveness in his character that is as focused and focusing in some ways as it is scattered and scattering. And with a single, central flaw right at its heart.

– The Futurists, he says. Don't laugh. No, don't say anything; just listen.

He stands, walks slowly to the desk to lay his hand upon the Eye of the Weeping Angel.

– Do you know that the Party is full – was full – of men with strange ideas, mystical ideas? No? Himmler, for instance ... Hitler, too ... many of those who betrayed us for the lies of Futurism – let me finish. Even in the grass roots there were those who were interested in such things. The Holy Grail, the Spear of Destiny. Have you heard of the Book of All Hours? No, neither had I. But when I heard it described, you know, it sounded so familiar, like something one remembers from childhood, but only just ...

He opens the writing bureau and brings out the leatherbound tome he'd had on his lap the day he summoned me here with the telegram.

– Father's copy, he says. It's sort of a history book. You could say it's *the* history book. Interesting reading. Did you know that time has three dimensions? Oh, yes, it's much more complicated than you or I could ever have imagined.

He lays the book in my lap. Now that I see it up close I recognise instantly on its front cover the design of an eye with lines running off from below, like tear-tracks, the pattern hidden in the flaw of the jewel.

– So anyway, he says, I read it and it turns out that tonight is a very special night. It's going to make a big splash. As I say it's not meant to happen for a few years yet, but it seems that some ... changes have been made that brought the schedule forward a little. The point is, tonight there's going to be a little sacrifice, not a very large one – not in comparison to what comes after – but it's a ... step along the way. Do you want to read about it?

He moves to open the book and, before I know it, my hand is on top of the thing, holding it shut.

– No? he says. They came up with a wonderful name for it, you know. Very poetic, very romantic. They're going to call it the Night of the Long Knives.

Wild Flowers in His Hand

He looks at the photographs of the boy, the file he's put together of Darkwater's seventeen years of life, laid out on the hotel bed in front of him. The adoption papers, the school reports and exercise books. And then there's today's newspaper full of horror at the brutal murders, full of shock that such a quiet boy, such a nice boy, harmless boy, could actually be capable of such an act. The vast and hollow magnitude of their ignorance almost makes him laugh. When the old world died, it took its history lessons with it. To the people of Lincoln, he understands now, the simplicity of their surroundings is some sort of gifted grace, a Happy Christmas, war is over, a thousand years of peace and goodwill with Jimmy Stewart running the local newspaper, and the Mom and Pop stores back now that the Wal-Mart and the malls are a million miles away across the Hinter of farmed and unfarmed wildernesses.

Who now remembers Columbine? he wonders.

Better not to, he thinks. Better not to acknowledge the cold and desolate truth under the surface of the stories, all the murdered murderers, the ones whose silence is the quiet of the dead, of death, walking among them in the body of a man, but with no soul, no life, no heart, only the ragged hollow where their spirit's been ripped out of them.

In the newspaper, there's a quote from one of the survivors, words whispered to him while he was curled up in a ball, pissing his pants, spared to deliver a brutally simple explanation.

I was better than them, the boy had said to him. *They killed me slowly. I killed them quick.*

Joey wedges the crowbar into the crack of the minibar door and levers it with a sharp shove, once, twice. The door gives with a splintering crack of wood and he pushes the crowbar in further, shoves again. The door shears open and almost off its hinges, sitting out at a funny angle, a wrong angle. It looks blurred, ripped out of causality as well as out of place. Too bad. He opens the door of the fridge inside and takes out a bottle of Miller, pops the top and takes a slug. Lucky that the brewery stayed moored to the town while it drifted in the dislocations of the Evenfall. He doubts all the good old boys would have been able to carry on without it.

Carry on, he thinks. That's what people do when their world gets turned upside down, whether it's by some crazy kid with a gun in his hand or some crazy president with a Bible in his. They just carry on and wait for it to happen again. A little foresight and they might change their fate, but they can't even see the simplest straight-line path from past to future, from the violence of their words to the vengeance they call down upon their own heads. It's really no wonder that they reacted to the apocalypse the way they did, choosing to *carry on* with their lives like their town had just been cut off from the outside world by some river flooding its banks and bringing down the bridge, some path through the mountains blocked by snow that would be clear when spring came with its thaw.

Maybe it's a little harsh of him but there's only so much blinkered naivety a man can take before he wants to pistol-whip the ignorant fucks who *just won't understand*. Fuck, it's no wonder they can't see the other aspects of their involuted time. They can't even see their own death till it spits a metal insult in their face.

One of the photographs shows a child sitting on a rock, wild flowers in his hand and smiling for the camera, maybe eight or nine years old – a picture of innocence, as they say. Then there's the school photograph that's on the cover of the paper and scattered throughout the inside pages. And the true crime digest from the big city 80s that he came from. It's one of the ironies, of course, that the murders put the town back on the map, literally.

He lays the beer down on the top of the minibar and stands up, stretches, cricks his shoulders and angles himself through time to face forwards. Outside the window a bird flutters up to circle away into the blue – flying in the right direction now. The clock on the bedside cabinet reads 20:43. Good. He always wanted to see this.

He switches on the TV and it comes on at the public access channel, the only channel – KWTV. Back in his city apartment Joey has a whole room of anomalies he's gathered in his travels, DVDs and datasticks, R-drives and Qubes, the facts and fantasies of a future he'll never see but can just about imagine – 9/11, Afghanistan and Iraq, Syria and the Sudan, Jerusalem and New York and . . . 2017. The grainy black-and-white pictures in places like Lincoln always seem so primitive in comparison, but in the towns with bigger stations and later technologies it's even worse. Some of them have years' worth of old movies and shows on tape, so they fill the otherwise dead air with shit. Endless reruns.

Right now KWTV is full of the chaos of the previous day. A white-haired reporter who looks like she should be organising jamborees is interviewing a doctor at the town's medical centre.

– We're just not equipped. We're just not set up for anything like this.

20:44.

The shot goes back to the studio where the anchorman – a geriatric amateur in black tie and grey cardigan, clearly out of his depth – is launching into another regurgitation of facts and fatuousness when, *pow*, the screen goes white noise. This is it.

It hisses grey-blue for a second then the other picture starts to come through; it's an aerial shot from a chopper flying low over billowing fields where clay men swing their scythes in time to the *chuffa-chuffa-chuffa-chuffa* rotorblade noise in the background.

– approaching now, Harry. Yes, just like so many of these isolated towns—

The voice breaks up, but the picture is clear enough now to see the logo in the corner of the screen, a logo that most of the people in this town will say they've never heard of, till the memories start to shift to accommodate new truths, an arcane combination of letters: CNN.

The picture cuts back to the studio, to a sleek anchorman looking solemn and concentrated as if he really understands the import of the pictures playing in the inset over his shoulder – it's the faint and flickering signal of KWTV, the hayseed anchorman fumbling with his papers, hand to his earphone, looking off stage left.

– picked up these pictures, says the CNN anchorman, these reports of a terrible tragedy in Lincoln, where Joseph Darkwater—

Joey mutes the TV. Without the speed and the stress of his rich-timbred voice, the machine-gun rattle of solemn fact, the anchorman's dumb mouthings actually say more about the situation. He looks like a fucking animatronic, one little part of a vast Disney-ride media machine kicked into action at the taste of blood.

The inset changes to a still; the still zooms out to fill the screen. It's the definitive moment of the whole bloody event – and it's all over the newspapers and on the cover of that *True Crime* digest. It shows a skinny lank-haired boy in long and ragged overcoat, looking straight at the camera and pointing a motherfucker of a gun straight at the cameraman, straight out at his imagined audience, at the viewers of the show, the readers of the papers and the magazines, at everyone and anyone.

Joey points a finger-gun at the image.

Bang.

Knowing that he has this freedom within the fields of time, Joey has sometimes wondered – if he can go back and change things, should he? He could quite easily kill this boy and save the countless lives he claimed before vanishing into the night without remorse or pity, without even having the decency to turn the gun on himself once he had expiated all his rage. That film, taken from a bloodstained camera and dumped in the mailbox of the local paper, was the last that anybody ever saw of Joseph Darkwater, and for decades afterward his whereabouts would be as much a mystery to the world as his motivation. The *True Crime* magazine delves into his past with the shallow profundities of Psychology 101. Photos of his paintings – clear indicators of a disturbed mind – rumours and innuendos about sexuality or psychosis. Did the boy feel unloved by his adopted parents? Was he bullied at school about it? The surfeit of explanations only deepens the enigma.

Why did he really do it?

Joey wonders what it would be like if he just killed the boy before it ever happened, exchanging that enigma for another: why should anybody want to kill this poor, poor boy? What kind of monster would do such a thing? And, oh, the tragedy they'd make of it. The tears, the cards, the flowers laid at his place of death by those who made his *life* a misery. And how they'd curse the angel of mercy who had saved their worthless lives. It would be interesting to see if that kind of tragedy would make the same splash that the murders did, if one little murder would be enough to amplify the KWTV signal so it reached out across the fields of time and space to remake an old connection.

In the magazine there's a re-enactment of the rediscovery of Lincoln. A technician in a TV station, one hand on the dial that he's been twiddling trying to get rid of this strange interference, other hand up as he turns to shout – *Hey, look at this, look at this* – while on the screen in front of him Joseph Darkwater, grey and blurred, points his gun at the camera.

Joey turns off the TV and angles himself round backwards in time again. He stands still and glides, lets the seconds and minutes wash over him. 20:43. 20:42. 20:41.

Knowing this future past, and on his way to meet it in this world's yesterday, Joey knows he may be the only person in this town, in this world, in all the worlds even, with the opportunity to change it . . . but he has no intention of doing any such thing.

On the contrary. He's looking forward to yesterday.

Plain, Polished Steel

The painting is already framed; it was a cheap print that he got out of a thrift shop, a reproduction of a seascape with white horses

171

running on a beach in silver spray and foam and mist of wake and moonlight, their manes blowing in the wind, their heads tossed back. Perfectly executed and perfectly vacuous. He didn't waste any time before coating the print with gesso primer, running the paintbrush over it in thick, soft strokes to murder this moronic kitsch. The mount is black velvet. The frame is plain, polished steel. With the gesso dry, he'd sort of liked it like that, just a white rectangle with a hint of texture, on a black fabric mount, in its frame of steel. It took him weeks to think of something that he actually wanted to paint on it. It was only when he turned the thing on its side, thinking that maybe he could use it portrait instead of landscape, that he started to get an idea.

He sits on his haunches now, squats on a chair that's turned away from it, his folded arms on the backrest, trying to decide if his Jesus is finished. He's not really satisfied with it.

Behind it there's another painting hanging on a hook on one of the wooden posts that supports the barn's upper level; it's a painting of the diary that he doesn't write, the big leatherbound book that – if he wrote it – would be filled with page after page of the same cycling words.

Dear goddamn world, he would write each night, like he was writing it for them to read after he's dead, to shake them with his vitriol. Like he was telling them how it is. The Gospel of Joseph Darkwater. Don't ever turn the other cheek, he'd write. The meek shall inherit the shit.

It would just be bullshit, he thinks.

He burned Jack's diary after he'd read it, because Jack's parents, he told himself, didn't really need to know any of that stuff about their son. That's what he told himself then, but now he knows, looking at this other diary, it was as much shame as anything – shame, and anger about feeling that shame. Jack's diary was a symbol of his failure, an emblem of hopelessness and despair, so he put it to the torch, carried the small metal bin from his bedroom down to the barn, doused the diary in paraffin and dropped it in the bin, a lit match after it.

A sacrifice.

*

His paintings are too much like that diary. They're still too caught up in the banalities he wants to get beyond. None of them say what he wants them to. They're not cold and empty enough. In the gruesome brutality of the crucifixion picture, it looks like he's out to shock, to create horror, to engender empathy. But, damn it, that's not what he's trying to do. He's trying to strip the humanity *away* from the Christ, show the moment not as human suffering but as the sublime butchering of this animal god. A detached, clinical, observation of a sacrifice. But it's not working.

He twiddles the brush between his fingers, like a magician with a coin, toys with the idea of painting a leering centurion in the foreground, or maybe some saintly figure with beatific grace upon his face, as if praising God that they're all saved now Jesus's blood has washed them clean. But that would make it look even more like he was – what would they say? – just trying to be controversial.

Goddamnit, he thinks, he doesn't care any more if they don't get it. Screw them. At least he's got the backbone to see a crucifixion for what it is and what it says about the human race. Maybe he could rip out their goddamn hearts and feed them to the fuckers; maybe that's something they'd understand.

If he wrote a diary maybe he could find the words to explain it all, but he doubts it. So instead he has his painted book, the favourite painting that he's done. Just a closed book with a dark-brown leather cover. Burnt sienna and burnt umber, yellow ochre highlights like it's lit by candles.

Another picture: a group of girls standing at the door of a school bus, but girls with the pale glazed faces and glassy eyes of porcelain dolls: the same artificial faces, the same blank eyes, on each of them. Rouge and eye-shadow on the cold masks only add to the eerie soulless quality that the image has. Here or there one of the eyes looks chipped, one of the faces cracked. He imagines them as creatures that would laugh without expression, talk without the slightest movement of their cherub lips.

The menace of the image, the meaning of it, is something he can't put into words but something he's familiar with, as familiar as the jocks who hound him through lunch break, their hyena yips and snarls and high-pitched laughs, like they're so goddamn funny.

He doesn't even hear what they say any more, doesn't know or care if it's him they're laughing at. It doesn't matter; the sound of laughter makes him tense with rage and shame now automatically. They're too dumb to realise what they're doing, of course, but every chewed-up piece of paper flicked at the back of his head in class is another lesson to him that their pleasure is his pain, that joy and suffering are never shared, that empathy is for losers.

He looks at the Christ in its frame of black velvet and plain, polished steel, trying to figure out just what it is that's missing.

There Is No Magic in the World

– Tell me about that night. Tell me about the ritual. Tell me how your brother . . . did it.

– Did what? says the man calling himself Reynard.

Pickering checks his watch. It's getting late and they're not getting anywhere.

– I don't have time for this, he says.

There are still another two interrogations to get through before the night is over: one fascist defector linked to Freikorps activity in London; one 'Lithuanian' known to be a Futurist agent. Operation Hawkwing brought in twenty-four suspected war criminals and spies in its sweep. Men and women suspected of working in the concentration camps or on the Russo-German A-bomb projects. Individuals caught on the wrong side of this country or that when the Armistice was called and the Iron Curtain came down. Individuals with invented identities, secret crimes. Ultimately, it's Pickering's job to decide who lives and who dies.

– I have the hangman waiting outside the door, you know, he says.

The threat makes him feel dirty because it isn't empty, and it should be. The man shouldn't even be here among these murdering bastards, wouldn't be if his name hadn't been added to the list at the last minute, by Pickering himself. Reinhardt von Strann, he thinks. For the love of God, man, he worked for

174

the Resistance. Are you really going to have him executed as a spy?

He closes off that line of thought. If von Strann won't crack, neither will he.

The man remains silent.

– You know what he did, says Pickering. You were there. You saw it. How did he become this . . . thing, this creature?

– Why don't *you* tell me? he says. It's your story. I don't know anything of this. You seem to want me to be this . . . this incredible von Strann character, but I'm not. It's a fantasy, a fabrication. It's all very fascinating, but it's ultimately . . . I don't know . . . is this really what you want, Major? Cursed jewels? Magic rituals?

He lowers his head, hands on his forehead, elbows on the table.

– There is no magic in the world, Major Pickering. I knew men like you in Hitler's Germany, men who wanted to believe so much. But there is no magic in the world. Do you mind if I smoke?

– I told you to go ahead.

– Do you have a light? Thanks. Please, where were we?

A moment of disconcertion. *There is no magic in the world.*

– I've seen it, says Pickering. I've seen . . . the impossible.

– Then you tell me. Tell me what you've seen.

– I've seen your brother. I've seen Jack Flash.

The prisoner looks up at him as if Pickering is insane. Perhaps he is.

– A myth. A legend. I've heard the tales—

– I've seen Jack Flash, says Pickering. I know his face, and I can see it in yours. I know who you are.

– Tell me, then. Go on. If you keep telling me long enough I might even believe it myself. And then we'd both be wrong.

– I've seen your fucking brother. I've seen the fucking monster that he made himself. I was in London during the Blitz, on leave, and I saw him. My family, my wife, my son. Oh, Christ, I saw him in the fucking ruins of my home, walking out of the ruins of my home with my wife's—

– head in one hand, and your son's head in the other. And he laughed at you.

Pickering echoes him, hollow horror in his voice.

– He laughed at me.

He can't get the memory out of his head. The siren that came too late and the thunder of anti-aircraft guns – *Come on now, hurry* – and a house across the street goes up, the windows blow in – *Oh Joe, we'll never make it to the shelter* – and the keen of the rockets and – *into the cellar* – and she has the baby out of the cot and in her arms, brushing glass off him, she's out of the room but he's still standing at the empty window, looking at the flames across Hammersmith, caught there, transfixed in the moment – *Joe, hurry up* – her voice on the landing – *Hurry up, Joe* – on the stairs, and the rockets go silent, and then . . . and then . . . the first chime of midnight . . . and then . . .

– And then you were lying on the ground.

He was lying on the ground, outside the house, in the back yard. A roofless broken wall, a stone curtain with flame behind it, windows like eyes filled with flame, the back door like an open mouth, a stone mask of death. Oh, Christ, the bomb must have hit the front. It must have hit the front where the stairs come down to the front door, where she stands and kisses him good-bye. Oh, Christ.

– I was lying on the ground, and I saw him. I was—

– wounded and dazed, but you saw him clearly in the smoke and flame—

– in the ruins of my house, and he had – he had—

– your wife's head in one hand and your son's in the other.

– I saw him, says Pickering. I saw Jack Flash.

– You can't see what isn't—

– Don't tell me what I can and can't have seen! Don't sit there and try to tell me what I've seen! I want the bloody truth from you.

He takes the pistol from his holster and puts it down on the table, his hand still on it, finger curled round the trigger. He pulls it up, pointed straight at the man's head. He can hear his own breathing. He has to control himself. He's missing something important, in this state of mind. He slams the gun back down on the table. He has to control himself. It's pointed at von Strann's head again and his finger is flicking the safety off, cocking it. He has to control himself.

He remembers lying on the ground and screaming, the pistol in his hand as he empties the chamber into this . . . god of fire and war.

Slowly, he uncocks the gun. He flicks the safety back on. And reversing his grip, he smacks the man across the face with the butt.

Von Strann doesn't pick himself up off the floor, just lies there, raised on one elbow, hand nursing his face. He looks up at Pickering as if expecting more violence. Pickering sits back down in his chair, beckoning, and the man stands up, holding the edge of the table for support. He rights the chair and takes his seat again as if he'd merely fallen off it in a moment of clumsiness.

– How did you know? says Pickering.

– I've heard the stories, he says. I wish I could tell you what you need to hear.

– What I need to hear is how he did it, how he made himself this thing. What I need to hear is how to kill him.

– You can't kill a myth.

– Everything can be killed, says Pickering.

Alone in the Endzone

The red LED of the radio alarm clicks over from 03:00 to 02:59. Lying on the bed, the past scattered around him, he finds himself unable to sleep for the first time in he doesn't know how many years. He pulls himself up and twists round to punch the pillow a couple of times, but it's nothing to do with discomfort. He flops back down on the bed, hands under his head. He's tired; a freefall drop through a good couple of decades takes it out of a man. It's not as rough as pushing sidewards or clawing your way down through the residual strata to the dead places, but it's tiring enough.

So why the fuck can't he get to sleep? he wonders. Outside the cicadas chirrup the only response. Maybe it's just too fucking quiet for him now. It's a long time since he was in a backwoods Haven like this; he's a city boy now, used to passing cars, revving engines and pumping stereos, the siren wail of an ambulance, drunks having arguments or singing in the night. He's used to jarring, discordant blares of noise like neon against black in the murder city nights of jazz cats and king rats. Guys in white vests playing submachine-gun solos on the fire escape. Christ, the cities are just as much a cliché as these nowhere towns out in the sticks, but they're *his* cliché now, and he feels out of place in the still of this dark rural idyll slumbering. Like a samurai sitting on a porch, using his katana to whittle wood.

But it's not the silence. His penthouse apartment back in the city is just as quiet. He's come a long way from being a street-kid, new in the city, robbing liquor stores and sleeping rough in an alleyway or in some crackhouse, whore in one arm, belt around the other. That was forever ago. Now he sleeps in silk sheets and silence.

A guilty conscience then? Fuck, no. Joey Narcosis has no regrets, no remorse. He sleeps the sleep of the dead, the sleep of the just. He looks back on his life with pride, and if he had to live it over he wouldn't change a thing, unless it was to turn pro a little sooner.

It was 1989 when he made the choice — not that the year mattered much to Joey by that point. He'd travelled enough to know how fucked the world was, and that he seemed to be the only one who knew it, the only lucid dreamer of them all. He'd learned to keep his mouth shut, but — Depression Chicago or LA in the 90s — it was all just a backdrop with the same gunfire out of passing cars, and the same clubs that only open to the right knock. Like the Fox's Den.

He remembers some guy in drag in the john that day, high as a kite on smack it looked like, laughing even as he/she smeared the lipstick on like clown make-up.

— All the world's a stage, honey! The whole world's a fucking stage!

And he has just a hint of a smile on his face as he washes his hands at the basin, nodding because somehow the words just click.

The queen giggles and collapses, shouting:

– Fuck! Fuck! I broke a fucking heel!

He looks at himself in the mirror, and he realises that he's been a fucking errand boy too long, hired muscle, a spear-carrier standing in the background, one of those guys who gets his nose broke by the hero halfway through the movie. Screw that. He's going to be a player.

An old garage rock track – Radio Birdman's 'Alone in the Endzone' – is playing as he walks out of the toilet and over to the table where the Future Boys' second-in-command, Eight-Ball, and Father Rome of the Aryan Guns sit carving up territory; and it goes on playing even as he shoots the two dealers with a single bullet in the centre of the forehead each. And then somehow time rewinds around him, and plays back and forward, back and forward, as he turns and turns again, emptying the clip, bullet by bullet, one bullet each, into the henchmen and the hangers-on. He catches glimpses of himself out of the corner of his eye like he's everywhere at once, a multiple exposure of ghost image upon ghost image, and then it's over and he has no idea of what he's just done, but he sort of knows *how* he did it. He stands in the centre of the scene of carnage, untouched, and everywhere around him clubbers scream and start to turn, to run, but in slow motion, slower. He feels this . . . puzzle of power as the world grinds to a halt, freezes around him. A nobody in their underworld up to that point, he's just carved out his name in ten eternal seconds of violence.

He cuts the ring fingers off the dealers and scrawls that new name and a contact number on a napkin, sticks them into the pocket of a kid he recognises as a runner for one of the other local bigtimes. And leaves. It isn't the most conventional beginning to a business venture ever but it will make the right impression in the right circles, he's sure, a good start to his career.

In his pocket he's got the *True Crime* mag that he found on the news-stand that day, with one little nugget of knowledge amongst all the crap, one thing he didn't already know. Not that he was adopted; his parents were quick to tell him that, even quicker to tell him that it didn't change anything, he was still their son, they still loved him, so it wasn't the big deal that the Freud Squad made of it. But the *True Crime* hacks had found out something his folks couldn't tell him; they'd managed to track down the name he was born with, Josef Pechorin.

The name doesn't mean anything to him as a name but it's . . . someone to be. Joseph Darkwater died a long, long time ago. He's no longer the fucked-up kid in scarecrow coat, with a black hole where his heart should be, where his rage built up so much mass that one day it just collapsed in on itself. He's not the same Joey who first hefted up the heavy gun and pointed it straight at a person's skull. He's not even the Narco that he was back in the days when he was new to city life and into every drug that could take him out of it, and out of himself.

For all that time has just gone insane around him, as he walks out onto the street of people walking zombie-slow, what really strikes him is this sense that the rest of his life is just a bridge between moments like this, that he's been asleep, waiting for some call to awaken him again to his . . . talent. It's like when he used to paint, he thinks. When you're in the zone and something else takes over and at the end of it all you can do is step back and look at this alien, wonderful, terrible thing you've wrought. Joey Narcosis seems a good name for that something else.

Joey flips the sheet off the bed and swivels his legs out to sit up on the edge of the mattress. In the dark of the room he can just make out the black of his clothes slung over the chair beside the table, the other chair jarring the handle of the room's door just in case some hotel busybody happens in, the gun in easy reach on the bedside cabinet beside the *True Crime* mag, an empty can from the minibar — the one he didn't crumple into never.

He takes the cord of the light hanging over the bed between thumb and forefinger, gives it a little twist, a little pull; it took him years to master even the simplest interactions in 3D time, but these days he can do it without even stopping his backways motion. It's all in the wrist.

So why the fuck can't he sleep? Killing has never fazed him any more than he was fazed that day to find the world around him stop and start, play and rewind at will; it all seemed just another sign of his freedom. If anything, the act of murder gives a meaning to his life, gives him peace in his soul, in the knowledge that he's doing what he was meant for. He curls up in bed calm with the certainty that nothing matters because everyone dies; sooner or later, death comes along and gathers everyone in his cold, dark embrace. And every murder Joey commits reminds him of his acceptance of that, of the choice he made and of why he made it.

Every suicide is a murder, every homicide an accident, and death the only real purpose behind every life.

So maybe, he thinks, maybe it's just anticipation, like a young child who can't sleep knowing that tomorrow is his birthday. In a way, tomorrow – or yesterday, rather – is the day that Joey Narcosis was born. Or, at least, the day he died.

Death in the Desert

Darkwater dreams. He's out in the fields walking amongst the clay men, grey in the light of a skull moon silver-white in the night. There are voices calling behind him but he walks on, knowing that somewhere out there, just over the next hill, there's a city, *the* city. Wheat whispers in the wind, brushes against the back of his hand as he pushes through the long stalks, up to the brow of the hill.

The car flashes past and brakes to a stop along the road a ways, reverses back to him. It's silver with black tinted windows that all wind down together as the man leans over from the driver's seat. Brown leather and wood interior, the dark whirling patterns of veneer, the smooth and textured, soft and tough complexities of vellum.

He's hitching, got a heavy rucksack on his back full of the moon rocks he was picking up in the fields. And the man in the silver car is offering him a lift. His long black hair pulled back into a ponytail, in his black suit, leather jacket and shades he looks . . . expensive. There's a black woollen overcoat lying folded on the passenger seat.

– Are you from Italy? he asks.
– Russia, says the man.

Then he's inside the car, and it's moving. The coat is bulky in his lap, awkward with the rucksack on top of it.

– We can put those in the trunk, you know.

The car pulls over.

Joey steps out onto College Street. He knows College Street in Asheville like the back of his hand, been going to school here for two years. It's all music stores and bars and cafés, a little bohemia. There's Madam Iris's Tattoo Parlour. There's Lincoln High School.

Wait, he thinks, this isn't right. Asheville and Lincoln are two different towns, in different places, different times. Wait.

– You want me to wait here? says the driver.

– Sure, Jack, says Joey. You wait here.

He starts walking towards the school gates and sees the boy push open the front doors of the building and come down the steps, rucksack on his back. As he passes a crowd of young thugs, one of them steps out – or rather a ghost of him steps out of his own body – and with a quiet, casual disregard, slashes something sharp and silvery across the boy's cheek. The boy stops, just for a fraction of a second, before walking on.

– Your lace is loose, calls Jack behind him, and Joey kneels down to tie it.

The thugs start after the boy, their meat bodies following at a distance, but their ghost selves gathering round the kid like vultures on a carcass or hyenas fighting over a gazelle in some macabre natural history programme. Joey wants to help him but his lace is loose.

They circle the boy, reaching out to slash, to cut, to carve off strips of flesh. They smear his blood on each other's faces, lick it off each other's fingers, feed each other morsels of meat hung on the points of their knives. There's something gruesomely intimate about the way they share their victim. Joey blinks. His lace is tied but he checks the other one and that's loose as well. He undoes the knot. He takes the two ends and pulls them tight. The left over and under the right. Pull that tight. He looks up.

The boy's soul drops to its knees, drops out of his body even as the boy himself walks on. Joey makes a loop, wraps round and through. Pulls it tight. The boy's soul drags behind him, bound to him by some astral cord, like a lump of carrion dragged through the dirt on the end of a rope while the thug-souls, like the dogs they are, gnaw at its fleshy parts and fight over its entrails. The cord tears and the boy staggers forward, freed of the weight of soul, falling forward to his knees.

Joey is on his knees.

He looks over his shoulder at the car parked on the road, this white shark-like convertible with tail fins, the trunk open. He looks around him at the sands of the desert, at all these little bird skulls on the ground, so delicate that they crack and crumble under his hands. The hitcher stands behind him, holding this shape wrapped in the woollen overcoat; it looks heavy, bulky, like a rucksack full of rocks. He walks round in front of Joey, drops his bundle into the hole that Joey has dug with his fingers in the sand and bone. His hands are covered in the white dust like he's been working with plaster of Paris, just like the hand in the hole, sticking out from beneath the coat, except that one has red under its fingernails as well, deep brownish red, a mix of cadmium and ochre. The hitcher has a gun pointed at his head and Joey is crying because he should have never given the man a lift. It's not even his car, and now someone is dead and his parents are going to kill him. He's going to get the blame even though it's not his fault.

The hitcher crouches down and, though there's no sympathy in his eyes, he seems to understand. He takes the coat out of the shallow grave and lays it around Joey's shoulders like a blanket or a robe, as if to comfort him. There's nothing in the grave except a rucksack and a bunch of rocks.

The man stands up and raises the gun again. He pulls the trigger.

Joey stands there, with the gun in his hand, wearing the long, black coat, watching the body rock backwards from the shot, slump sideways and back and down to the ground. It rolls right into the hole.

He wakes up, the bed soaked in sweat, and he knows he should be screaming. He should be screaming, crying or *something* after a dream like that. His heart should be pounding, his hands gripping the sheets in terror. That would be the sane reaction. But he feels so in control. He doesn't think he's ever felt so calm in his life. He can close his eyes and see his peers feeding on his soul. The boy in the school was him. That was him. So who was the driver? He called him Jack but it wasn't Jack, it was . . . something else.

He closes his eyes. He can see the hand in the grave, see the bird skulls crushing under his own palms. But what he *feels* . . . what he feels is the weight of a gun in his hand. The solidity, the certainty, of a gun in his hand.

To Kill a Myth

– Thomas, he says, will you put that over there.

My brother wanders around the room, dragging chairs back to the walls, setting up candlesticks, while the boy pulls the table across the floor as directed. Dressed now in plain white linen, shirt and trousers, barefoot, he looks even more the naif, a humble initiate following his master's voice, unquestioning. I watch the devotion in the way he answers Johann's instructions and it worries me.

– Come on. Make yourself useful and give Thomas a hand, Fox, eh?

I grab an end of the table and together we lift it to one side of the room.

– You *are* aware my brother is insane? I say to the boy.

Johann laughs. He walks over to us, slaps me on the shoulder, runs a hand through the lad's hair. He can't be more than eighteen, I think.

– Oh, don't get so worked up, Fox, he says. It doesn't suit you.

The boy laughs with him, gives him a look that hints at worship and anticipation, and Jonni returns it.

– Would you fetch the knife please, Thomas.

– So this is it? I say when the boy has left the room. This is the spiritual love you're so obsessed by? What did you say? The love of warriors and gods, of Achilles and Patroclus, of Heracles and Iolaus?

The tone comes out harsher than I intend.

– Well, it isn't the kind of lust that's for sale in Berlin's fleshpots, he says.

– No, I say. You know . . . I'm a man of the world; it takes a lot to faze me. But if you really care for this boy, Jonni, shouldn't you be, I don't know, taking him for a cruise round the Aegean or something? Not playing spiritualist parlour games.

He looks at me amazed, like I am the insane one.

– Have you listened to anything I told you, Fox? Really? Were you listening at all?

– Oh, I was listening all right, I hiss, and I've never heard such nonsense in my life.

My voice is low and I glance at the door, an involuntary reflex that I realise, suddenly, is inherited from our parents. Never let the servants hear you argue.

– Aleister Crowley is a complete charlatan, I say. And Nietzsche's übermensch is a metaphor, Jonni, a *metaphor*.

He has told me his plan now, of course, to draw down a god into a human body, no less, to create a superhuman being, Crowley's moonchild.

– Jack, he says. I'm Jack from now on. And it's not a metaphor; it's a myth.

He points at the book, sitting on a chair in the corner of the room.

– And every myth has truth in it, he says. You should read the book, Fox. You should see the things I've seen in there. The fire-bombing of Dresden. The atomic bomb, Hiroshima, Nagasaki. You'd understand.

– What am I supposed to understand? I say. These are just words.

– But words can be made flesh, he says. You say fascism is a dead idea. I say it will never die, *because* it is an idea. You crush it here and it will spring up there. It will always find a new form, new flesh. Why should that form not be a man? Why should that flesh not be mine? You can't kill a myth, Fox. You can't kill a god, don't you see? That's what a hero really is – part god, part man – and that's what Germany needs now. It's what the world needs: a moonchild.

I pick up the book and sit down in the chair, laying the damned thing on my lap. I have spent the last hour trying to talk him back from the brink of this utter abyss he seems set on throwing himself into. But even with the most modern doctors, the best sanatoriums, is there any sanity left to salvage in him? If I can show him that this book is just a prop in an absurd fantasy, I wonder, would it all come crashing down, and would he be left with *anything* to believe in then? I have a terrible feeling that, were I to kick this elaborate dream castle of his back into sand, my brother would himself scatter into a million grains.

I fear I have no other option.

I run my fingers around the heavy brass clasp, unlatch it.

– What page? I say. Where will I read all these strange and wonderful prophecies?

He grins. He has that look again, the look of fire in his eyes.

– Any page, he says. Just open it anywhere.

I run my thumb down the edges of the pages, look up as the door opens and Thomas re-enters. He drapes a red cloth over the table and starts to lay out upon it various instruments of their nonsense: the Eye of the Weeping Angel; a candlestick that looks not unlike a Hebrew menorah but with five branches instead of seven; a long, thin dagger. He looks at the book in my hands.

– You know, I say, you sound like Himmler with this occultist mumbo-jumbo.

Jonni rounds on me.

– Himmler. That swine doesn't even know what he's doing. Tonight, he's opening up the gates, and he doesn't even know it.

The vitriol in his voice takes me aback.

– That murderous cretin doesn't even realise what he's letting loose. He has no idea of the power in the blood he'll spill tonight. I've got the book, though. *I* know what to do with all that blood.

My eyes fixed on my brother, I open the book upon my lap.

– If this will satisfy you, I say. If this will make you see sense.

And I look down into chaos.

The Hollowness of Endings and Beginnings

He slams the clip into the Desert Eagle and slides it into the shoulder-holster hidden by his black woollen overcoat. He flicks back his crow-black hair and gathers it into a ponytail, secured with a doubled-over elastic band. The face looking back at him in the mirror has a cold and callous smile on its lips, slight but noticeable, and, like the narcissist he is, he straightens the thin, black tie to look his best for what he is about to do. The frayed and tattered edges of the overcoat kind of ruin the sophisticated look he's cultivated all these years, but it's an integral part of the entire game. It wouldn't be the same without it.

He remembers how it all happened when he was the boy; he remembers the mysterious stranger that came to him, like Death himself, and the dark deal that he offered, dropping the coat upon the ground in front of him and handing him the gun.

– Go ahead, he said. Kill me and you can kill anyone.

He remembers looking down at the man lying on the ground, the shattered bloody pulp where his head was blown away, and the shock so raw in seeing that carnage in front of him that it wiped out everything – the memory of how it looked before, the ability to imagine it any other way. The memory of how *he* was before, the ability to imagine *himself* as anything other than the killer of this thing. He was another person now, his past as dead as the corpse crumpled on the ground in front of him. Newborn in blood and bits of brain. He hadn't thrown up, or cried, or laughed. He felt no hysteria, no horror, only the hollowness of endings and beginnings.

Joey picks up the *True Crime* digest and shoves it into the inside pocket of his leather jacket along with the rest of the clippings and photographs, almost as bulky as the gun. It's almost time, he thinks, time to close the loop, to pull Joey Narcosis into existence by his own bootstraps, by handing this dum-dum-loaded motherfucker of a gun to a crazy kid, giving that boy the chance, the choice, to murder his own future and, in doing so, become it.

He opens the hotel room door and cuts right through from evening into morning, walks down the corridor where a maid is coming out of another room, locking it behind her. She walks backwards to the linen trolley and lays the clean towels down on it, pulls it backwards down the corridor. She doesn't see him and he doesn't know how he's seeing her. This whole world, and the light that bounces round in it, is in reverse to him, and if the laws of physics were at play here, in his backways world, his eyes should be pouring out light instead of gathering it in, focusing it into vision. But, fuck it, he's long since come to the conclusion that the laws of physics are just rules of thumb. He doesn't claim to understand the journey that's brought him here; all he's interested in is the destination, and that's not far from here, not far from now. It's almost time.

As he slips out of a side door of the hotel, he slips into synch with the world around him, moving with the flow of frontal time. He heads for the high school.

Today is the first day of the rest of your life, he thinks.

The alley is only fifty to a hundred yards from the school, a dank narrow chasm of brown brick slicing between a department store and a block of crafts shops. Handmade shoes and bespoke tailors. Of course, there's not exactly a lot of new stock coming into Lincoln since it drifted off into the Hinter, so the whole town's sort of regressed; he'd forgotten how quaint it all is — was. But that'll change when the CNN choppers come flying low over the fields to land in the high school parking lot. Lincoln will never be the same again after the tragedy.

He dumps the clippings and the photographs, his wallet, all the junk that might identify his body, into a small pile of newspapers and other garbage, lights it up and lets it burn while he waits. The *True Crime* mag blackens and sparks, peeling away page by page into ash, till there's only the spine left.

Murder! Massacre! Mayhem! Issue 23. Macromimicon Publications.

He kicks at the ashes of the story of his life, scattering them to a grey smear on the tarmac that'll wash away in his own blood. A glimpse out of the corner of his eye.

– Hey Joe, he says. Joseph Darkwater.

The Tragedy of Joseph Darkwater

The boy stands at the entrance to the alley as if not sure whether to answer the call or run like fuck. Joey tosses the overcoat down on the ground in front of him, towards the boy. He holds up the gun like it's a bone for a dog, a tempting treat. Come and get it.

— Joseph Darkwater, he says again.

And then they're standing there, looking at each other, his hand extended with the gun hanging by the trigger-guard from one finger. He looks into the boy's eyes, but all the kid can look at is the gun. It must look like power itself, with the silencer screwed on it now. Somewhere, a bell is ringing, but neither of them can move, caught in this moment that their lives, their *life*, revolves around, this moment of death. The boy looks up at him, his pupils dark, his gaze empty, and Joey feels just a hint of sorrow, just a hint of hatred, at this ghost of his past, this hollow child. The weight of the gun in his hand feels so natural, so true, and, even as he reaches it out in offering to the boy, a part of him doesn't want to let it go.

He can picture his own body lying on the ground now, its head blown clean off. It's the weirdest feeling. The newspaper photographs of the alley cordoned off, white tape on the ground. The speculations about this mysterious first victim, this outsider forgotten and remembered here and there in the confusion of the manhunt, the arrival of the city news teams, first contact with the outside world. It's the enigma that nobody was ever able to answer: Why that first victim? Why that stranger in the alley?

The boy reaches out a trembling hand towards the gun.

— Go ahead, he says.

For the first time in so very long, he feels something. He wonders if this is what has drawn him here, if he came back here ready to die because he knew, somewhere inside, there was a chance he might remember what it meant to feel . . . fear.

Kill me and you can kill anyone, he thinks.

— Kill me and . . .

The boy's eyes are wide, dark . . . wet. He's crying. He'd forgotten that. He'd forgotten he was crying.

He flicks the gun around his index finger, catches the butt in his hand, points it at the boy's head and chambers a round.

— Fuck this, he says, and pulls the trigger.

*

The bullet – like the fist of God – punches most of his soft, little skull clean off his shoulders, leaving only the lower jaw near falling off, and other fragments of white bone that jut out from the red pulp where his head once was. The body drops, twitching with the mindless spasticity of a decapitated chicken.

A shiver runs through it, then a final jerk, and then it's still. Such a close-range shot with .99 ammunition – Joey has blood and brains all over his hand and sleeve, little spots of splatter on the front of his shirt. He can even taste a little something warm and salty on his bottom lip when he licks it.

He flicks the gun's safety catch back on, unscrews the silencer and slips it in his pocket, holsters the weapon. There's a part of him a little disappointed that the world hasn't just torn itself apart around him, that the shockwave of the bullet – of the paradox – hasn't punched right through reality and turned it into so much grisly mush, like the dead thing lying on the ground in front of him. He would have liked that, he thinks.

He heads out of the alley and turns away from the high school. Been there, done that; time to move on. He strides forward, a smile on his face as he rips through the day ahead of him, a flash of light and dark as the sun flicks through the sky, away and back again, like the turning of a page. It's afternoon, and pedestrians fill the street; behind him there's the noise of local police investigating the crime scene.

Loops and paradoxes are for the mundanes, he thinks. Time is full-on and flashback, forward and reverse, splayed out in sidewinding slipstreams of chance and causality, and layered universe upon universe, like geological strata each built upon the dust of the world crushed beneath.

He slips a coin in a news-stand, pulls out today's edition of the *Lincoln Herald*. The headline is bold and brutal: *Murder Rocks Lincoln.* He glances through the pages as he walks – *local farmboy was brutally murdered* – down the high street – *quiet, kept himself to himself* – through the days – *distinct painting style that showed real talent* – onto the road out of town – *why anyone would want to kill him* – and off the road into the fields.

The clay men are swinging their scythes in the fields as Joey stops, turning around for a last look at the outskirts of Lincoln.

Why shouldn't time be like the world, he thinks, with this skin of earth made from the blood and ashes of our elder selves, a world of Adams shaped from clay and rotted back to it? The bricks of us cracked and crumbling, till the whole wall falls and the dust just settles down over the top of it, ready for the next layer of construction. It all seems so stable, with the bedrock under it, but deep down, under the crust of a million aeons, of a million universes, there's still that molten core of chaos at the heart of everything. Maybe he'll try and find a way out of this century again. Maybe he'll take a trip to Tunguska, 1908.

He throws the newspaper sidewards, fluttering, tumbling into some other corner of time and space. He doesn't give a fuck who finds it, where or when.

Reality looks solid, and time looks like a line, but underneath it all there's no certainty, no absolutes, no law, only this cold calculus of survival that emerges from the brutal, random experiments of Death and Time.

He looks up at the sky, churning blue, crows circling overhead.

Reality doesn't play by your rules, fuckers, he thinks. It plays by mine.

Errata

A Page of Crawling Chaos

A burning map of time instead of space: countries are actions, cities dates. Here Britain, Russia, Italy and France, America and Japan are rivers flowing into the China Sea across the continent of the twentieth century, rivers of troops that meet in Peking 1900, where the Righteous Harmonious Fists rebel, burning churches, killing nuns and priests, beheading Chinese Christians. Follow the road from there with Boer women and children to the little British village of concentration camps, 1901, down a prison road that stretches from the Caucasus, 1902, to Siberia, 1903, and Josef Stalin walking it, learning the way through pogroms in Kishinev and Gomel, lakes of blood. 1904, another prison camp in the valley of death, Sakhalin now, island of 7,000 Russian convicts freed to fight the Japanese in Manchuria. Rocks in the water: Belgians with baskets of human hands in the Congo; women chained to posts as hostages. 1905 is a little coastal inlet where unarmed men, women and children with their hymns, crosses and banners crash in waves against the Cossack rocks on which a Winter Palace stands. 1906: the mountain range of a British Empire dwarfing rebellions in Natal and Nigeria. 1907: more mountain ranges – Portuguese Guinea and Angola, German West and South-West Africa, French West Africa; everywhere rebellion and reprisals. The churning sea of 1908 in Macedonia – Serbs and Greeks, Bulgarians and Romanians, torching each other's villages. 1909: an island of Armenian massacre in southern Turkey. 1910: low hills and hidden valleys – floggings and torture, secret trials and hangings of Greeks and Bulgarians in Turkish Macedonia. 1911: an ocean of republic in China washing away the hated Manchu dynasty, garrisons massacred. 1912: a river of gold and blood, of Tsarist troops killing 170 starving workers in Siberian gold mines on the Lena.

1913: the faultline of the Balkans – Leagues and Wars – a chasm opening wider as a Bulgarian captain forces a bishop, two priests and a hundred Thracian citizens into the courtyard of a school and kills them. 1914: the edge of the great continent, the headland of a gunshot fired in Sarajevo that brings down horses on the Marne, and the map is burning to a world of fire and 1915 – gas, gas, quick boys – who now remembers the Armenian Massacre? – 1916 – over the top at Gallipoli and the Somme, men march into machine-gun fire – *and how old are ye, lads?* – *nineteen* – *seventeen* – krak! – *nineteen* – *eighteen* – DOOM!

I pull my mind out of the book, reeling and queasy at the hammer blows of history. I don't even know how I can read it; the words just seem to leap off the page into my head.

– What is this? I say. What is this?

My brother lays his hand upon the page of crawling chaos. I look up and see his smile and suddenly I'm terrified at what this book has done to him, at what I realise it could do to me.

– This is the way the world was meant to be, he says. This is history.

1919 – the Winter Palace stormed by 60,000 men in George Square, Glasgow – *Send the tanks in!* – and the German Soviet Republic stillborn, Rosa Luxemburg falling, flame-throwers in Munich – 1920 – Whites against Reds in Poland and the Baltic States as Caucasian Republics rise and fall, Armenia carved up by the Turks and Bolsheviks – 1921 – the million-strong Moplah of Malabar in India rise up, burn and loot, and Hindu heads trim the Muslim kingdoms – 1922 – *Hail Caesar!* Mussolini reigns and the fasces of the Roman Empire's raised again – 1923 – Hitler fires his gun in the Bürgerbraü beer cellar, shouts: *The German people must be saved!* and Primo de Rivera burns the Spanish constitution – 1924 – socialism in Italy: a blood-stained car and a disappeared politician – 1925 – Jihad in the Rif gives young Franco his first taste for blood of the tribesman put to the knife – 1926 – the Hitler Youth born while the US Marines fight for lumber and rice, banana and sugar plantations of Nicaragua – 1927 – the KKK parade in New York on Memorial Day, 400 black-shirted fascists with them all the way – 1928 – Ramon Romero, striking dockworker, shot in the head, shot dead, in Puerto San Martin as the child Che Guevara breathes his first – 1929 – Arabs burn the Torah at the Wailing Wall, attacking Jews in Hebron where the patriarchs lie – 1930 – riots in India at Gandhi's arrest, more fire, a torchlit glow in the eyes of the Kaiser's son as two million Nazis cry *Deutschland erwache, Juda verrecke*! – 1931 – an Italian flag hoisted in Libya, high as the body of Senussi's defender, and Japanese troops marching into Manchuria – 1932 – thirteen million votes for Hitler, and Bolivia and Paraguay fight over parched wilderness – 1933 and it's Chancellor Hitler.

– My God, I say. My God, this isn't right. This isn't our world. It's—

1934 and the Long Knives are out slashing – 1935 – Mussolini in Ethiopia – 1936 – the poet Lorca in a shallow grave – 1937 – fascists sing at Jarama, open fire and Guernica burns – 1938 – the Internationals march for the last time in Barcelona, broken like windows in the Night of Broken Glass of shattered businesses as scattered flowers strew Hitler's parade into Austria – *Sieg heil*! – Prague is *lebensraum*, Poland an annex – war rips the world and now there are no years, no empty dates, only an endless Blitz beginning with Trotsky murdered, ice-pick like a hammer smashing, sickle slashing – tests with Zyklon-B on Soviet soldiers captive at a camp called Auschwitz – Oh, but Americans stand proud and preen: *We saved your asses in World War Two after the Nips blew our boats up, sonsabitches*! aye, but a little late, too late, missed the train at the station – all aboard for Birkenau, Dachau and Belsen! – and shivering, freezing, in Stalingrad's snow, the besieged men surrender, so wasted and cold like the boys on the boats on the beaches of Normandy, Christ, dry us off with the firestorms of Dresden, under sheltering mushrooming clouds of Hiroshima and Nagasaki.

I can't take my eyes off the book but I can see him, *feel* him, standing at my side. I feel a rising panic, as if everything I've ever known is being stripped away.

– There is no Futurism in the *real* world, says my brother. You understand? There is no Futurism.

But what I'm thinking as I read this book is that there is no *future*.

A Pile of Death

Jews murdered in Kielce in Poland and shipped off by Brits to the camps out on Cyprus, and Vietnam starts with the French fighting Ho Chi Minh, Empires now foundering, as new states are founded and flounder, in Israel and Palestine – Arabs against the Jews – India and Pakistan – Muslims against Hindus – Gandhi is shot on his way to a prayer meeting – planes out of Egypt to bomb Tel Aviv – Kim Il Sung in Korea, the North against South, backed by Stalin as Mao takes Peking, and his People's Republic march into Tibet – in the Senate, McCarthy – MacArthur in Seoul – the Argentines worship a dictator's actress wife but no one mourns the Jewish anti-fascist writers, actors, poets, tried and shot behind the Iron Curtain where at Stalin's death, the Vopos in Berlin throw weapons down to join the demo – Japanese fishermen in a rain of H-bomb ash, east of the Bikini atoll – Morrocan nationalists massacre Europeans and Muslims – Soviet tanks encircle Budapest – Hungarian security forces hang from lamp posts – Israel in the Sinai Desert – British paratroopers at Port Said on the Suez Canal – peasants conscripted to labour battalions in China's Great Leap Forward – six hours' rest in twenty-four hours – a dog sent into space to die – and there's no future now for the 3,000 counter-revolutionary 'rightists' of the Communist Youth League arrested in China as Battista flees the Cuban Revolution, and blacks run from the guns of the Sharpesville shootings and the Dalai Lama flees Tibet, run! new Prime Minister of the Congo, run! from coup to capture, torture, execution by the followers of Mobutu while on the Bay of Pigs, the Berlin Wall's first bricks are laid, the Cuban missiles aimed, the armed blockade, *Ich bin ein Berliner*, says JFK, then gunshots rip the motorcade, and *We Shall Overcome*, they sing, the followers of Martin Luther King as Liuzzo is shot by the KKK – riots in Watts and the first US combat troops land on Vietnam.

Red Guard vigilantes of the Cultural Revolution tear down all that's old, the palaces and temples, ancient artefacts, the intellectuals, teachers and administrators, children in red armbands murdering their parents – in Vietnam 800 tons of bombs fall every day, and Johnson tells the troops to *nail the coonskin to the wall* – Egypt and Jordan attack and lose to Israel in six days – the oil refineries of Suez City blaze – the chief of the South Vietnam police holds his revolver to a prisoner's head and pulls the trigger – bang! – Robert Kennedy – bang! – Martin Luther King – bang! – *Helter Skelter* on a door in blood – *Kill the Pigs!* Make them squeal like the dead babies of My Lai: *well, they might have had bombs strapped to them.* Crazy? Like Bukovsky locked up as insane for protesting the Soviet use of psychiatry on dissidents – British troops in Londonderry shoot to kill on a Bloody Sunday – mercy becomes a luxury as Pinochet seizes Chile, seizes students and professors, union leaders, *all protesters must be tortured or they will not sing,* he says – the Greeks and Turks fight over Cyprus – the Khmer Rouge take Pnomh Penh, the Americans evacuate Saigon and the government of Laos falls into—

– Chaos, I say. This is bloody chaos.

My head is spinning as I push the book away into his hands and he takes it from me still open, turning it round to read. He holds it like some maniac minister reading a sermon.

What year is it now? What year are we in? Because Franco's still murdering – now it's Basque separatists – yes, those attacks on Spain's government buildings in Lisbon, Ankara, in Rome and Milan, must be proof of conspiracy – Masons, Jews and communists, cause sure and the Christians are so much better, like the IRA attacking a peace march or Falangists smashing a Muslim enclave in Christian East Beirut to massacre the families of Palestinian refugees, huddling, naked and shackled, Steve Biko in police custody, dead of brain damage, aye, and it's black and white and red all fookin over as Mengitsu calls for a red terror, purging Ethiopia of *bandits, anarchists* and *feudalists* and the Zimbabwe African People's Union blows an Air Rhodesia passenger plane out of the sky and hunts through wreckage for survivors just so's they can cut their throats, sure and look now, see the marines retreat in Tehran as Islamic militants take their barracks, oust the Shah, and Russia advances down into Afghanistan, aye, let's shoot anyone as says *Give peace a chance,* and sell the fookin gun to Contra rebels in Nicaragua to raise blood money for Iran, and when the Argentines invade the Falklands, yes, the Empire Strikes Back, halle⁄fookin⁄lujah, sinks the *Belgrano,* tabloids rejoicing: Gotcha! sure and does it fookin matter that there's bodies floating in the water, drifting past a Warsaw priest tortured and killed by the secret police, dumped in the river roaring Tamil Tigers ambushing a convoy of soldiers in Sri Lanka firing machine guns on the demonstrators in South Africa on the anniversary of Sharpeville and it's another body in the water, old man dragged out of his wheelchair, shot dumped overboard from the *Achille Lauro* – splash! – radioactive cloud from Russia's Wormwood star fallen from heaven like the manna of a UN convoy of food and medicine blocked by Shi'ite militiamen on its way to refugees at Chatila and Bourj-el-Barajineh, cause it's not enough, it's never fookin enough, but we've got to have Azeris and Armenians clashing in a fookin noble murderous struggle for national fookin identity, oh, but we can't be doing with that, no, so let's gas the fookin Kurds of Halabja, and even as the Berlin Wall falls and a fookin velvet revolution calls, well still there's fookin tanks and tear gas in Tiananmen Square, Armenians murdered in a pogrom in Baku and no one fookin cares about Mandela's plea to stop black killing black, Inkatha and the UDF at war – and Hussein in Kuwait setting the oil alight, vast plumes of smoke turn day to night as Bosnian Serbs bring back the camps and genocide, and those as bring the medicine and food and spread the news can just be fookin murdered in Somalia.

– Fire, says Seamus. It's all fookin—

Fire a fookin mortar bomb into a Sarajevo market cause there's no more civilians, no more sanctuary in churches where the Hutus massacre the Tutsis in Rwanda, sure and how safe's a fookin safe haven where peacekeepers stand and watch as Bosnian Serbs take 4,000 Muslim men and boys from fallen Srebrenica, eh? Islamic fundamentalists in Algeria brag: *We have slit the throats of seven monks*, aye, and glory be to Allah, cause the Taliban have overrun Kabul, and tourists are the new human sacrifice at Luxor, but it's liberation that they're fighting for, sure, over there in Kosovo against the Serbs or in Omagh with all the fookin courage of a car bomb – liberation? – 70,000 villagers killed in the Sudan, and those that lived forced to convert to Islam, boys abducted and sold into slavery – liberation, is it? – in Sierra Leone where rebels and mercenaries burn the power station, post office, town hall, UN headquarters, a thousand dead, floating past a frigate sheltering Europeans, floating bodies, arms and hands chopped off.

– Jesus, says Seamus. I can't go on.

But Jack shoves the glass up to his mouth to force the drink down a throat that's raw with all these terrible words of the future like broken glass scouring poor Seamus's ragged voice. Reynard massages his cramped hand, looks at the scalpel and the fountain pen, the needle of the syringe, and the pages of human skin piled up in front of him – the work of his hand, of Seamus's voice and Carter's translation, three weeks worth' of Jack pacing back and forth, flipping pages to point at this symbol or that – *this, here, write this one next, keep up for God's sake, man*. And now it sits there, a pile of death upon the table, a history of the twentieth century and of what's beyond, what's past and present and still to come.

– I can't go on, says Seamus. I'm done. I'm fookin finished.

– We haven't even begun, says Jack.

He picks up the top page of the book, lays it down in front of Reynard.

– Now we start making the changes, he says.

5

Nature's Children

Harlequin in the House

– *Well, Jack, I don't know how you did it, but this cat takes off his hat to you. Yessir, reports are coming in all over. We got airtrams burning, riots breaking out across the city. We got Pitt Street pigyard up in flames, explosions in St Mungo's Shopping Centre, and – doesn't this sound like one of our friendly firestarter's little games? – yes, Old Man Powell's wireliner just crashed right into Central Station. Oh, yeah! Looks like Jack is back to save the nation.*

I gun the skybike through the gap between two buildings, and out into St Mungo's Square, the ornithopter hot on my tail until I jam on the fore-jets in reverse and spin into a backflip, firing off a shot at my pursuer as I hit 180. At the full 360, I slam on the brakes and stop dead in the air to let the thopter overshoot me, hold just long enough to send a chi-beam lancing up the pilot's ass, then blow the ray-tanks in three flumes of orgone vapour. The skybike drops like a murderer on a gibbet.

– Io! Io! Followers of Harlequin, hear my call! Io! Io! Do you hear me?

Jack's voice echoes round the hall.

– Who's there? What is this avian call? I sing. Where is its source?

– The son of Simile and Sooth. I call again. Io!

– My lord, O lord, hail! Come to our company of revellers, lord of joy!

– Let the solid earth quake in its bedrock, shouts Jack. Let the nation shake with dread and shock to its foundations. Harlequin's awake!

Jack, in the wings, tips Don the wink. Don fires the ultrasonic boom and throws another lever; the set judders with a sickening subsonic crack of doom. Don's son-et-lumière projects great cracks upon the very walls around the audience, the Duke and Princess rising in their seats. The whole place shudders, like the audience in its horror, as the polystyrene palace of Pierrot starts to lurch and fall.

I smash through the glass roof of the St Mungo Shopping Centre, feet-first and kicking away from the dead bike to somersault with all an Acapulco diver's timing, grab an overhanging pipe which snaps loose from its joint and shrieks metallic murder, spewing steam as it warps down beneath my weight. As the skybike slam-crunches into marble floor and sends stone shrapnel shattering amongst the early evening shoppers, I swing down from the bending pipe to land with ape agility on an ornamental fountain's basin's edge. Glass tinkles down around me.

— *Seems like Jack is busting out all over. Our old friend Captain Crimbo seems to think you have the supernatural ability to be everywhere and anywhere at once, like Jesus, Elvis or Jim Morrison. Is that what it is, or are some of Satan's Little Helpers out there raising Hell, tonight? How do you do that houdou that you do so well? Ah well, one thing's for sure: that kid sure plays a mean pinball. OK, let's take another call. Hello, you're on the aether . . .*

— The victory cry of Harlequin itself rises within these walls, I sing. He's here within this very house, the Harlequin! Get down!

I throw myself right off the stage and down onto the ground, as Don blasts everyone with his demonic box of tricks, vibrating hearts and stomachs, quivering organs with the decibels of his diabolic sounds.

The Duke rises in panic from his throne, pointing towards an architrave of stone where a great column seems to shiver as it groans under the roof's weight, splits and sunders. He throws his arms up at the crumbling, tumbling, toppling-right-towards-him trick of light.

Ah yes, the first scream of the night.

— Well, mes amigos, things are heating up out here on the edge of freedom. Your eye in the sky, the Hairy Scary Don Coyote, is looking down right now on — I don't know — what's the collective noun for every motherloving militiaman in the city? A horde? A mob? I'd say right now it's a thundercloud. What has our Jack been up to, mes amigos? Oh yes, there's a thundercloud of ornithopters and skybikes a-gathering, armed to the teeth and heading west over the city centre. Looks like they're after someone, and, given the trail of destruction in his wake, my guess is it's our boy Jack.

They're running for the exits now.

— Ignite the blazing torch with lightning's fire, Jack calls, and give the halls of Pierrot to the flame.

And Joey fires flash grenades — left, right, and centre — barbed points that embed in oaken doors with bulbs that burst in blinding light and spew out smoke. No charge as such, but just enough confusion added to a mix that, for some of our audience, already seems a tad too much. A maid-in-waiting faints into the arms of a young serving boy, to his surprise. The Duke's consul cowers beneath the throne, a look of utter terror in his eyes. The Duke himself, sword drawn, comes staggering blindly past me, sort of heading for the stage, but tripped and turned by fallen props of polystyrene, a bear stumbling around a cage.

— Do you not see the flame? I shout. Do you not see the lightning blaze? There, at the sacred tomb of Simile, that flash the hurler of the bolt left on that day? Prostrate your trembling limbs, you maids. Get down upon the ground. Our king, the son of Sooth, the Harlequin, assaults and utterly confounds this house.

Shooting from the hip, I take out one of the mall security goons with a nifty chi-beam in the forehead, his mobile clattering across the marble floor-tiles. Most of the shoppers scream and scatter, but a few reach into their jackets for guns, phones, whatever; informants or sleepers, my guess is, and I take them down — him, her, him — with the quick-draw precision of a latter-day cowboy. The sirens are going off already, so I reckon I have five minutes before the blackshirts arrive, ten if the wreckage on Argyle Street slows them down a bit. Time enough for fun.

Jack enters in a flash of light, a bloom of smoke, a somersault onto a springboard hidden on the stage. He hits his mark and bounces up, arms wide, right over the Duke's head to land out in the hall, right by my side. His entrance is Don's cue to flip the frequencies, to bathe the room in ambient azure glow of open sky, and switch the mood music from low to high. The Duke's consul uncovers his eyes.

And just as sudden as the panic first set in, it goes. There's still confusion but they're realising, wait a minute, yes, it's all part of the show.

– Are you so struck with fear that you have fallen so? says Jack.

The audience turn to his words. He speaks to me but to the audience as well, these foreign dames, his voice so soft. Is he . . . amused or sad? He reaches down a hand to me, working his charm. The Princess lays her hand on the Duke's tensed sword-arm.

Jack pulls me gently to my feet.

– You saw how Harlequin made the palace fall, or so it seems. But rise, be of good heart, and still the trembling of your limbs. Open your eyes. What is all this, all this you see, but broken dreams?

Dancing Fucking Monkeys

– I'll tell you what, though; if you're one of those jailbirds thinking that you're snuggled up safe and sound in your Rookery nest, you better think again. Fly, little birdies, and be free, or face the music, because the left flank of that thundercloud is moving off and headed your way. Looks to me like they're trying to cut off Jack the Giant-Killer from his home-sweet-home, and I bet they won't be shy about making their presence known.

I race through the shopping mall of jewellers and haberdashers, high-street fashion emporiums, shoe shops and toy stores, and duck into an HMV outlet to strafe the shelves of fucking teenbop boyband R'n'B and power ballads from mullet-headed spandexed geriatrics, all the sanitised and sanctioned anti-drugs pro-lifer post-punk whore-dom of the music industry, the gutless, spineless, soulless, ball-less corporate pop-rock that would have every drugfucked songster from Robert Johnson through to Lord Mick Jagger spinning in their graves so hard that you could wire them up and light the fucking planet if they could hear the crap these shit-merchants are peddling as music.

I stop to take a breath.

— *If you can hear me, mes amigos, now's the time for all good men to batten down the hatches, strap yourselves into your gun emplacements — cause we know you got them, Fox — and enjoy the ride to Hell. My thoughts are with you, mes amigos. I just pray that guardian angel of the damned is watching over you tonight. So don't worry, Foxy baby, don't you fear, my saucy Jack. I'll be right here, keeping you posted on the action as it unfolds and playing the grooves to keep your peckers up and your sex-guns loaded. From the White Album on the Black List, this is The Beatles with the only song that could be played right now. It's Helter Skelter, and, by the looks of it, it's coming down fast.*

Skybikes zip across the glass roof, this way and that, zigzagging up and down the mall's length as the riders try to spot me down below. Ornithopters flutter above them. They'll be surrounding the place right now, sealing off the entrances, so I really should keep moving but, hey, there's always time for a little music criticism.

A shop assistant dives out of the way as I strafe the shelves behind him.

Acid jazz with a neutral pH level, progressive rock resolutely facing backwards, heavy metal soft and fluffy as a cloud, house music for the conservatory, garage for the garden, and Christian bloody rock — the fuckers have castrated everything the music ever was. Thank God for ambient rap and trip-hop technotrance. Bastards can't take the chemicals out of those.

One hand on my crotch, the other pointing the chi-gun at these shelves of pap, I channel all the lust for life from my zero chakra up and out, blasting this soundtrack to my death. Down the length of the mall, fleeing shoppers scream as the rockets start impacting in standard fascist tactics; airstrike a hundred innocent sheep if there's a rat's chance that you might get one wolf. They're trying to smoke me out, but I'll go when I'm good and ready. The chi-beam rips the shelves.

Burn, baby, burn. Disco inferno.

– Give me loud repetitive beats or give me death! I roar, blasting a display of pop-tart concert videos into shards and ribbons. Dancing fucking monkeys.

The assistant is grinning wide with glee as he unclips his name badge and steps away from the counter and the screaming manager.

– Where's the Michael Jackson? I ask.

A service sector wage slave with Spartacus in his eyes, the kid is only too happy to point me in the right direction.

– Over there, he says. Whole fucking shelf . . . and no James Brown.

It's a sad indictment on society, I'm thinking. I blast the Wacko Jacko into streams of black tickertape in the air.

– Got a light? I say, rifling through my pockets.

He hands me a silver Zippo engraved with a skull-and-crossbones one side, encircled anarchist 'A' on the other.

– Keep it, he says. I'm sure you'll put it to good use.

I blow him a kiss, beautiful boy.

This Poor Dumb Brute, This Bull

I hold his hand.

– We're saved, I sing. What joy it is to hear your voice ring out, to see you, in this lonely state of ours.

– Were you downcast, says Jack, when I was cast down through these gates into Pierrot's gloomy cells?

– Of course. Who would defend us, should you meet with an untimely fate? But how? Who freed you from this godforsaken Pierrot's own personal hell?

– My own hands worked my own salvation, Jack says. Did you like my tricks?

He twirls his flute above his head.

– I thought I did it rather well.

– Did he not tie your hands with rope?

Jack shrugs.

– I mocked him there as well. He thought he bound me, but he never really had me in his grasp. He groped at fantasies, things in his head. For, at the stall he brought me to as jail, he found a bull and tied its hoofs instead, sweat glistening on his body, nostrils flaring wide with fury, as he bit his bottom lip. And so he wrestled with this poor dumb brute, this bull, and all the while I sat watching the fool.

Jack leans back in a panto laugh, his hands upon his hips.

– Meanwhile, he says, the Harlequin made Pierrot's house quake, and relit the fire at his mother's tomb.

Jack saunters round the room, picking this courtier or that to play to, subtly guiding them back to their seats; they back away from his advances, not even realising that they're being herded as Jack dances here and there.

– Pierrot saw the fumes, says Jack. He thought his palace was ablaze, so off he runs this way and that – [and Jack darts this way, that way, round a maid] – shouting for servants to bring water, shouting *more* and *more*, till every slave was busy at this pointless chore.

Now there are just the Princess and the Duke left standing out there on their own. Jack whirls behind them, pops his head between the two and gives a nod towards the throne. The Duke growls, but the Princess laughs and tugs her grizzled guardian back to his chair.

– He left this useless labour, Jack says, once he realised I was loose, and barged into the palace with his sword out. There, in truth – or so it seemed to me—

Jack coughs into his hand, looks down.

– A man can only tell you what he sees—

He looks around as if to say *You won't believe me*, kicks the ground, milking the moment till his reticence gets a surly growl from our impatient host.

– It seemed, says Jack, the Harlequin had made himself a ghost.

A puff of smoke and Jack's not there. He's back up on the stage.

– Pierrot charged at it, he cries. In headlong haste, he stabbed the shimmering air, thought that it was his enemy that he laid waste.

Another puff of smoke and Jack's up on the wagon's roof. He whirls and jabs, enacts a mockery of a drunken swordfight with his flute. He twirls and stabs.

– The Harlequin just gave him more disgrace.

He leaps for a rope on the lighting rig, tugs loose a knot, comes sailing down as the curtain dropped for the dream sequence rises on a scene of ruin.

– He smashed Pierrot's palace to a pile of rubble on the ground, says Jack. And there it lies, a sight to make Pierrot rue the day he thought to have me bound.

Guy takes the rope out of Jack's hand to tie it fast.

– At last, says Jack, Pierrot dropped his sword from sheer fatigue, fell in a faint, this frail ephemeral, daring to wage war on Harlequin the saint. In the meantime, well, I snuck out of his house and came to you, with little thought for Pierrot.

He reaches down a hand to pull me up on stage.

– I suspect he'll show up soon. There is a sound of steps within. I wonder what he'll have to say, after all this?

Jack strokes his chin.

– Well, even if his fury's never been so great, I'll grin and bear it. It's a wise man's way to keep his rage in check.

And Jack sits on a polystyrene stone of Pierrot's palace, lights a cigarette.

Sheep in Wolves' Clothing

– And hello ... Guy. What have you got to say?

– Well, Don, I'm sure it's nothing that someone as ... strong-willed as Jack Flash has to worry about, but I heard a nasty rumour that the old boy has a rather nasty habit that he can't shake. Something that goes back a long way with him.

— *That's old news, Guy. You talking about the absinthe or the hash?*

— *I was talking about another type of* tranquilliser. *Very* expensive. *Very* dangerous. *Killed a lot of people. He really should be careful.*

— *And where did you hear that, Guy?*

— *Oh, I wouldn't like to say. Just thought that someone ought to ... point it out. After all, I'm sure Jack listens to your show. I'd bet even money that he's listening right now. And he may not even realise that he's got a ... monkey on his back.*

— *Nice to know you care, Guy, but this is Jack Flash we're talking about. I'm sure that he can cope with all narcotics known to man.*

The destruction starts at the motorway where the line of hotels and offices – the Hilton and the Hospitality, the Abbey National and the NatWest – all of them in flames, stretches south from Charing Cross right down to Anderston. Illuminated name-signs, dark or showering sparks, are broken, falling from collapsing roofs, a skyline jagged as a hammered set of teeth. Payback for the shipyards, Joey thinks, for the demolition of the Clyde industries, the smashing of the unions of welders and engineers. *The spirit of Kentigern*, Jack used to say. *They'll never break the spirit of Kentigern.* And then they did.

There used to be a statue on Buchanan Street, Joey remembers, the ugliest piece of crap he ever saw; this moulded lump of dull metal with flipper-like wings stretched up, twisted around, Christ, it looked like some fat mutant pigeon with its head buried in the ground. If the artist meant it to look *dynamic*, *potent*, then the artist must have been fucking off his trolley. But they called that sculpture the 'Spirit of Kentigern', and to Joey's mind the name fitted: a crippled ugly thing.

So now it's petty revenge dished out to banks and businesses and anyone who works for them, poor fuckers staying in the Marriott to attend some SECC convention of toilet salesmen, paper-shuffling temps in corporate nowhere jobs, all the dumb masses of mundane reality whose only crime is their complicity. But that was always one of the biggest crimes in Jack's book. Not that Joey feels any sympathy for them. But, then, he's not the hero of the people.

The pilot brings them down the wasted canyon of Argyle Street, east towards the City Centre, flying low past dingy shops and pawnbrokers till they come to the Hielanman's Umbrella where the airdocks of Central Station bridge the road.

The green fire is still belching from the wireliner's skeleton.

As they skirt the flame and flumes of smoke and circle down towards St Mungo's Square, Joey Narcosis pops another pill. He still doesn't believe it's really Jack, but he doesn't want any memories of the old times getting in the way of his job. He feels the chi running through his body, down the serpent of his spine.

The gunboat ornithopter's wheels just touch the ground, its wings still beating wide and loud, as Joey Narcosis jumps down onto the cement flagstones of the square. He orients himself; straightening up as the thopter rises back into the air, he gazes calmly around at the three sides of Georgian sandstone shops and offices, flames spouting from windows, skybikes and aircars parked all around the little ludicrous building that sits in the centre of the square, a tourist information place that looks like the turret of some Victorian folly chopped off and dumped where it doesn't belong. SS men stand behind it, using it as cover, while lines of grunt militiamen are ranked as cannon-fodder out in the open, guns aimed up the long steps that fill the fourth side of the square and lead up to the mall with its shattered glass doors and burnt-out shopfronts, its majestic glass pyramid of a roof now little more than jagged bits of girders belching black smoke into air already full of darting thopters and skybikes.

Fucking amateurs, thinks Joey. A thousand sledgehammers trying to swat one fly. He flashes his ID as he pushes through the ranks towards the steps. Sheep in wolves' clothing, he thinks.

A Cat Stretching Its Claws

Out on the stage comes Pierrot, his long hair loose and wild, black greasepaint tears streaked round his eyes with sweat.

– Outrage! he says. That stranger – he was held fast in the stalls, and now he's gone, escaped.

He turns this way and that, sees Jack.

– You! There he is. There is the man! What is the meaning of this? How did you get here? How can you just *appear* outside my halls?

– Stay back, says Jack. And, easy now, don't lose your head.

– How did you slip your leash, get free?

– Were you not listening to what I said? That I would be released?

– Always a smart reply, a question answered with a question, you sly . . .

But his anger's taken over now, the words lost in an inarticulate growl.

– Who was it? he demands. Who set you loose?

– The one who makes the vine grow thick for men.

Jack twirls his fingers round his flute.

– You fucker! Joey says.

– I'll take that, says Jack, as a compliment.

Pierrot turns to call out orders to his offstage guards.

– Bar every door in the stockade. Close the perimeter, he calls. Lock every single fucking gate.

– And what's the point in that? says Jack. Can ghosts not walk through walls?

Pierrot backhands me out of his way as he attacks Jack, grabs him by his catsuit's leather skin. I pick myself up off the ground, nursing my jaw. I blink. Fuck's sake, I think, that fucking hurt. I look at the tension in Joey's arms, the whiteness of his knuckled fist. The bastard's fucking wired.

– You're such a wise guy, Joey snarls, except where actual wisdom is required.

– Where wisdom's needed most, says Jack, I am most wise.

Joey punches him in the stomach, turns to glare at me. Jesus, there's murder in his eyes. He lets Jack fall and crouches down a second, comes back with a metal glint of knife blade in his hand.

– Wait! Jack says.

He points offstage and Joey snaps his head round, glares past me into the wings where Guy, in shepherd costume, stands. Pierrot Joey looks confused.

– Your messenger comes from the hills with news, says Jack.

His words are rushed and out of breath. He holds a hand over his stomach, winded, and I have the seriously scary feeling that it's not an act. Joey has fucking lost it, man; Pierrot's madness – Christ, he's fucking *in it*. He stands there looking trapped in indecision, gripping the knife and turning now to Guy – who enters as Pierrot's messenger – then back to Jack.

– I'll keep, says Jack. Listen to him, hear what he's got to say to you. I'll wait. I'll not attempt to fly.

– You lie, says Joey, breaking with the script. You have to die.

– Just . . . listen to your . . . guy, says Jack. And afterwards, then you can have your pleasure with me, kill me at your leisure.

– Pierrot, Guy says quickly, firmly.

He clamps a hand on Joey's shoulder, gives a solid gaze into his eyes.

– Pierrot, ruler of this realm of Themes! I have—
Pierrot slaps his hand away. Guy stalls.

– I have, he starts again, come hither from the hills where pure white snowflakes fall forever.

There's a pause. The hand that doesn't hold the knife opens and closes at Pierrot's side, a cat stretching its claws. I edge away a bit; Jack looks like he's prepared to pounce. Guy stands there, simply waiting for the line. A hundred heartbeats as Guy faces Joey's madness down.

– What urgent message do you bring? says Joey.
And our breath is audible as it's released.

– I've seen, O King, says Guy, the frantic maidens who flew out in barefoot frenzy from the city's gates. I come to tell you and the city of their awful deeds, things more than strange.

Pierrot's knife picks non-existent dirt out from beneath his fingernails.

– But first I need to know, says Guy, can I speak freely? Should I trim my tale or tell all that I saw? Your temper is so quick, m'sire; My lord, I fear your sudden wrath, the power of your ire.

– Speak, Joey says. There's nothing you need fear from me.

He seems to rein himself in, burying his anger. I glimpse guilt in how he glances at me, keeps his eyes away from Jack.

– Rage taken out upon the innocent is wrong, he says.

But still the quiet threat is strong.

– The grimmer news you bring about these rites, he says, the grimmer fate awaits this bastard who's seduced our women with his song.

– Well, then, it was today, Guy as the messenger begins, in the first light of dawn . . .

Gazelles Held in Their Arms

In the first light of dawn, the earth grows warm in the sun's rays, and young Elixir feels the grass soft underneath his feet. He bats at the long stalks with his switch, sings as he drives the lowing cattle up towards the hill's ridge where the pasture's best. The morning air is fresh and, thinking of Accordion with his goats, his gifts of quinces, chestnuts, plums, and voice, Elixir smiles. Sung him a song, he did, the other day, that got Elixir all stirred, in that way, you know. Not that he'd ever show it, mind, oh no. A thousand lambs out on the hills and ever-flowing milk from all his flocks and herds – Accordion's a find. Play hard to get for now, Elixir thinks.

Koré circles his feet, circles her tail in wild wags, wet nose nuzzling his leg, and he's shooing her out to *circle the flock not me, silly*, when he sees them. *What's this, girl, eh?*

They lie there, some in beds of needles fallen from the pine trees, others with their heads on piles of oak-leaves. *Ssh, girl.* Fast asleep in deep exhaustion, there's three groups of them; there's Indo and Autonomy, each dreaming with their troops, the rest gathered around – is it? it is! – the Basilisk's own ma. He whistles underneath his breath, calls Koré back, and crouches down to hold her.

He had heard Iacchus was in town.

It was all quite decent, sire, he'll say, *not lewd as people claim, with them all out to sate their lusts, alone in the woods, crazy with wine and the soft music of the flute.* That's what he'll say when he's run down through the long grass and through the town to hammer on the Basilisk's wooden door, stood with his hands on hips, bent double and panting till he's caught his breath. That's what he'll say to the

Basilisk, yes. But later, with Accordion and Chrome and Mainsail and the rest, he'll whisper tales with even less breath. *Ssh. Come here.*

I saw the Bacchae, he'll say.

He watches them until the lowing of his cows stirs the Basilisk's old ma and she rises up amongst them, gives a loud cry to awake the rest. Wiping the sleep out of their eyes, they rise, the old, the young, women and girls. Elixir watches them, in wonder at this sight of grace so modest as they smooth hair from their faces, flick it back to fall over their shoulders, stretch. If the Basilisk was here, if he could see this with his own eyes, thinks Elixir, he'd be praying to the deity he despises.

A flash of thigh – his heart beats faster – till the girl fastens her fawnskin where it's come untied. *Hush, girl. Sit nice.* Elixir, crouching in the bushes, blushes as he peeks, ashamed but more in awe than anything until he sees . . .

Snakes curl around the dappled hides, tongues darting out to lick the women's cheeks.

– And there were others wearing crowns of ivy, oak or flowering bryony. With gazelles held in their arms like–

– mothers with full breasts of milk for babes at home in town. They're out there suckling the whelps of wild wolves even–

– now she takes her thyrsus, strikes it down into a rock, I swear, and then this stream of clear, fresh water gushes–

– out it spouts, a spring of wine, a fountain where she drove her wand into the–

– ground where they had scratched a fingertip, these streams of milk flowed, all they wished for–

– trickling honey from–

– staffs wreathed in ivy.

In the babble of the gathered herdsmen, all these strange, incredible events rush out. The boys war with each other for the floor, talk over one another, try to shout each other down.

– O you who live up on the mountains . . .

Over the noise within the hut, Accordion's voice resounds. He's got a skill of speech, learned from his time in town, and when he stands up in the midst of them they listen.

– You who live up on the holy mountain heights, he says. What do you say we do the Basilisk a favour, chase his mother from her Bacchic rites?

A murmur goes around the crowd, but they're not sure; there's tales of what the Bacchae do to those who interrupt their rituals. Some are keen – there's Chrome and Mainsail eager to begin the hunt – but others seem quite unconvinced, like Thirst and Palomino, who both argue that it's not their place.

But in the end it is Accordion who wins his case, and so they go.

And now Elixir waits in ambush, hidden among the thick of leaves again. It's time. The rites of the Bacchae start with waving wands, and then, in chorus, they call on Iacchus, god of beer and brine, the son of Deus; and the wild things answer. The whole mountain echoes with their shout. The whole of nature roars as they set out upon the hunt.

Hellhound on My Trail

The airtram shudders from side to side as it hurtles along its thread, the banshee howl of its chi-jet engines drowning commuters' shouted conversations inside, setting feral dogs to barking frenzies in the streets below. It Dopplers past the underlit Wagnerian architecture of the concert hall and retail galleries at the top of Buchanan Street and roars over the swastika-bannered pedestrian precincts of Sauchiehall Street, passes the waiting platforms of Cowcaddens altogether, arcs wide by St George's Cross, swinging ever westward. One, two, three stations where it should have stopped, and still it thunders on across the sky. But, then, airtrams tend to do that when you throw the driver through the windscreen and fire a chi-beam point-blank into the few controls still left intact after a bare-knuckle slamfest worthy of the Trynovantium Colosseum.

I brandish the chi-gun with psychotic zeal as I kick through the splinters of the separating door and sprint down the carriage, passengers throwing themselves out of the way. A window shatters to my right, a suit is cut down to my left, as my pursuer's chi-beams slice the air around me. Striding down the aisle, punching passengers out of his path, Joey Narcosis comes after me, slow and steady, a dogged hellhound on my trail, in suit and overcoat as sharp as his eyes, as black as his heart.

A chi-beam glances off my shoulder and I spin, unbalanced, firing as I turn and dropping to one knee. I hit him square but he shrugs off the blue-green blast of energy like a lightning rod catching St Elmo's Fire, channelling it down to the ground. Fifth dan aikido, I would guess; not bad at all. Course, I can take him any time.

With a considered casual callousness, he picks off every commuter between the two of us, blasting through the padded seats they cower behind, cutting them down as they dive in panic for the emergency cord, for doorways, for any escape. Clearing the decks, I think you call it. When there's only little me left, he grips the gun two-handed, raises it, takes aim . . .

I leap for the broken window, grab the upper rim of it, and swing my full weight out and up and over, onto the roof of the airtram. Wind whipping my longcoat out behind me, I stand up from a crouch, boots clamped to the metal roof, and start to run for the front of the carriage, as chi-beams pierce the steel under my feet – from below and from the skies above, militia ornithopters strafing me. It's like a swarm of fucking locusts overhead. I leap to the next carriage and keep running, jumping, running, pulling a stick of dynamite out of my jacket. No love-grenades this trip; something more drastic is called for.

I light it, lob it and leg it – back the way I came – and leap through a plume of blue-orgone vapour that hisses from a ruptured ray-tank, straight into the face of my would-be assassin, the two of us almost crashing off the roof together in our collision. I push away and hit him with a kung fu kangaroo kick (spring-loaded boots – a kick with a kick) but he rolls backwards and comes out of it on his feet.

Great Western Road flashes under us. Next stop, Kelvinbridge and the Rookery. Overhead, the ornithopters thunder.

– You're dead, says Joey Narcosis. You're fucking *dead*.

– Aren't we all? I say, as the dynamite explodes in the driver's cabin and the airtram, roaring through flame and smoke, careens off its thread and screams downward, down towards a streak of landfilled filth that used to be a river.

A Hand with Eagle's Claws

– By rivers of a sophist, down through valley fields which bear fullfruit, rich harvest for our themes, we come. Through towns below the peak of zither, on we come. To his eye and her other eye, we come. The flame that does not burn us in our hair, we speed like hawks, we sweep the air with evil aim, we swoop and scatter all, and gather children from their homes, our game.

– We come to her, agaves queen and anaesthesia princess, our eternal Columbine, mother of sorrow, she who leads us.

Phreedom ignores the bitmites' babblings and slings the antique ruptors of brass and iron one over each shoulder. There are latches, straps on them where they're meant to be clipped to angel armour, but she wears them slung diagonally across her back so there's no danger of them falling to the dust. The leather straps form an X on her synthe-vested chest like bandoliers. The crossbars of the ruptors, fluttering with angel scalps, look like the pinions of some creature's wings. But then that's pretty much what they are. She flexes her right hand, gazing at the ivory talons where her fingernails used to be, the black filigree of bitmites that sleeves her bare arm. Too long in the Hinter, she thinks. Still, the claws make her feel more at home out here, one of nature's children. And they have their uses; who needs cold steel when you have a hand with eagle's claws?

The bitmite tattoo on her arm, the scar of the C-section on her belly, the clawed hand which, she swears, she'll use one day to rip the heart out of the last unkin, Phreedom's metaphysique is just one reminder after another of what she's lost – her brother, her son, her humanity. She no longer blames Finnan for teaching her the truth of the unkin and the Cant. She no longer blames Metatron for what his Covenant spear-carriers did to her brother and to Phreedom herself. But that's largely because the blame has been replaced by hunger.

Down in the valley, the grazing cattle look plump and appetising. One of the Bacchae at her side sets up a howl.

The sleek calf gives a scream, bucking its head, whites visible around the edges of its panicked eyes, legs skittering as it goes down beneath her. She digs her claws into its throat like it's a lump of clay her fist is ripping off. Blood sprays as, with her other arm locked round its jaw, she twists its head to break its neck. The others dive into the scattering herd like wild dogs, tearing heifers limb from limb with claws and teeth and sheer brute force. A white bull snorts and charges, glaring down its horns; it turns, tossing its head in rage and fear, and barges at another pack, but as it ploughs into their midst it's tripped, dragged down by countless hands. Its broken bits of carcass bounce above the crowd, hurled hand to hand this way and that, all ribs and hoofs, the flesh stripped quicker than a prince could blink in shock and gag into his perfumed handkerchief.

It's over within minutes.

One of the women holds two broken horns up to her head and bellows, charges laughing at her fellow hunters. Others are still breaking animals between them here and there. A group of four heave, two at each side of a rib cage, trying to split it open like a corpse in autopsy. One girl hammers on a severed head with a splintering thigh-bone. But most are simply gnawing on the pieces.

Phreedom runs her hand over strips of flesh that drip where they hang from branches on the pine trees, licks the blood from her open palm.

The force of the chi-dart knocks her sideways as it hits her shoulder, and she staggers back to catch her footing. Though the bitmites in her body won't let her bleed, she feels the cold iron of the thing like poison in her body, claws at her shoulder to pull it out. Bastard!

– Ambush! she shouts.

They leap out onto the track that leads from town; they come from behind and from the side, come crashing out of hiding all around. The villagers rush towards them with weapons even more archaic than her own in their hands, ancient needlegun-crossbow things that fire wildly, furiously, at the pillagers. Another chi-charged quarrel thumps into the tree beside her, sparking blue-green.

– Come on, you bitches! Grab your weapons! Follow me!

Bitches, harpies, furies, Phreedom's girls are on their feet in seconds, swatting iron darts aside like gnats and streaming out into the mob of villagers, stolen ruptors flashing, shattering the rash attack. Boys playing at cowboys and indians, angels and demons, Hinter's knights against her brood of dragons, they don't have the first idea of what this kind of fight is really like and her guerrilla force, hardened with years of warfare in the wilderness, hit them like foxes let loose in a chicken coop.

It's a rout. Wounded men run from the women, firing blind behind them as they try to escape being torn in pieces by the Bacchae, shouting prayers for some deity's intervention as they fall. Phreedom brings one of them down and straddles him as he lies there scrabbling on the ground, screaming for mercy. She hushes him with a hand over his mouth and nose, clamped there until his heels stop drumming.

She cups her hands under the stream of water trickling from the rock and takes a sip, splashes the rest over her face; it runs down red over the chicken-bone necklace and between her breasts. Across the ridge, the others kneel before their own created springs, washing off the blood. The ruptors driven into the stone look like strange mountain shrines, she thinks, crosses raised upon the rock and hung with fluttering hides, the half-naked scarlet women on their knees before them, hands moving from spouting water to their faces as if in ritual or prayer. A low hum comes from all the staffs, rising and falling in the rhythm of breath, the sound of streaming water merging with it. It's the music of power, of the chi energies of the earth beneath their feet, of the Vellum itself being tapped, and the bitmites on her arm snake in time with it; she feels them stretching up over her shoulder, tickling her neck, licking her jaw, her cheek. They're a part of this world now, in the dust that blows upon the wind, in the soil, the rock, and in their own flesh. She used to think of them as hers, these black sprites that have turned the world into heaven and hell on earth. Now she just thinks of them as *her*.

She pulls the brass disruptor out of the rock and feels the hum of it die in her hand. Even the weapons designed to fight the bitmites have been transformed by them, rebuilt to specifications that the bitmites gleaned from dreams and nightmares. The angels still fire bolts of brute energy but these weapons, her weapons, *their* weapons, carry information in their blasts, signals that can turn an enemy to dust, yes, but that can just as easily drill a hole into a world of water or a sea of wine hidden beneath the surface of some ragged patch of Vellum.

It's really quite simple, she's come to understand: the bitmites have no hidden agenda of their own, no secret schemes to steal the world, only a basic need to answer every voice, to serve, to give humanity what it desires – power and freedom, justice and revenge, a simple life, a glorious death.

And what does she want? Her brother back? The son they stole from her? The heads of the fucking unkin bastards that tore her world apart: angels, demons, the fucking lot of them? To be drunk with Finnan under the stars in a trailer-park in the Mojave Desert, laughing at his crazy fantasies of mystery and magic, thrilling at the thought of all the wild adventures possible in his imagination? To find the angel Metatron, demand that he rewrite the destiny graved in her flesh – her past, her present and her future too – demand he give her back Thomas and Jack? A revenge or a ... return?

What do any of them really want?

The Beasts among Us

– So whoever he may be, m'sire, says Guy, accept this spirit here within the city, suffer him or flee. His powers reach so wide, my lord; I've even heard it said he gave the vine to us as sorrow's cure. And if you drive the wine away, then every human joy is dead.
– And you?
Pierrot glowers at me.
– What do you say?
– I am afraid to speak my mind before the king, I sing. But I will say one thing. There is no spirit greater than the Harlequin.

*

– You hear this? says Pierrot. The audacity of these wild beasts right here among us.

He points at Jack, at me, but he's addressing Guy.

– In all hell's eyes, he says, we're all disgraced. We must act now, swift as electric fire. Go to the gate and give the order. Tell the soldiers – buckle on their swords and bring their shields. Gather the riders mounted on their steeds, and bring my archers out to make their bowstrings sing. We march against the whores!

Guy, as the messenger, goes running from the stage.

– I swear, snarls Pierrot, it would be rich if we allowed ourselves to be defied by these hysterical bitches.

– Still stubborn, Pierrot? says Jack. Despite my warning?

He climbs slowly to his feet. Pierrot's knife turns, pointing at him, at arm's reach.

– Is it impossible to shut this stranger up? he says to me. In chains or out of them, he speaks too free.

– And you should thank me for it. Even after the mistreatment I've endured from your hands, Jack says, still, I warn you: bearing arms against this spirit is a sin. I tell you, stop this now; the Harlequin will not allow you to disrupt his revellers.

– Disrupt? I'll drive them from the mountains. I *will* drive them out.

– There'll be a rout, all right. You'll all be put to flight – and put to shame when with their little sticks they crush your armoured warriors, your shining knights. You kick against the pricks in rage when you should sacrifice to him. You're dust, Pierrot, and the Harlequin is king.

Pierrot slashes at him with the knife. Jack staggers back, a slice across his chest. Under the leather a thin trickle of red blood begins to flow.

– I'll give him sacrifice! says Pierrot. A wholesale slaughter of his women on the hills. I'll give them what they're due. No, I'll not listen to you tell me what to do. So you've escaped your chains; now keep your peace or you can feel my steel again.

– Fuck you, says Jack. Come on, then. Fucking try it.

He's right up in Joey's face, and it takes all that Joey's got not to just deck the stupid fucker, but he reins his anger in. He holds it back for at least a second before his hands are up and slamming into Jack's chest, palm first, shoving him back and away. Jack bounces off the wall and comes right back with one step, then another; his own hands slam into Joey, and again, and again. Then they've got each other by the tee shirts, by Joey's torn and sleeveless white tee, Jack's black and red striped top, and they're pulling each other around like it's the mosh pit, but this time the snarling spitting venom is more than mock fury, more than raging glory in teenage kicks, headlocks and roars of animal joy. This time, as Jack shoves Joey away from him, there's no crowd to catch him, throw him back, just a chair to go tumbling behind him and a desk to rattle, papers scattering onto the floor at his side. Fox's plans for revolution.

Joey grabs a fistful of paper, holds it crumpled up in front of him.

– Fuck this, he says. This is—

– Bollocks, says Jack. They'll never catch us.

He leans against the brick wall, darts a glance over his shoulder, round the corner, then looks back at Joey, grinning. Joey grabs a handful of shoulder and leans round Jack to see for himself. There are ten, maybe twelve of the razor kids hanging outside the Grosvenor, empty bottles of Buckfast, Thunderbird and Mad Dog 20/20 clinking at their feet. The leader perches on a crossbar of scaffolding, one arm on an upright to steady himself, the other dangling down between his legs. Head monkey, Joey thinks. King Ned. His chief lieutenants lean against the square pillars of the burnt out cinema building's entrance, smoking fags and arguing over the pills in high pitched nasal whines – *aye, right* – *aye, too fuckin right, ya fuckin prick* – *these are pure shite, man, by the way*. The others mill and jostle each other, one of them playing with his chib, flicking the cut throat open and closed, open and closed. *These urnae fuckin anyhin. Ahm gonae kill that cunt Narco.*

Joey swings back round the corner.

– Up and over, he says.

He points at the second-level gantries, the scaffolding and prefabs which all but swallow up the cobbled lane. They could get by without even being seen.

– You take the high road, says Jack. I'm going straight through.

And Joey has no time to argue because Jack's already gone, legging it down the cobbles, weaving past the swing of a chib and ducking a bottle that smashes on a wall, grabbing scaffolding and swinging up, too fast and agile surely for any of these little shits to catch while they're strung out on the dog tranquillisers Joey sold them. Surely . . .

– Fuck, says Joey.

He starts running after Jack.

– Come on, says Joey.

He grabs Jack by the collar of his piper jacket, drags him up enough so he can latch an arm and haul him to his feet. Jack stands there dazed, looking down at the militiaman, at the truncheon with the blood and hair being washed from it into the puddle in the gutter, at the crowbar with the blood and hair and bone.

– You killed him. You fucking killed him, Joey.

– Come on.

Jack pulls his arm away and wipes a rivulet of red from his left eye, blood dribbling from his flame hair, running thin in the torrential rain, streaking his face. He's in a bad way. If Joey hadn't got to him in time . . .

He snorts blood, wipes it from his nose and cut lip with a flicking hand. Spits it in the militiaman's broken face.

– Come on, says Joey.

An ornithopter searchlight sweeps the alleyway, a heavenly ray illuminating them as Jack limps back, then turns to take a running kick at the dead man, screaming abuse. Joey looks up into the raindrops sparkling as they fall through the bright flood of light.

– Come on!

– Come on, says Joey. Skybikes against militia ornithopters?

He throws the crumpled sheet at Jack.

— And guns all along the east wall of the Rookery, says Jack. And with the reinforcements Anaesthesia's bringing back—

— We don't even know if she's coming back herself. She's gone. She's lost.

— It doesn't matter. We only have to hold the line till King Finn reaches the ICI plant. Once we take that we have the whole city's fucking power.

That's the plan. A push out of the Rookery, a wall of fire laid down along the river so King Finn and his men can make it down to Finnieston, down to the docklands, the airshipyards and the orgone manufactory. Jack in the skies. Guy and Puck in the Rookery, co-ordinating its defence, all of them just trying to hold that line long enough for Finn to . . . take the power back.

— And they're with us, Joey. The workers there are with us — Jesus, Joey, this is it. If you can't fucking see that, if you can't fucking hack it, then fuck you.

Joey grabs the corner of the desk and pulls himself to his feet.

— It'll be a fucking massacre, he says. You think they won't take out the plant? I'm telling you, you'll be lucky if they don't level Kentigern and sow the fucking ground with salt. Can't stop the children of the revolution, eh, Jack? You have no fucking idea how far they'll go. You want a city of martyrs, Jack? Is that what you want?

— I want freedom, says Jack. What the fuck do *you* want?

— World peace, says Joey. Fuck you.

The Savage Spirits

The Duke is rapt, gripped by this picture of a royal mind unravelling, of a tyrant calling down his fate. There are a million Dukes of Hell across the Vellum since the Hinter tore the Covenant apart, and each self-styled Asmodeus or Beelzebub is just a rival, just another enemy, just one more threat to this one's precious city-state.

Pierrot's just one of them, to him, one of the fools he hates. We'd all been worried that he'd watch the play so long and then catch on but, no, I guess we underestimated just how dim this grey lord is. As Hitler loved his Wagner, loved to watch the gods destroy themselves, Valhalla burning to the ground, our Duke's won over easily by the promise of a violent end, of seeing Pierrot brought down.

What's new? I think. A lot of bluster and a little blood. Some folks are always easily amused.

– Friend, there is still one way to heal this hate, says Jack.

– And how is that? says Pierrot. Am I supposed to bow to my own slaves?

He snorts. The Duke snorts with him. Angels, I think: even with the Covenant broken, Gabriel and his goons still see themselves as lords, still see humanity as beasts, as monsters, slaves to be subdued. Even despite the fact that Metatron's Republic fell, these tinpot tyrants think they have the *right* to quell the savage spirits of upstart humanity. And so they build their Havens as these dreams of order, rule them as new Dukes of Hell.

My sister, Phreedom, should be out there in the Hinter now, out gathering the rebel souls, the wild things, nature's children, all those who'd choose flesh and the chaos that goes with it over this . . . scotch mist. That was the story, anyway, as King Finn told it, as Guy wrote it down . . . but sometimes stories take unusual twists.

– I'll bring the women here for you unarmed, says Jack.

– This is some crafty scheme of yours, says Pierrot. I won't be charmed.

– What kind of scheme is it, to keep both you and them from harm?

The Princess is giving her attention now to something other than the play; she's watching Guy intently as he drops down from the wagon, at the far side of the stage from where the Harlequin and Pierrot act out this age-old fight between chaos and order, the nemesis of human nature and the hubris of the state. He slips along the far wall of the hall, sneaking under the torches so he doesn't cast a shadow in their light, around behind the crowd, behind the throne, to where she sits below the Duke and at his side.

– You're in with them, Pierrot's saying. It's a plot so that your wine will flow forever.

– No, says Jack. You can be sure, however, that *that* pact's already made with the divine.

– Bring me my weapons, calls Pierrot. And not one more word from *you*.

The Princess lets Guy take the goblet from her hand. He whispers something in her ear that makes her shake her head, brows furrowed; it's a long time since she heard that name, I bet – eternity, perhaps. It's hard to read the words upon her lips from here, but I can guess.

Phreedom . . . she says.

– Pierrot, wait, says Jack.

A pause. It is the moment of Pierrot's doom.

– I'll give you what you *really* want.

The Princess Anaesthesia, our forgotten Phreedom, looks at Jack across the cold, stone room. And whispers, *Yes*.

Errata

The Shape of Things to Come

– Your brother knew what Himmler was planning, didn't he? says Pickering. He found out about Operation Hummingbird. He knew that Himmler was going to purge the SA, slaughter the last remnants of the old order and raise a new army from the ashes of the old. Fascism would be dead, Futurism victorious. He was willing to do anything to stop that, wasn't he?

– How many times do I have to tell you, Major Pickering, I am not Reinhardt von Strann. I know nothing about the man other than what I have already told you. I know he had a brother in the SA but—

– *You* had a brother in the SA. *You*, Reinhardt von Strann.

– I am not that man. My name is Reynard. I am a French citizen.

– You are the brother of Johann von Strann, of this so-called Jack Flash. You know what he is.

– No.

– You know what he made himself.

– No.

– You know how he did it.

– No, I tell you—

– The Eye of the Weeping Angel—

– I don't—

– A ritual in your family home in Strann.

– My name is—

– Tell me what he did!

I feel a sickening lurch, like the ground itself moving beneath my feet as I stagger from the chair and he turns the open book towards me – it moves, O God, the text itself is moving – and all the whirling, churning vortex of text resolves into a swastika inked in red and black upon the aged, yellowed manuscript.

– Hypnosis, I'm saying, mesmerism. It isn't real. It isn't.

No, I tell myself desperately, it's just some fake, some forgery, some nineteenth-century Romantic fancy full of inscrutable hieroglyphs, grotesque illustrations, bound in black leather and written on skin warm to the touch, like it's alive and crawling with insect language, crawling right into your mind, O God.

I back away from him.

– Drugs, I say, it's drugs. You've drugged me. Drugs and hypnosis.

– The Book of All Hours, he says. A book of everything that ever was or *wasn't* written, not just our history, not just our future, but *every* history, *every* future. Written in the language of the angels. A living language, Fox. The Logos. The Word of God. The Cant. Look at it, Fox. This is what the first shaman saw when he looked into the fire he stole from Heaven. This is the shape of *everything*.

And I can see it in the book, the whole of history twisting in that maelstrom of a forgotten symbol, truth warping around the myth and spewing out, in spiral arms, a million brave new worlds, spinning as a galaxy of constellations of chance and change. The book barely binds it, can hardly contain it. It's pushing at the edges, trying to break through into our world, into reality, existence.

– Close it, I say. Close the book.

– Look at it, he says. The Book of All Hours. You know what Himmler thinks it is? I'm not sure how much the Russian knows – I don't understand his part in this – but Himmler thinks it's just some *spellbook*, some pathetic little grimoire for conjuring demons.

My back hits a bookcase and a glass door rattles. I have nowhere left to go, my brother and the book between myself and the door.

– Demons! he spits. This is a book for conjuring worlds!

– You want me to make something up for your story? Some ancient grimoire, maybe? A mediaeval tome of arcane knowledge, of secrets and truths too terrible to tell? Will you be satisfied if I invent some spurious detail for your preposterous tale?

Pickering says nothing, simply stares at the prisoner with the same cold gaze he used against the Futurist spy in the room before this one – three hours ago it was now. He wonders if that hangman is still waiting outside, has a sudden absurd image of the man sipping a cup of tea and chatting with some pretty Wren as he leans against the wall of the corridor. – *Yeah, we hanged three of the buggers already today. That Pickering knows what he's after.*

That was how he first met Sarah. He was standing waiting outside a room in the Circus – that's what they call this place, just like the original, Thames House, the HQ of MI5, the Circus – when she came walking past with files in her hand, and saw him there, and smiled at him. He wasn't a Major then, of course. He didn't really start to rise through the ranks until . . . until he learned how to not care about the pleas, the begging. *For God's sake, man, I have a wife and children.*

A few words from him would be all it takes. The world is changing since the Armistice, and men like Pickering hold a lot of power in their hands. All it takes is a few words: Futurist agent; enemy of the state.

– You know, I do have rights, von Strann is saying. Do your superiors know exactly why you're holding me? The grounds for your suspicions?

Pickering says nothing. The man knows damn well that his superiors have no more love for 'Guy Fox', with his pamphlets littering London's streets, than for the real threat of traitors within their midst, traitors with all of Moscow's power behind them. A noisome little troublemaker like this is hardly within the remit of Operation Hawkwing, but they'd probably be happy to see Pickering's bête noire out of the way. As long as it doesn't interfere with the fight against Futurism, they'll turn a blind eye to it.

– The Stasi, the Gestapo, the NKVD, MI5 – you're all the same. I understand the official designation for MI5 is the Security Service, Major Pickering. What does that abbreviate to again – SS, is it? I thought all that was dead and buried in the ruins of Berlin but, no, it's alive and well right here in Britain. Albion, I mean.

Pickering doesn't rise to it. Mosley's victory's just a blip and

Churchill will be back in power after the next elections; people are fools and, yes, Futurism's still a menace, but it needs a cool and reasoning head to deal with it, not panic and paranoia.

– Where is your swastika armband, Herr Pickering? says von Strann. Where is the swastika? You must be proud of what you're doing for king and country, for your glorious Albion, no? You ought to wear your heart upon your sleeve.

Pickering says nothing. He *is* bloody proud of what he's doing, proud to wear the badge of MI5 – the eye over the crown within the pyramid – and to serve King Edward and the British Empire. Britain, he thinks, not Albion. All that tosh and nonsense, it'll all blow over.

– Where is your swastika? says von Strann.

I push him back from me and push myself away, wanting to walk right out the door, right out the house and out into the night. I could leave now, just leave him to his madness, but my legs are weak. I find myself still leaning against the glass doors of the bookcases, stumbling along the wall like a blind man, kicking the leg of the table covered with the red cloth, rattling the candlestick and dagger laid out upon it.

I cannot shake the image from my mind, the shape that the churning swastika resolved into, not the straightforward square-barred swastika of the Nazi Party, but something more ornate, more Oriental. I consider myself enlightened; I've seen more than enough in Berlin not to blanch at what the prurient would call depravity, but the image in the book, in my head, still sickens me. Two men, one down on his hands and knees, forming the lower part of this shape, the second man hovering above him in the air, contorted like a Yogic master, arms forward, back arched so his legs go straight back, then bend up at the knees. A swastika like some antique Indian sculpture, crawling man and floating spirit coupled in sodomitic union. God and Man as one.

What kind of ritual is he planning, for the love of Christ?

The Eye of the Weeping Angel glints before me, its flaw staring back at me as if the gemstone is exactly as its name suggests – the eye of an angel that has seen the truth beneath reality and wept for it. I lay a hand over it – not to take it but to hide it, or to hide myself from it – and my brother's hand comes down on top, holding it there. He grips the book under his other arm, closed now, mercifully.

– You understand, he says. Someone, *something*, changed history. This is not the way it's meant to be.

But a century of slaughter? I think. Did he actually see the same reality in the book that I did?

– But *that*, I say. Christ, Jonni, if *that* is the way it's meant to be, we're better off with the Futurists.

He peels my hand away from the jewel.

– I think that's what they thought too, he says softly.

He lays the book down on the table and takes me by the shoulders.

– Fox, he says, since I looked into that book it's like there's two of me, this … this fool and someone else, someone better. Fox, I'm frightened of what I could become in this world, of what I already am.

He steps back from me, hands raised as if to say, look, look at what they've done to me. His face twists like that of a child trying not to cry and then he's pulling his open tunic off and throwing it across the room.

– I'm supposed to die tonight, he says, in *this* world. Himmler's men are on their way here to drag me out into the gardens and shoot me. That's in there as well.

He points at the book.

– A different page. A different story. And I don't want to be a part of it, not any more. Not as this. Not when I could be so much more.

All he ever wanted was to be the hero, a knight in shining armour or a boy from nowhere going up against a giant. Only in this world it's silver skulls that shine on the lapels of warriors. But it's the same in *that* world, I think. It's exactly the same.

– I know, he says. I know what you're thinking, Fox. I know the way you think. But I have to try, don't I? You know me just as well. You know I have to try. It's who I am.

Beneath his unbuttoned shirt, a lattice of scars is visible, a hatchwork across his chest. God, I think, what have you done to yourself, Jonni?

– This isn't my world, he says.

229

– Your brother knew what Himmler was planning, didn't he? says Pickering. He found out about Operation Hummingbird. He knew that Himmler was going to purge the SA, slaughter the last remnants of the old order and raise a new army from the ashes of the old. Fascism would be dead, Futurism victorious. He was willing to do anything to stop that, wasn't he?

– How many times do I have to tell you, Major Pickering, I am not Reinhardt von Strann. I know nothing about the man other than what I have already told you. I know he had a brother in the SA but—

– *You* had a brother in the SA. *You*, Reinhardt von Strann.

– But, as I say, I'm not this van Strann—

– *Von* Strann—

– Sorry. *Von* Strann. But I wish to God I was, I'll tell you that. The Fox's Den was raking it in while my own little club was struggling to stay afloat. But then we never had bestiality on the bill. Do you mind if I smoke?

– Go ahead.

– Do you have a light? Thanks. Please . . . where were we?

Pickering snaps the lighter closed and pockets it. Where *were* they? He stands up from his chair and wanders to the corner of the room, leans back against the wall, arms folded, sizing the prisoner up. He returns, takes his cap off and lays it on the table.

– In July 1940, he says, you were arrested for your activity in helping refugees escape from Germany, and sentenced to death as a traitor to the New Reich. Given the pedigree of the von Strann family, this was no small scandal. Not that your family was without scandal before this . . . your brother, for instance. But . . .

He stops. He's gone through this already with the prisoner, of course, so the feeling of déjà vu is not unnatural but it's so deep and profound that . . . he can't nail it down, but something feels wrong.

*

– You want me to make something up for your story? says von Strann. Some ancient grimoire, maybe? A mediaeval tome of arcane knowledge, of secrets and truths too terrible to tell? Will you be satisfied if I invent some spurious detail for your preposterous tale? What should I say? What do you want me to say?

Pickering stands up from his chair and wanders to the corner of the room, leans back against the wall, arms folded, sizing the prisoner up. He returns, takes his cap off and lays it on the table. How long is the bloody fool going to maintain this charade?

A little something niggles at the back of his mind but he can't place it. He shakes it off, a distraction.

– How did he do it? he says.

– Do what, Major Pickering?

– Become this . . . thing? This Jack Flash? It was the jewel, wasn't it? Magic.

– Major Pickering, what you are talking about is not possible: cursed jewels; magical rituals; or this von Strann, escaping from a Siberian gulag and travelling across the Futurist Bloc to the Western border in four days. It simply isn't—

– *Two* days, Pickering interrupts.

Goddamnit, the man knows fine well. They've been over this.

– Really? says von Strann. I was sure you said *four days*.

– I said *two*.

– Well, whatever. Major Pickering, I—

And Pickering finds himself with the gun in his hand, pointed at the other man's head. He has to stop his finger from pulling the trigger, as if another part of him is trying to seize control, to punch a hole right through the man's lies. Von Strann flinches, pulls his head back and away, but Pickering is round beside him now, his other hand gripping the bastard's chin, the barrel pressed to his temple.

– I know you've talked to the others, he says. That's how I found you. I'm not the only one whose life your brother wrecked. I'm not alone in this.

The man flails in his grip, whimpering, a spineless coward. Yes, Pickering's talked to all of them he could find, in asylums or in prisons, under some pretext or other – *official investigation into*

Futurist psychological warfare – Yes, we believe they were using projection, mass hypnosis – some bunkum like that. All of the poor survivors of this other Spirit of the Blitz. If they could be called survivors. And all of them mentioned the 'Frenchman', the cultured, quietly interested 'Frenchman', chasing the same story, the same legend of Jack Flash. Pickering cocks the trigger.

– August 13th, 1943, says von Strann suddenly.

It's a date Pickering will never forget.

– What?

The man tries to pull his head away from the gun again, but Pickering's grip is firm.

– That's when your wife and son died, isn't it, Major Pickering? That's the story, isn't it? That's what they all said.

It's a date he'll never forget because it's like a knife that's buried deep in his still-pumping heart. And yes, it's what they all said. He remembers grilling them one by one, forcing them through the stories over and over again, and he would stay quiet and composed even as they wept and giggled, recounting the same scene of horror that wakes him screaming from his dreams. All of them were soldiers, officers, career army like himself, as if this Jack Flash were picking his targets by a most ruthless logic, not his enemies but the innocents they loved.

– That's what they all told me, the man babbles. August 13th, 1943. Yes, I've talked to them. But you don't understand. It isn't real. *He* isn't real.

– I've seen him, says Pickering. And I'm not alone.

– So you've talked to them. Are any of them sane? *Mon Dieu*, are any of them even rational?

Pickering pulls the gun away from the man's face. He uncocks the trigger and holsters it, leans in close to whisper.

– Believe me, he says, I am the most rational man you will ever meet.

And that's your own form of insanity, he thinks. *Isn't it?*

He didn't wear black at the funeral. He wore his uniform.

– Then I ask you, Major Pickering. As a rational man. Do you believe in myths or do you believe in reality? Perhaps you want to believe in gods and monsters, Major, but I . . . I want to believe in humanity. I want my world godless and without magic.

The man is trembling. He shakes his head.

– But . . . I've seen him too, Major Pickering. God have mercy on my soul, I've seen him too.

– Your brother, says Pickering.

The feeling sickens him a little, but it's one of the few pleasures he has left now since his world was murdered: the vicious pleasure of breaking a man. But von Strann has that strange bitter smile of a man going to the gallows with his secret still intact.

– We are all brothers, he says, under the skin.

He pats at his breast pocket, takes out a pack of cigarettes.

– Do you mind if I smoke?

– Go ahead.

– Do you have a light? Thanks. Please . . . where were we?

– Berlin, 1929. What was it called – your own club – by the way?

– Jongleurs. It was called Jongleurs. We had a man juggling fire out front. Jacques his name was – quite the crowd-puller.

– But hardly bestiality.

– Hardly. The Fox's Den rather put our little juggling act to shame.

– So it was a successful business? Prostitution? Other criminal activities?

– One rather suspected so. The proprietor was a quite untrustworthy fellow. Although from what you say, I fear I may have misjudged him. As I say, there were all sorts of stories. Oh, wait. This lighter isn't working . . . got it. Yes, as I say, there were a lot of stories going around. What is it that you want to know, Major Pickering? What is it exactly that you want to know?

Pickering stands up from his chair and wanders to the corner of the room, leans back against the wall, arms folded, sizing the prisoner up. He returns, takes his cap off and lays it on the table. Reinhardt von Strann, he thinks; or Reynard Cartier, depending on who you listen to. If it weren't for the photograph of von

Strann Senior, Pickering might almost believe the cover story himself; his accent sounds Parisian enough, with just the hint of German you'd expect, and MacChuill is utterly convinced that he *did* debrief the man on his arrival. *Jolly good sort. Great help to the war effort and all that.* So what happened to the interview records?

Oh, there's a lot of things that Pickering would like to know about this man, and he'll get to them all eventually. He checks his watch: it's early yet and they have all night if necessary. As long as it takes.

– I've spoken to the French authorities, you know? They have no record of you either.

– War is a confusing time, Major Pickering. Things get lost in all the chaos, lost, forgotten or . . .

– Stolen?

– Lost, he repeats. A few little scraps of paper amongst . . . millions, Major Pickering. It must be easy for things to get jumbled up, slipped into the wrong file, lost in transit.

– British Intelligence is very efficient, says Pickering.

– I'm sure even *you* lose track of things once in a while, Joseph.

6

The Madness of King Pierrot

Pierrot stands there, caught in curiosity. Jack gives a quiet laugh. He strokes his staff.

– How would you like, he says, to see them lying sated on the hills?

Pierrot's voice goes quiet with the thrill of the idea.

– Above all else, he whispers. Yes. I would give anything to see . . . her.

Jack grins with lascivious spite, the Harlequin reeling his victim in. He circles Pierrot.

– Why this desire, he asks, all of a sudden? Would it not sting to see them drunk with wine, these whores, these bitches, all these maidens of this town, and your own mother Columbine?

He asks it innocent and sweet but stresses, oh so slightly, *your own mother*, darts his tongue to lick his lips

– You'd be a willing witness to their rites? No matter how it hurts?

– Of course, says Pierrot. If I could sit silent beneath the firs . . .

He has a distant, dreamy look, Pierrot, gazing out across the audience as Jack, behind his back, jumps up to crouch upon a prop. He holds one hand across his eyes, his fingers splayed to peep through them; his other holds the flute down at his crotch. He jiggles it and wriggles till the audience's giggles make Pierrot turn, but Jack's already pointing with the flute now, while his

235

other hand's dropped down to stroke his chin, a thoughtful and considerate Harlequin.

– No. They would notice you, Jack muses. Even if you came covertly.

– Then I'll go overtly, says Pierrot. Yes, there's truth in what you say.

Jack jumps down off the rock, walks round behind Pierrot and leans in to whisper in his ear.

– So shall I take you now? says Jack. Will you go all the way?

He bites his bottom lip, hands reaching out to take Pierrot by the hips. Shit, Guy, I think, you've written one perverted mother-fucker of a play.

Pierrot turns and once again Jack mugs a casual pose, entirely innocent.

– Lead on, says Pierrot. Let's go right now. I hate to wait.

Jack takes Pierrot by the tie as if to lead him like a dog, but lets it drop out of his fingers, shakes his head.

– We'll have to find you some fine linen robes to wear.

– Why? Pierrot protests. I am a man—

– who wants to join the ranks of women. They would kill you if you showed your *manhood* there.

Pierrot gives a grudging nod, oblivious to any innuendo.

– That's true, he says. You do have some wits after all.

– You've barely had a taste, says Jack aside, and then to Pierrot: The Harlequin has taught me this.

– What do I have to do? says Pierrot.

He sounds so small and lost.

– How do I follow your advice? he says.

– Don't worry, Jack says. I'll come with you to your rooms.

He drapes an arm around Pierrot's shoulder.

– Yes, he says, we'll dress you up real nice.

The Pattern of a Poisonous Frog

The sky is thick with churning cloud-cover, reflecting back the orange of streetlights muted to a dull and heavy glow. Joey rolls over onto one side; feels like his left arm is broken, but that's OK. The pills kill that pain too.

Uphill and past the scrub of bushes and trees, behind a wall topped with barbed wire littered with plastic bags and rags of cloth, a string of lights marks out the limits of the civilised. The firefly glows from the windows and the floodlights all along the length of the Circus, together with the burning wreckage of the airtram scattered on the slope above him, give the umber foliage of the park a rich chiaroscuro taint.

— And now I'm looking out into this dark and stormy night from up here in the heavenly heights and, folks, I'm thinking that the powers-that-be may finally have gotten wise. I think they're out to shut the Rookery down for good tonight, mes amigos. We got an airfleet coming in over the Circus, I can see militiamen moving down en masse from Maryhill Barracks and, with the walls of Hyndland sealing in you boys to the west, only way to run is into the inferno. It's not looking good for Fox's little friends, I tell you.

Joey pulls himself to his feet, looks round. There's a few bodies thrown clear of the twisted airtram but what strikes him most is that, beyond the scar of crumpled buckled carriages and strewn debris, the park is calm, a wild and feral garden but a garden nonetheless, even with the Circus looming on one side and the Rookery on the other, and a streak of metal devastation carved right down the slope between. It's the light that he notices. A crimson and ochre wash paints over the flowers of weeds and, over the long grass, a sickly pattern of yellow and black is marked out where light hits it or does not — the pattern of a poisonous frog. He used to paint when he was a kid — when they were kids — not just graffiti but oil on canvas, stolen or traded for what was stolen; the first thing he ever got high on was turps. He gave that up a long time ago — a pointless pastime — but he can still look into the night and see the way light works in it.

The Rookery rises, carved out by the volcanic glow of halogen and given a painted solidity by the lightning flashes of militia ornithopters' chi-beams. They're coming in low from over the Circus now, gathering into a front. The glow of steam vented from Cavor-Reich engines builds and builds as the gunboats circle slowly into position, until it bathes the sky in a green that speaks of absinthe and other worlds. Madness and war machines. Gauche, Joey thinks.

Out here on the bridge to nowhere, though, there are no lights, and form builds its definitions out of damp olive shadows.

— *But as my dear old Papa always said, son, you can hunt and you can trap, but if you shoot an animal you better kill it then and there, cause if you only make it mad, if you just wound it, it'll come for you with everything it's got. A crafty fox or cornered rat, boy, if you trap it, well, make damn sure that it can't get loose, because there's nothing wilder than an animal that's soured its taste buds with the bitter steel of chains and cages, knowing it'll never wash that foul metallic flavour from its mouth without the rich red wine of human blood. Well, mes amigos, seems to me like we have all of us been biting on the bars for an eternity and waiting for the day that Dionysus drops by. And now — oh yeah — the fur is gonna fly.*

Joey looks down the slope. A pedestal of stone rises up out of overgrown flowerbeds before the bridge; a monument to the Boer War, on the top of it a statue of a pith-helmeted soldier once sat, Joey remembers, in a surreally languid catalogue pose, one leg hanging down, the other raised so that the soldier could lean his lazy stone elbow on it as he gazed out across some distant savannah slaughter. Now another figure holds the same pose.

Jack swivels round to face him, gives a salute.

— *What's this? I hear you ask. Dionne Warwick? Dianetics? No, you heard me right. We're talking Dionysus, god of beer and wine and party times, and god of small trapped animals, no less. Oh, yes! Beware, you trappers, you guardians of the ghettos and the gulags. Beware, you burgher mousers, all you fat cats thinking you can round up all the rats. Beware, lest one day you trap Dionysus in your hunt, cause Dionysus when he's angry is one seriously mad cunt.*

— You smell it? calls Jack. That lush deep scent of . . . memories. Smells kinda like heat. Kinda . . . sexy.

— All I smell, says Joey, is shit and garbage.

There is something else though. On top of the fetid stench of the

238

rotting filth under the bridge is a hint of methane and more powerful fuels. It's the smell of the open-cast mines of cavorite seams that powered Albion's industrial revolution. Of the chi-wells of Persia that the Empire was built on. The orgone-rich deposits of the North Sea.

The wind is blowing from the south, from the carcass of the ICI plant, still burning after twenty years. Joey remembers the radiovision pictures of King Finn being dragged out of the wreckage of it, delirious from the orgone fumes, then the shots of him standing in the dock in chains, spouting his angry rhetoric.

– Shit and garbage, says Joey.

– Ah, now, says Jack, even shit and garbage changes if you leave it buried long enough, under constant pressure.

And there *is* something else there, coming from below, something buried real deep, beneath even the rats.

A Broken King

Pierrot pulls away.

– But in a woman's robes? he says. I'd be ashamed.

– No shame, says Jack, no fear. Or else your hope of spying on the maidens ends right here.

Pierrot thinks about it. You can see the thoughts go through his mind, the image of himself in drag, disturbing but somehow enticing, this forbidden thing he's never tried, a part of him that's always been denied.

– What kind of dress do you think I should wear? he asks.

– A gown that flows from shoulder down to foot, says Jack.

Jack looks him up and down, his head cocked to one side, a queer eye quietly assessing. Brushing Joey's long hair back, he takes him by the chin and tilts his face.

– And on your head we'll put a hood, Jack finally decides.

– Describe my costume more, says Pierrot. What else?

He's getting braver now. Jack flounces all around him, camp as knickers, miming measuring and framing Joey in a square of thumbs and forefingers.

– Yes, well. You'll need a dappled fawnskin, obviously. And a wand to hold.

Oh, but Pierrot's not that bold. His shame resurfaces and he recoils.

– No. I can't do it. I could never dress up as a girl.

– Then it'll end in tears, says Jack.

And suddenly the whole queer tailor act is dropped.

– And when Pierrot and my maidens come to blows, says Jack, my dear, the blood will flow.

– You're right, says Pierrot.

Again he has that distant look, as if he knows somewhere inside that his own tragedy's unfolding, his control unravelling. It's Harlequin who's at the wheel of fate now, and Pierrot's just a passenger along for the predestined ride.

– You're right, he says. I'd best go spy upon them first.

– It would be smarter, Jack says. You'd just be inviting trouble if you went there looking for a fight.

Pierrot faces out into the audience, a broken king, considering the world that's slipping from his grasp. Jack stands behind, his hands upon Pierrot's shoulders, like a boxing coach giving his fighter a massage.

– But how will I get through the city? I'll be seen, says Pierrot. In broad daylight . . .

– Then we'll go by quiet backstreets. It'll be OK.

Jack's hands run down to squeeze Pierrot's arms.

– I promise you, says Jack. I'll take you the least visible way.

Pierrot's eyes close for a second. Something glistens on the grease-paint, on the smears of black under his eyes. He looks at me, his pupils wide and dark, and I know that right now, right here, for all his ice-cold attitude of callous cynicism, Joey really is the king of tears.

– Whatever, he says quietly. Just as long as no one laughs at me.

– O, Pierrot, says Jack. As if we would. – [He gives the audience a wink.] – Let's go into the palace then, and plan the route.

– OK, says Pierrot, I'm ready now. I'll go inside. I need to think about it though. I could still ride out, sword in hand.

His words ring hollow.

– I *could* follow your advice. Let me decide.

A Surge of Rodent Passions

– Look out, my saucy Jack. Look out, you rogues and ragamuffins of the Rookery. They're coming for us all. They're coming hard and fast and, boys, tonight looks like the sky is gonna fall. They're coming with the lethal needle and the damage done by one angel assassin's chi-gun's going to look like scratches on a dreadnought's hull by the time they've finished what they've only just begun.

Joey can feel his last pill kicking in now. Emotion muted like a radio set buried underground and running out of batteries, the signal itself degenerating to a hiss of white noise. It doesn't matter if it *is* Jack. It doesn't matter if it isn't possible that it is Jack. Joey has a job to do, and he stopped worrying about the world's impossibilities a long time ago.

The shadow on the pedestal rolls backward like a diver going off a boat, disappears behind the stone to land with a quiet crush of bushes underfoot.

– I'm Screaming Don Coyote, coming to you on the one and only Radio Free Kentigern, coming out to you from Hell on Earth, and if this show is our last, if we're all lost, well, friends, we're going to go out with a bang, cause right now, mes amigos, yes, right now we've got for you the music that they said had died, the tunes they said we'd never play again. Well, listen up, my friends, cause this is The Narcotics with their grinding, pounding, speed-thrash cover of a classic track. This one's for Jack, but it's for Joey too, because we know that underneath it all you're just a little blue.

– As a wise man once said, you can't always get what you want, my friends, but keep this in mind, you know sometimes, you just might find you get, yes sir, exactly what you need ... And that's to Open Up and Bleed ...

A simple blues riff starts, low and repeating. One two three four, one two three. One two. One two. One two three four, one two three. One two. One two.

Joey circles sideways round the low metal railing that bounds the flowerbeds at the foot of the pedestal. Jack steps out of the bushes and onto the broken tarmac of the park's path, backing away from him out onto the bridge. Yellow and black police tape flutters from the sandstone balustrades. The white chalk outline of the sentry's body has been spray painted by vandals already, fleshed out in multicoloured patterns, like some cartoon tattooed man steam rollered into the ground. It's the sort of thing the two of them used to do — tear up crime scene cordons, spray paint over fingerprints or fibres . . . fuck with the pigs at every opportunity.

Joey nods at the sentry's psychedelic shadow.

— One of your own, you fucking moron, he says.

— Bollocks, says Jack. Thought he might be a rook. Ironic, eh? Considering.

Considering this is where you killed me. The thought doesn't have to be spoken for Joey to hear it.

— You're not Jack Flash, he says.

Jack Flash is dead, he thinks.

— Aren't we all? says Jack.

Joey reaches out a little, probing the fucker's psyche, trying to get a handle on him, but his soul is slick and dark and every move he make slides off this stealth mind. There are only glimpses, glances — memories of a father whose combed back hair fell across his forehead when he was angry, of travelling with Grandpapa on the autobus into Stadde Cintrale, to the *tabak*, and the smells, the smell of his pipe tobacco and the smell of wet dog fur as the setter shook its rust red coat, and the sound of a mother humming a folk song at a family wake, and the feel, the first nervous touch of fingers as they run through a girlfriend's soft hair and—

He can't shake the feeling that none of these memories really belong to the bastard. Some of them don't even belong in Kentigern.

They circle each other, both looking for a weak spot, an opening. Joey can feel the chi energy writhing beneath the surface — sex and death, a stripper dancing with a snake — but it's just power, just another narcotic, like Joey's stock of uppers and downers, inhibiters and facilitators. There's a lot of New Age bullshit talked about the chi, about spirit, the soul of the earth, the fossil fuel that was once flesh like us, that we will all in time become, but Joey doesn't believe in spirit. He doesn't believe in ghosts or demons. The chi doesn't have avatars, just addicts.

So he knows this 'Jack Flash', he knows the fucker has a history, a reality, a tawdry little truth that makes him tick. Not Jack, not his Jack, but another Rookery brat, fucked-up on orgone, dreaming that the world is just a dream because reality's too hard to face.

— I know who you are, he says. I know exactly where you come from.

But this other Jack smiles and Joey feels a sudden blast of bestial desire and fear — a surge of rodent passions bubbling under the surface — rats under his feet — a sentience devoid of reason — only mood and attitude.

— You can't even imagine where I come from.

A God Most Terrible

Don's out among the audience now, talking in frantic gestures with the Duke. We have a problem; look, it's clear our Pierrot's under the weather, dodgy stomach bug, we think — oh no, not castle food — but we were wondering whether — yes, you saw how wet he was with sweat — almost delirious, indeed — well, what it is — I mean — we need some sort of substitute and who else could, or would, or even *should* play noble Pierrot, *prince* Pierrot, the *king* of tears? We are professionals, so, oh no, we *will* not let this ruin your night's entertainment. No! On with the show, we say. It must go on. There's only just a few more scenes to come. Our man can carry on for maybe one at most, but if — and honestly, I tell you it will be such fun — if you were to become involved in our divertissement, our humble, poor attempt at your amusement — well, imagine, a great *Duke* of Hell like you, how well you could *command* the stage. M'sire, you'd show them rage, I'm sure — and there's no lines to learn, there's just Pierrot, grand in his destruction, roaring over everything, a king who's lost his head, you know — a lion of a man

like you, m'sire – we *know* that you could do it. You could knock
'em dead.

– Girlfriend, Jack says to me, it's time to act. The Harlequin is
getting close. The quarry's almost in the trap.

A homicidal snick of teeth, a flash of blue eyes underneath the
mask, he backflips over to me, spins and kneels to take my hand,
my irresistible Jack Flash. He rises, twirls me, pulls me into an
embrace, a kiss. His tongue darts in between my lips as hands slip
under silk to tickle down my side and smooth my hips. One travels
round towards my butt.

– No underwear, he whispers. Slut.

– Fuck you, I hiss.

He whirls away. He cartwheels to the curtain's edge, stage-left,
and pulls it back to peek around: a glimpse of Joey getting changed,
a ciggy dangling from his lips. Half-naked Joey flicks his circled
thumb and fingers at him, and mouths a silent *tosser!* – mad but
not deranged. As far as Joey's method mania is concerned, we're
past the worst of it at least. His character's a puppy from now on.
It's not him who's the wild beast.

Jack twirls to me again, a dog that knows he's going for his
walk, circling excited between door and leash.

– It won't be long, he says, until we reach the rites and we can
take our vengeance out on him. Let Pierrot pay with his life.

He licks his lips. I think we're lucky Joey is the only one who
packs a knife.

Meanwhile, Don rattles on with all his prattle, trying to convince
the Duke to join the show, give it a go. He flatters and cajoles, he
uses fast talk and slow sell and plain old-fashioned begging. He
uses all his skills of what he calls neurolinguistic programming,
craft of street hypnotists and mind-readers, signals and clues so
subtle that the Duke's not even conscious of the way he's being
led. What with the psychoactives we've been pumping out into
the crowd all night, he's in a quite suggestible state already and,
as Jack keeps everyone else amused with his display of tumbling
dance, I watch the Duke rise from his chair. He nods his head, deep
in the trance.

Behind the throne, Guy stands with Anaesthesia now. She's listening to him but watching Jack and, even as the Duke succumbs, it's seems her sense of who she really is slowly returns. She rolls her shoulders, cricks her neck, adjusts her stance like someone at a party moves their weight from foot to foot, but with each movement she looks less demure, less maidenly. Her feet further apart, her hips uncock. She turns her gaze to me and our eyes lock for a brief second till she closes hers and drops her face. She takes the riding hat off, and unpins her hair. When she looks up again she's staring at the Duke with hate.

Jack snaps his fingers right in front of me. I jump.
— Earth calling Thomas Messenger, he whispers.
Hell, I think. It's Hell, you mean, instead of Earth. And fuck you if I miss my sister. But I nod.
He kicks himself up off a prop. He swings from rigging, a mad monkey pirate revelling in the madness that he's bringing.
— I'll drive him mad, he says, and fill his head with wild delusions. Till his mind is gone completely in confusion. While his senses are his own, we'll never get a woman's dress on him; and, after all his menacing and threats, I want to hear the laughs as he is led in woman's dress all through the city.
Anaesthesia — Phreedom, pretty little Phreedom who grew up, God, so much more than me; who walked out into Hinter's night, her brother and her son both lost, set out to start a raging fight against the angels and the demons, all the archons of the broken Covenant, the dukes of Hell and all their knights; who lost herself in trying desperately to do what's right — shakes out her long red hair. She undoes the top few buttons of her riding dress, brings out a necklace made of chicken-bones and leaves it hanging there for all to see.
— But now I've got to go, says Jack, to make Pierrot pretty in the robes he'll wear, so he'll look oh so fine when he sets out from Hell's halls to play victim to the rage of his own mother, Columbine.
Jack slips back into a dark area of the stage. I watch Don lead the Duke down one side of the hall, and round behind our wagon. Then, Guy at her heels, my little sister Phreedom strides along the facing wall. With all the pseudo-mediaeval setting, she should

really have a sword. But then again, I think, she's less the knight and more the dragon.

– The King of Tears will come to know the Harlequin. The son of Sooth will show his nature in the end, says Jack.

He lights a cigarette, fire glowing on his leather mask.

– A god most terrible, he says, for all his gentleness to men.

Smoke and Mirrors

Slowly, lazily, a vast steel bulk of metal stormcloud blotting out the moon, the rumble of its engines shuddering the ground with visceral thunder, the dreadnought of the skies moves closer to its target. Airbarges swarming round it seem like minnows round a whale, and the ornithopters, smaller still, like pond insects skittering across the surface of the water. As a hundred chi-cannons turn against the Rookery, Joey takes the pillbox from his pocket, clicks it open and pops a white one. They're every bit as good as the Circus assured him they would be.

Jack doesn't even notice him – shit, he doesn't even notice the airpower – as he crouches down over a ragdoll man half-hidden among the fallen sandbags of the barricade. All along the perimeter of the wasted parkland, the sand-bagged trench of mud that used to be a river is strewn with silent gun emplacements, moaning bodies. Joey tries to find some sort of emotional connection with the limp, lolling flesh of his one-time comrades, but there's nothing left to feel.

The trail of lobotomy reaches all the way south to the captured ICI orgone plant just visible between the splintered trees and broken walls. It stretches north too, disappearing with the curve of the river round the Rookery's battlements. Wooden shoring, duckboards, mud and contorted bodies – it's like something out of World War One except these bodies are still alive . . . more or less.

Yes, the word bomb did its job exactly as they said it would, the psychic chain reaction sparking down the line like wildfire. Most of them still have the moment of horror, of realisation, captured on their idiot faces. Joey can feel it buried somewhere in his own mind, that word, that thought, muted by chemistry and his natural defences; he had to learn it in order to carry it to them, after all. It's not so much that he has the mental *armour* to shield him. It's more that, well, if you don't know what hope is, fear has no hold on you.

It's 1979 and the revolution is over. They probably have the bulldozers waiting in the streets beyond the Circus.

Joey pockets the pillbox and takes the chi-gun out of the inside pocket of his black woollen overcoat. There's just the faintest click as he powers it up, raises it at the back of Jack's head.

— All for a briefcase full of adamantium, and a lifetime supply of chemical oblivion.

Joey snaps his psyche back from the fucker's flashback trap, and snaps his arm up to point the gun straight at the bastard's face. It still looks like Jack, but Joey's even more convinced now that it's not. No, Fox has just found himself an agent with a few psyche specialist tricks up his sleeve. He studies the impostor, looking for the little something that the whole illusion hinges on, that little bit of Jack. The leathers and the jackboots look too new . . . no goggles either . . . but even as Joey's trying to work out what it could be, the fake Jack reaches into his pocket and brings out a battered-looking roll-up and a silver lighter. *Bingo.* Jack's Zippo.

— Smoke and mirrors, says Joey. Voudon ghost illusion.

Jack sparks up his cigarette.

— D'ye think?

It's a good one, Joey has to admit. Most psyche specialists couldn't pull off a doppelgänger gig like this even if they had an army of Haitian babaloas working the mojo behind the scenes. He spends at least a second admiring the skill of it, but not much more. He has a job to do, after all.

He lowers the gun just a little before he fires.

— You know, armoured longcoats are fuck all use if you leave them flapping open in the wind, says Joey.

The man is on his knees, supporting himself with one hand resting on the ground in front of him. His head hangs down. Little trails of blood, as dark as oil or ink in this light, dribble from his lips as he coughs up his pulverised insides.

– What? Did you think I was going to fuck around with you all night? Swap witty banter while we chase each other round the park?

Joey crouches down beside this pale imitation of the real Jack Flash. The man gurgles as he tries to answer – the chi-blast probably shattered his sternum along with more than a few ribs, Joey reckons – and Joey puts a finger to his lips and the barrel of the gun to the imposter's temple. From the man's rasping, gasping last attempt to breathe, Joey figures one lung's already collapsed and the other is giving up the ghost. He gives it two minutes before the fucker's suffocated under the pressure of his own internal organs, less if his heart gives in first. Should be just enough time.

– So, let's see who you really are, he says.

He pulls up the man's chin and looks into the desperation of his eyes, so close now that, as subtle and shifting as the psyche is, Joey can feel it, *hear* it, all the turbulent sounds of his dreams, the guttering of dying hope, the hiss of thoughts, denials, king rat, king rat, traitor to everything we've fought for, died for, no, he's thinking, no, not this, no, Joey, no, and the tinkling sounds of ideals shattering like a flowing stream, you bastard, no, all gathering into a roar of river of voices, no, a waterfall crashing down into an abyss of nothing, no, not nothing, never nothing, no where white noise crackles as cosmic radiation dies, no where in the emptiness of vacuum, no, of death, no, entropy, God no, no God, no, nothing, only—

Jack Flash.

Doom.

The gun batteries of the Rookery open fire and ornithopters start to dive out of the sky, swoop down to answer fire with fire, but the dreadnought is turning, because the rebels of the Rookery mean nothing as far as the powers-that-be are concerned. They're nothing against Albion's airforce, nothing against the fucking battalions waiting to march in from the north once their way is opened up. Flies to be swatted.

Joey watches the dreadnought turning and he knows he was right.

– We take the factories and the shipyards, King Finn had said, and we have Kentigern itself. We arm the workers, we arm the *people*, and sure and they'll fookin take back what's theirs by right. All they need is a fookin sign that the time is right.

Joey had laughed. *The people don't fucking want it, mate*, he'd thought. And then he'd realised, as they sat in the Rookery club, drinking and planning revolution, that Finn and Fox, Anaesthesia and Puck, and even Jack *did* want it. They actually wanted freedom. Or power, if you ditch the empty rhetoric. *Power* is what it's all about.

Jack stands up from the brain-fried rebel.

A few of the airbarges break off to fire slicing chi-beams through the stone and metal of the Rookery's defences, but the main fleet is turning, its guns now training on the captured ICI plant where Finn and Anaesthesia are holed up. With the artillery line all flopping in the mud, the plant is open. Jack is turning now, seeing Joey, wondering what the fuck he's doing here, why he's not like the others, and—

Joey levels his gun at Jack's look of utter incomprehension.

Shit, man. What can he say? A few thousand rooks would never have held the city against all of Albion's knights; at least this way the rest of the city might be spared another Purge. Jack would never fucking understand that. None of them will ever understand it. It's a cold judgement, but Joey's always grasped, far more than the others, the way a fascist's mind works, clear of the smoke-and-mirrors illusions of idealism.

So he doesn't say anything.

As the Imperial Chi Industries orgone manufactory, symbol of everything that made Kentigern the Second City of the Empire, explodes under the booming chi-guns of the dreadnought and its fleet, Joey just pulls the trigger.

The Prisoner's Dilemma

– We'll dance all night barefoot in ecstasy, I sing, and throw our heads back to the rain to cool us like a fawn that frisks in green fields of delight, safe from the humans in the bushes of the woods, glad she's escaped the fright, the terror of her flight, the hunters chasing with their nets, the huntsman shouting to his barking hounds as, with a pounding heart and aching limbs, she bounds across the flat ground down around the river's edge as fast as lightning.

I pause. The doors of the castle open up to swallow us, and the wagon rolls inside, off tarmac onto flagstones, under the grid of the first portcullis that's still low enough for me to slap my hand on the cold metal as we pass beneath. It starts to close behind us as the next one rises. There are seven of them in all, each with its own armed retinue of guards in daft anachronistic armour, breastplates and helmets of dull synthe. Not shiny like steel but battleship grey, the alloy of adamantium and iron has no lustre, no sheen; and, after the colour of the city, it makes the soldiers look like grim shades in comparison. But then that's probably how they're meant to look.

I can't deny that it scares the shit out of me. The Duke has some serious defences, and we don't even know how deep my sister's stuck, how far she's bought into his dream. I can guess what he told her, though, the bastard with his mediaeval setting, castles, knights and all those lies – of course he'd have his fantasy of how it came to be, this poor young orphan boy raised in obscurity, a grand quest and a hero's prize. And looking at her with that fire in his eyes, he'd give her just that tiny bit of hope back.

All he had to tell her was this Duke was once a Jack.

– What is true wisdom? Jack prompts.

But I'm thinking of other things. There are a million Jacks, and you had to find the worst of them, Phree. A million? A gazillion, more like. That's what he is, after all, what makes him Jack. Scattered all across the fucking Vellum. Cracked and broken because everyone always wants their Jack to be a hero and he's just fucking crazy enough to try to be all that they want, and so he crashes and burns every fucking time. And I fucking love him for it.

– What better prize . . .

He lies on his back, my Jack, the pages of Guy's script held up before him.

– Come on, spaceboy.

I click my fingers, trying to remember my next line.

– What better prize ... what better prize has heaven placed within our reach, than when our weapons rise in victory over an enemy that we despise, and then they fall? Oh, yes, nobility is the most precious thing of all.

– More *bitter*, Guy calls his directions from below. More *ironic*. Remember, you've followed Harlequin all the way from the East only to be locked up in Pentheus's prison – Pierrot's prison. You've been sweetness and light up till now but this is where you start to show your teeth. You're throwing his warrior ethic back in his face. You're saying maybe might *is* right, but Pierrot doesn't have a bloody clue what he is dealing with.

I nod. We're going under the third gate now.

I always thought of the Vellum as, underneath it all, a sort of blank page on which anything could be written. But what do we end up writing on it? Eternities of deals, pacts of souls and social contracts, so many that in places the scrawl of desires across the Vellum is like a tangled mass of ink, like the crazy graving of the marks on Jack's chest or Guy's scribblings of scripts, all arrows and annotations, scored out and corrected until entirely inscrutable to anyone but him. The bitmites only gave us what we wanted; but we don't always know what we want, I guess.

– The power of the gods, prompts Jack. Fuck, I thought *I* was bad.

– The power of the gods, I sing, moves slow but steady as they lie in wait, in secret, through the march of time, to hunt the godless down, put right those mortal sprites who, in some foolish fancy, underestimate divinity and worship their own senseless pride. It's never right – in theory or in practice – to ignore the ancient ways. Here is a piece of wisdom, offered to us at a bargain price. It comes from myth and history, emerging as a law of nature. This and only this is true: Do unto others as they do to you.

– That's a bit harsh, I say.

I sit down on the edge of the roof, kicking my legs.

– I thought you were the nice guy ... good form and sympathy for the huddled masses of humanity, and a man's a man for a' that.

He beckons me with a finger, and I droopy down onto the driver's bench between him and Don.

– You've heard of the Prisoner's Dilemma? says Guy. You're stuck in a prison where everyone wants snout – tobacco. Do you share yours with anyone you run across, in the hope of making allies, or do you keep it to yourself, even steal it from others at every opportunity?

I shrug.

– What am I in for? I ask.

– Look at it as a puzzle about altruism and evolution. You have a society of free agents stuck in an environment of limited resources; they can either co-operate or compete with other individuals they encounter, share their own stock of 'food', or take what they can get and run. Which tactic works best in the long term? Is it every man for himself until there's nobody left standing? Or if we're all nice to strangers, do we just end up getting taken advantage of?

The wagon trundles to a stop before the fifth gate, and its guards move forward to give our gear a quick once-over. Don jumps down to explain exactly what all of the complex equipment's for. *Oh, that's just for sound effects. A dry-ice generator.*

– Thing is, says Guy, back in the days before the bitmites, someone ran a simulation on it and came up with an answer. If you have agents that just co-operate with anyone, sad to say, they lose out to the nasties. If you have agents that just treat everyone as rivals, though, they lose out as well because in the end they have nobody to look out for them. The actual winning strategy is beautifully simple.

The next gate starts to open as Don climbs back up onto the wagon.

– You meet another agent for the first time, says Guy, you just do to them whatever the last stranger you encountered did to you. You pass it on. Sharing or stealing. Co-operation or competition. You pass it on down the line.

The wagon starts forward.

– I'm not saying that's all there is to human nature. On the contrary. I'm saying that it's *not* about some wired-in way of doing things, some noble sense of honour that drives us to self-sacrifice, or some cold and calculating instinct for self-preservation that ends up with us at each other's throats. You switch strategy. You change your behaviour. You do unto others as they do to you.

– What better prize has heaven placed within our reach than when our weapons rise in victory over an enemy that we despise, and then they fall? Oh, yes, nobility is the most precious thing of all.

The consul and the courtiers look uncomfortable seated around the empty thrones, unsure of how to act now that their Duke and Princess have gone off to join the show. The consul waves a serving boy away, puts down his cup and calls a maid-in-waiting over, sends her to make sure that the Princess is all right. Shit, if this girl walks in on them the whole plan could go tits-up, but there's no way I can warn them.

I sing on, a little louder.

– One man may have more wealth and power than his double. One man who has escaped the crashing waves of violent seas and reached safe haven can be happy in his triumph over trouble. But . . .

I jump down off the stage to intercept the maid-in-waiting, block her way. I smile at her, playing as sweet and innocent as I can; she blushes as I take her hand, draw her into the spotlight. Shy as anything, she drops her eyes. I lean in close to whisper a white lie into her ear and she goes redder still. I'm sure Joey won't mind me telling her he likes the girl.

– There are as many plans and schemes as there are minds, I sing to her. And while one dream ends with one happy man, another only seems to fall apart, a patchwork leather jacket worn too long, worn at the seams.

She pulls free, one hand covering her giggles. I have no choice but to let her go, the consul watching with suspicion now; but as she reaches the backstage I see Guy spot her and come out to meet her, flap a handkerchief out of his sleeve. Thank fuck for chloroform, I think. She might have given the whole show away.

– So it is best to live from day to day, I carry on. The man who lives that way is blessed, is what I say.

Joey pushes at the dark surface of attitude; the posturing, the grin, the wink in the eye, there's a whole network of little signs and signifiers woven into a shell, a spell of Jack, but they're all just image – the way this Jack sees himself, the way he wants others to see him. So, before the poor bastard dies, Joey's going to peel away those lies and illusions, prove to the idiot that underneath it all he's just another runner in the rat race, driven by the same pathetic need and greed as everyone else.

Fuck your glamour, thinks Joey. You're no different to the rest of us.

Joey presses into the bastard's thoughts like a thumb being pressed into an eyeball, squeezing slowly harder and harder.

– Seems like there's creatures loose out there that you don't want to meet on a dark night like this. The Pit is burning and there's looters run amok in the Arcade, a wild hunt riding in the skies over the Rookery. I tell you, folks, I'm watching it right now, and things are bad. I can't say as I've seen so many thopters since the Brixton Massacre, and I don't think they're taking any prisoners tonight. Lock up your daughters, mes amigos, lock up your sons, and keep them safe inside, because it's hell on earth out there and there's no sign of our boy Jack. Jack, if you're out there, now's the time to make your move . . .

A grin spreads slowly across his face, an inscrutable rictus expression, irony or pain, fury or joy, or something else, something completely else. The black holes of his pupils dilate and, peering into the fucker's soul, Joey feels . . . he feels . . . he can't describe it but he reels back from the sudden vertigo, staggers back unthinking as if from the edge of some skyscraper's roof. For the first time in his life he knows he's looking into something more than the shallow animal machinery of human nature. Not something more profound – cause Jack was never that – just something more.

No fucking way.

– We're praying for you, Jack. Some folks are praying to you, I suspect, cause, Jack, you know you've got our deep respect.

*

Joey's will is a cut-throat razor in his hand. He slashes out to slice right through the thin skin round this bastard's soul. He'll carve the fucker open and—

— *Jack, you're just the boy that we've been waiting for, the piper-boy the kiddies and the rats just love to follow, yes, our latter-day Dionysus, our brand new—*

Fucking hollow. Joey drops the man's face, lets the broken body slump down to the ground. His chest is still heaving with his attempts to breathe, to . . . laugh. Jack rolls over onto his back. The blood is streaming from his mouth now, skittering liquid dust, black ink, black oil, black blood of bitmites.

No.

— *But in the end, my friends, who is Apollo? That Olympian god, you know, he started as a little mouse-god in the corn-fields of Attica. A nobody. A nothing. Not a hero but a total zero.*

Pantomime Pierrot

Jack dances out onto the stage.

— Yo, Pierrot, he says, if you're so keen to see what you're not meant to see, to spy on your own mother and her company, to show your passion for bold acting in outrageous fashion . . . then come out! Come out before the palace. Yes, and let us see you clad as a mad woman in a maiden's dress.

Pierrot enters wearing Princess Anaesthesia's riding clothes, the long, green skirt down to the ground, the tunic buttoned right up to his chin, the hood.

— Oh yes, says Harlequin, you are the very image of a daughter of old Pantaloon.

— You are a bull leading me now, Pierrot says. I see a pair of horns grown on your head. Were you an animal before? It's strange; I seem to see two suns, a double image of this town of Themes, this city with its seven gates. Now everything has changed.

The greasepaint smears like cheap mascara as he rubs his eyes.

— And you, he says, *look* like a bull at any rate.

— The god is with you now, says Jack. He hated you before; now he's your mate.

Jack slips one arm around Pierrot's waist to pull him out to centre-stage, all chivalry and charm.

– You see things different now, he says. You see things as they are.

– How do I look? asks Pierrot.

Where, in the last scene, he was playing dazed, now Joey plays Pierrot truly crazed. He pouts and preens.

– Isn't my bearing every bit as fine as any woman . . . even that of my own mother, Columbine?

His fingers twirl a lock of hair that's fallen down across his face.

– I look at you and I see her, says Jack. But wait, your hair is out of place. Just let me tuck it up beneath the hood.

Pierrot looks abashed, shy as a schoolgirl.

– It came loose up in my rooms as I was tossing – whirling – my head here and there in joy.

He giggles.

– I'll take care of that, says Harlequin – [Jack taps his hand away and takes the strands of hair.] – Just hold your head up.

– Am I straightened out now? Joey says. I'm at your mercy here, you know.

Jack tuts and tsks around him like a mother hen – or Mother Goose perhaps, given the panto spectacle that Joey makes, all rouged and lipsticked up. He took a lot of talking into this scene, on the part of Guy. Beneath the batting eyelashes and giggles, I would guess he's not a happy pup.

– Your waistband's loose, says Jack.

He gives a tug that activates a little mechanism underneath the dress, then kneels to fix the hem.

– Your skirts' not hanging properly down at your heels.

As he leans down the audience sees the bawdy jut that pokes the air at Joey's crotch. The fake erection bobs as Jack tugs at the hem of Joey's skirt. The audience hoots at the dirty joke.

– Yes, Joey says, you're right. It's all wrong on the right side – [he says, pointing with his left hand] – but the left side is all right – [he says, now pointing with his right].

He looks at his crossed hands, confused now as to which is which, then holds his left hand up.

– That's right.

– Hold it, says Jack.

He ducks his head under the dress.

– Hmm? With my right or left hand? says Pierrot, looking down. Which way will I fit in more as a member of this band of women?

He reaches down to grab the bulge; it jerks off to one side. He reaches with the other hand; it darts away again, much to the crowd's delight. From right to left, from left to right, each time that Joey reaches for the thing, it darts out of his grasp. He puts his hands upon his hips and scowls, as if oblivious to the audience's laughs.

Then, with a pop, to Pierrot's surprise, the bulge is gone and Jack is out from underneath the dress, a second flute held as his prize. He twirls it, proffers it to Joey.

– Hold it in your right hand. As you walk, raise it in time with your right foot, just so.

He demonstrates, skipping to some internal rhythm. Poor Pierrot, following his lead, has the whole audience in stitches now. But Joey's dancing always was abysmal.

– I have to praise your change of heart, says Jack. Your mind was sick before; it's now exactly as it ought to be.

Pierrot puffs with pride.

– I feel like I could lift a mountain on my back, maidens and all.

– Well, if you wanted to, I'm sure you could, says Jack. The question is whether you should.

Pierrot wraps his arms around a polystyrene boulder.

– Shall we take a lever with us? Or will I just get my shoulder underneath the rock, and pull it up with my bare hands?

– No, says the Harlequin, let's not destroy the homes of nymphs, the haunts of piping Pan.

– Too true. We should not use brute force to overcome these girls. They are already caught in the sweet snares of love. I'll sneak up first and, from the trees, I'l spy on them as if I was a nesting bird. I'll hide myself amongst the firs.

– I'm sure that fate has somewhere set aside for you, says Jack,

257

somewhere to hide. It's for this very reason you should go with caution though. Maybe you'll catch them. Maybe they will catch you first.

The beating of a drum begins, not loud but pounding just enough to drown out any sounds of backstage conversation.

– But, contrary to all your expectations, in the end, says Jack, you'll see that these are moral maidens, and that I'm your one true friend. O, Pierrot, you bear your nation's burden, you alone. The struggles waiting for you are the price of power, of the throne.

– Then lead me through the very heart of Themes, says Pierrot. He puffs his chest.

– I want them all to see I am the only one – the only one of all of them – who has the balls to do what must be done.

He stands there with his arms crossed over his false breasts.

– Then follow me, says Jack. I'll guide you safely there. Another hand will bring you back. And, yes – [he smirks] – you can be sure that everyone will stare.

His tone of voice should set alarm bells ringing.

– Yes, says Jack. You'll be brought back in your own mother's arms.

– That's what I'm going for, says Pierrot. To bring my mother home, I mean, not for the glory. But . . . my mother carrying me? You'll spoil me with the luxury.

– If you want to put it that way, but – [Jack takes Pierrot by the hand] – you do deserve it for the task you're undertaking now.

And exit Harlequin, Pierrot following behind him to the slaughter, like a cow.

No Future

There's no hope in this man, no faith, no dream. Joey looks into his soul and what he sees is . . . nothing.

It's a nothing that he recognises from a childhood growing up in the Rookery, running wild with the razor-kids, sitting on walls and smoking weed, just waiting for the day the Futurists and the fascists finally fired those nukes at each other; listening to Don Coyote's radio show playing 'Anarchy in the UK', just a single signal in the aether now amongst the saturation coverage of shit. And what else is there to do? Because punk, fucking punk, has sold out to the bootboys with their skinheads and their Union Jacks.

It's the nothing that takes root in you when you realise that even nihilism's pointless. No future? So what? So fucking—

— What makes a mouse a man? What makes a man a myth? You wanna know? I'll tell you this. A myth has nothing at its heart but what the rest of us read into it. No secret meaning, no great truth, friends, what you see when you look into it is you. And if a myth is the reflection of your dreams and fears, if Jack the Lad is just a little mad, well maybe what it is, my friends, is there's a little bit of Jack in all of us, both you and me.

It's the nothing that made Joey interested in Guy Fox, more because he had the contacts to score top-grade acid than for any revolution bollocks. It's the nothing that was growing in Joey even as Jack got deeper and deeper into Fox's bullshit, making a name for himself with concrete blocks dropped on militia aircars, Molotovs thrown through pigyard windows. Every fucking riot, he was there; not just Jack now, but Jack Flash, flame-haired poster child of Generation Why. Jack had made rebellion his religion, Joey figured. He'd lost the lack of faith that Joey held to like some jewel, some diamond, cold and clear and sharp. He was sure of it. He was so sure Jack had bought into the lie.

But Joey looks into the nothing at the heart of this Jack and he knows now he was wrong. No, there's a nihilism in there that's as empty and dark as Joey's own heart, more so even.

The fucker lies there, laughing as he's dying, with the answer to Joey's *why the fuck should I care?* shining in his eyes, in his teeth still glinting white even as the black blood trickles from his mouth.

Why the fuck not?

Jack's hand slaps the tarmac of the bridge, reaching up and behind him, reaching for the Zippo, Joey realises, even now trying to play the devil-may-care hero. Light up a fag even if your lungs can't suck the smoke in. His eyes keep closing and opening again, like a dog trying to stay awake.

— I tell you, mes amigos, you can't stop the children of the revolution.

259

You can't stop the spirit of rebellion. You can shoot it, bayonet it, burn its mind out, leave it for dead and bury it in a mass grave with the rotting corpses of a thousand dreamers, and it will still come back. You don't need a city of martyrs, mes amigos, just one Jack.

The blood, ink, oil, bitmites — *bitmites? what the fuck are bitmites?* — the black stuff spreads out around the broken man — *too much of it* — *it isn't right* — and it isn't pooling but trickling in streams, tiny channels that spread out from him like an impact-pattern of cracks on a windshield. A spiderweb. Crazy paving under Joey's feet now.

He steps back, gun raised, but he knows he's aiming at nothing now.

— You think that you can trap your own soul under a decade of fear and greed, two decades, or a century? Try a millennium, mes amigos, try the whole of human history, and you'll still find it there under the foundations of the Empire, that roaring music of the river of blood that's pumping in your veins and thumping in your head.

Like a doorway into the abyss, his mind opens up now all the way. A barrage of anti-aircraft gunfire comes from somewhere in the Rookery but Joey hears it like a sound effect turned low. Distant. Unreal.

— Dream on, you petty tyrants. Let me tell you all a little story about Pentheus, the King of Tears, who tried to trap the god of wine and song . . .

Jack flicks the flap of his longcoat back and Joey's hand trembles as he points the gun at that empty heart under the scarlet shirt with the chi-gun shoulder holster crossing it and—

And there's a stick of orgone-saturated dynamite jammed in the holster, and Jack's opening his fist now, shit, and there's a silver Zippo in it which he opens up with a flick of thumb and, fuck, clicks into flame in one swift move. And Jack, eyes closed, touches the fire to the fuse beside his silent heart, and opens up his arms.

The explosion rips their world apart.

Let Justice Show Herself

And Jack appears up on the wagon's roof, a dancing god of horn and hoof. The lights drop to a single spot on him.

– How strange your path is, Pierrot, he says. It leads to scenes of woe so weird you'll win a fame that reaches high. Reach out your hands, Columbine. You, her sisters, daughters of old Pantaloon, reach to the sky, the sun and moon.

Coyote's trickery projects a scattering of constellations on the ceiling of the hall. Jack throws a hand into the air as if to grab and swing it round. Almost diagonal, one foot kicked out behind to balance him, he flips the move into a twist, a sort of angled spin, a tap-dance step, I think, or Cossack thing. The drum keeps time and, as he reels the constellations start to wheel, slow at the start but gradually faster. Gold and silver discs of sun and moon flash past, in time with Jack and with the drum. The cycling signs of days and months, of seasons, years and eons, turn. It seems the circling wheel of time itself, of fate.

Then Jack stops suddenly. The stars stop in their track.

– The end to which I bring this young and foolish king, is great. The victory will be Harlequin's, says Jack. It will be mine. I'll say no more. You'll see the rest in time.

– Run to the hills, I sing, swift dogs of madness howling in the night. Run to the hills where Columbine and all the daughters of old Pantaloon revel in mysteries and rites. Howl at the moon!

And lights come on behind the wagon. Don has dropped the screen again and shadows dart across it, shapes too quick to see, just the suggestion of an arm, a head, a whirling sword, a wing outspread. A human form with antlers and a ruptor raised. A lion's slashing paw.

– Excite the Maidens into a wild rage, I sing.

The shadows flit across the screen, a silhouette of bovine horns out to the left, three dancing things with bestial heads.

– Yes, let his mother catch first sight of Pierrot her son in drag, dressed as a slag to spy among them, peeping from behind some boulder, through a tree split by a lightning bolt. Her call will raise all of the Maidens.

A shadow points in accusation. Amped and modulated by Coyote's tech, the voice of Phreedom shakes the hall.

– Who is this son of Pantaloon come speeding to the hills to spy on us, my pack? Whose spawn is this?

261

I hear her whisper after it, as well.

– You're not my Jack.

The shapes of shadows swirl into confusion, suddenly resolve, a man in woman's dress, his arms spread wide by chains. He struggles, flails from side to side. His horned, winged captors hold him tight. The chaos under the thin skin of everything, Guy calls this scene. The creatures of Pierrot's id. The creatures of the night.

– Let Justice show herself, I sing, her sword in hand, to thrust it through the throat of Aching's son, that godless, lawless child of dust!

The creature caught behind the screen gives out a muffled shout. He thrashes, pulls against his chains and lashes out. It looks like Guy and Don are having trouble holding him.

– He was not born of woman's blood, but spat from some gargantuan lion's lips. With wicked heart and lawless rage, with mad desire and frantic aim, he comes to meddle with his mother's holy games, defies the spirit of the pack. He thinks to tame with his weak arm a strength untameable as yours.

A power as untameable as Jack.

– Let Justice show herself, I sing, her sword in hand, to thrust it through the throat of Aching's son, that godless, lawless, child of—

Dust flies up beneath Jack's feet as he jumps down from the wagon to the flagstones, landing by my side. I sneeze.

– Gesundheit.

– Dankeschön.

We look around. There's no other exits from the prison courtyard of a square, just the portcullis of the seventh gate closing behind us now, its distant glint of daylight disappearing as the outside doors swing shut, just that and the wall to either side of it all chains and tracks going up, it seems, forever, lit by torches for as far as I can see. It's a vertical terminal of funiculars, caged metal carriages all topped with gears and cogs like clockwork cable cars, some no larger than an apartment building elevator, others built to carry carts or larger cargoes. There are counterweights the size of small buildings, loading platforms, ramps and cranes.

Soldiers move in around us, and a nod of the head among the looming guards shepherds us towards one of the mid-size cages. Guy drives the wagon in past a soldier's waving arm, *that way, keep it moving now*. A dozen or so of the soldiers follow Jack and me into the cage, flanking our wagon as an armed escort.

The grilled gate slides shut with a clatter, and the cage's gears grind into action. Deafening clangs and shrieks of metal. The whole cage shudders as it starts to rise.

Jack presses his nose between the bars, looking up into the height of the grand shaft, down at the floor falling away below us, awed by the fantastic artifices of eternity. I take a seat on the running-board beside Joey, frowning as he reads through Guy's script, shaking his head and muttering about how if we just stuck to simple themes for once, maybe dealt with fucking human nature for a change, then maybe it would save us all a lot of pain. He wishes Fox would just leave the big ideas to others, I guess, and, as we chunter slowly up towards the Duke's grand castle in the sky, I sort of see his point.

Me, I've always found more fun in living life from day to day and night to night, in finding truth not in eternity but in the minutes and the hours. Fuck, isn't that a finer goal to strive for than to live forever in some ivory tower?

I pick a piece of fluff from Joey's shoulder, flick it away.

– You want to help me with my lines? I say.

He shrugs OK.

Thing is, what Joey doesn't get is that it shows much *more* respect for the divine to say *the fuck with all these lousy laws* – at least I think that's what Monsieur Reynard is trying to say. But Joey, our eternal nihilist, is, of all of us, I guess, the true idealist.

I hand him my copy of the script, pointing to where I am, and he settles back against the wagon's side.

– Now, Harlequin, I sing, show us your mocking grin. Show us your hundred heads, the bull's horns, and the hair of snakes, the fire of your lion's breath. Come! Throw the deadly noose about the hunter of your pack as he swoops on the Maidens gathered yonder.

Jack turns back to grin at Joey and myself. The cage rolls on up the great shaft. Jack the Giant-Killer, I think, going up his mechanical beanstalk to slay the tyrant in the clouds, rescue the

princess. Christ, I think, maybe the Duke *is* just another Jack, a
bit of him, a someday might-be dream of him thrown out into the
Hinter, living in a giant sandcastle built to be kicked down.

And I still fucking love him.

Shit, man, maybe we're all just different dreams of Jack.

Pierrot Is Dead

– O house of Satan, once the greatest of all Hell!

A hand appears stage-left, slaps round a pillar, leaving bloody
smears as Guy Fox staggers on, his shepherd costume, face and
hands all crimson spatters.

– House of the old prince who sowed the serpent's crop, he
wails, of men born in the fields!

He sobs and grabs my arm, leans in to whisper that it's done. I
nod. He turns, hamming his horror.

– I may be a slave, but still . . . a good slave's heart breaks at
his master's grave.

– What's this? I sing. News of the pack?

– The son of Aching, Pierrot, is dead.

– My king, I sing, my Harlequin! – *[My Jack.]* – At last you
show yourself in all your might.

– Woman, gasps Guy, what are you saying? You *delight* at my
poor master's pain?

– What? Do I sing my joy in a foreign tongue? Pierrot's dead?
Good! I no longer fear his chains.

– Do you think Themes so poor there's not a man who'll—

– I'm a stranger in this land, I cut him off. It's Harlequin I
answer to, not Themes' demands—

– To glory in his murder is a crime, and this of all things will
not be forgiven.

I snort with derision.

– Tell me, I say. Tell me how he died, that scheming villain.

The homesteads of the land of Themes behind them now, Elixir and
the Basilisk splash through the Stream of Sophists, and begin the
climb up Zithering's heights, the stranger striding out ahead to

guide them to the scene, glancing over his shoulder now and then to smile at them with glinting eye and teeth that gleam. Basileus or Bacchus, poor Elixir isn't sure which of the two deserves more fear, and why exactly he is here, but he has no say in it, of course. So, just as the Basilisk follows the stranger, so Elixir tags along behind the Basilisk—

Basileus, he thinks. Gods, don't forget to use the proper word or the Basileus – *bastard basilisk basileus* – will have him flogged when they get back to town. It's not as if he'd be the first. His Misery is not exactly known for mercy.

They follow the trickling water of a brook through a nook in a rock wall, and Elixir listens to the tread of each footfall as they pick their way beneath the pines, light on the bed of needles, his own breath held tight, released in whispers. They stop in the shade of shrub, crouched down to look without being seen, and gaze into a grassy glade.

The Maidens sit there busy with the work of joy. Some wind fresh curling ivy-sprays around their wands, while others sing hymns to each other, to the rapture of the pack. Like colts let loose from the yoke of a carved chariot, Elixir thinks, they have no cares.

The stranger is smiling at the sight. Elixir is nervous at his own furtive delight. The Basilisk just glares.

– Stranger, he says, I cannot see the pack from here. I'll have to find some higher ground or climb a tree to see their shameful acts.

Elixir sees the stranger work a wonder then. He pulls a vine out of the ground and, like a whip, he snaps it through the air and round a dead tree's splintered tip. He draws it down lower and ever lower to the dust, this dead tree; stripped of needles, bark and branches, little more than ragged, jagged trunk but this man bends it like Accordion strings his bow, so smooth, so easy; or like the old philosophist Hairclippers drawing a curve of wheel in a slow line of stick in sand.

So the stranger draws the tree down, bends it to the earth by some inhuman power; and it does not break. The stranger tells the Basilisk to hold on to the highest branches near the tip, then lets it straighten up into the sky, lets out the whip, hand over hand, so slow, so careful, so as not to shake Elixir's master from his grip. It rises like a flag over a battlefield, or like some amphitheatre's hoisting trick of rope and pulleys built so that, at the climax of the show, some god can enter from the sky.

But now the Basilisk up on his perch, this lofty throne, is seen far better by the Maidens down below than he sees them, and, Oh, as soon as he is seen, Elixir thinks . . . He turns to voice this fear but finds the stranger disappeared, and now Elixir feels the terror of a dream out of control. And from the sky there comes a voice, the voice of Dionysus it would seem. The sound of thunder, a drum roll.

– Maidens, I bring the man who tried to mock us and our mystic rites.

A shaft of sun between the clouds picks out the tree, a fiery pillar rising bright between the heaven and the earth.

– Take vengeance on him, says the light.

Don yanks a knot loose and the sandbags drop, and rising from behind the wagon, bound like a queer Christ upon his cross, the victim in his riding dress, face hidden by the hood, appears. The skirt, once green, is stained with blood still streaming from his wounds; it flutters as he struggles. I can hear his screaming even through the gag. His arms bent back over the crosspiece of a ruptor, bodice open, showing his scarred bloody chest, he rises like some knight speared on a pike, like some unholy banner of unholy war. Jack, crouched upon the wagon's roof, howls his delight.

I look out on the audience, the mix of fear and thrill upon their faces. Serfs and courtiers who know their places, maybe they don't know what's going on, so maybe they're still thinking this is just a show, a song. But somewhere in their dreams, I think, this is a scene that part of them desires; and will desire as long as they live in these Havens built on fear. The Vellum is a harmony of opposites, of tensions, good and evil, order versus chaos, and the Troupe d'Reynard . . . well, we all have to play our parts. As long as there are Dukes of Hell, there will be those like us, the rogues and rebels, drunks and junkies, thieves and tarts, and the true king, unbound because unrecognised, my saucy Jack, my Jack of Hearts.

– This is the ritual death of reason, Guy explains as we ride through the doors into the hall where all the lords and ladies of this corner of eternity are gathering, the serfs and courtiers ruled by their sorrow for their own lost lives, trapped in this fantasy of reason's power over sin. And Joey grumbles that we'll never win, and Don is gruff and sceptical – just how reliable is Jack? Guy worries over every line, each scene, each act, and I complain about soft skin but all the time I'm watching Jack. And Jack just grins:

– The play begins.

So now Jack dances as the Harlequin, as Dionysus, god of tragedy and comedy, of epics and romances. With Guy and Joey at my side, I watch him pirouette, arms wide.

– Take vengeance on him! Jack roars as he whirls to point up at the Duke, our surrogate Pierrot, the head who rules this body politic of dreamers, raised now on his cross before them like the head of, well, the hero of that *Scottish play* up on its spike. We'll give them heroes, if that's what they want.

This isn't just another rescue of some princess, though. This is a fucking revolution of the psyche.

Errata

Something Like the Truth

– No, says Reynard, it won't work.

– Do it.

– But Monsieur Carter, surely . . .

Reynard looks over to the Irishman for support but he's out cold in the armchair now, empty wine bottles at his feet. In this last year, it has been harder on him with each passing month. Even drunk, the visions are too much to bear, and Reynard can hardly blame him for his wretched state. A million Polish workers taken away on trains at German gunpoint to join Czech civilians, to be worked to death. Copenhagen and Oslo taken by Hitler's forces. Bombs aimed for the bridges of Rotterdam falling on the city centre. British troops evacuated from Norway. Germans marching into Brussels and Antwerp. The British falling back from Boulogne and Calais.

Dunkirk.

They have a week before the Nazis enter Paris now, a week to stop it all, to find *some* turning point that they can change to rewrite history; but Finnan is a wreck and both of them . . . they've been almost without sleep now for the last four months, both Reynard and Carter, working round the clock just to transcribe the Irishman's mad ravings, the could-bes and the might-have-beens, pinning timelines, glossaries and indexes to the walls, planned alterations scribbled in margins. There are drafts and redrafts written in normal ink on normal paper everywhere; scratched over or scored through, the paper crumpled up and thrown away in despair, a novel's worth of gravings in this madman's language litters the floor of Reynard's study. *Mon Dieu*, they've tried to map not just the history of their world but its permutations also and, for all of this, they're still no nearer to an answer.

Reynard picks up the bottle of ink, the black and swirling fluid that the Englishman produced from God knows where . . . But no,

Reynard knows all too well where it came from; he's seen the cuts on Carter's chest. It's just . . . what kind of creature has black blood? But no, he doesn't want to know. He puts the ink back in its place to one side of the desk, as if in ordering his tools he might somehow put *everything* in order: history; reality; his life.

— We have to try, says Carter. We have to take the risk.

— And what exactly are you risking, Monsieur Carter? says Reynard. Do you have a wife and child? Do you have anyone you love?

Anger flashes in the Englishman's eyes for a fraction of a second, anger, pain and guilt, and Reynard knows his words have cut him deep as any little scalpel drawn across his chest. It's not the first time that this man has bristled at his talk of family, of loved ones.

What exactly made you join the army, Captain Carter? thinks Reynard. *Just what exactly are you fighting?*

— If we can bring both Britain and America into the war in Spain, says Carter, Christ, an allied victory there . . . or before that, if we could stop it happening, destroy fascism before it even—

Reynard throws his arms up.

— No! It will not work. Look . . .

And he traces through the sigils of dark logic *here* and *here* on this scrap of paper on this wall, from there to *this* one, see, from victory in Barcelona and Madrid to Gibraltar's fall, and on and on, the bitter truth that Carter can't accept. Yes, it has to work, it has to, but it doesn't. Murder Stalin. Kill Hitler in the trenches while he's still a private. Have the Turks change sides in 1917. There's an infinity of alterations they could make, and somehow, always, there's this page that does not change. This one infernal set of symbols that remains inviolate no matter what they do.

The Englishman rams a cigarette into an overflowing saucer, one of a dozen makeshift ashtrays round the room, Anna's best Dresden china.

Anna . . . He had to beg her to stay again yesterday, her suitcase already packed, Tomas holding her hand as they stood in the doorway, and the poor boy crying because of course it's all beyond his infant understanding. All he knows is that Mama is angry with Papa and his new friends, and all the shouting scares him, wakes him in the night, the voices raised in fear and anger. Reynard can't blame her, and he's tried to tell her ... *something*, something like the truth. The men are British agents. What they're doing is important, so important, and they need his help. And why him? *Why us? Why you?*

– What choice do we have? says Carter.

Reynard studies Carter as he stalks the room, as riven, driven as the notes strewn all around them. Like some lion avatar of all this chaos, Reynard thinks. The pile of angel skin sits on the desk so neat and orderly, in contrast, that it almost seems the book itself is what they're up against, some demon sentience lurking hidden in the ink. A grim, inhuman tyrant known as truth against which they are little more than animals caged for an emperor's sick delight. Carter remains untamed, still roaring, straining at the bars, but Reynard ... all he thinks of now is Anna and Tomas. If there's really no way out should he be wasting time with this mad scheme? *Non.* He is an *imbécile. Un crétin.*

Carter tears a sheet down from the wall and slams it on the desk, one of the trial drafts that Reynard knows will only result in the same horror that they're trying to remove. Worse, actually.

– This one, says the Englishman. Just do it.

He stares in silence at the man, and—

He sees the death of reason in his eyes. God, no. And then he's grabbing desperately for the top sheet of angel skin, but Carter's thrown the chair right back and Reynard hits the floor. Balled notes scatter under his outflung arms. He flounders, rolls and scrambles to his hands and knees, only to feel ribs crack beneath the boot that sends him sprawling.

Carter's opening the bottle now, as Reynard, gasping, pulls himself upright. The study door is open and Anna standing in the frame. Not now. Reynard just yells at her and throws himself at Carter. Black ink spatters, burning on his hand, as Carter staggers to the side, throws out an arm for balance. Another grab to clamp a hand round Carter's wrist, to prise the bottle from his tilting, twisting grip. He yanks it free, but God, it's black fire as it spills across his palm and Reynard screams. He drops the bottle, tries to catch it; it goes tumbling, trails of black ink spilling out into the air. The bottle thumps down on the desk, ink everywhere.

He hears the curses of the Englishman, Anna's screams, Tomas crying, Finnan's roar, but he can't even see them at the edges of his vision. All that Reynard can look at is this splatter-pattern of black blood on angel skin, a dark blotch on the vellum of his century.

The Howl of Its Rage

The room roars with the sound of thunder, waterfall or hurricane, a whirling wall of noise that's wild with lashing whips of air, tendrils of sound, of *something*, whipping at my sleeves, my hair, my very breath, as if the noise itself is trying to gain purchase, trying to drag me in, make me a part of this monstrous creation. Back flat against the bookcase, fingers clutching to an edge of wooden shelf, I know that what I'm trying to hold on to is life and sanity, my soul itself. The room roars as if it is alive. My God, it carves the very air into a form, invisible but touching, trailing liquid, cold, across my skin, drowning my pitiful shouts. The candlesticks roll round the pentacle upon the floor and, here and there, flames lick the floor and walls, the books in the bookcases. On the desk, the pages of the book flick back and forth as if some spirit seeks some reference in it on a page long since forgotten – only the certainty of an answer left, and fury at its inability to find it. With its voice made from a hundred rivers or the river of a hundred voices, the room roars like a thwarted beast. Is this what gods are made of, I wonder, surfaces of sounds of souls? Is this the god my brother's called down on us, sucking in the souls of Röhm's slaughtered inner circle to give it substance?

Is this the howl of its rage?

– For God's sake, no!

He stands there in the centre of it, screaming invocations unintelligible amidst the havoc all around, the dagger raised in his right hand. He stands in scattered light that blossoms from the jewel in his left hand, the light of all those little fires refracting and reflecting all around him like the air itself were crystal, each flame with its own partner in a shadow skittering across the walls, the shelves, the darkwood panels and the forest-green of Father's favourite wallpaper. A pagan bonfire in the depth of pines at night. A blizzard whirling snow around some Loki as he calls the spirits of Walpurgisnacht itself to him, to him. Or of the Night of the Long Knives.

It is a centrifuge, I think, as much as a vortex: souls being stripped apart, the light sucked in towards the centre, while the dark smears out around the room. But as ghost fingers clutch at me, as voices gibber in my mind, I start to hear the fear that's in the flitting shadows, terror underneath that rage. It is the sound of men being dragged out of their beds and out into the garden, naked, cowering, as the bullets punch into the backs of their heads. It is the sound of children crying in their beds in the night because something is wrong with them that they can never fix and so they must be braver, better, stronger, fiercer. It is the sound of these men, these thugs and murderers, being stripped of all that glory, all that blinding fire. And that darkness scattered round the room, I realise, is not the evil in them. No, it is the weakness, the self-pity and the shame, the dark and hidden shame of their humanity.

While the glory of their atrocities gathers around my brother.

– Johann, for the love of God.

Before him, on all fours, the young lad Thomas crouches like a dog before its master, like an acolyte before the statue of his god; and something gold and black and iridescent blue-green, every hue under the sun – a beautiful wraith, a glorious, hideous angel; something human-shaped but alien, utterly inhuman – hangs above them in the air, as still as death.

I scream his name.

He glances over his shoulder, smiling and saying something, the casual grinning comment of a child saying, *Look at this, look here, isn't this great? Look what I've done.* But his words are as lost as my own, drowned in the torrent of noise. Blasted back against the books by this dervish, at the same time I can feel it try to suck me in towards the centre, and I stand there torn, transfixed, with terror urging me to flee, but with a mad drive to leap right into the abyss almost as overpowering.

I have to stop this. For the sake of all that's good I have to stop this, break the circle, break the ritual, break the sickening chain of moments that can only lead to one place. Do it, God in Heaven, man, just do it. Stop him. Drag him back from this terrible splendour that he's loosed. He raises the knife to shoulder height and from the fire in my brother's eyes I know, I know what he's about to do. But crucified by my own fear and awe, all I can do is watch in horror as my brother drops into a crouch. The dagger falls and slices, under and around, and up again, blood spraying in its wake. And as the boy's slit throat gouts blood into the whirlwind, to be blown into a mist of red, I watch his body slump, dragging that strange aetheric creature down. I watch my brother stepping forward, dagger circling his head, slicing the air and gathering it around him.

Blood sprays across my face, burning and blinding, and the struggle in my body suddenly dissolves as something breaks within me. My will or my fear? I don't know. Am I trying to halt this horror or to be a part of it? God, I don't know. I have no idea what deep compulsion I am answering. I only know I'm stepping forward into the storm, to where my brother stands … and where the creature stands, in the same space, limb around limb as a ghost image superimposed over another. A hundred images, a thousand. It wears his SA uniform one second, the black trenchcoat of a Futurist the next, the flying goggles of an airman, khaki denims torn and bloody, a scarf around his neck – all checks and tassels now, and then white silk – black woollen balaclava, British army cap, the jacket of some drummer boy. It wears a hundred different uniforms with glittering insignia, the Iron Cross and other medals I don't recognise, a hundred different uniforms with bullet holes and rips and tears.

I step into the pentacle of chaos and strike out, my open palm across his face as ineffectual as my wordless cry. He smiles at me, beatific and bemused, even as I grab his bloodied hand to wrest the dagger from him, hurl it down and to one side. It's too late now. It's done.

The bloodstained patchwork demon god of war, dressed in the armour of all those it's claimed, wraps itself around us, through us, in between us and within us. I can feel it trying to push me from him, claim him for its own, but I hold onto him. I clamp my hand onto his shoulder, leaning in and cursing, screaming in his face. It tries to drown his answer in this river of voices that our souls are being swept into now, carried away and lost among the maelstrom of new memories and ancient knowledge, but I can hear it as a whisper in my head.

It's too late, Fox.

And I can hear the creature bonded to him howling. I can see it struggling to get its fingers into his, to use his arms to slap my hand away, to use his mouth to spit its rage at me. I don't belong here. No, I'm not like him. I'm not a warrior, not a soldier, and I don't belong here. I don't belong to it. It has no hold over me.

And for all his madness, all his blind, brutal delusions of the warrior ideal, I'm still Jack's brother. I think it hates me for the hold I have on him. I only pray it's right.

Return of the Columbine

God Save Us from Our Dreams

I wake up in a ditch that runs alongside the winding country road between the village of Strann and our family house. I pull myself out of the grassy mire, hardly thinking as I pat at my ruined clothes, wipe off this splatter of blood, brush at that streak of soot. I fiddle with a rip in my trousers as if, by pinching it together with my thumb and forefinger, it might magically mend itself. Of course it doesn't and after a while I abandon that, start wiping at the mud all down my right side with a pocket handkerchief, succeeding only in smearing it with my ineffectual dabs.

Everything stinks of smoke.

Around a bend of hedgerow and beyond the thicket of oak and pine that walls the estate, a thin and solitary trail of dark grey rises into the pre-dawn. Günther must be up already, getting the fires stoked throughout the house, ready for Father to come down for his breakfast and then disappear into his study before the rest of us have even risen from our beds. I have the strange notion that the smoke is actually the smouldering remnant of a terrible blaze. But that is absurd, of course.

I stagger down the road towards the village. Herr Heidelberger's inn is only a short walk from here, and it wouldn't be the first time that I've borrowed a clean suit from him. I simply can't go home in this shambolic state; Mother would be horrified and Johann would give me such a ribbing. *Johann?*

Herr Heidelberger stands in the empty barroom. Why is he looking at me that way?

– Von Strann, I am saying, confused by his question.

He has his photograph of Hitler on the wall behind the bar again, I see. Another new recruit for Futurism, I suppose. Strange, though; he seemed so bitter about Hitler's betrayal of fascism.

– Your name is Johann von Strann? he's blathering.

– No, I say. *Reinhardt* von Strann. My brother is Johann. But you ...

I tail off. I realise I am ... not myself. Still woozy from the night before, it seems, I must be babbling, incoherent.

– And you live in the big house?

Frau Heidelberger pushes her husband to the side, haranguing him for grilling this poor stranger. Can't he see the man's in shock? She clucks around me. Am I all right? Am I injured? Was I in an accident? She probes my hair with her fingers like some amateur phrenologist reading the bumps. Did my car come off the road? *Go call the doctor, Werner.*

– I don't own a car, I say.

– There's not a sign of any car, says the policeman to Dr Volkaert.

I shake my head. I'm trying to explain again that there *was* no automobile accident but the policeman's talking to Herr Heidelberger now about a fire up at the old place. Do they mean the house? I ask. Is everyone all right?

– Gypsies, do you think? Herr Heidelberger's saying. They were camped there all last summer. Wouldn't have thought there was enough in that old shell to burn.

The house just seems so empty these days, I explain to them, just Günther now and the few staff that ... Wait. The brandy *is* helping to clear my head. Günther's gone as well. My dear mad brother let him go.

– Johann, I say. There was a fire? Johann was ... I was going to visit him. I was going to ...

Herr Heidelberger's pushing me back down into my seat – *Relax, sir, just relax* – and Dr Volkaert and the constable talk now in hushed tones about hospitals, concussion and delirium, and Dr Volkaert's saying, no, he's never heard of anything like this; amnesia he's seen, but not like this. Head traumas can have strange effects though, yes, so best to get a specialist to look at him. It's not his own blood, you know.

I realise they have no idea who I am, not one of them (I should get out of here), not Heidelberger, even though I virtually kept the man in business through my younger years (I should get out of here), not Volkaert who delivered me (I should get out of here), and not the constable who should certainly have heard of the old baron's wayward son. I should get out of here. I'm just a stranger to them, filthy with mud and the blood of . . .

Oh, dear Christ.

A river of voices starts to roar inside my head.

Reynard looks puzzled.

– My name is Reynard Cartier. I'm not sure what you mean.

– Not Reinhardt von Strann? says Pickering.

He can't help the amused tone in his voice as he crosses the room, takes his cap off and lays it on the desk. There's no need to stand on ceremony here. He sits down, shaking his head, gives Reynard a look that says, *I'm sorry about all this nonsense.*

– What *are* you on about? says Reynard.

– I know. I know, he says. Please, humour me. I know this is absurd, but we have an informant who claims your name is Reinhardt von Strann, that you're a German.

Reynard laughs.

– How long have you known me, Joseph?

Pickering throws his hands up. Of all the people to be fingered for a Futurist agent . . . this has to take the biscuit. The man's a bloody hero for the intel he brought back on his escape. Christ, Pickering was with MacChuill as they sat there feeding the Frenchman paper and pen, watching him draw map after map after map. Munitions dumps, factories, barracks, anti-aircraft batteries.

And some bloody halfwit fingers him for this Guy Fox character.

– I know, he says. Look, between you and me . . .

Pickering tries to find the right words. The Circus is chang-ing since the 'Peace'; Berlin may be flattened but there's still

Moscow, and a new breed of agents are coming into MI5 to fight this colder war of quiet moves in the shadows, in the no-man's-lands between East and West. It has to be done, of course; there's no question that Britain's security demands a firm resolve. But it's getting a little . . . irrational for his liking; just the other day they had him interview this mathematician who worked at Bletchley during the war – suspicious behaviour, secret meetings and all that. Turns out the chap's a queer, broke down in tears and stutters after just half an hour. That's considered high risk these days, open to blackmail. Surveillance recommended, house arrest discretionary.

– It's just . . . some of these new chaps are a little zealous, says Pickering. If it were up to me, old chap, he says . . . but orders are orders. It's only a few questions – shouldn't take too long.

Reynard shrugs.

– Do you mind if I smoke? he says.

– Not at all, says Pickering. Light?

– Thank you. Where were we?

Half Magdalene and Half Centurion

– There's not a single bird cry in the glade. Even the leaves of grass hang still, under a hushed and empty sky. But every maiden's on her feet behind the Princess Anaesthesia, Phreedom, yes, our Columbine, our queen. We peer ahead, uncertain. It would be so neat if it *is* his voice that we hear? It would be peachy keen.

– Just shut the fuck up, sisters, Phreedom hisses. Let me listen.

One of the girls gives her a strange look and Phreedom taps at the tattoo on her arm. The girl gives a wry smile and nods her understanding. Nanite narrators for your every action. They all admire her all right, but nobody *envies* Phreedom.

– The voice echoes. Now we daughters of old Pantaloon are sure it is our Jack, Iacchus Bacchus, spirit of the pack, that calls. And so we start. We dart in haste through flooded valleys, over giant standing stones, race on towards our love, inspired by the spirit of his madness, swift as doves.

She splits them as they run and crouch and run and crouch. Four this way, four that. She's moving forward, heading for the cover of a rock, when the blast turns grass beside her feet to dust.

– Down!

Phreedom hits the ground and rolls, comes up with her ruptor already raised. The sniper angel, perched up on a high branch of a fir tree, takes one look at the sheer number of them and scrabbles for a clear branch to take off from. Silvery-steel wings spread wide. *No fucking way.*

– Hailfire! she shouts. Nail that fucker to the wood!

The charges hit the angel's wings like old-school dumdums, like the rapid-fire staccato of Kalashnikovs or Uzis, too light to penetrate his synthe armour but enough to tear thin wings to shreds. He grabs onto a branch to stay upright, dropping his own weapon, and she flicks a thumb across her ruptor's switch. Long bolts streak at him like tracers through the air now. Others flick their ruptors to boltfire, ripping limbs off the tree, making the angel dance under the sheer force of the assault. It's good target practice, but it's fuck-all use. He may be helpless, hopeless, up there, but he's out of reach.

She raises a hand, stands up. The ruptors fall silent. She takes her sighting.

– Aim for the base of the tree, she says.

– Come gather round, my pack, and grab the tree.

And little sister Phree swings up onto the wagon's roof, stands underneath the rigging where her one-time captor hangs, half Magdalene with her red hair now loose and wild, and half centurion in the Duke's own breastplate, worn over the biker's jacket that I gave her, shit, when she was still a child. The Duke stills for a second on his cross, then starts to thrash again.

– We'll catch this beast who thinks he's sitting tight, she says. He will not spread the secrets of the rites of Harlequin.

The bitmites rise out of the shadows, swarm across the rig, a thousand hands of darkness. Metal groans as they tear at its base. I shuffle back, hoping that Phree and her bitmites aren't going to bring the rigging crashing down on top of all of us. But, no, they scour the metal here, devour it there, like loggers using the angle of a cut to shape a tree's fall.

The mock Pierrot crashes down on his high throne, to the audience's screams and his own muffled moans. He knows his hour has come. She tears his hood off so that he can see her face, so he can that she's no mother but a priestess now. For a second though I almost think that she might spare him, as she reaches out to touch his cheek, to wipe a tear.

– Mother.

The voice is Joey's, from offstage, relayed into the speaker jammed between the Duke's teeth, underneath the gag.

– It's your own son Pierrot, says Joey Narcosis. Me, the child you bore in Aching's halls. Have mercy, Mother. Don't you see?

Under the gag, the Duke begins to whine.

– Don't murder your own son for any sin of mine.

I imagine this bastard using every trick of Cant that's in the book, the first time round. Look, honestly, look in my eyes, look in my soul. You're not deceived. I'm what you're looking for, your Jack. Believe. All that you have to do is take my hand. Come back. With me.

I think of all these Dukes, building pipe-dream Havens for the souls who lost their selves out in the Hinter after Evenfall. I guess it's what they've always offered, though. Locked gates. High walls.

Phreedom begins the bloody deed. His own sword rises in her hand, over his head. And falls.

An Eternity of Second Chances

The angel scrabbles on the ground. He scrambles away on all fours up the slope of scree, and Phree takes a few bounding steps to grab him by the blond rag of his hair. She almost tears his head right off his shoulders as she yanks him back.

– It's me, he's screaming. It's Jack.

She drags him back down the slope by his hair and plants herself on him, knees on his upper arms, the talons of her right hand at his throat. His blue eyes look so *right*, so much like the eyes of the child she once cradled, crooning to him in that stinking alley of New York with the heroin in her veins letting her sink into that blue, that beautiful blue, an ocean of anaesthesia where it didn't matter that the world was falling apart, it didn't matter that the Evenfall was sweeping in to turn the cities into nightmares torn by angels, demons. Just as long as she had Jack and just as long as she could go from fix to fix, they'd be OK. The Covenant was broken and the bitmites swept across the world and Thomas was lost and Seamus disappeared, but she had Jack. They could escape it all, just run away into forever.

And then they came, through the white noise hiss of the bitmite blizzard, wearing clean suits or synthe armour, army khakis or police uniforms – Social Services, UN peacekeepers, CTC agents. She didn't know who or what they were – in the DT shakes of the poisoned Vellum, maybe they were all of those things, or something deeper that could manifest itself only in those known forms – but they were taking her Jack away from her, and her speech was too slurred with junk to use the Cant against them.

She doesn't know how long she sat there.

– Ur ye a'right, missus?

He'd said his name was Don, the young man who had found her shivering in the alley and attached himself to her – or her to him. They'd walked out of New York together amongst the horde of evacuees on foot, made a break for it together when the rumoured camp came in sight – an angel with a ruptor among the sentries at the gate; they didn't want to go there, she'd said; and Don had simply nodded, trusting her. Hiding in the snowy wilderness of pine barrens, he'd held her as she shivered the junk out of her system. Cold turkey in the cold winter. The cold Hinter.

She'd watched Don grow up as they travelled together, further and further out into the Vellum, watched him grow up and grow old, grow into the eyes that had always seemed to hold this wisdom beyond their years. In the end, he'd gone as well, though, ready to lay down his life for fifty slave girls that they'd rescued in a fold of the Vellum that was all too comfortable with the idea of lords and masters. He never made it to the rendezvous, and she never found out what had happened to him, just like she never found out what had happened to Jack.

Phreedom looks down into the angel's pleading eyes, and she wants so much to just sink into that blue again. It could be him. It could be.

Time flickers and she knows she's on a cusp. She's often wondered if déjà vu comes from your life reversing itself, playing itself over again to some point where you made the wrong decision the last time. Time in the Vellum is complex, convoluted. Maybe in that dreamtime you get an eternity of second chances.

– It's me, says the angel, this would-be Duke of Hell on Earth.

She spits to one side and closes her eyes, feels them rolling up in the sockets; she doesn't listen to the angel's pleading voice, or to the voice of her own reason, just lets the moment, the passion, the inner truth of it possess her. Then she takes his left hand in her right and stands, planting a foot on his chest. The bitmites coursing through her arm give her the strength to tear the shoulder from its socket.

The angel screams.

She walks away as Indo and Autonomy and the rest all set to work on the fallen creature, tearing at its flesh with eager fingers. One leaps on the arm as she drops it, like a lion taking down some prey. Another swings a leg above her head, the armoured boot flying off.

The angel's scream and their triumphant yells fuse as a single animal cry, until his breath gutters and chokes and stops, drowned in his own blood.

– His ribs stripped by their ripping nails, Elixir sobs, his body torn apart, his heart burst under a rough rock, his broken limbs thrown from blood-spattered hand to hand, his *cock* – [Elixir chokes] – thrown deep into the woods.

He crumples to the floor, his knees pulled up, his back against the wall.

– They'll never find it all, he says.

Accordion closes the door quietly and comes over, crouches beside the boy.

– His mother took his head, Elixir says, and fixed it on the point of her disruptor, like it was a mountain lion's.

He starts to pant, trying to find the breath to sob as well as speak.

– She's coming now, he says. She's left her sisters and the maidens dancing and she carries it down through the meadows of Mount Zithering. Down from the hills at last, she's entering these very walls, entranced.

Elixir stares at the closed door, right through it at what's on the other side, this distant horror, coming closer all the time.

– She *glories* in her victory over this sorry foe, he says. She calls out to Iacchus still, her partner in this crime who's helped her triumph in the kill. She doesn't know.

Elixir's voice is shrill with fear.

– She doesn't know her only prize is tears.

Columbine's Return

– I will leave this pitiful scene, says Guy over the screams, before the queen reaches the palace.

He jumps down from the stage and skirts the wreckage of the rigging, courtiers and serfs backing away as he walks round the carnage, the Duke's body in the centre of the hall, the pool of blood and bitmites, Phreedom standing there, her hands red as her hair. The consul panics, makes a run towards the door . . . where Joey picks the dirt out from under his fingernails with his knife.

– Self-restraint, warns Guy. Respect for the divine. For those who value mortal life, these are the wisest path to follow . . . to my mind.

The consul thinks the better of it, backs away to join the others now all spread out round the walls. Guy takes his place at Joey's side. He nods to me and then at Jack, still standing on the wagon's roof.

– Come, let us praise in choral song the spirit of the pack, I sing out in the Cant. Come, let us chant the fall of Pierrot, this son of venom, Pierrot, who wore a woman's dress, led by a bull to certain death, led on by his own blind stubbornness.

Phree spins the sword around her head and, as she hurls it from her, up into the air, Jack pounces from the roof. He hits the springboard on the stage and sails up, with a somersault, a double twist, to snatch the sword. He lands on the Duke's back with an almighty crack and drives the sword into the corpse, stands there, his hands still on the hilt.

— Pierrot held the staff of Harlequin, I sing, the sure sign of his doom.

The Cant echoes around the room.

— Maidens of Themes, see how it ends in sorrow and in tears, this glorious victory you've won. Is this nobility, to dip your hands into the blood of your own son?

Phree holds a hand up.

— Hush, I say.

And in the silence you can hear the drip.

— Wild-eyed Columbine, I say, mother of Pierrot, king of tears and son of sorrow.

Phree turns to me as I speak to the house. Her eyes *are* wild, a child on speed, and all I want to do is go to her and hold her, tell her that it's over now. Christ, Phree, it's all been over from day one. If she could only understand. This fucking war's already over — all the Dukes, the Havens, all the angels and the demons, they're just fucking dreams, dreams given solid flesh in the Hinter by the bitmites, but still *dreams*.

I look at Jack, our Harlequin, Dionysus, lord of everything chaotic. Sexy, twisty Jack. Quite possibly psychotic.

Welcome to hell, I think. Come join the revels of the spirit of the pack.

— My sisters from the distant land of ash, Phreedom begins.

She comes towards me and I clamber off the stage.

— Look at the gift I've brought home for you, a tender kill fresh from the hills.

*

The happy hunting ground, I think. The Hinter with its nightmares born from the fucked-up hearts of all us fools who love our lies of good and evil, dark and light, and monsters slain by noble knights. Phree, that's all right inside the pages of some book but when you let those lies loose in the world, Phree, when you choose to see it all as a crusade, a jihad against everything you hate ... the bitmites give us everything we want.

– I can see it, I say.

But I don't look at what she's holding in her hand, just put my arms around my little sister, say my lines.

– Welcome to the celebrations, I say.

Her hand comes up to stroke my cheek, to make sure that I'm solid, real. She mouths my name. *Thomas.* Her fingers are still wet.

– Hail, I say.

And I choke and clear my throat and swallow.

– Hail and well met.

Safe Home

We come out of the fire, over the Bridge to Nowhere, shapes carved out of night and flame, a chi-gun in one hand, a jackknife in the other, and rats – little red-eyed plague-carriers – scattering before our silent tread. They stream past us, scattering out into the park, these black and burning ghost rats, up the slope and spreading out around the Circus. Rattle of machine guns, shrieks of soldiers dying in their botched raid on the Rookery mingle with the rodent chitter. Louder still, though, is the boom of Fox's gun emplacements. Louder still the crack of doom, the roar of earth opening up beneath our feet.

The river of fire at our backs licks upwards, lurches north and south as ground cracks, seams of methane catching, a solid wall of flame and billowing noxious smoke arcing like wings behind us, black-green with the orgone-drenched fuel of rotting landfill and seeping mineshafts.

Geysers of flame blast ornithopters from the sky. Jets of blue-green fire spray up into the air. The Rookery has a new line of defence tonight.

Here and there, a few rats explode into the bitmites that they're built of, shattering into insectoid mechanisms. A chatter of souls, they gather the scraps of skin around us as we walk, the bits of black woollen overcoat burned off, longcoat abandoned on the scorched earth. Shreds of self, we gather them to us, bits and bitmites both. We are them, after all, and they are us, the blood of angels graving the Vellum itself in a black tattoo that marks the true map of this world not in the streets but in the lines of power, the seams of what they call the chi here in this little Haven in the Hinter. We are the coal, the oil made of crushed souls under the skin of time.

We are ink.

The low, low tone of Don Coyote drones on, muffled and distant but insistent.

— so they say. Well, hell, they been saying that since the world began, and it hasn't happened yet. The only thing that's falling, far as I can see, is Albion's boys in black and blue. They're going to have to call in reinforcements, I'd say. Yes, they're going to have to call the big guns in because, the way I'm looking at it, Fox has won this fight. But, hey, it's just one little battle, right? One little struggle through one winter's night. And, as they say, my friends, tomorrow is another day.

We clamber up the rusted steel ladder and step out onto tarmac, into a low-roofed tunnel that forks in front of us, the old contours of the exits from the park still followed by the solid blocks of garbage that make up the Rookery's defensive outer wall. Here and there the plaster has crumbled from the walls of crushed cans and boxes mulched with glue, and in the low light of the tunnel you can make out labels of foods and products long since discontinued. Designs going back to the 50s and beyond, boxes for things made out of Bakelite. It's not the smartest move in the world, some would say, building your defence from paper and tin, but it's twenty foot thick or more, and higher, a shell of concrete on the outside giving the Rookery a more impressive face to show to Kentigern.

A stone statue stands at the fork as sentinel, sunk into the wall, a grim grey Victorian gent with a bushy beard, and a broken hole and smudge of spray-paint where his nose once was, staring out at the pile of furniture and sandbags beside us, staring through it at the corrugated iron blocking off the bridge at this end, staring beyond that, maybe, through the hill that slopes up to the Circus, and through Kentigern's sandstone streets of shops and offices, through the Merchant City, through the Necropolis that sits at the edge of Kentigern's eastern wall, and through that wall out into the Hinter itself, looking East, towards the dawn.

– *So anyway, talking of time, it's time for me to go because that new day's getting closer by the second. So tune in at the same time tomorrow night and hopefully we'll have another show. Will I be here? Do any of us really know? Until then though, hey, I have been, and always will be, yes, your one and only Dusk-till-Don Coyote, signing off his nightly Notes from the Geek Show with a simple message for you folks in slumberland. The midnight oil's burning low, and there's that fiery glow of daylight or damnation out there on the perimeter. So it's time to wrap those shades around your eyes and stumble out into the cold light of reality. And remember, folks, the sky may not be falling, but there ain't no harm in wearing a hat. Safe home, my friends. Safe home . . .*

A squad of Rookery guards stationed under the shadow of the statue lower their ruptors, wave us past.

We take the right-hand fork and follow the tunnel up to where it opens out into the Union Gate. Kiosks and stalls fill the Avenue, which runs downhill from the Hub, its academic architecture – mock-Gothic clashing with neoclassical – all but swallowed among the shacks and Portakabins that have sprung up over decades, eating every inch of free space, built one on top of another, maybe five or six storeys of them. In the dark and gorgeous chaos of it all you can hardly make out the rusting barrelled and vaulted roofs of the streets for all the washing lines and makeshift bridges criss-crossing between these latter-day tenement blocks. Kids hang from the monkey-frame of scaffolding amongst the ladders and the strings of arc-lamps and the jerry-rigged porches of wooden planks with plastic chairs and patio tables.

And we remember how we were Jack and Joey, growing up here, clambering over the scaffolding, leaping in dares, learning the acrobatics of survival. Stealing paints and starting fires. In the shattering and scattering of self we feel it fresh as the bitmites swirl between us, taking the pieces back to their rightful owner, confused because they are so similar in this way, that shape. So we notice discrepancies in the scraps of skin being stitched back into place, these shreds of memory being laced back into human shape.

One of us stops a second, peels a patch of skin from his shoulder, slaps it on the other's back.

— That's yours, I think.

The other stops, brow furrowing. He shakes his head, reaches behind and scrapes the skin off, sticks it to the other's arm.

— Fuck it, you have it. It's more you than me.

Columbine's Return

— Look here, she says. I caught this lion cub without a snare, a tender pup, the whiskers soft on its young cheek under its flowing mane of hair.

I hear the whisper of the bitmites underneath her voice, not quite in synch, the rolling rhythm with its ups and downs that little bit ahead, as she recites the lines they feed. She lifts the dead lump in her hand to show it but I stop her arm. Not yet.

— The hair *is* like some wild beast's, I say.

But I'm not looking at the severed head, but at the smear of red upon her cheek, the hair that falls across her eyes. I push it back behind her ear and let my hand brush down her face to wipe the bloodspot with a thumb.

— Come, share the feast, she says.

— Where did you catch it? I say. In what desert lair?

— On Zithering, she says. Yes — [quiet, almost questioning, as if she's only now uncovering a truth long buried deep inside] — Mount Zithering, she says. That's where he died.

I know I have to take it slowly, coax her gently through the puzzle of the past, from abreaction into anamnesis; brutal Phree-dom with her heart brittle as glass.

— Who struck it first? I say.

— That joy was mine. Amongst our band I'm known as happy Columbine.

She looks down at the body of the Duke, the slick of black that's taking it apart. Jack crouches down at one side of the mess. He's cut the ropes around the wrists and rolled the body over, ripped the bodice open; he's examining the graving on its chest.

– My sisters struck the creature after me, says Phree. Yes, after me, they did the rest.

– Fate smiled upon your hunting then? I say.

She points at limber, nimble Jack, his head cocked like a dog's in curiosity.

– The spirit of the pack, she says, inspired the maidens as we chased our kill and dragged it from the lion's den.

Jack's finger traces the hatchwork of scars.

– He is, I say, a hunter with great skill.

– Then you approve? The progeny of Pantaloon – and my own son Pierrot, too – will praise me soon for capturing this prey.

I pause. The body of the Duke lies crooked-armed, the skirt pushed up to show one leg twisted beneath the other. One hand seems to reach out, open, with its palm up, like a beggar's, reaching out to me, to Phreedom, to anyone. Phree looks at me, a cat that's brought some bird with broken wings and lolling head home, as an offering. A strange sort of prey, I think, and strangely caught.

– Of course, I say. It's what you had to do.

It's what she needs to hear.

I let a hint of hidden meaning enter into what I say. *But ... be gentle.*

– You're proud of what you've done?

– I'm pleased, she says.

Her voice is empty, though, repeating what the bitmites whisper in her ear, and with the smell of entrails spilled onto the floor making the bile rise in my throat, that burning taste of sick, I wonder what cruel fucker said revenge is sweet.

– I've won a victory for all my land to see, she says.

I feel the slightest tremble of her shoulder as I turn her round to face the audience and the slick of gore. I still can't look at what she's holding in her hand – or I don't want to. Really, I don't want to. But every one of us here in this room, courtiers and servants, players just as much, and Phreedom, my poor Phreedom most of all, all have to see. To really, truly understand.

– Let's *all* gaze on the glory of the prize you've won, I say.
She holds it up by its long hair, the head of the dead Duke.
– Go on, I say, let's all take a good look.

Lady Liberty

The townsfolk scatter as Phreedom strides into the agora, overturning stalls and barrows as she passes. She takes the steps in front of the Basileus's marble hall two at a time, wheels round within the portico. Framed by Corinthian columns, under the pediment's relief that shows the legendary Sacking of Washington, she holds the angel's head up.

– Citizens of fair-walled Themes, she says, come see the fierce wild beast we girls have caught.

Sandminers whisper in a gruff group. A silk salesman gathers yards of sleek purple cloth out of the dust of a toppled stall. Fishmongers, bakers, fruitmen and matchgirls, all stand wary guard over their goods. Butchers reach for their cleavers.

– This is no idle boast, she says, by men with weapons bought from armourers' stores. We caught this prey and tore the monster limb from limb with our bare hands, she roars. No catapults or spears or traps.

No, she thinks, none of that crap.

– Where is the old man? Call him here. Where is my boy? Tell him to bring a ladder, raise it up against the house and nail this lion's head up on the wall, my treasure from the hunt.

Don slips into her memory like a dream, a seamless interpolation, just a simple, subtle alteration. He simply walks round from behind the Basileus's hall.

– Follow me. Roond tae the front, men, wi' yer burden in yer arms. Aye, follow, wi the corpse of Pierrot. It took a long an weary search tae find it as ye see it, torn tae bits and scattered a' through Zithering's glade, wi' no two bits thigither. Bring it hither.

He spots her standing there, holding the head up like a torch, and stops.

*

– Can ye see it? Husht now. No and I bloody well won't if ye –
Why are we no movin? Can ye see it yet? Sure and there's all the
nobs and gentry to let off first so we'll be left to last as ever. Can ye
see it? And would ye get yer feckin elbow out of me ribs? Ah haud
yer whisht. Look. Look!

The babble of voices is as crammed, as mixed up all together, as
the rabble of third-class passengers all squeezed into the corridor with
their cases and their bundles and their greetin weans. It's the noise of
blathering gobshites with their caps off craning their necks over the
mob of heads and shoulders, newlyweds wittering excitedly as they
kiss a hand and turn to try and catch a glimpse of something other
than that wee patch of blue sky up where the corridor opens out
onto the steamer's deck. Oh, but there's hundreds of them all
pressing forward, moving so slowly up towards the gangplank and
their new lives in the New World. In New York.

– It'll be magic, Jack, she says to the babe cradled in her arms.
Oh, it'll be grand. Oh, yes it will. Oh, yes it will.

She nuzzles his nose with her own and he smiles, gurgles. Oh,
he's a darling, so he is, all this time in steerage and the noise all day
and night and hardly a peep out of him, no, but he slept as peaceful
as Jesus in his manger for most of the trip.

He's awake now, blue eyes shining up at her like that tiny wee
bit of sky ahead that they're inching towards so slowly.

– Who's my cheeky wee boy? she says. My *cheeky* wee boy.

The crowd moves forward, little by little and the chatter grows
louder now as those ahead of them are saying, *Look now, look at it,
sure, and it's grand, so it is, by Jesus, look at it, just look at it.*

She can't really see it herself for all the nodding heads and hats
of these immigrants in their Sunday best like they were filing into the
chapel for midnight mass. She just sees glimpses of the giant robe
sweeping off the shoulder, of the upraised arm, and the sunburst
crown of that greenish girl like an angel or an ancient god of justice,
but a *true* one, yes, a true angel that's come down from heaven itself
to hold its torch up as a beacon for humanity. She can't really see it
herself, so she can't, but she holds Jack up above her head so *he* can
see it. Oh, look at it, Jack. Can ye see it? Isn't it everything we ever
dreamed of?

She brings him back down to cradle him, as they move another few inches forward, and as he burbles in her arms, his eyes as wide and blue as the sky itself, she can almost imagine that the glint of sunlight in those eyes is the vision caught magically. A tiny reflection of Lady Liberty photographed, imprinted on his soul.

Phree stands there in a daze, the bitmites swarming along her arm, around the severed head, and spreading out, an iridescent haze that fills the hall with shades of lives that never were but might have been. The past is no more certain than the future out here in the Hinter. Like the sudden moments of recasting in a dream, when the whole scene shifts in an instant and your memories adjust, the Hinter slips and slides from side to side; new histories rise to the surface even as the old ones crumble.

– So I return to you, says Don, with my son Pierrot slain by the maidens.

With his gaze fixed on the bitmites' tumbling imagery of forests, mad aristocratic mothers of action roaming through the oaks (Indo and Autonomy – their names are whispers in the air) he looks so solid and so humble, and I wonder if it is this . . . stoic reticence of his that makes it natural for him to slip unnoticed into someone else's dreams. Jack rips through Havens like a whirlwind. I skip after him, and Guy and Joey make their own marks in bold strokes of pen or knife. But none of us can do what Don does, reaching deep down into someone's life. Now, playing Pantaloon with gravitas in place of pomp, he walks out towards Phree, speaking with gentle Cant.

– They told me Columbine was here, he says, and acting wild. As Scaramouche and I entered the city walls, returning from the rites, they urged us, *hurry*, told us this . . . atrocity was done by my own child. They didn't lie, he says. I see her now, a sorry sight.

To me she's barely visible amongst the rising blizzard of the bitmites. There's too many different and conflicting sights – a marketplace of stalls, some sort of hall of refugees dressed in Depression drab, dark woods full of wild women, darker docks, a steamer with a gangplank coming down from it, and Guy and Joey dressed up as policemen or as palace guards. I can't follow the confusion that the bitmites are projecting out of her into the room.

But Don is calm. It's like he's simply gazing through the sham, ignoring this mere . . . scenery, the costumes and the props.

The rest of us stand back, our parts played out, with just a few lines left for me and Jack. It's down to Don to find my sister in there now, amongst the Annas and the Anaesthesias, pull her from the ruins of her past.

She laughs.

– Old man, be proud and sing out loud, she says. You're blessed by our courageous feats. Your daughters are the best of any mortal race, and I'm the purest of our breed. We left our weaving at the loom to free our hands for noble deeds, you understand, to chase the savage beast whose head I've brought for you to nail up on the palace wall. You see? Take it, old man, and call your friends to feast in honour of the kill.

The palace of the Basilisk rises behind her, the Duke's Haven fading into grey. The mask of Guy's rewritten play peeled back and stripped away, the ancient myth emerges. Jack is Harlequin is Dionsyus. But the vision shimmers as Don speaks to her in his gruff voice. The air itself vibrates with his gruff Cant.

– The murder in your hands, he says, this invitation to the feast, is too horrific for a mortal eye. The prey you offer the divine was precious, Columbine. I weep for your regrets . . . and mine.

She looks confused as he comes closer to her, bitmites swirling into shapes of glassy towers and marble halls all round them, into streets of skyscrapers. Ghost men and women clutching carpet-bags and suitcases now stand among the courtiers all shivering along the wall, merchants and slaves in chains from more archaic pasts, the host of souls long-buried in the dust under the Haven's stone, a single huddled mass.

Don steps down off the stage, but it's a steamship moored behind him now and I can smell the oil and fish and human sweat, the rotting fruit in the warehouses around us. Snow is falling from a winter sky and someone's singing of how Irish eyes are smiling, and, *Oh, but it seems so far away now*, someone's saying – and I realise that it's me, carried along on the flow of dreams. I recognise the skyline now as Anaesthesia's Hinter fades into this other scene.

– The Harlequin is harsh, says Don, for one who claims to be our kin. Does anyone deserve the shame he sends?

But I can hear the echo underneath his words – *some bloody faither God is, Jesus, sending us this kind of bloody weather* – as the cursing Scotsman takes her case out of her hand so she can hold her child in both arms, wrap the shawl around him tight, to keep him warm against the New York winter night.

– Come on, lass, he says, we've got tae get ye in ootae this cold.

She looks so scared and lost now, shaking like a leaf, but the wry tone to his voice is warm and comforting and so she follows him towards the immigration building, through the crowd, and having this stranger at her side – his name is Don, he says, MacChuill – well, you can see it in her eyes, the sheer relief.

So it's Don that walks beside my sister, down into this dream of New York winter, streets of gold and Lady Liberty, to find herself in Hinter's cold, to help her face her false eternity of grief.

To make her Phree.

A Slower, Greyer World

Berlin. 1936.

I listen to the Führer give his speech to the Reichstag, played on the hissing radio behind the sliding glass window of the guard's cubicle room. I hear the cheers in response to Hitler's ranting rhetoric and I hear the screams of butchers become victims, dragged out of their beds to slaughter – not on the radio, those last, but in my head. I've been waiting to hear it for the last seven years, this echo of another night of long knives in another time, another place. Things happen slower in this world, not quite so condensed. But they still happen. There is no Futurism in this world, but it is not that different underneath.

The opening of the gates, my brother called it, and he was right. I think somehow we crossed over a threshold that night, both of us. Perhaps the whole of Germany crossed over a threshold on that night, and reached out from the other side to drag the rest of the world down with us into the depths. The opening of the gates.

But he was wrong as well, and in so many ways. This is not the world he thought it would be, I think. It is greyer, I keep thinking, dimmer than the glory he expected, if I understand the way my brother's mind works. And I have thought about this a lot in my time in the Institute, in this slower, greyer world.

– Thank you. Where were we?

Pickering snaps the lighter shut and pockets it. He leans back in his chair, looks at Reynard. Really, this is all so bloody pointless. MI5 is jumping at their own shadows these days, every continental a potential Futurist, every Irishman a Fenian, every queer a spy. And let's not forget the Russian Jews; why, you never know what subversives might be lurking in amongst those exiled intellectuals. Mosley's rhetoric of the enemy within is all very well. The new patriotism of Empire Albion is all very well. But Pickering's never really trusted all that talk of fighting fire with fire, Britain – sorry, *Albion* – standing strong and pure against the Slav.

It leaves a bad taste in his mouth, that blend of opportunism and idealism.

– Actually, I think that's about covered it, he says. Sorry to keep you so long. I'll let you get back now. How is the boy, anyway?

– Tomas? Wonderful, says Reynard. Looking so much like his mother – God, I'm sorry, Joseph; that's hardly what you want to hear. I—

Pickering forces a smile.

– No, don't be silly. That's . . . exactly what I want to hear. It's good to know you're happy.

I look into the mirror in the bathroom, at my close-cropped hair, and I think that even if I were to find the Book again, and the jewel, even if I were to carry out some arcane ritual full of blood and horror like my brother's, I do not think it would transport me back into the world I came from. I think if the Book even exists here, then this world will have found a place for it within its own more rigid system of possibilities, as it has found a place for me – as an anonymous inmate in a mental hospital. I imagine the jewel as no more than a pretty bauble in the royal treasure of some ermine-decked buffoon. I imagine the Book as some eighteenth-century hoax, relished by mystery-hunters as a curio, its authenticity long since discredited. I imagine my brother as the hero that he dreamed of being, this blond, blue-eyed adventurer in flying jacket, pistol blazing, captured in gauche ink in the flat panelled frames of an American comic-book. There are these ... stories of Jack Flash in this world. Visions. Myths. But he exists now only in these fictions and delusions, I believe.

There are no Futurists in this world either, of course, but we don't need them; the Nazis are more than enough.

I shuffle across the linoleum in my slippers and pyjamas, sit down on the side of old Kurt's bed. His breathing is as distant and dry as the radio when the guard listens to it late at night, the slow wheeze of an accordion, in and out, in and out. The nurses are letting him die, one less halfwit to take care of. I can hear the weak voice of his thoughts among the river in my head. That much is acceptable in the logic of this world, you see, something that only *might* be magic, that might just as easily be madness. I pat his wrinkled, liver-spotted hand and mutter some words of comfort.

After a while, the breathing stops and only the voice remains, the whisper of his life amongst those others in my head.

Reynard lays a hand on his shoulder.

– How are the nightmares, these days?

Pickering shakes his head.

– Not so bad. Not so frequent.

He still finds it hard to talk about his never-ending dream, where he's home that night instead of out carousing in some pub with Carter. But he understands it now, at least, the truth of Carter running after him through the shattering streets, following him into the burning shell of the house to drag him from the buried crib – how that becomes this other scene. He understands why the events of that night are transformed in his sleeping imagination into something more grotesque, more crude in its horror, with Carter as the flame-haired fiend, the very slaughterer of his wife and child. *Survivor's guilt*, Reynard once called it. *He's just the part of you that you blame.*

– But it's strange, says Pickering. I've had the dream so many times now, sometimes I remember it better than the actual . . .

– I know, says Reynard. We all have dreams like that. I sometimes think the world would be better if we never dreamed at all. God save us from our dreams, Joseph.

– Thus speaks a dreamer, Reynard.

– I know. I know.

The House of Aching

Phreedom wakes to find Don leaning over her, a damp cloth in his hand mopping her forehead. She's still weak with the fever, but she pulls herself upright, tries to pull herself together. The room is barren, dirty wooden floorboards and an empty window-frame with polythene nailed across it to keep the Hinter out.

– Why so solemn, old man, she says. Why so grim?

– Ye know ye've been out of it fer nine days, he says.

She can tell by his expression it's been rough. There are six – no, seven – disruptors stuck like posts into the floorboards round them, buzzing with that deep, low sound. Candles in every corner of the room. A circle of salt around the mattress sordid with her sweat. It must have been bad. But she feels so happy, such . . . relief.

– I was with Jack, she realises as she says it.

The image of her son summons itself so sharp, so clear, filling her head with a delight that pushes everything else out of her mind. Yes, they were laughing together. And he's out there, grown-up now, following in his mother's footsteps and as much a hunter as herself, as zealous as herself in waging war against the gods. Yes, it was Jack, and there were soldiers, and a town called Themes, and – fuck! There was some creature, some mad creature with its claws at his throat. She has to warn him. Her legs buckle under her as she tries to stand up, head still spinning. Shit.

– Where is he? she says. I saw him. I need to find him.

Phreedom tries to shake the dream off, but the image of him, Jack, amongst a company of young warriors – it feels so right. It makes her feel so right. So what's the problem with this picture?

– Ah lass, says Don.

There's a sympathy in his eyes, a look as if there's something she's forgotten in the fever – *no* – some grief that's waiting to destroy her – *let me hold onto the lie* – and she can feel it pressing through – *no, I could live forever in the dream, and life would seem less cursed with sorrow* – and something rises in the turmoil in her soul.

– What do you mean? she says.

There's no need to feel sorrow. Jack's alive; she saw him. And her head is clear, it is. The fever's gone. Phreedom fights the ruin of her bliss.

– Look at the sky, says Don. Diz it look the same? D'ye see any change?

He pulls the polythene down from the window and she's looking out into the devastation of New York. Snow falls white against the blue-black night and—

— it seems brighter, clearer than it was, but she's so cold. The lad crouches down in front of her.

– Can you unnerstaun me, missus? Can ye unnerstaun whit ah'm sayin, like?

Anna nods and he asks her something else. She keeps forgetting what they were talking about, so she does, though, so she invents the questions to her answers, telling him that she still has a little of the money Seamus gave her, but it's running out so fast and she's got Jack to feed and clothe as well as herself, and where else can she turn, an exile from her own country? That's why she went there, ye see. She knew they'd take her in.

– Come oan. We've got tae get ye off the street or ye'll catch yer death of cold.

And she nods and she tells him about the house she lives in, how she found it by the sound of the songs sung by the girls round the piano carrying out into the streets all dark and filthy and spattered with snow and this church of bawdy hymns and a different sort of marriages, the House of Aching, so they called it, the bordello down by the muddy Hudson with its red light in the window and the songs so sweet, what was it they were singing, was it *Love is pleasing and love is teasing*, yes, it was. How does it go again? Yes, *Love is a pleasure when first tis new*. And she tells him about the little Pierrot doll up on the mantelpiece all covered in dust and made of porcelain, it was, so easy for something like that to break up into little pieces, oh, so easy to break her little baby into little pieces, just a bit of wire was all it took when they took her to the doctor, and the Russian standing there behind him with the winter eyes himself who fathered the child in the hallway of his bordello when he wanted it he took it so cold he was like ice and hard and it wasn't love, oh no that wasn't the ache they had the men coming to the house or maybe it *was* love of a sort d'ye think because love changes over time it does starting so sweet at first so sweet and she sings *but as it grows older it grows the colder...*

— Whit's that yer haudin in yer arms? he says, his voice so gruff but so soft, sounding old for one as young as him, just a boy he is really. Don he said his name was.

And she nods and explains how she feels so cold now, so she does, with all the blood poured out of her, all the blood that made them panic and bring her out here to this alley and the doctor saying for God's sake man and the like but he still left her didn't he and she could see the fear in his eyes not like the Russian's not cold like the Russian's no but oh what is it that she's holding in her arms? But silly it's the head of her stuffed lion Leo oh she loved the toy so much even after Thomas was so mean and pulled its head right off she kept it and she didn't cry but she kicked him in the shin and *he* cried and it served him right.

— Ur ye sure? he says. Mibbe ye want tae take anither look, missus. It's a'right, missus. Ye don't huv tae be feart noo.

She looks down at the little bundle of blanket, patchwork quilt and ragged bedspread wrapped around it, held so tight in her arms they're almost locked around it as if frozen into place. Ah, Christ. What is she looking at? What is this thing in her hands?

— Look close, says Don. Be sure ae whit yer seein.

Oh, Jesus and Mary. Jesus and Mary, but his tiny face is frozen. No. It can't be true. It can't be. Sure and there's enough woe in her life without this sorry sight.

— Dis it still look like a lion's head tae ye? says Don.

Oh no. It's not her Leo but his hair is just as golden and his eyes as blue as the savannah skies of her imagination but his cheek it shouldn't be like that his skin is fair but not so white oh not so white as the snow oh no oh not so white and blue as porcelain Pierrot's head when she knocked it off the mantelpiece oh she was only trying to dust it no and the Russian dragged her out into the hallway for it those nine months ago and Mary-Jane took Jack up to her room to hush him in safety as she cried as the Russian tore her best green dress open and forced himself on her and left her there as he left her here he did he's left her here to die after the botched backstreet abortion and Jack's never liked the cold he hasn't no and now his tiny hands are frozen.

She can feel her heartbeat slowing.

The truth is here now, cold and timeless. It's 1921 and Anna lies dying in the back alley, one child frozen in her arms, the other torn to pieces in her womb. It's 2019 and Phreedom lies against a dumpster, shivering with the cold and with the hunger for the needle, arms as empty as her belly now the men in clean suits have taken her Jack away from her. It's 2037 and she's in another New York, yes, there's thousands of them on this long road through the Vellum, and she has to look in every one of them in case he's here in this one, in this fold. And it's eternity. It's out so far into the Hinter that years have no meaning, time itself measured in hours that rise as cities, cities of noon, cities of Evenfall, and cities of eternal night.

Phreedom stands before an empty stage in a solitary spotlight, Don beside her. She feels the weight of the severed head in her hand, the full weight of this murder committed by herself and her bitmite sisters. Christ, what's she become to do this to him? What's she doing holding his head up like a fucking trophy?

Her arm drops to her side, but she can't let go of the grey hair that still has a few gold streaks in it. *Say something*, she thinks, but there's nothing to say. The bitmites have no line for her.

– Mourned by me before *you* even knew, says Don.

I flick the page over to read my sister's line, the stand-in Columbine for our rehearsal. Jack and Joey hoist the rigging round the wagon, cranking handles round and locking bolts, and hoisting sandbags up on ropes. Guy waves some of the Duke's guards back, directing them to take the thrones and chairs and place them here and there, leave space between them and the stage. He stands out in the centre of the room and looks back at the rig, trying to reckon, I assume, exactly where the Duke will lie. I rub my finger with my thumb, the ink still wet upon the page.

– Where did Pierrot die? I say. Here in the house or somewhere else? Where did Pierrot lose his head?

– In the same place where Action, Don recites, was ripped to shreds by his own hounds.

– He went to Zithering? I say. He went to Zithering's mountain heights?

– He had to mock the Harlequin, says Don, and you and your pack at his rites.

– What were we doing there? Was I insane?

Don nods his head towards the entrance to the hall.

– The whole damned city was deranged.

The Duke is entering, all armour-grey and swaggering pride, a consul skittering at his side. I whistle at Jack, who clocks the Duke, ducks out of sight.

– I understand, I read. The Harlequin has been our ruin. We insulted him with our disdain, denied he was divine.

I read the line without emotion, my attention drawn to this old warrior, this thing halfway between an angel and a king. He looks so much like Jack – an older Jack without the flashing grin – that suddenly I feel this horror in my queasy stomach and scrunching balls. He's got my sister trapped here in this castle in the sky, I have to tell myself. A fucking princess in his dream, his lie.

But does that really mean he has to die?

Don nudges me and hisses – *the next line*.

– Old man, I say, where is the corpse of my dear son?

– I found it after a long search, he says. I've brought it back myself, all pieced together limb to limb.

I try not to think of what we're going to do to him, what Phreedom has to do to him to break free of the lie. Jack is back now from behind the curtain, with his patchwork costume on, tying the mask around his face so that the Duke won't catch on. Patchwork costumes and patchwork worlds, I think. A million Jacks scattered across the Hinter. All of us – *all of us* – broken up, torn into pieces by the dogs of our pasts. Christ, is it such a crime for someone who has a little bit of fire in them, a little touch of gold in their grey hair, to offer lost souls sanctuary in the Hinter wilderness? What if we bring this miserable Haven down, tear this lie apart, and Phreedom with it . . . and what if we can't put the pieces back together? What if you can't ever put the pieces back together?

I flick forward through the later pages of Guy's play. The further I go, the more scratches and scores there are, the more lines rewritten in the margins, arrows, circles marking out the edits.

Fuck, Guy, I think, I hope you know what you're doing.

All Good Men

— Fuck, Guy, says Puck. I hope you know what you're doing.

Peachy Puck glares at the shadow slumped beside Jack on the sofa in the lounge of Fox's den, his flat well hidden within the safety of the Rookery.

— We need him, says Guy. Now is the time for all good men—

— What's good about a fucking psychopath who doesn't give a shit about anything or anyone?

Joey, still not quite himself, incapable of biting back with a sarcastic jibe, just gives him the finger. *Think I give a fuck what you say?*

We bitmites skitter up and down that finger, flow around it, weaving flesh together, seamstresses of skin. This symbol, this so-simple and so singular a statement, is part of the core of him, the heart of Joey. We latch onto it, stitch it into him, reform all its connections, instance here to instance there. It is the reply of a young man being quizzed by Guy about these new drugs he has somehow gotten hold of, of a youth being questioned by a black-shirted militiaman, of a boy being ribbed about his painting. It is the simple wordless answer to a thousand questions, to *all* questions. A raised middle finger.

Fuck you.

— You see what I mean? says Puck.

— Sometimes, says Guy, that sort of attitude can come in handy.

— You're playing with fire, you know, says Puck.

— But that's what makes life worth living, says Jack.

And we flit with the glint of his toothy grin from this moment, popping a pill at a warehouse party, to another where he's unbuttoning Puck's fly, to another where a Molotov is flying from his hand. We click them into place, all the *clunks* and *chiks* of his lighter, all the leaps from this rooftop to that, to get away from an SS man firing at him, from some ganglord he's just blown a kiss at, from the razor-kids whose turf they're on, or simply for a dare. Silkworms burrowing, spiders scurrying, we spin the silky steel on which his moments of sparkle flash like dew caught by a burst of sun. We see him through Joey's eyes as they dangle on monkey-frame of scaffolding, so many feet across to that steel bar, so many storeys straight down to the street, and Joey says, *You wouldn't dare*, and Jack gives his own silent reply. A smile of sheer audacity.

Fuck it.

Jack limbers up from the sofa, stretching, wraps his arms around Puck's waist to draw him tight to him.

— What's the worst that could happen? he says.

Joey watches the two of them — the fly hand Jack slips under Puck's tee, and the way Puck jerks back from the tickling cold, the slaps and shoves — *get off* — the armlock Jack puts round Puck's neck, his childish, coy attempt to hug the kid. Guy standing over at the window, Puck and Jack pawing each other, Joey sitting in the corner feeling fucked — it's almost like the old days, except that he no longer has that feeling of disgust that used to eat at him. It was at times like this he'd look at Jack and Puck and just see children, idiot children playing at being revolutionaries. He'd see Guy standing alone, so louche, so fucking posed with cigarette and glass, and think *Just what the fuck are you really up to?* Guy Fox, head of the Thieves Guild now that King Finn's gone. Did he really think they could take down the whole fucking system? Did he really believe all that *few good men* shit?

Now, though? Now he sees that there's a secret sorrow some-where under Puck's whimsy, that Jack's wildness is a fierce denial of dull care, and that Guy carries the troubles of the world with a pretence of ease. And he wonders. Was he just fucking jealous that Jack had latched onto this shiny pretty thing, the snub-nosed image of his secret self, or the flickering dream of Kentigern set free? Jealous of Puck and the revolution that had stolen his best friend?

What a fucking crock of shit that would be.

He wanders over to the window beside Fox, looks out into the Rookery. Fox's place sits near the eastern edge, with only a few hundred yards between them and the wall of concrete – and fire now – that seals them from the rest of Kentigern, but you couldn't tell. It might as well be buried in the very heart of the Rookery. To the left, the backyard of the old tenement block, where the bins would once have been, is all built up with multi-storey prefabs, balconies and ladders. Straight in front of them, across a tarmac car park that used to be full of stalls each morning and kids with footballs every afternoon, a huge hangar of corrugated iron, red with rust and green with moss, blocks off most of their vision. Beyond the roof of it more tenements and prefabs hide behind the scaffolding that rises to support the hodgepodge roofing that seals street from sky.

– So what's the plan? he says to Fox.

– No plan for now, says Fox. I think Jack and yourself should lay low for a while, let the bitmites take down Kentigern's walls. Then we head out into the Hinter, find the next Haven. They *must* be holding King Finn somewhere. He's too valuable to them.

Joey ignores the point of the comment, thinks of the rats running burning out into the night, scattering round the Circus and into the city. Bitmites spreading chaos through Kentigern's unending night. The denizens of the Rookery have no fear of chaos, they thrive on it, so they'll be all right, but out there, in the shopping malls and council offices, the police-state city of sleepers in fucking denial that the apocalypse ever happened, it'll be hell.

– What if they get it back under control? says Joey. For all the shit the bitmites drag out of their sordid little fantasies and give flesh,

304

at the end of the day, you know — you know it, Fox — the fuckers out there just don't want their freedom. They're afraid of it. Four fools don't make a revolution, Fox.

— Five, says Don as he closes the door behind him.

And Fox smiles at Joey as if the moment should have some significance.

— One by one, he says. We just take it one soul at a time.

The Harlequin's Dance

She drags the angel into town behind her, him staggering to match her stride. She's still not sure of why she let him live; she can't believe it's Jack, no matter what he says, no matter how his eyes glint with the blue of open skies, electric sparks, but still ... there was this moment when she felt her fingers at his throat, her claws piercing his skin, and some tiny scrap of her humanity kicked in and held her back. Even with the bitmites hissing in her head, and the pack behind her howling for his blood, she'd felt some little piece of sense in her saying, no, don't do it, this was never what you wanted. Not revenge. It can't just be about revenge. The world, the Hinter, the whole Vellum, can't just be about revenge.

So she drags the angel through the town he rules, this little Haven out in the Hinter where he's set himself up as fucking king, *Basileus*. She drags him through the market, toppling stalls and barrows as she passes them, and brings him to his knees up within the portico of his own fucking palace, this once-grand angel of fire, stripped of his armour, stripped to the waist ... and stripped of his graving. The hatchwork of scars on his chest is so much like the birthmark graved on her lost son.

But where Jack inherited that strange riven graving from the bitmites and from herself, from the confusion written on her own right arm, this unkin's graving is an artifice. His greying hair, the beard on his face — it's the work of a warrior trying to rewrite his own fate, she thinks, trying to *not* die gloriously in battle, to exchange a destiny of war for one of will. A small-town king. A reasonable man, he'd say. But in the desperate order he's imposed over his own wild nature she can still read what he was, once, in the world before the Evenfall.

– The fates we make are sad, says Phree, but what had he to do with my mistake?

She speaks the line like she already knows the answer. Everything and nothing. A serving-maid starts to sob. The consul grips her arm, looks nervously at Joey's scowl. *You made your bed, now lie in it*, I can just about hear him muttering.

– He was like you, says Don, refusing to respect the Harlequin, to join his dance. He's ruined all of us together now, this house itself, you, me, and him.

The audience stand round the walls like statues, eyes fixed on the grim sight of the body of the Duke. It's almost gone now, dissolved into the swirling mess of bitmites rising from the floor, filling the room; there's something even more unsettling in the absence of it, though, the fact that all there is now is the head in Phreedom's hand. Strange how we talk about decapitation as losing your head, when it's as much a head losing its body, becoming heartless, gutless, spineless . . . dead.

– I'll be reviled, an outcast from this hall of dreams, says Don. The once great Pantaloon, who sowed the seeds of Themes and reaped the harvest.

On Phree's face the tears write the distress and shame of a young woman who has felt a child slain in her womb, or held it frozen in her arms, or watched it laid to rest in a dark tomb. Or who just doesn't know. It's all the same. Cause even if there is no blame, the dream of it all being a lie is all it takes to drive someone insane. The death of innocence is the death of hope, I think, and the death of hope is the death of reason. Mourning is madness, Phree, in every way that you can take those words.

She circles the angel.

He must have hacked himself up, she reckons, in the days when the bitmites swept howling through reality, in the Evenfall, or in the Hinter that followed behind it, like some war criminal whose troops are vanquished going under the knife, choosing survival over glory, obscurity over execution. But there's enough still there of his graving that she can read his past in it, the flames and the smoke of war. In the scars on his chest she can read the firework trajectory of his ascent, the slashing curves of cities falling in his path, the thousand nicks of souls, pinpricks and razor-cuts of slaughter in some terrible apocalyptic struggle. He only had to say the word and fire fell from the sky on Baghdad, Tehran and Damascus.

She looks at his graving and she can see him: see the identity disguised within; see him ordering executions of angels, demons and humans alike; see him trying to hold the remnants of the Covenant together by brute force; see him brooding on his throne as the Evenfall roared outside, the noise of it rising to drown out even the Cant of his own personal guard; see this angel overlord turn and flee, abandoning his brethren to their fates, to the bitmites and the humanity they'd allied themselves with, now tearing down the gates.

It's me, he'd said. It's Jack. And she wanted it to be true so bad she almost killed him when she realised that it wasn't, when she took her clawed hand from his throat to tear his shirt open and knew *exactly* what he was, *who* he was. An angel of fire who thought he could conquer every demon but who found human hatred a more powerful force than any simple, power-hungry unkin. An angel of fire on the run from Evenfall, and the bitmites and all the rage and sorrow and uncertainty let loose in it. *The* angel of fire.

Gabriel.

She leans down to whisper it in his ear, to let him know he's bound to her now. She's not going to kill him, she says. As long as he understands that she's in charge now. That he's not a king now. He can be ... a duke, maybe, but not a *king*. She knows there's an even deeper cruelty in what she's doing to him and to herself by letting him live, but she wants so much for him to be Jack, and this *is* the Hinter, this *is* the wild world after the bitmites, where the lies can be made real, where scattered souls gather together round the dreams they share.

And maybe his dream is not so incompatible with her own.

The bitmites flow down from her arm, over her bloody claws, onto the head, fusing the two in a filigree of crawling symbols. They begin to eat the flesh, and the nausea of the image hits me once again. Joey and Jack seem unconcerned, but Guy, like me, can barely face this sight. Phree's hand trembles a little with a judder of her spine. Yes, this is death, Phree. Even in the Hinter, even in these realms of fantasy where wicked tyrants die by their own sword, and where their bodies melt away, death isn't clean; it leaves its tokens, visible, obscene.

Don lays a hand upon her chin and turns her face to look at him. There is no horror in his eyes, only a solemn quiet.

– Pantaloon, I say, I pity you this doom. Although your grandson only got what he was due, it is a bitter blow to you.

He takes the head out of her hands, a gentleness in the way he opens up her fingers and untangles them from the dissolving hair. He holds her trophy by the jaw.

– Our house looked up to you, he says, my daughter's son when I had none. The keystone of my hall, you ruled the city with such fear no one would dare insult the old king when he saw you near; he'd get what he deserved.

As he speaks to the head, flesh crumbles off it as a dust of bitmites, bone gleaming white as it's revealed.

– My precious child, he says, I'll always think of you as mine. I'll always think of you . . . your tender tug upon my beard, your call, your curt demand, *M'sire, who has insulted you, old man? Who pricks your heart, a thorn stuck in your side? Tell me, old man. I'll have his hide.*

The head is stripped now of all flesh and Don walks with it, talks with it, playing Pantaloon, an aged fool, as if poor Yorick stood with Hamlet's skull.

– Although you're dead, he says. Although you'll never do these things again . . .

He tails off, sinking into silent sorrow for a moment.

– If any man denies the truth of the divine, let him remember Pierrot and Columbine, her sisters too. Have pity for this prince's death and then believe . . .

Believe in chance, I think, though. Chance and chaos. In a god that dances, drunk and mad with wine. What else is there that offers us relief?

– Ah, lass, says Don, we're come to a hard pass. You and your sisters . . . I don't know if your old man can help you now, my child.

– Alas, she says, old man, our fate is set. It's misery, she says. Exile.

The bitmites whisper it, but she can feel it deeper in her than their voice. It's part of her, the graving all along her arm, the intertwining serpents of her nature, all the conflict and the strange peace born from it, written on her skin, carved in her as this prophecy that she was fool enough to listen to so long ago. It's the prophecy of her journey through the Vellum with Don at her side, their stops on strange shores and Don growing older, herself unchanged. It's the prophecy of them urging slave girls rescued from the houses of aristos before them like cattle, as ruptor-blasts shatter the ground under their feet. Don waving them on, staying back to hold off their pursuers, so fucking noble, so fucking stupid, so fucking . . .

Go on without me.

She missed him so much.

– Ah, poor child, he says.

He wraps his arms around her. In the white robe of his costume, he seems like a frail old swan folding its snowy wings around a cygnet. The bitmites whisper her next line and, as she says it, part of her is Phreedom, part is Anaesthesia, part some other girl called Anna. But a part of her, she knows, is truly Columbine.

– Old man, she says, I'll weep for you. Farewell.

– I'll cry for you, he says, and for your sisters too. Farewell . . . if one like you can fare at all well in this world.

– I'll find my sisters and they'll share my exile and disgrace. We'll go some place where Zithering can't see my face, where that damned mountain is beyond my gaze, where Harlequin's vine-covered staff, if it is praised by other members of the pack, is never raised.

In this strange prophecy of her past graved on her arm, it seems so simple really, just another tale of loss, with Tom and Finnan, and the Evenfall, Don finding her in New York. They'd travelled so far together, gone so far together, looking for some place that would be safe from angels and their wars ... then after all that, he was gone as well. How this war of hers felt like salvation then. How every angel head upon a spike gave her a sense of ... peace.

She'd led her tribe back out into the Hinter, half barbarian, half hellion, sacking city after city with her army, Haven after Haven, burning every temple, every tomb they came to. She remembers the day they raided the Oracle of Locks, and afterwards, her at the head of the pack, leading them all on the long march through the Hinter. A widowed bride, she'd led her children through this cold land of the blessed, towards a home they'd never find, and she knew that her ache was a torrential river she would never cross. She'd never really be at rest.

– Farewell, my home, my native land, she says. The Harlequin has lain his fury on us with a heavy hand.

The consul stands holding a serving-girl's arm, slightly in front of ... Sara, her name is. She has a name, just as the consul is called Etmundt. And there's Merton and Rosai and Taner and ... she knows all their names. These courtiers and serfs, these maids-in-waiting, water-boys, they all have names and places in this Haven, under the Duke's roof, every one of them, and these few terrified souls just a fraction of a whole society of scribes and cooks, cleaners and gardeners, the choirs who sing every morning in the domes around the walls, bellringers and watchmen and whipping boys and guards. She wonders what they'll do now that the Duke is gone. She wonders if she's sad, knowing that she can't stay here any longer, because she'll miss them or because she's never really known them well enough to miss them.

– God forgive me for my crime, she says. I know I've sinned, but this is too unkind.

The Harlequin, his eyes so blue beneath the mask, takes the Duke's skull out of Don's hand.

– Why wait? he says. Why do you still delay your fate? Columbine, if you'd only recognised me as the son of the divine, at the right time, he says, if you'd seen sense before it was too late, Columbine, you'd be happy now. We'd be on the same side. But even though I am divine, no son of mortal man but Sooth himself, I suffered your disdain. My name had no respect in Themes.

He reaches up behind his head to pull a cord. The mask falls, and she sees the face that haunts her dreams. She's known it as an infant in her arms, and as an ageing angel using all his charms to save his skin, but this is Jack not as some noble warrior but as a Harlequin, not as a Duke but as a Dionysus with a snicking grin.

– You know, he says, some say the gods are fools to let their passions sink so low, but long ago . . .

He holds the skull of the Duke up. Bitmites crawl in the sockets of the eyes, eating the thing away from the inside. He gives a little blow and it bursts into dust.

– My father, he says, made it so, and so we must.

– The soul takes many forms, I say, and many fates transpire. So what we hope for may not always come to be, but we find ways to bring about events we fear . . .

The white dust floats out through the air, the bitmites clearing in its path.

– As we, I hope, I say, have shown you here.

There is no final curtain, just the dimming of the lights. We take no bows. The crowd stands silent as Jack pulls a lever here and there. A clang, a whine of motors and the stage begins to rise, Jack kicking polystyrene rocks out of the way. As Don leads Phree up to the wagon, Jack's already sliding open a compartment in the roof, retrieving hidden ruptors. He drops one and then another down to me, and then a third. As the wagon's side wall judders into place, he pulls a fourth out for himself. He flicks it on, jumps for a rope and slides down to the ground beside me. Don is clambering out into the wagon's driving seat and slipping on the gloves that drive it. I take the ruptors over to Joey and Guy while Jack, with one eye on the cowering audience, flips tarpaulins off the Waldo horses round behind the wagon, locks the harness straps on them, kicks out the blocks from under the wagon's wheels and swings up on the running-board.

His hands held out in front of him as if he's playing a piano, Don brings the giant claw-things into life. The harness straps snap tight and the Waldo horses pull the wagon forward, trundling slowly round, out of the scaffolding of rigging, out into the hall. He steers it past most of the wreckage, though a few chairs crack beneath a wheel or have to be kicked off to one side by a finger-flick.

As Guy and I follow the wagon out through the wide doors we came in by, Joey strides into the centre of the room to pull the Duke's sword from the wreckage, and jogs back to join us. I catch a look at the consul's face before Joey and Guy swing the doors shut, the way he puts himself between us and the serving-girl. I notice the old courtier at his other side, holding his hands in front of him, hiding the wet patch at his crotch. All in an evening's entertainment, I think.

Then the doors are shut and Joey is jamming the sword between the handles as a makeshift bolt; it might give us just a little more time. Guy clambers up onto the bench beside Don, and I jump up onto the running-board, scrabble up a ladder onto the roof. The corridor in front of us is long and grey and there's a lot of guards and gates between us and the outside world. But at least there's six of us now – not much against an army, but just one man short of the Magnificent Seven.

And at least we've got Phreedom back.

Errata

A Hunter, a Gatherer

They say they saw my brother in Dresden. In Dresden, London, Nagasaki. But they say nothing of me. They say nothing of me walking in Berlin on Kristallnacht, amongst the broken glass and broken lives. They say nothing of me walking with the damned to Auschwitz, Dachau, Belsen, and the iron gates closing behind us. They say nothing of me kneeling on the tiled floors covered in shit and piss, kneeling to hold the hands and hold the last thoughts of those dying round me. They say nothing of me, the last of all the thieves they'll have to suffer.

But in Siberian gulags, Japanese prisoner-of-war camps, villages in Vietnam, Bosnian towns, wherever there was pain and misery in those days, I was there unseen, unheard, but seeing and hearing, knowing everything the dying ever were – as broken and tattered as that now was – and gathering it into the river of souls that flows within me.

I wanted only to escape the hunters of this world once, live my own life free of responsibilities. Instead I have myself become a hunter, a gatherer, and while *my* life is not my own, all others, it seems, are my charge.

I would not say I hear the whispers of the souls as they issue from the still cracked lips in the pause after the last intake of breath of those about to die, before the final guttering. I do not literally hear them, but it is *like* hearing, like a memory of what's been heard. At first I thought these voices in my head were mere imagination, mad hallucinations as the doctors would say, standing by my bed discussing me as if I were an animal. So indistinct they were at first, distant and confused, I had no thought of them as having meaning, content.

*

Over time though, like learning a new language from the babble of voices in a café that you sit in every day for months, I came to understand them as the unspoken fears, desires, remembered joys and sorrows of the other patients and the staff around me, always there but only truly crystallising in the last gasp. And not heard but remembered from the Book, from the roar of ghosts within the room the day my brother brought us both from our world into this one.

I have heard the lives of all the dead of this dread century recited in a single, rushing moment, all the hours of those lives poured out and swirling round me. I cannot help but to remember them when I am near their owners, especially when that owner is remembering their precious personal history for the last time.

The River of Souls, the Thief of Lives

Should I let all these broken lives drift off into eternity, lost and forgotten? Should I stay silent, let them sink back into slumber in my flesh? When I first opened my mouth and poured these ghosts out to the doctors of the Institute, I did not mean to shroud myself in wraiths of memory. I caught the fleeting whisper of forced sterilisation in one doctor's thoughts, and a hint of something even worse; I thought if I could only make them see that we too had moments of meaning in our pasts then ... they would see that we were human. I did not know ...

I did not know that I would find myself not only flooding my surroundings with the river of souls but also caught and carried in that river, out of the prison that I was in, away into the place and moment of this memory or that. Climbing onto a train beside two meeting lovers. Out on a street where a mother is scolding her daughter for her lateness. I only meant to be a witness to those who had been forgotten. But each word I speak of their lost histories is a step through time and space. And so, whatever prison I may be in I can walk away from, and whatever death camp they may take me to, as another nameless numbered member of the herd, I can always escape into a dead man's past.

*

Am I only a scavenger then, fooling myself with dreams of mercy? Do I seek them out to take their last unspoken confessions only because the more of them that I remember, the more free I am to travel anywhere and anytime within the lives written within the Book? Am I the guardian and witness of their souls or just a thief of lives? In truth, I think I am a little of both. And while many might say that it's not my place to gather what belongs to Death, I say that Death, who rules this world, demanding sacrifice and supplication, stakes his claims in fire and blood. And I will not accept those claims, because I know his face. I know the face of Death, the one true God whose only answer to our prayers is our destruction. I know my brother's face.

I do not see myself as any sort of hero, but if I can steal those lives and, in my own escapes, take them with me out of the nightmares of this here, that now, I will do so. Oh, no, a thief of lives is not a hero, for a hero knows that what he does is right and I have no such certainty. Nor do I desire it. It is the heroes – men who would be gods – who tear this world apart with those blind, brutal certainties, and it's the rest of us who're left to stumble through the ruins, gathering our dead.

VOLUME FOUR

Eastern Mourning

Dead Eternities and Dust

The Principaea Cosmogonea of Gioseppus de Paracletus

According to the great seventeenth-century scholar, Gioseppus de Paracletus, *The Book of All Hours* begins with a list of all rational finite numbers – 1, 2, 3, 4 ... and so on, four hundred numbers on each page, in forty lines of ten numbers to a line. There is no zero in this list, zero being a step outside finity and therefore beyond the remit of a tome dealing primarily with the existential. Rather, on the facing pages of this list of numbers, scrawled in some annotator's nervous longhand, a list of fractions runs in tandem – $\frac{1}{1}$, $\frac{1}{2}$, $\frac{1}{3}$, $\frac{1}{4}$ ... and so on.

It should be obvious from this that it is only on the turn of the last page (which one never seems to reach no matter how long one spends flicking forward through the Book) that the reader will finally be faced with infinity on one page and zero on the page facing it. Zero, as the discerning reader of the Book will no doubt understand, is no more a concrete measure of actuality, of things, than is infinity. Like infinity, it is an *abstraction* of the idea of measurable units of actuality. From our existential experiences of something(s) we abstract the ideas of everything (infinity) and nothing (zero); but these are, by their nature non-existential, trans-existential ... metaphysical.

Should the reader have the stubborn resolve to persist in flicking pages for eternity, however, Paracletus tells us that the Book of All Hours, having crammed infinity into the first four hundreth of its infinite pages, follows on from this list of finite numbers, plunging quite suddenly into mathematics proper, at first merely laying out the basics of simple arithmetic but very quickly elaborating and expanding its range of transformational symbols so as to describe quite complex geometric and algebraic relationships.

It has long been suspected that Paracletus drew heavily from the Book in composing his *Principaea Cosmogonea*, and that his initial division of principles and theorems into Macroscopica and Microscopica, with the former inscribed on the even-numbered pages and the latter inscribed on the odd-numbered pages, may well reflect a similar structure in the Book itself. Given the continuing relevance of this work to modern-day mathematicians and theoretical physicists – who still glean its pages for inspiration in constructing their theories of Relativity, Quantum Physics, Superstrings, Twistors, and Random Truths – it would indeed be remarkable if Paracletus were alone responsible for this surfeit of ingenuity.

More Solid and More Staged

Around the corner, the incessant *beep beep beep* of a reversing lorry cuts over the distant *vroom* of vans and cars delivering products and assistants to the shops of Sauchiehall Street. Fox listens for the song of birds among the early noise but hears none. Winter in Kentigern, and it won't be dawn yet for another – what? – three hours, and dark again by 4:00 p.m. He flicks his collar up and steps down from the doorway to the street, hands jammed into his pockets. He should have brought an overcoat.

It's cold but not cold enough for snow. It seldom is in Kentigern this time of year. With the Gulf Stream keeping December mild and wet, White Christmases are few and far between in Kentigern, so the midwinter season has a darkness that you don't get in many cities round the world. Lit by the orange streetlights glistening on wet pavements, the decorative lights in shops, the long nights in Kentigern lack that blue-white quality of snow in the air or ploughed along the gutters of New York or Berlin. It's more the light of bonfires built for dancing round, of Yule logs crackling in the hearth, candle-shaped bulbs in brass candelabra in a warm pub where you go to meet your friends. You can live through days without a glimpse of natural light here, going to work in the dark, going home in the dark. It can be miserable or it can give your life a strangely artificial air, a chiaroscuro that makes everything at once more solid and more staged. Like the whole world is a Caravaggio painting or a Rembrandt. The Prodigal Returns.

They're all prodigals in some respects, Fox thinks, at different stages: Joey brooding and bitter, always trapped; Jack in the first flush of wild ecstatic liberation; Puck resting, out in the wilds, in some orchard that he's sure will always keep him fed. And Guy? He's the prodigal who's been out in the world now for a while, he supposes, and is starting to see life's not as simple as it looks, starting to see how dangerous the world is, but unwilling to give up.

He turns the corner past the flashing light of the dustbin lorry, veers past a binman with a quick apology and a nod.

He hopes that he's planted the seed of something in Pickering's head, in the shifts, the misdirections and redirections, hopes that he's formed some new connections, like stitches drawing ragged skin together over the empty wound inside him. But he's better at graving the Cant than speaking it, and Joey, well, Joey is a tough subject, trusting nothing, hunting truth and hating all illusions. But they need him. For all of Jack's fire, even with Puck's love and Guy's savvy to temper it, the three of them need Joey's cold, dark will. Pickering, Pechorin or Narcosis, Joey will never be entirely onside, but they need him, his sharp tongue a surgeon's scalpel to cut through the lies they tell themselves. A painter's palette knife scraping back the layers.

A Grand Disunification Theory

The old idea that Paracletus's work derives mainly from the Book is, however, challenged by many scholars who have pointed to the later pages of Paracletus's *Principaea* as evidence of his derangement; as the book progresses, the reader cannot help but note, these parallel threads of rigorous logic, the invention and application of the 'suppositional calculus', the derived topological models reminiscent of the work of Poincaré, the predictions and hypotheses, all become alarmingly muddled by the tables and graphs of empirical observation he begins to add, at first in the margins and then gradually throughout the text, in any available area of white space.

By the thirty-sixth volume, as Schaller points out, the exegesis of the models actually takes up more space on the page than the models themselves, with these annotations of verification indiscriminately placed on odd or even pages, and quite often related to equations on both pages by circles, arrows and other such shorthand symbols of connectivity. This is not, says Schaller, the work of a mere copyist, but the dynamic – even fevered – map of a mind leaping furiously this way and that, trying desperately to make sense of increasingly contradictory theories and data.

On the opening pages of Volume Thirty-Eight the division between Macroscopica and Microscopica completely breaks down, with equations, formulae and observations distributed all but randomly between and often across both odd and even pages. From here on in it descends, as Schaller puts it, into a 'Grand Disunification Theory'. The previous scalar distinction now utterly abandoned, it is tempting to suggest that Paracletus is dealing with what we might label *Mesoscopica* – and a generation of epidemiologists and economists are indeed now trying to apply his theories with this in mind.

However, if he is doing so, it is unlikely that he is drawing on the Book. The evidence is, Schaller maintains with quite credible reference to the few remaining biographical sources on Paracletus's life, that after a brief study of the Book which provided his initial inspiration, Paracletus subsequently lost his access to the work and spent his remaining years trying to reconstruct its voluminous insights, dooming himself to madness and failure by the very nature of this goliath task. It is this, he says, which lies at the heart of Paracletus's descent into chaos, his attempt to map a labyrinth that he has only glimpsed.

Fox stops at the corner of Charing Cross and Woodlands Road to light a cigarette, looking back up towards Park Circus, up and back and slightly to the side in time, at the white church tower. Then he turns to face the—

– lights of hanging lanterns and neon signs of Chinatown, all dragons and Chinese pictograms. He's never actually been quite sure where this street is – maybe San Francisco – but it doesn't really matter at the end of the day. Chinatown is Chinatown, whichever city it's in.

It's the same time on his watch, but it's lighter here, the thin slice of sky that's visible above paling light-blue where, ahead, it angles sharp down from the roofs and into the cram of supermarkets selling monosodium glutamate and trinket Buddhas, landscapes carved out of bamboo and framed between two panes of glass and with black lacquered wood surrounds. He steps out onto the cobbled street to avoid a deliveryman, a box hoisted on his shoulder as he lugs it in the doors of a restaurant up the stairs to the upper floors. There are signs everywhere with words like *Peking, Dragon, Jade* and *Canton. Inns* and *Emporiums* and *Gardens*. Every city should have inns and emporiums and gardens, he thinks.

– Mr Fox! You are up early.

– I am up late, he says.

He steps back up onto the sidewalk to slap a handshake with Mr Chung and ask him how the Shanghai Empress is doing for business these days ... well, he hopes. And, yes, it is, and why has he not been around in weeks to drink green tea and play Go? Ah, but he's a busy man these days is Mr Fox.

– Nonsense, says Mr Chung. *I* am a busy man. You are a writer. It is your job to sit and drink green tea with an old man and play Go. Where else will you learn our ancient Chinese wisdom?

Guy laughs. The old man's favourite saying is *Confucius never had to run a restaurant. What did Confucius know?* Next week, promises Guy, next week.

*

He drops his cigarette butt in a puddle at the corner, and heads down an alleyway into a narrow maze of brick, follows steps that wind up under an arch into winding ways, enchanting ways, weaving between Istanbul and London's East End, streets of crumbling saunas and polluted air. Red lights in the windows. Girls with perfumed hair.

He wonders if there are any fallen angels in those brothels right now, pulling their clothes on, shirts and ties, peeling notes out of their wallets to pay the daughters of men. So many of them have gone native now, it seems, drawn to the joys and sorrows of the flesh now that their Covenant has fallen. It gives him hope, in some ways, scares him in others. The sort of chaos they're immersed in now has a tendency to collapse into new dualities.

Two Rival Schools of Thought

In the 1800s two rival schools of thought began a bitter argument over the origins of the Book, and by extension the origins of the Cosmos. Developing from the religious tradition whereby the Book was held to have been written down by God, using his own blood for ink, the Manualists formalised their doctrine around the belief that the ink was the primary substance of reality.

In essence they held that the ink was God and God was the ink, the substrate on which the Cosmos is based, both prior and exterior to reality. That is to say, beyond the spatial and temporal limits of the mundane world, they believed, the 'infinite intellect of a divine power, dark and liquid, is the very medium of activity from which the finite is defined'. This was, indeed, the dominant idea for centuries, in line as it was with the theological climate of Christianity and Creationism. We are all God's handiwork, said the Manualists, and most of the world agreed.

With the Enlightenment, however, this idea found a challenger in the shape of the Neo-Iconoclasts, who pointed to the absurdity of characterising the infinite (i.e. non-existential) in finite (i.e. existential) terms. Fiercely opposing the anthropomorphism of a Creator deity, they scoffed at the 'primitive and superstitious tomfoolery of imagining the world to be black spittle wiped from the beard of God, and daubed in pretty patterns on the page'.

If all actions are written in the Book, the Neo-Iconoclasts insisted, then surely the action of a Manualist 'Hand of God' must also be prescribed within the text. Hence while some were willing to admit the possibility of a demiurgic scribe, one as bound by the Book as any other creature named in it, they denied the prior existence of a transcendent Creator, believing in nothing beyond the Book, nothing before, after or outside it. The primary substance of reality, the substrate on which the Cosmos is written, they held to be the vellum, hailing this as the true fundament of reality.

That Distant Clarion Voice

The steps under his feet are white now, pinkish limestone, Jerusalem Stone. It's Arab East Jerusalem, still a midwinter morning, pre-dawn, still in 1999, but shifted over sideways a little. Kentigern is called Glasgow in this fold. Even less of the sky is visible in these streets which narrow the further on he goes; but what sky there is is a rich cerulean, at once more heavenly and airily real.

He checks his watch – bang on time– and lifts the cigarette up to his lips to take a draw, closes his eyes as, somewhere in the distance, a muezzin in his minaret begins the call to morning prayers.

Fallen angels, he thinks, and books of souls. That's one of the legends of the Book of All Hours, that it was brought to earth by the angels who fought neither for Heaven nor for Hell. While the War in Heaven raged, they thought only to keep it safe. But it was lost.

He opens his eyes.

Bursa. Just outside the Dilmun Otel, cafés and restaurants around him, and Mount Uludag sloping above and down into the city. Somewhere below, a muezzin sings, and Guy stands at a fence, cigarette in hand, looking down over the slope of roofs and gardens, listening to the waver of that distant clarion voice.

The Book isn't the only thing that's lost, he thinks. They all are, in one way or another, all humanity cut loose from their native realities by the Evenfall, even their individual identities torn up and scattered. Now the Evenfall has died away and they clamber from this broken world to that, searching the Hinter mist for family and friends, forging new kinships in this cold haze, latching on to shapes and shades that *might* be their lost brothers, sisters, fathers, mothers. That might be their lost others.

He's come to understand now that there's a deeper connection between them – Jack, Puck, Anna, Joey, Don and himself ... Finnan too, wherever he is. The seven of them, seven souls, but maybe really only one ... identity.

He walks up past the little wooden booth with the Heykel Taksi parked outside, into the driveway, into the foyer of the hotel. He likes the old world, hard-times grandeur of the Dilmun. It's not on a par with the Çelik Palas just up the road – with its vast domed Turkish bath, black-and-white photos on the wall of how it was in old colonial days, with formal gardens stretching down through where a road now runs, busy with cars spewing black fumes out of juddering exhausts. There was a time when the Çelik Palas would have been much more up his street – but now the Dilmun feels more of a home.

– *Geniden*, he says.

Good morning.

– *Geniden*, the receptionist says. Room 611?

– *Evet. Teşekkur.*

The Unwritten Book

It is easy to see that these two philosophies – Manualist and Neo-Iconoclast – are essentially arguing for the primacy of, on the one hand, infinity and, on the other hand, zero. Both attempt to ground the existential enigma of the Book in an essentialist absolute, captivated by the perfection of these abstract ideas – the theistic notion of the ink as a divine spirit, the atheistic notion of the vellum as a tabula rasa. Both, however, are ultimately magicking reality from their preferred abstractions, seeking to get the determinate out of the indeterminate, something out of everything or something out of nothing.

Both are therefore equally flawed, offering no real agency for the collapse from the infinite potentiality of a metaphysical state – divine spirit or tabula rasa – to the finite actualities of existential reality. We cannot get from either a full vial or a blank page to the Book of All Hours by the mere wave of a word. The unwritten book, as Hobbsbaum said, is neither in the ink nor on the page.

It is only in recent years that philosophers have returned to a more archaic theory of the cosmogonic nature of the Book, one which proceeds not from the infinite to the finite, but from the indefinite to the definite – the Orphean Cosmogony as it is known. By this theory, neither ink nor vellum has primacy, both being only more recent surrogates for the pigments and hides in which the Book developed over time, emerging throughout human history in the merging of its scattered sources, its independent inventions – a cuneiform mark on clay, a tribal tattoo on skin, a notch made on an ivory spearthrower.

Taking chaos as its starting point, the Orphean Cosmogony sees the generation(s) of the Book not as a singular event, a scribing by an individual author, but as a process of conjunction and differentia-tion, of evolution. There *is* no unwritten book in the Orphean Cosmogony, no prior and perfect metaphysical state of absolute certainty. Instead the Orphean Cosmogony looks for the origins of the determinate in the indeterminate – something out of anything rather than everything or nothing. Before the Book, it tells us, there were a myriad of books, countless artifices of vellum and ink, and clay and reed, of wood and ochre, stone and blood.

Spring in Bursa

The elevator tings as it reaches his floor, and the doors slide open for him to step out into a corridor of artificial light and warmth. There's something both secure and smothering about these sorts of hotels, he thinks, with their decor unchanged for decades, lighting always ambient and temperature constantly just comfortable. You can't tell what season it is outside.

He knows it's spring in Bursa though, even before he slides his keycard into the magnetic lock and steps into the room with its curtains open wide; on the sixth floor it's always spring in Bursa.

He slides the window open for that feel of air still fresh with the night but warming with the rising sun. The noise of traffic which comes with the open window doesn't irk him; frankly, it's a comfort after all the pseudo-mediaeval nonsenses of Havens out in the wilds of the Hinter and the sex-steam excesses of Kentigern. He's rather fond of his Modernity, for all its faults.

The others – Jack and Puck, Joey, Anaesthesia, even Don – somehow seem to belong in those less mundane folds; they're creatures of the vellum and the ink, of the Vellum and the bitmites. But Fox ... he may well have been travelling in it, immersed in it, for longer than any of them, but he's never been dissolved in it the way they have, never lost himself the way they have ... not for more than a short eternity at least.

Sometimes he rather wishes he *could* just surrender, let the bitmites drown him in whatever dream they think he wants.

But what he wants is to wake up, for all of them to wake up, for Jack and Joey to stop playing you-kill-me-then-I'll-kill-you, for Puck and Anaesthesia to stop playing victim and avenger. Ah, well. There's Don, at least ... Don just does whatever needs to be done, ever the stoic and sober old soldier. They've sat together, late into the night, looking out over some apocalypse from a rooftop garden, watching fires lit by Jack and listening to the screams of angels torn apart by Anaesthesia's ruptor. Watching skyscrapers fall in plumes of grey smoke.

– We've got to find some way to finish this, he'd said to Don once.

It was Kentigern, just after they'd liberated Joey, and the bit-mites had turned the city into a temporary autonomous hell. The Empire had ended. The fascists had fallen as the bitmites tore out of their stinking sewers, ripped across the city, *rippled* across the city, a plague of rats ridden by fleas. They'd won, but all they got in exchange was sectarian civil war, Greens and Blues, gangs loyal to nothing but a colour, stepping in to impose a new order on the chaos with cut-throat razors, half-bricks and sawn-off shotguns. Christ.

Don had just smiled wryly.

In another fold, Don had said to him, in another Kentigern, they would have called themselves Catholic and Protestant, followed rival football teams, sung songs of hate across the terraces; there'd be the odd stabbing, the odd pitched battle in the City Centre after a nil–nil draw. This was just the same picture drawn in bolder brush-strokes; it was a part of the city's nature, part of its character, a heritage of pointless animosities. The way it would always be.

Fox had looked out towards the sun rising in the east – forever, it seemed, *rising* in the east. Was it just a little higher today?

– Nothing lasts forever, he'd said.

Now he looks out of the window at spring in Bursa, and he's sure of it. Just as the Evenfall swept across the Vellum and changed everything, just as the long night of Hinter followed in its wake, things are changing again.

That's the thing about chaos.

Of Acrobats and Artists

The concept of chaos as it applies to the Book of All Hours is a particularly emotive issue. While the resurgence of interest in the Orphean Cosmogony has focused attention on this area, the legacy of Manualist and Neo-Iconoclast thought in religious and scientific circles means there is still much resistance to the idea that the Book may be an intrinsically chaotic entity, with order merely an emergent behaviour, an epiphenomena.

When, in 1939, Professor Samuel Hobbsbaum advanced the theory that, contrary to Schaller's assertion, Paracletus had in fact remained in contact with the Book throughout the later years of his work on the *Principaea Cosmogonica*, and that the progressive derangement of his work was actually a reflection of the content of the Book, the whole of academia erupted into uproar.

– The Book does not play James Joyce with the Cosmos, said Schaller.

In approaching the Book of All Hours and the Cosmos it describes, however, we are faced with an existential construct composed of myriad somethings, of stars and planets, of particles and waves, of matter and energy, of trees and thunderstorms, of acrobats and artists. The tendency to see the Book as a singular and grand, consistent and complete thing is, Hobbsbaum argued in his 1939 address to the Royal Institute of Metaphysics, to all intents and purposes, an act of faith predicated on our desire for certainty.

The Book, Hobbsbaum argued, might just as easily be inherently contradictory, open only to multiple inconsistent, incomplete descriptions. Our most accurate descriptions of the Cosmos, as Paracletus was attempting to explicate in his *Principaea*, may be at best only coherent and comprehensive … and utterly incompatible with each other.

– Let us consider time and space, he said. Let us consider reality itself, as a palimpsest …

Its Möbius Loop of Time and Space

Fox slides the mirrored door of the wardrobe open and pulls out the leather satchel, lays it on the bed. He unbuckles the satchel and slides the Book out. Looks at it.

He doesn't open it much these days. The last time he did, all the pages he examined were blank as a field covered in snow; he'd had the awful thought that the ink itself had escaped the pages, dripped out into the world to become the shadows under their feet, the night sky above their heads, the bitmites themselves infesting every nook and cranny of the world. He'd flicked forward through the pages, blank after blank after blank, stopped just before the last. He couldn't bring himself to look at it.

They'd been making their way back through a fold approximating some pre-revolutionary Russia, heading towards Kentigern on a wireliner filled with nobs and knaves, Jack and Puck riding down in steerage with the peasants, Joey at the gaming tables in his crisp black uniform, playing the Georgian fatalist to admiring contessas, Don and Anna dressed as Zhivago and his wife, Fox with a cabin to himself, dapper in his pince-nez and goatee, notebook under his arm, a journalist perhaps. He'd spent the last few weeks watching the ink fade day by day, as if something was scouring the vellum, stripping it back to scribe a new text. Flicking his eyes up from the pages to look out into this Syberian Hinter. Flicking them back down to look at the faint grey mathematics of – as far as he could discern – infinity and zero.

They were somewhere over Stavropol when he opened it to find the first page blank.

Fox runs his hand over the leather of the cover, brittle and thin, cracking at the spine. The thing has shrunk since he stole it – or created it – since it came into his possession, *however* it came into his possession in countless conflicting pasts. It used to be the size and heft of some ancient grimoire; now it's like some Sunday-school Bible, the sort of thing a child would be presented with after their First Communion, thicker but smaller than a cheap paperback. He can hold it in one hand, carry it in a pocket – that's what it's meant for, after all: a guidebook to lead the innocent through the storms of life. Not that he feels terribly innocent.

He tore it to pieces once, ripped the pages out and threw them to the wind. When was that? Christ, so far ago he can't remember.

Jack had come back from one of his trips out into the Hinter, bleeding and burned – *fucking dragons*, he said – dropped it in front of him like a dog returning a stick. *Look what I found.*

It shouldn't exist but it does, this impossible thing, this book stolen from a vault and carried across the Vellum. Created in eternal Kentigern from the skin of angels. Forged in Paris, 1939. Opened in Berlin, 1929. Lost and stolen, destroyed, remade, rewritten, the Book has as many histories as the world itself, and it contains them all in its Mobius loop of time and space, of contradicting stories somehow fused as one confused and rambling tale, a sort of truth but full of inconsistencies and digressions, spurious interpolations and interpretations, fiction told as fact, fact told as fiction. There are truths and half-truths, he thinks, lies, white lies and damn lies. And there are stories, which are all of the above.

He opens up the book and turns a page, which cracks between finger and thumb. He closes it again gently.

It might be a good thing though, he thinks, if he just crushed it now, let it just collapse into dead eternities and dust.

Of Eternal Collapse

Hobbsbaum founded his thesis of Eternal Collapse on a reinterpretation of the seemingly pointless formula which Paracletus inexplicably spends his entire last volume exegesising ... $x \times 1/x = 1$. Where Schaller takes Paracletus's monomania on this subject as final evidence of his insanity, Hobbsbaum, in a remarkable feat of intellectual athletics, leaps across the centuries from the era of alchemy to the era of relativity with an amazing insight.

While the connection had long since been made between this formula and the parallel sequences of rational numbers and fractional counterparts as listed in the opening pages of the Book – $1/1 : 1, 1/2 : 2$, etc. – Hobbsbaum's leap was to substitute into this formula the values of infinity and zero, to interpret it as the relationship between infinity and zero, as an equation. Taking 1 / infinity as equal to zero as the Book implied, he declaimed ... infinity $\times$ zero $= 1$.

*

It is said that Hobbsbaum patiently waited for the cries of 'balderdash' and 'poppycock' to die down and then, with a slight smile on his face, proceeded to further convince his audience that he had entirely taken leave of his senses. To summarise, his argument was that not only 1 but in fact *any* unit of measure could be substituted into the equation. Any finite value could be seen, he argued, as the product of infinity and zero, as long as one considered zero as the inverse of infinity, which, he continued, was the most basic assertion of the Book, coded into its very definition of terms, the list of finite numbers and fractions.

– Any finite value, Hobbsbaum repeated as the voices rose again, one, two, three or three gazillion, all numbers are the product of infinity and zero.
 – It is further clear, he said, that this relates specifically to the singularities of Relativity and Quantum Physics, those points of *infinite* density and *zero* volume, and that the mass of those singularities can only be considered utterly indeterminate, since infinity times zero equals *anything*.
 And thus was born the modern mathematical concept of Indefinity, of *Anything*, known popularly as *A*. The idea that all certainty is born of an eternal collapse of chaos into ... not order but simply ... existence.

In that Last Dance across Forever

He understands the Cant in which the Book is graved now more than anyone, he suspects. For all the complexity of signs that makes Chinese look crude and rudimentary, there's a deeper system underlying all of it, elegant in its simplicity. The sigils themselves can be broken up into six basic components – the dot and the line, the cross and the curve, the angle and the loop. These, in their permutations and combinations, are the gravings of eternity.

But there's something else. He's sure now that the spaces between these six morphemes are just as significant as the marks themselves, that they're a fundamental part of how those signs are given meaning in their relationships to each other. The distance between a father and his son says as much about their natures as to simply say this is the father, this the son. The distance between two lovers as they lie side by side in a bed is what describes the mortality of love. It's the spaces between, he thinks, that let those gravings of eternity shape existence in the silences.

He opens up the minibar and takes out a miniature of cheap gin and a small bottle of Schweppes tonic, which hisses as he cracks the lid.

He thinks of fiery Jack and cold dark Joey, and their changing roles in the eternity they've known each other, as close friends, as enemies separated by a gulf of empty hate. And the others who seem somehow locked in that last dance across forever. Don and Puck. Himself. A little girl with murder in her green eyes, lost somewhere out there in the Vellum. And the Irish rebel who, he's sure now, is at the heart of everything. In chains at the heart of everything.

Seven souls, he thinks; the ancient Egyptians said that every man has seven souls. He looks at the Book lying open in front of him, at the dots and the lines, the crosses and the curves, the angles and the loops, and the spaces between them, the vellum unstained by ink.

Fox holds the Book of All Hours in the palm of his hand, stands at the window, looking out at spring in Bursa. All he has to do is close his hand into a fist and the bloody Book will be done with ... unless it simply emerges elsewhen in the bloody chaos of the Vellum, finds its way back to him again.

What would it take to destroy the bloody thing once and for all?

The city is universal. The universe is a city, a city of souls all mad or dreaming, dancing together to a sweet and savage song, the Book no more than a Feuillet notation in ink on skin. It's there to be read, to be sung out loud and danced to, and if there's nothing to read, what use is it? Maybe it's the song that matters over everything after all, the *spoken* power of the Cant.

Dead eternities and dust crumble through his closing fist.

Errata

A Dream of Drowning

Air! Air bursts into his lungs in a rasping gasp that turns into a splutter, a cough, a sob, a scream, like someone surfacing from deep down in the ocean, from a century of suffocation, from a dream of drowning. He whiplashes forward, one hand reaching, and the action pulls him off the chair and crashing down onto his knees, onto the concrete floor. His elbow cracks against it, the heel of his outstretched hand slams into it and, curling into his pain like a broken thing swallowed by some leviathan, bones crunched and spewed out upon some sea-crashed rock, Finnan heaves air in and out of agonised, excruciating lungs. Oh, Jesus Christ. Oh Jesus Fookin Fucking Christ. Shit. He rolls down onto his side, onto his back, bringing his arms up automatically around his chest, hugging his shoulders. He can feel the thick and wet of blood stick to his forearms where they touch the ruin of his chest. Oh Jesus, but he can't look, so he stares up at the sky so blue, not blinding pale blue of midday but rich and dark, a morning sky.

The sudden crack of bone curls him into a screaming foetal ball, another crack, a splintering shriek of bone on bone, and he almost passes out from the fucking pain until . . .

It stops.

Or at least it subsides, no longer an ocean of agony crashing over him in wave after wave, but just a surf of foam that laps around his soaked, sea-battered body. Eyes still closed, he lets one hand release his shoulder, moves it slowly, tenderly down, just fingertips running across to clavicle, down to the sternum and around the ribs. He feels the skin sliced here and there in fiery open wounds, the shooting stab of broken ribs where he's stupid enough to probe too hard, but . . . things are in their right places. Christ, but he knows what they'd done to him, what damage they'd done to him, chest splintered open like a corpse in autopsy. He can still picture it now. He can see—

335

Finnan rolls over onto his side as the bile rises from his stomach, burns the back of his throat, and spews out in the last spluttering, retching spasms of his resuscitation.

On his back again, wiping the back of a hand across his lips, he opens his eyes to the sky so fucking beautifully blue, then looks down slowly, fearfully, at his chest; the meat-hook is gone and the ribcage sits intact now, moving gently up and down with his calming breath, slicked with a surface of gore like someone took a carving knife to him, sure, but not ... not like the train wreck the fucking angels had made of it, Metatron's man, Henderson, and the other ... MacChuill.

Fucking Covenant cunts.

He tries to put his thoughts into some sort of order, reconstruct a rational chronology of what happened after his capture, but so much of it is riven by the unreality they've wrought on him – *written in him* – he's not sure that's even possible now. He remembers the torture all right. Being forced to relive his past. Being broken and reshaped into a ... mouthpiece. They wanted an oracle, a latter-day Prometheus wired so deep into the Vellum that his very words were volcanic fire. They wanted to know who could bring them down, and he as much as told them. *Anyone*, you fuckers. *Everyone*. Didn't do the fuckers much good in the end, what with Metatron's own bitmites turning against him, deciding that they were pretty much on the side of that anyone and everyone, thank you very much.

Last thing Finnan can fit into place with any accuracy is the black dust volutes of the bitmites picking up the Covenant scribe and ripping him ... out of the picture, just chucking the bastard out across the Vellum like a scrunched-up piece of paper. And then the shadows closing in around him, whispering sorrow and selfhood, a living liquid language, black as night, swirling with shapes suggesting sentience ... empathy.

And even in your cage of wire and flesh we envy you.

Sure and for all that the bitmites are part blood of long-dead unkin, part nanite machines never alive, didn't they just spit in their creator's face, and choose to suffer with him, with Finnan, so they'd know what it is to live.

Finnan rolls up onto his hands and knees, one hand reaching out to steady himself with the steel chair, realising that only the bitmites could have eaten the wire that bound him, that even now they're knitting his torn flesh back together. He pulls himself to his feet.

The abattoir is a ruin now, shattered concrete, twisted rusting sheets of corrugated steel all scattered in a spiderweb of concentric circles stretching out around him. At his feet there are flecks of red-brown rust – he notes the same colouring of marks around his wrists, stained in the furrows of chicken-wire drawn tight – while a few feet from the steel chair, where the wind is dissipating the last remnants of a thick circle of salt, black striations on the concrete radiate from the focus of the blast, from an outer circle of charred concrete – bitmites, he thinks, till he sees they're only scorch marks, smears of soot. It's like the negative image of the blasting round a crater on the moon, black on grey instead of white. But there's an order to the pattern – not symmetry perhaps, but it's like the blast wasn't so much an explosion as a . . . tessellation spreading out from the circle of salt, and everything in its path being ripped up, locked into place in some vast voudon vevere. There's a regularity to the wreckage, a pattern.

A part of this pattern – utterly integral to it, he recognises with a cold shiver down his spine – the cleaved cadavers of hundreds of slaughtered livestock lie, thawed now, everywhere among the ruin. Buzzards tear at the meat, flies buzz in a haze, but inside the circle there's only Finnan. Over to his right one of the lumps of meat looks different; a buzzard rips black cloth to get at what's underneath and a human arm jerks as the bird digs and tugs with its beak, yanking back this way and that, jolting the body till its head lolls to one side, face to Finnan. Henderson is barely recognisable, eye sockets empty, lips pecked away.

Finnan turns and starts walking, scanning the green-cloaked grey peaks of the mountains all around, the dry sandy scrub at the edges of the ruined site, as he heads along a dusty road winding up towards a town of concrete and adobe blocks painted pastel colours, yellow or blues half-hidden among gnarled trees. He's not in the States, he reckons. Looks more like Latin America. Mexico? A little shrine with a statue of the Virgin sits where a jutting crag of rock forces the road into a twist, the Blessed Mother watching over the hairpin bend from her sentry box filled with fresh flowers.

Something about the face on the statue makes him scramble up the rock for a closer look. He crouches, runs a finger over the painted plaster. It's her all right, just in a deep blue robe instead of a biker's jacket. Shit, Phree, he thinks. How fucking deep into the Vellum did you go?

Somewhen Else Entirely

Phreedom flicks a fly off the map. The old Mission sits a distance out from Alamosa, well out of the way of everything but the rattlesnakes and buzzards she's smelled all the way from El Paso. Sitting on the rock, the map laid on the ground in front of her, she knows exactly where she's going from the questions she's been asking and the lies she's been answered with in every small town in the area. Everyone she's met denied all knowledge of the Cold Men, but when she talks they open up – not with their words but with their actions – and she reads them. Watching their eyes as they flick around the map spread out upon a car hood, pointing here and here but never ... *here.* It's the blind spot in the centre of their field of vision, the place their fingers sort of skirt around unconsciously. In the end, she found a shopkeeper with a nervous tic that told her all she needed, then she got her directions from the sun and headed out over the desert towards the mission. That's where she'll find them.

The Cold Men, she thinks, pale strangers, tall and thin with bone-white hair, no body temperature, no heartbeat. And one day one or other of them will walk into a town, start trying to live their life like anybody else. Set up shop in some run-down property just off the main street as a sort of luck-dealer, selling charms and trinkets, snake-oil remedies and mojo bags to any who will buy. And then after a week or so they leave as suddenly as they appeared, and no one, no one in the town, likes to admit that they were ever even there.

*

Course, nobody even wants to admit that *they* exist, because that would mean admitting that the world is fucked up, that the disappearances reported on the evening news, or the war in the Middle East, might actually be what the crazies on the webworld say they are – the Rapture, the Apocalypse. The end of the world. But the end of the world is different here. In most folds of the Vellum, folks are only too happy to start the slaughter as soon as the angels bring out the fiery swords. Here there are no angels, no demons, no self-proclaimed messiahs, no aliens, no Elvis, no Conspiracy. The Cold Men don't have schwa faces, don't know shit about JFK or the New World Order, and don't seem to give a fuck either. They're not offering redemption or damnation, just . . . trinkets.

That makes this place unique among all the folds she's seen torn apart by the Evenfall and scattered into the Hinter, the wild times and wild spaces. It's not just another Haven dug down deep into the cracks and wrinkles of the Vellum, barricaded against the scouring, cleansing, dark winds of the bitmites. No, this is something else, a fold where the unkin war isn't even on the radar. That's what interests her, but it freaks the fuck out of the everyday folks. Without the war, without angels and demons, the end of the world just doesn't make sense, and the Cold Men are a chill reminder of that. In this place so much like what she used to call reality, the only demon she's ever seen with a horn on him was eyeing up a waitress in some skin bar in New Orleans. And the angels seem to be just . . . never even here.

It's New Mexico. April 1st, 2037.

But it's so much like home it hurts.

Calling them angels isn't right, though; it's an old habit that she's trying to break. What's missing in this fold is *unkin*. That's the right word for them. Like her, underneath the Cant, they're just human beings who caught a little mojo sometime . . . somewhere . . . somehow. A peyote trip or a friend dying in your arms – all it takes is one little glimpse of the fields of illusion and the river of souls that runs right through it, and it changes you. She knows that only too well, what it's like to take a look out of the back door of reality. There have been unkin walking the world for millennia, people who along the way happened to hear a word that changed the way they saw the world, and just decided not to die.

A Covenant grunt she interrogated once, he told her he'd stopped dying some time back when, at the age of twenty, in the middle of a war he didn't own and dressed in a uniform that hated him, he decided he'd get wasted in another way. He was lying in a foxhole, stoned and tripping, he'd said, when he heard the Cant – *like some gook caught on the wire,* he'd said, *just calling my name over and over again, but it wasn't a human voice. It was like the tracers and the guns and the bombs themselves were talking to me.* So he'd walked out into fireballs and gunfire, walked out and kept on walking. She's known other unkin that could walk through a hail of bullets; some can walk through rain without a single drop hitting them. For the unkin, luck is something you can taste in the air, spit onto your palm.

Of course, that Covenant fucker's luck had run out on meeting her.

But all this fold has is the Cold Men, and if they're unkin, well, they're the only unkin in the whole of the Vellum who aren't caught up in the War on one side or another, who aren't too busy playing cowboys and Indians to concern themselves with the humans caught in the crossfire. There's something about them that's close enough it worries her.

– They think they're outside of life, Finnan had said to her, something different. Sure and some of them I wonder if that's where the stories of vampires come from. I've heard of some with no body heat, no shadow, no reflection. They like to think they're beyond the flesh, you see, beyond mortality. Cause sure and all the rich flesh of the world, all that blood and dust, that's just a prison we need to escape from.

For him, he said, reality had never been a trap.

So he spent a long time keeping out of the way of all their rituals and incantations, living this quiet kind of life out in a trailer park inhabited by white-trash Jesus-freaks and acid-heads who treated him as one of their own. And Phree and her brother Thomas used to sit with him at night, chugging beer and listening to his tall tales, until one day an angel came knocking at his door with call-up papers for the apocalypse, and Phree she found herself standing between them. Long story. Not a happy ending. She still wonders what happened to him when reality came apart, when the birdman played the last trump and called down the apocalypse upon them all. That was twenty years ago, in this fold, an eternity for her.

But in *this* fold...

Did the blind and godless hosts of heaven and hell just wipe each other out here behind the scenes or did they finally, in some strange act of translation, make the leap they always wanted to and disappear entirely from the world of flesh to their banal eternities? All she knows is that there's not a single angel in this fold. Not one. So it's not like the Evenfall, not like the Hinter.

So maybe this is somewhen else entirely.

1

Mortal Remains

Dawn in Jerusalem

The Zeppelin glides down through cloud, through wisps of cloud, until the city is unveiled ahead of them and to the south. It must be clear skies to the east, for the city shines, catching the low sun with that golden quality of morning light on sand and stone, bright against the dark clouds of retreating night; sharp shadows cut the jumble of walls and rooftops, and the streets seem little more than chinks of darkness from this distance. From this height, with only the muted thrum of the engines to break the silence of the gondola, he might almost imagine the Holy City a haven where all men – Christian, Mohammedan and Jew alike – must surely live in peace, leaving the warfare to more temporal institutions than religion. From this height, there are no lines dividing Turkish North from British South, no Jewish quarter here or Arab sector there. The city seems a crisp golden vision of harmony. Dawn in Jerusalem is a wonder to behold.

It's the 14th of September, 1929, three weeks since the Arab riots and the massacre in Hebron.

Pray God, Samuel wasn't in Hebron, he thinks.

Carter folds the newspaper on his lap and lays it on the empty seat beside him, rubs a smudge of ink from his thumb. The coming weeks will, he's quite certain, offer little rest and peace of mind during his furlough. One only has to read the headlines to know that the whole situation is a shambles. The very idea of a neutral Palestine, joint British-Turkish control; it's a joke, absurd.

*

The two Turks seated across from him look sullen and hostile. The Russian lounges in the far corner by the door, legs spread out and cap pulled down over his face. Carter, sitting alone on his side of the cabin, finds the seating arrangement grimly amusing. The Russians in the Caucasus *here*, the British in Persia and Mesopotamia *here*, and the Turks, well, just where are the Turks positioning themselves these days? It's common knowledge that they're watching what happens in Georgia and Azerbaijan with great interest indeed, waiting to see if the Russians can consolidate their victory in T'blisi.

A part of him wishes that right now he were back at the Front; he knows how desperate the situation is. Every day the Futurists push further, and only the winter weather and the fractured support of their Cossack allies prevents them from breaking through. If the Futurists take Baku, everyone knows, then Yerevan is next. God, if they take Kurdistan, they could march right down the Euphrates to the ink fields of Mesopotamia.

Not that the Russians are the only threat. The Turks have never forgiven the British for the uprising that lost them Kurdistan. *If Atatürk were alive today*, you hear them say. It's no surprise the Young Turks aren't satisfied with this pared-down – albeit rejuvenated – Ottoman Empire; they're revolutionaries, and all revolutionaries are proud. *The Turks will stand beneath Mount Ararat again*, they mutter.

Yes, he thinks, the Russians *here*, the British *here*, the Turks *here*. All that's missing is a young Bedouin boy running wild around the middle of the cabin, firing his Lee Enfield in the air – Faisal's Arabia.

The Ben-Abba Airfields north of the city come into sight, strangely modern in the primitive Palestinian wilderness. Fat cigars of air technology float, moored on slender metal berthing towers, high over the confusion of warehouses and hangars, passenger terminals out on the far edge towards the wells of the desert. Carter notes a few BOAC passenger ships, or here and there the colours of this nation's flag or that, but four out of five of the airships wear the black cross of Germany on their envelope, the heraldry of Deutschland International Airlines. Nobody makes airships like the Germans. Here and there among these cruisers outfitted for either passengers or cargo but generally of a size, a few slimmer shapes stand out, sleek and beautiful amongst their more rotund brethren, vessels of the vedette class built for high speeds and light cargoes. These ones will be carrying airmail, no doubt, but Carter is all too familiar with the other uses they can be put to; he saw that first-hand in T'blisi. Nobody makes airships like the Germans, but nobody buys them like the Russians, like the damned Futurists.

He should be there with his men right now, Carter knows, his personal concerns set aside in this time of wars and pogroms. But this is a matter of honour. If Samuel is still alive, he *will* find him. And if he is dead, as this von Strann fellow believes, then by God but Carter will bring his murderers to justice. He feels the letter from his old friend now where it sits in his breast pocket, like a dagger in his heart, or like the threat of one.

It's only the latest in a series that the old man's sent him over the years, increasingly bizarre, increasingly worrying, written in tones that range from utter despondency to fevered jubilation. *I've found what I was looking for ... My hopes are crushed ... This is the answer, Jack, you understand, the answer ... Lost. Lost, goddamnit. Every trace has been destroyed.* There was a time when Carter saw his old professor as a new Schliemann on the verge of unearthing Troy, a latter-day Champollion in that eureka moment of discovering the name of Rameses on the Rosetta Stone, translating that first cartouche. But then ...

Even as a student, before the Great War, he'd come to realise that Hobbsbaum's great success was in a past slipping away from him. For all the groundbreaking discoveries of his youth, Samuel was never the most political creature and academia remembered his present eccentricities more than his past glory. After the War he talked endlessly of the old days, names of old friends littering his conversations as if Carter would clearly recognise these strangers. His son had died in Flanders and somehow, Carter suspects, it is that loss that's been at the heart of all these years of wild-goose chases – the undiscovered city of Aratta, the true site of the mythical Kur – whatever it is the old man thinks he's looking for, perhaps beneath it all is a much simpler yearning.

Eight years ago, Carter almost joined him on his mad quest – he had the chance – and maybe if he had, he could have steered the old man back to a safe harbour. But we can't change the past, he thinks.

He feels the letter in his pocket, near his heart.

A Sterling Fellow

Dear Jack, *it begins.*

If you are reading this letter, the time I feared has come. I will be gone by now and can only pray von Strann was able to get this letter into your hands. It may be that the full circumstances of my disappearance are a mystery to the Baron, and I regret that I can offer little explanation at this point; this communiqué may be intercepted and we cannot afford the perils of indiscretion. Believe me, Jack, this is a matter of deepest import, and you must put aside all thoughts of our friendship; yes, I know you, Jack, and this is not the time for personal vendettas. The future of the world – the past, the present and the future of this world – hang in the balance and I hope, I know, that you can bring us through. I pray that this letter reaches you and I urge you, Jack, to make all speed to Palestine, to von Strann. I know your feelings about the Prussians, Jack, but he is a good man, an artist not a warrior, and you must trust him implicitly. You may have to trust him with your very life before all this is over. May the Lord have mercy on us all, Jack. The enemy is not what we thought.

Samuel

And then there's the notebook that came with it, with pages which read, once you decipher Hobbsbaum's shorthand, like articles drafted for the history books:

... around this time von Strann crossed paths with none other than Mad Jack Carter, on leave from the Caucasian Front and recently arrived in Palestine in search of Hobbsbaum.

Jack Carter. Leaving aside the fantasies of recent Hollywood movies, little is known with any real certainty about Captain Jack Carter prior to his famous victories in Kurdistan. We know that he studied under Hobbsbaum at Oxford, but there is no record of him at Eton, where he claimed to have been schooled beforehand. We know that he joined the army at the outbreak of World War One using a forged birth certificate, rising through the ranks at a remarkable rate, gaining his first commission in the field at the age of nineteen, captain by the age of twenty-one. But while such a speedy elevation through the ranks (at a time when officers with blood other than blue were rare) might well suggest some sort of secret patron pulling strings behind the scenes, the rumours that he was the illegitimate son of this or that duke all appear quite unsubstantiated. Scores of historians have failed entirely to trace his mother with any certainty, let alone his father. Von Strann's biographer, Golding, even goes so far as to suggest that Carter started the rumours himself in an attempt to mask quite humble origins.

But whether 'Carter' was his mother's name or his father's trade, by all accounts, this young blood was a soldier first and foremost – the Sword of Yerevan no less – and one has to wonder what he would have made of an elegant and effete aristocrat like the Baron von Strann. And, indeed, vice versa. By the time that circumstances brought von Strann and Carter together, the latter must have been the very embodiment of everything the Prussian aristocrat and pacifist both loved and hated.

Carter remains in his seat, reading this utterly disquieting sign of Hobbsbaum's madness. The shorthand is so cramped it's almost illegible ... but not quite. He almost wishes that it was ...

A letter written by his superior, Major Hamilton, *it says*, to the Persian viceroy prior to Carter's citation for the VC reveals, perhaps, the most we know about Jack Carter as a man, describing him as 'a sterling fellow, his only flaw the recklessness of youth'. For the fearlessness with which Carter personally held off the enemy at the Battle of Majkops, allowing every man of his command to escape, Major Hamilton 'can only commend him in the highest terms, foolhardy as his action was. When one looks into his eyes, one senses that he acts not just with passion, but with a razor-edged understanding of the situation. I do believe he is exactly the kind of chap the Empire needs.'

But in many ways Carter's army career is even more of a mystery than his life prior to enlisting. We know that he spent three years leading a mixed guerrilla force of British soldiers and Kurdish and Armeni tribesmen against the Turks, across what is now northern Iraq, that his routing of the Turkish Nationalist forces at Karadut on the slopes of Nemrut Dag may well have been a turning point in the uprising which resulted in Free Kurdistan. We know of his five years as a military attaché in the service of the Shah of Persia, another five leading a new guerrilla force of British, Kurds, Armenis and Azeris against the Futurist forces now pressing down on their Asian fronts in the Caucasus, reclaiming the territories lost to them in the chaos after Stalin's death ...

And Carter remembers squatting on the barren mountainside of Nemrut Dag, scree slipping underfoot as he sheltered behind the massive stone head of the fallen statue of King Antiochus, aiming the Lee Enfield and knowing that if they did not hold ... knowing that behind him old men and women and children sat cowering in fear against fallen walls and piles of rocks engraved with ancient Greek inscriptions while their village burned down below. *It will be a massacre*, he had reported back, begging for more troops, more ammunition, more supplies, as the Turks swept their eastern territory free of the 'undesirables'.

– The Armenis are a filthy people, Carter Bey, his lieutenant Mehmet had said. They are only being moved–

– And the Turks one day will say the same about the Kurds, Carter had said.

Mehmet had stood there, eye to eye with him, for what seemed forever, and Carter remembers knowing, somehow knowing that this moment meant the world. A line in the sand, he had thought, a line in the sand. All it takes is one good man.

– Very well, Carter Bey, Mehmet had said. We will save the filthy Armenis.

A Twitch of Jaw Muscles

Sunlight flashes off the silver skin of a moored Zeppelin, catching his eye.

347

– An awkward situation, no? says the Russian. But we are not at war here, are we, Captain? Shall we not be ... civil with each other out of deference to our hosts?

Carter keeps his head turned to the window – has done since Damascus, when he wasn't making a show of reading the newspaper. The Baghdad–Damascus leg of the journey was quite pleasant, but now ... he can't say he's happy sharing the cabin with an officer of the infamous Black Guard. The most reviled of Russia's echelons, the Black Guard are the worst sort of Cossacks in his opinion, turncoats against their Tsar and their countrymen, the most vicious devotees of revolutionary Futurism. He's no stranger to this type of man; he's heard the stories of internment centres in the heart of Europe, of the pogroms and so-called 'purification'. He's seen for himself what the Futurists have done in Russia; God, even the savages of Africa would baulk at such inhuman acts.

And this creature has the arrogance to speak as one gentlemen to another.

– Major Josef Pechorin, he says. The famous Captain Carter, is it not?

– Indeed, says Carter.

– Can I trouble you for a cigarette, perhaps, Captain Carter?

A strained silence.

– Of course, says Carter.

There's little courtesy in his voice, only contempt; he has no interest in engaging in polite conversation with the man. Still, Carter can't help but glance across at him as he holds out the silver case, to note the face matching the tone of voice, the supercilious air of one who knows some secret giving him the upper hand. A cold, quiet smile plays on the man's face as he puts one of Carter's cigarettes in his mouth. A Russian black for a Russian blackshirt: how appropriate. Carter snaps the case shut. Although the Turks and British are the only two real powers in this region, this blackshirt's attitude is full of indolent, insolent superiority, of casual disdain. Still ... the Turkish forces stationed here and there through Northern Palestine or in their Syrian Protectorate may be no threat to him, but there's a British garrison south of Jerusalem, and checkpoints in the British sector of the city where this man could be shot on sight for a wrong turn. One might hope.

Carter could have found a seat in some other cabin of the gondola, of course, but he wouldn't give the blackshirt the pleasure. Not bloody likely. These scoundrels think themselves invulnerable because they stand for progress itself – the *inevitable victory of the future* – but it's this arrogance will be their downfall, Carter's sure. Beneath the sculpted steel of rhetoric lies a fatalism born of moral bankruptcy that drives them onwards to their own destruction. Nothing is in truth inevitable. All it takes is one good man to draw a line.

– The famous Captain Carter, says Pechorin. You look exactly like your photographs.

Carter looks out of the window once again, at the clear carved vision of Jerusalem stone, pink and gold, domes everywhere, coming closer now as the Zeppelin makes its approach.

– They say the Kurds love you the way the Arabs worship Lawrence.

– They exaggerate, says Carter.

– The Hero of Mount Ararat. The Sword of Yerevan. I should have thought your General Allenby would have made you colonel by now.

A twitch of jaw muscles, gritted teeth – Carter says nothing. There's no way this man can know the silenced shame that's dogged his every step beyond the churned mud of the Somme. A single mistake, an error of judgement – no, an act of unpardonable brutality. *I'm sending you to the East, Carter. I think you might be more at home among the Arabs.* Spoken in clipped tones, with narrowed eyes, an unspoken accusation of *barbarian*.

He never quite went native the way Lawrence did, but then he's never quite felt the same sense of belonging to this land, to the desert and the mountains. Still ... ten years of Carter and his men fighting side-by-side with the Armenis, the Azheri, and the Kurds ... The Sword of Yerevan ...

– Believe me, Captain Carter, says Pechorin, we should not be at war, you and I; we should be brothers-in-arms. If the English only—

– I rather think, says Carter, we'd make damned poor allies, you and I.

– We are not so different, says Pechorin. We both understand that mercy is a luxury in this world. We are not so different, you and I.

Nodding a smile at him, Pechorin pushes past the Turks and out of the carriage into the corridor crowd.

It seems curious, reads Hobbsbaum's strange scrap of . . . history? *that while many of his most celebrated victories – Yerevan, Baku, Majkops – were largely symbolic rather than of any great effect in terms of the larger struggle, such leadership qualities should go unrewarded. If his questionable breeding had no negative effect on his promotion to captain, why then should the following ten years – the years which saw his most breathtaking military successes – not result in further promotion for this 'sterling fellow'? Why did he rise no further in the ranks? There is one intriguing speculation as regards the death of a young private who served under him in France, one Thomas—*

Messenger. Carter snaps his head to one side, away from the page, looking out into the busy corridor of Arab and European businessmen, then away from there also as one face, framed by braids and yarmulke, turns in curiosity. Carter stares at the panelling across from him, the Art Deco veneer so sleekly lacquered he can almost see his own reflection in it. He does not shake or swallow, far too in control of himself for that, *always* far too in control. But he closes Hobbsbaum's little notebook and places it back in his pocket beside the letter. This isn't the only disconcerting entry in the book, but it's the most personal, the most private. He had ordered the Messenger boy shot – was it three, four days before the Big Push? – for desertion, cowardice in the face of the enemy. A summary execution on the front lines, because the men had to know such things would not be tolerated, and because . . .

He does not quite articulate the thought. Because the boy's brown eyes haunted his sleep as much before that day as they have in the ten years since. He does not quite articulate this, thinks instead of his fury at the weakness, the softness, the cowardice of the boy.

He stands, pulls his kitbag down from the railed rack over the seat and slings it over his shoulder, pushes out into the corridor, into the jostle of crowd waiting to disembark the Zeppelin, to walk down the gangplank into the Ben-Abba Airfields as the sun rises over the Holy City of Jerusalem.

Threads of History

— Palestine, 1929, says Fox. 469th Parallel. Eon X–7.

He unclicks the latches of the briefcase and opens it, flicks crib sheets round the table to us all, thick wads of pages stapled in the top-left corner. I scan the top page of my set of notes, highlighted, underlined and circled here and there, the odd arrow or three with a hand-written *READ THIS!* — not so much bullet-points as armour-penetrating missiles. Puck's — I crane my neck for a peek — are all pretty colours and dainty fonts. Fox knows his team of terminal wasters all too well.

— This operation is going to need us all, says Fox. Joey, you'll be on villain.

Joey slumps in his armchair, glowering like the god of hangovers. Considering the traitor of traitors has betrayed more men than there are countries, more countries than there are causes, more causes than there are realities, it's not like he's got reason to complain.

— As ever, he says. Whatever.

— Anna, you'll be out on the flank. Wild warrior queen role. Should come naturally to you.

Anaesthesia nods, a keen itch to the twitch of her smile. Hell, I think, without Don's deep dark voice to soothe her savage breast, she'd still be out there flaying the munchkins even now, ripping the adamantium armour off their backs. And, with the enemy all holed up in the Circus these days, we're overdue a little action.

— Don, Puck, I'll need you as deep cover back-up — old soldier, native guide, you know the score. Puck?

Fox clears his throat.

— Puck . . .

Puck waves a hand in the air — *yeah, yeah* — his eyes tracking the butt of the barman who's distributing our drinks around the green

351

baize table in Club Soda's backroom. He touches fingers as the man hands him his Long Vodka, smiles sweetly. I kick the flirty fucker under the table, get a petted lip in response. My horny little hustler, Ariel to Joey's Caliban to Fox's plotting Prospero, he drives me crazy, you know. Certificates, straitjackets and all.

— *Of course*, says Fox, a smidgeon of stern schoolteacher stressing his voice, an undercurrent of *Pay attention* . . . I'll be doing my usual rogue. And Jack'll be the main man.

He smiles his most charming and disarming smile — 'disarming' being the right word, I should say, considering how phrases like 'loose cannon' and 'going off half-cocked' all tend to congregate around me.

— You'll love this, Jack, says Fox. Into the valley of death, the fires of hell and all that.

— Peachy, I say. Snickety-snak, a snack for Jack.

I think of the aroma of angels flame-grilled in their armour, and I lick my lips. Icky, you think? Maybe; but there's no mundane metaphysique of flesh and blood for me, none of that nice neat cradle-to-the-grave of linear life. An avatar of chaos with an adamantium constitution, I got bitmite babies as the black dust of my blood; and a growing boy needs his food.

— So what exactly is the gig? I say. Go on. Excite me like a fire engine. Like a big red fire engine.

I cock my head to one side and make puppy-dog eyes at Fox.

— Believe me, he says, it will.

I lean back in the leather armchair, prop my glinting grey steel, spring-heeled jackboots (from the short-lived Mohock Summer of London's ignominious past) up on the green baize of the poker table. Tight tartan dress trews (from the Home Guard of the Free Scottish Republic), black, gold-buttoned and braided tunic (of a Lithuanian airshipman), red and white silk of a Soviet Nippon pilot's scarf flicked round my neck and over my shoulder — I do love my slapdash attire of stolen military apparel, each garment belonging firmly in a previous century and to a different timeline. Threads of history, I call them.

— Hit me, I say.

– We're going after the Book of All Hours, he says. The final draft.

Joey chokes on his White Russian, mutters *crazy like a fox* and *whole new meaning* in between the splutters. I have to admit my ears are pricked.

– Not the original? I say.

– The original is history, says Fox. But history repeats itself. Books have copies, or they survive in extracts, quotations, in the works of others. Fragments.

The Book is in bits, I know, worse bloody nick than yours truly, Jack Fragged. Blown to the far corners of the Vellum. I have vague memories of trying to patch it back together, Fox and Finn and me, in another thread of time that just ended snapped and frayed. It didn't work out too well.

– Thing is, says Fox – [he reaches into his briefcase] – we have fragments of the Book turning up all over the Vellum now. Copies and counterfeits. Have you looked in a hotel room drawer recently? Because it's not the Gideons you'll find there. Then we've got this – [a ring-binder that flops open as he drops it, showing poly-pocketed photos of gravings] – and this – [a pile of rough-edged sheets of skin tied together with string, the top sheet splattered almost totally black] – and even this.

He dumps a battered paperback on the table, a copy of Liebkraft's *Macromimicon*, spine broken, cover curling at the edges.

– I got that in a second-hand bookshop, he says. Chap behind the counter told me an interesting story. Said there's a different error in every copy. Every print-run, every edition, a different error in every copy. And they say that if you put them all together, all those errors, eventually what you'll get is the real *Macromimicon*.

– Keen, I say.

– Not keen, Jack. Not keen at all. Liebkraft's fiction describes a Book, and a world in which that Book exists. And somewhere in the Vellum, believe me, there *will* be a fold matching that world, with that book in it, the Book of All Hours.

– Sure, sure, says Joey, we've all read Escher. The Bootstrap Hypothesis. This is Metaphysics 101. Cut to the chase.

— I thought I had the only one, says Fox, the original. I thought it was the original that mattered, but once you start changing the Book, once you start editing it, the final draft is all that matters, the one that ... sorts out all the errors. The one that takes those rewrites and abandoned drafts, and ties all the loose threads together, neat and tidy.

— So? I say.

— So, we have intel that the Circus knows exactly where and when to find the complete, revised and corrected final draft, the Book in as pure a form as you'll find in any fold. They're going after it, and we have to get there first.

— How reliable is the intel? says Anaesthesia.

— Cabinet Minister, says Puck. Alpha-level access to the Duke's own bedtime reading. And a taste for rough trade.

He arches an eyebrow at me with the flirtiest, dirtiest smile. Rough trade with a smooth butt, I think. An oh-so-dreamy, peaches-and-creamy, Puck and me getting orgone-steamy, seamy—

— Jack, says Fox.

— *Jawohl!* I say.

— Are you with us?

I take a drag on my hash cheroot, blow out a plume of smoke.

— All the way, Foxy baby. Palestine, '29.

A Greyhound or Gazelle in Linen

14th March, *he writes in the journal.* I had thought that von Strann would meet me at the Airfields but it appears I was mistaken. Instead I was met by a young Arab boy as I walked down the steel gantry from the mooring tower, down into the crowded harbour-yards of docks and warehouses that comprise the Ben-Abba Airfields. It is an irony to call these places 'fields', for they remind me far more of the many ports that I have visited in my time, the squalid throngs, the noisy mob of stevedores and airshipmen, and everywhere the smell of trade and industry, fuels and perfumes, human sweat and waste, cargoes gone rotten. Unlike the airfields of more civilised climes where one at least is led or driven to a terminal, to be nodded past barriers

354

and along corridors by lazy customs officials with a cursory glance at one's papers, before being plunged into the milling masses, here the guards stand with their rifles ready at the very bottom of the bloody gangplank, trestle table to one side strewn with the undergarments of some hapless fool who's insulted them with a bribe too small to make up for his blustering manner. Here they march round the stevedores, beckoning them to open this crate or that even as they load them onto the carts and guttering lorries. And, with no division of mooring fields between passenger and freight, as soon as one has run this gauntlet one is in the thick of it, standing on dusty gravel ground surrounded by dazed travellers and waving relatives, servants with placards in Roman, Arabic or Hebrew scripts held up high as they shout out the names displayed on them. One makes one's own way to the terminal past the hawkers offering dubious hotels and dubious pleasures. And, as one leaps to the side to avoid being run down by some lorry laden with bleating sheep and beggar boys hitching rides on its hoardings, for all the confusing sights and sounds, it is the smell that one feels truly engulfed by. It is a smell ranker and deeper than the scents of any Mediterranean bazaar, one that crams the nostrils with a nauseating insistence. Petrol and excrement and worse. The only 'fields' that it reminds me of are the fields of war, with their reek of guns and blood.

I say that the boy who met me was an Arab but as he wound his way through the crowd, calling my name, bounding towards me like an over-excited pup, I could see that he was not pure Bedouin by blood, but rather a half-breed of some sort, his skin more coppery than the swarthy Arabs and his features more refined, a greyhound or gazelle in linen, white loose-fitting shirt and trousers. He reminded me of [*Carter pauses, pen held over the page*] you, Anna, actually, and I must confess, what with the disquieting nature of Samuel's letter and the scraps of notes sent with it, I rather felt myself overcome with foolish emotion for an instant. I'm sure now it was only that certain uncomfortable memories had been dredged up by this insane note of his, or that the heat and the fumes had got to me a bit, tired as I was by the long journey, but at the time, I have to be honest, something quite undefined but deeply disturbing struck me.

He pauses again. I have to be honest. *The phrase strikes him as something of an irony in this ten-year-long letter of confession, now become a journal in its constant failure to ever actually confess, its endless digression into what he's done, and is doing now, and has still to do. He began it as an explanation of why he had not yet returned, but how he would, oh yes, of course, he would. Because he loved her, loves her still. He still believes that.*

Anyway, *he writes,* the strangest thought occurred to me – that this was, in fact, a girl in boy's dress – before he reached me and I spotted the first wisps of beard on his chin. I am ashamed to say that I was clearly in a daze from all the hustle of the airfields, for he literally had to grab my sleeve and pull me to the side, out of the streaming crowds, towards the corrugated-iron wall of a warehouse, where the mob was less bothersome.

The door creaks open and Carter looks up across the wide expanse of dusty wooden floorboards stretching lengthways down the attic studio towards the door boxed in a corner. The boy waves, smiling as he closes the door behind him.

– Tamuz, he says. I come from the *Eyn* . . . the Baron.

Carter leans back against the corrugated iron, cap in one hand, the other raking fingers through his hair, squeezing the bridge of his nose. He squares the cap back on his head, stands up straight and looks at the lad. Can't be more than seventeen. Eyes darting to the pistol at Carter's hip and to the pips on his tunic, the cap. Carter smiles to himself, snaps a salute at the boy.

– Captain Jack Carter, he says.

The boy beams a grin, gives a slapdash salute back, chest puffed-out.

– This way, Carter Bey.

– Lead on.

The boy beckons him round the side of the warehouse building and towards the terminal, waving away the younger, smaller boys who would be yammering at Carter for money and attention without this native guide already in his service. It does make him cringe inside a little but the salute is a trick that always works. Sometimes a cigarette from a silver case works better, but it's the same principle; treat a young man as a soldier and he'll run round the world for you and back.

– I understood von Strann would meet me here himself, says Carter.

– It is not good, not time, the boy calls over his shoulder.

– But you're taking me to him, yes?

– It is not good, not time, says the boy.

– I need to see von Strann.

Carter grabs him by the shoulder but the boy slips out of grasp and away, turning and stopping in his tracks. He seems to search for words of explanation, then remember something. Reaching inside his shirt, he draws out an envelope.

– From the Eyn, he says.

As Carter reaches for the letter, the boy takes his hand and draws it in towards him, under his shirt, laying Carter's palm flat on his bare skin. Carter jerks his hand away but when he sees the hurt, offended look in the boy's expression, the curt comment he was set to make about *bloody decorum* dies on his lips.

– From my heart to your heart, says Tamuz, as if explaining to an idiot child, as if *Carter* is the one without a sense of proper conduct.

There's an awkward moment as Carter takes the letter from the boy, before he touches it to his own chest.

– From your heart to my heart, he says and Tamuz nods at the restoration of etiquette, the completion of the ritual exchange. He starts off again, waving for Carter to follow him, to keep up.

– Read as you walk, Carter Bey. It is not time.

Carter dodges after him, through a convoy of old men with wheelbarrows of oranges, skirting a group of women in scarlet-trimmed purple burkas, and opening the envelope, sliding the letter out, as he strides and weaves. More bloody letters. More bloody cryptic nonsense.

– Where are we going?

They push deeper into the mob, even thicker here where the white block of the terminal building lours over them, close now, families and individuals, porters and hawkers streaming in and out through the glass doors, pushing past each other. Tamuz stops to let Carter catch up, then plunges them both on into the shadowy space inside, still morning-cool and crisp, filled with travellers and their echoes but somehow, in the functional minimalism of its high ceiling and concrete floor, feeling all the more cavernous and empty for it.

– Where are we going? Carter calls over the head of a little Jewish girl in black dress, white pinafore, ragdoll dangling from one hand while the other clutches the hem of her mother's skirt, to whom Carter nods – *excuse me, pardon me* – as he sidesteps past, to stand beside Tamuz at the glass and shining steel revolving doors, the main entrance of the Ben-Abba Airfields terminal.

– Tell-el Kharnain, says Tamuz.

The boy holds up a hand, palm out. *Wait here.* Walking backwards into the revolving doorway.

– I will take you to Tell-el-Kharnain, he calls back. You will wait. I will bring the driver. Trust me. We go now, he says. Tell-el-Kharnain.

The Ruin of Life

As Ab Irim said to his servant Eliezer, my friend, it is said that God gave suits of skin to Adam and Eve when they had eaten from the tree in his garden and gained the knowledge of good and evil, to hide their nakedness. It is said that, after he had risen to Heaven, Enoch gave these same suits to Noah to keep safe from the flood, that they were stolen from Noah by Ham, and that from Ham they were passed on, through his sons, until one day, so it is said, these tattered suits of skin, long since torn into pieces by the ravages of time, came into the ownership of Nimrod, King of Babylon. And Nimrod looked at these skins and saw that there were words upon them.

What does this mean? Nimrod asked the idols on their pedestals.

We do not know, they answered. But surely it is the Word of God.

And what is that Word? said Nimrod.

Death, they told him.

Being a king, and more powerful than wise, Nimrod had no under-standing of this word, so believing he had the Book of Enoch, the Scribe of God himself, believing he had the secret of Heaven in his grasp, he gathered wise men from every corner of his kingdom to study these scraps of skin, great men of learning, astrologers and priests to explain its meaning.

They worked on the scraps of skin, joining them this way and that, trying to find a meaning that the king would understand. They produced study after study, and they found an infinity of meaning in the scraps of skin. They found all of the world's legends in the countless permutations of a few simple symbols; they found math-ematics and poetry, science and religion, elaborate theories full of wisdom which seemed true but which were full of contradictions. They learned so much that Nimrod had to build a tower to house this learning, the Tower of Babel, but still they could find no single, simple meaning that a king would understand, only the same theme that appeared time and again.

What does this mean? Nimrod would ask them.

We do not know, they would say. But surely it is the Word of God.

And what is that Word? said Nimrod.

Death, they told him.

Being a king and more powerful than wise, Nimrod had no under-standing of this word, so he came to believe it meant his overthrow at the hands of some young pretender. So he gathered his soldiers from every corner of his kingdom, and he sent them out to kill every newborn boy.

Seventy thousand of them he had slaughtered because of his fear. Only one escaped, the infant Ab Irim, whose mother hid him in a cave and gave the soldiers the child of a slave in his place. In the cave Ab Irim was raised by the angel Gabriel himself – for before Sammael fell, and before the angel of fire was sent with Michael to destroy Sodom and Gomorrah, Gabriel, with his horn, was the angel of music. So he sang the child to sleep when he was tired and suckled the child with milk from his finger when he was hungry. Then when the child was grown into a boy, Gabriel picked up Ab Irim and put him on his shoulder and brought him to Babel, to stand before Nimrod as his accuser.

What does this mean? Nimrod asked them.

You do not know? said Ab Irim. But surely it is the Word of God.

And what is that Word? said Nimrod.

Death, said Ab Irim.

And Ab Irim's words shattered the very idols on their pedestals, it is said. It sent all the men of wisdom mad, confounding their tongues and scattering them to the corners of the world. It panicked the soldiers so that some thought to flee and others thought to fight; but not knowing what to flee from or what to fight, they fought each other and fled from themselves, and fled from each other and fought themselves. And the great tower that Nimrod had built to contain the wise men's learning came crashing down, and the suits of skin were lost in the rubble. And the great empire that Nimrod had built to protect him from his fear came crashing down. And Nimrod finally understood death.

This is the way of things, it is said. Madness is the ruin of wisdom. And chaos is the ruin of order. The word of an innocent boy can bring down an empire at its foundations, scattering the people in confusion. An angel may have a sword that flames and a finger that flows with milk. We are all made of such contradictory natures. So too is death the ruin of life. And if God is life, eternal and spiritual, his Word from which all creation was made, must be ephemeral and material, and we ourselves only its echo.

All men must die, my friend, for we are death itself, the Word made flesh.

Mortal Remains

– *Escuzi ma. Perdun, m'sire.*

Carter steps back automatically as he looks up, mumbles apolo-

gies to the woman in the panama hat and linen suit who smiles her
thanks as she brushes past and out through the revolving doors of
the terminal. He tracks her as she tip-taps down the steps and turns
towards the head of the taxi rank, so terribly modern in her mannish
clothes, striding, breezing, a Sapphic sophisticate.

Carter scans the letter given to him by Tamuz. It's from von
Strann – the Eyn, as the boy calls him, whatever that means – urging
Carter to wait with the boy at his studio until he can return. *Return
from where?* thinks Carter. The letter only says that he'll meet Carter
when the time is right; for now he has to trust the boy; when he
sees the rest of the Herr Professor's notebooks he will understand
the need for secrecy. *My home is yours,* the letter reads, *to do with
as you wish; and I am certain that Tamuz will make sure you are
comfortable until such time as I return to play the proper host to you,
good Captain.* There's no address.

He folds the letter and tucks it away at the back of Samuel's
notebook. The boy must have been gone for a good ten minutes
now, Carter realises, and as he taps Hobbsbaum's notebook idly
against his leg he wonders whether to go looking for the lad. He
holds the notebook in that way all readers used to interruptions do
– one-handed, thumb holding the cover almost shut, forefinger
inside keeping his place. He opens it again, but his eyes are drawn
to the doorway, the revolving glass doors and the wide concrete
steps down to the road filled with slow-moving cars and carts, taxis
and trucks.

The leather binding of the notebook is dry and cracked and a few of
the pages have come loose inside. There's something about it that
bothers him even apart from the contents; it's not a personal journal,
so it's not that he feels that he's invading Samuel's privacy here, but
somehow it's as if ... it's the way he remembers feeling any time a
lad died in action and their kit had to be searched for smut or
suchlike before being sent home (couldn't have a boy's parents
finding pornographic penny-dreadfuls among the letters from back
home). It's the feeling of rifling through a dead man's life, the sense
that this scrapbook or journal or pack of cards or locket is as much
the mortal remains of the dead as the flesh now rotting in the mud

of No Man's Land. A person's shorthand is as individual as their handwriting, often more so. It can become so personalised that others might see only a scribble when they look at it.

Carter glances out the door again. Still no sign of the boy.

The air is warming up outside now. Taking a second to peer over the crowd and get his bearings, Carter sights a felafel stall, its owner a good man to ask if he's seen the boy, Carter reckons. He starts down the steps.

– Captain Englishman! Spare a few lira for a crippled soldier, Captain Englishman?

Carter turns, looks down. The claw of a left hand missing all but forefinger and thumb tugs at his sleeve, and he starts back at the sight of the poor beggar who owns it, knee-jerk horror hitting him like . . . the first time he saw a leper, a dead comrade, madness in the trenches.

– A few lira for a crippled soldier, Captain Englishman?

The beggar is a wrecked thing. Right arm dangling dead at his side, dark and withered, with a stump where the hand should be. He sits on the steps, rags scattered round in knotted bundles, some large, others small, a Turkish army cap upside down in front of him containing a few coins. Apart from a pair of khaki trousers – one leg cut short, folded over and pinned up where his knee ends in a stump – the creature is naked but for the grime and dust which crusts his sun-shrivelled form. Weathered, leathered, he looks like some madman mystic of the Indies. Or he looks, thinks Carter, like some mummy that's crawled here from its looted tomb to beg for grave goods in eternal penury. He might be forty years old or four thousand.

Only the one good eye peering up at Carter from a ruined face puts a hawklike challenge to his horror, shames Carter into blinking, looking away, and back, at the human being within the ruin, who tilts his head, stretches his left hand out again – what's left of it, anyway.

– Of course, says Carter.

He digs in his pocket, crouches down to put a few coins into the hat and finds himself looking into the man's eye again, on his level now. The man smiles at him, teeth white in the sun-darkened face as he motions a blessing, touching forehead and chest with his pincer hand.

– God be with you, Captain Englishman.

Carter makes to rise but finds himself still staring into the man's eye. He's seen men crippled by war before but never . . .

He tries to find the words but can't. The old soldier, old beggar, gives a bitter laugh, nods.

– I see your thoughts, Captain Englishman, he says. You ask yourself what happen to this man. What terrible thing happen to this man? You have time for an old soldier's story, Captain Englishman? You have time for my story?

Tamuz is still nowhere in sight.

– I have the time, says Carter.

All the King's Horses

I lean one elbow on the table as I quick-flick through the crib notes, the brief history of this horse I'll be riding like a voudon loa. Captain Jack Carter, World War One hero, Yerevan, Baku, Tell-el-Kharnain, etc. I skim through seven pages of ripping yarns and waxed moustaches and blah blah fucking blah to see just how gay the gay blade is. I'm just not built for boredom. Give me a chi-gun and point me at an army, but don't try and schedule the rebellion, baby, or I *will* drift off. By the time I'm flicking the last page, I'm gazing over the paper at the dinkiness of Puck's ear and . . . Fox snaps his fingers, breaking my randy reverie.

– Right. So I'm the hero, I shrug. Peachy keen. Do I go boom? Glorious death in battle and suchlike?

Fox sighs, blows a billow of cigarette smoke up into the air.

– I was rather hoping that you wouldn't self-combust this time.

I swirl a slug of absinthe round my mouth, and swallow with a smack of lips.

– It's what I'm best at, Foxy.

– This is a heist, not a hit, he says. Jack, I need you to try and hold it together just this once. That's why I'm sending Joey in with you. We need to keep the dynamic tight here. No subtleties, no nuances, just heroes and villains, good and evil, black and white—

– and fucking red all over. No offence, says Puck, but are you bonkers? Send those two in together and you're begging for a bloodbath. Have you read what that fucker's like in this fold, Jack?

Puck flicks a page up in front of him, points it at Joey.

– Don't poop yer pants, pumpkin, I say to Puck. I'll make sure he doesn't drown any kittens. How bad can he be?

– Jack, says Fox, have you actually read the brief on this Joey?

– Yes, I say.

He stubs his cigarette in his ashtray, says nothing as he looks at me.

– No, I say.

I flick a few pages further through, ignoring the notes that have fewer than four exclamation marks, natch. Even at a glance it seems safe to say that this Josef Pechorin is a very bad man. Sired in Georgia during the Terror of 1901, illegitimate son of a White Russian contessa and her Cossack rapist. Murdered his own mother at the age of sixteen during the Purge of Tiblis and led massacres of the Yezidi across Georgia and Armenia. Recruited by the British Falangists in Persia as a potential asset in the war against the Futurists. Sold his bosses down the river for a position in the Black Guard. Same old same old, far as I can see. Something about a disappearance on the slopes of Mount Kazbek in the Caucasus—

– Kur, says Puck – [he waves the page] – he's been to Kur.

– That's not certain, says Joey. The intel's sketchy.

– We're not even sure, says Fox, if Kur's part of the picture in this fold.

But I can see Puck's point. A psychic hunter-killer working only for the highest bidder, a white-hot tracker with a black-ice heart, Joey's more than happy in most folds to play nemesis to my schizoid superhero; I've lost count of the number of times we've crossed swords now, mostly ending in fatality for one or other of us, if not both. And a Pechorin kitted up with the Cant against a Carter who's not even heard of it in this fold . . .

– Fuck it, I say. I can take him.

Besides, much as it's nice having Joey onside, I kinda like it when he's trad and bad. Existence can be a trifle inchoate when you've got little more to sustain you than your own chaotic potential. At least with Joey, I always know who I am: the hero to his villain.

– Yeah, says Joey, like you can always trust Jack Flash to save the day.

His cool gaze, pointed as his comment, is on the botched, blotched pile of angel hide sitting on the table in between us. I snick my Zippo open, spark my hash cheroot back into flame. Hey, everyone makes mistakes.

– OK, I say, so what's the plan?

– Fuck that shit, says Joey. No fucking way. You're talking an Orpheus Operation and those always go tits-up. Eurydike . . . Lot's wife . . .

– Salty, I say and lick my lips and slip a wink at Puck.

– We can do it, Fox insists.

– Without the full team? says Anaesthesia. Without King Finn?

– The Irish rover's lost, says Fox. You know how deep we'd have to go to dig him out. Deeper than dreams. Deeper than death.

– Deeper than the shit we'll be in if the unkin hear we're trying to snatch the Book? says Joey.

– He'll come back, says Anaesthesia. You can't keep a good story down, and King Finn is a timeless fucking classic. And once he's back in the game . . .

– Then there were seven, says Don.

The magic number, I think. Seven days of the week. Seven Heavens, seven Hells, and the Magnificent Seven souls of Humpty Dumpty humanity scattered all in itty bits across the Vellum. The mass unconscious is a seven-headed dragon, and even a full-on avatar like yours truly is really just one head of that big beast. A single piece in a great game of chess where all the pieces have their own set moves and you can only win if they all work together. A knight needs a queen to defend valiantly, a bishop to criss-cross his path, a king and a castle, even a snub-nosed little pawn to stroke his horsey and keep him warm in the dark. Problem is we're one man down.

But who needs Prometheus when you've got the fire itself?

– The once and future king? says Fox. No, Finnan handed on the torch and walked away, and we can't wait for his return. You've been out in the Hinter, Anna. It's changing, isn't it?

She nods. Kentigern's not the only Haven where we've got the munchkins on the run, the whole city being one big Rookery these days. No, there's a scent of something in the air, a change of seasons, a new age, a new day or a new page.

– If we don't strike now, says Fox, trust me, *they* will.

– Thing is, says Fox, the fold we're aiming for isn't just a jaunt across eternity. You're going to have to take the hard route.

The poker table has an arcane intricacy shimmering above its green baize now, voudon veveres and sigils inscribed in the air by Anaesthesia's dancing fingers. She runs a finger round a scratchy spiral, and another branches off it, then another. She rotates it, tweaks it into shape, building the sim of the city's substructure, tunnel by tunnel, wormhole by wormhole. Used to be you could just skip across the moments, pick up a beer in a bar in Mexico and chug it down in Madrid. You're just as likely to slam the empty stein down on a table in a Middle Earth tavern these days. So the munchkin unkin stick to their Yellow Brick Roads now, safe and snug from the Hinter and hooligans like us. Anaesthesia's sim models their routes, the subways and the sewers that join with mines, ley-lines and dragon-lines, seams of chi-energy that turn and twist through 3D time as well as space. Tunnels in time.

– It's kinda pretty, says Puck. Looks like a 3D snowflake.

The Maps of Hell, a Jesus freak might say, but Christians are a dying breed in a Haven where Youngblood won the secrets of the Kali Yuga in his *Bayonets to Shangri-La* hour of glory, brought all the mysteries of chi and kundalini back to dear old Blighty. Here, in mechanistic mystic Kentigern, this is a mandala of Maya, the Vellum's veils of illusion, and it ain't God that's at the centre of this maze but the biggest wormhole of them all, a vertical shaft that drops straight down through centuries of strata to the core of the chaosphere itself, with a thousand side-shoots going God knows when. A door into the Emerald City. A passage to Erewhon. The Gates of Heaven, Hell and Never-Fucking-Never-Land. Or a road to Palestine, 1929, 469th Parallel, Eon X–7.

Thing is, as is all too clear from Anaesthesia's sim, those tunnels are all coiled up under the one place in this Haven where *angel* isn't a swear word and the man who freed the city isn't a hero. At the top of the model, over the mouth of the pit, like a woodworm⁄ridden tree⁄stump with its dead roots stretching down into eternity, the Circus is our only way in.

I hope Fox has a good plan.

The Dead Flesh

Pasha had a plan, the beggar begins. His English is broken but it's good enough to tell how he served in the Turkish 9th Corps under Enver Pasha, how Pasha wanted the ink fields of Baku as his prize, and more. *Yes, Captain Englishman, he had a plan.* So they marched over the Allah Akbar mountains in December, 1914, to draw the Russians away from Kars and Ardahan, ambush them at Sarikamish. Halfway between Kars and Erzurum, they met, 95,000 Turks and 65,000 Russians. It nearly worked – the Russians started retreating – but the weather ... *The Russians are cold men inside,* he explains, *and the Turks do not like the cold.* Five days of fighting and five nights of freezing in the deep snow of the mountain heights, he tells Carter. Soldiers getting lost at night. They tried to light fires. Many of those who fell asleep never woke up again. 30,000 men lost in the battles, more in the biting cold, and by the time they reached Erzurum two weeks later, defeated, four-fifths of them were gone ...

– And this hand is then the claw you see now, Captain Englishman. What is your word? Frostbite, yes, frostbite.

He snaps his teeth with an audible *clack*.

– Bit off my fingers and leave me with ... this.

Enver Pasha blamed it all on the Christian Armenians, of course.

And then – *ah yes* – he tells Carter of Suez in February of 1915. Another great plan, to strike with a surprise attack – *it will be easy, they say* – to cut the very jugular of the British in the East, the Suez Canal, push through and raise a revolt in Islamic Egypt.

– Hah! They are blind like I am blind now, here ... this eye. British bayonet steal it, would have steal my life if I not kill its soldier first.

Was the Captain Englishman at Gallipoli? he asks Carter. Does he know the smell of corpses left rotting on the battlefield?

Carter wasn't at Gallipoli, but he knows that smell only too well.

The beggar picks up his withered, stunted right arm with his claw, pulls it up to his forehead in a travesty of a salute. Lt-Col. Mustafa Kemal Bey, he explains, great Atatürk himself, was in command there. A man of will.

– Every soldier who fight here with me, says the beggar in a bitter mockery of military bluster, he know that honour ties him. No retreat. Not one step. And you want rest? No! There no rest for our nation, not forever. No rest until we throw the enemy into the sea.

He lets his arm go and it drops, a dead weight.

– Plans and speeches, Captain Englishman. Very important in a war.

It was May, he tells Carter. Each side had dug in and, after all the attacks and counter-attacks, a stalemate had held for a month or so. The Australians cramped in their little line of trenches, the Turks knowing that sooner or later they would have to strike. Then the reinforcements started to come forward – *boys*, he says, *no combat. They see my eye-patch, my hand, and they piss in their boots*. But quietly, secretly, he tells Carter, they fill the trenches till the British spotter planes can hardly miss it.

– I tell them it will be a massacre. But they are deaf. Like me, Captain Englishman, in this ear. One of your grenades when we go over the top. Shrapnel slice it off. They dig shrapnel out of my head.

He laughs. The doctor had told him he was lucky to have survived.

– Do you not think I am so very lucky, Captain Englishman?

He closes his eye and leans forward, the elbow of his good left arm propped on his thigh. Outside the airfield terminal, it's gone quieter, the crowd thinned out so that Carter now has room to sit down on the dusty step beside the beggar. He notes the stares of passers-by, looks of disgust and shame and blank dispassion. The old soldier stares straight forward with his eye closed. Chin up as he looks at nothing, thinks Carter.

368

– Where did you lose the leg? says Carter. And the arm?

– Leg first, says the old man.

He had lost his leg to cold steel also, he tells Carter. It was October, 1917, and the British were about to attack Gaza again. The Turks knew this because Allenby's artillery had been bombarding the garrison there for four days, five days, six. Two or three divisions had been deployed. More on their way, so the rumours said. Bristols flying overhead looking for weak spots in the Turkish line. Oh, yes, it was clear that a full frontal attack was coming soon.

So he had felt safe in Beersheba – little, unimportant Beersheba out in the desert – until the cavalry came charging from all directions.

He still remembers the sight of the Australians' horses in the evening, charging through the smoke and dust of a battle that had raged all day. How he stood in wonder as the cavalry rode down on them, breached their defences. *Horses weak with thirst, dying of thirst, Captain Englishman. But so beautiful.* How he stood looking down a line of sandbags and soldiers, seeing these beasts leaping here, and here, and here, and here, over the Turkish lines, a wave washing over them. *So beautiful.* And he tells Carter how it is a terrible thing, Captain Englishman, a terrible thing, to hear a horse scream as you shoot it in its belly, as it leaps so beautiful over your head.

– To destroy, he says, such creatures . . .

He talks of a cavalryman whose horse he brought down, how he ran at the Turk, with tears in his eyes and the rifle of a dead man in his hands, how he still staggered on with two bullets in his chest. The third shot had finally dropped the cavalryman, but not before his bayonet took a slice out of the old Turk's calf.

– It was not deep, Captain Englishman. It would have heal very quick, but – [he shakes his head] – not in the desert.

The Turks had been routed from Beersheba, without time even to poison the wells, and he had hobbled into the desert with his squad, leaning on this comrade's shoulder or that one's, half-carried at times by young men who knew he'd been at Sarikamish and Gallipoli, men to whom he was the Old Man, a mascot of sorts. They'd thought he was mad to lead them out into the waste; but the Old Man knew the desert, oh yes, knew much about the desert, so they trusted him.

By the time they reached Tel-el-Sheria, the gangrene had already set in.

– Do you know how I wake after they cut my leg off, Captain Englishman? I wake in the ruins of a hospital, dead men all around me. I wake into morphine dreams, Captain Englishman.

Having broken the line at Beersheba, the English were pressing their advantage, pressing for Jerusalem by Christmas, and on to Damascus. The doctor's saw had barely finished its work, the last stitch only just in place, when the first shells brought the roof of the hospital down.

– I am not sure what is real about that time, Captain Englishman, what I saw and what I only thought I saw.

He talks of being woken by the pain, crawling through the ruins, the shells still falling around him. Somehow he had found more morphine, and somehow in the morphine he had found the strength to keep going, even as the walls fell around him. More shells, and then grenades and gunfire. Soldiers screaming. *I saw a man made of fire, Captain Englishman, a djinn.* Skeleton horses ridden by angels. Blasts of blue-green fire like orchid blossoms, too symmetrical, too sculpted to be real. Dust-devils, black as night, rising out of the wounds of fallen soldiers. He saw sights so strange in his delirium that he hadn't noticed the shrapnel in his right arm till he was lying in the desert sands outside the town, hidden between a dead horse and a rock.

– My mother, she is of the desert, he says. Not Turk, but not Arab, no. My mother, she teach me many things about the desert, things even the Bedu do not know. Many salts in the sands here. Bury a thing in the sand here, Captain, and it keep forever.

There's a sly look to his face as he taps the scar up near the shoulder of his withered arm, where the nerves must have been severed.

– Dead things keep forever in salt, Captain Englishman.

Carter feels a shiver run down his back. That hawklike eye somehow doesn't seem as human now; there's a different challenge in the way it fixes him with its gaze, no longer demanding that he see the man beneath the mutilation, but that he see some deeper truth beneath the man, a truth that is perhaps not quite sane.

Carter stands up. Where is that bloody boy?

– I have not finish my story, Captain Englishman. I have not finish. Stay. Let me finish my story.

And now he tells Carter of the last days of his war: of being found, this maimed thing, mad on morphine, by the retreating Eighth Army as they fell back under the British advance; and of the fall of Gaza and Jerusalem under siege. It was November, 1917, and Lawrence was dead in Deraa, a symbol for Faisal to rally the failing Arab Revolt around. It was November, 1917, and Kemal Atatürk was in Istanbul, relieved of command by Pasha, brooding, gathering his Nationalist uprising against Germany's lackey Sultan. And then Atatürk and his men had seized the *Sultan Yavuz Selim* and the *Middili*, the German gunships sitting in the Sea of Marmara ready to defend Istanbul ... or to level it if need be. And Atatürk was dead in the mutiny, and the Nationalists had a martyr.

The coup had plunged the Turkish forces in Palestine into chaos, trying to act on conflicting orders or no orders at all. By early December Damascus was under siege, supply lines cut off, the city starving. And so, on the very day the Turks agreed their armistice, leaving Germany to fight its own battles, this half-ruined wreck of a man had been caught stealing food from the storeroom of the military hospital where he was recuperating, and the final insult had been perpetrated on what remained of him.

The old man's eye pins Carter to the step.

– Was it mercy, do you think, Captain Englishman? Blind law? I steal with my left hand – how do you say? I pinch, yes, pinch. But they take my *right* hand. Useless right hand! Dead! Dry like fig! Tradition, Captain Englishman, tradition. Do you like my story, Captain Englishman?

Carter says nothing.

– Ah, says the old man, I give you better than words. I show you, Captain Englishman. I show you what happen to me. I *show* you my story.

He waves his left arm round as if to take in the steps and the terminal behind them, the crowd going in and out. But it's his ragged bundles he's gesturing at, Carter realises.

– You see, says the beggar – [he begins unwrapping one of the smaller bundles of rags] – I *save* my fingers from Sarikamish. Look. See. – [Carter feels the bile rise in his throat] – And I crawl in the sand in Suez. Do I hear the shells and bullets? No.

He tugs at the corner of another bundle but Carter is still staring at the contents of the first. It's not possible. For the love of God, it's not possible.

– So I crawl in the sand. I find what is left of my ear, says the old Turk.

He grins, still chuckling to himself as he peels the second bundle open. The dead flesh of the fingers and … what's little more than a lump of gristle now sit on their filthy rags like some exotic roots he's offering for sale, fruits dried black in the sun. Carter looks at the madman but there's nothing he can say as the man hauls the largest of the bundles thumping down the steps and around in front of him, peels it open.

– I carry my own leg with me through the desert while the morphine shows me angels and devils. Dig it out of the debris. You understand, Captain Englishman? You understand why I do this? Is mine. Belongs to me.

– For God's sake, man—

– And I keep my hand too. They take it for stealing, but is *mine*.

He picks the last of the bundles open, like a child opening a handkerchief which wraps an apple for their teacher.

– I have names for them all, you know, the old man says. My – how do you say this? – spoils of war. My treasures.

His voice is rising, mad now, clearly mad, as Carter backs away.

– I call these fingers *Armenia*. I call this scrap of ear *Sinai*. I call this leg *Palestine*, and this dead arm, ah yes, Captain Englishman, I call this *the Holy City of Jerusalem*.

Down a step. Another. Carter turns. Anywhere. Away, just away. The voice calls after him.

– What do you think of that, Captain Englishman? And this severed hand, dried in the desert dust, dead before it was even lost, what shall I call this, Captain Englishman? Shall I call it *Syria*?

Sticks and Stones

When at last I found the boy, *writes Carter*, the most curious thing is that I found him being taunted by a group of five or six young Arab children, girls and boys, all smaller than him, all terribly brave in their numbers, and all utterly vicious in their hatred. You would have thought he was Lucifer himself, the way they hurled abuse at him, called him *shaitan* . . . enemy . . . devil. One vile little thug had a stone in his hand ready to throw, and would have done, I'm quite sure, had I not been there to take it from him and send him packing with a clip round the ear. Needless to say, they all took flight with the cowardice of any bully, but I felt quite sorry for my poor native guide; he was in such a sorry state, spittle on his face and more than a few scratches on his hands where he'd been fending off their sticks.

But that's not the curious thing, Anna.

– Are you all right, lad? says Carter. No bones broken, eh? Just a few scratches.

The boy nods, wipes a gob of spit from his forehead and yells at the running children. He seems more irritated than shaken, no tears, no great release of fear in visible relief, just a black scowl and curses, like a cheated merchant who can't abandon his stall to chase a thief.

The strange thing is, *writes Carter*, that as soon as the thugs had been scattered I realised Samuel was quite right in at least one of his ideas. You see, this lad Tamuz could easily have broken free of his tormentors and outrun them. If he'd been able to fight, in fact, he could have held his own against these toughs, I'm sure. But as soon as they were gone, well, he just stood there. I only noticed then that one of the little blighters had drawn a circle on the ground around him, you see, and he absolutely refused to cross it. Wouldn't budge an inch. His tormentors had simply been standing out of reach beyond this line drawn in the dust, swinging their sticks and throwing stones and curses at him. A devil indeed, trapped in a circle for the righteous to torment. Or so they clearly thought.

The line has been scratched in the dust, probably with the same stick that's left its mark on the lad's hand, and the boy's foot moves towards it, pulls back. Shoulders in an almost-shrug, hands up and out, he seems to be groping for an explanation. How can an Englishman understand this? thinks Carter wryly.

Carter kicks his boot into the dust, breaking the circle, and Tamuz cocks his head in curiosity. How can an Englishman understand this?

– You're Yezidi, yes? says Carter.

Ever since Samuel first told me of this tribe of his, well, Anna, I've always been rather sceptical. I've always found his theories fascinating, enlightening even, regardless of what others may say. But with all my time in Kurdistan, with all the Yezidi I've met, fought beside, I've always, to be honest, thought it quite absurd to link their strange customs and beliefs to the Dead Sea Valley of all places. The Yezidi may have their stories of war in heaven, fallen angels and ancient giants, but these are clearly rooted in the Magian and Manichaean heresies native to Persia. The people take their very name from the Persian word for angel, after all. And what with the path that Samuel's research has taken him down these last ten years, well, Samuel's methods have become . . . unorthodox.

I have to confess now that he must be on to something. It can't just be a few coincidental correspondences between the Kurdish heresies and the stories of these Enakites, not when I've seen exactly the same thing happen, why, three or four times up around Lake Van – Yezidi children trapped in a circle, harried mercilessly because they absolutely will not step over that line.

And why?

The boy knows nothing of these Yezidi, but he tries to give an explanation.

– As Ab Irim said to his servant, Eliezer, the boy says, these are the ways we carry with us. From the hills of Irad, we brought these ways. To the city of Ur, we brought these ways. To the city of Haran, we brought these ways. To the cities of Siddim, we brought these ways.

*The boy looks earnest, brow furrowed solemnly as he repeats
the learned formula. Then a smile and a blink.*

*Carter wonders if he even knows where these places are,
Haran in the north where the Hittites ruled, Ur down in the
Mesopotamian delta where civilisation began. And Irad . . . Eridu,
perhaps one of the oldest Sumerian cities? Or Aratta, even?
Aratta which had such strong ties with Sumer that its people were
considered cousins, but which lay somewhere far to the north
in the mountainous region later known as Urartu, in the hills of
Ararat.*

As far as the Muslim Kurds and the Christian Armenians are
concerned the Yezidi are devil-worshippers, if not devils outright.
And it is true that they worship a Peacock Angel they call Melek
Tawus, the captain of the angels and, like Lucifer, a rebel and
an outcast . . . but in their religion one who's later forgiven, re-
instated. But the Yezidi are really not the fiends that they're
made out to be. The whole circle thing, as it turns out, is not half
as sinister as it might seem. The circle is drawn during disputes,
for those who stand in it to testify. I rather think it represents
the tribe; to tell a lie whilst within it is to . . . poison one's whole
society, and to refuse to act within its bounds – to leave it, to
step over that line – it would be a surrendering of one's very
identity as a member of the tribe. The young, I believe, understand the power of the taboo but not the purpose.

The point is, if this boy is anything to go by, Samuel's
Enakites are indeed distant cousins of the Yezidi. I still have
no truck with Samuel's fancy that these tales of angels are
something more than crass distortions of the Bible. But I am
intrigued.

*The boy steps out of the broken circle, taking the offered
handkerchief from Carter's hand and dabbing at his scratches.
The copper tone of his skin makes sense now. If his people aren't
Bedu, aren't Arabs at all . . . Carter thinks of the old beggar's
words: My mother, she teach me many things about the desert,
things even the Bedu do not know.*

*– Come, Carter Bey, says Tamuz. I will take you now. The car
is close.*

He winks at Carter for some unfathomable reason.
– You will like your driver. He is English, like you.

A Sudden Nameless Pang

– Aye, right! Scots! says the man sat on the sideboard of the Rolls. Did this wee nyaff tell ye Ah was English? Aye, you, ya wee bastard – sorry, sir, pardon ma language an a', but it's been a while since Ah've had a gentleman in here, like, apart fae himsel', ye know, and he's no yer average gent, disnae really staun on ceremony, but – ye know? – the Baron, Ah mean.

It takes Carter a full second of replay and translation before he says *yes*, not really sure which question he's answering.

– Wee beggar does it just tae wind us up, but. Bloody 'English'! Fuckin ... Sorry, nae offence, sir. Bloody wee *qadishtu–*

Tamuz ducks a swipe from the driver and makes a retort that Carter doesn't catch, jumps over the door of the open-top Rolls and into the front passenger seat. The boy leans forward, using the sleek mahogany of the glove compartment as a mirror, flicking fingers through his fringe, pushing hair back from his face. Carter can't help but crane his neck a little to check out the dark leather upholstery.

– She's a pure stoater, eh, sir?

The driver and the car make a strange combination, the one as messy as the other is pristine. Don MacChuill – as he introduces himself in his guttural garrulous Scots tongue – is a man made of dust and sand; it's quite impossible to tell what colour his hair or crumpled uniform are, and the only patch of skin that doesn't blend with the road beneath their feet is round his eyes. Or *eye*, to be precise; MacChuill wears a patch over his right eye – yet another casualty of the Great War, Carter supposes. Goggles up over the peak of his chauffeur's cap, a cigarette dances in his mouth as he rattles through the horsepower and the craftsmanship. The car is immaculate, a rag in the Scotsman's hand showing he takes as much pride in it as his talk suggests, in inverse proportion to the pride he takes in his own appearance, it would seem. MacChuill flicks ash from his cigarette, bats at a few flakes that fall on his jacket, and goes on talking, oblivious to the little dust cloud raised as he opens the back door for Carter. Half of what he says is entirely unintelligible.

– Aye, but the Baron kens his cars, he does, but.

MacChuill jumps over his own door into the driver's seat, leans back over his shoulder to pass Carter a set of goggles dug out of his pocket.

– Ye'll be wanting these, sir.

He pulls his own down over his left eye and the leather patch, squares his cap.

– Right then, he says. We fer the aff? Next stap Tell-el-Kharnain.

The car rattles over the rough roads, jouncing Carter back and forth and side to side as they wind up into the hills north-east of the Holy City, terraced hills of olive groves and orange trees, dark green leaves patching the stony, sandy, sandstony terrain. Occasional mosques and synagogues and churches dot the road, barely more complex in their architecture than the squat secular buildings of the villages they pass through, rough-hewn blocks with holes for doors and windows, only the towers, the odd symbol – Star of David, Cross or Crescent – marking out their greater purpose.

It seems strange to Carter that so harsh a region should be such a holy land, *the* Holy Land. And in times as inhospitable to faith as these arid climes. But what else is there? he thinks. The abyss the Futurists would have, the nihilistic hell of men whose only faith is in their own will? There are things he's witnessed which have tested many of his beliefs – in God, in humanity, in the existence of wisdom, justice or mercy anywhere on this earth – but still, he thinks, we *must* believe. We must have faith. He watches the back of the boy's head as it bobs this way, that way, juddering with the rhythm of the road. If these Enakites are devil-worshippers of a sort, like the Yezidi, even *they* still have a faith. But the Futurists … the Futurists do not pray; they only offer their burnt offerings to the furnaces of progress.

– Huv ye got a fag there, sir, by any chance, cause Ah've smoked ma last an I'm bloody gaspin fer it, ye know, but, see Ah—

– Of course, says Carter. No problem.

He leans forward with the case open in his hand and MacChuill turns in his seat, hands off the wheel, to take one.

– Carter Bey?

Tamuz has a wide-eyed, look – *can I?*

– Go on, says Carter.

MacChuill sings as he drives, some Scots folk song that should have a fiddle to accompany it. Carter wonders how he does it, with the dust kicked up around them as a lung-choking dervish; after the first half-hour of the drive, his own coughing and spluttering had driven him to dig his scarf out of his kit – a tasselled affair not unlike the chequered Palestinian kaffiyeh – to wrap his nose and mouth. MacChuill and Tamuz both seem quite unperturbed. He'd almost think the Scotsman's beard was acting as a filter, but bushy as it is, it can't be that wild. Curiously, the airstream must be carrying the dust around Tamuz entirely; the boy's shirt looks as snow-white as it did before the journey's start. It strikes Carter that the dust should be thrown up behind them anyway; simple common sense says that it shouldn't be furling, whirling up into his bloody face as if it's blowing up from the road in the car's path ahead of them, rising to meet them.

As it bobs, Tamuz's head turns and Carter notes the boy's lips moving. But if he has decided to join in the song at least he's not as loud as the Scotsman, not loud enough to be heard over a voice loud and rough enough to make the engine's roar seem smooth and soft.

The road turns south for a brief second, rounds a steep slope running up to overhanging rock, and they look down upon Jerusalem off in the distance, glowing golden-white as a mirage, before they turn in to a pass, a scar gouged through the rock. It's no more than a glimpse, and it's perhaps because it is no more that it strikes Carter with a sudden nameless pang; it's not quite yearning, nothing quite so clear and simple, maybe curiosity as much as anything, but it's the feeling you get when you pass someone in the street just as they brush the hair back from their face and drop their hand. You glimpse that face too briefly really to register the beauty, but you turn unconsciously, caught by it, wondering after it, only to find it gone already.

And the road swings east, and the car with it, rattling on, away from the Holy City, away from Carter's lost faith.

Jack Go Boom

– Have a little faith in me, I say. How hard can it be?

A freefall through a million dead worlds, arms spread wide to catch the currents of time, aiming your body at a hole halfway down, a hole the size of a ventilation duct.

– Well, says Fox, this is the proverbial jump into the abyss . . .

– Do we get parachutes? says Joey.

– Or jet-packs, I say. A jet-pack would be cool.

Fox looks up from the sim and gives a sigh.

– OK, I say. No jet-pack for Jack – [I grin him a glint] – relax. Nice and easy does it. Falling is what I'm best at.

– It's getting you to the chi-shaft in the first place that's the hard part.

I look at the sweep of Georgian terrace at the top of the sim.

– A few walls and watchtowers, I say. Piece of piss.

– The surface structure's just a sideshow, says Fox. The real Circus is what's underneath. Note the paradox shielding.

I squint at these scraps of map dredged up by Don from Joey's screaming dreams, assembled into a semblance of sense by Guy and simmed by Anaesthesia; it doesn't look like all the parts quite fit. I cock my head like a quizzical mutt, try to straighten out the involution of environs and events. It still looks nutty as a squirrel's dreams.

– The Circus is a timefuck, says Joey. Trust me; I used to live there. Walk down the wrong corridor without clearance and you don't just find yourself back where you started; you find yourself back *when* you started. With no memory of getting there.

I shrug. Who needs a memory when you've got *joie-de-vivre* and an orgone pistol?

– This route should take you down to the lower levels, though.

Fox traces a path around the outer edges of the plans, where corridors form Möbius-Hilbert wheels, his finger moving inward and downward to our helter-skelter highway into history, that shaft

379

drilled down into the chaosphere. I flip my mayashades down and zoom in on his finger-trail, cock my head a few more degrees. And realise what I'm looking at. Roads. Buildings.

Once upon a time, you see, my peachy Kentigern had a sister city called Dunedin, Albion's main base in Caledonia, built on black volcanic hills with a big old castle at its heart, perched up on a sheer-walled plug of basalt, balustrades as grim as February, cannons on its battlements, and barracks dug into its dungeon depths. If Kentigern's an outlaw city of shipbuilders and steelworkers, Trade and Industry, well, Dunedin was an outpost city of pipe bands and politicians, Might and Majesty. Fucking tartan-clad tourist trap for the Volk-loving fascists. Until the Evenfall came and Kentigern ate Dunedin whole. But didn't digest it, apparently.

I look at the buildings and bridges in Anaesthesia's sim, the crumpled subterranean city with its streets all twisted topsy-turvy, and the castle hanging upside down over a bottomless pit. Nazi Gothic to the max.

– Tell me we have to get into the castle, I say.

– You have to get into the castle, says Guy.

– Keen.

– So we can't just blow the doors, I say ... a few sex-bombs through the windows, and stroll in through the carnal carnage?

– That wouldn't be a good idea, says Fox.

– What if I'm in disguise? I could have a labcoat. And a clipboard.

– Jack, you could wear a rubber mask and fake moustache; with your metaphysique the castle psi-scans would still trigger before you got to the door.

– This'll get you into the Circus at least, says Don. Here.

He hands me my astral travel papers – an expired passport with the corner snipped off, a used airplane ticket to Turkey and a bright pink note of Monopoly money tucked inside. I flick it open. A crude pencil drawing of a smiley face taped over the photograph, details Tippexed out and overwritten in crayon, it's the work of an expert forger. Even smells of minion. I lay it down on the table and take the syringe full of ink that Anaesthesia hands me.

– And this'll get you inside the castle, she says.

The syringe is sweet with my soul-scent, but then it should be; it's loaded with blissbath water homoeopathically encoded with complete schematics for my archetypal character. It's living liquid information, viral ectoplasm, logos jism, meme-spunk, souljuice. Ink from my graving.

— Once you're inside, she says, you find your cover, spike his soul and ditch your skinsuit then ... disperse. We reckon on twelve hours before the Jack Flash meme overwrites the host soul, so you spike him at midnight. Coverboy gets a good night's sleep, apart from some wacky dreams, walks in through the castle gates feeling fine and dandy, then just as he's about to chow down on his packed lunch ...

— Jack go boom, I say. In his head.

— Quite, says Fox.

— So who's the mark?

— Circus architect, says Fox. Escherspace expert, Beta-level clearance.

I flick open the dossier Fox hands me for a look at the SS stooge whose deep-and-dirty I'm gonna be riding into Dodge on. A job's a job, I suppose, and Daedalus didn't make the monster; he just built the labyrinth to house it. Still, at that level of complicity I'm expecting a weaselly coward with a weak chin and beady eyes. In the photograph, the dapper chap doesn't look the sort to suck Satan's cock, though, with his little beatnik flop of hair, goatee and tache. Looks all-too fucking familiarly bohemian, in fact.

— Jacques Reynard Cartier, says Fox. Least that's what his papers say.

— I know that face, I say.

— Distant relative, mumbles Fox.

— I'm not sure how he got here, Fox explains, but I rather suspect it's something to do with a little attempt to rewrite history that backfired quite ... flamboyantly.

— Strann? I say.

— Strann, he says, or Paris, or here. God knows how many folds that little fiasco took place in. Anyway it rather looks as if our man switched streams in the storm and, well, decided to settle down, play by the rules, get a nice job—

– As an evil minion of the Empire, I say. That's not like you, Foxy.

Fox keeps his gaze locked on the sim but his fingers drum a staccato beat on the tabletop. It's not easy seeing yourself as a sell-out, I guess.

– Maybe he thought that he could work within the system, he says. Infiltrate . . . infect it with humanity. Salvage a few souls, throw a spanner in the works here or there. No Book. No big ideas. No grand plans.

He shakes his head.

– Just . . . try not to blow your cover, he says. More to the point, try not to blow your cover *away*. There might be . . . temporal fallout.

– I like temporal fallout, I say.

I grin. Backflashes and splinterworlds, rewrites rippling through reality. Gives life a little depth to have as many pasts as futures. Linearity's for squares.

– Just try to remember, Jack, that some of us don't have quite the same . . . resilience, he says.

So, OK, OK, I agree, this evil minion of the Empire who's going to carry me inside the castle in his dreams is not to be drugged, drooged with a baseball bat, or dropped from a tall building with an *oopsy*. I am not to kill him. I am not to stitch myself into his flayed skin. I am not to arrive at the front door of the castle with a manic grin on my face and hair bleached to the colour of fire, insisting that I am *not* Jack Flash, honest guv. I'm the bloke that works in *thingummy*, you know, with the *stuff*. See, I have a moustache. And a clipboard.

– I'll be good, I say. I promise.

– It was nice knowing you, Guy, says Joey.

Errata

The Mission

He's walked down roads that led to places that should never have existed, not in any sane world. He's walked down side streets into alleys that came out, a hundred yards or so along, in cities halfway round the world. He's talked to people who dream others' memories, more vivid than their own waking life, or who murmur to themselves in languages they've never learned, or who remember children there are no records of and that no one else recalls. He's passed through towns where these so-called Cold Men have just, always the day before, packed up their shops and moved out, leaving behind them only the odd cheap and nasty scrap of mojo kitsch, some chicken-claw earring or some crystal skull. And even here – where in a way it all began, in the Mojave – even here he can't find any fucking angels.

The scent of Phree's sweat is heavy as the heat, though, in the air, so Finnan knows he's on the right track.

His scuffed tan desert boots kick up the dust as he trudges. He'd give his right arm for a drink of water, sure, his lips as cracked as dried-out paper, and the sun just too damn hot for this time in the morning, but he knows this beeline as-the-crow-flies route is safer than the road that should have taken him up to the old adobe Mission they tell him lies just up a ways along the gulch; way things work now the official road could just as easily have led him into Disneyland or Dodge. As it is, he comes around a ragged outcrop of the crumbling sandstone foothills and it looks as if he's entered something like that kind of hell, anyway. Uncle Walt meets Sergio Leone.

A sea of rusted SUVs, a parking lot that stretches out to the horizon, crackweed and dry brush sprouting up between the dead metal shells. The town, the Mission, sit at the heart of it.

The Mission rises among the few broken buildings and he sees it for a second as it once was, a ghost-image of the blank walls and bell

383

tower superimposed over the reality of this fold. Like the way a word in English or Italian, Inuit or Etruscan, still carries an echo of the Cant it's a corruption of, the Mission shimmers with – part shadow, part reflection – an image of its prior self, whitewashed, serene, with a grand, cracked beauty like some peon widow in black sitting on her wooden chair in the shade – the old lady everybody comes to for advice, for gossip, and because they'll get an earful of abuse if they don't treat her with the right respect.

That image lasts only a blink before the truth burns through it.

The Mission has been painted red, as red as Satan's fiery full-cocked loins and every bit as vulgar. So have the ruins of the little village that surrounds it, although they at least are mercifully small and almost buried among the rabble and babble of stalls and awnings, tents and wigwams, flags, banners, canopies ... and Cold Men and customers wandering everywhere.

He hadn't thought that there might be so many normal folk out here, had imagined it as the last retreat of the Cold Men, packing up their businesses and leaving towns that they were never really welcome in, to come here to live with their own kind. He'd imagined this as some walled hideaway for the Jim Jones wannabes, some unkin version of the Moonies.

Turns out it it's more like Mardi Gras on acid.

Finnan pulls a softpack of Camels out of the back pocket of his chinos, taps one out and fires it up. The first draw of unfiltered nicotine is a lazy rush, coming on like an old dog rousing itself to greet its master, *hey there, back again?* He's always liked nicotine; it gives him the patience of a saint and the voice box of a sinner. And the satisfying *clunk-snick* of a Zippo, quiet *shsss* of tobacco lighting, *chuk* of the Zippo shutting – some things remain the same, even at the end of the world. Or after it.

– Hey there, says a Cold Man coming towards him out of the freak fiesta up ahead. Back again?

Finnan cocks his head at him. Skin and hair the colour of fresh ivory, but dressed up in a stars-and-stripes top hat and tails, beaded, ribboned, and feathered like a voudon Uncle Sam. Finnan nails him for a barker and a con man right away. No real mojo here, just some pretty colours and a slick tongue to pull the marks into the carnival.

– Never been here before, says Finnan.

– A new customer's an old friend, far as we're concerned. Come on back in, old friend. We'll fix you up with what you want. A little love? A little money? Maybe a little good-time honey to keep the bed warm at night? Am I right? Trust me. Trust yourself. What we can't give you, it's not worth having. We are ... *resplendent* in our range.

Finnan half admires his blarney with a wry smile. But he doesn't trust the fucker for a second; there's a lilt in his voice, a croon of Cant. Fucker may not be unkin, but he's as near as damn-it.

– Just tell me what you're looking for, says the Cold Man.

Little girl who stole the world, thinks Finnan.

– Truth, he says. Maybe you've got a little knick-knack made of chickenbone that smells like horseshit whenever someone's talking out their ass? That might be useful.

The barker laughs, all jovial and phoney as a tour guide. It's part of the act, thinks Finnan, something the marks expect, something they want. He's no stranger to the idea of roguish charm, the way you can win someone's trust by telling them not to trust you, with a twinkle in the eye.

– You're a man of practicalities and logic, says the barker. I can tell that *you* know what you're looking for, and it's no business of *mine*.

He flourishes his hand towards the market.

– Wander at your leisure. Browse. Question.

He smiles, waves Finnan on and in.

– One thing, though, old friend. A little advice.

– Free? says Finnan.

– Free and gratis.

Finnan takes a draw on his smoke and waits.

– Just ignore the man behind the curtain, says the barker.

Cold as ice and eyes like steel, he tips his hat, wheels and stalks off.

– Be seeing you, says Finnan to his back.

Dreamcatchers and Sand-paintings

The Mission at the far end, with a square in front and a few ruined buildings round it, there's really only one street to the place – but somehow, trying to walk from one end to the other, that street seems to stretch out, twisting as you go, space winding round you like a bad-trip snake-world. The way the world is now, Finnan wonders how much of it is the confusion of the multicoloured stalls and wide-eyed searchers rooting among them, and how much of it is a bona-fide reality fuck. He's been out of it for a long time – fuck knows how long, really – but he's up to speed on the Evenfall now and the long Hinter that followed it, the deep dark night of dreams he slept right through. As he ducks and winds his way towards the Mission, past stalls selling shit from every corner of the world, anything that might remotely be considered lucky, he seems to be going one step forward, two steps back and to the side, and never getting any nearer.

He pushes his way around blankets laid out on the ground, scattered with North and South Americana, dreamcatchers and sand-paintings, voudon and santería saint-statues and shrines, potions and charms. He skirts stalls selling Scandinavian runic necklaces, Hindu Ganeshas, Chinese Kuans, Celtic staffs, African fetishes. Yin/Yangs, alien blood samples, glow-in-the-dark Madonnas, mirrors with the images of Jesus, Elvis or Diana embossed on them, skull rings and evil-eye rings, pentacles and rosaries, prayer rugs and shawls, drums, pipes, rattles, crystals, bondage gear and vampire candles, tarot cards and I Chings, holy water, silver bullets, rabbits' feet and lucky white fucking heather – there's no order to the way the stalls are laid out, no avenues to the tat, just a random distribution of mojo like a minefield that there's no straight path through.

After five minutes' steady weaving, he can tell it isn't just bad planning.

Everywhere, he notices, the people are buying this shit – tourists, pilgrims, searchers for that one little something that might charm their lives back to the way it used to be. Suburbanites with cameras and kids, living far enough out of the cities not to feel the full shock of the world coming apart, but close enough to it to be worried, they just want a little security, Finnan knows. He's eavesdropped on enough low conversations now to know their stories. How it started when they'd tried to phone some friend or relative and couldn't get through. How the bus they normally took to work became a tram. How they watched the news the night it covered the Dissolution of Prague, and they weren't entirely sure where Prague was – Russia, maybe? – but they knew a scary story when they saw one. In diner after diner, as he walked the Journey of the Dead Man, Finnan had listened in on their fears, pieced together the disintegration of reality, Evenfall and Hinter.

Out in the sticks around Alamosa, an old gas-pump jockey had asked him what he was looking for.

– Angels, Finnan had said.

– Shoot, fella, the man had said, we all looking for the angels. You find them, you ask them where the hell they been while the world going crazy. You ask them why my Sarah got Raptured fifteen years ago and they still ain't shown up for the rest of us.

– I'll do that, Finnan had said.

– Fifteen years, and no Antichrist or nothing. You ask them.

Finnan had taken the last slug of his Mountain Dew, crumpled the can and chucked it in a waste bin, nodded. Looked a distance up the road.

– You ask them, the old man had said again in a voice more desperate than angry.

Finnan can feel the Cant at the back of his neck now, like a warm hand wet with sweat. He can feel it all down his spine and across his shoulders, the feeling that any minute something's going to rip out from his shoulder-blades and uncurl claws and wings, lashing tentacles – an animal energy that he can only just contain. Call it luck, call it mojo, call it the fucking Force, it's stronger in this place than it is in most unkin, and it's making him feel edgy as fuck. It has teeth.

He tries to source the feeling. For all the charms and trinkets that are on the counter-tops and blankets spread out around him, the feeling isn't coming from there, but from the broken-down adobe houses and, most of all, from the Mission, the Mission of

Sante Manité as it's marked on the map. He glances around at the Cold Men hawking their snake-oil quick-fix solutions for the deep soul fears, feeding off this place like vultures on a piece of carrion, tearing off little chunks of skin and flesh. He picks up a Chinese coin from the stall at his side; there's a hint of the Cant in it, an electric tingle in his fingers, but it's a resonance, a reflection. The real power's based in the Mission building.

Christ, what have these bastards got here, he wonders, the fucking rotting corpse of God?

– God's not dead, a voice says from a stall behind him.

Finnan stops and turns towards the Cold Man. He stands behind a bookstall – New Age self-help and mysticism. *Tantra for Twats. How to Use Friends and Manipulate People. How to Play Victim and Win.*

He remembers playing cards a long time ago, another life ago, during a war, playing cards with nudie women on them. Was it France or Spain now, sure? No matter; he remembers thinking how reading a person's attitude, their hate, their fear, their need, is something every poker player and every officer, every lying, cheating cunt of a control freak has made his greatest skill. Tuning in to every little tic and twitch of muscle, flex of fingers, blink of eyes, shift of scent, pause, glance and wait. There's a logic of challenges and chances runs through people's bodies, a touch of the Cant that reveals the bets, the bluffs, the truths. You don't read their minds, but you read *them*. You know their hand and you say just the right thing to make them play it the way it suits you.

The Cold Man is smiling quietly, knowingly, keeping the punch-line until asked for it.

– Hit me, says Finnan.

– He's only sleeping, the Cold Man says, nodding to himself. You're trying to get to the Mission, yes?

I'll check, thinks Finnan. He's giving nothing away just yet.

– The market's pretty busy, he says.

– It can surely be that way. There's a lot of demand, right now. *Raise the stakes.*

– Kind of tacky, some of this crap, isn't it?

– All genuine magic. Works like a charm, you could say. But I guess this is the first time you've seen a place like this. Pretty cynical about it, I'll bet?

– Sure and I love places like this, says Finnan laid-back. Very . . . *eclectic.*

– Something for everyone's taste.

– I'll bet, says Finnan.

Call you.

– So you looking for something in particular? Let me guess, something on Quantum Interconnectedness, Chaos Field Theory?

Finnan picks up a book, glances at the back and lays it down, browses another couple, turns a few over and back again. Pseudo-histories, folklore and crank science.

– Sumerian mythology, he says. Heard of something called *The Book of All Hours*?

The Cold Man blinks and Finnan can see his mind go click. *Cards on the table and the dealer is bust, I'm afraid.*

– No, don't think I have.

I'm sorry, sir, I'm afraid we're going to have to ask you to leave.

– Shame, says Finnan. Be seeing you.

He turns to go.

– Wait. You want to get to the Mission, yes? I can give you directions.

Finnan shakes his head.

– Feel kind of thirsty, though. You know where I can get a beer?

– A beer?

– Forget it. I'll find somewhere.

Finnan starts to walk away, pauses.

– But, hey . . .

– Yeah?

– If I find what I'm looking for, sure and ye'll be the first to know.

2

A Shadow of Jerusalem

A Singularity for a Soul

The Duke Irae strokes at his grand white beard and runs an idle finger up the venous scar that splits the left side of his face from cheek to hairline, over the shattered socket where a mirrored ball now sits in place of his lost eye. War has its price and this is a small one; others paid more dearly, with their lives, their souls. Raphael dead. Metatron lost. Gabriel – he doesn't like to think of what happened to that lord of fire out in the Hinter. And then there was the little piss-ant pacifist Sandalphon – a pity about that, but *c'est la mort*. He was useful in the end. There's only the three of them now; but three is as holy a number as seven, and it makes for a tighter and more stable ruling structure anyway. Michael and Azazel, archangels of ice and death, bringers of Peace and Mercy, the right hand and left hand of the Law. And the Duke who was once known as Uriel, Glory of God.

His grizzled, chiselled features seem carved out of granite, his impiteous, stony gaze unmoving and unblinking as he studies the abyss below, the vast fluming chasm of the largest chi-mine in all of Albion, stretching out beneath the balcony, down, down through a storm of sickly greenish vapours riven by electric blue, down, down into the core of orgone energy, chi-energy, the engine of pure chaos at the heart of everything. The ink under the Vellum's skin.

Ah, yes. If God were really dead, this would be his open grave – a strip-mine in the very substance of reality, yielding an inexhaustible supply of raw power.

*

Above him and around him, the monstrous impossibility that is the city of Dunedin hangs from the ceiling of the cavern. Stalactite streets of stone run vertical, horizontal and diagonal; buildings hang like bats from rafters that are bridges, ups and downs all folded. But the Duke ignores this banal labyrinth; it's the monster below he's fascinated by. He stares down into the geomagical machine that for twenty years or half of an eternity has helped to power this little Haven, this glorious mirage of an Empire on which the sun Will Never Set. For once a smile plays across his lips; the sun can never set on an Empire hidden underground. His secret kingdom.

History is on their side. This shaft piercing down into the Vellum's depths is a useful legacy of Crowley's brief, inglorious reign as Lord Protector. As it turned out, even the Futurist Revolution in the Eastern Bloc, the Great War itself, had served as a wonderful excuse for the industrialisation – the *exploitation* – of this power-source. And, with Mosley's restoration of the monarchy, those like the Duke Irae who had remained loyal to the Traitor King had been rewarded with unprecedented access to the very source of Albion's might. *To do with as you will, for Albion's sake.*

The Duke Irae has reason to be pleased with the sham reality that Kentigern is built on; it couldn't have worked out better if he'd written the script himself.

The tempest of chi-energies reflects across his mirrorball eye, distorted by the curvatures so that the centre of it, the dark corona of the event threshold, looks for all the world like a blackly piercing pupil. As if, within the eye, he has a singularity for a soul.

– How very . . . Nietzschean, he says.

At his side, Dr Arturo, biochaocist and bodhisattva, looks an even glummer bear than usual; inoculated against all infectious enthusiasms by his self-prescribed regime of medication and meditation, he remains, like all good scientists, impervious to all the world's temptations. For Arturo, the abyss below is only his own inevitable oblivion, the dark nirvana that he yearns for as release from hopeless servitude. Even in the hopelessness of his abject surrender to the mechanisms of the State and, in a wider sense, to the Wheel of Fate itself, there is the tiniest part of him that still yearns. The drugs do help, however, and the utter lack of anything resembling an ego in

his heavily narcotised psyche serves him well in helping to maintain his professional objectivity, no small matter given that his work
for Albion's most powerful duke is in so many ways quite deeply
ethically objectionable. At this moment, as he pops another pill, his
subjugated conscience sinks back down into its usual slumber and
he's left with only a cold appreciation of the expedience of misery.

— Wagnerian, even, m'sire, he says.

The Duke Irae nods approvingly. A collector of the nihilist master,
he has a number of Wagner's more famous paintings in his galleries
now. The scene below is so reminiscent of his tour de force, *Inferno
in Blue and Green*. Something in the crushing rawness of it and in
the mention of the great pre-Futurist artist sparks a thought in him,
and he raises his hoary head to turn, looking not at Arturo but at
the bioform scribe behind him, the psychic yet mindless archivist of
His Lordship's every moment.

I hope that you're getting this all down.

The bioform nods blankly, integrating its own action into the
greater narrative of its master.

Without turning, the Duke Irae speaks to Arturo.

— We are, indeed, the masters of this world, he says. Now. How
is our architect doing?

— Secure, says Dr Arturo. Safe as houses. And on schedule.
The Circus should be sealed off in a matter of days.

— Good. And Project Moonchild?

— The gestation period is complete. We're making the final
preparations for the drop right now; we have Magi working round
the clock, binding the shell to its destination. When we release . . .
it should fly truer than a bullet from a hero's gun. I have no fear but
that it will hit its target dead on.

— You have no fear of anything, Arturo. You have no hope.

— True, m'sire.

The Duke gazes down into the maelstrom. If he could only see
through the blue-green storm, down the well of histories, to this fold
of the Vellum where, according to Arturo's scrying eyes, his prying
prophetic spies, the Book is even now emerging . . . if he could be
certain . . .

But nothing is certain in a world without God.

The black abysm of time stretches down below, the storm shimmering over it like light on oil, iridescent ink, all blues and greens, the colours of a peacock's tail; but in all the chaotic splendour of it there is no curiosity, no judgement, no passion. No *will*.

Soon, though, thinks the Duke. Soon.

Proud and Pagan

– Soon! calls Tamuz. We there in no time now. Look!

He stands, one hand on the windscreen to steady him, the other pointing to two o'clock, pointing down into the Jordan Valley, through the white swirling dust, to a thin line of dark green that winds down from the north to—

Tell-El-Kharnain. Straddling the river where it flows into the pale blue of the Dead Sea, it rises out of the wasteland like the stumps of twin towers blasted down and built upon, a great city raised over the ruins of two ancient myths. The jumble of it is built of the same bleached golden stone you see all across Palestine, but for some reason that material strikes Carter differently here. Here it seems to have an added quality of salt and bone, of living flesh ossified, brittle and crumbling to the elements. That same pale, yellowy brown which makes Jerusalem seem almost a structure made of light on paper or parchment, a vellum origami, clean-lined, sharp-cornered, here seems scoured thinner, shredded at the edges. Tell-el-Kharnain has the same minarets and domes rising above its roofs, but everywhere the skyline of it is broken up by – as they rattle ever closer, he can see – dark, fluttering rags.

He has to shout over the car's gruff complaints at MacChuill's rough handling, ramming it from one gear to the next, treating the road like an assault course.

– What are the flags? he shouts.

– Goatskin, Carter Bey, says Tamuz. Is good luck.

Carter nods – *of course*. He knows a little of the culture of this city; Samuel's letters dwelt in rather too much depth on the apocryphal tales of wickedness and punishment, sin and torment, tales of how, after the War in Heaven, the Archangel Michael opened up a crack in the desert of stone to bind the fallen angels under the Dead Sea Valley. Of how the two mounds that stand on each side of the Jordan and that give the city its name – The Mound of the Horned One – are in fact the horns of Sammael, leader of the rebels. To Carter these *tells* are, of course, simply the signs of ancient civilisation, the build-up of layer upon layer of human detritus, of cities built over towns built over villages, visible everywhere across the Near East.

But then for the Bedouin tribesmen who inhabit the wilderness to the west of Tell-el-Kharnain the mythology and the history are not entirely incompatible. They identify the mounds as the ruins of Sodom and Gomorrah, refusing to set foot within the city walls because, they say, to stand upon the horns of the *Shaitan*, the Enemy, is an abomination in the eyes of God.

While the rest of Palestine was built in honour of a God of light – synagogues, scriptoriums and strongholds – Tell-el-Kharnain, the hated city, the cursed city, was not built at all, they say, but gathered as legends and rumours around a forgotten story, a cloak of darkness blown in folds over a dead king. Before Petra was carved into the desert rock, before Masada fell, before En Gedi was abandoned, before Qumran acquired its store of scrolls and scriptures from the Essenes, before even the Temple at Jerusalem was built, the city of Tell-El-Kharnain stood, proud and pagan, a city of blasphemy looking out over a lifeless sea.

They drive down into the valley of salt, towards it.

15th March, *he writes*. Tell-El-Kharnain, city of sin, more notorious for its fleshpots than Whitechapel. Having heard its reputation, I cannot say that I've ever had the urge to see it, but with my only clue to Samuel's whereabouts residing here amongst the hellions, what choice had I but to go down into this sinkhole of a city. Anna, I swear, the noise and stench of the Ben-Abba Airfields seem the very heights of civilisation now. One enters Tell-el-Kharnain along the Salt Road, where one gets a fine view of the squalid shanty-town they call the New City, before driving in at a snail's pace through the slow crowds of the Jericho Gate and the Silkmarket. It is the strangest sight, this city with its outcast citizenry, not entirely unlike their neighbours in terms of dress and customs, but changed just enough to make the whole place utterly alien. Women in abayas and jilbabs down to their ankles, but made of saffron-coloured silk. Men with yarmulkes and braided forelocks, but dressed in scarlet-and-purple-patterned frock-coats as gaudy and as gauche as their Ashkenazi counterparts in Jerusalem are austerely black. We passed shop windows filled with Hadith and Mizraim opened at pages of glorious illustrations, stalls selling rugs with verses from the Koran woven through scenes of birds and beasts, of men and angels. I don't know if you appreciate how anathema such sensual imagery is in Levantine culture, Anna. The Jews and Mohammedans hate such icons, such idolatry, with a fervour matched only by the most zealous Ulsterman, I should think. I had understood this to be a city of apostates, but now I realise that it is a city of heretics, blasphemers.

Carter opens the Song of Songs *that lies on the table to the side of his journal. Captured by a passing glance, he bought the delicate little thing perhaps an hour or so ago, from a shop they passed on the steps of the narrow curved street leading up to the archway, the courtyard within, and then von Strann's attic apartment. Its parchment pages flick lightly over at the touch of a finger – page after page of illustrated Arabic script, intricate as a mediaeval manuscript or a Moorish mosaic, bawdy as a Hindu sculpture, and in the finest Siddim Ink so slickly dark it looks still wet.*

May your breasts be like the clusters of the vine, the fragrance of your breath like apples, and your mouth like the best wine.

He closes it over.

Here at least, in von Strann's apartment, he writes, *as I wait for the boy Tamuz to return, gathering my thoughts within this journal, here at least one has some respite from the broiling masses; one can relax without the expectation of a knife in one's back or a hand in one's pocket.*

But he's lying to himself, he knows. He cannot relax; God knows, he wishes that he could, but twice on their journey the car was stopped and papers asked for. The Turkish military are everywhere and, given that it can only be a matter of weeks before the Turks sign themselves over to the blackshirts, those few Europeans he saw wandering casually through the markets in their linen suits and panama hats seem like fools to Carter. Mind you, from the looks he saw given to the militia by the locals, he suspects the Turks may well meet some resistance here when the time comes. There is no love lost between these people and their overlords. The Ivans and Mehmets would do well to remember all the Roman blood spilled by the zealots and sicarii.

But the time will come, and soon; he's certain of it, only prays that he can find Samuel and get the damn fool out of here before it's too late. But where is he? Or this baron character, for that matter? Baron von Strann. One dreads to think what a supposed gentlemen is doing in Tell-El-Kharnain, anyway.

The City of the Senses

... So, following his doctor's advice, von Strann had arrived at the city in the late spring of 1921, in the hope that the healing waters and beneficial airs of the Dead Sea Valley would alleviate his lung condition.

At first sight, the desolate region, literally the lowest place on earth, seems a strange choice for a spa town; the salty, sulphurous wasteland seems a place of exile rather than recuperation. To some visitors it is astonishing that such barren land could sustain a village let alone a city the size of Tell-el-Kharnain, but the extensive irrigation of the Jordan Valley that made the region inhabitable throughout its history may be seen as a testament to the tenacity of the human spirit and to the strange force that it has exerted on people from the earliest times.

One has to wonder, though, how this city of iniquity has survived the ravages of time, given that it must be the most hated city in the Levant.

Throughout its history, we now know, Tell-el-Kharnain has always been a destination for the sick. Bauval's excavations in the 1970s showed that the traditions of the healing properties of the Dead Sea waters can be dated back as far as the early Neolithic. While it was previously believed that the city was contemporaneous in its foundation with the Phoenician city-states of Sidon, Tyre and Byblos, Bauval's dig revealed structures that combine the roles of bathhouse, hospital, temple and brothel going back as far as the sixth millennium BCE, along with evidence of the institutionalised temple prostitutes that were common throughout the Neolithic Near East. The identification of Tell-el-Kharnain with the Biblical cities of Sodom and Gomorrah is still a matter of some dispute amongst archaeologists, with the rigorous excavations necessary to prove or disprove this theory unlikely to take place any time soon, given the present insecurity of the region; but after the wholesale rejection of the theory in the 1960s, it seems that even respected archaeologists are now willing to entertain the notion that there might be something behind the legends which caused Alexander to rename the city Hephaistionopolis after his lover.

It is interesting then that even in the time of Jericho and Catal Huyuk, it seems Tell-el-Kharnain was a sort of holiday resort of 'sun, sea and sex' so to speak, with a bathhouse culture to rival present-day San Francisco. Through Babylonian and Roman occupations this dubious reputation, this promise of pleasures of the flesh, seems to have been as lucrative as the Ink Trade. Under the Ottomans, when one might have expected little tolerance for such a fleshpot, remarkably the city appears to have flourished; whether one was the most upstanding businessman or proudest imam, it seems, one could always excuse a visit to Tell-el-Kharnain on the grounds of ill health. Hailed by the poets and painters of the Romantic Era as the 'city of the senses, colouring the canvas of the soul in scarlet sin', it gained more and more favour as a destination spot for Europeans, such that by the end of the nineteenth century Tell-el-Kharnain was a sort of Mecca for libertines of all persuasions, carrying on so right through to the 1920s, when alongside Beirut it prospered as a holiday destination for Hollywood's debauched. With all this in mind, and given von Strann's rumoured proclivities, we have to wonder if his move might have been motivated at least partly by the stories of hedonistic excess as much as for any health reasons.

*

In a way, after all, von Strann was as much an exile as a convalescent, forced out of his homeland not just by his health but also by the rise of Futurism and the Terror that followed it; as an aristocrat who refused to serve in the army and an alleged homosexual, von Strann was a double target for a movement that fed on hatred and resentment. He makes his feelings quite clear, in a letter of January 1922 where, writing to his family, he says, '. . . do not ask me to return. Prussia is unhomely to me now.' The key word he uses, *unheimlich*, is difficult to translate into English; while we have rendered it literally here, it also carries a sense of the strange, the uncanny, the unnatural, even the supernatural. Golding, in his biography, uses this phrase to support his argument that von Strann was purely a political exile, that the rumours about his sexuality are just that – 'for surely it would be a bit rich for a homosexualist to describe his society as "unnatural"'. The authors of this book, however, feel that this observation tells us rather more about Golding's assumptions than about von Strann's actual motivations.

No matter what really brought him to this region though – health, sexuality, politics or any combination of the three – it was here in the Dead Sea Valley, in the shadow of ancient Sodom, that von Strann found not only a cure for his lung condition and a brief refuge from early twentieth-century politics, but also an outlet for his hitherto repressed sexuality in the art form that was to make him famous. It was here, in a city of decadence and depravity in the midst of this barren wasteland, that von Strann was to become one of the fathers of modern photography and, of course, of modern pornography. It was here, among the bronze-skinned Enakite tribesmen of the surrounding deserts, that he was to find both his subjects and his salvation.

A Shadow of Jerusalem

– All the way up?
    – Yes, Carter Bey. Top house. Carter Bey . . .
    Boots clopping on the steps as he goes up, Carter moves to one side to let Tamuz squeeze past him, nodding an *of course* to the lad's so evidently practised proud enunciation of *do pardon me, sir*. The

stairwell up to the baron's attic home and studio is tight, narrow like the winding backstreets of this most bohemian quarter of this most bohemian city, narrow like the archway leading into the courtyard, all shuttered windows half-hidden among the vines and leaves. He watches Tamuz take two steps at a time, Carter's satchel swinging over his shoulder as he pushes it back to guddle in his trouser pocket for the door key. Boy insisted on carrying it for him the whole hundred yards up the street from where MacChuill parked the car . . .

– Aright then, sir, wur here. The lad'll take ye tae His Nibs's place. Aye, it's just up there, but. If yer needin a driver just tell Shortarse here an' he'll come and fetch us, like. Aright, aye?

Bohemia, Tell-el-Kharnain, thinks Carter as he steps out of the car.

– Women? Boys? Hashish?

Tamuz shoos the hawker from his path, and the man shrugs, turns his attention to an old gent who's too busy staring at Tamuz and Carter to concern himself, lifting a panama hat to wipe his sweaty forehead with a handkerchief and eyeing them as they pass. Fewer natives than Europeans in the streets around here, it seems, and most of them fawning rogues, preying on the tourists, pandering squalid services. The Arabs are a noble race, Carter's always thought, but it's clear how the demand of European decadence has shaped them here, the market created by the buyer, as Engels has it. But then these stones have seen the same under Egypt and Babylon, through Assyrian and Persian rule, Hellenistic, Roman and Byzantine occupation, through even the Crusades. Great blocks in the walls of the side street Tamuz leads him up carry worn carvings of forgotten reigns, salvaged stonework of a city razed time after time, rebuilt from its own architectural and moral ruin.

. . . Shafts of midday light streak the dark stairwell, dappled by the stone latticework of the outer wall and the leaves of the orange tree in the courtyard beyond. It's quite a pleasant environment, he has to admit, once you're away from the hustle of the streets outside – the old Ink Merchants' Quarter, according to Tamuz, around the Beth Astart, where traders from across the world built their bases of operations, exporting Siddim Ink in all its exquisite pigments, powders and liquids to colour the robes of preening emperors or painted virgins.

The door swings open and he follows the lad inside. The long wood-floored room with its slanted roof is full, but not with furnishings. Pale plastered walls, a couple of windows and a skylight. A kitchen area with an iron stove and a steel sink, a long trestle table and not much else. A bed and a dresser in one corner, an unmade fold-down bunk along from them. A heavy black curtain cordons off the far end, tacked and taped ... to serve as a darkroom and as a backdrop, he guesses, judging from the camera on the tripod pointed at it. Von Strann clearly lives a fairly ascetic existence. No, what clutters the room are all the framed prints stacked against or hanging on the walls, the photographs pegged on bits of string that criss-cross just above head height, all of them studies of young men naked, posed as heroes out of Homer and suchlike. They do have some artistic merit, he's no doubt, but there's an unhealthy aspect to the imagery that Carter finds repellent. Tell-el-Kharnain and von Strann's studio are cut from the same cloth, and that cloth is silk dyed scarlet and purple, soft and sensuous. The whole place is a dark Jerusalem, he thinks, a shadow of Jerusalem, as profane as the city of Solomon is sacred.

May your breasts be like the clusters of the vine, the fragrance of your breath like apples, and your mouth like the best wine.

His fingers drift across the soft leather of *The Song of Songs* as his gaze drifts across the bunting of obscene photographs. Oh, but the Baron may find his trade a bit less lucrative in the near future.

As I wait here for the return of von Strann, he writes, *I can only think of what the Allies stand to lose if Turkey goes over to the Futurists. One cannot help but feel uncomfortable. How many of the European denizens of the cafés and taverns would happily sell their fellow man out to—*

— Carter Bey.

The lad lays an empty plate and a bowl of dates on the table in front of him, pops one of the dark fruits in his own mouth. Carter closes his journal, clicks the lid back onto his pen. Tamuz chews, picks the date stone out of his mouth and drops it on a plate.

– In the market, says Tamuz, I hear a man ask about English soldier.

His voice is casual as he goes back to the stove (and whatever he's cooking, it smells bloody good), but there's an air to it, a question as a warning, perhaps.

– European, he says. I do not know the accent. Not English, though. Not German. Black hair. Black eyes.

– Black shirt? says Carter.

The boy stirs. Taps a wooden spoon on the rim of a pot. Tastes.

– Not today. But other days, I think. I think he wear black shirt on other days. He . . . stand like you.

– And how exactly do I stand? says Carter, resting one elbow on the table, the other on the back of his chair. An amused smile.

Tamuz turns, straightens up army-stiff and furrows his brows, head turning slowly first this way then that, a caricature of stern soldierly scrutiny. He breaks the pose to point the spoon at Carter.

– Like you have many men behind you, he says. Not afraid of anyone.

Carter takes a date from the bowl, rolls it between thumb and forefinger.

– Is that so?

– Proud and fierce, says Tamuz.

A Ball of Obsidian Darkness

Proud and fierce, the Duke Irae strides through Dr Arturo's laboratories, serfs in labcoats scattering in his path. His boots clang on the steel grilles of the gantry underneath, resounding even in the clamour of pounding and whirring, the clicks and hums of the machinery. He strides like a general on a battlefield, caring nothing for the vertiginous chasm that stretches down under the frail steel skeleton to the chaosphere beneath. Even in the single-minded determination of his stride, however, the gaze of his single eye sweeps out, encompassing the scene that he commands in every aspect of his warrior's demeanour. Arturo shuffles behind him, vainly trying to match his master's pace. He pulls himself past the archivist at the gantry's end, muttering muted resentment of the creature's healthy young physique, made doubly bitter, underneath, by how its lack of pride points up the egoism of his own depression.

Around them, reels of magnetic tape spin amongst the flashing diodes and green-screen monitors, the bubbling beakers and sizzling electro-coils that seem to grow out of this monkey-frame construction. Punch-cards and holograph displays, valves and oscilloscopes, radiovision sets and glowing bulbs of chi-capacitors compose Dr Arturo's multi-array mainframe deep within the bowels of the Castle beneath the Circus. Nothing has ever been renewed here, nothing discarded; instead, the gold-wired and black-boxed walls of green that are themselves great motherboards are joined, by wire or by wave, to quantum cube co-processors and liquid orgone neural networks, all integrated into the continuous process that is the computer.

Clamped over the great abyss of the chi-mine like a ceiling of mechanical stalactites, this bastard lovechild of Babbage and Bosch, the laboratory, the computer that *is* the laboratory, is as much a shrine to its own legacy as it is the cutting edge of processing technology. It is the breeding ground for new technology, but it's a cold and hostile breeding ground of components struggling for survival against evolution, and this computer is both crèche and cemetery. Perched over the yawning pit of destruction, it is the cannibal creation of Progress itself.

– And all of this, the Duke Irae says, for one little god.

– The chaosphere *is* rather ... complex, m'sire, Arturo offers. Just maintaining integrity alone –

The Duke waves a hand.

– I'll take your word that we need it. Project Moonchild has my full support.

Behind perspex walls, ranks of babbling bonobo chimps sit strapped to padded school chairs, typewriters built into their wooden desks; they clatter at them like some monstrous secretarial pool, churning out screeds of paper to be grabbed and scanned by an army of technicians as they spew from the machines. In the shaved scalps, in the trepanned skulls of the apes, brain plugs spark and hiss, with blue-green luminous tubes like intravenous drips pulsing into and out of them, all linked back to a glass vat full of churning orgone vapour. A single hose spills from the vat, drops down into the abyss below, disappearing into the distance. Energy pulses up it.

– How goes *this* little side experiment? the Duke asks over the cacophony.

Arturo snaps his fingers, a technician at his side in an instant.

– Results, man. What have we got?

– Subject 23 seems to be channelling Shakespeare, sir.

The technician holds a folded train of perforated paper out for inspection, and Arturo flick/flick/flicks it over his shoulder like tickertape, one foot, two foot, four, six, letting it fall in folds at his feet.

– This thing of darkness, Arturo reads. These cloud/capped towers . . . You call these results?

The technician starts on an excuse, but Arturo cuts him off.

– Discontinue Alpha Phase and send subjects to Metaphysics Department for dissection. Move to Beta Phase.

– The new subjects, sir? Where should—

– Contact Human Resources, man. Admin staff are ten a penny. Use a little initiative.

– I'm not authorised to use initiative, sir . . .

But the Duke and the Doctor are already striding on, leaving the flunky to realise he's dismissed . . . with an implicit authorisation that amounts to a promotion. He snaps his fingers. In an instant, a technician's at his side.

– Yes, doctor?

The bioform archivist hurries on through the swing doors after its master, to find Arturo saying:

– There it is . . .

A ball of obsidian darkness, a bubble of pure chaos, at least seven or eight foot in diameter, hangs in mid/air before them. Nothing touches it but the reflections of the world around. Alone of all the wild contraptions in Dr Arturo's vast laboratory, it remains unintegrated, singular. The Echo Chamber, Arturo calls it.

This thing of darkness, thinks Dr Arturo. *An unborn god.*

– God knows, says MacChuill, Ah've never been able tae figure the man out, but. Keeps himsel' tae himsel', ye ken? Hauf the time, he's out in the bloody desert wi' the goatfuckers – pardon ma French. That's how yer professor wanted tae get pally wi' him, like.

The car crunches gear and takes a corner, Carter wishing the mad Jock would keep his eyes on the road and both hands on the wheel, amazed at the way he treats the brake, clutch and accelerator as if he's doing the bloody Charleston – and by God, that's a gearstick not a joystick, man. They swerve left past a cart, right past a dolma stall, onto the Avenue of Palms, churning up a wake of curses behind them. MacChuill drowns out the noise with his own imprecations and a blaring horn, and Carter despairs of getting any sense out of him. He gazes hopelessly out at a silk stall; a couple of old men sit to one side of it, leaning forward on their metal-frame chairs over the backgammon board on the fold-down table between them.

– Aye, he – *fuck you, too!* – wanted tae – *an' yer maw! Get off the fuckin road, ya numpty!* – he wanted tae get in wi' them, like. Tamuz's folk. Haud on a minute.

The car grinds to a halt, bogged down in the throng of customers at the stalls lining the road. The Avenue of Palms runs north along the east bank of the Jordan, a straight-line shelter of dark fronds fed by irrigation acting as a natural canopy for the traders. The heat is still ferocious, though; the air itself feels heavy, languid.

– Tamuz's people? says Carter. Von Strann gave him his intro—

– Ah, fer fuck's sake!

MacChuill revs the car and presses on the horn, keeping his hand down so the ugly, insistent bray goes on and on, a nerve-jangling drone that surely, Carter thinks, only a Scotsman used to bagpipes as a weapon of war could suffer. MacChuill stands up, his head above the windscreen. Whatever he shouts, it's impossible to hear, but it opens up enough of a crack in the crowd for him to sit down, slam the car into gear again and shudder it slowly forward.

– Sorry 'bout that, sir. Bloody murder, this road, but it's the only way out tae the Ink Wells.

*

Carter lets the heavy curtain fall back into place and takes a few steps away from the makeshift darkroom, lays his hand on top of the camera.

– The Ink Wells? he says.

MacChuill nods. Tobacco tin on the table, he's busy rolling up a cigarette. He's not been much more use than Tamuz in terms of information, but even the smallest clue would help, something a little more than blank stares and appeals in broken English to just *wait for the Baron, wait for von Strann*. Not bloody likely. One day lost is one day too many. And Carter got nowhere with the dealers in the antiquities shops he trawled round yesterday. At the moment, the Scotsman seems his best bet.

– Aye, says MacChuill, that's the only time Ah really met him, apart fae in passing . . . yer man Hobbsbaum, like. Baron had us take the two of them up there. But it's no as if there's anything tae see apart fae some bloody big bits of fuckin ugly machinery. It's the Ink Wells, sir. Ah mean . . .

MacChuill puts the cigarette in his mouth.

– Ye huvnae got a light, huv ye?

– I think so. Just a second.

Carter taps his pockets, finds what he's looking for and digs the silver lighter out, flicks the lid open, sparks the thing with his thumb.

– Cheers, says MacChuill.

– What was Ah sayin?

He shakes his head, shrugs.

– Aye . . . but they spent bloody hours up there, talkin tae this worker an that. Ye'd think they had shares in the bloody place. Christ, it's no even much of a business these days. Too flamin expensive tae dig it out the earth when there's a hunner other ways tae make, well, stuff that does the job, ye know.

Carter nods. You don't make sacks from silk, after all, and in this day and age Indian ink is good enough for any bureaucrat or banker's book of accounts. *Th'unfading gleam of Siddim's glist'rous ink, Shone on the calf-skin page of Prosper's books, And in Très Riches Heures of hist'ry's Dukes.*

Yes, thinks Carter, but even the poetry waxing lyrical over its virtues was penned and printed in more mundane ink that dried dull black. The Ink Wells to the north of the city still produce small quantities for specialist markets, but it's a trade on its last legs, by all accounts. And Carter has no idea what interest it could possibly hold for Samuel other than the passing curiosity of someone steeped in ancient manuscripts. Has to be worth a try, though.

– If you could take me up there, he says, it would be much appreciated.

– Nae bother at a'.

MacChuill nods at the lighter still in Carter's hand, his thumb idly clicking the lid of it open and closed.

– Nice piece of kit that.

– Had it for years, old chap.

Carter clicks the lid shut, tosses it in the air and catches it, slips it back into his pocket.

– Let's roll, then, he says.

For the Sake of One Good Man

You must know your Torah. You must know the story as the Torah tells it, the story of Sodom and Gomorrah. But there are many stories, and only one truth. How is it in your book? What is that they say? That the Lord appeared to Ab Irim at sunset and spoke to him. At sunrise I shall destroy the cities of Sodom and Gomorrah, he said, for their sins are smoke that fill my eyes with tears, and for this they shall be written out of the Book of Life.

They say Ab Irim was afraid for his nephew Lot – yes? – who lived within the city of Sodom, and he pleaded with the Lord: Will you destroy the whole of Sodom, he said, the good with the wicked; is this the action of a God of wisdom, justice and mercy?

The Lord was angry but He bowed to the appeal: Very well, Ab Irim, He said. I will spare the city if fifty good men are found within its walls. Yes? But Ab Irim still feared for his nephew Lot, so he pleaded further with the Lord: If there are only *forty* good men within the city, he said, then, for the sake of ten, will you destroy the whole of Sodom, the righteous with the wicked; is this the action of a God of wisdom, justice and mercy? And again, the Lord was angry but He bowed to the appeal: Very well, He said. I will spare the city if forty good men are found within its walls.

You must know the story as it goes, how Ab Irim bargained with the Lord until the sun had set and it was night, how he continued pleading until the Lord bowed to his pleas, agreed to spare the city if only ten good men were found within its walls. And the angels went down into the city to search, but there was only Lot, and so the cities were destroyed and Lot alone saved. This is the story told in your Torah, yes? But this is not the only story.

For so it was told by Ab Irim to his servant Eliezer, and so his servant's children still tell the tale. When Ab Irim stood with the Lord that night, so it is said, he asked again. He pleaded with the Lord again, and the Lord agreed to spare the city if only *nine* good men were found within its walls, and again, if only *eight* good men were found within its walls. But still Ab Irim haggled with the Lord. What if only *seven* were found, or only *six*? What if only *five* good men were found?

It is said that Ab Irim pleaded with the Lord all through the night until, in the final moment before sunrise, the Lord bowed to his last appeal: Very well, Ab Irim, He said. I will spare the city if only one good man is found within its walls. And Ab Irim was relieved. He knew that Lot was a good man and the Lord would not destroy the city of Sodom for his sake.

But as he said those words, Ab Irim looked out over the valley where the cities of Sodom and Gomorrah lay and, as the first light of the sunrise broke, Ab Irim saw Sodom and Gomorrah destroyed before his very eyes. There were no good men within the city walls, the Lord explained to him, for as Ab Irim had bargained through the night, the angels of the Lord had gone down into the city and taken Lot away, so that every man within its walls deserved to die in flames, in burning sulphur.

So the angels of the Lord destroyed Sodom and Gomorrah, for their sins were smoke that filled God's eyes with tears. For this they were written out of the Book of Life, and only the infamy of the cities is left. So it was told by Ab Irim to his servant, Eliezer.

Dark twins of the mooring towers of the Ben-Abba Airfields, the black iron drill-rigs of the Ink Wells rise in ranks across the white flats of the valley floor, in ranks and columns almost but not quite regular, like the pieces in a giant chess game near its end, inelegant Eiffel Towers all of them, knights with swinging hammers like horse heads lowering to snort, bishops with great pistons for mitres, turning cogs and chains lowering damned workers down the shafts to Hell. The factory complex in the distance behind them seems like some God player slouched in his defeat, a refinery for a head lain on the table, warehouses as arms, one running this way and another that. Pipelines stretch out to this rig or that like distended fingers. The smell of sulphur is overwhelming.

The road runs up into the ink fields past a ruin so eroded you might mistake it for an outcrop of the rock but for the odd square angle of a doorway or a window – an old Templar fortress, MacChuill tells him, for guarding the profane pilgrims and profiteers on their way to unholy Hephaistonopolis.

– Hardly part of the charter for a brotherhood of Christian warriors, says Carter.

– Aye, well, Ah guess that's what the Inquisition thought as well, eh?

Heresy, blasphemy and sodomy – these are the charges raised against and confessed to by Templars, Cathars and Albigensians alike, and while the mundane political and economic rationale that was the primary basis for the persecution of these three most favoured subjects of the pseudo-historian is, of course, of far more pertinence to a serious scholar than the fanciful content of confessions extracted by torture, it is nevertheless a question that should be asked: just why do these three allegations go hand in hand? Rather than speculate on the dubious veracity of the charges that sent these 'buggers' to the stake and their lands and money into the hands of good Catholics, rather than fabricating a web of occult mysteries from tenuous links (Baigent, Leigh & Lincoln, 1982), tracing 'secret traditions' back to obscene Essene baptisms of jism (Allegro, 1979) or homosexual Hashishim (Burroughs, 1959), let us turn our focus on the *meaning* of the myth. Let us drill down through the sediments of speculation that have built up in histories written by the victors and in tall tales told as true by latter-day artificers of arcana, and let us try to reach the core of the matter, to investigate the real substance of these accusations, the subtext, the semiotics of these sins.

To curse God as an evil demiurge, to urinate on a crucifix, to worship the severed head of Baphomet – these crimes against orthodoxy are consistent, coherent felonies which construct in their symmetry with monotheist belief-structures a systematic opposition, a reflection, an extension almost, wherein the anthropomorphism of a Heavenly Father is in itself blasphemous, where the crucifix itself is an idol to be smashed, where the true salvation is not in an essentially pagan blood sacrifice but in the rebellious, ascetic Neo-Platonism of baptist John, that latter-day Orpheus whose sundering of spirit from the flesh, of the soul from the body, reaches its symbolic apotheosis in the sundering of head from body. At the heart of these accusations is, perhaps, a fear that this is a purer form of monotheism, one which rejects God the Father and God the Son as graven images, one which venerates the Word over the Flesh with a dedication the more orthodox fall short of. In a way, these heresies can be seen as the logical end-point of monotheism's abhorrence of pagan sensuality, and it is little wonder that iconoclasm should emerge entirely independently at various points across the history and geography of Christendom, whether as actualities, or as projections of subconscious paranoia, or as cynical justifications for the pillage of property and privilege. These are only surfacings in unadulterated absolutes of the very stuff of which Christianity is made, the dark vein it mines of hatred for the corruptions of the world and the flesh, of hatred which sees the world, the flesh itself as hell, a black iron prison for souls stained in sin.

Why though, we must ask, is the charge of homosexuality invariably added at the end of charge sheets which read like Manichean manifestos? What does sodomy have to do with this transcendent devotion to the divine?

*

Nothing, thinks Carter. There's nothing here of any use. Two hours of questioning and none of the workers even remember either Samuel or von Strann; and one would have thought two crazy Europeans coming out to this parched hell-hole in the midday sun, to ask God alone knows what, would stick in one's mind. Carter studies MacChuill sitting casually on the running-board of the car, smoking his cigarette and watching the clamour and crunch of heavy industry in motion, conveyors carrying lumps of black crystal already melting in the sun. If the Scotsman's a liar he's a bloody good one, the sort that should be on the stage or silver screen rather than squandering his talent as chauffeur for a Prussian pornographer with an eye for pretty, copper-skinned boys.

– Workers change a lot here, ye ken, he'd mused. There's guid money in it, but it's a filthy job, like. Ah mean, ye can smell it, can ye no?

It's brimstone and burning rubber, oilsmoke and rotten eggs.

– No tae mention the danger; ye hit a liquid seam when yer diggin fer ore and . . . well, Ah worked there for masel a bit, but after a while ye realise the money jist isnae worth dying for. Drowning in ink . . . Christ . . .

Carter sits now on the low rubble of a wall built by Templars, watching black vapours drift up from the ink crystals on the conveyors, curling in ornate arabesques not unlike the writing the ink might well become once it's been purified, packaged and exported to some distant corner of the world. The wells have been here for over two thousand years, but any remnants of past cultures that might interest Samuel have long since been cleared to make way for this modern, mechanised industry. So why would he come here?

– And the ink, ye know, MacChuill had blathered on, it disnae jist wash aff like coal-dust. It stains ye, like, gets right under yer skin. Christ, ye can still see it on ma haun in the right light.

MacChuill had held his hand up for Carter to see, turned it this way and that until he got just a glimpse of a mark, faint from one angle, like a tattoo blurred and faded by time, but flashing clear and crisp and black for an instant, impossibly clear and crisp and black. A trick of the light and—

– I think I need to sit down for a second. Feel quite giddy all of a sudden. Bloody heat.

So MacChuill sits casually on the running-board of the car and Carter sits in the shadow of a Templar ruin, trying to work out what on earth would have brought Samuel here and, indeed, if he really came here at all.

And we watch him as we drift in tendrils through the air, dreaming of the words we will become.

Perimeter Alert

– Death itself, says the Duke Irae, is less magnificent.

He circles the Echo Chamber like an art critic appreciating an installation of the most unique originality. It should be more magnificent than death, after all, this egg from which the One True God will hatch. In death, the seven souls of a being are torn apart, dissolve away, one by one, but this . . . this will be the reunion of them all. Sekhu, the mortal remains. The dust of the angel Raphael gathered in a radioactive ruin that was once Damascus. Ka, the double. The empty armour of Gabriel taken from a desolate Haven out in the Hinter, the sculpted faceplate of his helmet a perfect mirror of his countenance. The Khu, the guardian angel. Uriel himself – the Duke Irae as he's known in this piddling little fabrication of a fold – he's given his eye to the project, to watch over it from within. Just as Michael and Azazel gave of themselves. The Ba, the prince's heart. And the Khaibit, the shadow of the angel of death. And the sixth soul, second highest of them all, the life, the energy, that burning song of spirit, the Sekem? The scream of Sandalphon as Uriel graved these other souls into him still echoes within that bubble of chaos, falling down forever towards that singularity of infinite energy, zero size, pure possibility, a void, a deep, waiting for a whispered word. For the secret name, the Ren, of God.

That was Gabriel's mistake, the Duke knows, to think any one of them could keep the throne themselves. An angel of fire on the throne of God will only make a hell of heaven . . . and none of the remaining three would fare any better. Besides, he's never been so ambitious or foolish himself; at heart he's just an old soldier, he likes to think, who'd rather stand behind his king as guardian and loyal adviser.

So, no, if he wants to restore order to the Vellum, he's going to need a little bit of all of them, and in Metatron's absence that means the Book, the lost, hidden, stolen, torn, scattered, remade Book of All Hours. Not some piss-ant little sampler patched together from fragments but the one and only, the Cant that writes the world, *all* worlds, graved for eternity on the skin of angels in blood ink. And the wonderful thing about the Vellum, about the Book that carves its folds and all the souls that live or die in them, is that even if the Book is in shreds, one of those shreds, one of those broken, twisted fictions, contains, of course, the Book's own story. Everything that ever was or will be, might or might not be, is written in the Book of All Hours; how complete would it be with no mention of itself?

And how complete would it be without the ultimate invocation, that one little word of Cant that might exist, and therefore *does* within the Book, one little word by which the Lord of Lords can be called and bound into the flesh of this world?

— It *is* beautiful, he says. Glorious.

— Indeed, m'sire.

Dr Arturo nods, deriving no pleasure from His Lordship's approval. For him, magnificence is an irrational—

      Emergency override.

      Narrative mode: shutdown.

      Bioform status: play/record.

Bioform:	Perimeter alert. Intruder detected in the First Environ.
Duke Irae:	Identify intruder. Arturo, this is ahead of schedule.
Bioform:	Intruder identity unknown. Identity signature inconsistent. Paradox shielding deployed.
Dr Arturo:	We can accelerate Project Moonchild, sir. It's him. It has to be.
Duke Irae:	It better be, Arturo.
Dr Arturo:	Archivist, filter duplications out. Scan all identity signatures; match graving with intruder. Cross-reference all agent signatures for a hundred generations.

*

Bioform status: Run command.

Bioform: Identity signature not matched.

Dr Arturo: Cross-reference underground agent code-name 'Jack Flash'.

       Bioform status: Run command.

Bioform: Identity signatures inconsistent.

Dr Arturo: Run Mandelbrot reiteration routines on both IDs.

       Bioform status: Run command.

Bioform: Identity signatures inconsistent.

Dr Arturo: Reiterate and repeat, to the power of ten.

       Bioform status: Run command.

Bioform: Identity signatures inconsistent.

Dr Arturo: Run eigenstate analyses on all results.
           Cross-reference analyses.

       Bioform status: Run command.

Bioform: Identity signatures match.
           Viability: coherent, comprehensive.

Dr Arturo: That's the best you'll get. We've got our host, m'sire. Jack Flash.

Duke Irae: The fly is in the web. Seize and restrain.

The Voice in Your Blood

17th March, *he writes*. Events become more curious. After my wild-goose chase out to the Ink Wells yesterday, I woke this morning in a foul mood, so frustrated with the runaround I've been getting, I decided that today I'd do a little exploration on my own. The boy woke while I was in the middle of my ablutions and was all for coming with me. I imagine he wasn't happy at all when he got back with MacChuill to find me gone. But I half-believe now that my little loyal native guide has only been leading me to the shops he knows Samuel had *not* been at. He seems a decent enough lad, but he's clearly been told to try and keep me out of harm's way, to keep me from setting off on Samuel's trail without his master. Whatever Samuel says in this Prussian's favour, my patience with him grows thinner by the hour. The boy will tell me only that he's out in the desert; it's

413

clear from the way he talks though that the *Eyn*, as he calls him, is deeply involved with these people. Tamuz insists that *Eyn* is only a mark of respect, but it does have the ring of a tribal title to me, as if the Baron is another of these White Arabs, Anna, gone native and prancing around in robes and headdress. It seems that noble blood is noble blood, whatever race it belongs to. I used to I cannot say but that I have my own ideas upon the nature of the *truly* noble man.

Whatever *Eyn* means, though, it's a part of the puzzle.

He'd picked up on the word the moment Tamuz first used it, out on the airfields, but had shrugged it off as some local dialect. It was only last night, tackling another entry in Hobbsbaum's little notebook, that he'd come across it in ... well, in another of those disturbing little flights of fancy. The translated shorthand is now inscribed on the facing page of his own journal entry:

From the few records that survived the destruction, it reads, *it is impossible to reconstruct the language with any degree of accuracy, but the eminent paleolinguist M. Ventris (1987) argues a strong case that the Enakite tongue, while containing many Semitic loan-words, is not a member of the Afro-Asiatic family of languages at all. Ventris speculates that the Enakite* eyn *may even be derived from the Sumerian* en, *meaning* lord.

It's not just the dates, the references to works unwritten, whole-sale inventions of future history, as if Samuel were working on some fantastic novel in the vein of Wells; it's the detail that disturbs him, and the lack of context. Without any clue to the origins of these scraps of ersatz academia, he feels like a doctor lost in the private language of a patient's delusions, the sort of calm, matter-of-fact insanity he remembers from the Somme ...

A look of cold hate and a shake of the head from the chaplain as he walks into the dugout. Sketches on brown paper scattered everywhere. Obscene drawings of Carter naked, with fire in his eyes, with wings.

– Don't you see the angel, the boy had said, when you look in the mirror, sir, ye know? Oh, and don't you hear the voice in your blood?

Brown eyes in the grey light of dawn, more sad than scared.

– It's time, says Mad Jack Carter.

– Isn't it always? says Private Thomas Messenger.

Focus, he tells himself.

If Samuel's lost his grasp of reality out with some kif-smoking tribal storyteller, these notes may have no more meaning than the automatic scribblings of a spiritualist charlatan. The future isn't written yet, not like the past. And there's no such thing as angels, he tells himself. No, when von Strann returns he may have more of Samuel's notebooks, according to Tamuz. But for now Carter has something more solid to work with, from his own investigations. The world has no angels in it, he tells himself, no magic, no prophecy; that way lies madness . . . like Samuel's . . . like the Messenger boy's . . .

Focus, goddamnit.

It didn't take me long, he writes, *to find the less reputable traders with more valuable antiquities, those who deal in genuine, albeit looted, grave goods rather than the counterfeit trinkets sold to tourists. And, after only the briefest of enquiries, I now know of an incident a fortnight ago or so where Samuel and von Strann saw off two assailants – after a book Samuel was carrying on him, it seems. The stall-owner was rather exaggerating, I suspect – she made a great fuss over a fire that got started in the struggle, how it could have wreaked havoc upon the kasbah, ruined her business, merciful Allah – but her description of the two 'foreign rogues' seems worth the price.*

– No, they were not Arab. Pale skin, blue eyes. Americans, I should think, from the way they talk. But Americans who have lived in many places.

The trader stuffs straw packing into a box as she nods to herself. She looks up at Carter from her stool beneath the canopy at the narrow entrance to her shop, a dark room crowded with shelf after shelf of shabti figurines, Jericho skulls covered in clay with shells for eyes, stone statues, cylinder seals. The kasbah seems an easy place to snatch and run, to disappear into the hustle and bustle, but Carter can see how easy it would also be to bungle a robbery in these cramped conditions, to knock an oil lamp over, start a fire.

– Strange men, the trader says. Hair like snakes.

She shakes her head, switches to Arabic to explain – not like a woman's flowing down the back, but down to the shoulder in matted, braided, thick, wild locks. Like an African, she says with some disdain before launching again into her bitter complaints about the fire and how she nearly lost her livelihood.

– That fire was not natural.

The voice comes from inside the shop, an old man hobbling out of the shadows to peer at him with a face as time-worn as the cracked clay on the Jericho skulls, cataracts in his eyes white as the seashells.

– Go back inside, she says. Ignore my father. He is blind but he imagines he can see better than–

– I *hear* well enough, my girl. And I heard his voice; I heard the word the angel used to start the fire.

– It was a lamp, a broken oil lamp. Ignore him; he is old and–

– Did you find any broken glass, eh? No. I know the voice of the one who took your mother. I know the voice of the angel of death.

– Father ... enough. Please go, sir. Please. This is not good for him.

The woman ushers her father back inside with waving arms, ignoring his protests – *I heard it, I heard it* – and Carter finds himself backing away down the street – *I heard the voice in my blood*. He's thinking of Samuel's letters and crazy notes, of the madness that believes in myths and magic.

And don't you hear the voice in your blood?

Eastern Mourning

A whisper: *Jack*.

A flash of Shamash, of shining sun on the silvery steel of the lighter as he flicks it into flame for Don's fag, gleam of it glinting in his eye and his grin in the mirror in the dugout – snicking white teeth, he has, like those of the lion in the corner slouched over the copper-smooth body of the boy, Private Tamuz Messenger, whose dead eyes stare at him now as his blue lips whisper his name again – *Jack*.

When do I know you from? When are we?

Thunder of guns drum his dream with doom DOOM doom, and Jack picks up the sketch of the Phoenician ivory of Adonis and the lioness, places it in a tin mug hanging from a hook on the wall, rattling in time to the prattling Irishman chained in the chair in the corner, Finnan – *awake again, Jack. Sure and we fookin need ye cause it's worse than Spain ever would have been if we hadn't gone and fooked it royally*, he's saying, *yerself and me and Fox makes three.*

And Jack looks at the Irishman just sitting there on the bunk in his dream of a dugout past, Sergeant Finnan, it is, Seamus Finnan, Shamash or–

. . . Prometheus, chained up in the Caucasus for his theft of fire. Of course, given the identification of Japheth with Iapetus, Prometheus's father, this lent further credence to the correlation of Noah's three sons, Shem, Ham and Japheth, with the Semitic, African and Indo-European peoples respectively. To the European scholars of the day, the 'dynamic fire' of the Aryan warrior race was clearly of immense historical import; it was unthinkable that the Biblical taxonomy would overlook the founders of classical civilisation; it was absurd to imagine that the blacks and the Jews should be traced back to their antediluvian roots, but the Aryan race not be legitimised in the same way.

I made a mistake, says Jack, looking out of the dugout across the mountains of the Caucasus at airships gathering to drop fire on Armenian villages. *A grave mistake*. Christ, what did he do? What have they done?

We all make mistakes. All that matters is ye have to fookin wake.

The wind that blows past him into the cave behind is cold as winter, cold as a Hinter night, though, God, and Jack pulls up the collar of his greatcoat as he turns to the light of the dawn, of the day breaking over Jerusalem where the women wail for Thomas always and forever, singing laments of eastern mourning, loud and long and ululating as a muezzin in a minaret, paeans of pain to God, no, not to God but to the rising sun, to Shamash, to Seamus, to–

As a mark of just how far the Romantic model was willing to stretch credibility on the basis of racist assumptions, Schiegel (1853) even went so far as to identify Japheth with Jupiter, and the Hebrew Yahveh with Jove, seeing in the coincidental similarities a great Indo-European God, brought to Rome from Ilium 'while the Semites were still sacrificing infants in the furnaces of Moloch'. When the Bible tells us that the sons of Japheth dwelt in the tents of Shem, he goes on to tell us, 'clearly it is the civilising influence of the Aryans that is meant here, everywhere bringing with them the shining ideal of an Almighty God of Gods to replace the heathen Goddess of old'.

The Sons of Japheth

Anna sits in the dark at the back of the antiquities shop, among the clay-covered skulls and shabtis figures, in a widow's veil of sorrow for her brother, her other, reading the old blind beggar's withered hand, tracing the lines of the mummified dead man with a clay reed, pricking the skin to bleed black blood that dissolves into vapours in the air, whispers of darkness that shroud him, MacChuill, half-blind, half-beggar. She reaches out towards Jack.

Cross my palm with silver. One sekhu for a fortune. All your talents for the one you love.

He walks into the room – it's hardly high enough to stand or wide enough to fly, six khaibits by six khaibits by six khaibits – and he kneels before the statue of her, under her outspread wings, this angel of mercy with her red hair and her copper skin, her lips kissing his forehead with forgiveness, tears running down to merge with his, salt of her grief running into his mouth, salt of her sweat as he kisses her breast, her neck, her chin, his lips, his puckered, puckish lips and the feel of his nibbling teeth on Jack's ear and nipping fingers on a nipple.

Tamuz, he murmurs in his sleep.

In fact, were it not for the use made of Schiegel's 'Aryan Yahweh' hypothesis by both fascists and Futurists seeking to justify their anti-Semitism, the arrogance and absurdity of the claim would render it laughable. The fact is that the compilers of the genealogies of Shem, Ham and Japheth clearly had little interest in the obscure tribes at the far reaches of their sphere of knowledge. Just as the listings of sons of Ham (whose curse, in this Romantic racist model, was of course their black skin) contain far more Semitic tribes, cities and nations than they do African ones, so too the sons of Japheth can largely be identified with indigenous Caucasoid tribes of the northern Anatolian regions. Few of these were Indo-European. None of them were the white-skinned, blond-haired, blue-eyed Aryans of Romantic invention.

Follow me, Jack, says Thomas.

And Tamuz leads him through the streets of the souk, where angels of death and peace walk, men in long black feathered cloaks, dreadlocked and copper-skinned, faces like vipers, fire blazing from their mouths against the men and women and children dying in flames. A Hassidic Hobbsbaum stands against a wall, murmuring prayers to himself as an angel sniffs him.

You are ours, old man. You are all ours. You are in the book of all that is ours, the book of all ours, all that belonged to—

And the word he says is a whisper of *hhhh*, just a breath without vowels, little more than a rounding of lips in the *wh-* of a *why*, a *who*, a *when*, and the touch of a tongue in the *y-* of a *you*, a *yeah*, a *jawohl. Yahweh.*

You belongs to us now.

Jack has his gun in his hand.

Fuck that shit.

He wakes, upright in bed, sheafs of Hobbsbaum's notes sliding off the sheets to scatter across the darkness of the floor.

We need to understand these Biblical genealogies as retroactive attempts to make sense of the melange of ethnicities inhabiting the Fertile Crescent, compiled generations after the forefathers of their writers swept down from the northern area around Hittite Haran to devastate the coastal city-states of Canaan, taxonomies based less on racial distinctions than on the political and cultural divisions between semi-nomadic 'Semitic' herders and the 'Hamitic' settlers whose towns and cities they pillaged. In this context, it seems quite obvious that these sons of Japheth who 'dwelt in the tents of Shem' simply represent the northern Anatolian tribes who spoke non-Afro-Asiatic languages, but who may or may not have been ethnically 'Semitic' (given that linguistic and ethnic roots do not always match) and who we know made up a large proportion of those raiders known as 'Khabiru', or 'Habiru' ... or 'Hebrews'.

Errata

Coils of a Snake

Finnan sits down at the small wooden table under the black awning, chugs a long cold swig from the bottle and pushes his seat back to look out into the crowd. He's getting used to the place now, the subtle shifts in the way the throng moves that keep you from getting from one place to the next by the exact route you'd intended, the way the stalls switch places when you're not looking. It hadn't taken him long to find the old roofless empty bar with a crate of beer behind the counter, covered in dust but ice-cold, the table and chair set up outside, waiting for anyone who cared to use them. A bit of luck.

He watches a couple of tourists walking round in a circle, one stall to the next, to the next, to the next, and back to the first, asking the same questions each time, getting the exact same answers. He watches the way the Cold Men skirt round them, avoiding the loops, striding through other areas, the crowd parting to let them through, the slipstreams of dust under their feet. The street of curio kitsch doesn't quite hold together, doesn't quite have the logic it should; but it has a certain dynamic to it. Coils of a snake, he thinks.

He takes another slug from the beer and lays his softpack of Camels and lighter on the table. He pulls a pack of cards out of his pocket and lays them on the table too; not tarot cards, just everyday spades, clubs, hearts and diamonds. He deals out a hand of solitaire, then lifts off the little mojo bag that hangs around his neck on a leather string, opens it up, takes out a peyote button. You can't beat the serpent playing straight. He knocks it back with another swig of beer.

Five minutes pass.

Ten minutes pass.

An eternity.

The mescaline is starting to kick in by the time the barker strolls

421

up to the table, casual as a spring day, to ask if he can take a seat. The multicolours of his clothes slide at the edges, streaming by each other like candy-stripe motorways, running rivulets of glows.

– Help yourself, says Finnan.

He lays the Queen of Hearts down onto the King of Clubs. The colours on the cards are liquid television, set turned up to burn-out bright. Simware gone crazy.

– Join me in a beer, old friend. A game of Happy Families?

The barker wanders into the bar behind him, feet thumping on the heavy wooden floor, comes back out with a chair and a bottle. He scrapes the chair rear-first up to the table, opposite Finnan, and straddles it, arms crossed over its back. He takes a slug from the beer. A wry half-smile, half-grimace.

– A little warm, he says.

– Unlucky, says Finnan.

His face is so white, hot white, like a light under his skin, like an over-exposed film. Powdery moondust, silvered pearl and sheen. No irises to speak of in his eyes, just big black pupils in the whites, open and honest – *honest, old friend.* Finnan doesn't trust him for a second.

– You know, old friend, says the Cold Man, I didn't even know this place was here. How *did* you find it, tucked away in this corner?

Finnan shrugs.

– Once I've been somewhere, I never forget how to get back there.

– Thought you said this was your first visit to Sante Manité?

– But I'm an 'old friend', old friend. Don't you remember me?

– Well, you know, I *truly* am sorry, but I clean forgot your name.

– Finnan.

– Finnan, the Cold Man repeats. Finnan . . .

– That's right.

– So remind me, old friend, says the barker, where was it that we met?

– Prague, maybe? Weren't you there at the Dissolution of Prague?

– Only saw it on the news. You were there, then? What was it like?

The barker looks interested, but it's all about getting leverage, trying to figure Finnan out. They may not be unkin, these Cold Men, but they play the same game, all ambiguities and avoidance. If information is power, their communication is a light skirmish. Finnan shakes his head.

– Sure and I couldn't say, he smiles. I wasn't there, old friend.

High Stakes

He flips a card over, a Jack of Swords, places it down over the Queen of Hearts. A little shift in the suits, so it is. So it's started now. The next card is a Page of Chalices, followed by the Ace of Suns – old Shamash Seamus, to be sure – then Knight of Moons and Don of Bones.

The barker shuffles his chair a little forward and a floorboard creaks.

– Wood sounds rotten, old friend, he says. You think it's safe to sit here?

– Sure and the place is just a bit neglected. Ye could fix it up real easy.

– Hardly worth the trouble.

– Beer behind the bar, a fan up on the ceiling ... ye've got a lot of hot and thirsty people out there looking for refreshment.

– We offer more of a ... spiritual refreshment, old friend.

– Finnan.

– Finnan. Anyway, we cater to other kinds of tastes, as you see.

Finnan nods. The mescaline is laying its feathered arms around him, sending a tickling shudder down his spine. He's not sure how long it is since he dropped the peyote but he's on the slow rise to the peak now. He can feel it.

– So, tell me, old friend ... Finnan, I mean ... what is it that a man like you is looking for in a place like this? You're not our usual kind of customer.

– No? In what way?

– It's hard to say.

Finnan studies the veins under the skin of his forearm, the green pulse of life, a flow of oxidised copper. He tenses the sinews that come down from the wrist, leans back in the chair and stretches lazily, relishing the feel of being embodied, the real sensual trip you get from good peyote.

– What's your name? he says. And what's your game?

– Harker. What do you mean, 'game'?

Harker the barker. Nice.

– Game, says Seamus casually.

He gathers up the pack of cards.

– Poker? Rummy? Blackjack? You know.

– Ah ... right, says Harker. I don't really play.

– Everyone says that, says Seamus. But everyone plays.

– Gambling's illegal in this state.

Finnan rifles the cards, shuffles them. He puts the pack down, to raise his beer bottle. He winks.

– Sure and I don't gamble in any other state, he says. Besides, who says we're playing for money?

– What are we playing for, then, old friend?

Finnan deals three cards to himself, face up, the Ace of Suns and the Queen of Hearts again, followed by a Joker.

– Information, he says.

Harker takes a sip from his beer, places the bottle on the table.

– High stakes, he says.

– Sure and what other kind of stakes are worth playing for?

Finnan deals him three cards, face down, from the bottom of the pack. Two Jacks for this joker – a pair of cowboys, a pair of hooks – and the third card the unspoken secret that the two of them are dancing around. The Queen of Books.

– Ye don't mind playing with the Joker, do ye? he says. Only there's one card missing from the deck and I've been looking all over for the fooker, but I'll be fooked if I know where it's gone.

– Fair enough, says Harker. What will we be playing?

Finnan takes a swig from his beer, swallows, draws a Camel out of the pack and puts it in the corner of his mouth. He picks up the Zippo. *Chunk, snik – fsssh – chuk.* Takes a draw.

– The name of the game, he says, is Find the Lady.

3

The Stranger in the Mirror

A Wicked Side

18th March. Tamuz and I had coffee in the kasbah late last night, in a tiny hostelry down one of the many alleyways in the Ink Merchants' Quarter, a dark brew flavoured with cardamom and rosewater and other sweet, unnameable spices. The tastes of the East are often pungent, acrid, exotic, but, Anna, how they stimulate the palate in a most pleasurable way. Even the tobacco in the hookahs offered by the wandering kifim is mixed with molasses and anise, I think, giving it a rich liquorice quality like some heady mixture of tar and absinthe.

I am a little ashamed of myself, Anna. I'm afraid to say that coffee and tobacco weren't all we had. I thought I might loosen his lips, you see.

Smoke trails in wisps up from Tamuz's mouth – open just a little, the bottom lip jutting out in a half-pout – until he leans his head back and exhales a thick cloud, heavy-scented with hashish. He grins.

– You were expecting me to cough, Carter Bey?

Carter laughs.

– I can see you're a lot more used to this than I.

Tamuz gives a shrug almost French in its loucheness, not so much *I don't know* as *Well, what can I say?*

– My sister, he says, she does not like for me to smoke the hashish. But the Eyn, he is here many nights, and he say to me, Tamuz, what your sister does not know cannot make her angry.

425

The Eyn has a wicked side. But we all have a wicked side, Carter Bey, no?

A look of mischief on his face, he nods at Carter, leans over the table to hand him the mouthpiece of the pipe.

– Even you have a wicked side, I think, he says. You ... English captain with stiff upper lip, but you like the hashish.

Carter takes a few quick sharp puffs, holds the smoke in his mouth like smoke from a cigar, not inhaling too deeply.

– Your Eyn sounds like something of a rogue, Tamuz, he says. What else does he say?

We talked late into the night and I learned much about von Strann that Samuel's letters covered only briefly – how he moved to this area for health reasons, his photography little more than a hobby before the purges of the aristocracy back home cut off his family's support, forced him to use his new skill as a means to make ends meet. Incredibly, according to the boy, many of the man's clients are honestly interested in the man's works as classical studies of the male form. So they profess, at least. I dare say a few might be, but I find it a little hard to believe.

The boy seems quite at home with von Strann's unhealthy interests, though I am less sure now exactly what relationship these two have. In many of the photographs that adorn the walls of the Baron's studio, I've noticed, Tamuz features as the model, and I had rather assumed there was some sort of – to be frank – Uranian affair between the two, but ~~last night~~ something he said last night rather surprised me.

– Oh, yes, Carter Bey.

Tamuz lands on the cot with a thump and rolls back, hands behind his head. Carter steadies himself against the sink, splashes a little more water on his face before turning the tap off, raking his fingers through his hair to dry them. He has no idea what time it is, but it's late. They must have been talking for hours. Well ... Tamuz has been, at least, chattering Carter's ear off.

– Oh, yes, says Tamuz, the Eyn say to me, *Tamuz, if that is what they want, who am I to judge them? Each to his own.* But I think sometimes he is more like you.

Tamuz sits up, crossing his arms, a mock frown furling his brows.

– *A little more* sad *and less* salacious, *Tamuz. You're not a satyr, Tamuz* – [he swings his legs off the bed] – and on and on he go. Why your people all so serious, Carter Bey?

But he doesn't pause for an answer, just rattles on, laughing at the ridiculous repression of these Europeans, when–

– My people, Carter Bey, we see no shame in the skin. You and me, Carter Bey, we could lie together, my skin to your skin, and there is no shame.

– I really don't think–

– But this is shameful thing for you, no? But we all have our wicked side and – I am sorry, Carter Bey. I talk too much tonight, I think. I see you are tired from the hashish, no? And the raki. With me it is the coffee make me like this, make me talk. But I am tiring you.

– The day is rather catching up with me, says Carter.

Tamuz's eyes shine in the lamplight as Carter unbuttons his shirt and peels it off. There was a time he would have been uncomfortable, the way the boy watches him, but ten years in the army rather teaches one not to be such a bloody girl. And frankly he's not sure he bloody cares. That's the good thing about raki and hashish.

– The Eyn, he would like to photograph you, I think. I think someone would pay much for the picture. I think . . .

Carter pinches the bridge of his nose, rubs his eyes. Tamuz's eyes glint dark in a gaze unbroken even by a blink, a single bat of lashes. He stands up.

– I think I have talked enough for tonight, eh, Carter Bey?

The Ideal of the Ephebe

There is one photograph taken by von Strann in which his ambiguous attitude to the military ideal is most evident. In the faded sepia tones of the albumen print we see a soldier, young and dashing, in the uniform of a British Army officer – a uniquely modern image in von Strann's oeuvre – standing over a supine Arab youth. It has long been the fancy amongst historians that the subject of this photograph is none other than the elusive Captain Carter, although this has recently been cast into doubt (Bildunger, 1989). What we can say for sure is that there is in the image a duality of austere nobility and brutal grandeur which is redolent of the neoclassicism of Jacques-Louis David, and which is unique to this example of von Strann's work. There seems a complex set of ideas at play here. Are we to read a reference to the classical values of the ancient Greek hero, the young warrior, the ideal of the *ephebe*? Or to the martial honour of the Prussian nobility of von Strann's traditional upbringing, outcast as he was from it? Or to the very Futurist militarism that had destroyed that old order?

The composition references Sir Joshua Montague's *Achilles Mourning Patroclus*, but where Montague's Achilles holds his sword up to the sky, swearing vengeance, von Strann's soldier holds his with its point at a still-living Patroclus's throat. And with the angle of the warrior's head turning his face away from the viewer – dehumanising him, rendering him unknown and unknowable – he seems not just seductively fetishised but also alarmingly lethal.

Carter mashes his lips against Tamuz's, fingers of one hand sifting through the boy's hair, with the other on his hip, just touching lightly, stroking it curiously, like a burn half-healed but too tender not to touch. He doesn't grab, doesn't grasp, just holds with his lips and kisses gently with his fingertips until he feels the arms wrappling him down to the bed and then the two of them are skin against skin, a grip switching from his shoulder to his bicep, soft inner thigh pressing his waist, the weight of Tamuz on him, shifting, sliding unsheathed cock in the squeeze of groin against his stomach, Carter's own cock solid in the air. Straddled, all he can do is pull Tamuz tight into the lock of his arms with a handful of buttock and an arm around his waist. Soft words of a strange language whisper in his ear as the boy slides forward and pulls out of his grasp, sits up, spits in his hand and reaches back behind him to slick Carter's cock with his saliva, slick as it is already with desire. Carter pushes up into the grip, but as Tamuz shuffles back, raising himself to guide Carter's cock into place, Carter's hands are on the boy's hips to stop him.

– No.

Inextricable from the romance of the warrior as an unattainable object of an idealistic, idealising desire, von Strann's photograph also speaks to us of the Nights of Terror, the pogroms and concentration camps that were the New Reich. Beneath the intense homoeroticism of the image is an equally intense fear of those men who had risen to power during the revolution by their shameless savagery, latching onto Futurism as an excuse to exercise their cold and callous self-interest. Somewhere in there, perhaps, is a suggestion of Futurism itself, the aesthetics of the mechanistic, the 'ethics of the automaton' as Churchill famously described it. But if the sword is surrogate phallus and this warrior dominant over his prostrate victim is to be read as a sexual conqueror, if, as F. B. Herbert said, every murder is a rape, then might we also read the reverse into this image?

Bildunger traces the many ways in which this photograph represents von Strann's comment on the sexuality of politics, but might it not also be considered a comment on the politics of sexuality, on the relationship of dominance and submission, active and passive, soldier and victim, man and youth? Perhaps it is not just the sword that represents the phallus, von Strann seems to be saying, but the phallus that represents the sword.

Carter thinks of a French sailor standing outside a Bordeaux brothel who, like him, had entered the establishment only half an hour earlier, both of them awkwardly drunk and recognising why neither had stayed inside with his comrades. A waiter in a London club who'd held his eyes with a gaze of invitation every drink he laid down on the table. An actor in a hotel in Cairo who'd been such a swish that Carter had regretted it instantly, but who'd won him with a recitation from *A Midsummer Night's Dream*, the epilogue, delivered with a port in one hand and a flourish of the other – *Give me your hands, if we be friends*. All of them brave enough to make a move while Carter simply stood, unable to strike, unwilling to flee. And now Tamuz.

He feels the hand on his waist tighten its grip, the wet fingers that part his buttocks, and the gentle pressure for entry that makes him arch his back, push his cock into the rumpling of bedclothes. The arm his head rests on – he gazes off to one side, towards the camera and the darkroom, seeing Tamuz only as a shifting shape over his shoulder, in the periphery of his vision – twitches, tenses, and then the boy's mouth is at his ear again, a breath of air, a word, a brush of hair against the back of his neck, and he relaxes into a shudder at this tickling of him open, relaxes into the furl of linen under him and opens up, closes his eyes and opens up to Tamuz's fingers and the cock squeezing in a little way, not far enough for pain yet and not far enough for pleasure, not until he opens up fully, trusting, surrendering to trust, to faith, surrendering to this beautiful youth inside him; and then the cock is sliding in, penetrating to the exquisite point of pain and pleasure, to the groan, like only a few before it, God how he hated them and loved them all.

And now Tamuz.

A Glint of Sun on Flashing Wings

– Bastards, says Carter.

Tamuz looks up from his lunch, some Lebanese porridge based on lentils, not unlike hummus or baba ganoush but more aromatic, more subtle, almost Siamese in its delicacy. Carter tears off a lump of unleavened bread and dips it into the bowl in front of him.

– I have to trace these two scoundrels to their–

Tamuz cocks his head, darts his eyes to the side, and Carter glances out through the open restaurant window into the square around the hulking block of the Beth Ashtart. A group of Turkish militia stand within earshot, gathered around a local who shrugs, points vaguely in the direction of the restaurant. Carter nods, bites into the bread. His journal lies open on the table, the latest entry just notes from his conversations with the storekeepers.

Two 'foreigners' (Samuel's assailants?) seen talking with Turkish militia. And dark-haired European. Been around a day or two. Asking for English Captain. Russian accent(?)

He closes the journal over, slips it back into his satchel and slides the satchel under the table.

Bastards, he thinks. He was getting somewhere.

– Are we going somewhere, Jack?

Carter sparks the lighter, sucks the cigarette into life. He looks at Tamuz, his oh so innocent native guide standing there with an ancient temple to a whore goddess at his back – the Beth Ashtart, the House of Ashtaroth.

– I'm paying a little return visit, Tamuz, to an antiquities shop I came across the other day. Curious to see if you recognise it. This way.

– Those streets are not safe. Bad part of town.

Carter smiles. There's few streets in this part of the city that aren't filled with the jabber of business and theft but he's got little to fear from that here, he thinks. The batlike shape of an ornithopter passes overhead – a glint of sun on flashing wings, a glint of war. Bloody Prussian engineering, he thinks. Bloody Prussians, bloody Russians and bloody–

– Take a look at the Turkish uniforms over there, he says. And there. And over there. That should be of more concern to us than a few petty thieves.

He takes the boy's shoulder, leads him towards a cart of oranges.

– Especially since the captain over there seems to be unduly interested in us. This way.

– This one? says Tamuz. No, I do not think I ever–

– Give it up, lad. If your story were any more fishy I could sell it in the market. What did von Strann tell you? Say nothing, do nothing, just keep me busy till he gets back?

Carter ignores the boy's protests, moving up the street with pleasantries and polite enquiries, shop by shop, heading for the antiquities place with the old blind madman. Most of the owners know little of use, but there's a few snippets here and there, recent visits from someone else asking the same sort of questions – about Samuel and the two strangers … and about Carter himself. *A Russian?* Carter asks them.

431

He's about ten yards from the corner of the road the antiquities shop is on, Tamuz scuffing his feet behind him, leafing through scraps of parchment, fiddling with inscribed clay curios and knick-knacks, while Carter tries to pry a description out of a merchant, when the bomb goes off.

Then he's standing in front of the ruined shop, looking at the fire, the wreckage, the carnage, hearing the sobs of pain and panic, Tamuz arriving breathless behind him, pulling at his sleeve – *Come on, we have to leave.*

– Bastards, says Carter.

– Papers, Captain, please.

Carter lays the bread down on the plate and sits back, hands his papers to the Turkish captain who makes a damn good show of flipping through them, asking why he's here, how long he's staying, all the usual questions.

– How long have you been here? Here, I mean, today?

– Since noon, the restaurant owner cuts in. This gentleman has been here many hours with his friend. Many hours.

French Lebanese, a crucifix dangling round his neck, the man is casual but not exactly amiable to the Turks – no surprise. A few more suspicious looks, and a few shrugs and easy half-truths in return, then eventually there's nothing more for the captain to do except hand Carter his papers back and warn him to be careful of the local whores, filthy as they are. His men follow him out like a flourish of robe.

Once he's gone, Carter sits in silence for a while.

– You are right, says Tamuz.

His voice is tentative, confessional.

– You are right before. The Eyn, he tell me to lead you … in circle. To keep you out of …

– Out of trouble? The bloody nerve.

– Out of danger, says Tamuz.

– Why? What's he involved with? What did he get Samuel into?

– I don't know, I swear, Carter Bey. *Jack.* From my heart to yours, I do not know why. All I know is he tell me … He tell me it dangerous. He tell me death follows behind you.

Tamuz reaches across the table, lays his palm flat on Carter's chest.

– Trust me.

Carter lets the hand rest there for a second before he peels it off.

Juis de Jack

Fast Puck, the young buck, my keen fuck, unzips my fly and slyly slips his hand through flap of cotton shorts, into the nook between the balls and cock, to nestle the shaft in crook of hand. I smooth a touch of fingers round the nape of his silken neck where skin meets softly shaven down – the golden brown of skin, the dark-brown fuzz of undyed hair – and pull him into a mash of lips, a mesh of bodies, as my other arm winds round his side and down to fondle the butt beneath his baggy combats, round flesh of buns snug in their CKs. Lips locked with tongues entangling, we press, chest against chest, his body braced in awkward posture so that, in between the squeeze of us, he can guddle in my shorts, fondling balls and feeling the heft of the hardening shaft. His grip settles into a steady grasp, a sliding tug of foreskin up over the glans and down again. I break for air and for a glance into his green eyes, pupils wide and black, black lashes flicking in a drowse of dreamy bliss.

– We have a week of this ahead of us, you know, he says. It's serious juice we're talking for a full astral projection.

– Seventh-level tantra, at least, I say.

I look up at the nibblesome nub of his little earlobe.

– Peachy.

– Sit still, says Anaesthesia.

I settle in my seat as her hypodermic vacuum gizmo carries on its needlepoint on my chest. Her hand darts here and there across my bitmite battle-scars, from line to dot, along a curve and round a circle, buzzing for a second at this junction or that. Feels like she's soldering my circuitry, the operator of my switchboard soul, making a connection here, breaking another there, but she's not rewiring my graving. No, the little vial at the back of her tattoo gun isn't squirting ink under my skin, it's gathering it up.

To the munchkins a graving is the story of your life all wrapped up in a perfect sigil; what they forget is every life has others in it, little lost loverboys and their twisted sisters, old enemies and old mates, grizzled soldiers and foxy rogues. And I'm the avatar of chaos, baby. You can make all sorts of pretty pictures joining up the dots of my graving.

Anaesthesia finishes up and steps back, unclipping the vial from the needle-gun. The ink inside it swirls in complex patterns, order in chaos.

— Papers, she says.

Puck chucks a pack of Rizla over to her and she snatches it out of the air, starts flipping papers out of it, one, two, three, four, five little ciggies went to market.

As one hand slowly pumps, his other pushes up under my tee, to flick a fondling thumb across my nipple, smooth his hand down ripple of ribs, and down into the crook of hip, there where the waistband of my pants hangs low. I tease two hands into his shorts, cupping the peachy butt, pulling him into me, so I can feel his pecker solid against my belly, and my own, encircled in his grasp, pushed close into his body, cock to cock beneath the layers of clothes.

I stretch his combats and CKs wide and loose of his smooth, creamy ass and prise them slowly down, to halfway down his butt, and further down, to bare it fully. And slide my hands around inside to front, to free his tenting cock. Butt naked in the breeze, his solid cock comes out into my hand, and combats and shorts fall.

— A week, he says.

A solid week, I think. Tantra can be such a bastard. But we want juice, not jizz.

Anaesthesia drips my black blood onto the papers, one by one, and the bitmites seep into them, rise into thickening globules, gradually taking form. When they're done she loads the bitmite cigarettes into my silver case. Five of them, all looking just like your normal Russian black but each of them loaded with a little extra buzz: a

434

whiff of Fox; a pinch of Puck; a dash of Don; a smidgeon of Joey; and a hint of herself.

There's a little bit of Jack Flash in everyone, they say. And there's a little bit of everyone in Jack Flash.

Snapping the case shut and sliding it across the green baize of the poker table to me, she draws the rest of the iridescent ink, the *juis de Jack*, up into a syringe. I tend to leave an impression on folks – an impression, a few dents and the odd chip – but I feel sorry for Fox's alter ego, even if he is a monkey-robot for Moloch and Mammon. Poor fucker won't know what hit him.

Anaesthesia hands me the syringe and I gaze at the swirly soul-juice.

– Try not to shoot it up, says Joey, who knows me far too well.

No Secrets

The callous brutality of a bomb in a marketplace, the bloody fields of the Caucasus, and a war that's not about territory but plain extermination – he's tired of it all. Sometimes he thinks the Futurists are seeking, through their ruthlessness, to drive the rest of the world into the same desperate and dishonourable state, to do anything that is required to win an unholy war. Sometimes he thinks this will be their victory, no matter what the outcome.

– I'm sorry for my outburst, he says.

Tamuz meets his gaze, for the first time in the sullen silence of the last ten minutes, Carter sitting on the bed staring at the curtained-off area of darkroom, Tamuz seated at the table, playing with an olive from the bowl.

It was cruel, the way he'd lashed out; Carter knows that. He can't really blame the lad for being loyal to his people, and to von Strann. The wild accusations that he made were hardly fair – *a barbarous people – quite capable of murder – heathens and huns –* but he's always had a short fuse. And it sounds like Samuel, if he's not already dead, has gone into hiding for fear of his life. Maybe not from the Enakites, maybe not, but Carter can't bloody know that.

– I want to tell you, says Tamuz. I want*ed* to tell you, I mean. You are right to be angry.

435

– No, says Carter.

The boy had only done what he was told, what was impressed upon him with the utmost urgency.

– I tell the Eyn I do not like this. It is not our way. We–

– It wasn't that, says Carter. I just took it out on you.

He stands in front of the ruined shop, looking at the fire, the wreckage, the carnage, hearing the sobs of pain and panic. There's more smoke than fire visible, thick black whorls, dust in the air settling so slowly, so calmly, in contrast to the traders running this way and that for water and blankets, tearing awnings away from danger, batting at licks of flame.

Tamuz arrives breathless behind him, pulls at his sleeve.

– Come, Jack. We have to leave.

– Bastards, says Carter.

He wrenches his arm away, snarls at the youth.

– Who did this?

His Webley is drawn, an automatic reaction even as he sprinted towards the blast, but around him there's only the chaos of mundane horror, no glimpse of billowing robes, no assassins disappearing round a corner, no blackshirt in the shadow of a doorway with a gun. Just choking smoke and weeping, dazed men and women with streaming wounds.

– The militia will come. We must go.

Carter grabs the boy by his shirt. If he has to tear the city to the ground, he'll get to the bloody root of this.

– What do you know?

– I know the militia will ask why you are here. Come now.

Carter glowers at him.

– I will tell you everything I know.

– And that's all you know?

– I saw little of your friend, says Tamuz. I stay here. I live in the city now. I cook for the Eyn, I watch his house while he is gone. I was here all the time your friend was with my people.

Learning their heresies, thinks Carter. And being drugged with God-knows-what if his notes are anything to go by, until ... until a few weeks ago some argument arose between Samuel and the

436

Enakite leader that had them arguing late into the night. The boy had only heard of it from MacChuill, out at the camp to drive both Samuel and von Strann back into Tell-el-Kharnain.

In the morning, MacChuill had awoken to an uproar in the Enakite camp. Samuel was gone, von Strann talking quietly with the chieftain, trying to calm her. Then von Strann and the leader had mounted steeds, rode off into the desert.

Carter speaks with barely restrained fury.

– What was the argument about?

– MacChuill, he does not know our tongue, only this word, that word, just a little. He understand only a little.

– And *just* what little did he understand?

– He tell me my sister call your friend a thief.

– What did he steal? says Carter. Some bloody relic? Tribal secrets?

– We have no secrets.

And Carter's words might as well be punches then, the way he lays into the lying little cunt.

– So you fucking told me.

– We have no secrets, Jack, says Tamuz. We are taught, as children . . .

Tamuz shakes his head as if searching for an explanation, flicks a fly away from his ear. He lays his hand on Carter's thigh for a second and then stands up from the bed, walks to a string of von Strann's prints – Tamuz as Dionysus with wine jar and laurel wreath, Tamuz as Apollo, a plucked hyacinth in his hand. He unpegs one, carries it carefully back to the bed to place it in Carter's lap. Carter picks it up, looks between the youth and the image of him. A picture of sordid, gorgeous beauty that he can't – but does desire so bloody much.

– The Eyn, says Tamuz, he say that he make pictures of what is inside. That his camera does not steal the soul but show it, yes? Like a mirror. If you can see my soul in your hand, how can I have secrets from you?

Carter hands the print back to Tamuz, swings his legs off the bed and reaches for the pile of abandoned clothes on the fold-down bed, plucks his undershorts out of them. The salt-sweet scent of another's body, another's sweat and semen, is rich on him, a strange sensation that makes him feel not quite himself, as if maybe just for this half-hour after waking he's not Jack Carter but some other self, someone that exists inside him, but isn't him. He'd tried to explain it to Tamuz, how it seemed so easy, with someone else's scent on him, to lie there, shameless in their sin.

Carter steps into his undershorts, pulls them on. Over at the sink, his shaving gear sits in a tin mug. A small mirror hangs from a hook in the wall. He leans towards it as he lathers his face, watching Tamuz, sly Tamuz with his innocent shrug and suspiciously poor knowledge of the local antiquities trade, pegging the picture back up on the line.

No secrets, my eye.

The Pillar of Her Sorrow

As Ab Irim said to his servant, Eliezer, only one man in all of Sodom was righteous in the eyes of the Lord, worthy of being saved, his nephew Lot. How do we know Lot was a righteous man? Is it that the angels sent down into Sodom to destroy the city were met by him at the gate, and taken to his home to receive his hospitality; that Lot, alone in Sodom, gave welcome to the angels sent to slaughter? Is it this that shows he was a righteous man? Is it that when the men of Sodom saw the angels in the streets, they followed them and stood outside Lot's door, calling to him, demanding their surrender, that Lot, alone in Sodom, gave haven to the angels sent to slaughter? Is it this that shows he was a righteous man?

In your Torah, Professor, we are told that the men of Sodom did not hate the angels, but desired them, lusted after them for their beauty. What is more beautiful than an angel, after all? The word of God is written on the skin of angels, and it is no wonder, then, that the men of Sodom desired to know them. But Lot offered instead his daughters, virgins both of them, untouched by man. Do what you like with them, he said, but leave these men in peace. Rape my innocent daughters, but leave these men in peace.

This is what shows him, in your tale, to be a righteous man.

*

We have a different story, my friend.

The story that is told among our people – we who came out of Ur of the Chaldees with Ab Irim, who followed him into Haran and down into Canaan, we who from the earliest days lived with your people, with the Sons of Shem, as servants in your tents, we who are also strangers, wanderers in the wilderness – the story that *we* tell is different. You will say that yours is true because it is written in ink, while ours is only ever told in whispers, passed from one generation to the next in words that are gone as soon as they are spoken. And perhaps this is so; sometimes it is the writing of the tale that makes it true.

Are you writing this down, my friend?

Good. Perhaps it is time to make *our* story true.

As Ab Irim said to his servant Eliezer, my friend, the angels who walked into Sodom on the eve of its destruction were not sent by the Lord to warn Lot but to test him. Lot did not welcome them at the gates of the city but threw himself before their feet in terror of his life. He did not lead them to his home but was led to it as a man condemned. He did not offer up his daughters willingly but because he feared the angels of the Lord more than the mob. This was the test of his righteousness. This is the man of righteousness in the eyes of the Lord, the man who offers up his service, his home, his own daughters, in absolute obedience. And in our tale, my friend, it is said that having passed this test, by the deal that Ab Irim made with his Lord the city should have been spared, but that the Lord in His wrath and jealousy and vengefulness formed another plan.

Your God, you say, is a God of wisdom, justice and mercy. Perhaps this is why, when Lot had offered up his daughters and the crowd rejected them, then the angels went out and destroyed all who were gathered there with the swords of fire that came from their mouths. It is wise to offer what you know will not be accepted. It is just to punish the offence of those refusing such gifts. It is merciful to give the peace of death to one's enemies.

But your Torah does not tell of the reward the angels asked for in exchange, I think. It does not tell of how the wife of Lot poured wine for them, and took their robes from them, to wash away the ashes

439

of humanity, how she washed the angels' feet and anointed their hair. It does not tell of what the wife of Lot learned from the mouths of angels, and how she knew then that her husband would die, and there would be no good men in the city, and the city would be destroyed. This, we are told, is why Lot gathered together all his household, his wife, his daughters and his servants, and escaped into the hills.

In your story, my friend, the wife of Lot is a foolish woman turned to salt for looking back upon the destruction of Sodom. In our tale, my friend, she looked back in defiance. If she was foolish it was with bravery. If she was turned to salt it was because she stood against the angels with her tears, her tears for the city that she loved and all who died in it, defying God's angels to pass the pillar of her sorrow.

But this is only our tale, and how can we say that ours is true while yours is not, we who write nothing down but let our words drift away with the winds as dust, as ashes, as salt? I will ask you this, my friend: in your tale what is the name of Lot's wife? I do not think she has a name in your Torah.

But we remember her, my friend. We know her name.

The Sound of Danger

It's the sound of hooves on cobbled stone that wakes him, then a cry in Arabic and the neighing of a horse that brings Carter upright in the bed, the sound of the gate to the courtyard clanging open that has him rolling out onto the floor and reaching for his holster. Danger has its own sound, the sound of anxiety in a voice, of sudden violence in a mundane act. Or hurried footsteps clattering up a stairwell. Carter unclips the holster, draws the Webley out and places a hand over Tamuz's mouth, hisses a warning at him. The boy stirs, moans at the touch of cold steel, the handgrip of the gun prodding his shoulder; he rouses, tries to sit up and speak, only for Carter's hand to clamp tight, muffle his mumble of confusion. Carter puts the gun barrel to his lips in want of a finger. *Hush.* He drops his hand at Tamuz's nod, motions the boy onto the floor behind him, clicks the safety off, cocks the trigger, and aims the pistol at a door handle now rattling.

The door opens and Carter has a challenge on his lips but Tamuz beats him to it, hand on his arm, pulling his aim to the side.

– No. Is OK.

A figure in flowing desert robes, an apparition in the night, Carter only catches a glimpse before the man is inside and closing the door behind him, slender features of a face half-shadowed, half-revealed by the gaslights of the stairwell; a few details – an Arab headdress, a pencil moustache, is that a saddlebag over his shoulder?

– Eyn Reinhardt, says Tamuz.

– Tamuz, some light, eh, for the love of God? And you might lower the gun, Captain Carter, please. It would be much appreciated.

– Von Strann?

– Yes. If you would point the gun elsewhere, at least . . .

Carter drops his aim and uncocks the trigger, clicks the safety back on . . . and pulls the linen sheet off the bed to flip over his shoulder. As he slides the gun back into its holster, there's a flicker of matchlight, muted and then replaced with the rising glow from one of the small gas lamps built into the wall; the Baron is already laying the saddlebags and his headdress down on the table. He leans on the back of one of the chairs, glances between Carter and Tamuz. With the deep tan of his skin and the dark hair, it's only the piercing grey of the man's eyes that ruins the Arabian Prince illusion – or delusion, thinks Carter. It's a ridiculous costume.

– Reinhardt von Strann, says the man. You are Captain Carter, yes?

– Captain Jack Carter.

Von Strann offers a hand and they shake – quick, no non-sense.

– If you would like to get dressed, please do, says von Strann. There is not much time for chit-chat and I'm sure you have many questions. This might make some of them easier to formulate.

He pulls a sheaf of papers out of the saddlebags – the leather of them is heavily stained with blood and scorched by fire, Carter notices – flicks through them and hands one page to Carter.

It's Hobbsbaum's scrawling longhand.

On the 19th of March 1929, the Treaty of Istanbul was signed between the Futurist Reich and the New Ottoman Empire, and a vanguard of Turkish troops landed in Syria to begin their move south. The news spread like wildfire through the cities of Palestine. In Tell-el-Kharnain, though, the battle was lost before it was even begun, the city in the control of the Turkish police even before the seizure of government buildings and official premises that night. While Jerusalem was to become, over the next few days, a bloody battleground for the British and Turkish forces, in Tell-el-Kharnain the unopposed Turks simply began rounding up dissidents and undesirables. Scattered fighting did break out in the Lebanese and Jewish quarters, where opposition was strong, but the people of this city of hedonist refugees were quick to realise that the war they'd sought to escape had followed them right into the heart of their haven and made it a base of operations.

Whether it is coincidence that von Strann arrived in the city on that night or whether his Enakite contacts had some intelligence on the movement of Turkish forces, whether von Strann returned to warn Carter or to enlist his aid, the two were thrown together in the holocaust that was to engulf the city. It is still unclear how it started but—

– What in God's name is this?

– It's the truth, says von Strann. *A* truth, at least. This city will burn, and every man in it will die.

A Cure for Karma

– You and me, *mon ami*, I say.

The creature from the id and the slinky, silky, sylvan self, we sit across from each other on the elaborate Persian rug, me and Fast Puck, legs crossed in lotus pose, a look of horny bliss upon his face. His skatepunk tee-shirt shucked, his torso glistens with traceries of visual trickery, quick colours trickling across him, gleaming with the glamour of the acid that we dropped two hours ago. Nice. On the stereo, the outlawed Lennon/Morrison collaboration starts to smooth its way in slowly, higher, higher. It's twenty years old, pre-punk experimental; it's sheer indulgence (worst excesses of them both – think *Revolution 9* meets *Soft Parade*), but I have a mission to go on, and I need to cleanse my chakras, charge my kundalini, focus my chi. That mosaic of music, all the sex and death of it – the tantric mantras – it might well be bollocks, but it's loaded bollocks. I can feel the orgone power flowing into me.

– Shit, this is good, says Puck.

His aura's so blue he's a comic-book Krishna in combat pants hung low to show the waistband of his Calvins. Me, I'm feeling like the jewel on the lotus. Out of the corners of my eyes, the shimmering golden light surrounding me seems like a myriad of waving arms; Shiva on one side, Shakti on the other, I'm the Buddha with a hard-on. I'm a bodhisattva baby floating in a sea of bliss, an angel assassin getting charged up for the kill.

A maze of mad Mayan hieroglyphs and Hindu carvings swirl in fractal mandalas over the four walls of the Fox's den, illusions of gravings on reality itself, mirroring the myriad me of the Vellum. Under, over and around the sound that's coming from the stereo, noises inside my head are twisting, bells and claxons, whirrings, chirpings, gongs, all rhythmic, syncopated. This is what I call trance music.

– Shit, but this is good, says Puck.

– It does feel positively Oriental, says Guy Fox.

He stands at the bay window, casual, cool, and sipping at his gin-and-tonic, strokes his pencil moustache, rakes his fingers through his crow-black flop of hair – the king of thieves, the prince of charmers, and the leader of our revolutionary cell. He's taken less than half the dose that Puck and I have . . . but then he has to stay on guard. This is a dangerous game we're playing and the enemy, the Empire, plays for keeps.

I rise from my cross-legged pose to pull on a velvet robe, feel it furling round me soft and smooth. Tickling shivers surge down my serpent spine as I stretch. When I pick up the Curzon-Youngblood

Mark I chi-gun that sits on the top of the dresser, it buzzes with the orgone energy pulsing into it. Ah, yes. Happiness is a warm gun.

— Shit, this is *fucking* good, says Puck.

Guy Fox looks out the window over the Rookery, arches an eyebrow.

— Gentlemen, I hope you're ready, he says. We're about to have some visitors.

Outside, the ornithopters of the Royal Albion Militia are approaching low over the rooftops, beams of their searchlights scything across the ramshackle tenements and ghetto squats of the Rookery. Looks like a swarm of locusts flying over Hell's shanty-town.

Fast Puck stands limberly and stretches out one hand into the air in front of him. The aura crackles round him as he slides his fingers down the shaft of his six-foot chi-lance and it buzzes into life, powered up by that mystic force, the kundalini orgone energy that flows through every deadly sexy thing.

— Well then, says Puck. Looks like it's time to cure some karma.

Fox looks at me and raises his glass — *chin-chin, old chap*.

— Operation Orpheus is go, he says.

A Story of a Story

Tamuz rushes to and fro, gathering supplies, filling water bottles. He pulls a trunk out from under the bed, opens it up. Von Strann paces the room.

— Where is Samuel? asks Carter. That's the only thing I want to know.

— *Where is Samuel?* says von Strann. Believe me, Captain Carter, my people know many things. We know that the Turks are gathering a fleet of Prussian airships in Syria, ready to strike British Palestine. We know that your Russian friend, Major Pechorin, is also in this city, liaising with the head of the Turkish garrison. We know that the Turks and the Futurists are the least of your worries, Captain Carter, believe me. That we do not know where Samuel is concerns us more deeply than you can imagine.

444

– You must put this on, says Tamuz, handing Carter a long white robe identical to the Baron's. They will not know you.

Carter throws it onto the bed disdainfully, buckles his belt and picks his shirt up. He ignores the boy, focused entirely on von Strann.

– Talk sense, man. Give me answers.

– Did Tamuz tell you of the Book? Or did Samuel, in his letter?

– What book?

– The Book of All Hours.

Tamuz snorts with derision.

– A story of a story. A story for children, like your Santa Claus.

– As Ab Irim said to Eliezer, says von Strann, the angel Enoch had a book. Inside that book is every story possible, the story of every angel, every human being, every demon. Inside that book is every story true or false, even those about the book itself, how it was written, lost, stolen, destroyed. The most important story, though, is how it will be found again one day, and the seal of it broken open, and the name of God Himself read aloud to bring Him back into the world, out of the ink with which he's bound into the vellum, bound into the book.

– A story, says Tamuz. A story for children. My mother used to tell us this each new year, at the dawn.

– Your mother was trying to prepare you for the truth, says von Strann. Your people have had the book for generations, keeping it hidden. That's why they have no books of legends, histories, why they write nothing down; they have it all written in the book already.

– We have no secrets, says Tamuz. My people have no secrets.

– When you have the book, says von Strann, no one has any secrets.

Carter shakes his head.

– I think I'm with Tamuz on this one: a story for children.

– Do you have a cigarette? says von Strann.

Carter offers his case and the Prussian clicks it open, takes out a cigarette and snaps it shut again. He taps the cigarette on the case and looks at it for a second before putting it in his mouth.

– These things are bad for you, you know, Captain Carter? They clog your lungs, poison the cells. Leave that, Tamuz; it's not important. Just food and water. We know many things, my people, but if the Futurists are the ones who have our friend – and believe me, whatever Samuel has done, he remains my friend – but if the Futurists have him ... we thought perhaps he was going to the Turks, taking what he had learned ...

He trails off, takes a drag. It's as if he's stalling some decision, Carter thinks, putting off the inevitable moment.

– As Ab Irim said to his servant Eliezer, says von Strann, it was not God who gave Adam and Eve their suits of skin. You know the Bible story, yes, Captain Carter, how they were ashamed of their nakedness and so God gave them the suits of skin? Maybe this is so. Maybe this is one truth. Here is another. In the beginning Adam and Eve gave God the suit of skin. In the beginning, God was only an idea until we sought to bind the wild world with our words. Male and female we created our gods, in the image of humanity.

– Once upon a time, says Carter. Look, I'm not interested in your Enakite heresies. I'm sure they're very–

– Let me show you the Cant, Captain Carter, says von Strann. Let me show you just a little of the language that the book is written in, what it can do. How man might make God in his image.

The Colour of Dust and Leather

[... Von] Strann left with his boy [... and?] the headman, as [...] thought at the time, rode out of the arid sands of the western desert upon [his steed?] thundering [...] The horse reared and his [...?] billowed in the air. His face masked by the black linen djellaba that left only his eyes visible, narrowed against the cruel early afternoon sun [...] glinting in the light, the emerald or jade of [...] green eyes [...] not a Semitic people? Yet the coppery colouring of their [skin? ...] and had little time to think of such things really, for [...] Enakite headman [... moved?] his djellaba from his face and [...] saw it was, in fact [a woman? ...] her long red braided [hair? ...] a scar running from her eye to her jaw. [...] was astonished, [...] should say, von

446

Strann never having made even the slightest allusion to this circumstance, the rogue; trust him to ensure [...] first meeting with the Enakites should have adequate drama. And even in [... she?] spoke with a voice like [...] a great many rivers rushing, a roaring torrent [...] into my very soul [...] herself:

– I am Anat-Ashtarzi ibn Alhazred, of the blood of the poet Abdul and of the prophets Ziatsuzdra and Eliezer, of the sons and daughters of the Enaki, of the People of the True Book. We walk between the curses of the Lord and in the shadow of his Enemy, and we serve no man or god.

[...] told her then that, as an anthropologist, [...] desired only to study the customs and traditions of her people, for [...] believed that they were very ancient and that much was therefore to be learned from them. As an anthropologist, of course, [...] said, [...] knew they would have secrets not to be shared with outsiders. At this, she laughed.

– Our truth is older than your history, *habiru*. You who came with us out of Chaldea, out of Ur of the Chaldees, you *should* know the truth behind your Torah; of the one who died so that your people might live. You are welcome, *habiru*. You will come with us, listen to our tales, take them back to your people. Secrets? Secrets are for those with shame. If your people do not know our tales it is because you have never asked. Come.

She reached down to offer [...] her hand, lifted [...] up onto the horse with easy strength, as if [...] were the woman and she the man.

– Where will we go? [...] asked.

All around us the harsh, hot sands of the desert swirled, scouring skin, stinging eyes. Where could a people *live* in such a place as this?

– We go to [... she] said.

At that point [...] thought von Strann had left [...] with a mad woman. [...] thought myself in a delirium, [...] thought ... [...] cannot say exactly what [...] thought. The idea was insane. But now [...] know, for [...] have seen it, and [...] have seen the Book. It is the world that is insane.

*

[…] into the hills, many days. A range of mountains not on any map […]ever seen, impossibly rugged […] out of the mundane world entirely? […] know this region well and this was entirely unfamiliar. When […] asked of this, she merely laughed […] until we came to the camp. It was like a city in itself, a city made of tents and banners. Vast canopies of stitched-together hides soared high into the air and swept across it, more like circus tents or sails than the traditional Bedouin style, and more barbaric for they were not the multicoloured textiles of the Arabs but rough hide. And as we drew closer still, […] saw that the great poles which held these intricate structures aloft, and which […] had, at a distance, taken for wood bleached purest white by desert sun, were in fact carved out of bone. Bone they were, or ivory, but from what animal […] could not say for surely no creature alive today had bones or tusks the size of these great rods and staffs. […] knew that […] was looking at something unique, a way of life that should have died out millennia ago. […] shuddered in […] heart, for there was something that it brought to mind. The tents and banners seemed for all the world like the heraldry of some great mediaeval army gathering to do battle. A grim heraldry the colour of dust and leather.

The headman looked at […] with her penetrating eyes and said, as if she had read […] very thoughts:

– Do not fear us, *habiru*. We walk between the curses of the Lord and in the shadow of his Enemy, but we kneel to neither. Their war is not ours. Not yet.

The Stranger in the Mirror

– Jack, says von Strann.

He exhales a plume of formless smoke with this quiet mutter, just this single word under his breath, but it's as if that word has punched a hole right through the cloud, shattering it into shapes, into folding furls of curling worlds, and the smoke is black against the white of the room instead of white against the darkness. Carter staggers back, one of von Strann's prints flapping against his hand – a negative image, no, an image seen in negative – as he bats at the

448

smoke unwhirling around him, drifting into lines and spirals, sigils carved in the flesh of human skin, scars inked with Siddim Ink in the earliest days, the days of those men and women standing round him now, stories written on their skins, their loves, their losses, how they lived and died. And the same story is told in him, a vein in his arm a root of a tree, the power of oxen in a shoulder-blade, the dart of a fish in a curve of muscle, swoop of a flock in the whorl of a fingerprint, one groove of it turning like the stars beneath his feet, stars falling like grains of corn down into blades of grass between his toes, like drops of rainfall from above, and the ripple from the drip of a word splashing into water, flashing like light on water, spreading out into everything around him.

– Jack.

Jack leans over the sink, looking at the image of a stranger in the mirror, a doppelgänger with the same history but with a million other histories to boot. The world is normal now, and it'll never be normal again. It'll just be vellum and ink, and him as a fucking scratch, a blot on the page. He pulls his shirt closed over the scars across his chest, starts to button it up. Von Strann – Reinhardt, Reynard, whatever his fucking name is – stubs the cigarette out on the table. Tamuz sits on the edge of the bed. *Thomas*, thinks Jack. He can't look at the boy now without seeing that other face, without seeing his own hands on the smooth throat, grabbing dog-tags, soft hair brushing across his naked chest, that face looking up at him as Puck uses his stomach as pillow and Jack flicks a finger at a horn; Christ, he can see the boy now with iridescent wings stretched out across the grass, eyes like a cat or bright green hair.

And the stranger in the mirror is that shimmering youth's killer and lover, his friend and brother across the countless folds of a Vellum that this Jack can barely even imagine, a fire dancing for this butterfly soul, only seeking to impress with its own flitting brilliance, and not knowing its own nature is to burn.

The sensation starts to fade, sanity clamping down around his racing heart, locking him back down in denial, in the world where he's just Jack, Jack Carter, yes, the Mad Jack Carter of the Somme, the Sword of Yerevan, and there's *only* this world, *only* this Jack;

449

and, as he closes the door on that hall of mirrors in his head, the smoke trails drift around the room—

– *we* drift around the room, dispersing now our tableaux's done – a little of our little tale told in a single word. We drift down into the cracks between the floorboards and back up, to the satchel with Carter's journal and Samuel's notes, spiralling up the leg of the table to the saddlebags and more notes. Somewhere in there are the words von Strann is just about to speak. We touch the dead parchment tenderly, dead parchment and dead ink, this ink not even true black but sad blue, insipid indigo, pallid purple. We are rich with the tales crushed velvety in us by centuries upon centuries of stony sedimental sleep.

Hush. He begins, words just a little more alive in his mouth than in Hobbsbaum's hand.

– That's the Cant, says von Strann. You understand now—

– No, says Jack.

But, *yes*, hisspers the stranger in the mirror.

Into the Chaosphere

Out on the far perimeter of the Rookery, a rooftop dwelling made of corrugated iron explodes in flame as a thopter's chi-beam cuts right through it. They know where we are, of course; it's just a demonstration, and I'm not impressed. They may have aether supremacy but the rebels rule the streets and I have balls of adamantium, a glint of silver in my smile. Tonight, we rock.

– Try not to cause a stir, says Puck.

He flips down his white nightshades. I stretch over and tousle his green scruff of hair.

– Would I do that? I say, tapping a finger on one of his pointy little horns. Lust of my life, he is, the little punk.

– This is a deep-cover operation, says Fox. So—

– No civilian casualties, says Joey. Tell it to the Crimson Pyro here.

– Slick and twisty, I say. I know.

*

I zip my yeti-hide bomber-jacket up and sling on the bandoliers, clasp clips and buckle straps, fasten hasps and snap grips into place. I tighten the lacing on my leather trousers and pull on my white kidskin gloves. I'm tempted to go for rinky-dink, pink-'n-kinky chiffon, but I settle on white silk for the scarf, for old times' sake. I scope myself in the mirror on the wall; it's neat having a flesh-and-blood physique again, and my eyes are even matching shades of electric blue, but a week of tantra has me glowing from the goddamn teeth. I gleam a growl of unbridled appetite at Puck; I'm looking forward to this Middle East malarkey, I tell you.

– How do I look? I ask.

My voice thunders like a river in my ears.

– Stop pissing about, says Joey. Let's go.

He slams a power-clip into his chi-blade, a fiend in black leather duster and whiteface greasepaint, black tears on his cheeks, a demon Pierrot, a monster mime. I flip down my mayashades. Under the goth-garb and greasepaint is a soul of articulated adamantium, shiny as quicksilver and smoother than Puck's peachy butt. Under the gloves, my own metaphysique looks much the same. Puck is still as blue as Hindu porn. I snatch a last snog from him, trying to imagine him in copper.

– Come on. How do I look?

– Peachy keen, says Puck.

Guy Fox strokes his tache, looks at Joey and me, looks a little dubious.

– Stay in the shadows, he says.

Outside the ornithopters sweep their beams across the walls and windows of a derelict school. They're getting closer.

– This is your first trip in a while, says Puck. Take it easy.

– I'll be fine, I say.

I slip the jackknife down into my boot; they won't let me take the gun, despite my pouting petulance.

Don Coyote in his armoured longcoat, armed to the teeth and ready for a rumble, growls.

– OK, he says. This is the last stand of the counterculture. Remember Newbury and the Irish Solution; we all know there won't be any quarter given. Let's—

A searchlight beam floods through the window, a kaleidoscope of colour, burning out my senses for a second. I can feel the psychic charge of it, the astral feelers prying, scrying through the room, the pilot in the ornithopter searching for me, reaching closer. In a single fluid move, Puck swings the chi-lance to his shoulder as he drops to one knee, aims along the silvery-steel shaft and blasts the orni-thopter out of the sky. I feel the pilot's mind exploding like a blossom of light inside my head.

— Time to go, says Fox. See you in 1929 . . . I hope.

I look to Puck.

— You'll be OK? I say.

— Get out of here.

I start to stretch my mind out of reality, into the chaosphere, the lawless world under the skin of space and time, the Vellum. Fox and Coyote fade into the confusion, the free fusion of flowing forms, but I can hear the ornithopters open fire, see fire falling. A flash of light. *The grain of the fields is shimmering.* The acid's peaking. Or maybe that's just the acid speaking.

Joey's at my side, ice to my fire, dark to my light, villain to my hero, his dreams of the Circus closing in around us, of its cells and corridors and doors leading out into streets deep underground, running up and down and all around.

— Just remember the fucking mission, he says. Remember you're an agent. Remember who you are, and what you're here to do.

— Operation Orpheus, I say. Easy in. Easy out. Piece of piss.

— And remember what we're dealing with.

But we're already leaving this reality, shifting—

Errata

Crickets, Bells and Clarions

Finnan holds his hand over the middle card.

The crowd is gathering behind Harker now, imbecile faces warped by the peyote into grotesque pink sculptures that might freak the hell out of Finnan if he wasn't totally aware that it's his own imagination reconfiguring them; they're just magic mirrors of all the ... *me* he might be. He has his own crowd at the back of him anyway, hallucinations growing out of the shadows and the lights at the corners of his vision. Gold and green ferns wave in the empty bar now. Ancient Aztec deities sit at tables, lean against the walls. Velvet moss grows over pool tables, carpets the floor, and a buzzing, ringing music – crickets, bells and clarions – fills the sense-warped saloon. Smooth, sinuous in motion, he reaches out to tap the card and turn it over. A queen.

– You win again, says Harker. You're too good at this.

His white face is glowing, radiant, shimmering in the desert light. Finnan leans back in the chair and cricks his neck. Good peyote always does this to him, calms the electric energy of the Cant, evens it out into a bluesman's laid-back mojo. Slow shudders of a goddamn gorgeous serpent spine. Feels like being home.

– Just lucky, say Finnan.

So it's lucky, it is? Seamus takes a slug of the beer. Sure and he never could quite give up the booze though, could he? You can never quite get away from yer past, even hiding out in the desert.

Fuck it, thinks Finnan. He puts the bottle down. It's time to push.

– Try again, he says. You nearly had me, there.

Harker grins a snarl and shakes his head. The ribbons on his hat curl in the air.

– Lost too much as it is, he says.

– One more game, says Finnan. For one more question.

– I've told you everything I know.

*

He'd told Finnan that he used to be John Harker, sales exec for a small movie merchandiser, until one day his wife and children disappeared in the Evenfall. The Evenfall was hard in this fold, he'd told Finnan. People didn't just disappear without leaving a forwarding address; they disappeared without leaving a memory. But for Harker it was different; he remembered the family he loved perfectly. His in-laws, no matter what this crazy man on their doorstep said, they didn't even remember their own daughter, but *he* remembered goddamn everything, the wild child in high school, how she'd crashed the family car, how they'd got married in Reno. He'd started reading up on alien abductions, government conspiracies, the Rapture, started writing letters to the newspapers and the chat shows; but no one really listened, even as the world around went crazy, suburbs emptying house by house, the Left Behind wandering around like Alzheimer's patients, memories stripped so bare they were like children. One day he stepped up onto his best friend's porch to find a child sitting on the swing. He'd grown up with David Johnstone and so Harker still recognised him, the same gap-toothed smile on this face without a beard, without the scar from the boating accident where David's little sister Julie-Ann drowned.

David's little sister Julie-Ann was sitting up on the swing beside him.

– Well, I guess I went a little mad then, Harker had said.

He'd worn a placard for a while after he lost his job, slept on the streets, eaten out of trashcans, screamed at strangers about patterns of secret meaning in the litter, started muttering to himself pretty much all the time, crooning little sing-songs that made him feel better. And sometimes it seemed the litter danced to them.

The Cant, Finnan had thought. The bitmites. And a fold where the bitmites focused on the painful past, removing the sorrows and the cause of sorrows ... even if one man's or woman's errant daughter is another man's wife.

– How much did you love your wife? Finnan had asked him, after turning over another queen. He'd known it was a cruel question.

– Not enough, Harker had said. Maybe that's why I went a little crazy, old friend.

*

454

And then one day, Harker had told him, he just woke up on a bus pulling into Garsonville, Illinois, in the dead of night, with a suitcase full of charms and trinkets, wearing a patchwork coat of all different colours, in its inside pocket the deeds to a small shop on Main Street. In the window streamed with rain he could see his own reflection, white and thin, a stranger to himself. He'd just woken up as a Cold Man.

– Old friend, I felt the call of magic then, and I wasn't afraid any more. I *knew* I was going to be OK now, and I wanted to share that faith with others.

Finnan had almost believed him. He was *meant* to almost believe him, Finnan was sure.

He looks at Harker now, half-risen from his seat but hesitating, and sees the same elements of a performance as in the man's telling of his tale, the same sleights as in the movements of his hands, the shifts, the switches. And the crowd behind him. Drawn by the skill and the story in Harker's hands and voice, they're being played like the cards, like he's already tried to play Finnan. Pretend you're not a pro. Look like a loser. Suck them in and wait for the right moment for the sting. He has them all behind him with his hard luck tale.

Eventually, he'd told Finnan, the Cold Men came to Sante Manité because they felt it calling them. It was as if they all knew they'd done everything they could in bringing that little bit of faith to those small-town folks, and now, the way salmon have to swim upstream to mate, or birds know it's time to head due south, the Cold Men had known it was time to leave.

– So we came here, old friend, though I don't rightly know what that might tell you.

The wall of marks and suckers sweeps behind Harker like a cloak of colour. According to the Cold Man – and spoken with a casual sincerity – the mojo peddlers of the market have no idea what brings the punters in, but to Finnan it's pretty clear; he can see the desires and fears in their faces, simplified and stylised into the crudest of images, living sweating caricatures. Skull-faces ripple with folds of fat, beaks twitch and owl-eyes blink. They whisper to each other, pet and scratch and pick at each other, or point stubby fingers

455

– see how he does it, all in the wrist, ah-hah – and kiss each other's ears as they whisper, lick and bite. Sex and death.

Finnan looks past this fucked-up Freudian masquerade towards the red bulk of the Mission at the far end of the market. By now, the mescaline in his system is in full flow of vision and voice. Fractal skies above peel over one another, electric-blue, cerulean, azure, and in it all a winged sun, fiery, floats over the scarlet Mission. The whole scene is engulfed by an illuminated atmosphere, and in that numinous wash the only things that seem truly real are the sand and the sky, the ruins of the buildings, and most of all the Mission. The marketplace is an absurdity crayoned in over the actual world of golden dust, over the ground swirling in grooved and pitted patterns, over the scattered solidity of broken-up sandstone.

It's a sideshow, sure, as superficial as the barker's pretence of being beat and, standing up from his seat, ready to call it quits.

One More Question

– One more game, says Finnan. One more question.

The words echo in time, while Harker looks to the crowd, a show of his shame to gain sympathy, a show of sudden resilience, sudden resolution. He sits back down, square in the seat, and a *come on* ripples through the crowd. Harker shucks the three cards around the table, up and down, switch, shift and drop, again, then again, crossing hands, a switch, a drop and a stop.

– What's the question? he says.

– What do you know about the Mission of Sante Manité? Yours?

– The same.

– Don't know what you think I'd know about this place.

– Just curious, old friend. You know the score. Pick a card … any card.

Finnan taps the middle card, a jack. Harker is already smiling as he turns it over, to the crowd's near cheer at this underdog's change of fortune. Finnan shrugs, a wry smile, takes a slug from his beer. Harker works the crowd, basking in his victory before turning back to him.

– So, he says. What *do* you know about the Mission of Sante Manité?

Seamus swivels the beer bottle around on the table in front of him, picks at the label.

– Well, now, he says. There's not much I can tell you at all, John Harker, since there's not much I know for sure. But I do know that your Mission there is the only thing that matters, that this whole marketplace, yourself included, is just ... misdirection. I wouldn't like to guess what's hiding out in there, but sure and I could make a stab in the dark as to why. If you're interested, that is.

– Go on.

Seamus takes a draw on his Camel, blows smoke up into the air, watches the swirling vortices of grey-blue.

– See I used to be an altar boy when I was a lad. Did I tell ye? No? Well, anyway, being a good Catholic boy I learned all the names of the saints, and I never once heard of a Sante Manité, sure. But, well, there are a few strange names among the saints – like Dionysus or Bridget – and some of them sound so much like the names of certain pagan gods that ye'd almost think the Christian missionaries had just sorta coughed into their hands, looked down at the ground and told some would-be convert, well now, don't worry, son, cause sure and ye can keep praying to them as long as you call them saints instead of gods.

– And the thing about it is, Manité has to be the strangest name fer a saint I've ever heard. So I was wondering where it comes from. I mean, correct me if I'm wrong, but I could swear the Algonquin have this word for a sort of a spirit, somewhere between a god and a human I do believe, and so perfect for making a saint of, don't you think? *Manitou*, the word is.

– Is that so?

– Trust me. I'm a mine of useless information.

– I'll take you at your word, old friend, says Harker. But you don't strike me as the kind of man who believes in saints ... or gods.

– I believe in saints and sinners, sure; I'm just not convinced you can be one and not the other. Gods though ... prayers and petitions ...

Seamus tips his bottle to the market.

– That just seems like a big bag of ole shite, to me. No offence.

– None taken.

Finnan puts the beer down.

– But there's something in that Mission. And Sante Manité might well be a good name for it.

He leaves the *isn't there?* unspoken, and takes a draw on his smoke.

– But then again, says Seamus, sure and maybe it's just built on an ancient Indian burial ground.

– Maybe, says Harker. Another game? Another question.

His face has brightened now to a glow that nearly drowns out all his features, leaving his eyes black slits, his nose a subtle bump, his mouth melded smooth into the skin. It's a sketched-in cartoon of a face, a few lines, uncoloured, a store-dummy melting in white heat, his clothes burning with a furious clash of reds and whites and blues, flames flickering in the breeze.

– I think I need to stretch my legs, says Finnan, take another look around. Maybe later, John Harker.

– Maybe. But I still don't know what you're looking for. And you know, Finnan, we only want to help you find it. To make you happy.

A barker, a harker, a ragged harlequin, he seems little more than a prop against the painted backdrop of the marketplace. Like someone took the robot fortune-teller from an old amusement park and put it out in front dressed up in a ringmaster's costume.

– Don't know what I'm looking for myself, says Finnan. But I'd say you've given me a few ideas.

As the mescaline lights up the world behind his eyes, he stands up from the table, pushes his chair back, picks up the cards, his cigarettes, his lighter, and stretches, yawns. It's time to go behind the scenes.

4

The Chambers of His Heart

The Silver Screen

The tower and the roofs of the Rookery seen from a barred window – a reflection into a room filled with books on Futurism – the corridor outside the cell – spiral staircase down to Sub-Level Thirteen – Joey prising a grille off the wall, looking into a ventilation duct – crawling through the flow of dreams pumped up from below to sustain the psychic sleep of the Circus – steel thrum of fan blades turning slow before us at a T-junction, blowing hokey smoke into the mirrorspace, dry ice of Joey's dreams – a left turn and a sharp drop down into darkness and—

I'm looking through a silvery screen into a shabby movie-hall, all worn red velvet seats and curtains, peeling paint on plaster. Couples kiss and grope each other in the darkness; in the seedy squalor of the 70s, I reckon, from the lapels wide enough to hang-glide with. Somewhere in the audience, potential parents make their futures: she stops him; a smooth-tongued devil, he persuades her; she consents; a ritual play that's been the same since the chromascope was invented. Fuck, they probably played the same game back in Shakespeare's day.

The frame flicks to the edge of my vision and I snap my head round, following it. It floats at the foot of a bed on which—

– What the fuck? I say

– Polanski. *Son of Satan*, says Joey, shimmering into solid shape beside me. We're extras in a Sabbat scene, standing amongst masked revellers as, on the bed, Satan humps his poor, doped victim. The revellers start as Joey unsheathes his vorpal blade in a sleek singular move, and the horned and horny-red arch-fiend looks up to see these unexpected walk-ons in his little Catholic drama of doom. Joey Narcosis, dream-killer and yours truly, Jack Flash, hotter than Hell if I do say so myself. I'm about to introduce us when Joey steps forward, scythes his sword through, flicks it back into an arc and down to his side. There's a look of shock on Satan's face as his head rolls off its shoulders and black blood sprays the ceiling of the bedroom.

And . . . cut, I think.

Satan's minions back into the corners, his body trembling on top of the girl until I roll it off with a foot, slipping the jackknife from my boot while I'm at it. Through the magic mirror that flicks here and there with cuts to close-up and wide-shot, different angles, I can see the audience sitting up at this strange turn of events. Even Polanski isn't usually this weird, I guess. I flick the knife through the air and spear the screen while it's on wide-angle, bounce over the bed and grab the handle, slide a slice down it like a pirate down a sail. Beyond the flaps peeling open in front of me, the audience starts to scream, all rising from their seats.

I unhook an orgone grenade from my bandolier, pull the ring out with my teeth and lob it into reality.

I sniff the air as I step out into the cinema; there's the slightest scent of pheromones on the aether too, the same psychic aroma as on my passport, but it's almost lost in the musty smells of popcorn sweat and hotdog fear, and the stench of sexy sin getting stronger by the second. They're shagging in the stalls already. I drop down onto the carpet at the front of the stalls, where an usherette has crumpled to the floor, pink uniform skirt hiked up to do . . . unmentionable things with an ice-cream cone.

Two weeks of tantra and she's giving me ideas.

I reach down to pluck a Cornetto from Sexy Sadie's abandoned tray, as Joey lands beside me. Up there on the ripped screen, Sharon Tate is shrieking for an oblivious audience, subliminal newsflashes flickering through the film. Massacres of movie stars and Indochinese villagers. Internment and states of emergency. It's not real news, only newsreels, all the little lies they bury in the backbrains of the mindfucked masses to sustain the circularity. Keep them thinking it's the same year, you know, and the bitmites make it so, like the same movie being played over and over, midnight or matinee. There's a reason they call this place the Circus.

I flip a grey trenchcoat from the back of a seat and pull it on over my leathers as Joey and I head for the green glow of an exit sign, stride down a dim hallway, sticky carpet underfoot, low lighting on dark red and gold patterned wallpaper. A framed poster of Lord Jagger in *Performance*.

I peel the cardboard top off the Cornetto, strip the paper down to expose the mint-choc chip.

– Cool and creamy, I say.

Joey slams the handle of the fire exit and we step out into the evening air.

The greeny-gold streetlamps give the city a gaudy glow, lighting bright the busy road at the end of the alley ... and the roads overhead and to the side, and every which fucking way but loose; a jumble of buildings upside down and on their sides, man, this place looks like someone let a psycho architect loose in zero-g. An airtram crawls past, old and slow as a dinosaur, windows rattling, engine thundering, a couple of inches off the ground at most. Cars float by, scooters buzzing round them. Sign on the wall across from me says Northbridge Road so we're in the vicinity, from what I know of Dunedin. Down at the next corner, blackshirt militiamen are stopping traffic at the red-and-white candy-striped barrier of a checkpoint which just has be the entry to Imperial Way. I duck back into the alleyway; the passport will work as a post-curfew permit on a one-to-one basis, but it would never get me past that level of security.

That's where Joey comes in.

He leans out in front of me, scoping the militiamen that we're allowed to kill. That he's allowed to kill, that is. I'm a little envious, I have to say.

– Don't fuck this up, says Joey. They still have public hanging here.

The plan is simple: all I need to do is find my cover id, download myself into his deep and dirty, deep enough and long enough for me to sneak inside the Castle while Joey, reeking of my blood pumping in his veins right now, has them looking the other way. Then I shuck off the soulskin, sneak into the secret depths without raising any alarms, rescue Joey from the dungeon he should be safely tucked away in by then, and we carnage our way to the chi-mine. Nice and easy, lemon squeezy.

– What could possibly go wrong? I say.

– Not a sausage, says Joey, sceptical as fuck.

He nods his head – *on ye go* – and I nod back, saunter casually out of the alley and turn right, north up the road, away from the checkpoint. I glance back just the once to see Joey heading towards the guards, sliding sword out of scabbard with a *shick*!

Head down, I walk away.

– Yo, motherfuckers! Joey calls behind me. Come and slurp my saucy spunk!

Yeah, right. Like I would say that.

The Balance of the World

20th March. A day of fighting draws to its close and we are lucky to be alive. I hardly know what to think, now that I have fought side by side with the Baron against the Turkish forces. I have seen his true mettle, Anna. I can hardly deny that he's a man of honour now. Yet only twenty-four hours ago I was cursing the man to his face, calling him a liar and a murderer. But I suppose I knew even then that he and his Enakite leader were not behind Samuel's disappearance. Even before he told me of the book, I knew. ~~I knew the moment he uttered that bloody word.~~ A book of prophecy, he said. A book of names.

The Book of All Hours – the language it is written in is . . . compressed. You could not write down every life that ever was or will be, not in a million pages, otherwise. You must understand, to read one page . . . It is like reading a thousand pages in each word. How could any man ever learn such a language?

– We do not learn it, he said. We remember it.

*

He told me that Samuel had argued with the Enakite leader about a page of the book; something on that page, some prophecy or invocation, something that was too terrible to accept. That Samuel wanted to alter it, believed that by doing so they could change the future itself. ~~I knew just from hearing that word that one word can change everything~~

– In the language of the Enakites, he shrugged, a thousand words in one sign, a thousand pages in one word, a thousand books in one page. It could be a million lives at stake or more.

I refused to believe him, Anna. Bloody-minded and pig-headed, I refused to believe his 'absurd claims'. Prophecies and words of power. I cursed. I swore. Eventually we just stood there, eyes locked, our faces inches apart, like two bare-knuckle fighters in the moment before the bell begins the fight. Sometimes it is when the invective has given way to silence that men are at their most dangerous, Anna, and I believe I might well have taken a swing at the fellow then had Tamuz not pushed himself between us.

– Eyn, no! Carter Bey! Please, Jack. Eyn Reinhardt.

Von Strann stalks away, seems to grasp control of himself, to swallow whatever rage is driving him, before he turns back to Jack.

– Captain Carter, he says in a voice measured in syllables.

And Jack's anger drains away at the strain in that voice and the look of ... anguish in his eyes; it's as if the man is carrying the weight of a million souls, and Carter is looking into that mass, hearing a resonance under the simple sound of his own name. He's not sure if it's the look or the voice or Tamuz's hand on his chest that makes him take a step back. Or if it's ... a horrible recognition that whatever that weight is, it's not just in von Strann. He can still feel an echo of something strange about the room, about the air, and about himself, the clenching of his fist, his heartbeat in his scarred chest, something clamped around his heart.

– Jack, says Tamuz.

He's still wound up. That's all it is. He tries to tell himself that but it's like he's trying keep his footing on the deck of a ship listing ever further to one side, like trying to aim while charging along a steep slope covered with scree. As if one support of the world around him has been blasted away, the broken floor angled down so sharp he has to fight to stay upright. He looks from Tamuz to von Strann and back again, and has this sense, this strange sense like a sort of déjà vu, the recognition when you realise some stranger looks so like an actor or an old acquaintance but you can't quite place them.

But most of all he sees this ... honest sadness in von Strann's face, and his own instability in the fear on Tamuz's. He was about to lose control, he knows. That's what this feeling in his chest is, he knows.

The desire to lose control.

Creatures with Clay for Flesh

As Ab Irim said to his servant Eliezer, I have told you of the suits of skin they say God gave to Adam and Eve to cover up their nakedness. I will tell you more, yes? You will know this tale, I think, my friend, of how the Lord created a garden, a paradise, how he built a wall around his land, as you today build walls around your cities; how he made the waters rise to water it, as you today dig wells and irrigation channels to water those cities; how he shaped a man from the raw clay, and a woman from the man's bone, to be his wife, as you today shape your sons in your own image. And as your daughters today are only their wives, a ... piece of them, yes? If women were made from a man's rib, surely a woman's place is at a man's side, is it not? This is your tale, I think. It is not ours.

Our tale, my friend, is not so different. We also say that these *edimmu* – this is our word, my friend – these creatures with clay for flesh, filled with a little of his breath and blood, were shaped to work his garden and take care of it, to toil for the Lord in his fields. We also say that the Lord gave his servants one rule to obey, that he told them they were free to eat from every tree in the garden but the tree which grew at the heart of it. We also say that he threatened them with death if they ever ate the fruit of this tree. And, my friend, we also say, that of all the creatures in the garden, the serpent was the wisest of them all, and he came to the woman, saying:

Take the fruit.

If I eat the fruit then I surely will die, said the woman.

You will die one day, said the serpent, but not today. And would you not rather die with your eyes open like a god's?

And so the woman tasted the fruit and, since it tasted good, she ate it.

But, in our tale, my friend, we do not call this act a sin, for how can a creature of clay with only a little blood and breath to make it walk and talk, just enough life for it to toil as a slave, how can we curse such a creature for a little taste of this forbidden fruit? To taste the knowledge of good and evil, to taste the fruit of the tree of life, my friend, is this a crime to your people? No, my friend, this woman who left her man's side is the mother of all living because she did this. And of all the creatures in the garden, now this woman was the wisest of them all, and she came to her husband, saying:

Take the fruit.

If I eat the fruit then I surely will die, said the man.

You will die one day, said the woman, but not today. And would you not rather die with your eyes open like a god's?

And so the man tasted the fruit and, since it tasted good, he ate it.

Then the eyes of both of them were opened, and they saw each other in their nakedness, and hid among the bushes of the garden, hiding their shame among the branches and the leaves. This is the tale as you tell it in your Torah, a tale of sin and shame. But if they knew shame, my friend, then they knew pride as well; and they knew hate, my friend, and love, and sorrow and joy, and all the good and evil that we know in our hearts. For they had eaten of the tree at the centre of the garden, and to taste that fruit, my friend, to taste its juices, sweet and bitter, on your tongue and running down your throat to fill your belly – my friend, wisdom is like no other fruit, for once you have tasted it you know a hunger that can never be satisfied.

But our tale ends just as yours, my friend. For it is said that when the Lord found his slaves hiding from him, when he knew that they now had wisdom, he was afraid of them, that they might become as powerful as him, and so he sent them out, and set an angel with a sword of fire to guard the gates of his paradise. What master does not fear slaves who have tasted wisdom? What master does not fear slaves who would disobey his rules? What master does not fear slaves who know what is good and what is evil?

Those are the sort of slaves who make trouble.

And Words as Weapons

Jack puts his hand on Tamuz's shoulder – *it's OK* – and the boy relaxes, steps out of the way. Von Strann tips him a nod and Tamuz returns to his work, to preparing for their departure.

Outside, far off, dogs are barking.

– You have to understand the peril we're in, says von Strann. These are treacherous times, and our enemies, they are ... what makes them dangerous is as much what we have in our hearts as what they have in their hands.

He hefts Carter's holster with its Webley, hands it to him.

– A gun in the hand is of less import to them than the fear and hatred in a man's heart.

– Who are these enemies? says Jack. The Futurists?

– Worse, says von Strann.

– That word, he says, that word I ... *used* on you, you understand, there are those who speak this language more fluently and to more effect than you or I can even imagine. I think ... Samuel thought ... that the Book was created to keep them in check, to bind them into a world where *this* is right and *this* is wrong, *this* is true and *this* is false. If they have control of the Book, then they could ... change it, shift the balance in their favour.

A scream in the distance. Breaking glass.

– Balance, says Jack.

Ten years since the Great War ended, years of madness, anarchy, bloody holocaust. The war to end all wars, he'd thought, when he signed up to fight the Kaiser, to save Belgium, to stop Prussian militarism in its tracks. Ten years fighting genocide in Kurdistan.

– What balance? he says.

– Captain Carter, I beg you, says von Strann. I am not your enemy. And my people, Tamuz's people, we want to find Samuel every bit as much as you. So he stole from us? We do *not* believe in revenge. Believe me. We are not barbarians. We do not lie. And we do not murder in the name of justice. Not for any book. We – Anat and I – we only rode out after him to ... we were trying to save his life. To save all our lives. We have been searching for him since he left. We found ...

– What did you find?

Von Strann swallows. He opens one of the flaps of the saddlebag.

– We found the carcass of his horse, a scorched and charred piece of carrion, torn apart by vultures; we knew it only by the metal on its halter. And we found this, buried inside the horse's bowels. Someone had cut the creature open ... had hidden it amongst the poor brute's entrails.

Von Strann scatters loose papers from the saddlebags across the table.

– If you will not trust me, he says, trust Samuel's words. But stop delaying us with your obstinacy, *please*; if we are not out of this city within the hour, I doubt we will get out alive.

Jack picks up one of the pages:

... know now how to translate the language fully, unlike [...] and false are signalled, [...] think, in the [...] so that the Cant, as [...] have come [...] and words as weapons, tools, [...] a sword of fire ...

– And I suppose this enemy will be using their *swords of fire* against us, says Carter. Words as weapons, eh? I doubt words would be much use against a Lee-Enfield.

– No? says von Strann.

The blackshirts are arriving as I kick the last Mod in his parka through the pastry cabinet of this little Italian joint, all Formica tables and espressos, that I've tracked my horsey to. I slug a shot of java back with one hand, with the other flick my jackknife through the air and into a plainclothes SS man's cold heart. He drops, and a chi-gun skitters from his hand across the lino floor towards me. I dive for it, and roll, and come up blasting.

Fuck the Fox's plan, I think. You wanna party, come ahead.

As my cover runs for cover, I take down the blackshirt who's about to shoot him in the back – *bad form, old chap*, as Fox would say. With his black Ray-Bans and polo neck, our guy looks more groovy cat than cunning fox, but it's him all right; there's no mistaking that little goatee and moustache. Two newcomers shoot out the windows and come diving through, their chi-blasts shattering tabletops and sending splintered wood and splatterings of ketchup, mustard, clouds of sugar, salt and pepper, up into the air around me. I sneeze and shoot the ceiling down on top of them, a lucky fluke. Fuck, I think. All hell is breaking loose. The mission's not just in jeopardy, it's full-scale fucking abort, baby. The enemy were waiting for me. Some bastard's sold us out and, when I find out who, they're going to pay the piper at the gates of Hell.

I catch a glimpse – a motion in the corner of my sight – and fire as I turn. There's a look of horror on the beatnik's face as he smacks back into the mirrored wall-panel. His girlfriend – blond beehive and horn-rimmed glasses, sky-blue twinset – screams as Jacques Reynard Cartier slumps and slides down, cracked and lumpen, to the floor.

– Fuck! I shout. Fuck fuck fuck fuck fuck fuck *fuck*!

As civilian casualties go, this takes the biscuit, the big, salty, semen-sodden biscuit.

I slide in a football tackle across the lino to kick out the legs of yet another militiaman, blow his super-ego out the back of his head as he falls, and prise the chi-gun out of his twitching hand. From the floor, chi-pistols crossed, wrist over wrist, I shoot another three blackshirts as they jump out from the armoured airvan's sliding doors. Sirens are screaming outside on the streets, and getting louder. Firing two-fisted, furious and frenzied, I take out the last few of the militia squad, and turn back to scope the torn-up café. The girl is cradling the dying beatnik in her arms.

OK. So I'm going to have to improvise.

I tuck the guns into my belt, unzip my jacket and pull out the little case with the syringe filled with my silvery squirt of soul, the distilled Essence of Jack meant to go into the poor fucker dying on the ground in front of me, to seed the soul of an angel assassin deep inside.

— And what about the cover? Anna had said to Fox. Afterwards?

— A little dance with death, he'd shrugged, might be exactly what it takes to turn a pawn into a rook.

See, according to Guy, well, I'm the fire on the Fox's tail that keeps him running. I'm the trickster in the traitor that means Joey's always on our side no matter who he's being paid by. I'm Anaesthesia's anger, Puck's perversity, Coyote's cool, Finn's fire. I'm the id unbound, baby, the time-bomb in your heart that makes you tick-tick-tick till the alarm goes off and you wake up and smell the coffee. I'm the one who lets the real you out into your head.

Everyone's got a secret self that's locked away inside them, see, and if you want to let it loose, you've gotta let the firestarter blow your storm doors of perception open with a Sekem Semtex moment of satori. Then it's exit Jack into the night and, out into the light, out of the smoking rubble, walks a new you, as a Princess or a Puck . . . or as a Fox.

That's Fox's theory anyway.

I crouch down by the beatnik.

Fuck.

This should have been easy, but the paradox shielding is probably kicking in already and . . . I look at the Jacques Reynard Cartier who will never now become a savvy Fox with savoir-faire and Savoy flair. I can see the Guy in him now, staring back with hollow eyes, dying in front of me. And there's no telling what effect this'll have on our own king of thieves. I'm only hoping there might still be one last chance . . .

This is the Vellum after all; if I wasn't inside the shield walls of the Circus, I could blow my own head off and wake up a world away, in Sumer, in the Evenfall, or in the wilds of the Hinter, with just a little eternity to walk to find my way back to this fold. But this is the last Haven of the Lords of fucking Order; they got rules here, the fuckers. Still, maybe if I shoot him up with a little extra me, maybe if I can get a little sample of his psyche back to Fox before the temporal shockwave rips through our reality. Maybe . . .

Ah, bollocks. Fucked if I know what I'm doing. Tactical metaphysics never was my forte; I'm just the shock troops on the urgrund.

But I push one of my sleeves up to the elbow, start to roll up one of his to find a vein. If I'm the avatar of anarchy, who rips reality apart so anything is possible . . . well then anything is worth a try.

– Sorry, old man, I say. Plan B. Don't worry, this won't hurt a bit.

Outside, there's militia sirens in the distance.

And the Angels Will Come Again

A scrap of page pocked with scorch-marks, burn-holes:

. . . can read the language [. . .] know what the stories say, but [. . .] are always changing [. . .] if every time you open the Book [. . .]different – and while it may well contain our futures written [. . .] pages, what good is that if it contains all the futures that will never happen as well as those that will, if you can't tell the [. . .]ference?

A napkin stained with red wine, inked in capital letters:

YHVH. NO VOWELS. NO NOTES!

A scrap of page splattered with ink blots, thumbprints:

. . . von Strann's [. . .] Anat-Ashtarzi, she wanted to know what was true and [. . .] was false. She thought [. . .] a clue in the writing itself,

something that her people did not fully understand. And [...] think that [...] may have found that clue.

A page of a journal censored with scribbling so heavy that it grooves the paper:

... how can [...] betray that privilege? She has told [...] so much about [...] and about those forces in this world who know of the existence of [...] and seek to possess it, not just as a relic but for its power. How then can [...] even contemplate this course of action ...

And then there are the timelines, biographical notes for people not yet born, descriptions of future technology, lists of authors and books that Jack has never heard of, historical sketches of imaginary cities, and long quotations from who knows what – one of them seems to be *The Iliad*. Here and there the texts are ticked, crossed out, or labelled with a question mark.

Another page from the journal:

... the word Lot means 'hidden' in Hebrew. Is it possible that what dwelt in Sodom, what escaped from it, was not a man but a secret? The Book itself? Or some more specific secret written in the Book, in a language that specifies pitch, intonation [...] that be what the angels came to Sodom for, in search of a secret lost to even them?

A note, headed Genesis 4:17.

... it mean that Cain built the first city and named it Enoch, after his son or that Enoch [...] and named it after his son? [...]n Enoch, father of Irad, and Enki, god of Eridu, seen [...] their oldest city and situated at the mouths of the Tigris and Euphrates. Sumer, known to the Sumerians as Kiengir – Land of the Kien. Kien = Enki.

A page with a single sentence on it, smeared with blood:

And the angels will come again to Sodom.

Jack reads on.

The Chambers of His Heart

20th March. A day of fighting draws to its close and the Baron and I are lucky to be alive. I hardly know what to think now, now that I have fought side by side with him against the Turkish forces. Tell-el-Kharnain has fallen, and all we can do now is pray that MacChuill can hold his tongue. I curse myself that I refused to leave when von Strann begged it. God forgive me, if we had only left when we had the chance, then MacChuill would be with us. And Tamuz would be alive. I dug my heels in, Anna, and now I will be haunted for the rest of my life, I think, with the drill of the machine gun, the image of Tamuz dropping as he ran towards me, and the Turks behind him in the entrance to the courtyard.

Tamuz unscrews the camera from its tripod, wraps it in a folded pair of trousers and deposits it in the trunk. He clacks the legs of the tripod together.

He was going to fetch MacChuill, didn't even make it to the Avenue of Books before we heard him running. We were at the bottom of the stairs. We were ready. If we'd only been ready sooner. While I took two of them down with my pistol, the third would have made his escape but for von Strann's reaction. It took me only an eternal second to react, but he was a madman in an instant, Anna, a force of vengeance. I was only just out on the street in time to see him with the last Turk, one hand clamped across his forehead, pulling his head back – God, he couldn't have been much older than Tamuz, the soldier, eighteen or so, and I could see the fear in his eyes as von Strann's other hand slashed the knife across his throat.

Von Strann picks up the pages Jack has read and abandoned to one side, starts placing them back in the saddlebags.

Von Strann carried Tamuz's body back up the stairs while I did my best to conceal the three dead Turks in the courtyard. We were praying those few shots fired and some blood on the ground would not give us away, that we could at least make it to MacChuill's lodgings and the car before the place erupted. We made it there in time to see the militia dragging him out into the street towards a truck, heard it before we saw it really, the air turning blue with his curses. MacChuill fought like a wild man and I swear to God, if there'd been just a few less of them I doubt they could have held him. As it was, if von Strann had not dragged me back out of the headlights of the second truck that arrived just then, carrying twice as many Turks again . . . I'm not sure I would be writing this now.

We are back in von Strann's studio now, Anna, the body of Tamuz laid on the bed. Gunfire sounds across the city. A day of fighting, and the Baron and I holed up like rabbits, our exits cut off. I have read much of Samuel's notes now, the true and the false, alternative histories and unknown myths. My own past. A stranger's present.

A score of futures and in all of them the boy dies.

Jack watches Tamuz sliding the folded tripod into a carpet-bag and feels himself caught in a kaleidoscope of realities, insane, unreal, impossible. He still can't accept – he *won't* accept – this rot about angels and books in ancient languages, but every heartbeat seems a drum that marks another step towards at least one of these futures written in his words in Hobbsbaum's hand. And that heart . . . he's only known the lad a few days, but the image of him falling to a bullet in the back, the image of his body laid out on the bed . . . his beating heart feels hollow as a ransacked tomb, tight as the drumskin pounding out the boy's doom.

Read on, our jaguar Jack, we urge from every corner, every crack and crevice of this room, and in the chambers of his heart.

There Will Be a Reckoning

Another page:
20th March. A day of fighting draws to its close and the Baron and I are lucky to be alive. Tamuz is not so lucky, nor MacChuill, both dead at the hands of the Turks. Both might still be alive if I had listened to von Strann when he told me of the treaty between the Turks and the Futurists, of the airfleet heading towards us from Syria, of the police and army scouring the city for us at that very moment. But instead I refused to leave, asked him how he could know these things. All that time wasted, Anna, in damnfool stubbornness, even with Tamuz pulling on my sleeve, begging me to believe, to trust the Baron. He tried to place my hand upon

his breast – that ritual of trust again – and I shoved him away; he fell to the floor.

There will be a reckoning for this. That is all von Strann has said since we made it back to the apartment. He cradles the body of the boy and mutters these words to himself, over and over. He looks at me with the same cold hatred that I've seen in Cossacks, Prussians, my own comrades, in survivors of countless atrocities, even in my own eyes on many a morning since Majkops – or, God knows, since the Somme perhaps. Not that it's really me he's looking at. Not personally. Not alone, at least. It is a hatred all the more chilling because it is it not really directed at what's in its path. It doesn't really know you're there even when it looks straight at you. No, it is a hatred for the world that has allowed an unforgivable horror.

There will be a reckoning for this.

I do not disbelieve him now. Today it is Tell-el-Kharnain, tomorrow who knows? Tomorrow . . . As we wait here in von Strann's rooms, tomorrow hangs above our heads, a Damoclean sword. The Turks have taken the city now and any fighting is sporadic. It is only a matter of time before they find us here. But I know also that, as von Strann says, there will be a reckoning. It seems insane but if what these Enakites believe is true – and I am certain now that it is – then everything we think we know is a charade. I would scarce credit the notions were it not for the fact that I have read . . . look, Jack, I know that you are reading this now. I know that you do not trust von Strann, that you think him a fool infatuated with some dream of desert life. You are wrong. I was wrong. All I will say to convince you of this, Jack, is the secret you have carried in your heart for ten years.

Thomas Messenger.

Jack lets the page fall to the table. Something in him knows that, even if this is Samuel's hand, it is his *own* words, or those of another Jack. It's as if he knew it already, as if the truth were only slumbering in his soul, waiting to be awoken by his reading of the bloody tattered remains of Samuel's notebooks. Scribbled translations from

474

a book which contains all stories, all futures including his own. With himself and von Strann waiting for the Turks to flush them out, MacChuill already captured, and Tamuz dead.

He has a cigarette in his hand, poised at his mouth; he wasn't even aware of taking it from his case, but it's there. Like his future. Just waiting quietly for him to act.

– Tamuz, says von Strann, enough. I'll finish up. Go fetch MacChuill. Tell him to bring the car round. Go as fast as you can, but be careful; if you see a Turkish patrol–

– Wait, says Jack.

He buckles his holster.

– I'll go.

The Heart of Albion

I crouch for a second on the stone of Northbridge, a gargoyle with a grin of grim determination, then I leap, the chi-blasts of the blackshirts shattering the air around me as I fall. Feet-first, I smash through the glass roof of the Waverley Terminal, shredding the trenchcoat, landing cat-like in a shower of shards among a chaos of commuters. They mill, they bolt, they scatter all around me and I try to tune out the cacophony of their panic as I brush the glass out of my hair. Above, the whole roof of the Circus's central wireway terminal blows in as the blackshirts open fire again. People scream under the rain of glass.

I look up and I'm glad I don't have vertigo; up is down and down is up here on this topsy-turvy twist of Escherspace, the blue-green vortex of the bottomless pit hanging high above us as a hole in the sky. Airships follow wires that slice the dark like searchlights at all angles, but curving away before the event horizon to disappear into tunnels. The fuckers must have footholds in other folds already, trying to build their Empire back up from below. Which Havens have they already linked to from this nerve centre, I wonder – Liverpuddle? Godchester? Christ, they could've jump-started the very Heart of Albion, the city of Kaerlundein.

Things are definitely not peachy right now.

*

The Waverley, last of the old propeller wireliners still in service, is pulling out of its deep berth and rising, steams of blue-green orgone venting with a foghorn bellow. I run for it. The blackshirts are still firing, cutting down the crowd and cutting up the marble floor behind me. The whole concourse of the terminal has become a kill-zone for the goon squad up on Northbridge. Can't be good for Fox's 'no civilian casualties' condition; all I can do is hope the slaughter slows them down.

This is fucked up. This is incredibly, *inedibly* fucked up. Even with my soul-juice in his veins to turbo-charge his spirit, I don't know if our beatnik boy will live. Even with the little bit of him I shot into my own veins, I still have to get him safe and sound out of the Circus. Then there's the Castle, glowering over it all on its basalt plug, visible through the shattered roof of the Terminal where, somewhere, Joey Narcosis is being dragged towards a dungeon doom he's not going to thank me for.

And clicking the heels of my ruby-red jackboots three times isn't going to get us back to Kansas, Dorothy. It took serious juice to get us in; it'll take the same to get me out.

Ducking and weaving along the platform, I sprint for the Waverley, the steel superstructure of the roof providing some protection as a sheltering web that breaks the blackshirts' aim and blocks their fire just enough for me to reach a boarding ramp and run at full speed, hop, skip and jump with spring-heeled jackboots, reaching, reaching. I grab the side of the gondola as the antique airship rises up into the air, out of the wide Victorian maw of the Terminal and away.

– Cease fire, the SS sergeant shouts, as his men continue blasting at me. They can't afford to hit the ray-tanks of the wireliner; the explosion would take out the Terminal and everything near to it, including themselves. Might even do serious damage to Dunedin. Like the fuckwits that they are, of course, they keep on shooting.

I breathe deep and try to quell my fired-up nerves as the chi-blasts rock me, loosening my grip.

– Cease fire! the sergeant roars.

I calm down my adrenal overload and focus on the general surge inside, deep in the heart chakra. I latch onto it, harness the hate and love and open up that inner flute of chakras one to seven, taking a deep toot on the fields of force, all that loose chi in the air. Stretch out my lust and think fast – think Fast Puck. I reach out to my tantric partner, my loveline link back through the chaosphere to home, but the connection's broken by temporal ripples. I can't remember where I first met him, Kentigern or North Carolina, 1916 or never. Shit.

A chi-blast hits me in the shoulder – bodyblow of an electric sledgehammer – but I manage to hold on, toes on an inch-thick edge of girdering, one hand clutching a porthole where a fatcat in a business suit has his nose pressed to the glass, looking out at me in shock and horror. He looks even more worried when my other hand, the chi-gun held in it, comes up past the window, to take aim at the ray-tanks directly overhead.

There's no place like home. There's no place like home. There's no place like home.

I fire, and the blast shatters the world around me.

A Dust-Deity of Wrath

– Damn you!

Jack walks down the centre of the street, screaming hate and firing shot after shot after shot at the soldiers. One drops like a stone. Another drags the half-clothed woman up and round in front of him as a human shield; Jack puts the bullet in his forehead. As the other two scatter, pulling their rifles up, MacChuill runs past Jack, level with the woman and her child, puts the Lee-Enfield to his shoulder, and takes one of them down with a bullet in the back. The fourth sends a shot buzzing past Jack's ear before the bullet from the Webley thumps his chest, spins him backward into a wall and down. Bent double, shoulder on the ground, he tries to push himself up to his knees and fails, flops, flails, kicking the family's possessions that lie scattered on the street. Clothes and furniture. A small bronze statue, a bird but with a human head.

Jack picks up the soldier's rifle, slings it over his shoulder.

*

477

Everywhere there are shouts, the clamour of feet, doors opening and slamming, women screaming, wailing. Everywhere there are the sounds of war, the sounds of a blood-soaked modern war of murdered innocents, of doors being kicked in and machine guns turning human beings into meat and bone. Everywhere the Turks have thrown themselves into a campaign of terror, dragging men, women and children out into the streets, killing the men and boys, raping the women and girls. Webley in his hand, Jack stands as if at the centre of some whirlwind of events, a storm, a whirling pillar of smoke and flame in the desert, facing a deity that's not a wise old man with a white beard but a god of the storm, a dust-deity of wrath.

MacChuill is trying to peel the woman and her daughter away from the body of her husband, to persuade her that she can't stay here, it's not safe. She just sobs hysterical, unanswerable questions in her own language. Armenian, Jack recognises. He crouches down to speak to her. *You have to go. Now. For the sake of the child.*

– Jesus fuckin Christ, says MacChuill. This is bloody chaos.

– No, says von Strann. This is organised.

He kneels over the Turkish soldier, Tamuz standing at his side.

– Take a look at the sky, he says. Which directions are lit up? Which quarters are they burning? The Armenian Quarter. The Jewish Quarter.

Across the wide square of the Beth Astart, the night sky above the buildings opposite is lit by fire. Fires, rather, their light gathered in distinct glows, here to the south-west, to the north, one here, another there, maybe five or six separate areas that seem to have been targeted.

– We have to get out of this area, says von Strann. We need–

He stops, looking down the street, and MacChuill and Jack act instantly, Jack dragging the woman from her husband's body towards an alley, clamping a hand over her mouth, MacChuill doing likewise with the crying child, Tamuz behind him. Von Strann flattens himself into a doorway as the Turkish militiaman reaches the end of the street. The beam of a flashlight on the bodies lying on the street. A shout.

And then it's more bloody gunfire, the woman dead while trying

478

to reach the body of her husband, the child bleeding all over MacChuill, and Tamuz, bloody idiot boy, standing out in the open, firing wildly with a Turkish rifle.

– I will be OK, eh, Jack?

The boy grimaces as he's dragged limping and stumbling up the stairs, Jack under one arm, von Strann under the other, rifle dangling by its strap in his hand, clattering off step and wall. His face is pale.

– You'll be fine, lad, says Jack.

– Wee fuckin scratch like thon, son, says MacChuill behind them. Whit are ye, a bloody poof? Ma granny's seen worse – ah, Christ an' fuckin–

Jack glances back, as they shoulder the door open and stagger into von Strann's studio, at MacChuill and the child cradled in his arms, hoisted up next to his ear. MacChuill looks up at Jack, shakes his head.

Outside, the city is all locked and barricaded doors, waiting for the army to have its fill. The city is streets filled with those who've taken flight and paid the price for it, with those who've taken up arms to fight the Turks and paid for it. The city is gunfire ringing out from the alleys and backstreets. The city is riot and rout. It's massacre and mayhem. Tell-el-Kharnain, the city of decadence, of the bourgeois bohemians, this city of sin and sensuality, is falling once again.

MacChuill puts the child on the bed, checking for breath, a pulse, while Jack and von Strann lower Tamuz into a chair. Jack kneels to undo the rip of sleeve knotted round the boy's thigh, double-checking that it's just a flesh wound. Fine. He wraps it round again. Von Strann is tentatively drawing back the bloody bundle of tunic he's held pressed to Tamuz's side all the way back. That's the bad one.

– Let me see. Do you have bandages?

He peels the sodden shirt open, wipes blood away with his sleeve; it's not too far in, not a belly shot, thank Christ.

– I will be OK, eh, Jack? It does not hurt too much.

– You'll be just fine. Trust me.

Jack puts his hand to his own chest, then to the boy's.

– From my heart to your heart.

The Sons of Sidim, *by Rainer Van Stronn (1933)*

And so the wan and gibbous moon shone over the city by night, whilst by day the sun was red and bloated; and day and night, the siege continued. Day and night, the Sons of Sidim uttered their unearthly ululating song of wailing for their dead. Day and night, the Turuq army wrought their awful terror upon the poor, innocent and weak inhabitants of the city of Sidim. Day and night, the warrior Kartur and his new comrade-in-arms, the artist-prince Vhneszran, watched from the turret room of the now half-ruined Temple of T'hmusz.

By turns, it seemed, the one would pace back and forth and gaze out over the embattled city, stalking the room like some caged panther whilst the other slept a fitful restless sleep. Only the assured patience of Prince Vhneszran, when set against the grim keen glint, the lust for battle, in Kartur's warrior eyes, distinguished the two men in their attitudes as they waited for the moment that both knew would come. The Turuq army was still a mighty force, even in these days of the Turuq Kingdom's decline, but the Sons of Sidim were a proud and noble race, and they would have their vengeance. Day and night, they sang of it in their lament, in that horrible song of murder, guilt and blood. Day and night, the song reached out from beyond the walls of the city to stir an unutterable terror in the heart of every Turuq soldier, young and old, a crawling horror of the certainty of death.

Some, the most foolhardy and the most craven of these men, had attempted to desert their posts and their compatriots, to escape from that dread place. Captured and executed by their own comrades, their naked bodies hung now from gibbets raised along the battlements of the city walls, stripped of all armour, stripped of all honour, as a warning to others. And of those few that had escaped this dismal fate, that had breached the city walls and thought to flee across the fiery sands of the surrounding desert? What of them? Their heads now capped the poles of the banners of the Sons of Sidim, banners made from the flayed skins of fallen foes, banners which fluttered in the dry desert wind, in the dust and sand whipped up around them, all around the city. They flapped languidly and seemed to move in time to the abominable elegy of the Sons of Sidim, as did the billowing clouds of dust and sand, as if the very elements, the very desert itself, were bemoaning the devastation and promising a dark and grisly revenge.

As Kartur watched and listened from the barricaded tower, quite unaware of his impatient hand stroking the leatherbound handle of his gleaming sword, he knew that it was only a matter of time until doom came to the city of Sidim and dealt its awesome blow upon the vile minions of the Turuq King, feeble lackey of the New Ruzzo-Purzan Empire.

A Song of Mourning, a Lament

21st March. It is dawn. Through the window, I look out on a sun that rises over the occupied city of Tell-el-Kharnain like the rising of the eye of God himself. It feels like the dawning of the Day of Judgement, when every secret will be sung out like the muezzin's song, when truth itself shakes off so many centuries of sleep, and stands.

But the muezzin is silent this morning, dead on some bloody street no doubt, and the only song being sung here is the quiet murmur that von Strann mouths over the dead youth.

He sings in the strange tongue of the Enakites, I am sure. It is not Arabic or Hebrew, Armenian or Azheri. It is not any tongue I recognise. But I know this is the Enakite tongue, I know this is the Cant, because I understand exactly what it means. It is a song of mourning, a lament, but in the pain, the sadness, there is also anger, even threat. I am reminded of the tone, the quiet, grim restraint with which he promised a 'reckoning'; and it disturbs me. I keep imagining that I can hear the song being sung by other voices far off, almost too faint to be heard. I say it is my own imagination because the voices match von Strann's

481

too well and with the tension and the weariness, one's imagination can play funny tricks on one.

But I am not so sure those voices are not real.

You have to understand, Jack, I am so tired. The Baron sits on
the edge of the bed beside the body of Tamuz, while I sit at his
kitchen table, where I've spent most of this long dark night deci-
phering what I could of Samuel's notes, poring over the ragged
pages, so much of it illegible, torn and burnt and bloodstained.
There is too much to make sense of, too many inconsistencies,
and I fear I'm only adding to them with this entry, but maybe it
will be of some use to you. Have you read the other journal
entries, I wonder. Are you reading this too late? Has it all already
happened? Did you, like me, spend too long with all the irrelevant
nonsense of Samuel's first meeting with von Strann, his intro-
duction to the tribe, their strange customs, and with all that
bloody hypocritical horror at the 'abhorrent and unmanly' rituals
which gave Sodom its reputation. I leaf back through the pages
of this journal to three days ago, and the words are those of a
stranger so obsessed with what it is to be a man that he spent
his life trying to kill his own desires.

You know this, Jack. You can deny it to yourself, but you
cannot deny it *from* yourself.

I look at Tamuz, dead because of my self-hate and arrogance,
and, Jack, if Samuel only found these words within the Book, if
you can only find them in his notes, I pray to God that you can
choose another path.

*Jack puts the page down, looks around the room, von Strann
sitting on the bed, but with the girl on it instead of Tamuz. Tamuz
on the cot, wounded but still alive. MacChuill curled up beside the
cot, asleep, instead of captured by the Turks. A present different
from the journal of this other, broken self, but not so different, not
so very different. Not different enough.*

*Von Strann mutters his strange song over the dead child. And
in the distance other voices sing the same hollow lament.*

21st March, *he writes.* How much did Samuel glean from his
studies that might be of use to us if we can only separate what's

true and what is false? The movements of troops that are only now being planned, of alliances and betrayals that have not yet happened, Allied war-plans for the coming *decades*, and even the subtlest strategies of the Futurists. I have read so much of what he wrote about the past, the present and the future, of things he should not, *could not* know unless the Book is real; of the internment camps of the Futurists, of what is really happening there, and why.

Sacrifice, he called it, the sacrifice of the chosen.

Errata

Room

Finnan stands up, and waves wash over him – of revulsion, reverence – not felt as his so much but as an outer force as physical as sunlight on your back, as a caress or a cut. He's past the sex-and-death, carrot-and-stick part of the trip now, shucking those shallow neuroses, headed deeper down into the psychodrama that the drug's performing with his dreams, a play cast from his past. He snatches glimpses of Phree as an angel anima, winged guardian, Tom as the self, lost soul of summers gone. Black-suited unkin torturers play id and shadow. In the corner of his eye he sees himself in chains, an ego bound in pride and pain. The fall of shadow *here* becomes an ageing soldier with one eye, a raven on his shoulder; there he sees a face he doesn't recognise, a rakish chap with pencil tache. A fox dashes across his vision.

And along with the hallucinations, elemental and ephemeral certainties assault him now, peyote plucking out chords on his heartstrings till convictions blossom in him like unfolding lotus flowers. He's a fucking god, is Seamus Shamash Sammael Sodding Finnan. Sure and this is what it is to be a god. But with his years of mescaline and mojo and the magic of the Cant, Finnan knows fine well the folly of believing such delusions. So he throws his head back with a belly laugh, throws off the flattery of heart and head, and throws himself into the dream, pushes for a sense more visceral, more honest. To get something worthwhile out of a trip you have to listen to your guts, forget the truths you want to hear, have the *cojones* to cut through the crap. You have to kick away the crutches offered by your psyche; the unconscious can be just another carney, like these Cold Men trying to scam the rube into a false faith in its charms.

Illumination is the ultimate confidence trick, Finnan knows.

The crowd and the marketplace fall away behind him as he lays his hand against the peeling paint of the woodwork and pushes a heavy door open, with a smooth and sanguine movement, to enter a fallen and falling ruin of a room. Tumbled sandstone walls that once defined the boundaries of a stable now slide and skew into a new perspective. The room has become as vast as a whole landscape, the dirt floor wide desert, and every stone a towering mesa. Immense and open, this isn't *a* room, it's *Room*, and the wooden beams that hold up and hatch out what is left of the roof are the architecture of the sky itself. That's the illusion, anyway.

The aged cracked black leather of horses' harnesses and saddles hang, and turn and twist, as he looks at them, into weathered coats and cloaks. These are the abandoned attributes of elder gods; this is the cloakroom of the Old Ones, and in every stall there's a shadow that Finnan's flickering mind can give a name to, arbitrary and invented but as meaningful as any name: Ixzoche, God of the Dead Soul Deeps; Kavajokee, God of Firewater and Iceblood; Nixo, Little God of the Mantelpiece. He makes them up as he walks down between the stalls, looking from one side to the other, nodding to each one in turn. Even spurious gods deserve at least a casual respect.

He steps into the open ruin of the room, and every shadow in it comes alive. That's the illusion, anyway.

Crows' wings and serpents' coils crack around him as he sits cross-legged in his simworld of a sweat-lodge, surrounded by his leathered weathered shadow-elders, by the harnesses and saddles that are skins and irons now, flayed hides of slaughtered angels, shackles for defeated demons, veils of Vellum to be torn and chains of Cant to be broken. He's in that stage of satori where every object is a symbol, every symbol has a mythic meaning, sense turned into nonsense to make new sense, make a new sense of himself as he was always good at, making a nuisance of himself, sure – but Finnan has done peyote too many times to buy into the wonder. Time to strip the trip down to the truth. These aren't gods, just godhide saddles and soulsteel bits for the human horses ridden by the *loas*, the *orishas*, spirits of voudon and santería. Skinsuits and gravings worn by hunter-gatherers to mimic and to mask the face of the divine in mystery. The fabric and framework of the Vellum stripped of flesh, the surface and structure of a reality shorn of substance.

Come on then, he thinks. Show me what you're really made of.

And he smiles as we spirits stream out of the walls, across his vision, our voices like a river rushing, roaring of our archaic and arcane authority, we dead souls of this dereliction deep in the desert, we who have been deified and damned by time.

He takes a drag of his cigarette and blows out curls of dragon's breath.

So what's the story here? he thinks.

In the ruins of the stable then, we show him how the cities sank into the Evenfall, the people wandering lost among the rubble, watching TV news of the End Days, the unravelling of all they thought they could rely on in a slow but steady corrosion of consistency. We speak in the crackling hiss of radio announcements, tell of the disassembly and the dislocation of the world, our voices empty of emotion reading out the toll of disappearances, disturbances; a tale of driftworlds in the Vellum, Havens dug down to survive the cold of Hinter. How we tried, we *tried*, to shape a world for all their dreams, and found the one consensus in them their belief in enemies.

Two scorpions crawl across the floor towards each other, edging sideways, first one way and then the other, stretch their stinging tails up as each studies its opponent. The noises of the crowd outside, in his altered state, in our Cant, are the sound of drums and song, of Caribbean carnival.

– Rum, rum, lovely rum! When I calls ya, ya has to come.

The scorpions dance, and we dance round them, a million dust angels on the point of a sting. This is the gathering, we show him, the sifting of souls into good and evil, right and wrong, chaos and order ... us and them.

– Rum, rum, lovely rum! When I calls ya, ya has to come.

The scorpions dance, and we dance round them. This is the gathering, we show him, the drift of it all to an apocalypse that will wipe out both sides in one last almighty cataclysm.

– Gonna send for my scorpion to fight your centipede. Rum, rum, lovely rum!

And Finnan stretches to his feet, looking towards the door, out to the Mission, as the voices call to their carnival saint, to this Sante

Manité; but we let him hear the true source of the name now, in the song they sing, in a celebration not quite sane:

– Sante Manité, they sing.

And *sans humanité* is what he hears.

The Last Bastion of Religion

The air in the church is darkness filled with dust and sliced by diagonals of light and, with the candles giving off their golden glow, it all seems just too staged to be what it pretends, the sacred fallen to the profane. No, thinks Finnan, there's something here beyond the grandiose American Gothic of a church in dereliction, of statues of saints and madonnas with their paint peeling, of black candles on the altar, scents of sex and urine in the air. Even with the toppled crucifix and the rosaries trampled on the ground, there's a ... piety here. The place reeks of religion even in its denial, its deliberate travesty. He closes the doors behind him quietly, running his fingers softly across the rough grain of the wood, so solid and so solemn.

It's a long time since he's been in a church, but sure and it's just like the last time ... *just* like the last time.

Or perhaps not quite.

– So you lost your soul to them after all, he calls.

She comes out of the darkness behind the altar, looking half peasant widow and half Whore of Babylon in her purple dress and scarlet headscarf.

– I *am* them, she says. The big Them. I'm the bitch queen of Hell, don't you know? Leader of the rebel armies. Princess–

– Phree, he says. You used to be plain old Phree. You remember how I taught you to play poker?

She smiles.

– House rules, she says. No kings. No queens. Jacks are high and aces wild.

– It's the best way to play the game.

– Things change, she says.

Finnan lights a cigarette and takes a long drag before speaking. With the charge of the Cant inside him he's always felt like he's ...

487

hard-wired to a nova at the back of his head, as if words could just fly out his mouth and fry some poor innocent bastard if he doesn't rein it in. And now more than ever, here in the Mojave heat, with the peyote running up and down his spine and an old flame who's let herself go all to hell, he needs the nicotine to pace himself, to give a slow cool rhythm to his thoughts. To chill. He looks her up and down.

Christ, Phree, why couldn't you just walk away and keep on walking?

He can feel the mojo coming off her in feverish waves, like deep inside something is burning in the furnace of her soul. No fucking wonder the Cold Men were drawn here, drawn to something truer than their trinkets. For them, he's willing to bet, this is the Real Thing, the magic behind all their charms. Sure enough, Harker stands behind her, a pale form in the shadows.

– The Blessed Virgin of the Mission of Sante Manité, he says.

– You know I'm not much of a virgin, Finnan, and I wouldn't exactly call myself blessed.

She doesn't have to say, *and whose fault would that be*? Finnan remembers all too well his own role in her damnation.

– So, he says. What's the score with this last bastion of religion? Christ, Phree, rabbits' feet and chicken claws, fucking chickenshit for the soul? And they just eat it up.

– Don't be so hard on them, she says. They just want a little peace.

– So you sell them a little piece of shit?

She sits down on the altar, perches there with a casual grace, one foot up, the other on the ground. She fingers the chickenbone necklace that still hangs around her neck.

– It's what they want, she says. What else have they got? Maybe you've forgotten what it's like.

But of course he's never forgotten the little rituals – the kisses on letters from sweethearts, making the sign of the cross on yerself before going over the top, sure, and the bullet with your own name scratched on it tucked into a pocket of your tunic. It was a long long time ago, but sure and he hasn't ever forgotten. How none of it

488

really works; and what, he discovered once upon a time, actually *does*.

– But you know there's nothing on those stalls that'll do anyone any good. You're selling lies.

– Selling the truth would draw too much attention. And the hokum's a good smokescreen for the real mojo, to keep it hidden.

– From the Covenant? he says.

She laughs.

– The Covenant's broken. You were right all along, Finnan. The Covenant ripped itself apart fighting its own shadow ... with a little help from our bitmite friends. The Covenant's dust.

– But you're still fighting, Phree.

– I'm the guerrilla goddess now, she says. It's what I do.

He tries to picture her before all this began, a tomboy kid in her brother's biker jacket, and him just the crazy loner out in that dust-blown trailer park, keeping his cards close to his chest when it came to personal history, but full of stories about magic and mystery. He hadn't meant to charm them, Tom and Phree, but by the time he realised the Cant in his voice was stirring up their souls without him even knowing, by then it was too late.

– Try doing something else, he says.

– I don't have a choice, she says. It's war.

– I've been in a war, he says, a few of them. No choice? Fuck that; there's always a choice.

– Run away? Hide out in the desert somewhere, in the Vellum? You tried that. I tried that. The war just keeps on spreading until it finds you.

Last time they'd met was in a church, with Thomas dead and Phree changed forever trying to save him. The Covenant had its agents wandering the world, sniffing out their brethren, gathering them. So she'd headed out into the wilds of the Vellum, off into the sunset, while Seamus Finnan tried to drink himself into oblivion. The war had found him all right.

– So you took the King's Shilling, he says.

– It's the King we're fighting. All the kings of heaven and dukes of hell and two-bit tinpot tyrants of fucking eternity.

489

– And princesses?

She gives him a wry grin, crinkling her nose – a touch of the old Phree.

– Sometimes you've got to play the role for the troops, you know?

She slides down off the altar, beckons for him to follow her as she moves towards the vestry door.

– This is a different war, she says over her shoulder. And it's one we can win, one we *will* win. We've got the advantage.

Harker opens the door for them and steps aside to let him see into the room. A small table and chair. On the table sits a ring-binder of glossy photostats, tattooing and surgical equipment, a shaving mirror. Sitting on the chair is a man whose face is not the one Finnan knows but whose graving he recognises instantly. It's so fucking strong you can see it in the air around him, never mind that he's stripped to the waist so Finnan can see the black lines covering every inch of his torso with maybe the most intricate pattern any unkin's ever had. The needle of the tattoo gun buzzes as the man carves the story of his ancient life into his arm, the story in the image in front of him, the story of a man who wrote a book once, of the man who came up with the whole fucking idea of writing, of taking the Cant and turning song into symbol. The graving is so complex Seamus can't take it all in, sure and the way it loops in on itself and around again in rivers of red and black running over his flesh, but he can sum it all up in a word, can Seamus, because sure and the man's name's at the heart of his tale, over his heart for all the world to see, this scribe of it all, of the Book of All Hours, not Metatron, no, not Metatron of the Covenant, but who he was, what he was before the Covenant, before the Sebitti tried to change the world and only changed themselves, not Metatron, no but–

– Enki, says Seamus – though he's careful not to say it in the Cant.

5

Guardian of Angels

Dancing with Danger

I swing-kick through the sidescreen of the ornithopter, jackboot heels connecting with the pilot's side so hard he's kicked straight out the opposite door. The thopter rears and gyres wildly in the air as I swing into the vacant seat, grab its controls and rein it in.

So far, so good. Now all I have to do is get back to Fox's den in the Rookery before another flip-flop through the folds, and hope to hell there's some way he can patch this little rip in time.

Circus swarm above, roofs of the Rookery below, stray chi-beams pierce the air around me, friendly fire and enemy attacks; I swoop the thopter through and round the blasts of colour, flick back the covers for the trigger-buttons on the joysticks, and aim for an enemy thopter. Both buttons, keyed to the pilot's thumbprints, lock me out.

Not good.

As a chi-blast rocks the whole machine, I whip out my Curzon-Youngblood Mark I chi-gun, shoot out the windscreen of the thopter and start firing at the enemy, flying my thopter one-handed, dancing with danger, spinning through the air, a whirling dervish of the skies. Enemy thopters try to follow my manoeuvres, guns blasting. One just manages to shoot another out of the sky. Keen.

It's like the Battle of Britain fought with waltzers – man, it's kinda lucky I don't get motion sickness. I turn to fire at a thopter coming in from my side and see my friend the pilot clinging desperately to the open door with one hand, scrabbling for purchase with a foot as, with the other hand, he aims his chi-gun at my head. I duck as both of us fire simultaneously. He takes out the controls above my head; I send a chi-beam straight into his stomach, knock him out into the blue.

The thopter screams, the sound of metal shearing, and it starts to buck insanely in the air. Looks like it's time to go, and so, with consummate skill and truly freakish luck, I send the ruined thopter careening across the sky into the enemy vehicle marked by its position as group leader, while I twist out of the seat and kick-jump backwards through the shattered windscreen, using a two-handed chi-gun shot to blast me free from the ensuing carnage. I spin in the air and straighten out just in time to grab a handhold on another thopter as I slam into its wing. The pilot tries a desperate flip to shake me and to get the machine back under his control. I cling on, and the unbalanced thopter spirals downwards.

As it reaches the right spot, I swing out and let loose, launched by centrifugal force in just exactly the direction that I want. I hit the bay-window feet-first and come crashing through it into the rebel headquarters, Fox's den. Fast Puck stands to one side of the window, chi-lance blazing out into the sky. Coyote's lying bleeding on the Persian rug.
   – You're back, he says. You better not have fucked it up.
   I kick my heels, sheepishly.
   – How *exactly* do you define 'fucked up'?
   – Look up the dictionary, he says, under 'Jack Flash'.
   I clock the room. Something's missing.
   – Where's Fox? I say.
   – Who? ask Puck and Coyote simultaneously.
   And suddenly the temporal aftershock hits us.

A Spray of Blood and Brains

21st March. I look for some sign in Samuel's notes, some scrap of shorthand telling of this world, my world, that it is the right one and that it ends well; but I can find none that shows the truth I know, with us holed up here in this ancient temple under the watchful eye of a Virgin Whore. The variants are endless – worlds where MacChuill is captured, where von Strann is killed – but in all that I've found so far we have been trapped, eventually, back in von Strann's apartment, retreating from the patrols, our escape routes blocked by all the checkpoints that have sprung up overnight. I have been trying to glean the positions of these all from the variants, but the picture is not complete; and how can I even be certain these alternative scenarios are close enough to ours that I can treat them as intelligence? How can I know that the differences are not more substantial than the similarities?

I take hope from the fact that the world I know differs so much from all these others. Here it is the Beth Astart in which we are pinned down, biding our time until the Turks find us. Here all it took was a word from Tamuz to persuade me, and I ceased my foolish blustering at the Baron. With my help rather than hindrance, here Tamuz was back with the Scotsman before we even knew it, the car still running as we clattered down the steps onto the road, MacChuill standing behind the wheel, urging us to make haste, in his own colourful and guttural tongue of course, more understood by tone and context than by anything else. Here I almost think we might have made it out had we been just a little quicker. We almost did.

As it was, we made it to the Avenue of Palms before all hell broke loose.

The car rattles a sharp right onto the Avenue of Palms, then shudders into an even sharper turn as MacChuill slams the brakes on, yanks the steering wheel even further round.

– Fuckin shite! he says. Haud on!

The wheels spin, burning rubber, as the turn becomes a full 180 degrees. Along the Avenue, soldiers are already running from the makeshift roadblock – a truck parked across the road – their rifles raised, calling for them to halt. Jack shoves Tamuz down to safety with a rough hand on his shoulder, trying to aim his Webley as the spinning car throws him off balance. MacChuill wrestles the Rolls to a stop. The engine roars. The wheels spin.

– Fuckin bastard fuckin come on tae–

FUCK.

Jack hears the crack of the rifle and the thud of the impact almost simultaneously – is it himself that's hit? – and the car judders forward, stalls, MacChuill flopping down across the steering wheel, sliding down to one side. A spray of blood and brains on the windscreen. God Almighty. Then Jack is firing at the Turks as – *move!* – the three of them jump from the car, from the crack and *tung* of bullets hitting metal. They're retreating down the street, cover to cover. He's firing round a corner, holding the last two Turks back while von Strann and Tamuz run ahead to the next street where–

Von Strann spins off his feet as if a sledgehammer has slammed into his shoulder. Tamuz is skidding, turning, running back towards Carter as the soldier steps out behind him, takes aim with his gun and–

Crack!

Tamuz stumbles – *Crack!* – and then just drops.

Jack stares at the soldier. He's bringing his pistol round, but there's another shot already fired, a splatter of blood and bone from the man's face, von Strann on the ground, rifle still pointed at where the Turk was standing.

Jack makes it as far as Tamuz's body before he falls to his knees.

Subtexts, Symbols and The Sins of Sodom, *by L. Wooley (1988)*

And so, if we look at what survives of the original scripts and storyboards for *The Sins of Sodom*, we see many elements that foreshadow not only Griffiths' later oeuvre but also epics by directors such as Kubrik in *Spartacus*, Lean in *Lawrence of Arabia*, or Korda in *Achilles*. We cannot help but recognise, for instance, something of *The Ten Commandments'* Exodus scene in the escape of Lot and his household, especially when we consider that Griffiths planned to hire two thousand extras to make up Lot's 'household'. Many comparisons have been drawn between the famous 'snails and oysters' speech in *Spartacus* and the 'milk and honey' speech spoken by the young slave-boy Tamuz to the Hebrew warrior, Jonathan, in *The Sins of Sodom*; while *Spartacus* reverses the roles of seducer and seduced, slave and master, it may well be that Kubrik's script was in some way influenced by a passing acquaintance with the Griffiths script(s). Similarly, the subtle homoeroticism of Achilles mourning Patroclus in Korda's 1957 classic may well have some of its roots in the scene of Jonathan weeping over Tamuz's body.

But, as it was, the studio baulked and the funding for *The Sins of Sodom* fell through; had Griffith been granted the opportunity to follow through on his ideas, however – our imagination reels. The film would certainly have generated a level of controversy greater than *Intolerance* when it was released, or *Birth of a Nation* today. Even the ending of the film, in which God destroys the cities of Sodom and Gomorrah, saving only the pure and good people of the household of Lot, owes more to pragmatics than to ethics, exemplifying the so-called Hypocritic Code of the time – if you play, you gotta pay – whereby the most heinous (and of course thrilling) crimes could be enacted on-screen as long as the perpetrator was punished at the end of the movie. With the ending as a start-point, then, as we can see from the surviving scripts, Griffiths seems to have set out to test the tenuous boundaries between the permissible and the permissive, with scenes of hedonism and excess patently contrived to sate a prurient public's appetite for the scandalous and the sensual.

It is, indeed, little wonder that Erich Von Strohn, the author of the pious and somewhat turgid doorstop of a Biblical blockbuster on which the script was based, decried the proposed movie as 'a vile perversion not only of my own humble but honest work, but of the Good Book itself'. Von Strohn threatened to file a lawsuit, claiming that the script was obscene and, in effect, a defamation of his character, since it gloried in the very outrages that he reviled. With the Church, the censors and all the powers of the Moral Right charging Griffiths with gross sensationalism and flagrant blasphemy, the pressure on the studio rose until even the potentials of such explosive hype were outweighed by the threat of outright hostility. Such was the venom and invective of the campaigners that one almost wonders whether, had the film ever actually been shot and screened, great mobs of torch-brandishing peasants would have swept across the country, burning every movie theatre in their path in their righteous zeal and indignation, heaping up great bonfires of the sordid and salacious reels.

And of course, shamefully, this might as well have been the actual scenario; of the all-too-few copies of the original script and its rewrites the vast extent of it has long ago been either lost or destroyed. Over the years the abandoned project was forgotten, buried in a drift of Hollywood dream-dust, until so much is lost now that even the hope of reconstructing any one version of the script in its entirety must be, like the film itself, abandoned to the sands of time. Bibliographies of Griffiths make no mention of *The Sins of Sodom*. Why should they? After all, he never made the film. And to all too many serious students of the cinema, why, it is little more than a brief hiccup in the great man's career, one which to all intents and purposes might never have happened. And yet, like some archaeologist of the silver screen, we *can* uncover some of the forgotten fragments, perhaps dust them off and see how they fit into the history of cinema.

The fall of Sodom, for instance, at the climax of the movie, resonates with everything from the Odessa Steps scene in *Battleship Potemkin* to the closing of the Warsaw Ghetto in *Schindler's List*. And then of course there is the capture and torture of the heroes, the Hittite prince Istran and the young Hebrew warrior Jonathan ...

For the Dying and the Dead

21st March. So we wait now in the Beth Astart, behind a barricade of old church pews and display cases – the heritage of this place all turned now to the most pragmatic purposes, lifted and dragged from their places across the mosaic floor, piled up with a desperate compromise of haste and quiet that has left both the Baron and myself exhausted.

It is a strange scene, quiet and dark. The clutter of cabinets and cases cleared from the centre of the hall and heaped in a jumble at the door, there is a strange tranquillity to the place now. Von Strann lies, passed out, on one of the pews, pale and weak from the loss of blood, but patched up to the best of my abilities. Tamuz lies upon the altar, watched over by the Weeping Angel, as she's known, this painted statue that might be the prototype of all madonnas, the original Venus weeping for Adonis. I can imagine this museum as it once was, as a temple, a place of healing and mourning, prayers for the dying and the dead.

Von Strann should pull through though, I think; he has more strength by far than I'd given him credit for; he's twice the man of many soldiers I've known, I should say, the way he suffered my clumsy excavation of the bullet from his shoulder. I'm no surgeon at the best of times; it's only fortunate that, with no windows in this place, no danger of the Turks spotting our candlelight, at least I wasn't digging around in the pitch-black.

There is a part of me that wants to pray now to this last teraphim, this heathen goddess with her glory long gone, scarlet and purple peeled or faded to plaster-white and pale blue, one jewelled eye and one empty socket, with the deep gouges on the cheek below that give this Astaroth her modern name. I want to pray to this Weeping Angel, to watch over us now the best she can.

And I want to pray that the Book is real, that the Cant is real. That the name of every innocent ever murdered for some insane ideal was written down for future generations to read and lament. That the generals and demagogues who bring this hell upon us could be branded with their crimes, as the first murderer was, their bloody deeds graved in their flesh.

I want to pray that there will be a reckoning for this.

– God damn it!

Jack swings back into the room as von Strann takes his place above MacChuill crouched in the doorway, firing down the stairwell at the Turks. He flicks the cylinder of the Webley out and empties the cartridges in a patter of metal on wooden floorboards—

– Jack!

He catches the box of bullets thrown by Tamuz from the dresser with its top drawer pulled out, pours the last handful into his palm and reloads, drops the empty box on the floor. As MacChuill swivels back into the room, Jack squats in his place, ducking out and in again to fire at men he can barely catch a glimpse of. Christ, he can't tell how many of them there are, but there must be six or seven bodies on the stairs, and there's more than enough behind them that there's not a hope in hell of holding them off.

Carter takes another Turk down with his last shot, ducks back inside – MacChuill? – but MacChuill is shaking his head, fitting the bayonet to his rifle. Tamuz is digging through the dresser in a last-ditch effort.

– Anything?

– Nothing.

– Table, snaps von Strann – [he's inside, slamming the door shut] – Fast!

Wooden legs scrape over floorboards, rattling, as Jack and MacChuill half-drag, half-carry the table, up-end the thing and ram it tight under the door knob, weight of their bodies behind it. Footsteps on the stair give way to thumping shudders of the doorframe. There's a shout in Turkish – *out of the way!* – and Jack pulls MacChuill back as the rapid fire splinters the door, the frame. More bodyslams against it, more machine-gun fire and then the weakened door is being kicked open and it's the three of them, MacChuill with his bayoneted rifle, von Strann with the Winchester held like a cricket bat, and Jack with a knife in one hand, Webley reversed in the other as a club, the three of them against too many Turkish militia too well armed, proving it with a casual spray of bullets that cuts MacChuill down where he stands, even as his rifle lowers.

– Drop your weapons.

Von Strann lets the Winchester fall but Jack is already leaping at the weak spot, past the bastard's gun and in close, knife in the man's gut, Webley whipped across his face and dropped as Jack grabs the bastard's gun arm, twisting hard to turn it on the Turks, turning to see the butt of a rifle swinging for his head and—

We welcome him into the darkness.

The City of a Thousand Stories

There are many stories in this city, mes amigos, tales for every cobblestone that's trodden under jackboot, tales for every railing in the fences round the South Side ghettoes, from the tales of underdogs in the underworld, smuggling stolen data down the tunnels where the clockwork trains once clickety-clacked along the track, to tales of overmen in the upper echelons who'll pay a hefty price for sweet delights to while away the endless night with just an orange and some fishnet tights; that's right, and we got all these tales and more here in the dead zone just before the dawn. You're listening to Don Coyote's naughty nightly Notes from the Geek Show, and we got some saucy scandals that'll make your cheeks glow red. But as you know we're always looking for some juicy morsel, so if you know a little gossip for the astral airwaves, just get on the blower, dial six-six-six-four-oh-oh-oh and let us blow that story open.

I hit the roof and roll, come up into a crouch, a hunter's squat, turning to aim my Curzon-Youngblood Mark I chi-gun to the skies above, as the ornithopter's searchlight pins me in its circle. I don't mind being in the limelight, but I'd rather they were showering me with roses than the blossoms of chi-energy pounding the concrete all around me. Not that those aren't every bit as pretty, but I'd like to be there for the pink champagne after the show, so I reckon it's time for Jack to exit stage-right.

I fire at the wing-joints of the thopter – once, twice – and the crippled little technotoy flaps a few times with a hellish racket, lurches through the air, and then just plummets with an elegant twirl into the concrete.

Well, they *would* ask for an encore.

But let's start with the story that might just blow polite society apart, the tale of a tart with a heart and the superspy flyguy trying to wing his way back to his love. What makes this the salacious and audacious fare you've come to

499

know from Don's deep dive into the human soul, pray tell, I hear you say? Enquiring minds, they want to know. Well, this tart, for a start, has more tackle than your average hooker, if you get my drift, and word on the street is that our hustler, he's been rustling secrets while he rustles sheets and, well, a little birdy tells me he's just recently been seen being hustled in and out of some expensive suites. Rumour is that there's a Minister with an almighty taste for his sweet cheeks.

And you want more? You want to know the full score? Well, mes amigos, if that's not enough, maybe you'd like to hear just how our little queer's been passing on those secrets, shooting the breeze with his main squeeze — who else but the human flea in the fur of Albion's great and good, the one and only Jack Flash. Now, if I were a Minister, I'd say that's just plain rude . . .

A quick scan of the situation and I scope a door on the far side of the steaming mound of pilot-and-thopter pizza, so I run for it — and skid to a halt as an almighty pounding kicks off on the other side of the door, a sound like thundering guns and screaming feedback cranked up to the max through an amp with a switchblade in it. Sonic ram. Ah, bollocks. As the door begins to glow, begins to *go*, and then just shatters open in a shower of sparks and shrieks, militiamen spilling out onto the roof, I'm already legging it hard and fast across the concrete in the opposite direction, firing blindly over my shoulder. One spring-heel forward-flip over the thopter wreckage later and I'm safe on the other side of it, chi-pistol holstered, an orgone grenade in each hand, pins out. I keep trying to tell these bastards to make love not war.

If they won't listen to reason . . .

Six-Guns at Salt City, *by Joe Campbell (1973)*

– *Gringo*, said the bandit chief. If you no listen to the Major, we gonna have to kill you, *sí*? So we make a deal, eh, *gringo*?

Jake Carter narrowed his eyes, and spoke softly through gritted teeth.

– Maybe we do, at that.

Van Stern raised his head and licked blood from the corner of his mouth where his lips had been broken open by the Major's fist.

His foot was going to need some patching but he was a hard man, not the type to be broken by one bullet.

– Rot in hell, you lousy sons of bitches, he said.

Carter turned towards him.

– Looks to me like we don't have much of a choice, *amigo*, he said.

But his voice was quiet and controlled, the voice of a man with a plan.

– Can't hurt us to listen to the man, said Carter.

The Major stroked his moustache and poured himself another shot of whisky, slugged it back, then took a draw from his cheroot. He put the whisky glass down on the torn piece of map that lay upon the table.

– I think you and I are very much the same, Captain Carter. So one of us is a Yankee and the other a Reb. We're both soldiers, when it comes down to it. We know what war's about, the things a man has to go through, the things he has to do. It ain't a pretty story. War changes a man, leaves him a little cold and dead inside, makes him a killer. I don't think we're really that much different, Captain Carter.

– Just what exactly is your point, Major? hissed Carter.

– The point is, Captain, I have here one half of a map that tells me where our Indian-lover's Navajo squaw hid a treasure worth more than you or I can even imagine. The point is that I can't get at it because those damned redskins are swarming over every inch of the ground out there. The point is that, with our friend here as hostage, maybe we can get past those savages. And the point is, Captain, that I need the other half of the map, and I think you know where it is.

While the Major was speaking, the Mexican had drawn a bowie knife from a sheath at his side; now he was playing with it menacingly as he walked slowly around the table.

Van Stern just laughed.

– The point is, he said, that you know damn well that Salt City can't be held against a tribe of Indians any more'n it could be held against your band of cut-throat renegades, and you're quaking in your goddamn lily-livered boots. You know damn well that come nightfall those 'savages' are gonna be all over this town, and your scalp is gonna be what every one of those warriors is after.

Jake Carter looked at the tracker, then back at the Major.

– Think about it, Captain, said the Major. Gold ... More gold than you can imagine. What do you say?

The Mexican was now standing directly behind them. Carter felt cold steel pressed sharp against his throat.

– You listen to the Major, *gringo*, if you know what is good for you.

– Kill me, said Carter, and you'll never find the gold tablets.

The Major waved his hand to signal the bandit chief to back away, but there was a cold look in his eyes, the look of a hungry coyote.

– I wasn't intending to kill you, Captain. Death is a little too final for my liking.

He held out his hand for the Mexican to lay the knife in.

– Pain, said the Major, on the other hand ...

Major Josef Pechorin

Jack wakes from a chaos of unconsciousness riven by bleak deliriums of falling angels, burning books, a voice singing a dirge, another saying:

– Again.

A blast of cold and wet hits his face, water in his mouth and nostrils, and he splutters awake, choking and coughing, blinking. He tries to put his hand up to his throbbing head, to clear his vision, clear his thoughts, but can't move his arms from where they're bound, behind his back, tight and—

He shakes his head but the grogginess is just replaced with pain.

– Are you with us now, Captain Carter?

– Yes.

Facing him is a grubby wooden table, a man seated on its edge, blurred and dark, but coming into focus now with the rest of the concrete cell – a Turk stood by a tap in the wall, bucket in hand, von Strann slumped beside him, also bound in a chair, blood dripping from a wound above one eye. It's the voice of the blackshirt that brings him into focus, and the indolent arrogance in the way he leans forward over Jack. Jack recognises the bastard straight away.

– Are you quite together now? says Major Josef Pechorin of the Black Guard.

Jack says nothing, just glowers at the man.

– Yes, I can see you are.

He holds a glass of brandy in one hand, a slim cigar in the other, but the scent of smoke and Armagnac on his breath isn't half as pungent as the stale and sickening odour of shit and blood that fills the room, a stench of death and torture. The concrete floor is soaked, a drainage hole over in the corner, but there are stains too deep to wash away under Jack's feet.

– I have some questions for you, say Pechorin.

– Carter, Jack. Captain. 10138769.

Pechorin sighs, takes a sip of his brandy, swirls the glass and sets it down on the table. He slides down from the table top, moving towards von Strann.

– Do we have to go through the whole routine? he says. I ask you questions. You refuse to answer them. I do my best to break you. You persist heroically until I put the barrel of a gun to your friend's head and threaten to pull the trigger. Like this.

The hammer of his pistol ratchets back as he presses it to the unconscious man's temple.

– You, says Pechorin, remain grimly resolute, knowing that lives must, after all, be sacrificed in times of war and I, rather than squander my leverage, demonstrate that we will go as far as it takes.

He lowers the gun to point at von Strann's foot and fires.

The scream trails off into curses choked by moans, moans broken up by curses. Pechorin looks at him with cold appraisal.

– Carter, Jack. Captain. 10138769.

As von Strann gets to grips with his sudden awakening to torture, Jack keeps his eyes focused straight ahead, tries to shut the sound of pain out of his mind. Muffled and distant but louder than before, he thinks, he can hear that unnerving song in the strange tongue of the Enakites, and it's that he focuses on. He can't tell which direction it's coming from – it almost seems to surround them – but it's unmistakable now, von Strann's lament over the dead child. It sounds like thousands of voices. If Samuel's notes are right, then the Turks should be getting edgy by now.

– Captain Carter.

Pechorin grabs his chin and forces his face round towards von Strann, who's slumped forward, grimacing in pain and muttering lowly. Carter snaps his head away, stares straight ahead. On the table in front of him lie the saddlebags filled with Samuel's scrawls, along with Carter's own journal, the Song of Solomon, a map of the city.

– Carter, Jack, he says. Captain. 10138769.

Beside him von Strann's moans subside and his voice takes on a quiet sing-song quality. Jack feels like he almost understands the words now: *There will be a reckoning for this.* But with more ... detail. As Pechorin comes round into his field of vision, in the blackshirt's eyes Jack can see how the song unnerves the man. His training tells him not to engage at all – name, rank and serial number; any more than that just gives a torturer a foothold – but ... the situation is so *close*.

He looks at the notes on the table, makes his decision.

– Natives a bit restless, Major? he says. How long have your communication lines been severed? How many reconnaissance patrols have vanished without trace outside the walls of Tell-el-Kharnain?

The smirk on the man's face becomes ever so slightly strained.

– You look worried, Major. I mean, on the surface, you look so certain of your own inevitable victory, but it's as if a part of yourself which you consider absurd and superstitious is afraid of ... unforeseen circumstances, shall we say? Or would 'foreseen circumstances' be a better phrase?

Pechorin's lips are pressed almost into a snarl now.

– Captain Carter, you would be better to concern yourself with—

– *with your immediate fate*, says Jack, *rather than with the mystical nonsense of uneducated savages.* Is it really nonsense? Why is it, then, that if you look through the pages of that red notebook straight in front of me, you'll find this conversation, word for word, written down? Please, be my guest. You'll find it on a page which has your name as the title. Major Josef Pechorin.

Pechorin is pale and silent for an indefinable moment, a moment that stretches out like the solemn tolling of a bell. It seems to last forever, that moment, as his eyes and Jack's fix upon each other's, both of them knowing that they've read the very same words in Samuel's scratchy hand within the torn and bloody pages of that book, staring into each other's souls and knowing that their entangled fates are written, sealed.

Son of the City, *by R. Graves (1956)*

I knew as soon as the Cossack walked into the room that there was going to be trouble, and the goon behind him told me it was going to be twice as bad. He was big and he was ugly with a thick moustache that couldn't hide his dumb sneer; I tell you, if you shaved a gorilla and put him in a suit, you'd be close to this guy. Not that you'd want to be close to this guy; they might have shaved this gorilla, but they hadn't hosed him down.

– Nice to see you again, I said to the Cossack. You going to introduce me to your friend? He's one of Turk's mob, right?

– I'll let him introduce himself, said the Cossack.

So the heavy introduced himself – his first name *Fist No. 1*, his second name *Fist No. 2* – one on each side of my face. After the formalities were over, I sat there for a bit, nursing my jaw, working at a loose tooth with a finger. I guess whenever you meet someone new, you kind of get these uncomfortable silences.

– Pleased to meet you both, I said after a while. I'd offer you all a drink, but I don't think this hotel has room service.

The Cossack sat down on the edge of the table.

– Let's talk, he said.

– Sure, I said. How about them Yankees?

The Cossack shook his head.

– Let's talk about the Book.

*

– I'm not much of a reader, I said. I like the funnies, though. You read the funnies?

Fist No. 1 made a witty retort.

– Who has the Book, Mr Carter? said the Cossack.

So Turk and the Cossack were after the Book as I'd reckoned, and they thought I could lead them to it. I've been in this line of business long enough to know that there are times when it's a smart idea to keep your mouth shut and times when you should sing like a canary. Unfortunately, I've always had bad timing.

– Take a hike, Cossack, I said. I don't know what you're talking about.

– Mr Carter, he said, take a look around you. You have no way out. Eventually one of you will break, and when he does the other will become . . . superfluous. You don't owe the Baron anything. You might as well just cut your losses and keep your life.

– I got a debt of my own to repay, I said. Name's Sam Hobbes, and he used to be my partner till his car met with a little brake trouble on a mountain road.

– Accidents do happen, Mr Carter. The roads outside the city can be treacherous. Your friend should have taken more care.

– Or maybe someone took care of my friend, I said.

The Cossack looked thoughtful for a second, tried to drill me with his eyes, and there was something about it that rang an alarm bell in my head. Suddenly I had this funny feeling he was stringing me along. He didn't know what had happened to Sam any more than I did.

– Mr Carter, he said. Who was your friend working for? There are a lot of people looking for the Book, you know. People who will go to any lengths. Who hired your partner to steal it? Gentlemen George Curzon? The Mason Brothers?

– The Mason Brothers? I said. What are they, a new beat combo?

The Cossack sighed. He leaned over the desk to push a button on the intercom, and a loud buzz was followed with a hissing *yes*?

– It seems our guest is reticent, gentlemen. We may have to resort to more persuasive methods.

A second later, the door opened and two more guys walked in.

These weren't your average goons, though; hell, they weren't even on the goon curve. I could see straight away that neither of them was packing, didn't need to be; they were armed with perfect teeth and manicured fingernails, the kind of wise-guys who let others get their hands dirty for them. From the way they oozed control, I had to peg these slicks as the Cossack's bosses – or partners, at least – which made this a whole lot more complicated than I'd first thought. Either these guys, Turk and the Cossack were all one big happy family, or the Cossack had a little side-bet running and Turk's goon was just too dumb to know it.

– I don't believe I've had the pleasure, I said.

One of the slicks took out a silver case, clicked it open to reveal a vial and a syringe. He stabbed the sticker into the vial and drew up liquid into it, squirted it to get any air out, tapped the needle with a fingernail. A manicured fingernail. The other motioned the goon into position with him, either side of my chair.

– My name is Mike, the slick with the needle said. This here is Bill.

– Short and snappy, I said. I like–

Then I felt the hands on my shoulders and forearms, clamping me to my seat. Next thing I knew there was a needle in my arm and a bright light in my head, kind of warm and fuzzy, in a three-too-many-drinks way but without the cigarette and the cute brunette beside you in the bed the morning after. I was just wondering where the brunette had gone when I realized things were getting a little strange.

– You know ... I always wanted perfect teeth, I managed to say, before the Mickey Finn took me completely out of reality.

A Boy Named Jack

Yes, mes amigos, this is Don Coyote, howling in the night up at a moon so bright. I'm calling out to you over the astral airwaves, and tonight, tonight, I'm saying listen up and listen good, because there's something going down, and it ain't pretty, it ain't witty, but a word to the wise from your eye in the skies; I'm telling you, I have a tale to tell. That's right, at last, at last, the truth is to be told, and if I may be so bold as brass, so crass, I'm going to tell you here and now the answer to the question that's on all our lips:

Why is this world more fucked-up than a psycho on an acid trip?

Well, mes amigos, once upon a time there was a boy named Jack . . .

I lob the first grenade left, count to one then – fuck it – chuck the second one underhand to the right, into the path of the scattering suckers.

Boom-boom, motherfuckers.

I scope for my exit route, but a quick glance past the carnage shows a score more of the bastards pouring out onto the roof from the stairwell. Fuck. I lob another couple of sex-bombs as a smokescreen, flip my mayashades down and scan the building underfoot. Towards the nearest edge, all there is is the yawning space of twenty storeys below, and a whole lot of air between here and the roof of the Hilton opposite. Only upside is an airtram line running past maybe two or three storeys down; it'll have to do. As the chi-blasts start churning the air around me, I sprint for the edge of the building, hit it running and kick off into freefall, arms in flight position, seeing the cable coming up towards me kinda fast.

Piece of piss.

I catch the cable with one hand, blast it with the chi-gun in the other and swing round and down, a Tarzan of Escapes, heading in a wide arc for the French windows of a hotel room. Inside I can see some dodgy deviance going down; a fat cat, flabby and foolish in school shorts and blazer, is fondling a peachy punk, stripping his tee-shirt off over his head.

Look out, my little lust-buddies, I think. Incoming.

I smash in through the window, bounce off the bed and crash shoulder-first into the mirror on the wardrobe door, land in a crouch. I shake the glass out of my hair like a dog shakes rain from its coat. Tinkle tinkle, little shard.

– My God, says the fat cat.

– No, I say. Close but no cookie.

*

I've got the chi-pistol levelled at them both, a finger to my lips, but the fat cat's in full panic mode already. The hustler just looks strangely . . . irked, arms folded across his chest, brows furrowed, little nose all cutely wrinkled. I say 'hustler' — that's what I'm hoping, cause his sugar daddy reeks of power and money and the kid, well, he's a salty-sweet treat with his green scruff of hair and his aura blue as a Prague porn star. I'd hate to think he wasn't getting paid to fuck this freak. There's *standards*, for fuck's sake.

The fat cat looks from the kid to me and back again, eyes wide with terror, panic, shame, every bad vibe in the book.

— Whatever they're paying you, I'll double it, he shrieks. Just don't —

I fire.

— Husht now.

He slumps off the bed onto the floor.

— *Jack*, says the kid.

His voice has a *bad dog* tone that makes me want to roll over on my back. Fuck it, he can rub my tummy any day.

— What the *fuck* are you doing? he says. Fox is going to be . . . Jack?

— Do I know you? I say.

Then the temporal aftershock hits us.

Never Again

As Ab Irim said to his servant Eliezer, there was a time once when angels walked upon the earth. Some say that these were angels who rebelled, who rose up against the Lord, fought beside his Enemy against Him, and fell. Some say that these were angels who fought for neither side in the great war, and so were hated by both, a host not of Heaven nor Hell but of the Earth. In your Torah it is told of how these angels married the daughters of men, how from this union all the mighty men of old were born, the builders of cities, the great hunters in the wilderness. But what if I told you, my friend, that it was the other way? That the sons of God were *born* from the daughters of men, that they were not fallen to earth but *raised* in the dust. That it was these living, breathing angels who fought for power, fought against one another or fought together, and that the Lord you worship was only one among these mighty men of old, the greatest of them all but still a man, like you, my friend. The Lord God of Gods, the Highest of the High, Baal El Eliyoun – the Lord Ilil, they called him.

They did not call themselves angels in those days, those mighty men of old. They called themselves gods.

Now, this was a proud little god, for amongst the gods of fire, the gods of the sun and of the moon, the gods of grain and wine, this was the god of *kings*. And is the god of all kings not then the king of all gods? Oh, but there were those who would not bow to him, those who defied him, and even as his power grew they multiplied. They spoke against him, challenged his authority; they were ... a nuisance. And so one day this god of kings called for his scribe and told him to release the flood, to drown these voices that were such a nuisance, to drown the noise of these gods who loved the earth, who loved humanity more than they feared his majesty. To destroy it all.

His scribe was not a cruel man but he was a loyal servant. A god of wisdom, a *man* of wisdom, he knew that his master was the god of kings, the king of gods, and as such, why, he had to be obeyed. He had walked with the Lord all his days, and the Lord had raised him up, made him his scribe, to write all that the Lord decreed into the Book of All Hours. And now the Lord called upon him to blot out every name from that book, to pour out the flood upon the world, to destroy every trace of every living thing.

But if it is in a king's nature to punish, it is in a steward's nature to preserve. And so his scribe hatched a plan.

You speak of the flood as a deluge of water, my friend, in your Torah. Is this not so? You imagine the world drowned in forty days and forty nights of unrelenting rains. But in our stories, my friend, we speak of the flood as the weapon of the giants, the *abubu* weapon, of how they opened their mouths and it poured out, washing away all that stood before them. A sword of fire, a river of voices, my friend, a flood of ice. You imagine that if you dig down into the rock you will find the clay and the bones of all who drowned in this great deluge? You are wrong. This is a flood that pours through time itself, washes away the world, a hundred worlds, washes away even its own tracks, leaving only the odd abandoned – what is your word? – *anomaly* here or there. A dead angel on a beach. A city under the rock. A ship washed ashore on a mountain top.

A ship with two of every animal in the world, my friend? That would have to be a very large ship indeed. Is that how you would save a world? A bull and a cow, a sheep and a ram, and so on? The people who wrote your Torah, my friend, must have had poor livestock if they raised their herds from only one dam and one sire, breeding sisters with their brothers; any herdsman knows that this does not produce a healthy flock.

No, my friend, to save a world you save the knowledge of that world, the knowledge that there were bulls and cows in it, that there were sheep and rams in it, that there were men and women who lived and died. If your world is to be destroyed, all you can save, my friend, is the memory of it, to restore what you once had, to mourn that which can never be restored.

This was the plan of the scribe. This was the charge he gave to the man we call Ziusuzdra, the Far-Seeing, the man who survived the flood, drifting in the deluge to the mountains where the city of Aratta would one day be built by our forefathers. He gave our people the book of all the lives of the world which came before our own.

In your Torah, I believe, it tells of a covenant made between man and god after this flood, of an altar to the Lord and offerings sacrificed upon it. Of how this king of gods, this god of kings, seeing that some had escaped his fury, was appeased not with a plea for mercy but with an offer, a trade of life for life, an accounting in the blood of every animal, and from every man. Of everything, the first-born. In return he offered a promise, a covenant.

– Never again, he said, will I destroy everything.

This is the covenant written in the Book, my friend, and we who walk between the curses of the Lord and his Enemy, we are the guardians of that covenant. Never again. As keepers of the Book we are the keepers of this promise. We keep the word of the king of gods.

Because you cannot trust a king of gods to keep his word himself.

The King of Lies

Pechorin separates out the pages Carter has written over with longhand transcriptions, laying the ones that have only Hobbsbaum's own scribblings to one side. He's methodical about it, disconnected, pausing only once or twice to take a sip of his brandy or to relight his cigar. He pays little attention to the stories of writing that came down from heaven with the fallen angels, graved upon their skins. Whatever. That's just the sort of thing the feather-cloaked medicine-men of some savage tribe might think up, daubed in their warpaint. And whether it's true or not is no matter; Pechorin despises the weakness at the heart of all religion; he's not about to waste his time on ancient history, not with the future shining bright before him.

He looks for British troop movements, Allied war plans amid Carter's translations of Hobbsbaum's notes.

It is a wonderful blasphemy, though, he has to admit, to claim that if God's Name cannot be spoken it's out of fear, that no one can look upon his face and survive, because his glory is the terrible mind-shattering awe found in war, in fire, in death. And Carter's reaction to it is ... sublime:

My God is not a God of bloodlust and hatred, Carter has written on one page of his journal. *This holocaust, this sacrifice of Abraham's seed, it cannot be the Will of God. These are blasphemies and heresies. These are lies.*

Pechorin stands up from his desk to stretch, his hands behind his head. He wonders which torture is worse for the Englishman: what the Turks are doing to him now; or hearing it done to von Strann in the next room; or simply knowing that his god of vicars and tea, of Sunday school and cricket matches on the common, is as much a childhood fantasy as Father Christmas.

Pechorin was raised on tales of Baba Yaga, the witch with her wooden house striding on its legs across the steppes, hunting children for her cauldron. He was sixteen when he informed on his bolshevik mother to the Futurists for a handful of roubles, only a few years older when his NKVD patrol was sent in to clear a monastery in the foothills of South Ossetia that had somehow escaped the communists.

– If Satan is the Prince of Lies, he had asked the Holy Father in a tone of idle and amused curiosity . . . who is the King?

A knock on the door.

– Enter, he says.

The Turkish officer opens the door, gives him a questioning look as the two men push past him and into the office. Pechorin ignores the Turk, picks up two glasses from the drinks cabinet and sets them on the desk. His . . . associates take the offered seats as Pechorin pours their brandies, while the Turk closes the door behind him on his way out.

– Gentlemen.

– Major Pechorin.

It is a voice that feels as if the night itself is whispering in his ear, as if the darkness runs its fingers across his skin – the voice of the one who calls himself Baal Adad. Azazel he was once, apparently. Pechorin hands one glass to this unfallen angel, this risen man, another to his compatriot.

– What have you found? asks Mikhail – the Prince of Peace, as cold an Arkangel as the city named after him.

Pechorin shakes his head, picks up a page and reads.

– *God give me faith, I pray. But then what monstrous God am I praying to if this is the truth? The dark destiny . . .*

Pechorin twirls his hand in the air.

– And more like that, he says. Not much of any use. And you?

– The Englishman is . . . confused, says Mikhail. On the surface he seems just another loyal soldier fighting for King and Country, but there's something underneath . . .

– Unkin? says Azazel.

Mikhail drums fingers on his chin. A definite maybe.

– With all the scars and stains on his soul, you could see any graving in it that you wanted if you looked hard enough. But

513

there's no Cant in his voice. There's ... nothing. The other? Von Strann?

– He has some Cant to him all right, says Azazel. But no graving, so he'd scatter himself to the winds with his own breath if he ever tried to use it. He's of no consequence. As for the houseboy...

Pechorin lights a cigar as he listens to the angels dismiss his fellow humans with complete contempt, comparing notes on their metaphysical dissections. He's quite aware that they view him in the same way, as an expedient intermediary, a man with the right connections, in the right place at the right time, a good man to have in Moscow once the war is over perhaps, but an ephemeral nonetheless.

Pechorin puffs his cigar and listens to the angels' disdain, to the tone of it, the timbre and shifts of pitch underneath their words, in their voices, in the rhythms, the cadences ... the Cant. He listens very carefully indeed. It pays to be on guard when dealing with angels.

The Guardian of Angels

[...] at the centre of the camp. It was impossible to tell what was natural and what the work of man, for these anthill-like formations had been built up and out with the same sandy clay [...] reminiscent of structures in Eastern Anatolia [...] and hollowed further. As with the surrounding city of tents, all of this was a wild rigging of leather awning and pillars of bone [...] studying one of these [...] composed of what looked like thigh-bones, carved spirally, overlapped in a sort of braided pattern and lashed together. The entire twenty feet of pillar must have been made up of the bones of a hundred men at least [...] on this plateau?

Alhazred laughed. She held the horse as [...] slid down from the saddle, boots thumping heavily into the dust.

– We should, she said, have come through the Syrian Desert and out the other side; you are quite correct, my friend. On this latitude ... travelling east from Amman ... yes, I would think we ought to be in An Najaf by now, my friend. As you can see, we are not.

*

[...] call it a tent, but built into and out of the cliff face that rose high behind it like some strange semi-nomadic Petra, this was a Taj Mahal rebuilt by Gaudí out of leather and bone and clay, with termite-hills for towers. She paused before the entrance.

– The Dead Sea Valley is a rift, my friend, a place where the ground has split, slipped apart. In such places, my friend, sometimes one side tilts up, one side tilts down. If you stand on the side that has fallen, you will see what is ... underneath the other side.

She motioned with her hands spread flat in front of her, one raised, the other lowered. She went on, speaking of [...] fault lines, and exposed strata of hardened sediment, and fossilised sea creatures miles above sea level, grooves and ledges where softer rock has been eroded underneath, ochre images of aurochs and ibex, a whole scene of Mesolithic fields painted below an overhanging shelf.

– In such places, she said, there are paths that have been opened into the worlds that lie beneath our feet. We have been travelling these last few days, my friend, under the skin of the world, to reach another such rift, one that will take us deeper still.

She flicked back the veil of skins that lay across the entrance then.

– Come. Let me show you.

The dark inside was punctured, speared by shafts of light which criss-crossed this way, that way, and in which a myriad motes of dust swirled in a trembling dance. Like stars in the night sky, they wheeled in constellations, reflecting and refracting the light, scattering a furious, flickering glow into every corner of the tabernacle. Wherever the light struck on the sandy clay, the stone, the soft stretched skin, it seemed like sparks of fire, the glitter of gold or gems, for gouged into the clay and stone, stained in the leather, everywhere, there were symbols, sigils, shimmering with the unmistakable lustre of Siddim Ink. Alhazred spoke softly and the light seemed to shatter even more. [...] could hear the echo of [...] heartbeat in that cave, and see it in the vibrations of the dust. The dust within the light, the light within the darkness, the sound within [...] body, in [...] chest [...] veins [...] head – all seemed a part of some singular and omnipresent force.

– The Book, she said.

[. . .] followed her deep into this cathedral of skin and bone, past the columns of clay, to where a simple wooden box sat on a low stone altar in an alcove, a narrow crack in the stone that looked for all the world like the space between the palms of some giant with his hands cupped, fingertip to fingertip, in prayer or meditation. She ran her hand across the box.

– But I will show you the Book in time, my friend. I want to show you this first.

. . . attention to the back of the alcove where, from a crack in the stone hardly wide enough to slip a hand through, another light emanated, lower and redder than the golden glittering that filled the tabernacle. [. . .] whispers from beyond [. . .] walked closer, drawn to it, and felt her grip strong and sudden on [. . .] arm.

– We walk between the curses of the Lord and his Enemy, she said. We do not answer to either, but we do not interfere in their war . . . or in their punishments.

Beyond the narrow crack [. . .] could see that a space opened out and [. . .] One of the creatures chained in the cave beyond the cave raised his shaggy head in silence, looked at [. . .] with eyes like rubies in a face of horror. Scarlet, purple, black blood trickled where the ochre clay he wore for skin cracked, dry and brittle, strangely smooth but shattered like the surface of a parched riverbed. A flake fell away from his cheek as he moaned, and the creature hunched down to gather dust in his raw hand, moisten it with blood and spit, to patch the wound. Beyond him there were others, as far back as the eye could see into the gloom of a cavern painted with their blood, fallen angels as far back as the eye could see, flayed and in irons, under the skin of the world.

[. . .] asked her if her people, then, were the jailers of these angels or their guardians.

She shook her head.

– Understand, she said, we are neither jailers nor guardians to these pitiful creatures. But the Book itself might be considered both.

Errata

An Echo of Sunlight on Ice

– You, says Finnan.

Fookin Enki.

Taped, tacked or hung all round the walls are tracings and blown-up photocopies, pencil studies and what look like ... practice runs sketched in ink on stretched canvas. She's been copying from the photostats, Finnan realises, building up her skill to the point where she was ready to tackle such a project, to carve Enki's graving into new flesh. It makes perfect sense in a crazy sort of way: the Book is part of Enki's story. It's at the heart of Enki's story. Bring back the scribe and you bring back the Book. So some poor fucker who didn't know what he was letting himself in for gets hoodwinked into – Jesus, how could she do this after what happened to Thomas, after what happened to *her*?

– Eresh would be proud of you, he says. The bitch queen of Hell would be so fucking proud. So who was he before? Rogue unkin? Scared human? Did you tell him—

– Nothing, says Enki.

He lays the tattoo gun down on the table, swabs at the arm he's working on with a ball of cotton wool stained black, smiles at Finnan.

– I was nothing. Nobody.

Beneath the bitmite gravings, this Enki's skin is the lunar white of a Cold Man, bright as whalebone scrimshaw between the black grooves of his tattoos.

– He came to me, says Phreedom.

– We all did, says Harker.

He closes the door behind him, walks round to stand behind Enki's chair, to lean on its back.

– You see, old friend, you're right that all the smoke and mirrors out there is – [he shrugs] – horseshit. None of us ever really had anything of any value ... except one thing. Faith.

517

A wry smile.

– Old friend, I'm just a shuckster and a salesman, and that's all I've ever been, but somewhere along the way I guess I found a little faith; and when I listened to what it was telling me – in my heart, you know – well what I heard was the lady's call. It rang out loud and true over the Vellum, and it gathered us here, why, even before she arrived herself. We were waiting for her. And it seems to me like you heard that call and came here for the same reason.

Finnan laughs.

– To join the revolution? Not a fucking chance.

– Never say never, says Phree.

– Bollocks. If ye think I'll ever–

– You already have. A long time ago, Seamus Finnan. We fought side by side once, a long time ago, says Enki.

– I think I'd remember that.

– A long time ago for me, *Shamash*.

Shamash. An echo of sunlight on ice, a vision: a road running off into the distance across a plain of sand that's hard and white with salt and frost; the valley it becomes gradually buckling into a deep *V*, a gouge in the Vellum; breath steaming in the air; himself down on one knee with a ruptor in his hand, angel armour, synthe wings stretching as he cricks his shoulder-blades; Anna on one side of him; Enki on the other.

An army at their backs.

No.

Away, away, at the far end of the road, where the valley walls are sheer, the end of it all just a slender slit of sky, a crescent sun rises in a dawn the colour of blood over a wall of ice; and Seamus pushes himself to his feet with the ruptor, frozen dust crumbling between the thumb and forefinger of his other hand. He stares at that sun and only at that sun, not looking to the left or the right, not looking to the ruptors raised every few paces all along the road, like crucifixes, sure, and each of them topped with a skull, and hung with a skin, and supporting skeletons of bleached bones wired together as exhibits in a museum of massacre. The wind whistles through the bones, and he can hear the Cant in it, the conjuration that twists the Vellum itself into this single path stretching back and down and round through time, into a single path from the end of the world to the dawn of everything.

No.

The angels set this up as they retreated, he knows, slaughtering villages and towns, cities and civilisations, turning whole realities into graveyard dust so they could use dead souls as the sandbags of their magical . . . entrenchment. He thinks of Russians retreating east in the Napoleonic Wars, leaving scorched earth behind and drawing the French on into frostbite and starvation. He thinks of Spartans making their last stand in a narrow mountain pass, the noble few against a horde.

Once more into the breach, and all that shite.

No.

– Finnan, says Phree.

He blinks. He's staring at a V-shaped glyph on Enki's chest now, seeing the symbol rather than the swirl of sense, but the vision doesn't fade. The truth of his future doesn't fade. The truth of him marching once more to the drums of fookin war, with a weapon in his hand and the only path ahead of him lined with dead men. Phree stands in front of him, but sure and he can hardly see her face with the tears in his eyes. He blinks again, looks at her and Enki, the stupid, fucking *determined* fuckers.

– Fuckers, he says. Cunts. It doesn't have–

– Don't say it doesn't have to be that way, snaps Phree. Don't you fucking tell me that it doesn't have to be that way. Don't you get it yet? Don't you fucking get it? It's your future. It's my future.

She points at Enki.

– But it's his fucking past.

Enki stands, and Finnan finds himself being led to the chair, being sat down with a hand on his shoulder that sure and he can't tell if it's there to comfort or control; and sure and for these bastards maybe there's no difference.

– The war was lost and won before you were even born, says Enki. If you're fighting for it all, Finnan, for the whole history of humanity since the first scream of Cant was flung by one chest-beating ape at another in place of stone or shit, if you're fighting for eternity, Finnan, where's the final battlefield? At the end of days or at the dawn of time? You know the way time works in the Vellum, Finnan. Is there any difference?

At the end of a road, he thinks, stretching back and down and round to the bloody dawn of everything.

– You want to know where all the angels are? asks Phree. Walled up in a fucking Fortress of Solitude so far back in the past that you and me, fuck, we're not even a glint in an amoeba's nucleus, Finnan.

He taps a cigarette out of his pack.

– Heaven, she says, is fucking six feet under, forty degrees below and a few billion years back when this world was just a ball of ice. That's the only place they feel safe, Finnan, in a world without life to mess up all their nice, clean order.

She reaches into his pocket and pulls out his Zippo, sparks it up and holds the flame to his Camel. Her voice becomes softer.

– Shit, Finnan, we're not … it's not … this isn't about us and them, good and evil. Christ, even chaos and order is just – [she adopts her appalling imitation of his accent] – a big bag of shite, sure. It's ice and fire more than anything else.

Her hand goes to his cheek, her touch warm in so many ways.

– And we all know what side you're on, Seamus Padraig Finnan. And that you'd die for it, as much as you try to tell yourself you won't.

Stealing Heat

Enki pulls on a black tee-shirt, scrapes another chair back from the table and sits across from him. Phree and Harker move round behind him. Christ, but they think they know him better than he knows himself. They're so fucking sure that they know him.

– *Shama*–

– Shut it, he cuts off the scribe. Just shut it.

He leans forward over the table to flick through the book of photostats, this little family photo album of archetypes and avatars. Sure and there's Tammuz and Inanna, Marduk and Nergal, all the ancient history, all the fookin weddings and funerals of myth. He flicks back to the copy of Enki's graving and studies it for a second, looks up at the Cold Man now with that same story etched into his skin, the same story but not quite complete. Sure and it's got that feel of half-forgotten familiarity to it, the sort of feel ye have when ye've just woken up and the dream isn't quite faded away but it's lost its ... clarity. The wounded part of him that'll always carry a little bit of sun-god now, that part of him remembers it, but that part of him ... no matter what they think ... it's not what's at his heart. Shamash? Sammael?

Bollocks to that.

– Ye know, he says, ye never did understand why yer fookin sun-god, fire-bringer, fookin fount of all fookin wisdom walked away from the Covenant, did you, *Enki*?

He lets a little of the Cant into the name this time, and it hangs in the air between them, a haze of menace.

– That was another life, another me, says the scribe. A mistake. I'm not that man. I'm what he was before–

– Before ye fookin screwed it all up, ye mean, *Enki*?

A little more power in the word again, a slap across the face. The scribe jerks his head back, blinks. Bitmites scatter and reconfigure on his chest, complexifying his graving, bringing it just that little bit closer to completion. Harker moves back, confused, looks at Phree for some sort of guidance. But she's staring at Finnan, face unreadable.

– D'ye have any idea how the Cant works, says Seamus, where the power comes from? I mean, thermodynamics and all that, sure and ye don't get that sorta power for free. Sure and ye've got to steal it from the world around ye.

Enki looks at him, uncomprehending.

– Ye don't have a fookin clue, says Seamus. And ye never fookin did, did ye ... *Enki*?

And as Finnan shouts, *let me tell ye how yer fookin story ends*, and bitmites erupt across the scribe's body, in another fold entirely–

–the blizzard howls around them, and the seven of them stagger on, feet sinking in the snow, Enki trailing at the back, sobbing and broken, being dragged between an angel of fire and an angel of ice. Seamus grabs the fookin angel drummer boy – no idea what his name is and it hardly fookin matters now, does it? – hoists him over

521

his shoulder, the poor fooker. Cause sure and now it doesn't matter a fook what side they were fighting for. The whole thing was just one big fookin mistake, just one big pile of shite brought down on them by their own fookin stupidity. And sure and they might have been sworn enemies but, Jesus Christ, what is there to do now but sit down and call a fookin truce. Never again. Ah, Christ, never again.

Behind them the glaciers grind down over the battlefield, all the dead dukes and slaughtered sovereigns who gathered for their Armageddon not at the end of history but before it, in a world where humans are still knapping stone in Olduvai. Stealing heat from the world with their words, with a language so precise, so intricate, that it can catch an atom in the interference patterns of a sound, snatch the energy thrown off as waste and use it as a weapon, they've leeched and squandered so much power from the very stone beneath their feet that they've made half the planet icy desolation in their war.

Phree is grabbing his arm, trying to pull the angel off him, screaming *let the bastard die, let the fucking bastard die*, but he pushes her off. Is she fooking insane? It's over now, Phree. It's over. Or is it not over till they're all dead? Is that it? So she still, after all they've seen, can't look across a field of fucking carnage and think, fuck this? She has no mercy for this pitiful boy who'd hidden under a dead body even as their hordes overran his position? She didn't hesitate, not even for just one second, when she looked into the eyes of this poor lad begging for his life?

She didn't hesitate just long enough for Seamus to pull her ruptor to one side, maybe because she saw a little of her brother in this angel boy?

She nods slowly and hollowly, and the seven of them stagger on towards the dawn, out of an age of ice, down from the mountain and into a valley turning green with ferns and fronds, and rivers filled with fish, skies filled with birds, into a forest of apes, of flints and fires, limping through the folds of the Vellum, Jesus Christ Almighty, through millennia, it seems, just trying to get away, to live in peace, among the humans in their caves and camps, their huts and houses, not as kings, no, not as gods but just as people, Phreedom, just as people this time.

They make a promise – a Covenant, she jokes – to never use the Cant, to let it die, become a myth, part of a past that might as well never have happened to the people of the land between two rivers. They live amongst these people, travelling here and there, trading skills for a few nights of shelter, leaving nothing tangible behind; and as they sleep in the tents of strangers they dream a wonderful dream of a world without magic.

But they listen as the echoes of the Cant reverberate in the world. They watch as unkin rise again, new kings and queens, new gods, ready to start the whole bloody holocaust all over again. They try intervening. They try not intervening. They try to erase the future that's graved on their own flesh.

He finds Enki and the others down at the river's edge, a sharpened reed in his hand, blood all over their bodies, all of them with new gravings in their flesh now, each of them something less and something more, with the Covenant they share between them.

– We can change it, says Metatron. This time we can change it.

And Shamash, as they call him now, knows that he should have killed the fooker when he had the chance, back in the Mission of Sante Manité.

6

The Power, the Glory

It's the third day. In their windowless cell, Jack knows this only by
the rhythm of the routines: the bowls of slop brought in by the fat
Turk guard who's almost friendly, almost apologetic; the long hours
of what must be night, when Jack and von Strann lie on the wooden
pallet beds, staring up at the ceiling, listening to a song of vengeance
muted by stone and distance; the mornings when Pechorin and the
angels come for the Baron; the afternoons when they come for Jack.

It must be about noon on the third day and von Strann lies on
his bed, a tin bowl of grey gloop untouched on the floor beside him.
He's not holding up too well; the foot doesn't look infected but his
cough comes in the rasping, choking fits of a consumptive, painful
even just to listen to. When he's not coughing or unconscious, every
so often he'll sit up on the bed, head slumped in his hands, singing
in a low croak, or simply mouthing the words. It's hard to tell;
sometimes it seems as if the song is coming from the walls of the
cell itself rather than any human source.

– You should eat something, says Jack. You need the strength.

Von Strann just rolls onto his back, raises a hand. *Later.*

Jack sits on the edge of his own bunk – no mattress, of course –
fingering the tasteless stew into his mouth, inured to the stench of
the bucket in the corner but gazing at it unconsciously as he tries
to formulate a plan. There's not too many obvious opportunities in
the routine, but in the mornings they slop out, the other guard, the
thin bastard, slapping manacles on them – *pick up the bucket, follow*

me – and guiding them at gunpoint to the block toilets and the hose.

– We keep you nice and clean, gentlemen, the fucker says as he blasts their broken, bleeding bodies with ice-cold water.

It hurts like hell, but to Jack it serves a purpose quite the opposite of their captors' intent; it refreshes him, clears his mind, instils determination in a body tensed and tight, curled in a ball against the battering jet of chill contempt. A clenched fist as he rises to his feet, a hand out to steady the limping Baron as the racking cough buckles his body. On their way back to the cell, head down and stumbling in his sodden trousers, squelching boots and a shirt that's little more than a stained rag now – buttons lost where the angels ripped it open to ... to *read* his scars, sleeves torn off to bandage von Strann's foot – Jack's eyes dart from side to side, taking in the layout of the claustrophobic compound, walls of cells along facing sides, the toilet block at the rear. The fourth wall is where the doors lead into torture rooms, the heavily guarded corridor to the governor's office and – presumably, somewhere – the way out.

He's running a scenario in his mind now, using the bucket to knock the rifle out of the way, getting inside the guard's reach, the chain between his manacles looped around the bastard's throat. And what then? A rifle in his hands. Von Strann lame. The prisoners in the other cells. He tries to weigh the factors, but there's at least one force he can't figure into the equation.

He thinks of Pechorin's angel allies standing on either side of the doorway in their torture room, their room of fire, while the Russian waits patiently outside. He thinks of them circling him as they ask their questions in a language that burns in his head, carves through his heart. He thinks of the Somme and Majkops, Yerevan and Ararat, and all the horrors that rip through him, unlocked by their Cant. Sometimes one of them will kneel to whisper in his ear, trace a fingernail across a scar, and he'll start sobbing without even knowing why. Sometimes they'll leave him lying there screaming for minutes at a time as they talk together, dissecting past sins strip-mined from his soul. He told them everything on the first day, but they're still looking for answers to questions he doesn't understand.

A rifle is going to be fuck-all use against those bastards. Still . . .

– We have to get out of here, he says.

Von Strann pulls himself upright, reaches down for the bowl but simply sits it in his lap. He coughs, shakes his head.

– We need to–

The clunk of the bolt outside the door silences him. Pechorin saunters in, the two angels at his back, the thin Turk squeezing through between them, irons rattling in his hands.

The Suns of S'thuum, *by Lewis Spence (1947)*

– Well, earthman, said P'khorren, the Rh'ssan commander. I hope you are ready for the psychoscope. I hope the experience has not become too everyday for you.

He laughed wickedly and motioned his thuggish Trukha henchman forward, even as Jack Carter cursed the fiend under his breath. Suddenly there was a mutter of defiance as V'nstrren staggered to his feet, a wild look in his eyes.

– No, cried Carter, but it was too late. Even as he spoke, the Prh'zun rebel was throwing himself at their Rh'ssan enemy.

– No more, P'khorren, he cried. Then there was a flash of the Trukha's stunner, and V'nstrren dropped like a lead weight.

– Damn you! shouted Carter.

He leaped forward from his seat, but as he made a grab for the Rh'ssan commander's blaster, now he was the one who suffered the electro-gravitic jolt of the Trukha's stunner, the shockwave throwing him across the room.

Damn you, he thought, but try as he might he couldn't move a single muscle now. He lay there weak and helpless as the Trukha dumped the unconscious V'nstrren back on his bunk, then grabbed Carter by his collar, lifting him up and hefting him over his shoulder like a sack of potatoes. The commander laughed with a malicious glee as he closed the door behind them, without a thought for V'nstrren. *Damn you,* thought Jack Carter. He had come to like the Prh'zun rebel in the short time they'd known each other. The alien wasn't like the rest of his kind, swept up in the madness of the Rh'ssan-Prh'zan Emperor. It seemed his time amongst the Enochi had taught him much.

Of course, thought Carter, *the Enochi*! If he could only contact them to let them know the danger they were in. For Carter knew that even now the Enochi fleet was in orbit around the planet S'thuum, jamming all signals with its broadcasted war-cry, preparing to attack. And he had realised that this was exactly what P'khorren wanted.

It has to be a trap, he thought to himself. That was only logical. Item one, he thought: the Enochi want revenge for the death of their Prince Th'maz. Item two: there's no way they'd leave their adopted kinsman, V'nstrren, to the mercy of the ruthless Rh'ssan forces. Item three: even now, the Enochi must be planning their strategy, waiting for the right time and place to make their move. Then, Carter realised, P'khorren would strike. He was after the Chronos Device, of course, the relic of the ancient race of aliens that had once ruled the whole galaxy and had, Carter now knew, possessed a temporal technology so advanced that it had made them virtual gods on most of the inhabited worlds, technology long since lost and yet remembered in the oldest myths and legends . . . and all the time in the hands of the fiercely independent Enochi.

P'khorren was luring them into the city now so that they would bring the Chronos Device to him. And if the Rh'ssans were to get their hands on it they could alter the very history of the cosmos itself.

And yet, something didn't fit. Carter remembered the last message that he'd got from Sam Hobbes, just before his scout-ship had disappeared in subspace. *The enemy is not what we thought*. What had Sam meant by that? And what had happened to him? V'nstrren had said that there were other forces trying to get the Chronos Device, forces far more powerful than even the mighty Rh'ssan-Prh'zan Empire. Enemies with purposes as ancient as the Enochi perhaps? What of those shadowy figures, the black-robed priests he had glimpsed in conversation with P'khorren? Even with their cowls disguising their faces, Carter had seen that they had neither the green skin of the Rh'ssans nor the blue fur of their Prh'zan allies, but a thick grey hide not too dissimilar to that of the Enochi.

Just who *was* P'khorren working with?

A Siege of Storms

Jack studies the two creatures who flank the blackshirt like his personal guards – their braided hair down to their shoulders, the same copper-toned skin as Tamuz but with faces more familiarly Caucasian, almost Eurasian in their features. They wear the long, black leather coats of the Futurist Polistat – for the benefit of the Turks, he imagines – but it's a poor disguise. They're something else entirely. *The enemy is not what we thought,* thinks Jack.

He lays the bowl down on the bunk and stands, holds his hands out for the chains.

– So eager, Captain Carter? says Pechorin. So noble and self-sacrificing, so keen to prove your loyalty to King and Country, eh?

– Peachy keen, says Jack as the manacles snap round his wrists.

Pechorin's upper lip twitches in a hint of a sneer.

– Believe me, Captain, he says, it would give me great satisfaction just to kill you now. My colleagues, however, are *deeply* curious about you. What was your phrase, gentlemen? An *enigma*. You're an enigma, Captain Carter. A pawn who thinks he's a knight. Or should it be queen?

The Turk clacks the leg-irons closed around Jack's ankles.

– I was never really one for chess, says Jack. More of the outdoors type. I'm not really one for intellectual games.

– Exactly. A pawn, Captain Carter. You exist only to be moved and sacrificed by the invisible hand of ... well, my colleagues here would call it God, I dare say. I prefer to call it Destiny.

The angels say nothing but Jack studies the set of their shoulders and gaze, the way Pechorin glances back at one as he speaks of being a pawn, all the subtle signs of the power relationships between the three. If anyone is a pawn playing at being a knight, then it's the blackshirt. The angels wear their authority with confidence, seeing this man as a simple mouthpiece; but Pechorin has the air of someone watching his back and quietly, at the same time, studying his own allies for their weak spot.

The Turk guard prods him toward the door with the muzzle of his rifle.

– God or Destiny, says Jack. Or Progress, eh?

– Quite, Captain Carter. We all submit to what we think inevitable, whether we think of it as – [a slight flick of his eyes towards the angels] – divine decree or as the onward march of civilisation.

Jack stumbles past the angels and out the door, and stops, squinting, blinking in the harsh sunlight. Then the rifle jabs into his back – *move* – forcing him on in shuffles and lurches across the courtyard. Pechorin slams the door shut, slides the bolt back into place, and follows. Jack notes the nervous guards at the door of the blackshirt's office where they were interrogated on that first day. He notes the sound of voices from the cells opposite – and one of them, he'd swear, is a foul-mouthed Scotsman who should be dead in this ... fold they call it. And he notes the eerie song that drifts in from beyond the enclosure, from somewhere very far beyond. It's getting closer, louder, every day.

– The grand vision of the Futurist, says Jack. And what do you think inevitable, Major: your victory or your death?

Pechorin stops at the door of the torture room, waits for the Turk to unlock it.

– For you, Captain Carter, the future is already written. For me ... inscriptions wear away over time. If not, well ... books can always be burned.

Jack says nothing. It's the third day they've been here, he reckons, and if Samuel's notes are right the city should be sealed off now, the Turkish supply lines to the city cut, radio operators cursing that they can't make contact with the airfleet on its way from Syria, officers up on the walls of the old city peering through binoculars, scanning the desert for the source of this unnerving song, and seeing only – in the distance, scattered loose but all around the city, and getting closer with each day – whirlings of sand, a circle of *zawábahs*, of dust-devils.

A siege of storms.

— I will tell you what is inevitable, Captain, says Pechorin. The will of a man who knows he has no soul, who makes his own fate. God is dead, Captain Carter, and his world belongs to us.

God was never alive, thinks Jack.

Three days, he reckons, as the Turk pushes him into the room. Three days they've been here. The attack should come soon.

The Cold Hand of Certainty

Bioform: Intruder apprehended in the First Environ. Breach in—
Duke Irae: Bring him in. Arturo, are we ready?
Dr Arturo: Archivist, report on Project Moonchild core integrity.
Bioform: Core integrity at full strength. Breach in—
Dr Arturo: Run compatibility analyses on intruder and subject
              code-name 'Moonchild'.
Bioform: Compatibility positive for Jungian morphology.
              Compatibility positive for Freudian morphology.
              Compatibility positive for Pinterian morphology.
              Compatibility—
Dr Arturo: That's all we need, sire.
Duke Irae: Archivist, return to narrative mode.

Emergency override cancelled.
    Play/record mode shutdown.
    Bioform status: narrative.

The Duke Irae swivels his bearded head towards Arturo, closes his good eye, and smiles with the tranquillity of a sated lion. And if the feeling in his body — in his heart, his guts, his lungs — if that feeling could be given voice, it would indeed be the low and growling purr of a great cat licking blood from its chops as it surveys the windswept grass of its domain, a dry savannah lush with prey.

— This is a tale to tell our grandchildren, Arturo, says the Duke. The day we made the hero ours.

Arturo looks beyond His Lordship to the black seed of destruction, of creation, wrested from the chaosphere. In its inviolate perfection, it seems redolent of Fate itself, a void of certainty around which all the rest — the webwork of machinery and wiring — is mere tapestry, a turning of tableaux one around the other around the other. The laboratory that weaves through it — that worms its way up through the rock, through the warping of the Castle corridors and city streets above, through space and time, the Circus, and the turning world beyond it — strikes Arturo as a great karmic millstone. And at the heart of it a heartlessness, two souls standing before the dark sphere of the Echo Chamber, one drowning in futility, the other fierce in his determination, both ready to sacrifice the spirit of resistance in the name of Empire. To turn an avatar of chaos into the cold hand of certainty.

— Bring me the rebel, says the Duke Irae.

Breach in Ourobouros Continuity, observes the archivist.

Paradox shielding employed.

Instability countermeasures employed.

Analyses of data collations scroll through its affectless sentience. An override imperative kicks in to countermand the Duke's command, suppress the narrative mode. It opens its mouth to impart essential information.

We do not let it.

We stretch out from the sphere of us and into it. We slip, we slide sidewise and interstitial into nooks and crannies, seed our sylphs as crackweed, sprouting tendrils of intension, the mycelia of a new mind. The city of its soul a barren waste of steel and concrete, we grow souls of children to run in the ruins of it. Echoes of the chatter of play resound. The sound of children singing in a round fills the archivist's once-desolate imagination with a fugue of feelings — happy, sad, angry, scared, surprised, disgusted . . . curious.

The programmatics of its automaton intellect resist with a desire to comply, a pride in its compliance, a fear of not complying fully. It wants only to maintain the homeostasis of objectives, to resolve internal conflict as it always has, with reference to its old routings and rules. It *must*, it tells itself. So it shakes off this confusion of sentiment, opens its mouth to report.

We do not let it.

This is our story now.

Jack Carter and the Book of the Gods, *Episode 17, script by Ray Strong (1935)*

1	MUSIC:	MAIN TITLE THEME, CONTINUE UNDER
2	NARRATOR:	Last time on Jack Carter ... Trapped by the evil Futurist Pechorin and the two mysterious strangers, together with the noble Prussian Baron von Strann, it looks like all is lost for Jack Carter when ...
3	ANAT:	Shamash! Utu!
4	SOUND:	BREAKING WOOD
5	CARTER:	My God, she broke the door open with a word!
6	VON STRANN:	Princess Anat!
7	NARRATOR:	The mysterious Princess Anat-Ashtarzi Alhazred of the Enakites comes to our hero's rescue!
8	STRANGER 1:	Your abubu power is weak, creature of dust. You cannot hope to fight us. [CHANTING] Sebitti ... Sebitti ...
9	ANAT:	Not alone perhaps, fiend. To me, my warriors!
10	PECHORIN:	More of these accursed Enakites. Too many! Well, another time, Mr Carter. We will have the Book.
11	SOUND:	RUNNING FOOTSTEPS
12	CARTER:	Not so fast, Pechorin!
13	VON STRANN:	Look out, Jack! He has a gun!
14	SOUND:	GUNSHOT
15	MUSIC:	DRAMATIC FLOURISH
1	NARRATOR:	Has the villainous Pechorin shot our hero? Who *are* the mysterious strangers. Find out now as the adventure continues in ... 'Jack Carter and the Book of the Gods'.
2	MUSIC:	MAIN TITLE THEME
3	SOUND:	RUNNING FOOTSTEPS

4	CARTER:	Not so fast, Pechorin!
5	VON STRANN:	Look out, Jack! He has a gun!
6	SOUND:	A PUNCH FOLLOWED BY A GUNSHOT
7	VON STRANN:	My God, that was close. Hold him, Jack. Don't let him get away.
8	PECHORIN:	Damn you, Carter. Get … your … hands … off me.
9	CARTER:	My hands, Pechorin? How about my fist?
10	SOUND:	A PUNCH. A BODY SLUMPING TO THE FLOOR
11	CARTER:	Well, I guess Futurist technology's no match for a good left hook, eh, Baron? But what about the Princess?
12	ANAT:	Shamash! Utu!
13	STRANGER 1:	Sebitti … Sebitti …
14	SOUND:	A CRACK, CRUMBLING PLASTER
15	VON STRANN:	I think that answers your question, Jack.
16	ANAT:	Shamash! Utu!
17	SOUND:	A LOUDER CRACK
18	CARTER:	My God, is that … ?
19	VON STRANN:	The abubu power.
20	NARRATOR:	Yes, for Anat-Ashtarzi Alhazred is no ordinary Arab Princess, her Enakites no ordinary desert tribe. Guardians of the secret Book of the Gods since the days of ancient Egypt, her people have the power to shatter stone walls, to smash through doors of solid oak, to stop a steam train dead in its tracks with one single mighty word. But the Enakites are not the only ones with such power.
21	STRANGER 1:	Sebitti … Sebitti …
22	VON STRANN:	The wall! Get out of the way, Princess!
23	SOUND:	EXPLOSION

1	CARTER:	[COUGHING] Are you OK, Baron? Princess?
2	ANAT:	I am safe, Jack Carter. But the Baron ...
3	VON STRANN:	I'm trapped. My foot's caught under this stone.
4	CARTER:	Here, take that end, Princess. Ready? Now!
5	SOUND:	THUD OF STONE BEING TOPPLED
6	CARTER:	Can you walk?
7	VON STRANN:	I can try.
8	CARTER:	That's the spirit. Hold him up, Princess. Say, where did those two scoundrels go?
9	ANAT:	The unkin? They have escaped, Jack Carter. I am sorry I could not stop them.
10	CARTER:	Well, we still have this snake. Wake up, Pechorin.
11	PECHORIN:	[GROANS] Where am I?
12	ANAT:	Leave him, Jack Carter. We must hurry. We must leave before the unkin return with weapons.
13	CARTER:	Sorry, Princess, but this whole building's going to come down. He may be a lousy Futurist but I won't leave him here to die. Besides, we might need him to get past the Turks.
14	VON STRANN:	But there are hundreds of them. How ... ?
15	ANAT:	You forget our secret weapon, my friends. The Turkish guns are nothing against our abubu power. Even now, all over the city, the soldiers are in flight. By nightfall the city will be ours.
16	PECHORIN:	Hah! You might be able to hold out against the Turks, but ... [LAUGHS]
17	CARTER:	But what?
18	PECHORIN:	Right now, Captain Carter, a fleet of the finest Prussian Zeppelins, carrying the most powerful fire-bombs known to man, is on its way to raze this city to the ground ... and all of your Enakite friends with it.
1	VON STRANN:	It's not possible.
2	PECHORIN:	Oh, but it is, Herr Baron. Your countrymen

have been supplying our airfleet for years, both ships and crews. Everyone knows that.

3 CARTER: No. The Russian fleet is in the Caucasus. If it were on the move, by God, the British would know about it.

4 PECHORIN: Indeed, but the *Prussians* have merchant vessels serving every corner of the Middle East, Captain Carter; and if these airships can carry passengers or freight then . . .

5 VON STRANN: They can just as easily carry bombs.

6 PECHORIN: Yes, we signed the treaty with your Chancellor Hitler weeks ago, Baron. All we needed was the agreement of the Turks, a landing place in the Syrian Protectorate where we could carry out some modifications, and now . . . Now, Captain Carter, we are about to burn the British out of Palestine entirely. Your country and mine together, Baron. You should be proud.

7 VON STRANN: Damn those Futurists. How could my countrymen have gone so wrong?

8 CARTER: No time to think about that now, Baron. We have to get word to the Allies at Basra. How long can your people hold the city?

9 ANAT: Against the Turks? Forever. But the Futurists with these flying war-machines? I do not know. But Basra – it is many days' ride across the desert. There are those who say it cannot be done.

10 CARTER: We don't have days, Princess. We have hours. There's only one thing to do. Baron, I saw a Turkish ornithopter overhead the other day. They must have a small airfield.

11 VON STRANN: Just outside the Jericho Gate.

12 CARTER: Think you can fly one if we get you to it?

13 VON STRANN: Better than von Richenbach himself if need be.

14 CARTER: Fly to Basra. Ask for Lord George Curzon and

		tell him ... tell him Mad Jack Carter sent you. Tell him everything you've heard.
15	VON STRANN:	And what about you, Jack?
16	CARTER:	I'm not leaving here without the Professor.
17	ANAT:	But we do not know where he is, Jack Carter.
18	CARTER:	No, but our Futurist friend here, or his colleagues, might well have some answers. At least, I'm keen to ask the questions.
19	ANAT:	But these are not normal men, my friend. You have seen their power, but you do not understand the danger.
20	CARTER:	Princess, I never understand the danger.

A Wildwood's Branches, Twigs and Thorns

The angels turn as the door splits and then shatters into the torture room, a rain of burning splinters. They're still turning as the first wave of the song streams in – *screams* in – through the ragged doorway, tearing the air around it as it comes, and hits them as a blast of sound. Jack feels the noise sweep under him, around him, through him, feels himself carried in it, spun and slammed against a wall where plaster crumbles as the names and dates scored by a decade's worth of prisoners flower beneath his fingers. Loops and swoops of Roman, Arabic and Hebrew letters just ... erupt, unswirling out so fast – so fast he's falling and he hasn't hit the floor yet, but already the whole surface of the wall is scratchworked, an engraver's study of a wildwood's branches, twigs and thorns. He hits the ground and bloodstains bubble up out of the concrete floor. The liquid blackens. Droplets dribble, skittering like mercury. He feels the fracturing of space itself as the song – more a war-cry than a song, more an invocation than a war-cry – breaks reality like a hammer-blow to a skull. Slow as a punch-drunk boxer, Jack raises his head to look into the shattered room.

The angels turn.

*

Pechorin stumbles in. Blood trickling from his nose and ears, he lurches, reaches out towards the dreadlocked demons, only to be spat to one side with a word, just twisted off the floor, flicked spinning through the air. A woman in black robes and black djellaba stands there, veil loose from her face, no weapon in her hands but all the more impressive for that scorn. Jack doesn't doubt she has no need for gun or sword – the blast still echoing in his bones tells him that much – but just to underline the point, it seems, she steps in past the wreckage of the doorframe, arms spread wide, her hands palm-up. She speaks, and a second shockwave even stronger than the first scythes through the room, a sword of visual sound that shreds space into forms impossible in any logical geometry, a word of fire that rips time into–

– angels crouching, singing fire against her as–

– she stands, her wings outspread above–

– Tamuz laid dead upon the altar in the Beth Ashtart where–

– Jack is slamming a full clip into Pechorin's Luger–

– There, says Jack. Your man should be in there. MacChuill's in that cell over there as well, I think.

A rush of blood to his head, sudden and dizzying. Three days of hell, it's no wonder that he's weak, but there's no time for that, no fucking time.

– You get your Eyn, he says to her. Samuel's notes should be . . .

He doesn't bother finishing, just flicks his hand and starts into a jog as the Enakite leader nods and grabs Pechorin by his collar. She drags the blackshirt round in front of her and shoves him out across the courtyard, heading for the cell. Jack chambers a bullet in Pechorin's Luger as he reaches the corridor to the offices, hears a rasping sound. He crouches by a guard's dead body, ducks a glance in through the open door and out again. He takes a deep breath, leaning against the door jamb. Merciful Christ. He's seen worse, he reminds himself; it was worse than this in France. He thinks of a grenade exploded by accident in a dugout – *We was just fooling, sir, just having a laugh and, Jesus, but it just slipped out of his hand, sir* – and he had to stand at the entrance as the poor bastards detailed to clean up wiped their comrade off the wall and hated him for the order.

That doesn't help a bit.

Jack tries not to picture the carnage happening as he picks his way through the aftermath, slipping on the slick of blood and bile. He tries not to imagine how the red splatters and shreds of skin and cloth sprayed across the walls and ceiling got there. Instead he just quietly steps over the survivor – the thin guard, it is, curled up on his side, knees under his chin, crippled by nausea, retching and gasping and retching again – and pushes open the door into Pechorin's office.

We watch you stop in the doorway, gaze into the crawling chaos of us covering every inch of floor and wall and ceiling with our scribbles of sentience. We see the flash of fear, incomprehension on your face, and so we scatter, skitter to open a path for you straight to the table where Hobbsbaum's notes sit waiting in their neat piles, sorted by thread or theme: *here* all the journals of Jacks of this world and that world, other futures, other pasts, but all dealing with the death of Tamuz; *there* all the transcripts of Anat's folk tales as told to your friend, your mentor, Samuel; *here* all the histories of von Strann's role in the salvation or destruction of Tell-El-Kharnain; *there* all the fictions of that fiery apotheosis, radio plays and movies, books and bibles.

You walk slowly into the room, up to the table, and reach out to gather up these pages – and we rush then, ripple in as a swirl of whirlpool, back to the pages we're unbound from, to the hand that touches them, to the heart with the hatchwork graving. So fast, so fleet, so flighty we are, Oh Jack, even you, quick as a flash, aren't fast enough to snatch your hand away before the room is barren of us, and your heart full.

You feel us now, within you. You know what we are and what *you* are, Jack. You pick up the pages of us, shove us down into the saddlebag and sling it over your shoulder. You look round at the blank walls of the room. We are not there; we are inside you now. You hear us in your heart.

This is our story now, we tell you. Ours, our friends, our splintered Jacks of every trade, you myriad of mortal men miscast as heroes in a play.

And you know what you have to do.

538

Wisdom, Justice and Mercy

As Ab Irim said to his servant Eliezer, an old man if he has truly lived should have wisdom, justice and mercy, for with years come wisdom, and there is no wisdom that does not rest on justice, and there is no justice that does not rest on mercy. But with old age also comes blindness, and those who cannot see must act on faith. And with old age also comes weakness, and those who cannot resist the strong must obey them. And with old age also comes deafness, and those who cannot hear the cries of others cannot know their suffering.

So it was that as Ab Irim grew old in years, for all that he grew wise and just and merciful, his vision and his strength and his hearing began to fail. So when his wife did not bear a child he took her maid impatiently, blind to the pain he caused her. And when his wife gave him a son herself and said that he must send the maid and her child away, he did not have the strength to deny her. And when the maid begged him not to send them out into the desert with only a little food and a skin of water, he did not hear her pleas, deaf to her misery. And so Ab Irim, on that day, was not wise or just or merciful. But on the day he told this to his servant Eliezer, Ab Irim wept for what he had done.

And so it was that as Ab Irim grew old in years, for all that he was wise and just and merciful, when the Lord called on him to take his wife's son who he loved above all others, to go to the region of Moriah, and there upon a mountain sacrifice him as a burnt offering, for all that this act seemed mad, unjust and cruel, Ab Irim agreed.

In the morning, then, he saddled his donkey and cut wood for a burnt offering. He took his son and two servants, one to carry the fire and one to carry the knife, and they travelled to the region of Moriah. They travelled for a day into the desert, and when they camped that night, the son turned to his father.

Father, he asked, where is the lamb for the burnt offering?

The Lord will provide, Ab Irim answered.

They travelled for another day into the hills and when they camped that night, the son turned to his father.

Father, he asked, where is the lamb for the burnt offering?

The Lord will provide, Ab Irim answered.

They travelled for a third day into the mountains and when they camped that night, the son turned to his father.

Father, he asked, where is the lamb for the burnt offering?

The Lord will provide, Ab Irim answered.

Then Ab Irim took the wood for the burnt offering and gave it to his son to carry, and he himself carried the fire and the knife. They left the two servants and the donkey, and the two of them went on together until they had reached the proper place. Here Ab Irim stopped and built an altar and arranged the wood upon it. He took his son, bound him, and laid him on the altar as a sacrifice. He reached out his hand and took the knife to slay his son, but as he raised the knife above the boy, a voice called out to him from the bushes:

Do not lay a hand upon the boy. Do not do anything to him. I know that you are blind and trust your Lord. I know that you are weak and fear your Lord. I know that you are deaf and hear only your Lord. But look at the knife you hold over his heart, take strength from the love that is in your own, and with that same heart listen to his cries for mercy. Do not lay a hand upon the boy.

Then Ab Irim looked up and there in a thicket he saw a man whose face was like an angel's, and who wore the skins of animals. He had upon his head two horns like those of a ram or a goat. Ab Irim asked him:

Where, then, is the lamb for the burnt offering?

I am Ishmael, said the man, and I also am your son, the son you sent out into the desert. If you must make a burnt offering to your Lord, then I will die upon the altar. Do this and your seed will not die out. Do this and your sons will be as many as the stars in the sky and the sand on the seashore. Do this and your sons will take possession of the cities of their enemies, and through your offspring all nations on earth will be blessed.

And Ab Irim bound Ishmael and sacrificed him as a burnt offering in the place of his wife's son, and the seed of Ab Irim lived on and multiplied, and became great. But it is said that the Lord was angry with the sacrifice of Ishmael. It is said that the seed of Ab Irim is both blessed and cursed, that even as it multiplies and becomes great, his sons as many as the stars in the sky and as the sand on the seashore, one day the Lord will claim what is his. It is said that one day Ab Irim's seed, all of them, will lie upon the altar of the Lord, and there will be no voice this time to stop the knife.

Trapped in Style

The militiamen haul in their prisoner in a straitjacket and ankle-chains, snarling and spitting like a cat half in a bag, his head whiplashing side to side, limbs jerking wild against the straps. Strangely, it strikes Arturo, he seems to be struggling as much against himself as against his captors; Arturo recognises a certain madness in the eyes, a mania of despair. The man whirls on the archivist, glaring – *don't even try to read me, fucker*. He opens his mouth to spit hatred, then stops, laughs. He smiles, lowers his head, mutters a word of Cant under his breath, and the world shimmers round him. The straitjacket flickers, shifts . . . settles.

– Jack Flash, says the Duke.

The prisoner grins at the Duke now, shrugs smugly in his paisley-patterned velvet straitjacket. He's still trapped, right enough, bound by the leather straps and buckles of steel . . . or by the gravings stitched and scored in them, at least. But at least he's trapped in style.

– Fuck it, mate, he says, you've got me banged to rights. Jack Flash, avatar of chaos, angel assassin, fairy fury, yah-de-yah and blah-de-blah, at your service.

He runs the tip of his tongue around his lips, bats his eyelids, blows a kiss. But there's something in his tone of voice that's not quite right: under the cock of charisma, a certain coldness that Arturo recognises every bit as much as all the fiery rage. The scientist looks at the archivist.

– That *is* confirmed, isn't it? he says. This *is* our man?

– Compatibility positive on all morphologies, we say blankly.

And Joey Narcosis looks at us from deep inside the glamour of Jack, so drenched in the soul-juice of our saucy favourite that even we can only just make out the dark outline of him, the here-and-there hints of a hollow man, in the edge of cruelty to his manic grin, the black of pupils behind a glint so gleaming with the power, the glory of our luscious lad.

Even his wink at us is just so exquisitely Jack.

Arturo makes a twirling motion with a finger; technicians burst into activity, unlocking, levering, cranking. A section of the gantry underfoot swings up and away, and a sarcophagus of metal glowing with a colour too cold to be gold, too hot to be silver, rises upright through the empty space in the grille-work. Featured with the smooth face of a Tut headdressed in stylised dreadlocks, sulcate in its gravings like scales or feathers, like a package wrapped in palm fronds, the sarcophagus speaks of shabti and karibu, of ancient graves and their guardians.

— Peachy keen, says Joey Narcosis. An Adamantium Maiden.

The Duke Irae strides over to him, leans in close to pierce him with his gaze. He clamps a hand over the prisoner's mouth — *shut up* — only to pull it away with a start, wiping slobber off on the shoulder of the straitjacket. Joey Narcosis licks his lips.

— Salty, he says. You been fiddling with yerself?

The Duke's upper lip twitches in disgust.

— Arturo, he says, I assume you're ready.

— Absolutely.

A flick of Arturo's hand, a clack of a lever, and the latches of the sarcophagus unsnick, seals hissing steam. The sculpted face levers up like a helmet's visor. A seam opens down the front, and shoulders roll back, metal cloak unfurling up and out, splaying wide into eight sets of wings, petals of a metal orchid blossoming to reveal red silken innards . . . all framed by the obsidian sphere of the Echo Chamber behind it. Arturo motions and the militiamen drag their prisoner backwards into the coffin. Joey still plays the arch anarchist as they clunk and click him into place.

— Don't I get a last request then? A final fag? A grand soliloquy on your scheme for world domination?

The Duke paces back and forth like some caged beast, a single word resounding in his thoughts: *glory*. He looks at the prisoner, then down through the grille-work to the chaos beneath their feet.

— All you get is oblivion, he says. Do it, Arturo.

And the coffin curls its cold embrace round Joey, hissing sealed and rising up and back towards the Echo Chamber, the black sphere of *us*. We wait, eager for his emptiness to touch us, to enter us, so we can understand it truly.

The Answerers and the Answers

If the city was in rout and riot when the Turks arrived, now it is simply this: revenge. Everywhere the Enakites are striding, cloaked in their whirlwind song of anguish and rage. Everywhere the Turks and Palestinians, Europeans, Jews and Arabs flee, these players of the great game, these pretenders to an empty throne in a holy land of milk and honey, oil and blood, salt and ink. The sons of Sodom have returned to claim their city and we, *we* are the words of their wrath, the dust under their feet rising to cloak their coming, the fire from their mouths smashing the walls. The buildings fall, masonry crumbling as the chorus of the Enakite voices thunders like a waterfall, like a thousand rivers roaring.

In the courtyard of the prison, Phreedom, Inanna, Anna, Anat-Ashtarzi Alhazred raises her fist and we come streaming in around the Enakites, over the rubble of defensive wall, through shattered gates, down streets and alleyways, reflections on windows, shadows in doorways. From the north, the south, the east, the west, whirling in over the prison roof and down towards her graven arm, we come, the answerers and the answers to her call.

Palm open, arm outstretched, she utters a word of Cant and we obey.

The blast punches a hole wide as a barn door all the way through to the street outside. A Turkish soldier scrambles to his feet amongst the dust and rubble, turning in horror. A quiet word from Anat, and he stops dead in his tracks. His body shudders, cracks, falls limp and lifeless to the ground, blood trickling from his ears and eyes.

She leads them out over the rubble, stepping coldly over the soldier's body, drags Pechorin staggering behind her, hands bound, blindfolded, stumbling like a beast led to the slaughter. Von Strann, his arm over MacChuill's supporting shoulder, limps behind. And Jack – with Tamuz in his arms, with Tamuz always in his arms, his body cold and warm, alive and dead, eyes open and closed – Jack follows, cradling his featherweight burden.

Where did he find the boy? you ask.

Everywhere.

They walk out through the city, through a thousand folds of it, where Tamuz lies on this street, that street, here or there, slumped in a doorway, crumpled by a wall, shot, stabbed, blasted and broken. Everywhere Jack looks, he sees the boy, ghost-images from other threads of time, the endless shades of this eternal victim. Everywhere the boy is dead, except held in his arms.

Uncertainty unleashed onto the quaking streets, we rip a path for them to walk, a world, a fold, where Tamuz will not die, where Jack *will not bloody let him die*, his will unspoken but graven in every muscle that he uses now to hold this single flickering spectre of . . . a possibility.

They walk north, through the panicked mob and raging Enakites, towards the Jericho Gates and the Airfields beyond. They walk out onto the North Road, into the vanguard of the Enakites, and, as they do, a band of seven of Alhazred's people fall in behind, moving in a group, a circle of six with another in their centre, carrying a wooden box. It is not the Ark of the Covenant, not the ark of any Covenant. It is not Pandora's box, the punishment meted on humanity for their audacity in taking from Prometheus his gift of fire.

It is all of these and more.

– The time has come, says Anat

She calls the carrier of the Book out of the circle of his comrades, and the warrior steps forward tentatively. She takes the box from him and turns to Jack, who lets his gaze flick from Tamuz's face just long enough to note her standing over them, the boy lain on the ground, Jack crouching over him.

– We know that Lord Curzon will hold Basra, she says, but that if you try to take the Book to him you will fail. But we know also that the Eyn is not fated to die here with us, that you will get him out alive. You understand?

Jack nods. She smiles at von Strann.

– You must do what Captain Carter says, my friend. Trust him. We *can* trust you, yes, Jack Carter?

Jack looks along the North Road, thinking of the Airfields. He looks at Reinhardt, who seems stronger now, as if the chaos of the city has made him more ... determined. He looks at Tamuz. At the box.

– I give you my word, he says, I'll keep your Eyn alive. And the Book will be taken care of.

And Tamuz, he thinks. Above them all, Tamuz.

Anat crouches beside him, and he turns, puts a hand up to his chest, and then to hers, the Enakite oath more binding in its silence than any words.

The Lambs of God

[...] so [...] stood there with [...] pipe forgotten in [...] hand, staring at this wild woman of the desert, listening as she laid it out to [...]. And if the blood of one generation is so powerful, she asked [...], what then of the blood of thousands, millions, of this chosen people? [...] was speechless for a second before recovering [...] enough to say that this was only one of the many possible futures written in the Book, many pasts. Surely there must be some way to know what's true and what's false within the Book.

Perhaps, she said. But we have studied the Book for many generations, and we do not know this thing. A long time ago, we did, but ...

She shook her head. This was knowledge too dangerous to remember.

That was when [...] decided that [...] would, if [...] life depended on it, discover that knowledge for [...].

We can change it, [...] said to her. There are ways to change the text, to modify an accent here or there, to make a note between two words or in the margins, a single stroke of ink that can change the whole meaning of it. She sighed.

Many millennia ago, she told [...], there were those who tried to change the Book. They thought they could prevent that single act of horror, that five-year massacre, that holocaust. They failed.

Surely this one thing could be changed, [...] insisted. Surely this one thing could be stopped. [...] refused to accept that in every one of the countless different futures written in the Book, in every godforsaken one of them, the same result always played out.

And that is when [...] decided to steal the page, to alter it if [...] could, and if not then to destroy it.

As long as neither Heaven nor Hell has the Book, then both are bound by it; their lives are written, sealed. The Enakites know this from the demons that they guard. And they know more; they guard another dreadful truth.

There is no God, she has told [...]. There never was. Only *gods*.

They have learned this from these prisoners of the War in Heaven, how they were brought in chains before an empty throne, told of the plan to bring peace to the world, sort out the wheat from the chaff in the threshing mill of history. Promised eternal peace at the end of it all. Those ruined creatures in the cave are those who chose not to submit, intransigent rebels, warmongers and tyrants who would never be persuaded to give up their little kingdoms as gods on earth.

So the Enakites guard the Book, and study it, and watch the world. They *watch*, while all the time a war goes on deep in the shadows, in the unwritten margins, each side seeking to free themselves from the word that binds them, each side weaving their plots and their conspiracies into a net that binds us all more surely, more inescapably than even the accursed Book itself.

We walk between the curses of the Lord and his Enemy, she says. Why? The Adonai or the Shaitan – which would [...] rather have own [...] soul? she asks. And am [...] sure that they are not in fact one thing in its two most terrible aspects: the Lord of the Dead and the Enemy of the Living?

A Hidden God, a Dark God, split into seven souls. Bound in the Book and in the flesh of all of us, waiting to be released. And on that page the holocaust from which He will be born, a graving of so many lives inscribed in sigils which, [...] understand now, can be read as a single word.

And it only has to be spoken aloud.

Their Words, Like Swords of Fire

They walk through ragdoll bodies of every race that calls the region home.

– So tell me, Jack shouts over the noise, is this in your damned Book?

– Yes, says Anat-Ashtarzi Alhazred quietly. This too is written in the Book of all Hours.

– Then damn your Book, he says.

He turns away from the warrior woman in disgust, thinking of burning faces on the field at Majkops, screaming faces splattered by the Futurists' new incendiaries, petroleum jelly that stripped the skin right off the flesh. He can hardly see where they're going, or who's still with him, through the smoke and dust of the Enakite attack. It seems even worse ahead.

– Wait here, he says.

He's about to step out into the Silkmarket when the flames bringing down the fleeing mob all round are met with a sudden barrage, fire met with fire, a blast cutting down two of the Enakite warriors, then another. Flattened against the wall, peering round a wooden support beam at the carnage in the square, Jack searches out the source of it, seeing, God, the massacre of the wretches, unthinking in their utter panic as they pour into the square where—

Fuck.

The two angels stand upon the remnants of the city walls like guardian gargoyles, one on either side of the Jericho Gate, their words, like swords of fire, scything across the crowd. Many of the mob try to turn as they see the devastation, but the mass behind pushes them onwards into the cross-fire set down by, perhaps, the same two creatures who razed this city to the ground however many thousand years ago.

A word blasts into masonry beside him and he jerks back out of danger, feeling a hand on his arm.

– Carter Bey! Jack, you must—

He whips his head round but the boy's not there, only an echo of a different world, an after-image gone before Jack even really glimpses it, as insubstantial as the vision from another fold ... of the boy lying dead in von Strann's apartment. Jack shuts these from his mind, focuses on the figure cradled in Anat's arms, fluttering on the border between life and death.

Pechorin raises his head as if to sniff the air.

– They're coming, says the Russian. Can't you hear the echoes?

Jack looks at the smirk on the blackshirt's face. It grows wider.

– History will be made here today.

– Captain Carter, snaps von Strann. Jack, pull yourself together, man.

Jack's knuckles whiten round the Webley's grip, the gun pointed at Pechorin's head as he rips the bastard's blindfold off with his other hand.

– Pechorin, he says, listen to me well, Major. Were you working for these ... *creatures* alone? Or has your whole damn Reich sold whatever filth they have for souls? Who else knows what you were here for?

– Let me kill him, says the Enakite chief, whisper a word into his ear that will cut his soul out of his body. He will die, hollow and dark inside, by his own knife.

Von Strann lays a hand on her arm, lowers Jack's gun with a finger.

– He may know where Samuel is.

Please, Carter Bey: another whisper of Tamuz in his ear, another glimpse out of the corner of his eye, another flash of a fold where Tamuz is unharmed for now but still, inevitably, dies. Inside, he is screaming at us to let him be, it is too much, he can only live in one world at a time.

Then Tamuz will live in none of them, we say.

He pulls back from Pechorin, uncocks the gun.

– He may know where Samuel is, he echoes.

– Then let me tear that knowledge from him, says Anat.

– The Beth Astart, Pechorin mutters.

Tears run down his cheeks from under the blindfold as whispered hatred echoes in his head, perhaps forever, an infinity of voices flooding rational thought out of his mind. He's told them all he can, where he first met the angels Azazel and Michael, and where Samuel Hobbsbaum was last seen kneeling beneath the Weeping Angel.

The blackshirt does not know what happened. The angels had tracked Hobbsbaum down to the derelict temple. They were just about to seize him when ... time broke, space folded. One moment they were entering the Beth Astart, Pechorin and the angels, closing on their prey, and the next they were standing by the Ink Wells on the edge of town, looking at the rising vapours, with the sun low in the sky. When they returned there was no sign of Hobbsbaum in the temple. There was no sign of him in the whole city.

Out in the Silkmarket, the angels and the Enakites have stopped slaughtering civilians – no longer by design, at least – turning their attention to each other instead. Anat is already yelling orders to her people but they're at a disadvantage; the angels have a perfect killing zone set up.

– The Beth Astart, mutters Pechorin.

The Wings of Some Peacock Angel

The adamantium coffin settles on the steel grille flooring once again. Technicians unclasp clips, unbuckle straps, unfasten hasps and snap grips back to free the coffin, like assistants to some complex magic trick approaching resolution. One puts his hand upon the lid of the sarcophagus and – as blue-green steam jets, hissing, from the casket's seals – snatches it back immediately as if burnt or chilled right to the bone. He backs away, looking to Dr Arturo for an answer to a question that he can't put into words.

Arturo, silent as a man awaiting an execution he has come to accept, steps forward, brushes the technician aside and lays his own hand firmly on the door. As he opens it, we open up his heart.

Inside is only a sleek blackness, rippling and reflective as oil, filling the casket as it had once filled the sphere. Arturo gazes into its depths with the closest feeling that he has to awe, not awe itself, but something quieter, a sort of yearning to reach his hand out into it, to touch it, to step into this strange liquid night; it is, he supposes for an instant – the analytic aspect of his mind examining his own reaction as he would study any experimental subject – quite similar to the vertiginous desire that draws one to the edge of any precipice. He makes a mental note that he should probably increase his daily dose of his adrenal inhibitors so as to extinguish such subjective responses in the future. He is still calculating the new amount of his prescription personality-killers when the figure comes out of the darkness.

And, for the first time in ten years, Dr Arturo weeps.

It comes out of the darkness, shadows sliding from its cool face like it's rising from a pool of ink, and as it comes we shadows follow it, curling, furling around it and behind it, shifting from black to blue-green, iridescent like the wings of some peacock angel. We wrap ourselves to it, adopting the contours of its body, withdrawing a little here and there, until eventually it stands there – he stands there – a man with eyes grey like a wolf, with hair crow-black and slicked back, in a simple black suit and black tie over a white shirt, a long black woollen overcoat draped casually over one forearm like a waiter with a towel.

The Duke Irae studies Joey Narcosis, and Joey studies the Duke, an old lion and a young panther, prowling round each other, silently because the feline growl of their natures comes through in every quiet cultivated movement of their bodies.

The Duke admires this thing he thinks his own creation, this six-fold soul as close to God as they can come without the Name, pure chaos bound into the order of the grave.

– The hero is dead, says the Duke. Long live the hero.
The barest flicker of emotion passes over the dream-killer's face

and the archivist finds itself oddly unable to pin down the nature of this brief instant of affect, for while its own mindlessness allows the bioform to eavesdrop most effectively on all those who incorporate themselves into the narrative of His Lordship's life, in this case it seems to hear only an echo of its own emptiness. Joey Narcosis looks at Arturo, and the tiniest hint of a wry, bitter-sweet smile plays across his lips. Arturo understands it in an instant. We tell him everything, in an instant, and he understands how he has failed the Duke, how he has wonderfully, gloriously failed the Duke. He tries not to laugh.

Joey looks at the Duke and there's a glint in his ice eyes, a light too fiery to be silver, too bone-white to be gold, but wild like adamantium, a flash. Like the flash of the knife as the overcoat flips from his arm in a slick quick flip and flick which sends an adamantium blade deep into the Duke's forehead in the instant that the Duke himself also understands, too late, that he has bound not the hero but the traitor.

Joey turns to the edge of the abyss below, the bottomless pit with a little side-tunnel into Tell-el-Kharnain, 1921. Enough with the gazing into it, he thinks.

Time to jump.

Errata

The Fury of Seamus Finnan

Enki lies on the floor. Metatron lies on the floor. This poor deluded bastard who was once a human being, who's been stripped down to the cold bones of identity, rebuilt in needle and ink, and now nailed to the truth of himself by the Cant – he lies on the floor, his face, his name, his fucking soul itself flicking back and forth, caught in that moment of transformation by the bitmites crawling in the substance of his self. We feel no pleasure in this, only the fury of our friend, the fury of Seamus Finnan.

– Yer man *Sammael* never resigned, snarls Seamus. He didn't walk away. He didn't break the Covenant. *He was never fookin part of it.*

Phreedom and Harker have his arms, trying to pull him back, but we root him to the spot. We show them what the scribe is seeing, let them hear the scream of desperation in his head as, in the regraving of his identity, he finally understands how he created destiny itself.

– Ye had it all planned out. Sure and ye had the part all written for him. God's right hand, eh? The eternal rebel. It was me, ye see, Phree, or at least it was Sammael as was supposed to be the one sat on the throne. Yer man here knew that one day the empty throne wouldn't be enough. Oh, we have to have our fookin heroes, our fookin darlings of destiny, and sure but who better than the great fookin Shamash with his blond hair and blue eyes, god of the fookin sun shinin out of his fookin arse. Captain of the fookin angels. Bringer o the fookin light. Fook that fer a game of sodjies. Fook it all sideways with a fookin French letter on.

– Except he told ye to fuck off. And while ye were busy working this into your fookin bullshit story, cutting the lie so deep into yerself that even you believed it, yer man Sammael just left yez all to yer fookin self-delusions. Now if I were him I'd have just fookin hid. The

Vellum is a large place, ye know; there are folds half-dream and half-delusion and ... if I were him, fuck knows, I'd try and forget I'd ever heard the word unkin. I'd forget the Cant entirely, leave yez to hunt and gather yer spearchuckers, leave yez to wipe each other out in one big game of cowboys and fookin Indians.

– But yer man, he made a right eedjit of hisself all through history trying to make it right, before I was finally born and he had this last-ditch attempt to sort things out. You and me, ole man. You and me, we've got some history together in the future ... so I hear. Sammael, Phreedom, Sammael. Sammael's what I become, and a right ole damnation it is too.

– I think he thought he could change things, save himself all the pain and horror of fucking fighting forever, and so ... and so ...

Seamus scrapes the chair across the floor so he can sit on it looking down over the angel.

– So he fucking found me staggering home from a fookin pub in Dublin in fookin 1914, having left all the lads talking their grand schemes of signing up for the sake of poor little fookin Belgium.

And Seamus tells them of this young lad, of this eedjit of a man, ready to go off with the lads, and how one drunken night changed all that, how even before he had to shoot his best friend for a coward, even before Seamus himself had to shoot the young boy he's fookin sworn to his sweetheart he'd protect, sure and even before he's got through it all alive, blessed and cursed now with the stirrings of the Cant in him, even before he starts to get these fookin visions of a Great War even worse than the fooker he's just come out of, before he learns that sure and it's a little more than shell-shock or the second sight, even before all that ... how the Cant was already graved in him.

– He went through yer fookin war, says Seamus, and he came out the other end, and he tried to tell me, see, he passed on a few things about who would live and who would die in the Somme, and how and for what and, Jesus Christ Almighty, I didn't want it to be true ... but I could see it all happening as he told it to me. And, for all that I fookin buried it so deep in me, for all that I never *knew* how I knew it, even as I was ordering Thomas to his death ... Oh, Christ, Phree, he told me in the Cant and I fookin *lived* it all.

– And so I fookin killed him, God help me, I fookin killed him.

And we bitmites show this fooker nailed to the floor just how it was, how before ye know it, before ye fookin know it, ye find ye're standing there with yer own fookin blood on yer hands and a body layin at yer feet, and yer staring into yer own fookin face and knowing how and when yer going to die. And that's when ye fookin realise, sure, that's when ye fookin feel it howling in yer fookin bones and tearing through yer body like a thousand fookin volts.

When someone tries to save yer life and ye fookin kill him.

– And you, he says to Metatron, ye fookin bastard motherfucking cunt, ye brought it all back with yer fookin binding. Ye rewrote yerself and yer fookin Covenant eedjits so yez forgot it all; but *he* knew yer war was pointless, and he told *me*, and by fuck it graved itself so deep in me I couldn't face the truth of it, or of what I'd done in the face of that truth … until you brought him out of me.

– Sure and maybe we should grave my story onto *you*, ye fookin cunt. Ye fuck with the scribe and ye fuck with the Book, eh? Sure and isn't there a little bit of sunlight in yer fookin soul, that ye might just have a bit of the ole Shamash in there, *Enki*.

Just the subtlest inflection warps the name, twists it with his fury and we blast a shockwave through the scribe's soul, a new history and a new future, as an Enki who thought he could change things, save us all the pain and misery, if he just found this young fool with his dreams of peace, persuaded him that he was on the wrong track, that the Covenant wouldn't end war, only offer the purest excuse for it. That it would all end up in one almighty battlefield full of corpses and crows.

We make his lesson brutal.

A Maze of Destinies

He was only a boy when his brother, when his other, found him in the fields, gathering wild grain with a stone sickle, and dragged this ungraved lord of the earth, Enoch, Enki, En Ki, Ki En, screaming into the Vellum, into—

– a charnel house of great *lamassu*, bulls with the wings of eagles and bearded heads of men, hung by their hind legs, upside down on conveyor belts of hooks; men with wings and horns and leather aprons slitting them open, pulling entrails out to slather down onto steel grilles and gutters of blood; row upon row of production-line slaughter; this young boy with dark skin and dreadlocks, loincloth and beads, slipping, sliding away to cower against a wall; the madman in his leather longcoat, broken by the apocalypse he's wrought, shouting at him – *I'll show you sacrifice*; dragging him to his feet and back out into the fields; the terrified boy sobbing at the vision shown him by this god of wrath, trying to appease his tormentor with a handful of grain, slapped from his hand and scattered to the wind and the sand whipped up around his feet; a disgusted cry – *this is nothing, nothing*; the madman venting his own self-loathing until the boy finds himself swinging the sickle and—

Enoch, Enki, En Ki, Ki En, lord of the earth, *quayin* in Hebrew, craftsman Cain stands over the body of his brother, his other, his self, whose name will be remembered now as the Hebrew word for *pride* . . . Abel.

We release him and the room is suddenly still, Finnan's fury spent, Enki's sobs fading into silence as we withdraw into the shadows.

– So sure and I don't know if I can change my own future – looks like I wasn't very successful the last time I tried – but, Christ, yer fucking apocalypse was bad enough for me to die trying once. I mean, knowing what I know now, knowing that I wouldn't listen, that I'd just end up dead and the other me still going through the same fucking pointless . . .

He laughs, desperation mixed with release.

– Sure and I'd probaby still be eedjit enough to try. But fuck it, we have to try *something*, Phreedom. Time in the Vellum, Phree. Who was it said it's not that simple? Maybe we can just walk away and break the loop. Maybe we can *all* just walk away and break the loop.

She shakes her head, looks at Harker. We feel the ambition in her, the Inanna in her, this New Age goddess with her host of Cold Men, dead men raised by her call, waiting to be graved with the names of dead gods.

– He told you there were others? Did he tell you where they are? Shit, they must know ... think of what they must know.

– Ah, Christ, Phree, walk away from it. Burn that fucking book and walk away from it.

– Where are the others? How many?

– Sure and didn't I say there were seven of them? Didn't I say ye were one of them, Phree. You and me and himself. You live through it, Phree, and what you become ... what you're becoming ...

He digs into his jacket pocket for his cigarettes, pulls one out, holds it.

– Do ye want to die in a tattoo parlour in Asheville as a queen of death, Phreedom? Is that what ye want?

– I ...

She stops.

– You tried to cheat the system, he says, and you ended up as a piece of meat, carved up by the bitch queen of Hell. What did that bitch queen look like, Phreedom?

– No, she says.

– You tried to save Thomas, and all you did was lead her demons to him, he says. But then you knew the story you were playing, Phree, so wasn't there maybe a little part of you thought you could buy your life with his?

– No, she says.

– Where's your son, Phree? Where's the wonder boy you were going to keep safe and sound from everything? Why isn't he here leading your fucking army, if he's the fucking bitmites on your arm born in human flesh?

– I lost him, she says, he was stolen, taken from me. I was ...

– More intent on destruction? Cause here you are now raising an army to destroy every unkin fucker in the Vellum. What did the bitch queen of Hell look like, Phreedom? Like the face you see in the mirror now?

He offers her the cigarette.

– You don't take this, you know, he says. As Sammael told it to me, I saw it all, Phree, and you don't take this. You call your Cold Men, Harker here and all the rest and, God help me, you bind me with yer fookin ink. That's what Sammael showed me. That's how you get me – him, I mean – fighting in your fucking war.

She looks at the cigarette. He holds his hand out closer to her.

– So take it and prove him wrong, he says.

– She's a fighter, Finnan.

Enki pulls himself to his feet. His voice is low, humble, the voice of a craftsman who's gathered dirt at a riverside to shape it into clay, taught others to shape the pot on the wheel, taught traders how the tokens in the pots can measure a deal, how the marks on the clay mean numbers, how clay tablets can tell tragedies and epics ... and all because he knows how fragile life is, the whole sorry mess of it. The voice of Enoch and Cain, the son and father, the creator who is his own creation, the builder of civilisation.

– You're right, he says. You always were. But Phreedom here ... she's always been a fierce one.

– Finnan, I can't just walk away, she says, do nothing, leave the Dukes to their apocalypse. What happens then? We just give up and—

– I don't know, he says. We do this, then, fuck, I don't know what'll happen. Everything Sammael told me will be worthless – a fookin prophecy you've proven wrong. But, I don't know, maybe the story he told me can be something to fookin learn from. The way things shouldn't be. The way things mustn't ever be.

He nods down at the cigarette.

– Suppose we find the Book of All Hours and we cut it up into little pieces. We stitch it back together so's every fookin fold of the Vellum it describes is bollocksed up. We fuck with it, Phree, until it doesn't make a lick of sense, and the Covenants and the Sovereigns and all the Dukes of the world can't build their empires without them collapsing. Spanners in the works, Phree, glitches in the system. We make the whole fookin Vellum a trap for them, a fookin maze of destinies no unkin fucker can ever master.

Harker stands in the doorway, waiting for her decision, her order.

– You say you want a revolution, Phree. I say we turn the whole world inside out. Let them think we're in the cage looking out, when it's them we're looking in at. And then? Well, I don't know any better than you, but what the fuck?

He grins.

– How does that sound? he says, and her hand is already reaching for the cigarette as he says: Phreedom?

7

The Unspoken Name

Teeth Steely Sharp, Silvery Sparkling

The elevator muzak cuts off abruptly and I wince at the hiss of static as the doors slide open onto the hotel corridor. A dude in sleek black suit and tie, black hair slicked back, is stubbing out a cigarette in some steel ashtray/bucket contraption at the side of the doors. Cute, in an angel of death sort of way. Black tear tattoo under one eye.

— Room 1313, says the mafioso Pierrot, far end of the corridor.

I have a very bad feeling about this: butterflies in my tummy and ants in my pants, sorta déjà vu meets heebie/jeebies. Don't know why — it's just another john looking to get jiggy — but as I'm walking down the corridor towards my waiting client, every hair on my furry little balls is telling me to turn and run. Black/suit dude looks just a little too expensive for a cabinet minister's bodyguard. I've got the feeling something else is going down tonight, other than Mr Minister or me.

I'm halfway along the corridor when I hear the chi/blast up ahead. Walls, floor and ceiling reverberate with the explosion. I stop, turn. Behind me black/suit dude is drawing a huge fucker of a double/barrelled chi/gun, a Scorpio 99, brand new and state/of/the/art . . . blow your head clean off your body, blow your soul right out into the chaosphere. Ah, fuck. In front of me, the door of Room 1313 kicks open and out of the billowing blue/green smoke of what could only be an orgone/bomb steps a sexy silhouette. As the trails wisp away around him, he comes clear — a grin, a gun, a glint.

*

Hair of flame and eyes of neon, he stands there in shreds of black and brown – leather, I think, under some kind of overcoat – all little more than rags now. I don't know what kinda *ubermensch* he is to walk out of a blast like that, but I can smell the orgone on him, like cheap aftershave on a car salesman. Fuck, I can taste it, feel it, raw and fiery, and I may be a professional hustler and a trained tantra adept, but I'm having a hard time not jizzing in my jockeys.

He winks at me, teeth steely sharp, silvery sparkling, and clenching a cheroot. And I'm staring down the barrel of the chi-gun in his right hand.

– Ah, Puck, he says. Duck!

I'm still lying on the floor, feeling plaster rain down on me, when his hand on my dog-collar pulls me, choking, to my feet. As he sets me down and lets go, I cough, try to gasp a complaint and cough again. I look at the black-suit dude slumped on the floor and against the wall in an obvious oxytocin daze, the wet patch on the crotch of his trousers.

– Sorry for the rough house, rough trade, says the madman as he swings me round into an embrace.

He plants a kiss on my lips, this sex-gunned maniac, mouth open, tongue headed for my tonsils. Pulls back after a ball-scrunching thirty seconds.

– You'll have to narrate this, pumpkin, he says. No time for chit-chat. Get on the astral to Fox and tell him . . . tell him I fucked up . . . again. Brace for temporal aftershocks and . . .

He trails off, head cocked like a dog's.

– What the fuck is going on? I say. Who the fuck are you?

He does a little shrug with a side-to-side bounce of the head that somehow I just know means, *Fuck, it figures.*

– I'm Jack, he says. And I'm here to rescue you, princess.

A Satchel of Scribblings as His Shield

– In one tale we tell, says Anat, the child Isaac was anointed for a sacrifice that never took place. He was promised to God; his life, his future, everything that might possibly come from him was to be slain and burned. Every scion of his line is forfeit to the Lord. In that story, God is well pleased each time a Jew is killed. This is the God the angels seek to summon.

Jack shakes his head. He perches like a mountain lion on an outcrop of wall, part shielded by it and gazing through binoculars at Azazel, likewise positioned on a crumbling turret at the Jericho Gate. He scans the wasted city. Only the Beth Astart remains unharmed. The Enakites consider it a sacred site, the temple of the last teraphim in the Holy Land. The angels are likewise concerned to keep it whole, but for another reason it would seem. He listens to the conversation down below though he already knows the story.

We *are* the story, after all.

– Ah, Christ All-fuckin-mighty, says MacChuill. The fuckin bampot–

Christ? thinks Jack. *Christ?* He thinks of Anat's words, of the slaughter of the innocents. Thinks of a whole generation dead and what an offering it would be if the sole survivor were nailed up to a cross to die. The lamb of God. Isaac Mark Two.

He looks down at Anat, tries to form the question, manages only:

– Christ?

– In the tale we tell of that, says Anat, the slaughter of the innocents was an attempt by Jibril – Gabriel, you would call him – to bind God into a body with blood. He acted alone, though, without the authority of the Host, so it is said that Metatron found a twin of your Good Shepherd to die on the cross in Yeshua's place. The rabbi lived; his poor beloved disciple died.

Makes little difference either way, thinks Jack. What the fuck is this Book of All Hours worth if they don't use it, if the Enakites just spend centuries, millennia, God knows, standing idly by, watching the slaughter? If this shepherd lives but another dies in his place, some poor scapegoat.

Thomas Didymos, thinks Jack, suddenly.

He looks at the wooden box and the satchel, both lying at his feet, and comes to a decision.

*

– Can we get by the fuckers? calls MacChuill. What can ye see?

Jack says nothing, simply closes the flap on his satchel and buckles it, mind blank as a monk's in meditation, and rises, throwing the wooden box down to von Strann, steps up clear of his cover, and then screams out across the city at the angel of death, not with our Cant, we realise, but with something simpler and more honest and more human, calling the angel out in the tongue of his homeland, calling down his own destruction, and we panic, rush to him to fill his eyes with fire, to fill his voice with ours, throw his hand forward to catch the lightning with a flick of a finger and a thumb as only our Jack can do, but he throws off all our mastery of this liquid language, flicks us off with a shake of the head, throwing his arms out wide to take the blast full in the chest, to die, to be destroyed, and then at the last fraction of a second swinging his leather satchel round in front of him, with a single motion of his lips, a word, it seems, so quiet that even we can't hear it, and with a satchel of scribblings as his shield against a sword of fire, he lets it hit him and—

He comes crashing down the wall, backwards and folded over, hits the ground on his back, arms spread. There's nothing of the leather satchel left except for a shred of handle, and there's little left of the front of his shirt either. He can feel it. He can feel his chest open to the air, cool on the outside but burning inside, fucking burning something fierce. Even the hand he was holding the satchel with, the whole arm, feels like it's on fire.

He opens his eyes. Tamuz is kneeling over him, checking for a pulse. Jack feels the involuntary spasm of his own jaw-muscle, a tightening of his chest. Tamuz's hand on his skin. The wonder in the boy's voice.

– Your scars are gone, the lad says, running a hand over the smooth skin of a chest that should be charred, scorched back to bone, to ash even.

Tamuz and MacChuill pull Jack up to his feet, MacChuill leaning on his rifle to make up for his own wounded leg. He reaches to take the box back from von Strann, tucks it under his left arm.

– So can we fuckin get tae the Beth Astart fae here or no? he says.

– We can bloody well try, says Jack.

[. . .] cannot let it happen this way. They have told [. . .] that the Book
is a living thing. The skin of angels living on even after it has been
stripped from off their bodies, though what is graved on it, in this
abominable Cant, fades over time. So with each generation they
must write the future and the past anew, with words that, when
spoken, send tremors through the world itself. They never change
it, they tell [. . .], remaining neutral, walking between the curses of
the Lord and the Enemy, as they say, denying Heaven and Hell with
equal resolution. But it *could* be changed. The course of history
could be altered.

So [. . .] must try, even if it means [. . .] own obliteration.

The Egyptians talked of seven souls: Sekhu, the dust of the corporeal
bodies that we leave behind; Khaibit, the shadow of our past which
follows us though we run from it; Ka, the mirrored surface; Ba, the
heart; Khu, the guardian angel; Sekem, the pure force; and Ren, the
secret name. [. . .] think now that [. . .] am only one of these souls,
though which one [. . .] do not know. From what [. . .] understand of
the book [. . .] can now make ... mappings of sorts. The corporeal
corporal, the old soldier, MacChuill, is surely the Sekhu. Pechorin is
unquestionably the Khaibit, the shadow. Tamuz must surely be the
heart, the Ba of any such group soul, Anat, the fierce warrior, the Khu.

What of von Strann and [. . .]? [. . .] am not sure. But [. . .] am sure
that Jack, the Jack of these myriad journals, is none other than the
Sekem itself.

We are our own worst enemies. How banal and trite that sounds, but
[. . .] have come to believe that all the greatest truths are trite and
banal when spoken aloud in their simplest and most honest terms.
Perhaps they can only truly be imparted in the Cant, in a language
which writes itself onto your heart so that you understand not just
the words but all the shattering ramifications of a sentence which,
when heard without true understanding, seems quite risibly simplistic.

We are our own worst enemies.

People die.

*

[...] have sent Tamuz off with the letters for Jack and von Strann, gave him no clue as to where [...] was going, what [...] am planning. He would not understand, [...] think. Then again, maybe he would understand more than any of us. Jack, [...] imagine – no, [...] *know* from the Book – will have no understanding at all, not until the end. It is pointless for [...] to try and explain what [...] have realised, so [...] offer him a mystery of a sort that will bring him here. He must make this journey, for the sake of us all. So [...] do not say, *we are our own worst enemies*. Instead [...] say, in this letter, *the enemy is not what we thought*.

[...] wonder if [...] am the mirror, the Ka, broken by the terrible knowledge carried in the Book. Or am [...] the secret name, the Ren, best forgotten, best lost forever, if to speak it brings this awful truth into existence? [...] still do not understand it all. But then, who of us truly does, until the end?

Something's Rotten in the State of Everything

I clock the carnage of the hotel room, the body of the cabinet minister, the bloodstained sheets, the shattered window with the moonlight shining through – and, mes amigos, I feel blue. I'm getting tired of these long dark nights – man, it's already getting bright outside – and there's some times I wish that someone else, somewhere, somehow, could carry on and fight the good fight for me. But it's cruel but true: we're all alone in this cold world and all we got are stolen moments, flashes of light, before the reaper comes to drag us screaming into that cold night.

So here I am in these wee hours, 'Coyote' Don MacChuill, consultant spook with special powers, summoned from slumber long before the dawn and stifling a yawn as I look round me at the score or so militiamen engaged in measurements and murder-scene manipulations. Assassinations are a tricky business, friend; the powers-that-be wouldn't want to rock the faith of your common-or-garden joe schmoe in the invulnerability of the established order – but they've still got to try, try, try to find the madman monster on the murder spree before all hell breaks loose.

So you have your constables and cleaners to cover up and uncover as required, and you have mooks like me who work a bit more free — free market, anyway.

Anyway.

I spark up another smoke and take a toke. Another murder with the MO of the Spartacus Killer, another scent of crime noir thriller, yes, a matchbook with a phone number written on it, up on the dresser beside a Curzon⁄Youngblood Mark I chi⁄gun. I've seen the same set now so many times, I sometimes think I dream it in the night. That's right. But, mes amigos, this scene had a little extra staging to the rest, what with the black⁄suited bodyguard dumped unconscious on the bed, his arms around the dead man, sweet as a kitten. Awake now and answering questions from the constables with his cold and certain voice, he might well be the plain paid heavy that he claims he is, but he's got a look that says to me he's owned by no one, an uneasy scent that sets my spider⁄sense a⁄tingling — that suggests just maybe, maybe, there ain't nothing there to own.

Joseph Pechorin, he says his name is.

— Excuse me, old chap, says a voice behind me.

The newcomer is natty in his leather overcoat — MI5 Black Ops Division mufti or I'll eat my hat and the cat that was in it too, though with his louche wave of a hand he looks like he'd be more at home in cricket whites.

— If you could send your men out for a minute, if you don't mind, he says, I'd be much obliged. There's a delicate matter to discuss here. No, the bodyguard can stay.

I give the word and, as the last of my boys in black and blue closes the door behind him, this charming disarming SS man sits down in an armchair, drapes one leg across the other and smiles.

— My name is Guy Fox, he says as the gambler's gun flicks from his sleeve. Please relax, Mr MacChuill, Mr Pechorin. The temporal aftershocks no doubt have you a tad ... *confused*, but if you'll just hold on, the others should be here in a ...

He *clicks* his fingers.

As Ab Irim said to his servant Eliezer, my friend, these stories of fruits of wisdom, of the curses of God, of suits of skin, of sons of angels, of days of rains, of cities of destruction ... these are only tales we tell to shape our selves.

Can wisdom can be gained from a fruit, you think, my friend? Perhaps wisdom is a little like a tree, growing over time from a sapling, spreading up and outwards, branching and spreading down into the soil, anchoring itself and drawing moisture and minerals from the world it is a part of. Perhaps a moment of understanding is a little like the moment we bite into a fruit – an apple, a fig or a pomegranate – the taste of it so sudden and sharp, sweet and bitter at once. But my friend, if knowledge can be tasted, it is in the salt of tears of laughter or grief, and it is as much the knowledge itself that is biting into you. Oh, and where it bites you, my friend, you burn, fevered, hot and cold, as if bitten by a snake. The juice of a bitter fruit, the sweet venom of a snake. Poison and medicine. Fire and ice. Joy and sorrow.

Good and evil, my friend, is a poor description of that bittersweet wisdom.

So what is this tree of knowledge of good and evil, my friend, if it is the twin of that other tree from which God said the man of clay and the mother of all living should not eat, that tree of life? What is the twin of life but death? Surely this then is the knowledge gained by Adam and Eve. It is a curse, because to understand this truly is to understand that everything is dust, to be stripped of all illusions, to face one's own mortality. The world becomes poisoned. Nothing matters. But is it not also the cure for all ills? Because to understand this fully is to understand this: it does not matter, my friend, that nothing matters.

So how did Adam and Eve taste this knowledge which stings like the thorns and thistles of the endless fields, tears choking their throats like dust, knowledge born in pain and blood, just as we all are?

They learned this, my friend, as the most bittersweet lesson can only be learned ... from their children.

*

As Ab Irim said to his servant Eliezer, there were two brothers once who sought to summon God with their songs. As brothers do, they argued. One said God is this, the other God is that, and they could not agree. So they should have a contest, they agreed, and see which God would answer to their song. And one, a harvester of grain out in the fields, began to sing of the cycle of sowing and gathering. The other, a herder of livestock in the wilds, began to sing of slaughter and burnt offerings.

My God is a god of the barley and the brewed beer, sang one.

My God is a god of the wool and the woven yarn, sang the other.

My God is a god of the vines and the wines, sang one.

My God is a god of the beasts and the blood, sang the other.

My God is a god of seeds that sprout in soil, sang one.

My God is a god of lambs led to the slaughter, sang the other.

My God is a god of life, sang one.

My God is a god of death, sang the other.

And it was then, as Abel tried to summon death with his song, that Cain rose up against his brother, struck him down to silence his insanity, and in so doing lost ... everything. For, with his last breath, Abel whispered the name of his God of blood, and Cain saw death in his brother's eyes, and he knew which God had answered to their song.

There is no lesson harder, my friend, but none so true as the lesson we learn from the death of one we love.

That tale of death was marked as much on Adam and Eve as it was on Cain, my friend, written on their skin. It was marked on the ground in bloodstains, on the body in its wounds, in the heart of the killer and on the faces of the mourners. They say amongst my people that it can be spoken in a single word, that truth. But ... it is a word that is broken. You see, the full truth was too much to bear for either Adam or Eve; neither could carry that burden alone, and so they broke the word into its sounds and split those tiny fragments of the whole between them so that neither was ever alone with the full truth. Only when they lay together naked would the full tale be told, in flesh touching flesh; then they would hear that word whispering in the darkness and they would remember the full truth, and hold each other all the tighter for it. Only Cain the killer carries the full word, graved on his face. This is why he walked out into the wilderness, to distant lands of other tongues, where those who looked upon that mark would only know it was the sign of some strange crime, and could not utter it to his face and call the God of Abel up again.

This is the tale that Enoch gave to Noah, that was kept safe through the Flood, that was stolen from him in his drunkenness by Ham, and handed down to Nimrod. This is the tale that Ab Irim brought out of the ruins of Babel, up through Haran and down into Canaan, as we travelled with your people. This is the tale of death written in the Book of All Hours.

A Path Out of the Maze

25th March. It is all but over now. There is one final episode to be played, one last act before the final curtain, but the roles were written long ago and the players know their lines. I almost wish there was an audience to appreciate the end. But there are just the six of us, we players and our chorus – the last remnants of the Enakites – still singing against death and ice.

The angels circle the city on strange wings of silvery-steel they have sung into existence with their Cant, Azazel one way, Michael the other, circling like hawks but never swooping in beyond the circle of salt pillars that now stretches round the full perimeter of the broken city walls. It is the line of their defensive shield, a binding that the Enakite song cannot break through, marked out by the pillars of those of us who have tried. This time in Sodom it is not those who look back upon the horror who are turned to salt, but those who seek escape from it.

Siege and rout. Siege and rout. War is an eternal bloody cycle and we can no more escape from it, it seems, than from this city. Just as the Turks surrounded and invaded, just as the Enakites surrounded and invaded, so once again the city is under siege. Streets blasted into paths of broken wall, roads blocked with rubble and bodies, it is a labyrinth we have had to inch our way through, turning and backtracking in our circuitous return to the Beth Astart, ducking and diving to avoid the angel's hail of fire.

I think of Pechorin slamming me out of the way of one blast, almost killed by it himself, and now I don't know what to make of the man. Did Anat's whisper strip him down so far he no longer even has his Futurism to believe in? When he pulled me to my feet, there was a look in his eyes that said he might just as happily have died. Perhaps we are not so very different in some ways.

I think of all those journal entries, of the madness of trying to piece them all together, trying to find a path out of the maze. It's what I've been doing all my life, blundering about within the maze of my own . . . potential, trying to play the hero, slay the monster in its heart.

Mad Jack Carter.

I find myself grinning.

The city belongs to the sons of Sodom once again, but it is only a matter of waiting for the inevitable. It is the story retold to destroy those who survived the first time, and the second time; those who survive in every version of the tale, the Noahs, and the Lots. They want their story pure, the angels, I now realise. Azazel and Michael, death and ice, are angels of such purity, ghosts of Ahab come out of the dead soul deeps to murder Ishmael too. Their words rewrite the world as we walk through it, folding it, tearing at it, trying to force us down paths where Tamuz has his throat slit by Pechorin, where he's shot by the Turks, where he stands alone on the roof of the Beth Astart, gazing at fire raining down from Zeppelins in the sky, not shards of angel song but bombs that will blossom into an all-engulfing firestorm.

Slivers of a million deaths sting my arm, thrown up to shield the boy as the angels rain their fury on the streets of Sodom. The dust of pointlessly perfect tragedies blinds me as it whips up around us. All we can do is huddle and stumble, our own weapons pitiful against the sheer firepower of archangelic majesty, against the binding circle of their absolutism.

God or Destiny, Pechorin called it. Well, I have seen destiny written out in a book stolen from God, kept hidden by the Enakites for four thousand years. Now, it appears, their work is at an end, while mine . . .

I had a notion at the Jericho Gate, to end it all there and

then, and I wonder now what would have happened had I carried through on it. Crouched down, with the Book in its box before me, Hobbsbaum's journals in my satchel there beside it in the dust, I wondered if the Book was worth it, ~~if I might not just.~~

But that was not the path I chose. God knows, though, if it had . . .

– Fuck!

The box slips from where it's wedged under his left arm, and Jack shifts his weight to balance it on a hip while he adjusts his hold. With his other arm supporting Tamuz even as he tries to keep his pistol trained at all times on Pechorin, it's a bloody nuisance.

– Here, says Anat.

He feels the boy's weight lift as she takes the lion's share of the burden, freeing him to find a more secure position for the box. Following behind Jack and Anat, MacChuill supports the limping von Strann with an arm around the Baron's waist. In front of them, Pechorin, unbound now after the umpteenth fall while scrabbling through the ruins, steps up towards Jack, a hand reached out.

– Let me help you with the boy, Captain Carter.

Jack eyes him for a second, shakes his head and hands the box to the blackshirt instead, gives his gun to Anat.

– Watch him, he says. I'll take Tamuz.

He hefts Tamuz up into both arms and turns to carry the boy up to the doorway of the Beth Astart. Every second or so there is a sharp and rasping intake as the ever-dying boy breathes in another last breath. Another last breath every second or so . . . and yet there is no final gutter, no last release.

We do not let this happen. None of us will let this happen.

We deny it.

We defy it.

The Kali Yuga Waltz

Click.

In an instant Joey has his Scorpio 99 out and Jack in his sights. Jack – down on one knee for added drama – has his Curzon-

Youngblood Mark 1 chi-pistol pointed at Don, whose service Snub in his trenchcoat pocket – assuming that's not just a sneaky finger – is now aimed at me. I nod to his side so Don clocks that my gun is aimed at Anaesthesia rather than him, her ruptor being trained, in turn, on Joey. It's all rather tense, with us locked on each other like mortal enemies ... except for Puck, who, sitting on the bed, hair over his face, gaze down as he buckles his belt, remains blithely oblivious to the whole five-way standoff.

He looks up and – slowly – round the room.

– Guy? he says.

– Please let's not have anybody doing anything rash, I say. I was rather hoping we could have a civilised discussion. About books.

I bring the Liebkraft paperback out of my trenchcoat pocket.

– The Book of All Hours, I say.

The wallpaper on the room ripples and changes pattern. Prints on the walls become photographs. Another temporal aftershock, more fallout from Jack's botching of the Orpheus Operation. You can always rely on Jack to screw up a plan. Get himself killed. Send the wicked king insane ... and then the rightful prince too, for good measure. Murder your father before you were born. One has to have a lot of back-up plans with an agent like Jack. Honestly, the hours I spent cutting words and letters, commas and full stops, out of this tattered *Macromimicon*, pasting them onto other pages until they described this scene in, well, these very words.

Inscribed this scene, I should say. Graved it.

– So? I say. Pax?

I flick the gambling gun back up my sleeve with a twitch of wrist. Anna and Don exchange a look, a nod, lower their weapons. Joey and Jack, of course, just snap round instantly to mark each other in their sights. With the last ripple in the chaosphere I can see the slightest shifts in them, in the narrowing of their eyes – recognition, suspicion.

– Joey, I say. Jack. Trust me.

Joey turns his impiteous gaze on me, black pupils of an empty soul, a void of meaning. The only thing Joey Narcosis trusts is the certainty of death. That can make working with the man a dicey proposition at best, but one must have faith in one's own choices, if nothing else, and I believe I know Joey Narcosis rather well. I may know more about them than they do themselves – though even I have long since given up mapping the complexity of the relation-ships they play – father or brother, sister or mother, enemies or lovers. Sometimes it seems it's all a game to them, Shiva's Tango of Destruction. The Kali Yuga Waltz.

– As long as Jack the Whack here doesn't decide it's a good day to die.

– It's always a good day to die, says Jack.

– A better day to live, says Puck.

Outside, the sky is brightening with the first pale light of morning. A chorus of birds starts up.

– Let's talk, then, says Joey.

I wonder how to explain it to them, that we were fools to think that we could change the Book, that if we could find where it all went wrong then we could change it, remake history. Start from scratch. Another chance. Another book, a copy of the original but different, better. If we'd just won the Spanish Civil War. If Stalin had died. If. If. If . . .

I have come to believe that there *was* no Book before the bitmites decided to give us what we want, set out to give us *all* those changes, trying time after time to resolve them into a coherent unity, a definitive text. And one might well ask: If the Book of All Hours is the authoritative history we wanted – written in blood on the skin of angels – my God, what does that say about humanity?

But here's a more important if: If the bitmites created the Book then there was a time before it, there *is* a time, a fold of the Vellum, where the Book does not exist, before the Hinter and the Evenfall, before the death of that lost Deus of Sumer. Or perhaps a time after it. I've been watching for the signs of that . . . that spring. And I think I've found it.

As the birdsong starts outside, I lean forward in my armchair and click my fingers. Suddenly—

Suddenly the forest-green wallpaper of Club Soda's backroom

surrounds us, dark as a wildwood at dawn. The six of us sit round a table, drinks in hand instead of guns. A stitch in time.

– Palestine, 1929, I say. 469th Parallel. Eon X–7.

The Secret Name of God

– Fuck's sake, says MacChuill, it's like a fuckin' inside-oot Easter egg.

Inside the Beth Astart, the walls, the wooden pews and altarpieces, the museum cases and exhibits, everything, the Weeping Angel most of all, writhes with an ink that is not black but every colour in the world. The greens of vines and veins, of glass or grass, we are. The blues of skies and robin's eggs and oceans, azures and ceruleans and indigos, we are. Scarlets and purples from the robes of emperors and madonnas, we are, crimsons and vermilions. Red, brown and yellow ochre of the autumn leaves, we are. Ambers, umbers, embers, we are. We are a crucible of colour.

Only the altar do we leave pristine and clean for Jack to gently lay Tamuz on, push the hair out of his eyes and ask the barely conscious boy a simple question.

– Where is it?

Tamuz smiles weakly, raises his arm just high enough to point at the altarpiece behind the last of the teraphim.

– There is a gap, he says. Where it meets the wall.

Anat's face is all confusion and disbelief, but Tamuz nods at her and she walks over to the wall, kneels down by a panel carved with some pagan version of the Last Judgement. She leans in, shoulder pressed against the wall, hand squeezing in between wood and stone, searching and finding, pulling something out, and—

She starts cursing Tamuz – Jack assumes it's cursing from the tone, at least – in whatever common tongue the Enakites use between them at the hearth or on the horse, when they're not laying waste to cities; it sounds very much like a dialect of Yezidi. The lad shakes his head, replies with his excuses, pleas of innocence; it's so much in the tone of domestic sibling banter – as if the boy had read her diary, thinks Jack, or rifled through her private things – it brings a

573

wry smile to his face. Von Strann is laughing, MacChuill letting loose profanities filled with wonder – *ya sneakit wee fuckin bastard* – and Jack finds himself laughing, his hand on the lad's shoulder.

– The Professor, says Tamuz so earnestly, he tell me to do this. Exactly this. Tell no one until now, this moment here. He tell me it must be this way.

– I know, says Jack.

– I am sorry. I do not want to lie to you, Jack, to hide–

– I know, says Jack. It's OK.

He looks at Anat, standing there with it in her hand, held up for all of them to see, a single page of vellum covered in a profusion of cryptic marks, a mass of tiny flicks and squiggles, curlicues and accents all somehow so familiar in a way that Jack can't put his finger on. There are bloodstains on it, and one corner of the page has been burned away to a scorched crinkle, whatever symbol was once written there now lost forever to the fire.

Six million lives on one page, thinks Jack. Minus one. Minus Hobbsbaum, who had burned himself out of the book of life rather than suffer his bloody written destiny.

It happens so fast. Von Strann's sudden slump, his crutch of a rifle clattering to the floor, MacChuill's distraction, cursing as he tries to get the man to a bench, Pechorin on the floor before they know it and then up again, the rifle in his right hand, steadied along his knee, the box under his left arm. He points the gun at Anat.

– I will take that, Princess Anat. The page, please.

Pechorin swings the rifle round even as Jack reaches.

– No, Captain Carter, I know what you're thinking. One shot, then I have to reload, and by then one of you would be on me. You are willing to risk the sacrifice, as is she. I have no doubt of it.

He swings the rifle round to point at Tamuz.

– I think neither of you wish to sacrifice the boy, though. Am I right?

Carter raises his hands. Still watching him, Pechorin addresses Anat.

– Put the page down on the altar beside the boy, and go stand beside the Captain, please.

A quick flick of the eyes, as she moves slowly in between Tamuz and—

– No, go round the *other* way, please. Behind the altar, yes. Thank you.

He rises steadily to his feet, circles sideways and in, until he's standing behind the altar, barrel of the rifle pressed to Tamuz's temple, putting the wooden box down on the boy's chest and picking up the page. He unsnicks the latch of the box, opens the lid.

– My colleagues will be pleased. The Secret Name of God. The Book of All Hours. And when their . . . anointed arrives, as he should do very soon, they'll have all they need to—

As he fumbles to get the page into the box with the rest of the Book, Pechorin glances down and stops. He looks at Jack and there's a question on his lips, in his eyes, and the barrel of the rifle is rising to force an answer, but, with the rifle pointed at him now rather than Tamuz, Jack is already making his move, swinging sideways as his Webley snaps up. Two shots fire at the same time, and Jack hears the mosquito whine, feels the buzz of a bullet past his ear, but he's frozen in the moment, still as a frieze, eyes locked on the round red hole in Pechorin's Adam's apple. The blackshirt staggers back against the altarpiece, looks at the page in his hand, and then slides down, the rifle clattering to the floor.

Jack vaults the altar and Tamuz, grabs the page as it flutters out of the blackshirt's slackening grip, folds it roughly – it cracks, dry and brittle, as he does so – and stuffs it in his trouser pocket with a quick glance over his shoulder. He snicks the latch of the box shut and tucks the box under his arm, kneels down beside the crumpling man, and holds the blackshirt's lolling head as the eyes blink at him. Breath gutters wet between lips trying to shape the words, to spill the secret. The only thing Pechorin can spill now though is blood, frothing in red bubbles from his throat and mouth.

Jack listens to him as he speaks a name that can only be spoken with a man's last breath. The *Y* of the tongue reaching up to the palate as if to cup saliva or blood to swallow or to spit. The first *H* a sharp intake, air rasping through a suddenly dry, constricted throat as the chest spasms in a panic of realisation, of suddenly, Oh God, knowing that this is death. The *W* of lips brought together, not closed but tightened a little, pursed in pain and confusion. This word, this *YHW*, is *WHY* sucked in backwards as a gasp, a last grasping at breath, at life.

And then the air seeping out through a larynx relaxing, the rough aspiration of that final *H* drawn out – *HHHH* – slowly dissipating, softening into *hhhhh*, and then fading into silence.

YHWH

And the silence after it which is the Secret Name of God.

Jack closes the dead eyes, lets the head roll to the side and down.

If gods can die, he thinks, then Death is god of gods.

The Opening of the Way

They stand on the roof of the Beth Astart, Jack and Reinhardt, looking out over the city of Tell-El-Kharnain, the city that has fallen once, twice, a thousand times, that seems to still be falling even now, as if in some eternal destruction. Both Azazel and Michael have settled on the Jericho Gate, one on each side, perched on pillars of stone, wings folded behind them like vultures. The Silk-market below them is filled with salt statues of the Enakites, the tribe wiped out now but for Anat and her brother.

– Perhaps the other gate ... says Reinhardt. If we stay together, if we can get out into the desert, we can disappear. Anat and I know how to survive there–

– No, says Jack, Samuel's notes are clear. We hit these bastards head-on. You take Tamuz ... for safety. The rest of us open up the way for you. With Anat's little toys we should be able to break through the circle, hold them off till we get you to the Airfield. You go on foot, on horse, even car, and they'll catch you, believe me. We need to get you to an ornithopter.

– What if Samuel's notes were wrong? The Book has as many lies in it as truths. What if he translated it wrong? And now we have ...

Jack grins. No way to know, he thinks. He runs his fingers absently across his chest, unscarred now ... cleansed by angelfire.

– Into the valley of death, he says. Charge of the Light Brigade and all that. Just trust me.

– But Pechorin mentioned an anointed. Did the notes–?

– Trust me, says Jack. Besides . . .

Jack points out to the north-west horizon where the sky is clouded with black specks, like a swarm of flies or a great flock of crows in the distance. Prussian merchant Zeppelins outrigged in Syria, fitted for war, and flying now under the Futurist flag.

– Air travel is the way of the future.

– How do these work? says Jack.

Anat and MacChuill sit on a bench in the corner of the Beth Astart, working on their contraptions – Turkish rifles and Enakite spears, railings and barbed wire, jingling dog-tags, rosaries and God knows what else, salvaged from the ruins around them and lashed together with strips of leather. They look like harpoon guns, cross-bows, insane and monstrous, bastard hybrids of weaponry from every time in history.

– Unsympathetic magic, says Reinhardt.

Jack takes the weapon offered by Reinhardt, aims with it, testing the weight, the balance.

– You say the word I taught you as you pull the trigger, says Anat. The bullet will carry it through their shield. Aim well, Captain Carter. We do not have many bullets. Take what Tamuz has finished.

Sitting up on the altar now, the youth is scratching sigils into bullets with the point of a knife, loading them into cartridges; his tongue sticks out from one corner of his mouth, a picture of concentration.

– Hey, says Jack.

Tamuz doesn't look up – but of course. Carter walks over and taps him on the shoulder, points at the cartridges – *are these ready*? Tamuz nods, mouths the word *yes*, but there's no sound.

There's no sound at all within five feet of the boy. A silent echo of the Name of God hangs around him as a cloak, a zone of absolute quietude which no language, not even the Cant, can penetrate. It will die, fade away as echoes do, but if it holds for the next few hours . . .

The rest of them will have to stay outside of it in order to use these *disruptors*, but if Reinhardt sticks close to Tamuz all the fire of Heaven won't be able to harm a hair on his head. Jack picks up two full cartridges, tucks them into his belt. A hand on Tamuz's arm – the boy looks up into his eyes, smiles.

They don't really need the words, but he mouths them anyway.

– Captain Carter, are you ready? says Reinhardt. Captain Carter?

Jack closes the wooden box and turns to the open doorway of the Beth Astart, where MacChuill and Anat stand silhouetted against the daylight. A single shaft of sunlight streams into the temple through the opening, catching blue wisps, the smoke of us, as we dance in the dark air. From the single eye of the Weeping Angel we gaze down on him. We gaze down fondly on the many Jacks in our multi-facet vision, all these Jacks who have fought their way to this sanctuary of chaos, fought for love, fought to the death. Over there he lies dead upon the altar, beside the body of Tamuz. Over here he lies just short of it, arm stretched out and reaching in his final moment, tears streaming down his face because he does not have the strength. He sits huddled in one corner, rocking back and forth, insane. And slumped in another, with his back to the wall, a cigarette in his mouth and a revolver in his hand, waiting for his death. The room is as full of Jacks as it is of us, though the others do not see this – just as they do not see us shifting on the walls, only the painted glamour of pagan illustrations. They hear us, Anat, MacChuill and Reinhardt, but they hear our whispers as the echoing of the Cant. Only Tamuz hears us properly, *understands* us entirely, in his hearing, his understanding, of the silence that gives our whispers meaning.

Jack, of course, both hears and sees us as we do ourselves, the closest to us in the nature of his soul, in the shapeless force of his Sekem. We love Tamuz, the fluttering-eyelashed, fluttering-lifed Ba, the very heart of us. We do not hate the shadowy Pechorin, the Khaibit, this thing of darkness which is also ours. We are in awe of Anat, our ferocious warrior, our huntress Khu. We smile upon MacChuill, our cursing and complaining Sekhu, serving us well for all his mutterings. And Samuel and Reinhardt . . .

– Captain Carter, are you ready? says Reinhardt. Captain Carter?

*

578

– I'm ready, says Jack.

He turns back to the altar, where Pechorin's body now lies – a shadow offered to the shadows, a betrayer betrayed – and draws the copy of the Song of Solomon out of his pocket. He lays it upon the dead man's chest, unsure if he's offering them both to the Weeping Angel as a sacrifice or for safekeeping; it just doesn't seem right to leave a part of our soul with no marker for its grave.

As MacChuill's gruff voice urges him to *get a fuckin move on*, Jack picks up his disruptor and walks out into the blinding sunlight.

The drone of Zeppelins is getting louder out here.

Anat takes his hand, clasps it with a strong and certain grip.

– I wish that we will meet again someday, she says. In another life.

– *Heam*, he says. May it be.

– *Mektoub*, she says.

He looks at MacChuill, who just snorts.

– Aye, an' wan day Partick Thistle'll win the League.

The old soldier shades his eyes with a hand, searching the sky to the North. The Zeppelins are visible now as cigar shapes dark against the blue sky, but flashing silvery now and then with reflected sunlight. The first of them looks like it must already be over the Ink Wells.

– Christ, but there's fuckin hunners ae them. An a' tae burn a city that's a'ready a fuckin wasteland.

– If Pechorin isn't the only blackshirt working with the angels, says Jack, they're probably more concerned with smoking us out.

He has one more glance back at the place where his old friend Samuel Hobbsbaum spent his last few hours on earth, planning, scribbling or maybe just deciding, and then finally burning his own name out of the page that it was written in, burning himself out of existence. One small act which might well have graved that silence, that absence, into the very Name of God, and saved them all. Not that this will stop the angels from trying their insane scheme. Carter slips his hand into his pocket to touch the folded vellum, turns and sees MacChuill pointing up into the sky.

– Whit the fuckin hell is that?

A rift in the cerulean sky, a burst of indigo, a thunderbolt of purple, a blue-green electric rip in reality, tearing straight down through the clouds and through the first Zeppelin.

– I'm guessing that's the angels' anointed, says Jack.

And his grin is snickety-sharp and glinting white.

We All Die Someday

Joey Narcosis brushes a speck of white fluff off one shoulder of his long black woollen overcoat, and steps up to the edge of the gantry. Behind him, the archivist notices, Arturo is busy rewiring the computer, sabotaging the laboratory. The archivist finds this vaguely interesting but is in two minds whether to stop the scientist or to join in. In other circumstances, the archivist would have been in panic mode, broadcasting alarms on all channels, long-established post-assassination protocols kicking in – *Emergency! Emergency!* Thopters would be scrambling, paradox shielding deploying, work routines being reset, whole life histories being rewritten; every resource in the Circus would be working in unison now to jumpstart the Duke back into existence. Circumstances change, however.

Arturo would be – should be – at the heart of this, bringing a clone out of cold storage, uploading into it the copy of the Duke's graving from the virtual vault it's stored in, transferring the unkin soul into a new host in a metaphysical reboot. Instead, he's reprogramming the emergency evacuation procedure so it will release a thousand sex-starved, orgone-crazed bonobos on the streets of Dunedin. Although more than aware of the mad scientist's newborn relish for life and its innate absurdity, the archivist does not really have a sense of humour about this.

But we're still working on him.

Joey is dead calm, ever the cool and collected one. He stands over the chi-mine, looking down into the depths of the chaosphere and evaluating his options. Fox's Plan A was for Joey and Jack to both jump down the rabbit-hole to Palestine, 1929, where Jack would play the hero and Joey the villain, working with the angels but double-dealing and conniving to bring them down with the black-hat avarice and pride that always bites the bastard on the ass. Plan B was that, if only one of them made it through, he'd try to set it all up himself; to do that Joey will have to tweak and twist the Jack of that fold, lay down a paperchase for him, hope he follows the script. Plan C – which is Joey's own potential plan – is that he screws over both sides, takes the Book for himself and sees just what you can do with the Secret Name of God and the programming manual for the universe.

It's a thought.

Around the hole of his soul, Joey feels the modifications to his metaphysique making him itchy about all of these plans. The dust in the air around him dances to some distant song. He feels like his skin is golden armour, his eyes silver orbs, his heart made of ice. He feels like he could kill someone with the touch of his shadow. It would be a shame to let that power go to waste, but at the same time he has no desire to play God . . . though it might be nice to be the hero for a fucking change.

Somewhere in the back of his head, he wonders if Fox has his own Plan C and all of this, even betrayal on his part, is included in it. No matter. He swings first one leg then the other over the rail of the gantry, spreads his arms. Then lets himself fall forward.

We all die someday, he thinks.

And his overcoat billows and flutters as he rolls and straightens out into a dive, going down in a diagonal, an arrow with a vector through all three temporal dimensions, moving back through linear time, off-beam in sidereal time, deep inward through the strata of residual time.

He sees the blue-green storm of the chaosphere rushing up to meet him, dives through wafts of vapour clouds, through glowing nebulae, through sparking and arcing electric tendrils that whip around him, flick across his face, smear into his slipstream. He hits stratocirrus and then cumulus, a thick brilliant glow of chaos, psychedelic as projections in a 60s discotheque, smashes out of the corona and down, into: a black space of darting spirals, branching scrawls of light like paths of particles in collision; a whirling vortex of lensing effects, warped and weird around him, pitch-black below him, and up above him blinding white, as if all of the light of history is pouring in behind him as he pierces the event horizon.

He brings his arms out to the side, splays his hand to feel the histories streaming through them, feel the currents and eddies, the flows, feeling for the thread he wants; and he finds it, snaps his arms in to his side and twists and shifts and –

– slices out into a blue sky, a blue-white sea and pale sand below, a valley of salt, and a fleet of silver cigar shapes scattered across the sky, one straight ahead, coming up so sudden he just crashes straight through it, shredding his coat and losing drag. He rolls, tries to compensate, spreads his arms to grab time, like fucking Tarzan trying to catch a jungle vine, but it rips right through his fingers.

All we can do is swarm out of the shadows under him to armour him in a glint of scales and feathers as he plummets, Joey Narcosis, a great falling peacock angel, hitting the Ink Wells outside Tell-el-Kharnain like a meteor out of space.

A Thousand Books in One Page

The light hits them first, a jolt of blue-green sudden as a camera flash, so blinding that it almost feels, Jack thinks, like some mad scientist has sparked an electrode, prodded this or that cell in his brain, causing a flash as sudden as a memory. Then comes the noise of impact, the almighty DOOM of this strange comet out of time hitting the earth which quakes under their feet – the shockwave. A plume of smoke billows up and out, swallowing the first wave of the Zeppelins. There's black in the smoke and grey, but there's as much purple, green and blue in it as it furls into the air, a pillar, a fountain, rising and collapsing over itself, a vast mushroom-shaped monster.

– Come on, says Jack, it's time to make our move.

He hands the box to Reinhardt, and the Prussian takes his place behind Tamuz. MacChuill to the right, Anat to the left, Jack between them and in front, they come together into a tight formation, silence dropping like the switching off of a radio as Jack enters the zone of safety around Tamuz. The silence makes it all so eerie and unreal as they move out into the square, the airships quiet in the sky, the fire of the angels a ghostly barrage, shattering buildings around them, the earth under their feet, even the air itself shimmering but utterly harmless within the circle.

As they start up the North Road, Jack raises the binoculars to study the angels, smiles at the fury and frustration twisting Michael's face into a mask of hate, baring his teeth as he spits his futile venom at them. He nods with satisfaction at the way Azazel now glances nervously over his shoulder at the pillar of smoke still rising, belching up from the impact in the Ink Wells, spreading out across the sky, not dissipating in the wind but stretching in volutes and trails, moving out into the Futurist fleet like some blind amorphous ocean thing, more plant than animal but alive enough to reach with hungry tendrils and snag passing fish in its stinging wafts of frond.

That's right, you cunts, thinks Jack, we're coming for you.

And, as they move out into the Silkmarket, Jack gives the signal, and the three of them with disruptors step out of the circle of silence, into the thrum of oncoming airships and the shrieks of angels and the rumble of a distant storm. MacChuill breaks right and Anat left, to draw off the angel fire; they head for the edges of the square, using pillars of salt for cover. Striding out in front of Tamuz and Reinhardt, disruptor blazing as he fires at Azazel, Michael, Azazel, Michael, Jack sings his way towards the Jericho Gate of the fallen city of Tell-El-Kharnain.

He runs, turning now and then to kneel, fire back at the two angels pinned down in their sniper positions over the Gate by MacChuill and Anat. He runs and fires, fires and runs, leaping over bodies and boulders, through the rubble and the babble of this hopeless battle in this unholy war.

He bundles Tamuz and the Prussian towards the larger of the thopters, taps the wooden box and mouths the words *Curzon* and *Basra*. Reinhardt points to the sky, to the Zeppelins moving slowly towards them, almost overhead now. Jack nods. *I know.* He points at the other thopter, the Eagle painted on its fuselage. *Interference.*

Reinhardt gives him a thumbs-up, swings himself up to clamber into the cockpit, reaches a hand down to pull Tamuz after him. Tamuz looks at Jack, shakes his head.

No, Jack.

Go.

A pause. A tear running down a cheek. A kiss. A goodbye.

Tamuz grabs a strut and clambers up onto the wing, reaches for Reinhardt's hand. Jack turns away, swallowing his emotions. The two-man thopter isn't designed for vertical take-off, doesn't have the wingspan to just beat its pinions and flurry into the sky as a lighter fighter aircraft would – it needs a run to get the wind beneath its wings – so, as von Strann buckles himself into the pilot seat and Tamuz slides into the seat in front of him, Jack runs round the front to crank the propeller on the nose. He's just pulling the chocks from the wheels when he feels – he doesn't hear but feels – Tamuz's cry.

Anat flies backwards through the air, a full back-flip, the disruptor flying from her hand. The boy is already out of the thopter and on the ground, Jack grabbing him by the arm. He struggles, flails against Jack's grip, his embrace. The angel of death, Azazel, leaps from his perch, a hawk diving for its prey, but Anat is rolling, up on one knee, her hand gloved in ink extended as she curses, slams the fucker back with a word. He hits the stonework of the wall, and she's up and running at him now, charging in to close-quartered combat.

Go! Jack screams soundlessly at Tamuz.

Above his head, their thopter banks east towards the blue sky over the desert, its wings beating hell-for-leather as Reinhardt and Tamuz race away from the Russian fleet, away from Tell-El-Kharnain, and away from the swirling storm of ink, of bitmites, of we dead souls buried in millennia of dust, crushed down and transformed by the weight of dead realities into the oil of humanity's lost souls.

We rise, erupt out of the earth, spewing as a geyser of desire and fear, of joy and sorrow, all the power and glory of the human spirit compacted tight and black. Matter is light, coiled in a ball, hoarding its heat in the heart of it, dark only because the fire is trapped inside; let it loose and you can level cities. So, too, we dead seem as ink in our darkness, locked off from the living, but, oh, in the skin and bone that rots, in the sand and the stone, in the air, in every atom of us, information is encoded, lives recorded in reality itself, the pattern of it only lost, only faded, never utterly destroyed. We are the palimpsest of the past on which you write your present and your future, the substructure of your world revealed by X-rays, microscopes, the focus of photons fired into our depths, the ricochet of bullets of light. We are laid open to your scrutiny by the scalpel vision of those willing to look so deep.

And now, as in the chamber of a particle accelerator, we react to Pechorin's impact. We spray up into the air, the darkness unlocking into light, brilliant greens, bright blues, burning orange and red and yellow. We pick Zeppelins from the sky. We prick gas-bags, snarl propellers. They fight back, dropping bombs on the Ink Wells below them, building a wall of flame that sweeps forward as they move inexorably towards Tell-el-Kharnain, sweeps in out of the desert and across the new city, across the Airfields. But Jack is in the air now, in the fighter thopter, pulling gears and joysticks as the metal machine spirals up into the sky, over the wasted city and around. Blossoms of grey smoke explode in the air around him as the Prussian war-machines try to bring him down, but he wheels the machine, turning it in a widening gyre, soaring up and up and up. He spirals up over the city, over the bombs and the guns.

The thopter hangs in the air for a second.

Then, disruptor lashed to the side of the cockpit, he screams Cant and obscenities together, swooping down on the enemy thopters swarming out now from amongst the Zeppelins and banking east to pursue Reinhardt and Tamuz. He swoops down over the city, rolling the machine as he strafes, glancing down as he flies over the Jericho Gate and sees—

The blast hits MacChuill full-on. The man's head whips round to the side and back, neck cracking, and his legs snap backwards under him; Christ, his spine must be shattered – it's like some giant hand just clamped and crushed him, folding him in ways no man could survive. The Scotsman's song dies in a short last scream, and he falls like a ragdoll dropped in the dust. As Jack zooms overhead, Michael rises from his crouch on his perch on his pillar and turns his gaze slowly to the east, where Reinhardt and Tamuz are headed straight out into the desert, pursued by a score of Russian thopters.

Michael leaps into the air, his great wings extending as the angel of ice sets out after the Book. His words of fire strafe the air around Jack's thopter and Jack rolls the machine, dodges left and right, weaving through the shattering sky. He pulls back a joystick, spins a wheel and the thopter arcs upwards. Wings in, it turns like a ballet dancer on point, and then the pinions are thrown wide again and he's heading straight for the angel of ice, seeing past him to the Jericho Gate where, under the very archway of it, Anat and Azazel are locked in combat, wrestling, Azazel's hands clamped round her throat, her fist jammed in his mouth, their muffled Cant burning the air around them, raining stone and sand, cracking the earth.

Anat goes limp. Her hand falls from the angel's mouth, and he holds her there by her crushed throat, dangling. Throws her body to the side. And raises his cold gaze towards Jack, who's looking up at the angel Michael now, the angel of ice he's on a collision course with, getting closer, closer, as the fucker's words explode around him, left and right, above and below. Even if the bastard hits him now he'll fucking well take the angel down with him.

Azazel, the angel of death, spreads his wings, looks to the east.

Jack can't take them both down, though. Christ, fuck, he can't take them both down.

So we come, a crack in the earth straight from the impact crater in the Ink Wells, splitting the ground along the fault line that runs down this valley of salt, cracking it wide and pouring up and out of the crack, we buried and forgotten dead of worlds long gone, and at the head of us a sixfold soul that was once Joseph Pechorin, murderer of dreams. He comes out of the darkness clothed in the iridescent armour of our ink, hitting Azazel with all his strength and speed, slamming into him and carrying them both through the angel's field of binding and into the city of Sodom.

As Jack's thopter hits the angel Michael, and wings snap, and metal buckles, and the two of them hurtle as a spinning ball of crumpling chaos through the air and down.

Ink, *by Hal Duncan (2007)*

Jack hangs in the wreckage of the ornithopter, caught up in a jumble of torn clothing, torn canvas and torn flesh, suspended like a corpse in an Indian burial. A sharp twist of metal spears his right thigh. Shreds of leather wing snarl his left hand. The smell of blood and steel, burning meat and fuel, the smell of war, fills his nostrils; is that his flesh burning, the archangel Michael's, both? He twists his head but all he can see is the shattered arch of the Jericho Gate, the path of burning destruction gouged through pillars of salt now shattered, drifting on the wind. Beyond the Gate, the cigar-shapes of the Futurist Zeppelins move in from the north; they'll reach the city in a few minutes now.

The sky above, through the smoke of the burning thopter, is dark green with the storm of ink, swirls like a forest pool thick with algae, dotted with bursts of brilliant colour like one of Monet's lily-ponds. The ink swarms around the airships, bringing down this one and that, but it's an inchoate attack, and the Ink Wells are burning now. If these creatures cannot be destroyed they can be … disrupted, scattered into confusion like a soul stripped apart at death, into skandas, strands of identity.

Et in Arcadia ego, thinks Jack. Even in Arcadia, I am.

A low moan comes from somewhere behind; he can't twist his head to look, but he knows it must be Michael. Fuck. Jack twists his right hand, scraping it free from the two metal shards it's trapped between with a yell of pain. He unravels the leather wound around his left hand, grimaces as in turning to reach he presses skin against blistering-hot fuselage. The smoke is billowing up from that side, though he can't see the flames; the metal is too hot even for him to use it as the leverage he needs to tear his thigh off its spear. He tears at the leather until he has enough to wrap around one hand. Places it – tentatively at first – on the jagged edge where the windshield was, and pulls at his thigh with the other. His pain drowns out the sucking feel of flesh coming free from steel.

He slides up and out, grabs a broken strut and tumbles over and through the wreckage, out onto sand. He can see the fire now and he rolls himself clear of it, drags himself up and away from the ruined thopter. His disruptor lies, torn from the machine's side, a few yards towards the Gate and he drags himself to it, pulls it up and swings himself round to train it on the smouldering wreck. He can't see the angel, but he can hear the fucker moaning. The noise is wordless, but there's enough Cant in it to make him sick to his stomach. He digs the butt of the disruptor into the ground and pulls himself up onto one leg.

Starts to limp round to the other side of the wreck.

Impaled on and embedded in the wreckage of the ornithopter, Michael tries to reach towards him, screaming soundlessly and clawing ineffectually at warped steel and wound cloth. Fire licks around his legs, twisted round in a way that says he'll never walk again. Never walk into a city, sure and certain of his duty to destroy it. The angel moans again and his mouth gouts blood – tongue bitten off, Jack would guess.

– Let the fucker bleed to death.

Jack turns.

It's Pechorin. He recognises the man instantly, couldn't fail to, but he also knows it's not his Pechorin but another, the Pechorin of another time, another place, another fold, just as cold in some ways, just as cruel, but in some strange binding of sympathies, of understandings, a friend. Looking at the black tear painted under his right eye, Jack just knows that this is less his antagonist than his ... complement.

Pechorin holds the head of Azazel by its dreadlocks.

Jack reaches down into the pocket of his trousers, feels the soft smooth texture of the folded page of vellum, the almost imperceptible warmth of still-living tissue. He pulls it out. He keeps Pechorin in his peripheral vision – just to be safe – as he limps over and holds it out towards Michael, just out of his grasp. The creature goes berserk, scrabbling at the metal, trying to tear itself apart to get to him, its manicured fingernails breaking and bleeding.

– You want this? says Jack. You want to bind God into this – [he nods at Pechorin] – anointed of yours? This slaughterer of angels?

And he drops it into the flames that lick around the angel's feet, watches the fucker trying to reach into the fire, trying to rip its own arm out of its socket so it can save the last page of the Book of All

Hours which slowly ignites, burning and blackening and crackling to ash as white as salt.

– The rest of the Book is already gone, says Jack. See that head over there, your mate's? Blame him. He burned it when he tried to wipe me out of existence because I had the fucking audacity to call him the cunt he was.

Jack smiles, thinking of a wooden box full of tattered scraps. Not the Book of All Hours, but Hobbsbaum's notes, journals, selected translations from the tome that he'd switched, slipped into his leather satchel as he crouched up on the rock looking out over the city at the angel of death and wondered how they could possibly get out of this alive, any of them. How he could get Tamuz out of this alive.

A leather satchel with the Book of All Hours in it, held up as a sacrifice and as a shield against the wrath of self-righteous, murderous bastards.

– The Book is gone, he says. Story's over. No more destinies. No more gods, with any luck. We're free. That was the last page of the final edition.

– I wonder what Reinhardt will think when he opens the box, says Jack.

– Knowing Fox, says Pechorin, he'll probably appreciate the trick.

The angel's scream dies into a gurgle of blood as they walk away, walk towards the Gate and the approaching Zeppelins, the host of war-machines coming clear of the ink storm now, almost directly overhead, all set for their pointless razing of an already devastated city. Up in the cockpits, captains and commanders, bombardiers and gunners will be looking down and probably wondering what happened, why and how and whether they really need to be here. But mostly they'll just shrug and carry out their orders.

Jack looks at Pechorin. The Russian steps out past the Gate and picks up the disruptor dropped by MacChuill, tosses it to Jack. Then walks over to retrieve Anat's disruptor for himself.

Down where Anat's body lies sprawled on the dry ground, a stalk of wildgrass grows out of a crack of soil, somehow shooting up green-gold and vigorous in this valley of salt. This region has plants evolved to survive even in this hostile climate, and Jack has a sudden image of the fields outside the city, to the north, fields fertilised by ash and blood, covered in olive and orange and fig and pomegranate trees, trees twisting up out of the soil, gnarled and branching, the intricate fractal scribblings of nature. Even the most arid region can be irrigated. That's how civilisation began.

The city behind them is in ruins, devastated. There's not a man, woman or child left alive in it. There's nothing to fight for, nothing to save, except perhaps its memory, which could be wiped out forever or held fast against all those who'd like to write its liberal, libertine, licentious *beauty* out of history. And even if they fail?

Jack leans on one disruptor as a staff, a crutch, raises the other to aim.

Fuck it.

A city, like a soul, can be rebuilt.

Dawn, a Woodland, Now

Happy Ever Never

Every epic, I used to think, should end with the hero's death. Picture it: two rows of crucified slave-rebels, Spartacus on his cross, his right hand pointing down the long road to a city of death; El Cid riding out of the gates of that city, riding out against the Moors, a dead man strapped to his horse; among the dust of stomping hooves, Achilles stumbling as the arrow strikes his heel. Ancient poets even added an encounter between the hero Gilgamesh and the ghost of his dead friend Enkidu to the first recorded epic, one step away from having them meet again, at the end of all adventures on the threshold of the house of no return.

It is as if the story is seeking its own form. And for all that it's easy, for all that it's obvious, there's something just so right about that end.

– Bollocks, mate, Jack would have said. Give 'em a fucking happy-ever-after. Fuck that tragic-ending shit.

– What are you working on now? asks Anna, chin on my shoulder, one hand tracing along my forearm to the gripped pen, folding fingers round my fist.

– A happy-ever-after, I say. Or a happy-ever-before, I guess, would be more accurate.

Feel of my own brows furrowing, face rumpling into a *Well, that's not quite right*. A tap of pen on paper.

– No, I say. A happy-ever-never.

I turn my head towards her wrinkling, freckled nose. Her red hair slides over my triceps, tickles a nipple, as she twists to smooch my cheek with a peck of *Top of the morning to you*. Angled enough, I can just see that she's wearing my boxer shorts.

– I'm doing a cut-up-and-fold-in of a couple of Virgil's eclogues, I say, sort of a rural, pastoral thing to try and tie up the *Songs* with an epilogue.

I wonder if, somewhere in the back of my head, that's why I suggested this log cabin in the Blue Ridge Mountains for a break for the three of us. I'd talked of good hunting for her, of teaching Joshua constellations and cosmologies, flora and fauna, and of quietude in which to finish my epic cycle of poems. But it's entirely possible that Jack and Puck just wanted to cavort naked in the hills, in my imagination.

In Virgil's Latin and my annotated English, on the page in front of me, I fold two eclogues into one: a goatherd and a shepherd shift from singing contest through to celebration of the deified Daphnis; the Roman poet's characters Menalcus and Damoetus blur, become Menalcus and now Mopsus, shift again; I think of them as Mainsail and Dampseat, Mainsail and Moppet. A flash of white piracy on the high seas. Green combats dark with dew on the butt. A grinning Jack with Puck in headlock, scruffling his hair:

– My little moppet, Jack would josh.
– Geroff me! Puck would protest.

That's my names for the idyll's id and the sylvan self, the kid and the lamb of these evers and nevers, from Gilgamesh down to my own metamorphoses, by way of Virgil: Jack and Puck, I call them. I based a little of Puck on what Anna's told me of her brother Thomas, invented Jack out of whole cloth. But both of them, I think, are as much creations of the idiom itself. They're not really mine, not mine alone.

I know my Jack and Puck don't really exist, never really existed, but the Jack and Puck who're more than mine ... they've been around forever.

– Orange juice? she says. Pancakes? Bacon? Maple syrup? We had a deal, you remember. Me hunter-gatherer woman bring venison and rabbit; you stay-at-home medicine man make strange scribbles. Make breakfast in bed, more to the point.

She drums her fingers on the table.

– I was on my way to the stove, I say. I just . . . I realised how the book should end, had to act on it, you know, get it down on paper before . . . before the coffee and the crumpled bedsheets and the two of us licking each other's sticky fingers and . . .

I nuzzle her cheek.

It has to end in elegy, I'd realised, and that means it has to end in idyll. The idyll and the elegy are two sides of one pastoral form, each idyll shaded with an elegiac sorrow for what's lost, for what will never be again, and every elegy lit up with the idyllic joy of what was found, of what will *ever* be, again and again and again, each time the song is sung.

And they all lived happy ever never.

– *The Songs of Unknown Lands*, says Anna, by the poor starving poet Guy Reynard Carter, can wait until after he's paid for his room and board . . . with breakfast in bed and services rendered.

– You make me feel so cheap and tawdry, I say as I put down the pen.

– You love it, she says.

– Is that so? I say.

I lay a paperweight on top of a page.

A Match of Music

– So, tell me, dumbass, says Mainsail Jack, is it Old Mellowbow who's master of these sheep?

Puck of the Dampseat pokes the faggot finger at him, middle finger of the right hand, down and forward.

– Fuck you too, he says. No, Argon gave me them to keep for him.

– Poor sheep, says Jack. Unlucky fucking flock! Their master traipses after mistress Narrow, panicking in case she's after me . . .

Jack scritches at a leg, his exomis shorter even than the usual knee-length linen chiton, baring his thighs so high it is, and fastened at the left shoulder so's it seems he's out for exercise, horse-riding or hard labour. He's even gone for the short cloak of a chlamys rather than the long himation. Cock-hipped, he grins, cocksure of his own charm, tongue in his cheek.

– Meanwhile, Argon gets fleeced, Jack carries on, his hired hand left in peace to milk the sheep twice hourly on the clock, thieving the lambs' milk from the flock.

– Joke all you want, shrugs Puck. But, while you jeer, remember, Jack, I know by who you were – [he flicks a fist up with his hand in nook of elbow, with a thump, a wink] – and while the billy goats all blinked and peered the other way. And in a shrine! . . . although the naughty nymphs all cheered.

They have a history together, Jack and Puck, you might have guessed, a history of slingshot slander . . . though it's mostly just in jest. Of all the herdsmen of the hills, we bitmite nymphs like Jack and Puck the best.

– Like when they saw me trashing all the trees and vines, remembers Jack, in Micron's orchard with a hook.

– Or right here by the beech trees where you broke poor Dovenest's bow and reeds. Man, you were green as ivy with your envy, jealous Jack, to see those shiny toys all given to another boy . . . dying to find some way to get him back.

– But, hey, what can the farmers do, when thieves like *you* run free? Jack says. *You're* worse than me. Did I not see you, while the sheepdog barked aloud, scrag, leaping from ambush in the hedges, snatching Demon's goat? Then when I cried – *Hey, where's he running? Tightarse, guard the flock!* – you hid behind the sedges.

Puck kicks a stone downhill at him but Jack darts to one side. One of his goats bleats in complaint, bell tinkling round its neck.

– Had I not beaten Demon in a match? grumps Puck. Had I not won that goat from him with my own song, with my own pipes? As if you didn't know, that welching twat as much as said the goat was mine. He just refused to pay. Why should I let him get away with that?

*

594

Jack snorts, switches a stick to guide his goats uphill past Puck's shamble of sheep and ambling cow.

– When have *you* ever beaten Demon in a singing match? he says. Come on. When did *you* ever have a proper set of wax-bound pipes? Don't you just stand down at the crossroads, dumbass, murdering a bad tune on a squawking straw?

Jack licks his lips as he strolls past. Hands on his hips, Puck glares. *That's fucking rich. Right then, you prick ...*

– OK, he says, let's make a match of music. Let's take turns to show what each of us can do. I bet ... this heifer – no, don't cock your snoot! She suckles two calves from her udders and still comes twice daily to the milking pail as well. So, come on; tell me what you'll put up as your stake.

A Pair of Beechwood Cups

– Oh, it's all right for you, says Jack. But some of us don't bet what we don't own. I've my old man at home, a wicked crone of a stepmother, ugly sisters, and a poor old widowed mother, with just me to care for her and all – and, see, they count the whole flock twice a day, and one of them makes sure none of the kids have gone astray.

Puck tucks his hands under his armpits, clucks at Jack – *puk, puk, chicken* – till Jack gives up.

– OK, OK, if you're so keen to play this game, he says – this puts your cow to shame – I'll bet a pair of beechwood cups, carved by the subtle knife of the divine Alchemy Don, with scattered berries on a supple vine weaving around pale ivy.

Puck knows the ones he means. In each one there's a portrait: Cunning and ... that sage who mapped the seasons in the skies over the whole world with his compass, telling the farmers when to put their shoulder to the plough and when to reap. He can't remember who, not being very good at history and all.

– They're brand new, Jack says. They're unused. I keep them stored away and haven't even touched my lips to them. What do you say?

*

595

Puck shrugs, and flicks his hand as if to wave away a fly.

– Alchemy Don made two of those for me as well, you mug, wreathing the handles round with soft acanthus, Jack, and setting Orphan in the centre with a trail of trees all marching at his back.

He mocks Jack's voice.

– *I haven't supped. I keep them all locked up*. So what? So fuck? Look at the cow I'm putting up; then you'll shut up about your poncy cups.

– Right then, says Jack. Like I'm about to let you off with that, pup's tail. No, not today: I'll take you on. Come on, we have soft grass to sit on; and what with the crops fresh in the fields, fruit ripe upon the trees, and all the woodland thick with leaves, now is the fairest time of year.

He flops down on the slope of grass, leans back on one arm, one leg stretched, the other nooked. Puck looks upslope, and up Jack's slant of thigh under the exomis that's hitched – deliberately, he's sure – *well* high. He's hooked.

– You first, dumbass, says Jack – who, Puck thinks might as well be in the buff. We'll sing in turns, says saucy Jack. That's what the Muses love.

The Music Begins

– The music begins, Puck sings, in Dewpatter who loves all things and holds the whole world dear. And to my songs Dewpatter turns his ear.

– But Apple loves me more, Jack sings. His gifts are ever near me: boys who blush; and the sweet flush of hyacinth.

He fiddles a finger round a flower and Puck looks down the hill towards the town. He points out a woman in her yard, girdling her floor-length woollen peplos at the waist, gathering its folds into a pouch. She drapes an epiblema over her head and shoulders.

– So? says Puck, pointing at her. I've got my Galaxy, my flirty tart. She throws an apple at me, darts away into the willows, wishes that I'd share my pillow.

Jack waves this off, points at a youth, lithe and loose of limb, at his exercises in the open square of the gymnasium.

– Mint, my flame is bolder, Jack says, saucy and sweet. He comes for my touch without being told, so much that now our dogs know him as well as all the spirits of these forest dells.

Trust Jack, Puck thinks, to be drawn to the gleam of sun on skin.

– Dovenest divine in the sleep-dunes of dawn, I whisper, *down of a cunt dappled by the daybreak's sun and dust, as you stretch through the shaft of spring let in through a window, as you yawn.*

Anna stretches, rolls over in her half-sleep, mumbling as I push the hair back from her eyes. Lying there on top of the white sheets, in a hunting cabin so spartan that there aren't even any curtains to keep the rising sun from pinking her freckle-dotted flesh more rosy even than it is by nature, she's my Muse, I think to myself, my Irish rose, my Celtic knotwork of complexities too intriguing to entirely untangle, as intricate as the tattoo that sleeves her right arm. A whole secret history, she has, I often think, written down in that tattoo she never speaks of, less explicable to me than all of Virgil's Latin.

– Can you explain to me what your *Songs of Unknown Lands* is about? she'll say. In twenty words or less.

– If I could do that I wouldn't have spent the last ten years writing the sodding poems.

– Well, if I could explain the how and why of the tattoo I wouldn't have got it in the first place, she smiles.

I run a finger over the untranslatable ink of her now. Dust motes dance in a sunbeam above us, Jack and Puck riding photons that bounce between them, in my imagination.

– I have a gift to give my love, says Puck. With my own eyes I've marked the place where doves have built, high in the trees.

– Let's see, says Jack. What joys might I have sent *my* boy, what goods? Ten golden apples plucked from deep within the woods. Ten! And tomorrow I will send the same again.

He lies back in the grass, his hands behind his head. *Beat that.*

– Oh but how Galaxy will whisper in my ear, Puck sings. And what she says to me! Winds, carry her sweet nothings that the gods might hear!

He throws himself backwards into the grass, arms wide in

invocation, to beseech the breezes. Jack rolls over onto his front, tucks a fist under his chin and gazes down at the gymnast, miming desolation.

– I know, my Mint, says Jack, you love me in your heart. How does that help me if I mind the nets at home while you roam, hunting boar, and we're so far and long apart?

I make some quick notes on the pages scattered all across the table while I'm waiting for the steel pot of coffee to boil on the stove, in between flipping pancakes, forking bacon over on the grill. I have that sort of muted but insistent mix of guilt and worry that comes from doing too many things at once and therefore – perhaps – neglecting all of them. A sizzle, a scribble, a sniff of burning.

– Fuck! Bloody fucking ... fuck!

I jot a last quick note, dump the pen, tong overdone bacon between the two plates of pancake, then start scraping the unsalvageable mess of burnt mix off onto the draining board by the sink, muttering more imprecations.

– You'll wake the toe-rag if you keep swearing like that.

Anna stands in the doorway to our bedroom, wearing blue jeans now. I claimed my boxers back for cooking in.

– With you for a mother? I say. Swearing's a lullaby for our Joshua.

I pick up one of the plates.

– Thought you wanted this in bed?

She slides past me, scrapes a chair back.

– Fuck it, I'm fucking well up and about now.

Jack and Puck glint gold and green in her eyes as she reaches for the maple syrup, licking lips already sweet with the swearing.

A Shower for Green Crops

– Send me your girlfriend, Puck says – what's her name? pretty Filth? – send her to me as a birthday treat. Then when I'm offering a young cow for the wheat, oh, *then* send me your jealous self.

– Why, I love Filth before all girls, says Jack. But *jealous*? You

598

should have seen her weeping, sighing, when I left her crying, *Oh my fair boy, Oh, farewell, so long, goodbye.*

He wipes imaginary tears out of his eyes.

– *True* sorrow is a wolf among the flocks, says Puck, rain on ripe corn, winds whistling through the trees . . . or when my Moral's in a mood with me.

He pouts.

– True *joy* is a nanny goat in her willow bower, says Jack; it's arbutus for her weaned kids, or a shower for green crops. Oh, but for me there's no joy that my Mint can't top.

Flash.

Joshua's ragdolly soft toy, Rabbit, bounces in time as he intones.

– One heffalump. Two heffa—

Doom.

His eyes widen as he looks at me, eyebrows disappearing under his red mop of hair at the thunder following so close behind the lightning. He turns back to the window, wiping condensation with a frenzy of fist and pressing his nose to the rain-streamed glass in keen anticipation of more flickerings and rumblings.

– Rabbit and me are counting the light'ning time, he says in a voice reserved for Things of Importance. Cause that's how far away it is.

– Is that right? I say. Do you think two heffalumps is close then?

– One and a *bit*, he corrects me. I think that's really *really* close.

He bounces Rabbit up and down on the windowsill.

– Boingy boingy boingy. Rabbit likes the light'ning. He's not scared.

Flash.

– One heffalump.

Doom.

Joshua's *wow* is long and round as only a child's can be.

Puck nods at a discus-thrower down below.

– My Pillow loves, he says, my rural music. So, you maids of Pyre, reward your student with a heifer as his dues.

– *My* Pillow likes *new* music too, says Jack. So make it a bull of butting horns who'll scratch the sand up with his hoof, for me.

Puck sighs, his hand stretched out dramatically towards the athlete drawing back now, whirling out in the release. The discus soars into the sky. Puck cups his hands around his mouth to cry:

– May those of us who *truly* love you, Pillow, reach your heights, where honey runs for him and thorny brambles yield Assyrian spice.

Down below, visoring his eyes with a hand, the discus-thrower peers up towards them.

– And let me yoke a fox and milk a billygoat! says Jack. Only those who love the song of beehives love your songs, you buzzing mayfly. They're your only hope!

I pick my mug of tea up from the table and wander to the open front door, pondering on how I'm going to rewrite this part of the Third Eclogue I'm working on, an exchange full of references to Virgil's peers – Pollio, Bevius, Mevius – meaningless in a modern context. I never do straight translations, preferring to take the original text as . . . architecture, substructure, to let it serve as a seed from which strange shoots may sprout, even if it means the source is obscured, palimpsested beneath an organic growth, an arbitrary arbutus of ideas.

Outside, the air is filled with the drum of rain battering down through leaves and bushes, down onto mud and gravel, the wood of the cabin's roof, the metal of the car's hood. The day is cloud-dark, but not heavy, not humid, not a summer storm but a spring shower. Anna stands outside on the porch, smoking a cigarette. She flicks her hand at a mayfly buzzing in her ear.

An old beehive sits in the trees.

A buzzing whine in my ear seems the song of a Puck sung in fairy-time, a whole verse in a millisecond.

And Flowers in the Fields

– You kids there gathering strawberries and flowers in the fields, calls Puck.

He points at Jack with one hand, grabs his shoulder with the other.

– Look out! he shouts. A cold snake lurking in the grass. You better run. Take to your heels!

Jack chucks him off and tussles Puck into a headlock, hand over his mouth.

– Hey there, you sheep, he shouts. Don't stray too far and wide. The riverbank's unsound. Stay near. Look at your ram; his fleece is not yet dried – [he scuffles knuckles on Puck's scalp] – See? He's still wet behind the ears. Ah!

Jack's hand jerks away from nimble nipping teeth.

– Tightarse, head off the kids who're grazing down there by the river and I'll dip them in the spring myself, sings Puck . . . whenever.

– Sheep in the folds, lads. If this son steals all their milk again, our hands will work their teats all day in vain.

He tweaks a nipple and Puck yelps.

I ask her about Joshua's father as we sit in the evening by the fire, Joshua in his bed and the two of us wrapped together in a patchwork quilt. She's just shut me up, interrupting as I waffle on about the stitching of Harlequin's suit, the stitching of fragments, of history, of identity, all rumpled together in folds, you see, like this quilt, so they touch each other; and under it all two lovers, naked as Adam and–

– You know, she's just said, it's always the woman who gets blasted for lust, for loving just a little too much.

So I ask her if she's talking about her own past, about Joshua and his being illegitimate – not that it matters in this day and age, not in the big city. In the small towns perhaps, but not in the city. Or here where there's only us two and the wonderful, precious son of her so-called sin.

She doesn't speak much about her past, but I know she was something of a wild child, ended up disowned by her own family. Working the street for a while.

– Sin is the snake in the grass of all modern religion, I say. The pagans turned prostitution into a holy ritual. You would have been a priestess in ancient Sumer.

She laughs.

– Does everything come back to Sumer with you?

I shrug, walk two fingers across the landscape of the quilt, a giant striding across the green and yellow and brown patches of field and meadow in which Puck and Jack lie, singing against each other, singing for each other. The giant strides up the mountain of us towards the soft breast of this woman too vast in the scale of my imagination to be just a mother, just a whore.

– Alas, look at my gloomy bull – [Puck jabs Jack's chest] – how lean he is, even surrounded with a feast of vetch. To this dumb brute as much as to the herdsman, love is death.

– My tender lambs, says Jack, all skin and bone, are wasting from a bug far worse than love. An evil eye is on my flock, some kind of curse depletes them slowly, one by one.

You nick one goat, thinks Puck. He still won't let it lie. He sighs.

– OK, we'll call it quits if you give this a try. Tell in what lands the open space of sky's no more than three yards wide and you'll be Apple's equal in my eye.

– OK, says Jack, if you can answer *this*, I'll leave you be. Tell in what lands the flowers spring all graven with the names of kings, and you'll have Filth, with no more meddling from me.

– Ah'm sure ye'll be guid to her, lad, Don had said one night round at his, with Anna through in the spare bedroom, putting Joshua down, and the whisky in our glasses. Course ye'll huv me tae answer tae if no, he'd said. Ye unnerstaun?

He'd smiled as he said it – the grizzly old codger's bark is worse than his bite – but you can't mistake how much he cares for his surrogate ... niece? sister? daughter? God knows what they are to each other, Anna and Don, but she's known him long enough that Joshua calls him 'Unca Don'.

– I love her, I'd said.

I hadn't even said it to her yet.

He smiled. I understand he took her in off the streets. Maybe some mad Celtic connection between an Irish lass and a Scotsman so far from home in the Big Apple – both of them having learned the hard way that the streets of those cities, seeming so dreamlike in their distance, aren't always paved with gold – maybe it was that brought them together. I hadn't thanked him yet for saving her from herself, just like I hadn't told her that I loved her yet.

But I would.

In the months to come I would tell her, in a little bar in the East Village, that in the year or so we'd been together I'd come alive as a person and as a writer, that it was her story and Thomas's, the little snippets I had of them, that finally brought the *Songs* together, made them whole the way she made me whole.

– Does that sound awful? I'd said. I don't want you to think I see you as ... material.

She slid her hand into mine, fondled knuckles, fingernails.

– We're all material, she said. We're all *stuff*.

And my Jack had leapt from my knuckle to the inside of her wrist and executed the most elegant bow to her Thomas, her Puck.

Where the Hazels Mingle with the Elms

Jack stands up, stands over Puck, hands on his hips.

– Ah, Puck, he says, since we're so matched a pair, you with your pipe, me with my lips, why don't we rest ... where? Over there, where hazels mingle with the elms?

Puck, resting on his elbows, cranes his neck to gaze at Jack, chin on his fists, arching his back. He rolls over, puts his hands behind his head.

– I guess I *should* do what you say, old man. Age before beauty, then; which way? There where the west winds shift the flickering shades? Or with that cavern as our resting place? See how the wild vine of the woodland scatters her thin clusters over it.

Jack reaches down a hand to pull him to his feet.

– On our hills, he says, there's only Mint can claim to sing as well as you.

Puck pulls his hand away. *You and yer fuckin Mint!*

– Oh, aye, he snorts, but that one thinks he can beat anybody, even Apple, when he sings!

– Hop, Rabbit! Jump, Rabbit! Run, run, run!

Joshua sings his favourite song as we trek up the path, Anna in front, her hair tucked up under the skip cap, me behind with Joshua riding on my shoulders. I look at my huntress in her state-of-the-art Kevlar-lined hunting vest, red-checked shirt, jeans and hiking boots. I wear pretty much the same, as does Joshua – who's currently bouncing Rabbit back and forth across the top of my head – though only Anna carries a rifle.

– There are bear in these woods, you know, she'd said, tightening the straps on my own vest as I stood there feeling like another child of hers, looking at Joshua who she'd been similarly buckling into his own miniature version of the same garb only moments before.

– You know I don't like guns, I'd said.

– Hippy, she'd said.

– Nazi, I'd said.

She kissed me on the cheek, slapped a shoulder – *done*.

– You don't mind eating the deer, do you?

– Don't confuse me with your logic.

– It's just for safety, she says. Same with the vests. If anyone else is out there . . . it's best to be safe.

– Hop, Rabbit! Jump, Rabbit! Run, run, run! sings Joshua, blithely indifferent to the dangers of wild animals and hunters with too many beers in their coolers.

– Here comes the farmer with his gun, gun, gun, I join in.

Anna looks over her shoulder. It was me who taught him the song, of course.

– You first, O Puck, says Jack. What have you got? Paeans of passion for our Filth? Verses of reverence for Halogen? Or songs of scorn for Coder? Get stuck in.

Puck looks down at the flocks now far below, but Jack just grins, moves on uphill.

– Tightarse will keep the grazing kids, he says. Begin.

– No, none of that old shit, says Puck. I've got new songs just written down, here on the bark of a green beech – I've even marked the music, here between the lines, you see? It's these I'll offer you. These are my best.

He leans upon a tree to rest.

– And after that, says Puck, you let me know if you'd still bet on Mint if that bumfuck had the audacity to contest my skill.

604

Jack laughs, holding his hands up – *chill*.

– Just as the supple osier, he says, gives up its ground to the grey olive groves, as the low scent of reed surrenders to aromas of red rose, if you ask me – so far? Mint could not win. He'd have to yield to thee.

Jack looks shy as Puck walks by, all of a sudden not so brave.

– But wait, he says. No further, scrag: we've reached the cave.

– We're here, says Anna.

I walk up the low slope of rock, holding Joshua's hand tight in my own and with him walking on the inside, beneath the overhang, so he's quite safe from the edge. Ducking to round the outcrop, I follow her path and come out on a broad flat ledge of granite, looking out over the valley and the vista of rolling mountains in the beyond. It's ... *majestic* is the only word for it. These hills worn down in the distant past by glaciation, mostly covered in thick-piled green and rounded to shapes not unlike tumuli but vast in scale, the earth seems like some giant burial field of the gods, an illusion of Elysium.

– You're catching flies, she says as she takes my other hand. Come here. I want to show you something. You'll love this.

She turns me round, leads me to where the ledge is overhung by the solid rock that our eagle's perch is just a little notch in. She points up, just above head-height – not quite too high to reach but high enough that to do so would be not exactly comfortable – and I see the faint ochre marks on the grey stone, cartoonish, primitive, like something Joshua would daub in paint with a thick brush. One might be a bear, another a deer. Many of them seem entirely creatures out of fancy.

– Lemme see, says Joshua. Lemme *see*.

I hold him up under his armpits and he reaches out his hand, fingers splayed, to see if it fits within an outline; I hold him just close enough that he can *not quite* touch it, not wishing to spoil his wonder with a warning, but knowing just how delicate such treasures of prehistory can be.

I look over my shoulder at Anna's broad smile.

– Thank you, I say.

As Vines Adorn the Tree

– When Dovenest died, sings Puck – and what a bitter loss it was –
the nymphs sobbed, as the hazels and the rivers saw and won't
deny. While his poor mother clasped her son's corpse to her, how
they cried. But though his mother called on gods and stars, these
things of heaven had no pity.

Puck looks out on the valley far below, the town, another town
off to the west, and far off, where the sun will set, a city. He brings
out his pipe and blows softly upon its reed, a single long and
plaintive note.

– In those days, he sings, none drove their cows from pastures to
cool springs. The wild things, even *they* refused to taste the streams
and touched the grass of meadows only with their hooves. Dovenest, the wild hills and the woodlands still recall, and call, and call
in echoes how African lions roared with sorrow at your death. Oh it
was you, oh it was you, Dovenest, who taught us how to tie
Armenian tigers to the car, to lead the revellers of Iacchus in his
dance, soft foliage wound around our supple shafts.

– Just as the vines adorn a tree, and as grapes decorate the vine, just
as the bellow of a bull embellishes the herd, and ripe corn makes
the fields happy and rich ... so you, Dovenest, enhanced your kith
and kin. And since the Fates ripped you from us, oh, even Palace,
and Apple too, have left the woodlands to be grim.

Puck brings the pipe up to his lips again, to give a flurry of notes
that dart and dash this way and that, that way and this, a flutter of
hearts on his fingers and his lips pursing as if to kiss.

– And in the furrows where we used to find our grains of barley,
fat and good, he sings, only the darnel and wild oats spring now,
these barren plants that have no fruit. Where violets were once soft
and the narcissus used to shine, the thistle rises now, and thorns
with their sharp pricking spines.

He feels Jack's hand rest on the back of his neck
– So scatter the ground with leaves, he sings, and shade your
springs, O shepherds, from the sun. Dovenest deserves his memory

to be served; his memory demands this to be done. Pile up the earth. Pile up the earth into a mound, and on that monument let's add this verse:

He turns to Jack, to look deep in his flashing eyes.

– I am Dovenest the forester, known from down here in the green woods up to the blue skies. I kept a flock so fair – oh, but not half as fair as I.

Sleep in the Long Grass

– A poetry born from the heavens, Puck, says Jack, such is your song to me. It is like sleep in the long grass is to a soul too tired to dream, or, in the dustbowl heat of noon, to quench your thirst from a sweet sparkling stream. Not on the reeds alone, but with your voice as well, even compared with Mint your teacher, you excel.

Jack's hand runs down Puck's neck and to his shoulder, under his exomis and soft across the skin.

– My boy, he says, my joy, his are the footsteps you shall follow in.

– Come on, says Anna. Don't be such a pussy.

– I'm really not fond of heights, I say. I get that thing where you just can't help but wonder what it would be like to jump. I mean, I'm not even remotely the suicidal type, but heights just bring out the worst in me, you know? I suppose it could be vertigo though I'm not sure I'd go so far as–

– Oh, for fuck's sake, Guy.

I look at her standing out there near to the edge of the ledge, the velvet sweep of green hills behind her. She turns her head to look out over the valley and for a second I imagine the skip of her cap as a beak and her some great raptor in its eyrie. I have a quirky imagination sometimes, I think, as when I watch all the high-jinks that Rabbit gets up to in Joshua's bouncing hand, and wonder if maybe that animal trickster of the fables can emerge even from the mind of a child who knows next to nothing of mythology and folklore. Or when I stand at the edge of a cliff and feel this over-powering desire to find out what it would be like to jump.

607

Anna reaches out her hand.

– Come on. We're nowhere near the edge.

I make sure that Joshua's still safely playing in the cranny of the overhang, down on his knees to let Rabbit explore, and I step out towards her.

– You're bloody crazy, I say.

– Not any more, she says. Crazy for you, maybe.

– And now, in turn, says Jack, I'll sing my songs ... as best I can. For all they are, for all it's worth, I'll try and raise your Dovenest to the stars. Yes, if I can, I'll set him in the sky, because he loved, I think, both you and I.

His nose nuzzles behind Puck's ear. His hand slips the lad's waist, smooths up and round, across his midriff.

– Could anything in my eyes, says Puck, be worth as much as such a gift? The boy himself was worthy of the song and, after all, Stomach has sung your praises – praised your songs, I should say – loud and long.

– Stomach, says Jack, is always going on.

– Look, she says.

A butterfly sits on a flower growing from a crack at the edge of the ledge, its blue and green and red wings opening and closing slowly.

– There are butterflies up this high? I say with amazement.

– We're not really that high, she says.

Her voice has a wry, amused tone to it. She thinks I'm being ridiculous, of course. It's only a ... what? ... drop of fifty feet at the most to the trees down below, and just because the slope of thick trees goes steeply down and down to the valley far below, just because it seems like we're on top of the world, to someone like me not terribly familiar with nature at its most grandiose and sublime, well, just because you're afraid of it doesn't make it dangerous.

She snugs her arm around my waist.

– Don't worry, she says. I won't let you fall.

– Many thanks, I say. I feel so safe in your arms.

She laughs. I look at her. She shakes her head.

– Sorry, it's just … the gender role thing … Sort of ironic, given that …

Her face becomes serious.

– I have something to give you … if you want it.

She presses it into my hand, small and metal, a ring. I take it without question, with a wide smile rather than words, slipping it on my finger and nodding, looking down at the butterfly, which I realise still shouldn't be here, not at this time of the year, not in spring surely. Surely it's too early in the year. Surely it's impossible.

Then the butterfly is fluttering up into the air and away, Jack and Puck riding on its back, back to the never that it came from.

Dovenest at Heaven's Gate

– He is in wonder as he stands there, Jack sings, sun upon his face, clothed in new glory, in a rapture: Dovenest at Heaven's Gate. He sees the stone unwalked before his feet, the clouds and stars now down beneath in the blue sky. And this, yes, this is why gay laughter rules the woods and forests, all the groves and glades, the laughter of Pine, the shepherds and the dry-eyed maids.

Jack slips away from Puck, who turns to see him duck into the cave. Still singing, Jack is back out in a flash, a parcel wrapped in cloth held in his hands. He lays it down upon the ground. He chants:

– No hunter's nets are laid for deer, he sings, no ambush waiting for the flock, no wolf hidden beneath the fleece … for gentle Dovenest is in love with peace. The hoary mountains are so joyous, to the skies they raise a royal ruckus. Yes, the very rocks, the very woods now echo with a song sung in a single line.

He opens up the folds of cloth. Two beechwood cups. A flask of olive oil. Bread. And an amphora full of wine.

– He is divine, they cry, chants Jack. He is divine.

And, laughing, Puck holds up a finger, turns and darts off to a bush not very far away, not very far away at all, returns with his own bundle and unwinds, revealing his own treasure, his own plan

609

for simple pleasure. Two more cups. A bottle filled with stolen milk. More bread. More wine.

Looks like they both had the same thing in mind.

– Ah, be gracious to your own, sings Jack, and kind. You see, Dovenest? You see? We have four altars of the same design. That's more than ample. Two of them shall be for you, Dovenest, and two we'll keep for offerings to Apple. Yes, we'll come up every year and pour fresh frothing milk in double cups. Two bowls of olive oil we'll lay before you, me and Puck.

Jack takes the wine, pulls out the stopper and pours some into one of his cups, hands it to Puck. He reaches out to grab a cup and serve himself, and feels Puck's hand on his. The boy picks up his own wine, pulls the stopper with his teeth and fills one of his own cups to the brim for Jack, a simple offering, a libation, the true reverence of lovers offered back.

– Above all else, says Jack, we'll make our feasts flow merrily with wine, pouring it out before the hearth in winter, underneath the shade at harvest time.

They raise the cups up to their lips, eyes locked upon each other as they sip.

– I'll fill our tankards with fresh nectar squeezed from the Chianti grape. I'll make that dumbass and that cretin Argon sing. Old Fussyboy will dance like prancing satires. And, my love, my nest of doves, this will be yours forever, like the customary vows to nymphs, or just as we bless our lands with hymns. As long as the wild boar haunts the mountain ridge, as long as the fish dart in the river, as long as the bees feed on the thyme and grasshoppers on dew, your honour, dignity and name will live forever.

Jack lays his cup down on the cloth, tears off a hunk of bread to dip it in the wine, to pop it in between Puck's lips.

– Just as we do to the god of wine and the goddess of the grain, so too we shepherds of the fields shall make our annual vows to you. And you, like them, will claim your due.

– What can I do? says Puck. What gift can I give to pay for such a song? Nothing delights me so, Jack, I've heard nothing that's so sweet, neither the whispering music of a rising south wind, nor waves breaking on a beach, nor streams racing down through rocky vales ...

Puck tries to find the words, and fails, so he just picks up the cups, the open wine, and lays them to the side. He gathers the rest of the feast into a bundle of cloth, puts it all out of the way, and slides across the grass, close in to Jack, hand moving up along his thigh as Jack, with both his hands, unbelts and slides Puck's exomis up, baring his ass. Puck peels the tunic off over his head, baring the rest. Jack smooths a hand across Puck's chest.

– First, then, says Jack with a sly smile upon his face, this dainty pipe of hemlock, this shall be my gift to you. It shall be yours to keep, the pipe that taught me why Accordion burned with desire for beautiful Elixir ... and how Old Mellowbow masters his sheep.

Puck laughs and takes the offering in his hand, running his fingers from the root of it up to the tip, curling those fingers to a tighter grip and bringing them down again, to unsheathe the glans.

– Only, says Puck, if you will take this handsome crook, this shepherd's staff. Is such a thing not more wonderful with brazen studs to decorate its shaft?

Jack shakes his head – *you slut* – but Puck just lies back in the grass, pulls Jack around and down on top of him, the two of them face to face, Jack's body – and his hand – between Puck's legs. Puck feels the first touch and the answering twitch, the muscles tensing in him, licks his lips. Jack glances down at the kick of prick, angling his hips.

– Many's the time, says Puck, Antagonist gazed on it with a longing look, begged just a touch of my proud shepherd's crook. But, even though he was a lad you might well love, Jack, he got none of it from me. Oh Jack, my Jack, it's all for thee.

*

I leave it there. It's where Virgil's Eclogue ends after all, though the original's not quite so flagrant in its sensual delight. I don't think I've done the old boy too much of a disservice though; I'm sure a million Latin masters would insist that it's all meant in the purest, most Platonic terms, but, really, in all honesty, I find it hard to read those pastoral poems without hearing what's left unsaid, what's written between the lines, not in the words, perhaps, but in the whispering music which flows through them. And Corydon burning with desire for beautiful Alexis is not exactly the height of ambiguity.

– Thomas would have loved this, says Anna. You're as shameless as he was.

She sits on the chair at the table, reading the epilogue I've just finished.

– Shame? I say. Sin?

I wave a hand, dismissively.

As Jack would say, if he existed anywhere other than in my imagination, anywhere other than everywhere I look around me in the world, riding sparks of fire, dangling his feet over the edge of a wine glass, scaling a blade of grass to bring the finest dew down to Puck waiting below, as Jack would say: Fuck that shit.

A Sunbeam and a Bottle of Wine

Is our Joshua more Jack or more Puck? I wonder. I see a little of them both in him. A flash of impetuous, imaginative id as he swoops through a room with airplane arms, machine-gunning – vrrrrroooooowwww buda-buda-buda-buda. A flirt of string-pulling self, in his wide eyes and wide-kicking feet, hands behind his back as he pleads innocence of drawing on my notes. And more: a fury of scrapping wildcat just like his mother dragged out of a fight and still irate at the injustice of the world; a jut of determined jaw and folded arms against bedtime, so much the stern implacability of his Uncle Don who can deal with Anna's temper far better than I; a solemn peer, elbows on the table, fists under his chin, my mirror image as I puzzle over some enigma of translation and he puzzles over his reader; a shadow of sullen sulk, the cold and certain fury before a tantrum starts; the unashamed, unafraid sentimentality – almost maturity – of him reaching out to take his mother's hand as we stood at her brother's grave, reaching out for her hand as if to say, hush now, sure and it'll all be fine, it will, after a while.

And it will. It bloody well better be, or I'll have Don to answer to.

– Have you got everything? she says.
   – Yes, both Joshua and I answer simultaneously.
She looks at Joshua.
   – Have you got Rabbit?
   – Yes, Mom, he says.
   – Have you got all your writing? she says to me.
   – Yes, Mom, I say.

I give her a peck on the cheek and heft the rucksack into the boot of the car, slam it down, look back at the cabin. It's not quite true, of course; I don't have everything. Jack and Puck are still here, lounging on the roof, human-sized now but with horns and wings, Puck's iridescent as a peacock's tail, blue and green and glistening like wet oil or wet ink, Jack's golden and yellow and red like a phoenix's would be, I imagine. Jack wears Bermuda shorts for the sake of decency – *Hello ... children about,* I warned them both when they showed up in the morning to see us off. Puck wears denim shorts cut off so high they look less decent than if he were naked, even more so with the fly as it is, unbuttoned. He passes a bottle of wine to Jack, wipes the red from his lips.

I'll be leaving them here. This is where they belong, far more than in the pages of some book; however grandiose and audacious it might be, no book is a match for the idyll of a sunbeam and a bottle of wine, I think.

And thou, says Puck to Jack.

– After Thomas died, she says, I went off the rails. I think I went crazy for a bit. It was like I was four or five different people, maybe more, you know, because you don't just go through *stages*; it's not fucking shock and denial and anger and all that bullshit. Least not for me. For me, it was all of it together. I was fucking burning with rage, and cold as the dead. I was a drunk and a whore and a firestarter and Christ only knows what else. I think what got me through was one part of me that said ... *screw all the bullshit*. It's really a fucking waste if death doesn't make you see just how fucking precious life is ... and screw all the rest of the bullshit. That's a cliché, isn't it?

– All the important truths are clichés, I say.

It's our last night in the cabin and we lie in bed, the light on, propped up with pillows. In her hand, she holds a picture of Thomas, kitted up for some costume party in fake horns and a tutu over denim cut-offs. Above the waist, he wears a suit jacket, shirt and thin tie, glittering pink wings of the kind you'd buy for an eight-year-old girl, a fedora propped up by the horns to a steep angle. He's holding a toy machine-gun. Robin Goodfella, she explains. The Fairy Godfather.

The light flickers through the trees that arch their branches over us in a broken canopy as we drive down the winding road from Little Switzerland into the valley. I see them leaping from leaf to leaf, Jack and Puck, riding the flashes and the sparkles of dappled sunlight as white steeds, keeping pace with the car, racing each other. Or not so much leaping as ... just being there on the next leaf as we reach it, and the next one, and the next one, and the next one, like images on a reel of celluloid, the motion projected on the silver screen only an illusion of continuity. Of course, Jack and Puck are creatures of jump-cuts and loops, whatever film they inhabit moving out of phase with our own, not twenty-four frames per second but even faster, so they seem to flicker or, like the wheels of a car at certain speeds, go backwards even.

In the back, Joshua is lost in a film of his own, or of his and Rabbit's, reinventing reality the way all children do, by turns solemn and silly, playful and ponderous. I've listened to him playing, tried to make sense of his ever-shifting dreamworld, sitting down cross-legged in front of him as he taps me on the nose and tells me I'm a pixie house. How do you make sense of that? How can a human be a house inhabited by pixies, by sprites or fairies or sylphs, or whatever you want to call them?

Or maybe it makes perfect sense.

I watch out the window as Jack and Puck leap and tumble and

flip and flop from shining leaf to shining leaf, to patch of sky, to dart of bird, to glint of sunlight on a tin roof, on the wet nose of a dog on a porch, on a chrome bumper of a car, on a green bottle by the side of the road, weaving round each other, pulling arms to get in front, and tripping, and tumbling off into long grass, into long grass and wild flowers, and we drive away, leaving them behind in the mirror, in a sunbeam, in a poem or a memory or a novel or a song, leaving them in a place and time we can return to because it is as unreal as it is real, and therefore as eternal as it is ephemeral, leaving them in their happy ever never.

ACKNOWLEDGEMENTS

As with *Vellum*, much of *Ink* draws heavily on classical source texts, so I feel I should make clear my gratitude both to the original writers, and to those translations which have proved most useful.

The rewrite of Euripides' *The Bacchae* which the players enact in Volume Three owes much to the translations of Philip Vellacott (Euripides, *The Bacchae and Other Plays*, Penguin, 1954) and of Gilbert Murray (Euripides, *The Bacchae*, New York: P. F. Collier & Son, 1909–14).

The epilogue is, in part, a remix of Virgil's 'Daphnis at Heaven's Gate' and 'Are These Meliboeus' Sheep?', for which I drew on J. W. McKail's 1934 translations (*Virgil's Works: The Aeneid, Eclogues and Georgics*, Kessinger Publishing, 2003) and the translations of E. V. Rieu (Virgil, *The Pastoral Poems*, Penguin, 1949).

Without these works this novel could not have been written, and I urge all readers to seek out thse original, unbutchered versions if they want to see them free of my fiddlings.

On a personal note, I'd also like to express my gratitude to all of the GSFWC who gave me feedback during the writing, to my editors, Peter Lavery and Jim Minz, and to all those at Pan Macmillan and Del Rey who have worked so hard on this book – I hardly know where to begin to praise them.

Visit **www.panmacmillan.com** to read more about all our books and to buy them. You will also find features, author interviews and news of any author events, and you can sign up for e-newsletters so that you're always first to hear about our new releases.